LASTLIGHT

THE AENIGMA LIGHTS
BOOK THREE

J.A. ANDREWS

Lastlight, The Aenigma Lights Book 3

Copyright © 2025 by J.A. Andrews

Website: www.jaandrews.com

All rights reserved. This book is protected under the copyright laws of the United States of America. No part of this publication may be reproduced, stored in a retrieval system, or transmitted in any form or by any means – electronic, mechanical, photocopying, recording, or otherwise- without prior written permission of the publisher.

This book is a work of fiction. Characters, names, locations, events and incidents (in either a contemporary and/or historical setting) are products of the author's imagination and are being used in an imaginative manner as a part of this work of fiction. Any resemblance to actual events, locations, settings, or persons, living or dead is entirely coincidental.

Ebook ISBN: 978-1-7362326-8-2

Paperback ISBN: 978-1-7362326-7-5

Cover art © 2023 by Saint Jupiter

for my family

MAPS

You can find printable versions of these maps at
https://www.jaandrews.com/printable-maps/

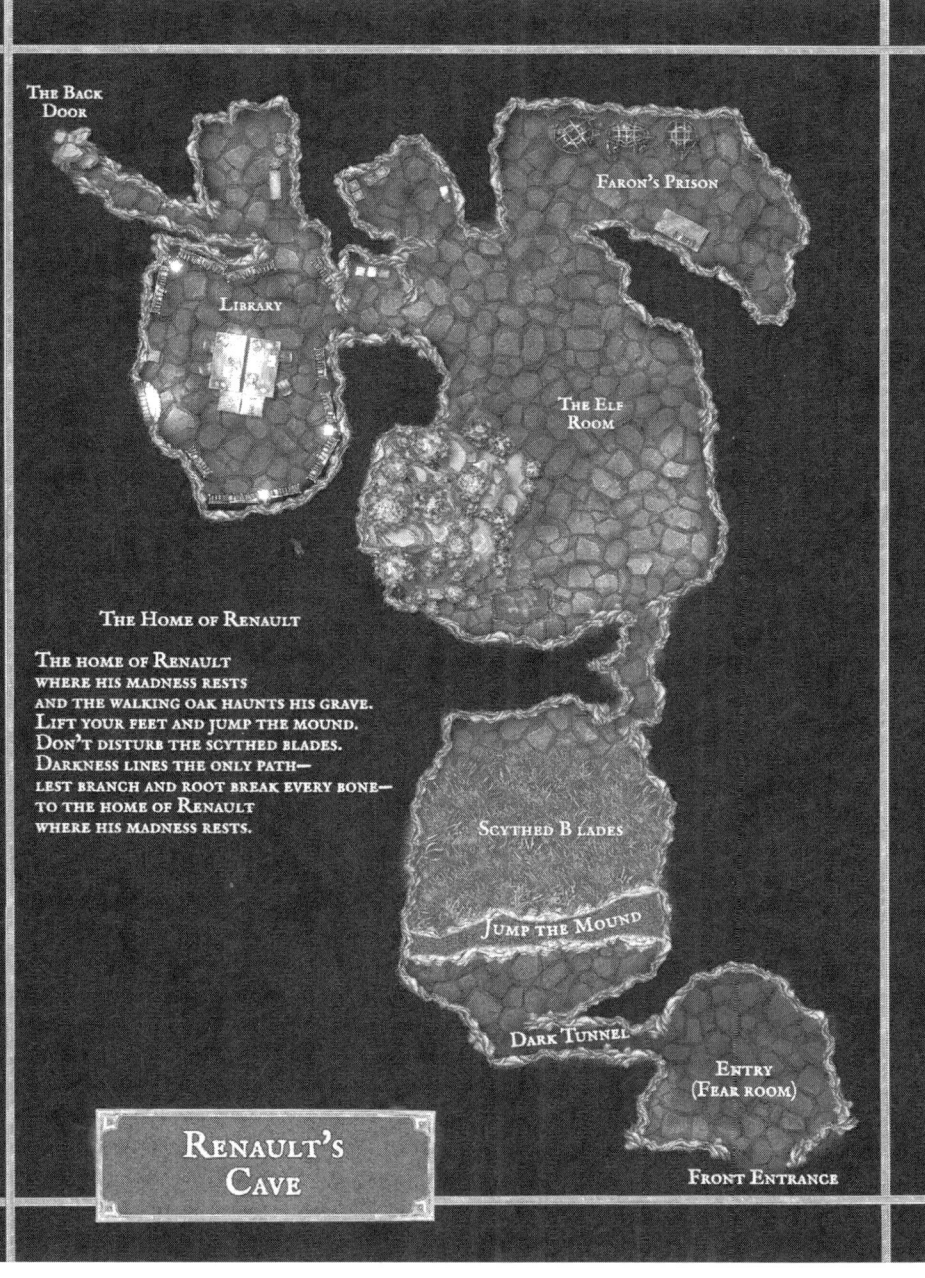

The Home of Renault

The home of Renault
where his madness rests
and the walking oak haunts his grave.
Lift your feet and jump the mound.
Don't disturb the scythed blades.
Darkness lines the only path—
lest branch and root break every bone—
to the home of Renault
where his madness rests.

Renault's Cave

An excerpt from **The Aenigma Box**
by Keeper Kate
Cygnus Cycle
20th year of the reign of Queen Madeleine, first of her name

I had always prided myself on seeing the whole story. Understanding the big picture. As a Keeper, for twenty years I'd pieced together historical narratives, searched through conflicting local legends to sift out the truth of what had happened, figured out how that truth had been altered by different groups.

But the story that played out in the White Wood when Venn and I arrived there…that I did not understand for so very long.

When we first reached the area where my brother, Bo, had disappeared in that odd ravine near the elven Wood and the human town of Home, I thought the local people's superstitions were just ignorant attempts to explain things they didn't understand. That the historical figure Renault the Mad couldn't actually haunt a ravine and bring death to people who ventured there.

But I suppose in some ways, their beliefs weren't far off.

Theirs were closer than mine were, anyway.

Bo disappeared, leaving behind the aenigma box we'd searched for our whole lives, after being attacked by a monster who resembled a tree, then chased by another made of shadows.

You'd think that would have made me focus on the more fantastical things around the area, namely the elven White Wood. But somehow, I thought the issues the elves were going through were unrelated. After all, what could they have to do with the disappearance of a random human man who'd traveled for weeks, following the trail of some ancient human emperor?

To be fair, Venn didn't suspect her people either, but they'd also hidden so much from her.

It was the elves I was completely wrong about.

I trusted Prince Faron, and he turned out to be the deadly shadow.

King Thallion forced me into a bond with the White Wood, a situation that drained my vitalle *slowly and continuously attempted to absorb me into its vast, eternal self. And the entire time it did, a part of me longed for it to. Longed to be part of something I'd never even imagined. To have the sense of community and belonging that Venn had every day.*

Thallion, I suppose, I was less wrong about. He was power-hungry and driven to find his missing wife, Queen Naevys, and would do anything—anything—to find her.

But I was most wrong about Naevys herself.

The beloved queen of the White Wood. The gentle Warden of the forest, tasked with safeguarding it. The elf who helped all other elves bond with the trees. The elf who had accepted the role of protecting the White Wood, knowing it would eventually take her mind and life and drag her fully into itself.

Even when we found her in that cursed ravine, half-dead in a cave she should never have been in, feeding a shield over the whole area with life she'd drained from the White Wood itself—even then I thought she was someone to be pitied.

Well, she was, but not for the reasons I thought.

The night we found her, we took her into the Elder Grove, healed her, and woke her from weeks of unconsciousness. King Thallion tried to relieve her of her Warden power, thinking that was what ailed her.

She woke enraged at the attempted theft of her power. She severed the connection between me and the Wood—and severed Venn's at the same time. She didn't recognize her husband, Thallion, nor her son, Faron. She didn't recognize anyone.

She fought us all. Nearly killed us all.

But she did recognize the aenigma box. The strange box full of pocket worlds, one of which held both my brothers in a valley where time moved tremendously slowly.

She snatched it up and fled.

We chased her the next day, not understanding at all what she was actually doing.

Time and time again, I had thought I'd seen the big picture. I'd tried to piece together the events around the White Wood.

That morning, I was still sorting out the events of the recent weeks. Trying desperately to make sense of them.

It wasn't those past few weeks I should have been focused on. What I had failed to take into account were the centuries that had passed before them.

PART I

THE CHASE

That connection to the forest haunts me still. I cannot walk under a tree and not feel the loss of it. There was a time when I belonged to the woods. I was part of something eternal and accepting. Something that valued my life as essential and meaningful.

Every once in a while, when I find a very old tree, settle between its roots, and lean back against it, I get the slightest breath of it.

Not stronger than the echo of faded memory—but it calls to me.

And it terrifies me.

CHAPTER ONE

"Does everything seem too…" Kate crossed the snowy glade toward the massive frost pine, her eyes lingering on a deep shadow tucked into the branches above her. "Dark?" The word was woefully insufficient.

Venn faced a frost pine, her head bowed, her palms pressed to the white trunk. The vivid reds and golds of her hair blazed like an autumn maple in the gloom. "The sun is still low."

The eastern sky was a pale lavender. The snow that chilled Kate's feet and sat on the boughs gathered the meager light until it seemed to glow a soft bluish-white. Despite this, the trees themselves stood like brooding sentinels, trapping the last shadows of the night under their branches and between their roots. "Is there a certain height it needs to reach before we can talk about how useless this is?"

"Shh."

Kate stifled a sigh of frustration and strode under the old pine's branches, which were so thick that the ground beneath them was clear of snow. She pulled off her pack and sank down. "Because this is useless."

Venn didn't answer.

A deep knot in a pine across the clearing sat in inky blackness. The nagging sensation that it wasn't empty crawled across Kate's neck, and she scanned the forest, her heart beating too fast for the quiet morning.

She forced her shoulders to relax, but the rest of her body was still tense. She half expected that any moment an elf would appear out of thin air to force her back into some elven crisis that would almost kill her and Venn. Again.

A hollow under a fallen log was black as midnight, and Kate studied it, watching for movement. "And everything is too dark." She glanced up at Venn. "I'd feel better if you loaded a dart in your crossbow."

This earned her a sidelong glance. "Because we're going to shoot the shadows?"

Kate gave a half-smile. "It's worked before." She sank back and surveyed the forest again. The trees themselves were anything but dark. Around the pockets of black, every trunk, branch, and needle shimmered with the elven queen's golden remnant. Rich and full and vibrant, even though it didn't banish a single shadow.

The trails of remnant she'd left in the past had been challenging to follow, but since Naevys had regained her full Warden powers last night, every inch of the forest glowed with it. Tracking her now was like tracking a drop of water through an ocean. An ocean that might arise at any moment and drown them. All in all, the golden lights felt…eerie.

And adding to that eeriness, the trees were merely silent pillars of wood and resin and needles, even though they *should* be more. They should be a massive, complex body. An overwhelming force of life and power, crowding around her with a warm vastness that welcomed and enveloped and consumed.

Instead, they were distant. Cut off.

Venn's silver-green remnant flowed around her like a delicate mist, slipping into the furrows of the bark. But it didn't seep into the tree like before. It merely hovered over the surface with a gentle longing. A finger of hopelessness trailed across the back of Kate's neck. If she felt isolated from the forest after the few days she'd been connected to it, Venn's isolation, after talking with the trees for centuries, must be… Kate shied away from the thought.

The distance between herself and the forest felt like a chasm of frigid night sky around her, leaving her with a hollow ache. A spike of fear rose in her at the terrible cost such a connection carried, but the longing for just a taste of it still gnawed at her.

She rubbed her face.

It wasn't the forest she needed. It was the box, and she had no idea how to find it.

"I've searched everywhere around here, Venn," she said, "and I can't track Naevys. The fact that you're still leaning against this same pine is leading me to believe you can't either."

Several heartbeats passed before Venn let out a long, controlled breath. Her jaw was set stubbornly, but there was something brittle in her expression. "It's like I'm a child again. I can hear the trees talking, but they take no notice of me. I can't ask them anything."

"We're never going to find Naevys or the box this way. We need a different plan. Or different tools. Or help from"—Kate winced before she continued—"someone who can still talk to the trees."

"Ayen is in the same condition as I am, and there is no one else in the White Wood I trust."

Kate's wince turned to a grimace at the other obvious option. "You could ask Faron—"

"No." The word snapped through the cold air.

"He's king of the White Wood now. Maybe he can—"

"We are *not* trusting him again." Venn held up a hand to stop

Kate's objection. "He looked for his mother for weeks, killing or hurting everyone—including us—in the process. And he never found her. He's as useless as he is deceitful."

Kate leaned her head back. "Well, we need something."

Venn gave a frustrated growl and turned back to the tree. "Just...give me a minute."

Kate's fingers tapped on her leg, and she fought back her impatience. She opened her pack and rummaged in it, searching for some distraction from the waiting.

Bo's journal was tucked along one side. She pulled it out and flipped it open to a random page.

>   *Ria,*
>   *Do you remember that catapult Evan made that was impossible to aim?*
>   *I found another one! There's a hermit who lives an hour's walk outside a rather small, rather humble town. He lives in his tower, which is so rickety I made any excuse not to enter it. Mounted on the slightly listing wall that surrounds it is a catapult large enough "to send the head of any wild man stupid enough to attack me back to his worthless bandit brothers." A gruesome but accurate description.*
>   *The hermit's name is Peltz, so of course the townspeople call him Catapeltz. The only way to safely approach his tower and not be catapeltzed is by singing. The man loves a good song.*
>   *I chose "By Old Down Donny Mill" because it was easy to change "flung by the brave Helonthrone" to "flung by the brave catapult." He loved it so much he gifted me a gnome made entirely of pine cones with a ghastly mouth made from a dead grub curled into a smile. It looks nothing like a gnome, but I named him Helonthrone. When I quit the area, I left him at the crossroads outside of town, his knobby twig arm pointing back toward Queensland, in case I ever lose my way home.*

But after my song, Peltz invited me to stay a bit, and I spent a long afternoon flinging rocks from his wall. His catapult can be aimed, and after a few tries, I was able to hit a target—assuming that target was a very wide, not-too-distant tree.

I won't hide from you that the entertainment of those hours was overshadowed by that almost-grief that thoughts of Evan always bring. My heart wants to grieve, but that feels too much like giving up, and so the hope always shoulders it away. At least, I call it hope. It's far more painful than I think hope should be.

That familiar painful surge rose in Kate's chest, and she closed the journal. Tucking it back in her pack, she took in Naevys's golden shimmers running along the large root next to Kate's boot. They moved with an almost mocking air. She cast out toward them, and the remnant itself didn't change, but the root lit up, then the entire tree, warming into a tower of burning life. Bright rivers followed each root into the ground. Venn watched as Kate's wave rolled away through the forest and lit every living thing for a dozen paces before fading away.

Kate reflexively searched for any sign of Naevys she could track, but everything, including the root next to Kate, was unremarkable. Full of life, just like every root of every tree in the world.

Kate spun around, clambering to her knees. "Venn!" She cast out again, this time focusing on the ground. The roots flared brightly, crisscrossing beneath the glade, filled with life and light and warmth. "Look!"

Venn frowned at the ground. "At the roots? They're—" She squatted closer. "Kate—they're normal!"

"*Perfectly* normal. Yesterday, there were thick veins of emptiness where the life of the forest had been drained away. But now…" Kate looked around the forest. "After all that effort to drain *vitalle* from the woods into the ravine, Naevys just... stopped?"

Venn's brow creased as she took in the roots in the fading wave. "Let's check. The ravine's not far."

They moved downhill, and the snow grew shallower. The white trunks of the elven frost pines grew more rare until they were far enough from the White Wood to be surrounded by only mundane, brown-trunked trees. Kate cast out every few minutes. The trees blazed into pillars, not as bright as elven trees, but still glowing with *vitalle*. Even the dangling moss that hung from their trees like old men's beards lit with a delicate warmth. The hollow paths among the roots that had plagued the woods for weeks still existed here, but they were filling.

The sky was now a bright pale blue, the sun only hidden by the ridge of hills to the east. Instead of the daylight banishing the shadows, they lingered under the thicker limbs and tucked in around the base of each trunk, watchful and waiting.

Kate peered through the trees, searching for a glimpse of the ravine where everything with Bo and the box had started. The fear that had wrapped around her like a fog since Naevys had stolen the box last night coalesced into a layer of ice-cold dread on her skin.

"Venn." The word came out so quiet it was nearly swallowed up by the woods. Even so, it held an unmistakable tremor, and the rest of her question got caught in her throat. As though merely asking it would shatter whatever small hope she was clinging to.

Venn glanced at Kate. "Your brothers are alive."

Kate stumbled to a stop, relief tangled with surprise. "How did you know I was going to ask that?"

Venn stopped too, and Kate closed her eyes, searching through the space around the elf for any sense of her. The connection the Elder Grove had forged between them had grown familiar enough over the short time they'd shared it that it felt isolating not to feel Venn's emotions emanating from her. "Can you feel my emotions again?" She opened her eyes to see the ghost of a smile on Venn's face, more resignation than amusement.

"No. Naevys damaged the connections I have with…" Venn gestured to the woods, including Kate. "But I'm still an elf and can still sense that everything inside you is humming with fear. I've only ever seen you really scared of two things." She raised one finger. "The forest overwhelming your mind when Thallion bound you to it—something we don't have to worry about since Naevys ripped you away from it too." She raised a second finger. "And the safety of your brothers."

"If she opens the box again—"

"Whatever Naevys wants it for," Venn interrupted, "she hasn't opened it." She reached up and pulled a broken twig from where it dangled from some moss. "I can still feel Bo. He's alive." Her face was almost calm, but Kate recognized the tension around the edges.

"But in danger?"

Venn rolled the stick between her fingers. "He's felt like he's in danger for weeks. Ever since he went into the box."

"Yes, but it grew stronger when Faron took it."

"It did." Venn met Kate's gaze. "I assume—as you certainly do—that was because the drawer had been opened again without the amulet to protect it and the pocket world had been damaged. Seeing as time is slower for him inside the box, in the time it's taken us to do the whole mess with Thallion and Naevys"—she gestured with the twig to the elven forest—"Bo has only lived a few minutes. Of course his danger level would stay the same."

Kate folded her arms. "And now? Is it still the same? Or has it gone up? Because you're being evasive."

Venn tapped a finger against the stick with a sigh. "It's gone up."

"How much?"

Venn tossed the twig and brushed off her hands. "It's not like there's a way to measure this, Kate. I don't know how much, but the life debt feels more urgent than it did before Naevys took the box." Venn held up a hand to stop Kate's next words. "No, I don't know why. If she'd opened it, I think he'd be in such immediate danger from the pocket world collapsing that I'd barely be able to breathe. At least that's how it felt when the shadow was chasing him and he called me for help." She dropped her hand. "It's not nearly that bad right now."

"But it's heavier than it was yesterday?"

Venn gave no response except a slight wince.

Kate looked up into the trees. "Why? What could the queen be doing to the box that makes it more dangerous for Bo besides opening the drawer?" She forced out the next words. "Or maybe she did, and you're feeling him dying."

"Did Renault's description of opening the Runelight Drawer make you think their deaths would be drawn out?"

The words from Renault's journal sprang to Kate's mind. *Massive destruction...destroy it completely.*

"If it's opened again," Venn continued, "I don't think anyone in there will survive long enough to..." She grimaced. "When a life debt snaps because the person you were bound to protect dies, it's supposed to be like having something ripped out of your chest. I don't think I'd confuse that with the debt just feeling heavy."

Kate studied her. "You'll tell me if it gets worse."

The crease in Venn's brow deepened. "Do you really want to know? You can't do anything about it."

Kate's arms tightened across her chest, and she ignored the truth in the words. "I want to know."

Venn studied her, then gave a reluctant nod. "It's staying steady since last night. And I have no idea what to do about it besides find Naevys, hope she still has the box, and hope…"

Kate blew out a breath, trying to dislodge the tension inside her, and started downhill again. "And hope she's lucid enough to reason with." She looked up into the trees around them. "Is it safe to assume that Naevys can track us in the forest like Thallion could?"

"Far more comprehensively than he could." Venn trailed her fingertips along a trunk as she passed, feeding a little *vitalle* into her tattoo. "When I lived with her, she could see any part of the forest and know what was happening there. But she could also see anything that *had* happened there." Venn's brow furrowed. "For most of my life, I've been able to ask the trees questions, but it can be tricky. They think a quick rain shower is as interesting as an elven council that happened beneath their branches. So getting them to focus on the right thing can be hard. But Naevys could do it easily. She said she could rifle through their thoughts and direct them to the thing she wanted.

"Her power lies in how connected she is to everything. Somehow, through those connections, she can almost read the trees' minds."

"Can she read elven minds?" Kate asked. "Or human?"

"Elven minds, to an extent. The more closely she is connected to them, the more she can sense. One of the Warden's duties is to mediate conflicts, because she can sense the truth from both parties. She was incredibly good at it. There were times that before I'd even greeted her, she was giving me advice on whatever was troubling me." Venn looked thoughtfully at Kate. "She might be able to do the same with a human mind. As the Warden, she's bound to more than just the White Wood. She's the heart of all the forests and growing things anywhere near here."

Kate's mind shifted from the queen to the box to Bo and Evan.

Her fingers itched for the notebook she'd left in Renault's cave. Last night, after fleeing the Elder Grove, she'd written down every question and idea she could imagine, but the thoughts refused to settle without being formed into a complete story, and none of the pieces seemed to fit together.

"Why did she take the box?" Kate asked finally.

Venn raised a single eyebrow. "Aside from the fact that it was Renault's, and she's been looking to replicate it for centuries?"

"Obviously because of that. But *why*? What is it about the box that she's so desperate for? She was trying to recreate the Runelight Drawer where time was slowed, but what use is more time to an elf? You already have centuries."

Venn moved quietly for several paces. "Maybe she wants something it holds."

"Like what? I doubt she knows my brothers are in there, nor would she care. And there's nothing else—" Kate stopped. "There is something else. Some*one* else. Or two someones. Renault's wife and daughter are in the box."

Both eyebrows rose this time. "I suppose if it's been around three hundred years for us, it's only been three hundred days inside the box. Depending on what sort of world Renault made for them, they could still be alive after a year."

"With all the effort he put into making it?" Kate said. "I'm sure they could survive this long."

"Why would Naevys want his family?"

Kate started walking again. "I don't know. The idea doesn't quite fit. Unless Naome knew more about her husband's work than any of their journals make it sound."

Low, rambling bushes filled the gaps between the trees, poking up through the snow with branches of dark green needles. A ripple of uneasiness crawled up Kate's shoulder blades at the glimpse of sharp thorns the needles hid. She shifted her shoulders, trying to shake away the looming sense of dread that hung over her.

"Whatever Naevys wants," Venn said, picking her way along a game trail, "I doubt she wants to destroy the box. She knows she needs the amulet, so why would she open it without it and risk destroying what's inside?"

Kate straightened. "Maybe she already has the amulet!"

"She's certainly searched more exhaustively than we have. And since she can't have been after Bo for centuries, if we can find her, we can maybe—by some miracle—convince her to let Bo and Evan out. Assuming you're good with her keeping the box for whatever she wants it for."

"She can keep it forever, for all I care," Kate said. "As long as we get my brothers back."

A rustle broke the quiet on the ground ahead, and Kate froze. Venn's arm with her crossbow rose slightly. Kate cast out, but nothing except low-lying brush lit up beneath the snow. It covered the ground ahead of them but concealed nothing. But the gaps between the snowy branches were thick with shadows as though they led into deep dark caverns.

"Venn, the elven wood has taken on a decidedly threatening feel in my mind." Kate started down the path along the thorny plant. Her leg brushed one, and a thorn caught on her pants, stabbing through the wool and snagging on her calf. With a hiss of pain, she reached down to extricate the plant. The branch was so riddled with thorns she could barely fit her fingertips between them. "Possibly because it keeps trying to hurt me."

Venn squatted down next to the plant, frowning at it. "Frenbrush doesn't usually have that many thorns." The bush filled almost every gap between the trees. "Or cover this much ground."

Kate yanked the thorn out. A scrap of bloody flesh hung on it, and Kate funneled *vitalle* into her leg. The pain dulled as the skin knit back together. Just below the branch that had snagged on her, the shadows were almost black. "Why is it so dark?"

Venn set a fingertip on the needles. "I can feel…something." Her brow drew together. "Anger. Just the barest hint of it, but I think the woods are angry."

A flicker of wariness grew in Kate, and she backed away from the brush. "Because Naevys is angry?"

"That would be my guess." Venn started downhill alongside the line of frenbrush. But before they'd gone a dozen steps, another patch of thorny brush blocked their path, forcing them farther to the left.

Kate searched ahead in the woods. "Was there this much of it a few minutes ago?"

"It can't grow that quickly," Venn said, but her voice was uncertain.

"Still," Kate said, "let's move along. Something about all this feels—"

A shout came through the woods from directly downhill, and they both spun toward it.

Another shout rang out. The voice was gruff.

And dwarven.

A third shout cut through the trees before it was abruptly cut off.

"Dangerous," Kate said, breaking into a run toward the dwarves. "Definitely dangerous."

CHAPTER TWO

The muffled shouts led to a small clearing enclosed on three sides by waist-high thorny frenbrush. In the midst of the snow, two massive mounds of dark green vines twitched on the ground, tufts of coarse black hair sticking out between gaps in the shoots.

Kate threw herself to her knees in the churned-up snow next to one of the bundles. The scent of spiced ale squeezed out between the bands of vine along with the glints of Silas's copper remnant. "Silas!"

He gave a strangled response.

"Twig?" Tribal's voice came from the other bundle. "Get us out of here! That thing's choking Silas!"

The thinnest vines were the size of Kate's finger, the largest nearly as wide as three of them. She yanked at a band around Silas's neck, but her fingers slipped off the slick green surface. "What are you two doing here? What happened to working on your forge in Renault's cave?"

"Less talking!" Tribal shouted. "More getting us free!"

"What did you two do?" Venn demanded, kneeling next to Tribal.

"Do?" He thrashed wildly. "Your blasted woods blocked our path, then attacked us!"

"Stay still." Venn set her hand on the vine.

"Hang in there, Silas." Kate pulled her knife out of her belt and sliced across one of the shoots where it came out of the ground before wrapping painfully tight across Silas's chest. The blade barely scored the surface. "Venn, can you get these to unwind?"

"Trying," Venn said through clenched teeth, both hands gripping one of the largest bands around Tribal's stomach. "They're not listening!"

Kate sawed at the vine, her frustration rising as she made almost no progress. "This is a very inconvenient time for Naevys to have made everything stop listening to you!"

"It was only the *trees* that stopped listening." Venn gripped a tendril with both hands. "Something as stupid and brainless as a tiny vine should listen!"

"Tiny?" Tribal's voice was muffled. "They're like massive tentacled monsters!"

"They're just vines." Venn grabbed another part. "What did you do to make them mad?"

"They're elven!" The vines tightened, and Tribal gave a grunt of pain. "They're probably always mad!"

Kate's knife paused. The surface of the bands around the dwarves glimmered with the same golden light that filled the entire forest, but… "Maybe they're not just vines." She set her palm on one and funneled *vitalle* into it. Deeper than the queen's sparkling remnant, dense trails of gold snaked along the vine, animating them.

"It's runelight! Naevys's runelight is controlling these!" Kate twisted to scan the clearing, casting out, but there was no sign of the elf queen.

Kate stretched out her own remnant from the end of her hand and poured *vitalle* into it, shaping it into a sharp knife of runelight. Her blade slid through the vine without damaging it but snagged on the queen's gold band. Kate sliced through it, and the band snapped, dissolving into a cloud of light. The vines quieted but stayed wrapped tightly around the dwarf.

Tribal gave a muffled groan, and Kate scrambled over to him, her knees freezing cold in the snow. The scent of roasting meat and the dwarf's copper remnant hovered around the vines. "Trade me dwarves, Venn. Silas's vines might listen to you now." She sliced her runelight knife through Tribal's vines, and Naevys's golden bands fizzled away.

"Hang in there, Tribal!" Kate glanced around again. Her gaze caught on the dark shadows lurking under the frenbrush.

"Do I have a choice?" he demanded.

Venn bowed her head over Silas, her hands gripping the vine. Slowly, the loops began to unwind.

Silas drew in a gasping breath. "Get these off me!"

"Venn," Kate said, "how is Naevys doing this if she's not here?"

Venn kept her hands on the vines and gave the forest a worried look. "What if she can use runelight anywhere in the forest now?"

Kate stopped yanking on the vine coiled around Tribal's head. "That's a terrifying idea."

"Twig!" Tribal grunted, twisting his shoulders. "Focus!"

"These won't move." Kate reached into her pack. "I'm gonna try some fire."

"Do *not* burn my beard!"

Kate grabbed a handful of the hanging moss and set her finger in it, pushing *vitalle* in until it caught fire. "You'll be fine." She coaxed a tiny flame from the moss and pulled it into her hand. Quickly, she moved it to her fingertips and set it against one of the thinner vines. The surface of the vine smoked and blackened.

"I thought elves," Silas said, through shallow, quick breaths, "could talk to plants."

"It's listening." Venn squeezed her eyes shut, her face pinched in concentration. "Slowly."

"Mountains grow faster than this," he grumbled. "Tribal, we have a defective elf."

Venn opened her eyes and glared at the vines. Then slammed her hand against the nearby trunk. "Ayen!" she hissed. "I need your help." Her scowl deepened, and she slapped her hand against the bark. "*Listen* to me! Call Ayen!"

Kate made the flame bigger, but the plant was too wet to do anything more than smolder. She gave a growl of annoyance and flicked her fingers, snuffing out the flame. "Any ideas besides blades or fire?"

Venn shook out her hands before putting them back onto the stubborn plant. "Not unless you're good enough at runelight to animate them yourself."

"No, I can't..." Kate paused, then took hold of Tribal's bonds again. "Or maybe I can."

She fed a snake of her remnant into the vine, then poured *vitalle* into it, but there was no way to anchor it to the plant. Her runelight merely slid through like a glittering red mist. "I can't connect to it." She crawled over to Silas and put her hands on Venn's, pulling the elf's glittering green remnant along the vine. It mostly pooled on the surface, feeling slippery and elusive. But occasionally a finger wriggled inside to connect to the plant. Kate followed one of the fingers with her runelight and felt it nestle into the plant.

Slowly, she tried to stretch along the vine like Naevys's

snakes, but most of the runelight seeped away into the vine and disappeared. "No, I definitely can't."

With a gust of *vitalle*, a tall elf appeared next to Venn. Ayen's rich remnant glittered with the dark blue of deep water and smelled of sap and moss and winding streams.

Venn let out a sigh somewhere between relief and exasperation. "Finally, something listened."

"Listened? You're so loud the entire forest can hear you." He took in the scene and dropped down next to Venn, setting his hands next to hers. "Are there dwarves inside these?"

"Yes, there are dwarves," Tribal shouted, "being strangled by your woods!"

"Isn't that the other elf who isn't connected to the forest any longer?" Silas groaned.

"I'm connected enough to loosen vines." Ayen grimaced. "I hope."

The two elves bowed their heads over Silas, and slowly the vine loosened until his head was free. He spit out a chewed-up mouthful of vine, then shimmied the rest of the way out.

The elves moved to Tribal.

Ayen's blue remnant slipped over the surface of the vine like Venn's, and Kate felt a pang at how weak it had become. "The queen took your connection to the woods too, Ayen?"

He nodded, keeping his focus on the vines. "I can only barely feel the trees. Can't even really hear them talking." At Venn's sharp glance, he tilted his head. "Can you?"

"I can hear them, but they pay me no attention."

"Well, you're better off than me." He glared at the vines.

"Why would she be?" Kate asked. "Naevys tore the Elder Groves's connection out of both of you."

Venn frowned, and she flicked another glance at Ayen before refocusing on the vines.

"How did you hear Venn's call?" Kate asked him.

"Not through the trees. I was on patrol, heard dwarf and human voices, and figured I knew who that was."

"You're patrolling in this condition?" Venn asked.

Ayen shifted uncomfortably. "I didn't exactly explain to Faron the extent of what the Warden took from me." He looked at Venn. "It's going to come back, right? It was like this when we were younger, but at some point the wood is going to recognize us, right?"

Venn kept her eyes on the vine.

A gap opened, and Tribal's arm squeezed out. He shoved at the vines. Tearing open a hole, he scrambled out and grabbed his axe from where it lay in the snow. Ayen and Venn backed away.

Spinning, Tribal smashed it into the vine. "Die, you wretched"—a thick band splintered under the blow—"murdery"—he slammed the axe down again—"weed! You should be chopped and used for kindling!"

Venn raised an eyebrow. "I think you've vanquished it."

Tribal pointed the axe at her. "You know what needs to be vanquished? This whole wood! Why is it always trying to kill people?"

"It's hardly always trying—"

"We just walked into this clearing, harmless as the day is long, and those bushes"—he jabbed his axe toward the frenbrush—"grew that tall in the space of a few breaths, and these cursed vines sprang up and grabbed us!"

"One incident," Venn said, "doesn't qualify as 'always.'"

"I don't know, Venn," Kate said. "I think I agree with Tribal on this one."

The dwarf flung up a finger. "The deadly black shadow who kidnaps and kills." He raised a second finger. "The mad tree queen who tears apart hillsides and kills people without touching them." He raised another. "The king who captured us and dragged us to your cursed Elder Grove where everyone almost died—*again*."

"To be fair, brother," Silas said rolling onto his back, still breathing fast. "None of that was the woods. It was all the elves."

"Of course it was," Tribal shouted, "because elves are entirely untrustworthy!" He jabbed a finger at the broken vine. "This wasn't the sniveling prince or the crooked king, was it? This was that mad queen trying to kill us this time!"

"It was definitely her runelight animating the vines." Kate surveyed the forest around them. "I'm just not sure why."

Ayen's frown deepened.

"Well, that rounds out the royal family nicely." Tribal pointed at Venn again. "There's something wrong with you elves." He stumped over to his brother and offered him a hand.

Venn rose to her feet with a sigh. "So it would seem."

"These two elves don't seem so bad." Silas rolled to his feet with a groan, pressing gingerly on his ribs.

Kate walked around the barrier of thorny bushes on the side of the clearing, only to find a nearly solid wall of them continuing up the slope, blocking the way south. "Is this normal?" An inky shadow near her foot seemed to stretch toward her, and she stepped back.

Ayen studied the nearest bush. "These never grow this tall or this…"

"Vicious?" Tribal offered. "Horrible? Murdery?"

Ayen considered the hedge for a long moment. "There is nothing like this happening deeper in the woods. Have you seen anything else strange?"

"Not this strange," Venn said. "But everything feels a little…"

"Vicious," Tribal muttered, "and horrible and murdery."

"It does seem to have a slightly malicious edge," Kate said.

Ayen took in the forest and the thorny hedge. "Will you all come with me to talk to Faron? If Naevys is doing something—"

"No," Venn said flatly.

A ragged hostility rose in Kate at the idea of getting dragged into another mess with the elves. "Absolutely not."

Ayen crossed his arms. "If Naevys is doing something to the forest, he needs to know."

"Then tell him." Venn said.

Kate stepped up next to her. "We have our own problems. This"—she gestured to the bushes—"feels like a problem the new king of the elves needs to deal with himself."

"Just come and tell him what you saw," Ayen said, a note of entreaty in his voice. "The dwarves can explain what they—"

"We were attacked, thoroughly unprovoked," Silas said. "And we also have better things to do than help the elves keep their forest—and their rulers—under control."

"Naevys's runelight animated those," Kate said, pointing to the vines, "to capture the dwarves, who were—" She took in the two dwarves. "What *are* you two doing here? I thought you were busy constructing your forge so we could make stonesteel."

Silas waved the words away. "That's all ready—we just need good wood. We gathered some, but it was a bit snowy. It's drying near the fire now. Crofftus and Fix are just tinkering in Renault's library, so we left them to keep an eye on things and were going to the ravine to check on our carriage of treasure when the mad queen attacked."

Ayen's expression darkened. "She's not mad."

"She's a little mad," Tribal said. "And she attacked us because she's scared of us and clearly didn't want us following her."

Kate straightened. "Following her?"

"We were going to the ravine to check on our carriage of treasure," Silas said, "when we caught a glimpse of her heading that way, past the frenbrush. We thought Kate might be interested in knowing where she was going, so we tried to follow—and she tried to kill us."

"Which is proof that it never pays to help humans," Tribal added.

"She can't have been worried about you following her." Venn said. "She can step tremendously far. Just seeing a glimpse of her would give you no idea where she was headed next."

Silas shrugged. "Well, the forest was just the normal level of elven creepiness until we tried to follow her, then all this sprang up."

Kate looked in the direction the queen had been heading, trying to get her bearings on the forested hillside. When she caught a glimpse of a rocky mountaintop between the trees, a cold chill crawled up her neck. "Venn... Can you think of anything in that direction besides Renault's cave?"

Venn swore. "She's back at the cave!" She started running uphill along the frenbrush.

"Venn!" Ayen called. "Faron needs your help sorting out this whole mess."

"Then he should have made many different decisions in his life," Venn called back over her shoulder.

Tribal started after Venn. "C'mon, brother. Can't let the mad queen mess with our stonesteel supplies."

Silas stumped after him, his shoulders slumped.

Ayen grabbed Kate's arm. "Can you talk to Venn? Convince her to help Faron—"

"After what he did to her?" Kate yanked her arm away. "No."

"What *did* he do?" Ayen asked.

"Ask your sniveling king," Tribal said over his shoulder. "Unless he commanded himself not to talk about it too."

CHAPTER THREE

Kate pushed her legs faster uphill through the ankle-deep snow, clinging to the thought of actually finding Naevys. Actually finding the box.

She tried to stifle the painful hope that kept boiling up inside her. No, the Warden hadn't been lucid enough last night in the Elder Grove to reason with, but she'd just woken from being buried for months, weakened almost to death. Woken to find Thallion stripping her Warden powers from her. Given the chaos of the Grove, it was no wonder Naevys had snatched the box and run.

Today, though, after time to recover, maybe...

The idea was smothered under the looming shadows the wood still held and caged by the long line of thorny frenbrush that constantly turned them from their path.

This wasn't the kind elven queen of Venn's memories. This was the Warden who'd nearly killed her husband and son, along with Kate and Venn.

No, Naevys wouldn't just hand over a box she'd sought for centuries.

She was hardly going to offer Kate some advice on how to find Renault's amulet to safely get her brothers out when just yesterday she'd been a rabid, cornered, feral creature.

Trying to ignore the growing dread at what sort of queen they were about to find, Kate extended her stride to keep up with Venn.

White trunks of the elven frost pines began to pepper the forest before Venn found a narrow gap in the frenbrush. Thorns scraped against Kate's hips as she squeezed through, and grunts of pain came from the dwarves behind her.

When they reached the bare slope beneath Renault's cave, the only footprints were their own from earlier. They hurried past the cave's front entrance with its traps and dangers. Instead, they climbed up the short rock face a little farther on and ran to the rear door—the narrow chimney leading down into the back of the cave.

Kate followed Venn inside, trying not to slip on the icy stone steps. At the base where the narrow tunnel began, she grabbed Venn's arm. On the floor of the tunnel sat a bright, fresh smudge of glittering gold.

"She's here." Kate clenched her hands against the warring hope and fear rising in her.

Venn moved silently along the tunnel until they reached the empty storeroom at the end. She crept up close to the brightly lit doorway into the library. A harsh, whispering voice came jumbled and echoing out of the library. The short bookshelf just inside the door was in disarray, books dumped on the floor or piled haphazardly on its top, all smudged with gold shimmers.

The terrifying power Naevys had shown in the Elder Grove locked Kate's feet in place. She concentrated on the box and started around Venn. "I'm not waiting for her to disappear again," she whispered.

"Don't—" Venn grabbed for her arm, but Kate stepped through the doorway.

The familiar sights of the library met her. Tables and bookshelves lit by hanging lanterns. Low burning logs in the fireplace. The glass vials and bottles with potion ingredients glinting subtly.

But instead of a library, it felt like walking into the forest itself—not just among the trees, but into the very soul of the woods.

The air shimmered with golden glints of light. Kate drifted with the wind over endless hills of pine trees. The delicate scratch of pine needles swept over her skin. Jagged maple leaves fluttered in blazing reds and golds. Roots nestled into the ground, brush sprawled across the forest floor, countless creatures scurried along hidden lanes in the fallen branches and logs.

Naevys, Warden of the White Wood, stood at the large table in the center of the library. Her dark auburn hair was tangled and windswept. She wore a long, sleeveless mantle of muted greens and golds that shimmered and shifted. Despite the snowy morning outside, there was no sign she'd brought a warmer cloak. Her skin had returned to its rich copper hue, although her cheeks were still gaunt and her eyes hollow.

Her gold remnant glittered from two other disheveled bookshelves and the floor. A chaotic heap of books lay on the table in front of her, but her attention was fixed on the rabbit she held in front of her face by the scruff of its snowy white neck.

Amidst the boundless forest sounds came the distant rumble of ocean waves, and the bronze glitters of Crofftus's remnant trailed away from the animal.

"Who are you?" Naevys hissed, raising her other hand. A sliver of wood slid out of her palm, sharp as a needle.

"Naevys," Kate said, trying to keep her voice steady as she entered the library with her hands held out. She scanned the table for signs of the aenigma box but saw only books.

The queen spun toward her, dangling the rabbit over the table. Her gaze fell on Kate, and her eyes darkened from brown to black.

Kate took a half step back. "Please put him down."

Venn came up next to Kate. "Hello, Naevys," she said with a note of wariness. "I see you've met our friend Crofftus."

Naevys's dark eyes moved to Venn but showed no recognition. She brought the sharp sliver of wood to the rabbit's neck.

"Wait!" Kate said. "What are you looking for? Maybe we can help you."

The queen didn't move.

"Are you all right, Crofftus?" Kate asked.

Katria, he said into her mind, his words tense, *please tread lightly.*

The quiet creak of leather vests sounded behind Kate, accompanied by the dwarves' rich remnants as they drew near.

"Do *not* draw your weapons," Venn whispered to the dwarves.

Silas's hand twitched closer to his knife. "Even if she starts stabbing people again?"

"No one needs to get hurt." Kate tried to infuse the words with a confidence she didn't feel. "If you tell us what you're looking for, Naevys, we can help you find it."

Naevys focused on Kate with an unnerving intensity.

"Maybe…" Kate searched the floor by the queen's feet and the two disturbed bookshelves, but there was still no sign of the aenigma box. "Maybe we can help each other."

Naevys set her free hand on the table, and a knot in the wood beside her fingers swelled. A new shoot erupted from it, snaking upward. She pulled a green ring off her finger, and vines burst out of it, wrapping around the branch. With barely a glance, she dropped Crofftus, and the branch caught him, coiling tightly around the rabbit, choking off its terrified squeak.

Crofftus made a soothing sound, and the animal stilled to a terrified quiver.

Naevys's eyes bored into Kate. "Who are you?"

Katria. Crofftus's uneasy voice slipped quietly into her mind, like a whisper in her ear. *The rabbit cannot breathe.*

The new growth from the table was thin and green like a sapling that should bend under the slightest weight, not stand straight up holding a rabbit. Kate cast out toward it, and Naevys froze as the wave rolled over her. The thin branch lit up with *vitalle* and the bright core of runelight that the queen had infused it with. Kate stretched a finger toward it, feeding out her own remnant, laced with *vitalle* in a long, sharp blade. When she reached the shoot, she sliced across the runelight, and the branch bowed under the weight of the rabbit. The coils loosened, and the creature tumbled onto the books. With a burst of speed, it leapt away from Naevys and off the far side of the table.

Naevys stared at the limp green branch. The copper of her skin darkened until it looked like smoldering coals. Flecks of deep, burning red shifted along her arms. Slowly, she faced Kate again, her face unreadable. "Who are you?" The words were deathly quiet, and a dagger of fear cut through Kate.

A rustle ran through Kate's mind, as though a door had just opened and an errant breeze had flowed in.

"Is she growing darker?" Silas whispered.

Venn rolled a dart between her fingers. "Do you know who I am, Naevys?"

The queen's attention turned to Venn, and her hands flexed. "You tried to steal my power."

"No," Venn said quickly. "Thallion tried to force your power onto me. I've never wanted to be Warden. You know this. You've known me for centuries. It was only Thallion who wanted to take the power from you."

Naevys closed her eyes, and her hands clenched into fists. The surface of her arms rippled, sending flashes of smoldering red across the darkness. Small barbs like blood-red thorns slid out of her skin, sprouting up to her bare shoulders like spikes of armor.

Kate forced herself not to pull back and searched the table again.

"We might want to consider leaving," Silas said in a slow voice.

Naevys's eyes flew open, so dark they were like two pools of the blackest night. *"Thallion."* She growled the word like a curse.

"A sentiment I can agree with," Tribal said under his breath.

Fear of the queen warred with the pull of the box. "Naevys," she said quietly, "there was a box." She held her hands out, showing the size.

The thorns on Naevys's arms grew, black at the base and blood red at the point.

"Naevys." An edge of pleading bled into Kate's voice. "Where is the box?"

"Safe," the queen breathed. The lock of hair hanging over her shoulder twisted, coalescing into a single strand. Streaks of dark, seething red raced along it while the rest of it blackened, as though seared.

"We should step back..." Silas whispered.

"No!" Naevys's voice came out rough as she spun to look around the cavern. The rest of her hair twisted in thick strands like vines of smoldering fire. "I will keep what is mine!" She snatched up four books from the table, the thorns in her skin glinting in the lantern light.

"Naevys!" Kate called. "Wait! We—"

The queen's eyes locked on Kate again, and a strange hunger filled the blackness. With a rush of *vitalle*, she disappeared and reappeared inches from Kate's face, snarling.

Naevys grabbed Kate's wrist, and the rustle in Kate's mind shifted to a prickle of fingers, digging and probing. Kate pulled back, trying to banish the sensation, but it only grew. Thoughts, memories, worries, hopes—all seen by Naevys. Kate flung up a shield, but Naevys blinked, and it dissolved. Fingers of the queen's awareness shuffled through Kate's mind, digging unimpeded into every corner.

Venn snapped her dart into her crossbow and raised her arm. "Kate?"

You know the worst. Naevys's voice echoed inside Kate's head, slow and thoughtful. *Not death—that at least has an ending. No, you know the ceaseless waiting. The suspension. The endless linger where you cannot bear to hope, but you dare not despair. The pinning of your soul to the wall in an empty grave. Life continues, but your soul is trapped. Waiting. The heavens could rend and all life bleed out of it— but there is still only the waiting for what might never come.*

The queen shuttered. *No, it will come.* The words snapped viciously across Kate's mind.

Naevys stared at Kate and Venn. "Don't run." Her voice slid out like a whisper with so much power that Kate stumbled back.

Venn tensed against the command.

Naevys let go of Kate's wrist, and one of the strands of her hair lashed out, a long, vicious thorn tangled in the end of it. The fiery barb snapped against Kate's cheek, stabbing into her.

The library darkened, leaving only Naevys, lit by her remnant, which had sunk to a dark, malevolent gold. Behind her stood a forest, steeped in brooding blues.

A creeping dread crawled closer, slipping through the trees like a slinking, sinuous creature with too many legs. Kate tried to take a step back, but her feet were locked in place. She twisted to look through the dusky gloom—except it wasn't dusk.

The treetops were bright with sunlight. It was only here, under the trees, that the woods were plagued with shadows.

The darkness bled out of Naevys and into the air around her. It slithered up the nearest trunk. Everything it touched curled and blackened.

Behind the queen, specks of colored light floated slowly forward.

In one clawed hand, Naevys held the aenigma box. Her other fist held Renault's amulet, clutched against her chest.

The specks of light drew closer with the flickering, erratic flight of tiny fairies.

A flash of yellow glinted through the dark trees—the brightly painted door, anchored between two massive pines.

A sliver of the ravine was visible to the right, crisscrossed with blazing strands of runelight like a cage. A brighter knot covered where Emperor Sorrn's carriage was buried, as though locking away a treasure.

A glimpse of Home could just be made out in the distance— flames and smoke billowing up from it.

The fairy lights flickered, and the woods began to fade just as the blurred shadows on the ground resolved into lifeless bodies.

An elf who looked like Faron. Two black-haired dwarves. A rabbit. A tiny gnoblin.

Naevys stepped over another—an elf with red and gold hair, her tattooed arm lying limp and bloody on the ground.

The light of the library rushed back in, and the forest scene disappeared. Kate stumbled forward. Naevys, whose remnant was again bright gold, twisted her head and yanked her hair back, tearing out a sliver of bloody flesh from Kate's cheek.

Kate's hand flew to her cheek, coming away wet and bloody.

Venn's crossbow twanged, but Naevys disappeared in a gust of *vitalle*, and the dart clattered against the far wall.

The lancing pain in Kate's cheek was swallowed by a strange numbness. She shouldered between the dwarves, stumbling into the tunnel and casting out toward the exit. At the far end, the queen's bright form lit for a moment before it disappeared again.

"Venn!" Kate started down the tunnel, but the walls tilted to the left, and the floor tipped underneath her. A huge hand grabbed her arm as the world spun.

"Steady," Silas said.

"Did the mad queen just kill Kate?" Tribal asked, his voice torn between worry and anger.

Venn grabbed Kate's chin, tilting her head up and peering at her with alarm. "Just put her to sleep."

"Go," Kate said, the word slightly slurred. She tried to push Venn's hand away, but her arms were as heavy as lead and a creeping darkness filled the edges of her vision. "Follow her—be careful!"

Venn ran down the tunnel, and Kate's legs buckled. Dwarven arms caught her as everything faded to blackness.

CHAPTER FOUR

The quiet clink of a metal against glass cut through the foggy darkness. Kate groaned, cracking her eyes to find a spattering of bright blurs. She blinked, and the library's lanterns came into focus. There was a quiet scurrying, and a small hand touched her arm gently. She turned to find Fix watching her with wide, worried eyes.

She lay on one of the cots that usually sat in a small room off the library but was now situated not far from the roaring fireplace.

"Welcome back," Silas said from where he sat at the table, working the wooden handle off a small steel knife.

Through the sluggish haze in her head, she caught the memory of the queen's face. Her cheek ached, and she found a jagged cut above her jawline.

Tribal squatted near the bellows of their newly made forge. The snowy rabbit emanating Crofftus's bronze remnant sat on the table next to a handful of glass vials and dishes holding liquids of various colors, his ears swiveled toward her.

"The queen?" Kate's words came out rough.

Gone, Crofftus said.

"Is she still the queen?" Tribal asked over the long whooshing gusts of air from his bellows. "Thallion isn't king any longer—thank the eternal roots of the mountains. Faron is. While he'll undoubtedly be just as awful at it as his father, it's a bit weird to still call his mother the queen."

"She is the *arymad* queen." Venn strode in through the doorway, her legs wet to the knees. She shrugged out of her thick cloak with an irritated motion. "The former queen. She no longer holds the position, but she will keep the title until she dies."

"The mad queen." Silas nodded. "That fits."

"The *arymad* queen," Venn corrected him.

Tribal kept fanning the flames. "I still hear 'mad.'"

"No luck tracking her?" Kate asked.

"No." Venn moved to the fire and held out her hands. "I found her footprints in the snow just outside, but from there she stepped. I searched every bit of woods that's visible from here, but there was no sign of her." She studied Kate. "She didn't put you to sleep for long."

Kate raised a finger to her cheek. "Why did she do it at all?"

"No idea. Why stop you, but not me? You couldn't have tracked her remnant any better than I could follow her tracks."

Crofftus's long ears twitched. *She knows Kate can see remnants?*

"Probably," Venn said. "We've talked about it in the woods. As the Warden, she's so intertwined with the forest that she knows everything that happens in it."

Fix held up the broken dart to Venn. The little node in the center where Venn stored the *ael'iza* that put things to sleep was intact, but the shaft of the arrow had a long split down it.

She gave a sigh. "That's what I get for shooting it into the wall. It's not worth trying to fix. It'll never be strong enough again to load into my crossbow. You can have it if you want."

He gave her a shy smile and sat down again, examining it.

Kate sat up and swung her feet down to the floor. The room spun, but, focusing on the bright fire of the forge, she stood and took a few faltering steps.

The sound of Tribal's bellows stopped. "If you fall and crack your head open, Twig, it's gonna make you feel worse."

She sank to her knees next to him, the light of the forge glaringly bright. "Just need the fire." She closed her eyes and reached toward the heat, pulling at the *vitalle*. It rushed into her like a river of warmth. She drew in a deep breath, her lungs stretching as though she hadn't breathed deeply in days. The fog in her mind burned away, and the cut on her cheek begin to heal.

Her face and neck grew warmer.

Tribal grabbed her shoulder, and her eyes flew open. She found herself slumped uncomfortably close to the forge. He pushed her back upright. "If you collapse and mess up the forge we've worked so hard on, I'm just going to toss you all the way into it."

She climbed into a nearby chair. "Then no one will be able to make stonesteel for you."

He went back to working the bellows. "We'll just find another Keeper."

She let out a tired laugh and ran her fingers over her cheek. It was slightly tender, but the skin was smooth.

"Why'd the creepy queen stab you with her creepy hair?" Silas asked.

"I'd be insulted that she didn't knock us out, too," Tribal said, "except she's an elf, and they're known for making poor decisions."

If she was going to incapacitate anyone, Venn would be the more likely candidate, Crofftus said.

Silas gave a dismissive snort. "Venn's not more dangerous than two dwarves."

Venn could overpower you both with ease. The rabbit hopped closer to one of the glass vials that was bubbling over a low candle. *Even without using her darts.*

"The poor bunny is delusional." Tribal took a pair of tongs and placed a stone crucible containing a small steel hatchet blade into the forge.

The image of the queen standing in the dark woods came back to Kate's mind. A shiver rolled up her spine. "She did more than just cut me." The creeping dread crawled back across her mind. "I saw...something."

"What sort of something?" Silas asked.

Kate paused. "Another Herald vision, I think."

Tribal exchanged puzzled looks with his brother. "What's a Herald vision?"

"Kate had a vision," Venn said, "given to her by the White Wood because...well, I'm not sure why she saw it, but she saw the yellow door from the Blind Pig, and Naevys was behind it. The Wood gives these visions to elves, sometimes, called Heralds. They're rare."

"The White Wood thinks Kate is an elf?" Tribal asked.

Silas's eyebrows rose in a skeptical arch. "Are you sure they were Herald visions, and you weren't just...dreaming?"

"She saw fairies in the vision," Venn said. "It's a known sign. Even Thallion believed that's what it was."

"There were fairies this time too," Kate said. "And I saw the yellow door again. It was in the woods, behind Naevys. The trees were dark—really dark. Not just like the extra shadows from this morning. There was a blackness bleeding out of Naevys. She held the aenigma box, and I think Renault's amulet. I could see the ravine, guarded by a cage of her runelight—especially where the emperor's carriage is buried. And I saw Home." Kate looked back into the fire, seeing the outline of buildings in the flames. "It was burning."

The room sat in stunned silence.

"Were the fairies trying to get you to do anything?" Venn asked.

"No, they were far away. It all happened very fast, mostly just an image and then Naevys taking a single step toward me." Kate's hands closed into fists at the memory of the corpses. "The last thing I saw was the ground, covered in dead bodies." She took in the faces around her. "Your bodies."

The rabbit and Fix both shrank into smaller balls.

"That's…" Tribal's voice rumbled slowly. "Bleak."

"And she was inside my head. When she touched me, she… crawled inside my mind and was sifting through my thoughts." Kate rubbed the back of her neck, trying to banish the creeping feeling.

The vision of the forest dying and Home burning niggled at Kate's mind. "This reminds me of a Flibbet story." At their blank looks, she continued, "Flibbet is a peddler the Keepers have known—or at least known about—for…" She blew out a breath. "About four hundred years. Although I'm not sure if it's been the same man all that time or if we've known generations of Flibbets." She waved the questions about the man away. "Anyway, he writes books and sometimes brings them to the Keepers. They're always fascinating, even if they're also always a little… peculiar.

"One was a story of a duke who loved his garden. He was a satisfactory duke, but he loved to spend all his free time caring for his plants, and since he lived far to the south, his garden produced things year-round. It became famous for the interesting plants he cultivated.

"Then one year, a beetle started killing the plants. He tried all the normal things to get rid of it, but nothing worked. He hired people to pick through his entire garden, killing every beetle they found. Within a week, they were plentiful again, and his plants were quickly being destroyed. He grew suspicious that his neighbors were the ones to blame for the insects, and he drove them all from their homes, then burned their property until there was a ring of razed ground around his holdings.

"But more beetles continued to appear. So he drove his people out of his city and set it ablaze until the only thing left was his own home and garden. And the beetles.

"Finally, in a fit of rage, he set fire to his garden, ran into his home, locked the door, and burned it down, too—with himself inside."

There was silence for a long moment.

"That's depressing," Venn said finally.

"Where did the beetles come from?" Silas asked.

Kate shrugged. "I have no idea. That's the end of the story. But it reminds me of Naevys. She loves the White Wood, and yet something is making her harm it and the things around it."

"So you had an elven Herald vision," Tribal said with the hint of a smile, "and now you think the mad queen is fighting beetles?"

Kate let out a laugh. "Probably not literal beetles, but maybe she has some figurative ones. Of course, I don't even know what the vision means. The last two Herald visions showed me the yellow door, and we found nothing important about that. Still..." She stood slowly, and when the room didn't spin, she moved to sit at the table. "We need to find out what Naevys is doing. Quickly."

Tribal's bellows began to slowly whoosh again, and Silas, with a troubled brow, turned back to his knife.

Neither Fix nor Crofftus moved, but Venn took a seat at the table. Kate focused on the golden glitters and forest sensations of Naevys's fresh remnants until the feel of the vision faded. Signs of the queen were everywhere. Smeared on each book. Settled in the gaps between them. Rubbed on the sides of pages she'd flipped through. Kate sifted through the scents of pines and the feel of maple leaves and found hints of Crofftus's ocean waves and the barest touch of the single plucked string sound from Fix.

At least a dozen books were sprawled open, all tossed haphazardly on top of each other. Pages folded and crushed between them. "Crofftus."

The rabbit twitched violently, and Kate hesitated.

Sorry, he said in a tense voice. *Rabbits are jumpy creatures.*

"My apologies to the rabbit. Can you tell us what happened?"

Crofftus shifted, his ears quivering. *Fix and I,* he said, his voice agitated, *were working on the solos potion when Naevys appeared in the doorway—*

"Wait, we can't make the solos potion," Kate interrupted. "I have no tenea serum left."

I may have solved that. His voice took on the professorial tone it so often held, even if it still sounded strained. *At least I was close when Naevys appeared in the doorway. She rushed into the room but paid us no heed at all, so we hid in the corner. She started pulling books from the shelves and muttering.* The rabbit's ears flattened against its back. *She was angry.*

Fix snuck up onto the table and crouched near Kate, wrapping his arms around himself and staring at the ground.

She kept muttering about "him" and how he was keeping things from her.

"Renault?" Kate picked up the nearest book, one of Renault's many journals.

I assume. Everything she looked through was his.

Kate closed the book and sifted through the others on the table. "These aren't about the box."

Not exclusively.

"Then what was she looking for?"

Ahh, he said nervously. *Hard to say. Hard to say.*

The handle of Silas's knife came loose with a snap, and the rabbit flinched. The dwarf raised an eyebrow. "You sound as skittish as the rabbit looks," Silas said. "I think its jumpiness is rubbing off on you."

You'd be frightened if she almost killed you, too, Crofftus snapped.

Fix shrank smaller, and Kate rubbed her hand over the gnoblin's back. The bones of his spine jutted against his patchwork tunic.

The queen was... furious, Crofftus said quietly, *and frightening.*

Kate shifted the books on top of the pile. "This one is Renault's notes on how much *vitalle* a kobold holds versus a goblin. This one has a chart of the power in wellstones of different sizes. That one is a record of the healing Renault attempted on a villager. An unsuccessful attempt." The stack of books sat mutely on the table. "I don't know what she was looking for."

Fix twitched, and his eyes flickered to Crofftus.

Venn studied the rabbit with a probing look. "If you were hiding with Fix, how did she get ahold of you?"

I hid at first, but then... The rabbit gave an agitated half-hop. *She tore pages from a book.*

"What?" Kate grabbed the nearest book. "Which one?"

I couldn't see from the corner, so I came closer. It had a black binding.

Kate sifted through more books until she found one with a black cover and the remains of two missing pages. "This is talking about Renault's amulet and mistlight. He was trying new magic with them. She tore out the records of the experiments themselves."

Silas considered the rabbit. "So you hopped up onto the table in all your terrifying, fluffy fur and tried to keep the mad queen from hurting a book?"

I... Crofftus hesitated. *I told her to stop.*

Fix cowered closer, and Kate set her hand on his back again, feeling him tremble. "I imagine she didn't take that well."

She was understandably surprised to have a rabbit speaking into her mind. She grabbed me by the neck and demanded to know who I was. The rabbit crouched lower. *Then she sifted through my mind.* He gave a little shudder. *Which is when you arrived,* he finished in a rush of words.

Fix leaned against Kate's leg.

She rubbed her hand over his back again. "Are you all right, Fix?"

He hesitated, then nodded with a jerky movement. Without looking at her, he moved over to the far side of the stand of glass vials and climbed up to the tabletop. He had no visible injuries, and he moved without any apparent pain, but his fingers shook.

Kate watched him for another moment then turned back to Crofftus. "And are you all right?"

Of course, he answered sharply. *The rabbit is merely having difficulty calming down.*

His words were still unsteady, but she let the bravado go.

A circle of green lay on the table, drenched with the queen's remnant. "This is Naevys's ring! The one that made those vines!" She picked it up and cast out toward it as though that would reveal where Naevys had been, where she'd hidden the box. As though it could tell her—

Kate spun toward Crofftus. "Did you say you can make my solos potion?"

"What's a solos potion?" Silas asked.

"Something I've been working on for twenty years." Kate set the ring down gently, kicking herself for disturbing any of the remnant on it. "It's what I was working on when Venn showed up at my door with the box. A combination of the tenea serum I had that let us store memories—the last of which was spilled in the Elder Grove—and my remnant amplifier. I believe, if I can do it right, I can make a potion that will show me the memories trapped in objects."

Silas's look grew skeptical. "Objects have memories?"

"I believe the remnants left on them do. I saw it used once by some Kalesh men the day they took the box and my brother Evan from me." Kate turned to Crofftus. "If we could make a solos potion, this ring could show us where Naevys has been—where she put the box! But…how are you creating more tenea serum? Tenea comes from a sea creature. I had to send a merchant all the way to Napon to get some. It's the essential part, and the only thing that holds memories."

Not the only thing, Crofftus said with an eagerness that was almost as intense as his agitation had been. He nudged a small bowl with his nose so roughly it almost spilled. A glint of light flashed out of the pinch of powder inside it.

Kate caught glimmers of green and orange and violet. "Is that…?"

Crushed wellstones. Fix ground down some of the fragments that the dwarves kept.

Kate cast out toward the powder, and it lit brightly with a chaotic jumble of *vitalle*. "This is just a disorganized mess. I think the crystalline form is essential for a wellstone to hold a memory."

I agree. But a crystal won't bind to your remnant amplifier. For that we need a liquid. He hopped over to a bubbling vial of liquid that was nearly clear but thick. Like transparent honey. *A tincture that will hold the wellstone's power.*

"A jumbled mess of powder suspended in a liquid is still a jumbled mess."

True. Unless we align the powder. Crofftus hopped quickly across the table and pointed his nose to a small chunk of stone. *The dwarves have a lodestone. If we bring them close to the wellstone granules and add some* vitalle, *they'll line up again.*

Kate considered the idea. "Not like they do in a crystal."

No. For our purposes, they'll do it better. Less rigidly. They'll be aligned, but free-floating, able to move with more nuance.

"A lodestone will affect a wellstone?" Venn asked.

With a bit of help from vitalle, *they affect more things than you'd expect. Not strong enough to spin a compass, but enough to serve our purposes.* There was a strange note in his voice. Almost pleading. *Put it near the powder.*

"All right." Kate held the lodestone close. A few granules twitched, and a flicker of hope lit. She gave the rabbit a smile. "Tell me what to do."

CHAPTER FIVE

Fix can add the powder and stir, Crofftus said, his voice growing calmer, *and he can hold the lodestone close while you add some* vitalle.

Kate pulled her chair close to the vial bubbling gently over the candle. "Go ahead, Fix."

The gnoblin poured the powder in and stirred it with a long, thin rod while holding the lodestone against the glass. Kate set her fingertips on the side and let some *vitalle* seep into it. Inside the fluid, specks of wellstone caught the light and drew the *vitalle* closer, wrapping themselves in the magic.

Slowly, each particle spun, drifting into something resembling order. The tincture gained a strange reflectiveness, as though it were made of transparent silver.

It's working!

The hope grew stronger inside Kate, and she allowed herself a small smile. "Are you able to move any *vitalle*?" she asked Crofftus. "This is using barely any."

I could once. Never in the quantities you can, but I have done this to more than one potion. I could heat things or light a small flame. Milton could do... His voice took on a bitter twinge. *He was always doing everything with it. Even when he didn't need to. Showing off all the time.* He fell silent.

Kate tried to imagine the wizened old Shield of the Keepers as a boy, flashing his skills about, but she couldn't quite make the image believable.

But when I inhabit animals, I can't do even the simplest thing. His voice was matter-of-fact, but the rabbit sat tense and still. *I'm not connected enough to their physical bodies. I've tried in creatures that I've bonded closely with, but on the rare occasions where I've succeeded, it caused them pain and...tattered the edges of my mind.*

"So if you moved a lot of *vitalle*...?"

It would undoubtedly kill the animal and undo my mind to the point where I doubt I'd have the strength to find another host. The rabbit's black eyes fixed on her face with an unnerving intensity. *Don't take the connection to your body for granted, Katria.*

Kate paused at his shockingly fierce tone and gave him a measured nod. "After almost losing the ability to move any *vitalle*, it does feel more precious." Despite the small amount of *vitalle* she was using, Kate's fingertips began to tingle. Beside her, Venn closed a book and picked up another. "Finding anything?"

"Not really." Venn flipped through some pages. "All these books are related to how Renault created the pocket worlds, but all different aspects of it. Since these are the ones she left, I guess she wasn't looking for information on how to calculate mistlight in a creature, or how to adjust the size of pocket worlds, or how to stabilize the boundaries of them."

That should be good, Katria. Crofftus hopped closer to the vial. *I'd like to let the wellstone tincture simmer for a short while.*

Kate cut off the *vitalle* and rubbed her fingertips and glanced toward the door, as though Naevys might be lurking there. "How long?"

Just until it clarifies a little. Not long.

"Let me know as soon as it's ready." The new smudges of the queen's remnant left the cave feeling vulnerable, and she pushed herself out of her chair, looking for something to distract her. "Where is that book on recreating the amulet?"

On top of that short bookshelf.

Kate pulled her journal and a pencil out of her pack and crossed to the bookshelf. A black leather book sat atop a short stack. It began with a series of detailed colored drawings of the amulet. The outside was a circular disk of stonesteel, marked with runes along its edges. From the front, a glass teardrop was visible, holding a deep red potion. From the back, though, it was much more complicated.

Nestled inside a ring of stonesteel, an elegant net of golden wire caged a cut topaz. Centered over the gem was a spiral like a spring. The notes around it described how pressing a finger against the spring would let someone's skin brush the topaz for just a single breath before pushing it safely away.

Behind her, voices tumbled over each other, but she ignored them all, jotting notes in her journal.

Can only touch topaz for a moment, she noted. *Why?*

The following pages were filled with the description Crofftus had found before, holding a quick overview of the process Renault had gone through to create the amulet. It began with what he called "his topaz" and the fascinating blend of elven and human magic he'd used to create it.

Need elven assistance, she marked in her journal under a quick list of the other ingredients needed. *An elf who wields* ael'iza *more powerfully than Venn.* She thought briefly of Faron, but the memory of him cutting Venn's tattoo was too fresh in her mind to disregard.

A different elf, then. *Evay from the lakes?* Kate considered Venn's aunt for a moment. She was a good choice. Not as powerful as someone like Faron, but Venn trusted her. Not to mention that Evay had once had a life debt to a human who'd become like a sister to her and she had no loyalty to Thallion.

She flipped a few pages ahead, looking for more detailed instructions. A quarter of the way through the book, she found a drawing of the topaz again amidst a crowded page of notes.

> *Curse Vrestous for taking my notes. I'm not positive the quantities are correct for the poserevenn powder nor the infusion of blenseed. Another attempt at creating the imbuing solution will require countless trials to be sure, but as I see no reason to create another Oziv amulet, I leave these approximate quantities as a guide to whoever else seeks one.*

Kate turned more pages, looking for the beginnings of his creation of the amulet.

There were three distinct parts of the Oziv amulet. The inner amulet, which contained the topaz encased in the golden net; the teardrop of lienick potion; and the exterior shell of stonesteel engraved with a complex series of runes.

The first set of instructions covered the runes, which were simple enough.

The lienick potion formula was next. While it wasn't simple by any means, it was doable. The few ingredients that would be difficult to find were already here, labeled neatly among Renault's other glass jars. The entire process would take only a few days.

She read on quickly until she reached the page describing the topaz in the back of the amulet.

From the first diagrams of cutting the stone, it was obvious that the level of mastery needed was far beyond her skill. Far beyond the skill of anyone she knew. And even if she could find the correct type of topaz (which Renault had noted was essential) and find someone to cut it correctly, the potion Renault had infused it with was complex enough to require four pages of descriptions, with copious notes explaining how these details were recalled from memory, since his original records had been stolen by the mage Vrestous.

But worse, the magic involved in imbuing the topaz with power wasn't just half-elven. It was such a complex combination of human and elven powers that there was no way it could be completed by two people. The steps required intricate, nuanced blending of the two skills that could only be done by a single mind.

Kate's pencil stopped, and her heart sank as the description continued. Having the help of an elf would gain her nothing.

Perhaps, while she'd been connected to the forest, she might have been able to dabble in the edges of what Renault had done, if it didn't kill her in the process, but here? Now?

Renault's connection to the stone and the potion was as far beyond her as a connection to the moon.

Her hope guttered out. This amulet was not something she could recreate. Not without years of study and honing skills she could never attain.

She flipped past the end of the formula, her mind dully noting several more steps that would be impossible without elven magic.

At the end, a new section began.

Early Failures

The Oziv amulet works flawlessly to connect with a ha'lynae and, as far as I can tell, does not degrade with each use. I believe it could be used hundreds of times at least to access the time-slowed pocket worlds without negative repercussions.

In an attempt to record all my research in a single volume, the following are descriptions of the earlier ways I failed to open a door into the pocket worlds safely.

The next pages held descriptions and diagrams of a dozen different experiments, each with explanations of what didn't work, each labeled "Failure" at the top of the page. Until the sixth page, which was labelled "Partial success."

Trial 17 - Preliminary tests with wellstone slivers show promise.

Trial 17a - Embedding chips of wellstones in a stonesteel sleeve
Results: A slight disturbance in the time barrier at the pocket door, but unable to create stable interactions between the wellstones. Instantaneous damage inflicted on doorway.

Trial 17 b - Fractured a single stone, then arranged fragments around sleeve, keeping their original alignment with each other in mind.
Results: Interactions between fragments still unstable. No increase in stability from randomly aligned fragments. Damage to doorway begins immediately.

"Too bad you didn't have a rabbit to help you suspend the fragments in a liquid and align them," Kate said quietly, tucking a little slip of torn paper into the page to save her place. "Although I'm not sure that a 'slight disturbance' at the barrier constitutes a success."

It was a half-dozen more pages before she stopped at a "Near Success."

Trail 27 - Lienick potion infused into wellstone
Unlike the topaz in my amulet, a wellstone is easily infused with a potion as volatile as lienick. It takes minimal ael'iza to fuse the two, although it requires a stone at least as large as my thumbnail to

hold the fifteen drops of liquid required. A larger stone works better, but due to the destructive nature of this process, the cost of wellstones would soon outstrip the repeated testing of this solution.

Results: When properly infused (see appendix C, section 2 for infusion notes), the saturated wellstone takes on the deep red hue of the lienick potion but retains the distinct sharp glitter of a wellstone. (Earning it the name "bloodstone" by Naevys, queen of the White Wood.)

Kate paused at Naevys's name, so casually included in his research notes, shocked again at how intertwined she was with his work.

The wellstone containment extends the life of the potion from mere minutes to several hours before the solution degrades and loses effectiveness.

During that time, if the wellstone is brought into contact with the barrier of a ha'lynae, there is initially no connection to the slowed time inside such a pocket world. However, if ael'iza is applied to the stone, the potion activates and a gateway between conventional time and a slightly slower timeline is established. The increased application of ael'iza leads to an increasingly slowed timeline at the other side of the gate.

Initial tests of this process proved very successful.

With careful execution, when the gateway is calibrated to the correct time flow, a stable connection is formed with the ha'lynae.

The flicker of hope flared up again, and Kate flipped the page.

This connection requires a great deal of ael'iza to maintain. However, if the power is provided, the wellstone can hold the connection until the lienick potion degrades.

The limitation of the bloodstones is critical, however.

Once the gateway is calibrated to the slower time flow, it cannot be undone. There is no way to disentangle the gateway from the pocket world. The doorway remains open, destroying any security that the pocket world should provide.

When the lienick potion degrades past the point of potency, the gateway crumbles, destroying the doorway into the pocket world with it. From our observations, the interior of the pocket world does appear to sustain damage at the same time, but the world itself is still intact when the doorway collapses.

I hypothesize that the pocket world, if large enough, could survive such an event, but having the anchor to conventional time and space severed, there is no way to reconnect to the pocket world. Anything—or anyone—left inside it would be contained therein forever.

In our tests, the bloodstones were potent for two to three hours.

"Two to three hours!" Kate breathed. "Crofftus! Look at this!" She rushed back to the table, dropping the book down between the rabbit and Venn. "We can create a temporary gateway into the box!"

CHAPTER SIX

Venn leaned closer. "How?"

Kate pointed to the page. "With a wellstone and some lienick potion, both of which are actually attainable! We can open a door for a couple of hours into the pocket world!"

"Why didn't Renault just use that?" Silas asked, pulling a hammer out of his pack and setting to work dislodging the steel head from the wooden handle.

"Because you can't close the door. Once the potion degrades, the gate collapses, destroying the pocket world door as well."

Crofftus's nose twitched. *So no one could ever use it again?*

"After the destruction that the Runelight Drawer must have suffered by now," Kate said, "I think everyone inside it would be thrilled to get out. And I'm not sure there'll be much left for anyone to use again."

This could work! Crofftus nudged the page with his nose. *The lienick potion would be simple enough. Time-consuming, but every ingredient we need is here.* His beady black eyes looked up at Kate. *I'll need your help, though. Rabbits can't see red.*

Kate raised an eyebrow. "They can't?"

Most animals don't see quite like we do. Rabbits can see greens and blues, but reds and oranges look mostly grey. Your hair, Venn's hair, the fire...they're all different shades of grey.

Kate scanned the room for a moment, imagining losing the ability to see anything red, before she turned back to the book and ran her fingers over the list of ingredients. Everything was here. That luck felt alien in this part of the world, where every task she'd tried had felt like a battle.

She paused, mulling the magnitude of the luck. In all the world, the only other place she knew where she could make such a thing was the Keeper Stronghold. She'd have the equipment there, and the ingredients. A couple of components would have taken some time to prepare, but nothing would have been out of her reach.

Kate paused as the thought resonated with something deep inside her—working in the quiet of the library with the advice of the other Keepers. The seven stories of books for reference. No caves. No elves just appearing in the cave with their troubles and threats. No elven entanglements that endangered life and limb. No floundering around in a world she didn't quite understand.

The complex, layered remnant of the Stronghold called to her with the whispered promise of belonging and home. And safety.

Katria! Crofftus said, his voice sounding tight with excitement. *I think it worked!*

Kate blinked and refocused on Renault's library, with its ancient foreign books and the queen's looming remnant covering everything.

In contrast to the safety of the Stronghold, this cave—everything about this part of the world—felt vulnerable. Filled with monstrous creatures and powerful elves and ancient deadly secrets. She rubbed her face, pushing away the homesickness. There was no reason to even think of going home until she had the box.

Crofftus's liquid shimmered with a slow, viscous glimmer, and Kate cast out a wave at the vial. It brightened, the flashing particles of wellstone forming a fluid lattice that shifted in the simmering potion.

A viscid crystal! The rabbit's nose twitched in excitement. *Now to see if we can cool it very slowly to preserve its form.*

"If this works…" Kate sank into her chair.

Yes! Crofftus said, sounding almost giddy. *It should mix easily with your remnant amplifier.*

"I could have a solos potion!" She looked over the table, glittering with remnants, including the bright circle of Naevys's ring. "Crofftus," she whispered. "Thank you."

I merely followed your ideas, he said with a magnanimous air.

Silas looked up. "Did the mad queen change out Crofftus for some other talking bunny?"

"Yes," Tribal said. "Where's the real Crofftus who talks like a snooty tutor and takes credit for everything?"

I did fill in several large gaps, Crofftus said with a sniff of annoyance, *and created a type of memory potion that no one has ever attempted.*

"Never mind." Silas refocused on his hammer. "There he is."

But the bones of the work were completed by Katria.

Kate focused on the page in front of her. It was an account of Renault's kobold.

> He is a dark purple color with long, pointed ears that move with his mood and a long, narrow nose that is much sharper than his personality. His face reminds me vaguely of a goblin, except it is much more human and easier to look at. Every kobold I have seen looks similar. The top of his head reaches my knee, and his hands are remarkably dexterous.
>
> The ease with which the kobolds open pocket worlds is astounding. Any time they want to disappear, they create a transient pocket.

They call it blinking when they disappear into these spaces. The beauty of the kobolds is that they step into one in one place and step out somewhere else. Tumble insists no kobold can blink a very long distance, but it reminds me of the way elves step. My mother could, and she explained it similarly. No matter what I have tried, though, I cannot manage it.

Can you imagine the power? Opening up a space only you can reach? The little creatures have no idea how mighty they are. It is almost a shame that they are so easily trapped into subservience.

I asked Tumble if he could teach me, and he has tried, but his instructions make no sense. I cannot fold the world into a pocket.

Kate set the book aside with a frustrated hum. "Every kobold I've ever heard of is an amazing creature. Ingenious, kind, and loyal. Renault did not deserve one." She glanced at Venn. "I hoped his explanation of stepping would help you, but unless you think 'folding the world into a pocket' sounds like a reasonable thing to try, I think you're still on your own."

"Fold the world?"

A hint of forest remnant trickled in through the back door.

"Venn!" Kate whispered, casting out. Two forms lit up in the tunnel beyond it. The front figure—clearly elven—raised her hands with a nervous giggle. "You're hard to sneak up on, Kate." Aislin peeked around the corner. Her golden hair sparkled with snowflakes, and her honey-colored remnant spread into the room like a mist. "Hello!"

Venn crossed her arms. "I thought I sent you two home to the lakes."

"Did you?" Aislin asked.

Matlen stepped in behind his twin sister. "We just came to make sure our friends were safe." His remnant mixed with hers, only the barest shade darker. He pulled off his thick cloak and shook the melting snow off it.

Venn pointed to the door. "Get yourselves home. After everything that happened last night, you should know better than to be here with us."

Aislin moved over next to Silas and reached for the hammer. He gave it to her, and she set her fingertips on the handle, then handed it back. "Wood's easy to shrink."

He gave the head a quick tug, and it slid off. He raised one bushy black eyebrow, then handed her a small hatchet.

"But Faron's looking for Naevys too," Aislin said, "so being here is like helping the White Wood."

"Stay away from that elf," Tribal said gruffly.

"Why?" Matlen asked Venn. "What did he do?"

"Nothing we can talk about," Venn answered before either dwarf could. "And regardless of the problems between Faron and me, you two should stay away from him. He's king of the White Wood now, and while he's not technically king of the lakes, his authority can't be taken lightly. And you two are not good at taking orders from anyone. Defying an order of his would be very dangerous."

"We actually came to give you a report about what's going on in Home," Matlen said, settling into a chair next to Tribal.

"It's a bit of a mess," Aislin agreed, sitting next to Silas. She looked up at Venn. "Don't worry—we didn't go into it. Actually, the whole town is a little out of sorts about that whole thing with the diamonds yesterday. We ran into a merchant a ways outside of town who'd seen most of it."

A hint of guilt tickled at Kate's mind. "What happened?"

"Well, after we planted those wellstone fragments on that grumpy man and convinced that little boy that there were diamonds on the elven side of the river, everything went mostly as planned. Except a lot more people went looking for the diamonds than we expected. Whole families came."

Matlen nodded. "You humans really like diamonds."

Kate's stomach sank. "How bad was it?"

"It turned into two groups," Aislin continued, "both trying to claim the ground for themselves. One group wanted to uproot the trees"—she gave Silas a smile—"because we had let it slip that the diamonds might be buried. The other group thought that was stupid and said the diamonds would be found in caves. Well, I guess everyone got a bit angry and some fighting broke out, so when Thallion arrived, the humans attacked him and the rangers, who put a bunch of the people to sleep, but someone shouted that the elves were killing them, and it turned into a full riot."

Kate shrank back in her chair, the twinge of guilt growing stronger. "Please tell me no one was killed."

Aislin shook her head. "All sorts of people got hurt. There are broken bones and people with their heads all wrapped in bandages. Some people in town are blaming the elves for it all, and a few have decided it was actually started by dwarves, but most people are really mad at that old man, Griston, who we planted the fake diamonds on."

Matlen gave a nervous smile. "The merchant said he stayed in a farmstead outside of town last night, but when he passed near Home this morning, the whole town seemed...on edge."

"We thought we should let you know," Aislin said, "that there's a chance you won't get a totally warm welcome if you go back there."

Kate glanced at Venn, whose frown was tainted with regret. If the town had grown more hostile, a dozen problems could easily crop up. "Maybe we should..." Kate's words trailed off. What was there to do?

"Twig," Tribal said, "before you decide to go take on some responsibility that's barely yours, the steel is molten."

Kate dragged her thoughts back to the room. "Right." She pushed herself out of her chair. "Where's the dragon scale?"

"Over here." Tribal hooked a foot under a chair on the far side of the table and pulled it next to his at the forge. Kate dropped into it—and into a wall of heat. On the floor by Tribal's feet sat the chip of dark green scale. The firelight sent ripples over the surface, like slivers of the deepest blue of twilight infused with a million minuscule stars.

The moment her fingers touched it, the vast, ponderous remnant unfolded around her. Caverns of stone winding through the earth, unchanging and unrelenting.

Near the mouth of the forge, the stone crucible held a pool of molten steel. It blazed with reds and yellows like liquid fire.

"You'll want this." Tribal nudged a thick leather glove with his foot.

It was stiff, and while the fingers weren't overly long, they were so wide that she put two fingers into the first slot. She pinched the scale between those and her thumb and held it over the crucible. Heat poured off the melted steel, pressing hot against her arm where the glove ended, but the thick leather felt merely warm. She focused on the scale. It didn't hold *vitalle* like a living thing, or like the blazing fire in the forge, but there was something similar to *vitalle*. Some essence that contained the magic that made the scale nearly indestructible. A permanent, non-living—but still powerful—magic existing in a complex structure of nodes. Keeping her ungloved hand back from the heat, she sent out a tendril of *vitalle* and scraped it over the scale. A shower of deep blue nodes sprinkled down into the steel.

Tribal studied the scale. "Nothing is happening."

"Nothing that you can see," Kate said. "You stick to smelting, and I'll stick to magic. This is going to take some time."

"How long? The metal will cool and—"

"Then you may have to heat it again." Kate cast out and found nodes of the dragon scale sinking into the metal. "It could take an hour, could take three."

"All right." Tribal resituated himself on his chair. "Lots of time to plan, then."

Kate spared him a glance.

A smile quirked up the edge of his mouth. "When are we going to get back into that emperor's carriage?"

Kate let out a breath and ran her finger over the dragon scale. "That's hardly a priority."

"Maybe not *your* priority, but Silas and I are very much in need of some treasure. There was a lot of gold in there. You could smell it. We need that treasure, and you owe us."

"For what?" Venn asked.

"Saving your lives," Tribal answered. "Repeatedly."

Kate paused in scraping the scale. "We literally just saved your lives. Or have you already forgotten the vines?"

"Is there any limit to your greed?" Venn asked, turning to a new page in her book.

"We're offended," Silas said, his voice still remarkably carefree. "This isn't about greed. We just need a little mood-improving gift for the gov'nor before we can go home."

"What exactly did you do in Rullduin?" Kate asked.

"It's not about that," Silas said. "He's mad about a little misunderstanding with Tribal from years ago." He waved away her next question. "Just a dwarvish thing. Nothing a bit of gold won't smooth over."

The whoosh of Tribal's bellows faltered the slightest bit, but he kept his focus on the flames.

"I'm guessing it's not that little of a misunderstanding," Kate said.

Tribal winced. "Well, the amount of treasure in that carriage is also 'not that little,' so everything will be fine." His words sounded confident, but there was a tightness in his shoulders. He nodded his chin toward the dragon scale. "Can we continue now?"

The scale looked exactly the same as when they'd began, and when Kate cast out toward it, the millions of nodes that lined up within it were only disturbed in a few places on the surface where she'd scraped a few hundred away. Inside the molten steel, the nodes were spreading out. Already it held nearly as much dragon scale as the dwarves' stonesteel knives. "I think it's almost done."

"Really?" Tribal leaned closer to the molten metal, his face bright with excitement.

"I can do a little more." She began to brush *vitalle* against it again, knocking more nodes loose.

"Aislin and Matlen," Venn said, her voice firm. "I need you to go back to the lakes." She raised her hand to stop their objections. "It's not a punishment. The relationship between the lakes and the White Wood is going to be strained once they find out what's been going on with Naevys and Thallion. I need Evay to understand what's happened. You don't have to tell anyone else—she'll take care of that—but I need you to find her and tell her."

Aislin opened her mouth to object, but Venn spoke again. "I'm not joking. This is not a game. I'm giving you a serious job." Matlen straightened. "Find Evay before Faron or anyone from the White Wood gets to the lakes, and tell her everything you know." She gave her niece and nephew a stern look. "Don't make me regret giving you something important to do."

"Before you go," Silas said, "I need some measurements of your skinny elf hands. Don't want to make your stonesteel blade too unwieldy."

The elf twins huddled around him. And Kate returned to the dragon scale.

"When we get into the carriage," Silas said, "I'm sure there'll be something to decorate the hilt with. There were all sorts of gems in there."

"The treasure in the emperor's carriage will have to wait,"

Kate said. "First we need to find Naevys. Venn, we need to enlist the help of some elves."

"We're elves," Aislin said.

"No," Kate said at the same moment as Venn.

"You already have a job," Venn said pointedly.

"The mad queen is a bit dangerous," Silas agreed. "Best if you two niblings sit this one out."

The elf twins shared a sigh but, after some forlorn waves, headed out the door.

There was a moment's silence.

"Kate?" Venn tilted her head toward the door.

Kate cast out, and the two elf twins blazed into light in the tunnel, just past the door.

Aislin gave a nervous giggle.

"All the way home," Venn said.

With a puff of bright *vitalle* in the tunnel, the two disappeared.

"What we need," Kate said, "is someone who can still talk to the trees. Do you think Evay would come back here?"

There was a rustle near the back door, and Venn shot to her feet, her crossbow raised.

Kate spun, a shock of alarm ran through her. The hint of an elven remnant wafted in, and she clenched her hand around the dragon scale.

A longing to be back in the Stronghold—somewhere actually protected—rose in her again as Faron stepped through the doorway.

He took in the dwarves' axes and Venn's crossbow and raised his hands. "I can talk to trees."

CHAPTER SEVEN

Venn kept her crossbow raised. "Get out."

Large clumps of snowflakes melted on Faron's head and the shoulders of a thick fur-lined cloak. His skin was flushed with a coppery warmth, almost too bright just to be from the torchlight, and his russet hair was threaded through with a brighter red like glowing coals.

"I come in peace, Venn." He glanced around the room, his attention snagging for a moment on the work near the forge.

Kate set the dragon scale down, and he gave her a smile that was almost a wince.

"Hello, Kate. Everything good with the...arrow..." He gestured to his own chest, the shadow of the alarm and outrage he'd shown when Thallion had ordered the shot still in his face.

The memory of the arrow slamming into her sent a phantom pain deep into her chest, and she stood, taking in a deep breath to banish it. She could see Faron's face leaning close. His fear. She could feel him tearing out of the arrow, the gaping hole left behind, and the rich warmth of his healing that rushed in to fill it.

"It's completely healed." She stepped up next to Venn. "Thank you."

Venn's arm dipped slightly, but she raised it again.

The nod he gave her was awkward and self-conscious, but at his core, he stood straighter than he had before. The likable confidence that he'd shown at times, the ease he'd always struggled to hold, seemed closer to the surface now. But he was still the elf who had viciously attacked her and Venn in these same caverns, when any conflict he'd felt had been quickly overcome by obedience to his father.

She shoved away the complicated feelings.

His remnant floated around him in a mist of vivid, glittering yellow-gold. Brighter than his mother's. More noonday sun than her dusky gold. The citrusy resin scent of pine sap and the open, crystal-clear expanse of mountain skies flowed out of him.

It was stronger than before. Bolder. And…different.

The power of his elven authority was clearly visible. Where Thallion's had stabbed out from him like insect legs, Faron's remnant reached out in thin tendrils like strands of spider web caught in a breeze.

Kate glanced down at Venn's ankle. The dark green shackle of Thallion's authority had disappeared last night in the Elder Grove when the White Wood had stripped him of his authority, but now a slim one of yellow-gold encircled her leg like a chain.

She looked back at the elven king, trying to figure out what else looked different about him. His eyes were shadowed, and his cheeks looked a little gaunt. But it was more than that.

"You look awful, Your Majesty." Silas gave him a smug smile. "Had a rough time of it lately?"

Faron's jaw clenched, but he kept his attention on Venn and Kate. "I'm sure you two are still looking for that box, and I'm willing to help, but I need your help in return."

Kate tensed at the idea of being dragged back into elven problems.

"No." Venn kept the crossbow raised.

"Venn, my father's authority is gone." Despite his exhaustion, there was a spark in his eyes. An eagerness. "This is our chance. We can do the things we always wanted to—"

"No," Venn repeated.

"C'mon, Venn," he said, a note of impatience creeping into his voice. "If you were going to shoot me, you'd have done it by now."

"Maybe I'm savoring the moment."

Kate set a hand on Venn's arm, wariness warring with hope. "Wait, how would you help us? Do you know where your mother is?"

He lowered his hands slightly. When Venn didn't shoot, he dropped them to his sides. "I don't," he began, "but—"

"Of course he doesn't," Venn interrupted. "That's why Thallion had to drag us into the search."

"I couldn't find her then," Faron said, "but I was trapped under my father, only able to do what he wanted. Now I can truly help you. But, Venn, the situation with the lake elves is…delicate. I need to explain what happened with my father and mother—"

"That he got his crown ripped away by the woods, and she's a violent loon?" Silas asked.

Faron gave the dwarf an irritated look.

"No," Venn said, "he needs to explain why he and his father lied to them about Naevys."

A flicker of frustration crossed Faron's face, but he forced out a nod.

Venn dropped her arm. "Good luck. They'll be right to be mad."

"I know, and I want to work toward peace and unity. I'm willing to confess to what my father and I did, but…" He took a step forward. "I need to find a way to rebuild trust after all this comes out. They trust you, Venn. They like you. Come help me explain all this."

Venn shook her head, and Faron addressed Kate. "I need your help too. Humans were hurt during the altercation along the river with the fake diamonds."

Kate's guilt returned. "I heard."

He took in everyone in the cave. "That was your doing." He raised his hands to ward off the objections that both dwarves let out. "I understand why you did it, and it worked to get my father out of the White Wood, but it's also part of our current mess. Will you come with me to Home? Help explain to them what happened?"

The responsibility nagged at Kate, and she shifted her shoulders under it.

He gave an aggravated sigh. "They're not going to listen to me explain that my father was corrupt and that none of us dared to disobey him."

"You think they'll listen to us?" Venn asked.

"Maybe. You two healed the men the wellstone damaged. The town trusts you."

"Because we've tried to help them," Venn said. "You lied to them about what you knew, who you were, and what you were doing. You *knew* Naevys was missing and that she had something to do with the ravine, yet you said nothing. In fact, you hurt humans to find her."

"My father was *killing* humans!" The threads of his remnant stretching out into the room brightened and grew. "I stopped that! Do you have any idea what I was working against, Venn? Any idea of the authority my father had over me?"

"Yes," Venn said, her voice cold. "I was under it too."

Kate took in Faron's remnant again. "*That's* what is different! It's gone!"

"What's gone?" Faron snapped, his voice rough with anger.

A wave of sympathy for him rolled across Kate. "I thought your remnant was lighter, but it's just that the dark green of his is gone. In the Elder Grove, his authority was…" She turned back to Venn. "The authority covered him. Not with individual strands. It was…everywhere. He was drenched in it. His entire remnant looked darker."

Fix and Crofftus both crouched perfectly still on the table. Tribal kept a black look locked on the king, even as he worked the billows slowly, but Silas's expression loosened from a glare to something more probing.

Faron's attention stayed fixed on Venn. She crossed her arms across her chest and shook her head, the action so tight it was almost a twitch. A jaggedness filled her eyes. "You left me to die."

He held his hands up again. "No, I knew Kate could heal you—"

"You did not!" Venn hissed. "You knew barely anything about Kate, and yet you *cut my tattoo*!"

"Do you think I wanted to?" He strode toward her, flinging an arm out to grab her.

Venn swung her crossbow up, and Kate yanked the flame out of the nearest lantern, pulling it into her palm and feeding *vitalle* into it until it blazed up like a torch.

The whoosh of the bellows stopped.

"It doesn't matter what you *wanted*!" Venn's arm trembled. "It matters what you *did*!"

He froze, his face angry and guilt-ridden and imploring.

"I think you should leave, Faron," Kate said. *Vitalle* tingled through her palm until it blazed like a torch.

A scrape sounded as Silas pushed his chair up. "They've both told you to leave, now." He pulled his axe from his belt. Faron opened his mouth, but Silas raised his axe. "I don't care if you're king of the world. If you try to use that authority of yours to command Venn to do anything, we'll see how well you heal from multiple axe wounds."

Tribal stood at Kate's shoulder, his own axe in his hand. "One almost did you in last time you crossed us, and I doubt Twig will heal you this time."

Faron's hands curled into fists, and with obvious effort, he pulled the strands of his authority back to himself. "I'm not going to command anyone," he said through clenched teeth. He brought his gaze back to Venn, a hint of pleading in them. "I'm not my father, Venn." The words came out so low Kate had to strain to hear them. "You know that."

Venn's shoulders rose and fell with fast, furious breaths, but she kept her crossbow trained on him. "There was a time when I believed that was true."

A flash of something Kate couldn't quite name crossed Faron's face, and she stepped forward, drawing his attention. Her palm burned with the effort of keeping the flame lit, but she kept *vitalle* moving into it and held it toward him.

He schooled his features back to a barely controlled fury and faced Kate. "You're a Keeper. You're really just going to leave the White Wood and the humans to struggle, knowing you were part of the cause and knowing it's very close to dissolving into fighting—when you could help stop it?"

Kate felt another pang of guilt. If the humans decided to fight the elves, there'd be more than broken bones and a head injury. This was exactly the sort of situation a Keeper would try to de-escalate. Of course, it was the sort of situation a Keeper shouldn't have helped escalate in the first place. She let the fire shrink in her palm.

Faron looked back at Venn. "And you're willing to just let a rift grow between the lakes and the White Wood?"

Kate glanced over her shoulder and found Venn's crossbow trembling.

Katria, Crofftus's voice said, loudly enough that Faron flinched. *This is ready to test.*

On the table, the vial was filled with a thick, still liquid that shimmered with a silvery sheen. The anticipation that the wellstone tincture might work drove away the lingering pressure to help with the political turmoil the former elf king had caused.

"I'm sorry," Kate said to Faron, "but we have our own problems. Good luck with yours."

He grabbed Kate's forearm. His grip was tight, and the firelight cast his skin in rich copper shimmers. "You can't—"

Venn shoved her fist against Faron's chest, the dart in her crossbow only inches from him. "Let go."

Faron's eyes flickered between the two of them, frustration simmering in them like a cauldron about to boil over. He leaned against Venn's fist. "What is so important here that you'll turn your back on everything you used to love?"

Venn held his gaze. "I need to find Bo."

Dark, ugly jealousy crept into the edges of his face, and he struggled to control himself. "Then why are you still betrothed to me?"

Venn let out a grim breath that was almost a laugh. "Not out of any fondness. You tore away the last of that."

He looked at the air around Venn, tracing something Kate couldn't see. He blew out a low laugh more self-mocking than humorous. "It's keeping you connected to the Wood."

Kate glanced up at Venn, but she didn't appear surprised. "That's why you're better off than Ayen?"

Venn didn't answer, but Faron's eyes narrowed. "How bad is Ayen?"

"You can end the betrothal at any time," Venn said, ignoring his question, "if you want to complete the work your mother started."

Faron let go of Kate. "Sorry, Venn. I can't manage to shake that fondness as easily as you."

Venn dropped her arm. "You have an odd way of showing it."

Kate flicked her fingers, quenching the fire in her palm. "We have work to do, Faron, and you don't have anything to offer that can help us in that work. You know the way out."

He stared at the two of them, disbelief warring with vexation. "I didn't realize I'd have to bribe the two you to do the right thing." He turned and strode toward the door. When he reached it, he paused. "If either of you decide to set aside your obsession and pay attention to what the world actually needs of you," he said, the words cutting into Kate with another jab of guilt, "come find me." He disappeared in a gust of *vitalle*.

The weight of responsibility lingered around Kate, and the image of Home burning floated to the surface of her mind.

Katria, Crofftus said. *We should test this.*

She pushed away the troubles of the world outside. "Right, make the solos potion to find Naevys," she said. "And find the box."

Venn kept her eyes on the floor where Faron had stood, but she nodded. "Find Naevys, find the box."

CHAPTER EIGHT

Kate sat at the table, rubbing her palm where her skin still tingled from holding the fire.

The wellstone tincture resembled her old tenea serum somehow. It was thicker and more uniformly silver. There were no glitters of light from the individual particles of the wellstones, but somehow it reminded her of the first time she'd succeeded at making the tenea serum. Maybe it was merely the way it captured the light, holding it with more tenacity than most liquids.

She needed a memory. Faron's face came to mind. It was tremendously different than it had been. She glanced at Venn, who frowned, unseeing, at the table.

Kate dipped her finger into the vial, pressing a tiny bit of the memory into it.

A faint blur of light emanated from her fingertip, cloudy and silver. Ill-defined, like a line of smoke instead of the strands of moonlight that had floated in the tenea serum.

She pulled her finger out, and the hazy line sat still in the vial. Not swirling, not rising, not falling.

Kate wiped off her finger and set it into the fluid again.

Nothing happened.

The memory merely floated, unmoving.

She trickled *vitalle* into the liquid, and the silver sheen brightened. Sending the *vitalle* to the start of the strand of memory, lower down in the vial, she grabbed at it and pulled it toward the surface. With slow, sluggish movement, the memory twisted and rose until it touched her fingertip.

She closed her eyes.

Faron appeared amidst the shining specks of light in the Elder Grove. Whispers from the trees filled the air. The pressure of the Warden's *valoryl* power surged past Kate like a thundering river, her fear sharp enough to taste.

The memory ended, and her eyes flew open.

Does it work? Crofftus's voice was torn between eagerness and nerves.

It wasn't as clear as a memory from the tenea serum. This had a haziness, as though she were looking through clouded glass, but the sounds and feel and emotions of it were stronger. Kate let a smile spread across her lips. "It works." She turned to Venn. "Want to see a memory?"

Venn blinked at her but nodded, her silence feeling heavy.

Kate pulled the memory from the Elder Grove back into her mind, piecing a few parts together. She set her finger into the vial.

> *Venn lay on the ground of the Elder Grove, the floating lights shimmering around her, the river of valoryl turning away from her and rushing toward Ayen. She stared forward, unseeing, greenish light pooling in her eyes. A thick strand of Thallion's authority was wound around her leg.*
>
> *Faron tilted his head toward Kate. "Did she want this?" he asked, his voice pitched below the chaos.*

Kate gritted her teeth against the pressure of the valoryl and shook her head. Faron's expression filled with fury.

"Will you help her?" Kate gasped. "I can stop this, but I need you to move her away from the queen when she's free. I don't think she can move herself."

Faron turned haunted eyes to Kate. "I can't."

The strands of Thallion's authority locked around Faron's chest and arms, wrapped around his neck, and pulled tight against his skin.

Tendrils crawled up and dug into his ears.

Strands of green wrapped tightly around Faron's wrists and encased each finger.

"If you ever loved her," Kate said, "take her away from me when I say."

The memory faded, and Kate pushed out the next piece.

Venn slumped lower, all the power of the valoryl gone from her body.

"Faron," Kate whispered. "Now!"

Dimly, she was aware of the prince leaning forward, his face clenched in concentration. His arms moved slowly, as though he were fighting a great weight. He slipped them under Venn's shoulders and knees and pulled her into his lap.

Thallion flung a command to stop, and Faron shuddered to a halt.

After another short break, Kate added the final part.

Thallion reached for Venn's arm. "It is my choice! I have commanded it!"

Faron twisted her away. Thallion's words rang through the Grove, and the band of green light around Kate's chest shattered.

Across the Elder Grove, every claw of Thallion's authority burst out in shards of dark green that fell among the whirling lights, winking out before they hit the earth.

Every elf in the Grove flinched.

An explosion of green shot out from Faron, and his gold remnant flared brightly. The twisting bonds around Venn fell away.

Faron stood, holding Venn and backing away from Kate and the queen.

"Stop!" Thallion shouted, shoving himself to his feet and lunging after his son.

Faron hugged Venn to his chest and pulled back.

Kate pulled her finger out of the vial, leaving the long, hazy string of the memory inside. She handed it to Venn. "After what Faron did to you, it's natural, and probably right, to never truly trust him again. But there's a lot of space between hating him and marrying him. It might be interesting to see what sort of king he makes now that he doesn't have this. Even though I'd be perfectly happy to see all that from a great distance so I don't get dragged into any more of his White Wood trouble."

Venn's eyes narrowed, but she dipped her fingertip in.

"Pull the thread toward you with *ael'iza*," Kate said.

The thread of memory moved toward her finger. She closed her eyes and stilled.

The crease in Venn's brow deepened. When she looked up, there was an edge of horror in her face.

"It doesn't excuse the choices he's made," Kate said, "and I'm sure it grew to that level because he obeyed his father a thousand times when he should have pushed back, but I thought you should see what it was like for him."

Venn handed the vial back slowly. "That was..." She rubbed the liquid off her finger, her gaze locked on the shimmering fluid. She cleared her throat. "It looks murkier than the old serum, but I could feel the Grove and your fear and resolve." She paused. "Will it be enough for your solos potion?"

"I think so." Kate turned back to Crofftus. "What do we need to get that started?"

We've already assembled the items. Crofftus hopped over to a collection of bottles and little bowls. *Fix, we'll need the wide-bottomed flask set up over the candle. Maybe two candles.*

Fix hesitated just a moment before climbing up onto the table and sorting through the glassware.

Kate went to her pack and pulled the vial of remnant amplifier out of it.

"A potion that lets you see the memories from objects," Silas said. "Think anyone will be able to see them? Because I can think of a few uses for that."

"Let's hope the gov'nor never gets ahold of any," Tribal said with a grin. "He would not be amused by where we took that seal of his that one night."

Silas chuckled. "No, he would not. But his shoes could tell us where he hid that secret stash of his."

We will put it to better use than assisting your thieving, Crofftus sniffed.

"You say better," Tribal said. "We say more boring."

"No, it's better." Kate gestured to the thin ring of vines. "Like seeing everything Naevys did until she took that ring off—hopefully including where she put the box."

Crofftus stilled. *Did she have that ring in the Elder Grove?*

Kate paused. "No, but it's the only lead I have, and so as soon as we have the solos potion, I'm going to learn everything it can tell me."

You realize this is going to take some time to finish, and unless we get it right the first time, we'll have to redo all the—

"Then we should hurry." Kate sat next to the vial. "First, we'll stabilize the remnant amplifier so it will finally not decay when light hits it."

When Crofftus still hesitated, she glanced around the room. "Is there some reason we need to wait?"

No. The rabbit sat low on the table again, looking nervous. *But Katria, you're rushing through the steps of brand-new research. We should slow down, do it right. We need to write out the—*

"Crofftus!" She pulled the cover off the remnant amplifier. "I'll write it out later. Right now, we work."

CHAPTER NINE

Kate dribbled another few drops of her newly stabilized remnant amplifier into the flask of wellstone tincture. The liquid in the bottom simmered with a translucent silver that was slowly gaining a blue tint that looked remarkably like Kate had always imagined the solos potion to look.

"How will you know when it's done?" Silas asked.

"I have no idea." Kate wrapped her sky-blue remnant amplifier back into its scarf and pulled a little dropper off the table. "Let's see what this does."

The dwarves and Venn turned to watch her. Fix's nimble fingers stopped moving, and he set down the scraps of warm material he'd been given by the rest of them—a glove with a hole from Kate, a torn hat from Silas, a scarf from Venn. Over the past couple hours, the bits of fabric had been slowly transforming into a patchwork cloak that was perfectly gnoblin-sized.

She drew a single drop of the solos potion out and brought it close to one of the books Naevys had been reading. The Warden's golden remnant was smudged across the page alongside hints of Venn's green one and Kate's own auburn shimmers.

Not on a book! Crofftus protested.

Kate paused, but the possibility was too much to let go. "It's just a drop."

She let it fall in the midst of all three.

A haze of remnants rose from the book. Naevys's gold ballooned out with streaks of Venn's and Kate's. A barrage of scents and sounds rolled over Kate. Rustling pine boughs, burbling streams, the chirp of birds. Kate leaned closer, wading into the remnants, sorting out the smell of her own—wheat fields along the river—diving down until she heard something else.

A crackling fire set against the backdrop of a rushing river. Deep in the crease, a speck of dark blue glittered.

"What's happening?" Silas asked, straining forward to see over the table. "What do you see?"

Venn came closer. "A sort of mist."

Kate glanced at her. "You can see the remnants?"

"Only vaguely."

Something flashed inside the haze. Kate stretched her fingers out and brushed them through the edge of the cloud.

The cavern around her was swallowed up by a cacophony of forest sounds crashing into her ears. The resin scent of pines, sharp and citrusy, flooded her nose, so strong she could taste it. The jagged edge of maple leaves dragged across her skin. Jumbled voices pressed against her. Dizzying fragments of images slammed into each other, through each other, overlaid in a chaos of motion and sound and impressions.

Kate yanked her hand out of the glittering remnants, and the clamor cut off abruptly.

She shoved her chair back as a wave of dizziness hit her. Every inch of her skin tingled at the sudden void around her.

It worked? Crofftus asked.

Everyone in the room fixed Kate with expectant looks.

"It..." Kate shook her head to chase away the dizziness. The open book still held a thinning cloud of remnants, but she slid it farther away from herself. "It did…a lot. Let me try something with just one remnant." Every book in front of her shimmered with multiple colors. She glanced over the table at Fix. "Could you hand me a vial that no one's touched yet?"

The little gnoblin picked up a small bit of glasswork from the back of the worktable and brought it over to Kate. She reached for it just as Crofftus hopped closer, and Fix flinched at the two motions.

"Sorry." With a pang at his jumpiness, Kate pulled her hand back. She offered him a smile. "Could you just set it down?"

He did, leaving only a smudge of his delicate yellow remnant on it as he crept back. Kate got a new drop out of the flask and dripped it onto the sparkles.

The yellow haze that rose from the glass was fainter and smaller than Naevys's had been, spreading in a pale mist that stayed within a handbreadth of the surface. Kate stretched her fingers into it. A slightly hazy image filled her vision, accompanied by crystal-clear sounds.

> *Glass clinked loudly. Fix's long, knobby green fingers picked up the vial. He brought it toward her, a simmering worry sitting in his gut. Her face was hopeful, expectant. She reached forward and Crofftus hopped closer, and a spike of fear mixed with confusion jabbed into his chest. He twitched. Sympathy creased Kate's brow for just a moment before she drew back her hand and offered him a smile. "Sorry. Could you just set it down?"*
>
> *He kept his focus on that smile, trying to rein in the hammering of his heart, and set the vial down on the table.*

The moment Fix's fingers left the vial, the memory ended and the cloud of yellow glimmers faded away.

Fix crouched at the corner of the table again, his arms tight to his sides, his eyes locked on Kate with a sort of desperation. She slid out of her chair and knelt next to him. "It's all right, Fix. You're safe here with us."

He twitched slightly at the words.

She held out her hand, and slowly, he took it, gripping her fingers tightly. "I'm glad you're here with us, but if you want to leave, if you want to go back to more quiet parts of the forest where no elves appear out of thin air, angry and threatening, I would miss you, but I would understand."

He gripped her fingers harder and shook his head with a quick motion. The fingers of his other hand flickered a few signs. *Stay with Kate.*

She smiled at him. "It does feel like you belong with us."

The hint of a smile curved up his mouth, but he stayed huddled on the table. Kate squeezed his fingers then moved back to her seat, catching the others in the cavern watching with varying degrees of curiosity. She let her smile widen. "It works. The memory looks a little hazy, but I could hear everything and even feel what Fix was feeling." She gestured at the book she'd first tried. "If there's more than one remnant, the memories come all at once, layered on top of each other, but with just one..." She looked over the books on the table again. Every one of them had multiple remnants on them. Naevys's, Venn's, a paw print from Crofftus, a smudge from a dwarf. Kate's own remnant glittered in warm red over nearly every single one.

Kate reached for Naevys's ring.

Katria! Crofftus sputtered. *At least don't rush this! Try it several times on something else! What if it damages the only lead you have!*

A surge of irritation rose at the idea of the delay, but Kate glanced back at the vial Fix had brought over. The solos potion had washed any traces of yellow remnant away. "It does seem to use up the remnant."

On the open book, where she'd dropped the potion, the

remnants were also severely faded. Kate's and Venn's were barely visible, and the glint of deep blue from the crease was entirely gone—

Kate leaned closer to the book, looking for more of it.

It was a *new* remnant.

Old, and set deep into the crease of the book...

She spun to look around the room, searching for a volume not covered in Naevys's remnant.

Against the wall, the queen had spilled a handful of books onto the floor, and Kate rushed over to pick up one titled in Renault's hand. Keeping her fingers along the edges of the pages, she flipped through it until she found a page that held a faded sketch of the elven wood. A handful of paths were drawn through it, all leading to an arch in the corner.

In the crease was the faintest trace of midnight blue.

She brought it to the table and set it down. "I think I found Renault's remnant." Keeping her fingers off the page, she let one drop of the solos potion fall onto one of the glimmers. Blue mist rose quickly. Kate dipped her fingers into it, and the cavern around her disappeared.

The crackling of the fire returned, accompanied by the rushing of a river.

> *A man's hands held the book open as he finished the map of the elven wood. The ink was crisp. The room around him was quiet and too steeped in darkness to make out. His table was cluttered with papers and pens. A handful of candles illuminated the page.*
>
> *A sense of resolution filled him. He drew a cluster of trees, and an edge of something like regret rose in him. For a moment, his quill hesitated, but he drew in a deep breath, and the resolve strengthened, crowding the pang of self-reproach to the very edges.*

Kate studied the memory for a moment. It felt a bit like the memories in the Wellstone at the Keeper Stronghold. The thought sent another jab of homesickness through her, but she focused on Renault's book. Even though she could only see one moment of it, it felt like she was moving along the path of it, moving from Renault's past to his future. She stretched out a tendril of *vitalle* and pulled the memory along faster. Renault's drawing sped up.

With a quickened sigh, he closed the book, and the memory cut off.

Kate blinked at the cavern around her as the blue mist dissipated. She quickly dripped potion onto one of the other two specks.

The cloud of blue rose.

"Venn, look at this." Kate set her fingers into it, and Venn did the same.

This memory showed Renault's hands beginning the map. The room he worked in was dark again, except for the circle of candlelight on his desk. His quill scratched over the paper as he worked diligently, adding details and names to the forest, until once again, he closed the book.

Venn pulled her hand back, blinking at the bright library around them. "That…" She looked at Kate. "That was really Renault?"

"It's a man writing in his book, with his handwriting. Although…" Kate paused. "This remnant sounds like a campfire near a river. I've always thought Renault's remnant sounded like the bell I can always hear in the box."

What did you see? Crofftus asked, his voice sharp with impatience.

"Renault drawing the map on this page." Kate pointed to it without touching it, trying to keep her own remnant away.

"What does the mad half-elf look like?" Silas asked curiously.

"It's his memory," Kate said. "So it's from his eyes. His hands look like a normal man's hands. More human than elven." A surge of excitement rose in her, and she couldn't stop the smile that crossed her lips. "Crofftus, it works!"

The first two specks of remnant were gone. Kate dripped some potion onto the third, and a brighter cloud surged out of it. Venn's fingers slid into it next to Kate's.

Renault's hands held the book open, its page half covered with the map of the elven wood, the rest still blank. Restlessness churned inside him. The gnawing tension of too many unanswered questions.

Kate drew in a breath at the familiar feeling.

"How much will it take?" his voice muttered. He carefully drew a line from a stand of trees to the small, precisely drawn archway in the corner.

"Certainly less than the Wood holds," a woman's voice said from over his shoulder.

Naevys stood there, peering down at the book. Her face was younger, brighter. The rich copper of her skin shimmered in the candlelight that lit the cluttered room around them. Bookshelves were placed along the wooden wall behind her, packed with books and apparatuses and scrolls. Her auburn hair hung over her shoulder in long strands that almost glowed, and she watched with sharp interest.

His eyes lingered on her face for a moment, a spark of something too complicated to unravel rising up in him. Wariness replaced it, and he returned his focus to the book. "Maybe not much less."

Naevys moved next to him, leaning on the table. Her long hair brushed the edge of the book as she drew close. "Will it really require so much?"

A dart of the tangle of emotions stabbed into him again, switching swiftly to anger, although directed more at himself than her. "I don't care if it requires the entire world," he hissed, dropping his quill to the table. "I will do what I must."

The book slammed shut.

Kate sank back in her chair, Venn's frown mirroring her own.

"Naevys knew he wanted to steal power from the White Wood," Venn said slowly. "She knew the paths he would use. All those years she was supposedly fighting off that very thing."

Kate stared at the bottom corner of the map. "Where does this arch lead?" She carefully flipped to the next page in Renault's book, but there was nothing else about it. "We already know how much power the Runelight Drawer took to make. It took the lives of a lot of gnomes and a decent amount of power, but…" She turned back to the map of the White Wood. "Not this. And he drained the Wood after he made the box."

Maybe, Crofftus said, *the aenigma box is more than you think it is.*

A burst of *vitalle* blew in the back door of the library, and Faron stepped inside.

Kate shoved herself to her feet along with Venn and the dwarves.

"We really need a way to close that door!" Kate said through clenched teeth.

Faron merely held out his hand. "Is this enough of a bribe to get your help?"

Grasped in his long copper fingers was the aenigma box.

CHAPTER TEN

K ate rushed toward Faron, wanting to tear his fingers off the age-worn wood, but he held the box out willingly.

Amidst the light gold of Faron's remnant, the box itself was wreathed in shimmering lights. Glitters of greens and a dusky orange. A flash of blue. A hint of a deep violet.

She grabbed it and backed away, letting the sense of vastness emanating from it wrap around her. The spicy scent drove into her nose and chilled her lungs, and somewhere unimaginably distant, a bell tolled, haunting and mournful.

She cradled it against her chest, turning away from him, squeezing her hands until the corners bit into her fingers, just to prove it was real. The low hum seeped into her. It held a warmth like firesides and safety and *home*. Bands of tension around her chest loosened, and she drew in a breath deep enough to stretch her ribs.

The nails studding the metal straps along the edges glinted from their pitted, dinged surfaces. She ran her thumb over the runes carved into the lid, dribbling *vitalle* into them without meaning to. Threads of light followed the carvings, drawing out the now familiar runes.

The king brought to his knees.

The failing battlements.

The tangle of hope and despair and the endless, endless waiting.

"You were that king," she whispered, picturing Renault's hands writing his journals. His endless searching for a way to save his daughter.

Venn's hand touched her back. "Kate?"

Kate flinched, realizing she was hunched over the box. She straightened slowly but kept the box close to her chest.

"Is it all right?" Venn asked.

Kate pulled her eyes away from the runes. "It seems to be."

Venn shoulders relaxed as she faced Faron. "How do you have it?"

"I just found it," Faron said. "I was starting toward the lakes when I caught a sense of my mother and followed it to a clearing. There was no sign of her, but the box was sitting on the ground. The trees told me she'd come there, set the box down, then wandered for a few minutes."

The room stared at him.

"It was just…sitting on the ground?" Kate asked.

Faron nodded.

Kate held the box forward. "This box? The one Naevys wanted for centuries?"

He grimaced, his face troubled. "She was speaking nonsense."

"Like what?" Kate asked. "Things about the box?"

He shook his head. "She was muttering, 'Can't leave. Can't. Could be like him. Need it!'" He paused. "And, 'Hate him.'"

"Hates who?" Venn asked, some of the hardness going out of her voice.

"I don't know. And I couldn't follow her past there. The trees wouldn't tell me where she'd gone."

He continued talking, but Kate studied the box. The question of why Naevys would leave it grated at her mind, but the wave of relief at holding it again was so strong she felt dizzy. She pushed away questions she couldn't answer and took it to the table, studying every surface.

It felt warm against her skin, and she closed her eyes. Something stirred inside her.

A longing.

A brightness just out of reach.

There was a sense...

Something she couldn't see, exactly, but a sense. It emanated from the box itself, calling her forward like a lantern shining silver with moonlight, beckoning to her from the end of a long, dark tunnel.

Hope.

It was hope.

The image blazed up, painfully strong, like a shared memory or a new doorway opening in her mind.

Her fingers tightened. The box was actually here. Not lost to violent foreigners or taken by elves. It was *here*. Safe.

The silvery light of hope was too far away, though, down a tunnel like the dwarven passages in Rullduin. Narrow, dark, and winding.

Kate focused on the lantern.

It was out of reach, but within sight. All she needed was the bloodstone, and she could open the drawer. That would take a few days to create, but for now, having the box was enough.

Her fingernail caught on the metal edging, and the truth of her situation came into focus.

Her eyes flew open.

She had the box—and she had the solos potion.

Leaning closer, she studied every surface, ignoring the ongoing conversation between Venn and Faron.

Faron's light gold remnant was smudged along the sides where he'd held it, and Naevys's darker gold covered more of the surface, as though she'd gripped the box as tightly as Kate.

The thought made her pause. Why would Naevys just leave it in a clearing?

But the shimmer of remnants pulled her attention back to the box.

Remnants.

There were no other recent ones easily visible, so she unwrapped her remnant amplifier again. Carefully, she dripped some of the liquid on the lid. Naevys's and Faron's remnants burst out strongly, but underneath them, emanating from protected gaps beneath a lip of the metal or deep in the runes, other lights glittered. Kate's own red covered most of it, but there, just at the corner, tucked under the edge of a nail, was the blue of a clear summer sky. She focused on it until she found a hint of the wind that blustered over the southern hills in the late golden days of summer.

The smell of Bo's remnant sent a pang through her chest. The morning that had started everything came back to her. The spring day, the red flag flapping above the mine entrance, the two foreigners in Kalesh tunics. Bo collapsed near the end of the bridge, and Evan lunging for the box.

The Kalesh man in his blood-red tunic chanting words of power and opening the Runelight Drawer.

Evan had definitely grabbed the box, but after twenty years, there'd be no sign of him even in the sheltered space beneath the metal straps.

She studied the worn wooden front. There were no cracks, no signs that any drawers could possibly open.

Except one *had* opened. If the Runelight Drawer was anchored to the lower half of the front of the box, then maybe…

Faron's voice grew more frustrated, and Silas interjected something glib, but Kate ignored them all.

She dripped some remnant amplifier along where the side of the drawer should be. Naevys's and Faron's remnants rushed at her, but she ignored them, looking deeper.

A glint of sky blue glittered from what looked like just under the surface of the wood. There, next to it, was a fiery orange speck so minuscule she could barely make it out. The faint scent of pines after the rain wafted past, tangled in the elves' stronger remnants, and Kate sucked in a gasp of air.

The voices around her cut off.

Venn came up beside her. "What's wrong?"

"I found Evan's remnant," Kate whispered, barely able to believe there was any left after all this time. "I think it's caught where the opening of the Runelight Drawer should be."

Venn sank into the seat next to her. "And Bo?"

"He's there too." Kate pulled the damp sleeve of her cloak up from where it hung on the chair behind her, wiping off the traces of Naevys's remnant on the surface. The gold remnant cleared mostly away, while the bit of orange hovered just under the surface.

Kate took the dropper and pulled a single drop of the solos potion out of the vial. She let it fall precisely over Evan's remnant, and the speck brightened like she'd blown on a flame. A hazy orange cloud billowed up from it.

Kate shoved her fingers into it, and Venn did the same.

> *Sunlight flashed off the surface of the river as it rushed by only paces away down the steep slope. Hands—a boy's hands, skinny and dripping wet—grabbed the aenigma box off the ground. A burning desperation to take it warred with a growing fear and a rising fury.*

In a flash of red, the foreign man crashed down in front of him, wrapping his huge hands around the box. Evan shouted, hoping to drown out any of the unnaturally compelling commands the man might hurl at him. The metal edges were cold. The stranger yanked at the box, and Evan's fingers almost slid off the smooth wood.

"No!" Evan shouted desperately, as though the word would make his hands stronger. Past the foreigner, Bo lay limp on the ground, and a wave of fear drove back all other thoughts.

Kate's hand began to shake.

The stranger let go of the box with one hand and slid a dagger out of his belt. On his sleeve, the embroidery seemed to move—the dragon slithering around the sword.

A weak voice shouted, and Evan spared a glance in that direction. Kate lay in the middle of the bridge, small and powerless, shouting and stretching a bloody hand toward him.

Kate wanted to pull her hand back, the terror and helplessness of that day filling her as strongly as it had when she'd been powerless on that bridge, but she couldn't look away.

"Run, Ria!" Evan screamed, but the words came out hoarse.
The stranger began shouting in his guttural foreign language, raising his arm.

Kate sat forward. The man was speaking Kalesh. Words that had been unintelligible in her childhood were clear now. *Rivers of the night flow through me. Strengthen me with your endless power. Rivers of the night flow through me...*

Kate's mind raced. Those weren't words that held any power. The man hadn't been trying to work magic on Evan. That was a mantra that Kalesh monks used to steady their minds. A prayer of sorts.

But if the man hadn't been using *vitalle* to open the drawer, how…?

> *Kate's voice came over the water again, demanding and furious.*
> *A gust of wind hit the shore. A ripple passed over him that wasn't quite wind.*

A shock cut through Kate's fear. "That *vitalle*…" she whispered, "was from me!"

Venn's shoulder pressed against hers, and the elf's form became visible beside Kate, a ghostly shape amidst the memory. "What did you do?"

"I don't know." Kate stared at her tiny, weakened form lying on the bridge. "I just wanted to get the man away from him."

> *More ripples grew in the air around him. They distorted the hillside, the river, the glowering man in front of him—everything but the box.*
> *The box, looking perfectly normal, began to hum.*
> *The world grew wavier by the moment, and Evan pulled the box closer to his chest as the indistinct man raised his dagger higher. Everything past him was hazy. Bo's body was a blurred dark blob on the blurred shore.*
> *Terror clawed up Evan's throat. "RUN, RIA!" he screamed.*
> *But the bridge was only a curving strand of darkness over the muddled greens and whites of the water. A curve of darkness that threw a strange hot wind at him.*
> *Through the rippling air, Evan could just make out the man towering over him as he flipped his dagger around until the hilt pointed down. The man let go of the box, grabbed Evan's shoulder with a grip that dug into his flesh, and brought the dagger down.*

"Take it!" Evan shouted, shoving the box away. But his fingers stayed locked around the wood.

The hilt of the dagger plummeted toward his head.

A blinding flash of light shot out of the box, stabbing into his eyes. He squeezed them shut, but the light turned his eyelids to blazing red. His fingers released the box, and he threw his hands over his face and dove to the side.

Pain shot across his head, not focused like a strike, but tearing through his skull.

He landed hard on his shoulder, and the pain in his head blinked out. He scrambled up, backing away from—

The man was gone.

The river and the hillside were gone.

He froze, half-risen on a plateau overlooking a mountain valley, spread out under wide, perfectly clear skies.

A crack reverberated through the air like the side of one of the mountains had just broken loose.

Far in the distance, a fracture raced across the sky, splitting like a bolt of black lightning.

A massive chunk of blue broke loose, as though it were stone, not a piece of the sky. It tumbled down and smashed into a distant hill, leaving a gaping hole in its place.

The memory ended, and the wisp of orange mist dissipated into the air.

Kate stared at the box, the knot of guilt she'd always carried expanding until it filled every inch of her.

"It was me," she whispered. The library was quiet, and she could feel the weight of all the eyes on her, the unspoken questions of what she'd just seen. She turned to Venn, barely able to breathe. "I'm the one who opened the Runelight Drawer."

CHAPTER ELEVEN

Shock cut through all the other emotions Evan's memory had raised, and Kate sank back in her chair. "I opened the drawer."

All the years of fury Kate had held against the Kalesh man who'd taken her brother twisted around to point at herself. The men hadn't wanted Evan. They'd wanted the box. They'd been trying to knock Evan out, not take him. If she'd left it alone, the box would have been gone, but Evan would have been left behind, just like Bo. Just like her.

"That dagger was falling very fast," Venn said quietly. "You may have saved his life."

"No. I *wanted* to save his life. What I did was trap him in a box for twenty years." Evan's terror and desperation surged back up inside of her. The image of the fissure in the sky added a tangled dart of fear and guilt. "And I opened the drawer without the amulet."

"What exactly did you two just see?" Silas asked.

Kate waved for Venn to tell them, then dropped her head into her hands, trying to ignore the elf's words.

She'd opened the Runelight Drawer. Dragged Evan into that huge valley.

Kate's mind caught on the idea of the valley, and she pushed away the memory of Evan's terror and focused on it. It was enormous. The pocket world Renault had made for his wife and daughter was so large they could survive in it for years. There had been the glint of a river in the center of it, forests of pines and deciduous trees. Something that looked like an orchard and possibly the roof of a house.

The entire valley had looked perfectly real. Perfectly alive and thriving, despite the fact that Renault had created it three hundred years ago.

"But Renault was right," Venn said quietly. "Opening the drawer without the amulet damaged it. The sky at the far side of the valley...crumbled."

Kate pressed her palms into her eyes. A huge chunk of the sky had collapsed just in the moment she'd seen the valley. How much more of the pocket world had she destroyed that day? How much more had collapsed when the drawer had opened to let Bo in? Or when it had opened during the fight with Faron?

She dropped her hands and reached for the box again, drawing in the warm hum of the wood, letting it soothe the prickles of fear dancing along the back of her neck. She rubbed her fingers over the spot where Evan's remnant had been.

"He's been in the box since childhood?" Faron asked quietly from behind Kate's shoulder.

Kate flinched.

"According to Renault," Venn said, "time in the pocket world is slowed until they live about a day for every year we live. So for us it's been twenty years. For him it's been a few weeks. He's still ten years old."

Kate's mind shifted to her parents, who lived in the same farm near the river from her childhood. They'd never given up hope that Evan was alive, but, over the years, they'd talked about him with more remembrance and less hope.

Ten years ago, her mother had stood at her kitchen window, staring out into the darkness. "I always imagine him running up over that hill from the river," she'd said. "I miss that impish smile he has."

Kate had set her hand on her mother's arm. "Bo and I will keep looking for him until we find him."

"We know you will," her father had said from where he sat at the table. "It's just..." He'd given Kate a sorrowful smile. "Someone else raised our son."

She tried to imagine what their reactions would be at seeing Evan again, still the same age as when he left.

But the tangle of emotions that raised was too much to sort out, and she pushed them away.

What was important now was finding a way to open the drawer safely and get Bo and Evan out. There was hope now. A lantern of light from the box, hanging in darkness, luring her forward. It was weak, but it existed. Kate fixed her mind firmly on it.

"And..." Faron looked between Kate and Venn, his face unreadable. "Bo is also in the drawer."

"He must have been drawn into it when your runelight opened the drawer." Kate gave the king a level look. "You move a lot of runelight when you're wrapped in shadows."

Venn looked back at the box. "Is there a remnant of Bo's that would show us when he went in? We could see how much damage the pocket world had sustained from Evan getting in, and maybe a hint as to how much more Bo caused."

The effects of the remnant amplifier were fading, but there were two different glimmers of Bo's blue from near where the runelight drawer's edges should be. Kate dribbled some solos potion on one of them. The cloud of blue that rose from it was twice as big as Evan's.

Expecting to see the small grove peppered with aspens and junipers where Venn had found the box, Kate pushed her fingers into the mist. Beside her, Venn leaned against her shoulder and did the same.

"May I?" Faron asked.

"Sure," Venn said. "If you want to watch yourself chasing and terrorizing Bo."

Instead of the clearing, Venn's cloudy form appeared next to Kate just outside a low shelter made by leaning walls of pine branches, and Venn drew in a sharp breath.

Daylight poured down into the clearing, but the air held a slight chill, and a trickle of smoke rose from the top of the shelter. Bo stood looking down at the aenigma box gripped in his hands. He ran a thumb over the runes carved into the top. "What are you?" he asked. "Why do you feel so...big?"

A moan came from inside, and he squatted to see into the entrance. Near the back of the shelter, against the wide fir trunk, Venn sat up, pushing off her blanket. Her skin was pale, her brow knit together in pain.

"Ah," he said, feeling yet another flicker of awe that an actual elf sat before him. "She lives!"

The elf tensed, fixing him with a dangerous look. "Where am I?" she demanded in a rough voice.

Bo crawled into the tent but drew quickly to the side, to give her space and not block the exit. He set the box next to his leg, close enough that he could still feel the edge of it dig into him. "In my beautiful home. Not as fancy as an elven house, I'll wager, but it's warm and dry. Which isn't too bad for someone who can't speak to trees. Are you warm enough?"

Her eyes grew distant for a moment. "How far down the mountain are we?"

He paused at the question. "Only a few minutes from the river. I'm not sure how long an elf can bleed out and freeze in the snow before it actually hurts them, but you looked like you had a good head start on both counts. So I brought you down to my basecamp, since I figured a bandage and less snow might help."

She shook her head as though trying to shake something off, then gasped in pain and grabbed for her bandaged leg.

He cringed at the memory of the wound he'd wrapped. "The wolves left a mark." *A ripple of uncertainty rose in him.* "I thought elves could heal themselves, so I just cleaned it and wrapped it, but I can find you a healer if you need one."

"Wolves?" *she asked blankly.*

"Only three, thankfully. And apparently not terribly hungry, since they let me run them off without much of a fight."

"You..." *The elf stared at him, understanding dawning.* "You had the lantern. You..." *She flinched, and her face paled even more.* "You saved me from the wolves."

The words bordered on an accusation, and he faltered. "And probably the cold," *he said, forcing his voice to stay light and fixing her with a small smile,* "but I think the wolves would have killed you first."

"You're..." *She swallowed, her face torn between confusion and dismay.* "You're human."

The words were said with such disbelief that he couldn't hold back a self-conscious laugh. "Is it that obvious?" *The fire had died down, and he added two more pieces of wood.*

"Yes."

Her answer was so abrupt that another laugh slipped out, accompanied by a bit of consternation at the impression he was leaving on her. "There's soup from this morning. Just fish and a few turnips, but you're welcome to some."

"I..."

Another wave of uncertainty rose, and he grimaced. "Oh, do elves eat fish?"

She nodded and reached down to touch her leg. Her movements were labored, and she adjusted to sit against the trunk behind her. She closed her eyes, her expression smoothing slightly.

When she opened them again, he offered a smile. "I'm Bo, by the way. And since you're the first elf I've ever met, I apologize if I've done anything..." He gestured at her leg, and then the whole shelter. "Wrong. I couldn't leave you in the snow, but I don't know how to find other elves."

She gave a tired, pained sort of laugh. "You saved my life," she whispered, then clenched her jaw shut as though blocking off more words.

He waved the sentiment away. "It was nothing. I was there and heard the wolves. I have some ginger and nettle for tea, if you'd like, but I wasn't sure if that only helped with pain in humans."

She pinched her mouth shut, staring at him with an unnerving intensity. Her eyes raked over his face as though finding something horrifically wrong with him.

He shifted. "I'll leave you in peace, then. I'm working just outside if you need anything." He picked up the box and turned to go.

"Wait!"

The word tore across the shelter, and he stopped.

Her body was tense, her arms drawn close to her sides, her shoulders hunched, and one hand gripped her leg above the bites, her knuckles white.

"All I have is yours," she whispered, and the words shoved against his chest with an ancient weight.

He drew back and began to shake his head.

"Ask for my day, it is yours. Ask for my aid, it is yours."

He shook his head faster, holding out a hand to push the heaviness away, but the power of her words flowed around it.

"Ask for my blade, it is yours. Ask for my blood, it is yours."

"No," he interrupted. The words rushed into him, stinging like they were made of tiny shards of glass or a million pine needles. "Stop! What are you saying?"

"Ask for my life, it is yours."

"Wait." He set down the box and held up both hands. "You don't owe me anything. I ran off some wolves. Anyone would have done the same."

A flush of red rolled over her skin, and she winced in pain. "I vow this to you, until one or both of us lie beneath the trees."

The last of the words shoved into him, filling him with something foreign and abrasive that swelled, then faded, settling itself deep in his bones. "What did you just do?"

She let out a tired, humorless laugh, rolling her shoulders as though under a heavy weight. "You saved my life. I owe you a life debt."

"I..." He leaned back. "I release you from any obligation. Really, it was nothing."

The corner of her mouth twitched up. "My life is nothing?"

"That's not what I meant." He ran a hand through his hair. "You don't owe me anything."

"It is not something you can dismiss. It is done. The debt began when you saved me and will be repaid if I ever save you."

He opened his mouth again, but she held up a hand.

"I know humans speak of vows as something that can be chosen. Something that can be broken. This is not such a vow. The debt has been incurred. It cannot be removed. Not by me, and not by you. It can merely be paid."

Bo opened his mouth, but he could feel them still. The words were part of him, anchored to something deep inside. He shivered *and pulled his legs up in front of himself, wrapping his arms around them.*

"My name is Venn." She closed her eyes. "If you ever are in need, call me."

The cloud of blue faded away, leaving Kate's and Venn's hands stretched out over the box—with Faron's next to them.

"A life debt?" he hissed. "To a *human*?"

Venn yanked her hand back. "I told you I needed to find Bo."

Faron stared at her. "Why didn't you just tell me why?"

"You're going to censure *me* for keeping secrets?" Venn asked. "After all you've done?"

"I would have helped you," he said between clenched teeth. "I was looking for Bo too."

"Well, you weren't king then," Venn said. "I was hardly going to trust you to keep it from your father. He'd have killed Bo before letting a human have such a hold on the elf betrothed to his son."

Faron opened his mouth, but Kate raised her hand to stop him. "Yes, there's a life debt. Yes, Bo is in danger. I would like to know how much danger, so if you two could quarrel elsewhere, I'm going to try the other bit of remnant I can see." Without waiting for an answer, she dripped some solos potion on the other glimmer of blue near the runelight drawer.

The mist rose, and Kate reached in. The library began to fade, and the glade where Bo had been drawn into the box finally appeared.

CHAPTER TWELVE

The elven forest rushed in to replace Renault's cave, and Venn's presence lit up again at Kate's shoulder. Distantly, she registered motion from Faron too, but he kept from touching her, and she assumed, rather than saw, that he was watching as well.

Bo moved quickly into the clearing, pulling the aenigma box out of his pack and holding it to his chest. The grey-blues of late twilight draped the ground under every pine with shadows. A dark one to his left made him grab the box tighter. But the shadow wasn't complete. He could make out the roots that rippled the ground at the base of the trunk, the blanket of dry pine needles coating everything.

He scanned the clearing, dread crawling up his neck, looming ever closer behind him. He stopped, spinning, scanning the ground until he found a spread of juniper bushes clustered beneath some aspens. Casting a look over his shoulder at the darkening woods, he ran to the junipers and dropped to his knees. The greenish-blue branches formed a matted cover over the ground. He dragged up a section, shoving the box beneath it.

He spun, heart pounding, searching for a hiding place for himself, but there was nothing. The memory of the wounded elf rose in his mind. The weight of her vow lingered in his bones. A tether. A bond that had grown familiar enough to fade into the background—but now it pulled at him.

"Venn!" The word came out barely above a whisper. A wave of embarrassment rolled over him at needing her help, but the thing that followed him was unnatural. If it was elven, maybe she could—

A blackness moved deep in the trees.

"Venn!" he called, the growing dread keeping his voice low. "If you really can hear me, I think I need that help you offered."

Nothing else moved in the forest. Bo shifted, and his foot hit something solid.

The box.

It couldn't be lost, not again, not here in the woods where no one would ever stumble across it.

He spun, searching for a way out. The trees around him felt watchful. Almost aware of him. Could he be all the way in the elven wood?

"Venn," he whispered, dropping to his knees again. "Please find this." His hands trembled as he tore a bit of paper out of his journal. He wrote: Take this to Ria at the Keepers' Stronghold—please. The words were scribbled and messy, and he gripped his pencil tightly for a moment, tamping down on the flare of longing to go find his sister one more time. "You'll figure out something, Ria," he whispered.

He shoved the note under the branches with the box and took a few steps away.

Through the trees, the shadow moved again, closer this time. It wasn't deep blue like the gathering gloom beneath the trees. It was the inky black of a starless night. The emptiness of a hole so deep there was no end. It was a tower of moving, roiling pitch, its surface too dark to even reflect the dusky light.

Bo tried to draw in a breath, but it came fast and gasping. He pulled his knife from its sheath. The blade shook like a leaf as the shadow glided into the gap where a faint game trail left the clearing. The pocket of darkness clung to the trunks on either side, sliding across the ground like oil, streams of it running along the roots, pooling in the hollows.

Fingers stretched out from it, reaching across the clearing like grasping tentacles, tearing a void out of the evening light.

Bo staggered backward, and his knife fell from numb fingers. His foot hit the aenigma box, and the shadow lunged, grabbing for him.

A blinding light burst out behind him with a loud hum. The tendrils of shadow reaching for him tattered at the edges as though a wind whipped through them. Fragments of the blackness pelted toward Bo, and he dropped to his knees, throwing his arms over his head. The corner of the box dug into his shin.

A barrage of impacts, feather-light and ice cold, crashed into him —through him—like darts of snow. The humming swelled and the brightness grew until he squeezed his eyes shut against it.

The ground beneath him trembled. Bo tensed for an attack.

The thrum spread out until it faded into the air around him, and a breeze smelling of summer and grass wafted past.

Bo risked a look under his arm and froze.

He sat on a high rock ledge. Only a couple of paces away, a long mountain valley stretched out below him filled with trees and hills and the glitter of a river.

There was no forest around him, no juniper bushes. He sat on a bare rock ledge backed up to a soaring cliff face.

"No," he whispered, spinning, running his hands over the rock as though the box had merely turned invisible. "Where is it?" A deep, rending crack split the air, and he scrambled around to face the valley.

The sky was a rich, clear blue peppered with dollops of clouds — until the far end of his view. There, huge chunks of the blue were missing, as though they'd been wrenched out and thrown down onto the far end of the valley, where there was nothing but rubble-strewn hills. Where there should be sky, there was nothing but hollow, vacant blackness. No sunlight, no stars, no...anything.

Another crack like splitting rock shook the entire valley. A fissure rent out from the starless expanse, branching into a dozen cracks speeding halfway across the heavens toward him.

Terror clawed up his throat as massive slabs of sky toppled down. One smashed into the side of a mountain with a deafening roar. The mountainside crumbled beneath it, and debris exploded out in a cloud that billowed into the air and tumbled down into the valley.

Another chunk dislodged, and Bo scrambled back. The edges of the valley began to darken, the sights and sounds fading.

A bit of motion flashed on the valley floor, and he leaned forward to see a figure running out from a stand of trees, shouting and waving their hands, their voice lost under the thundering collapse of the sky.

Bo's terror filled Kate's chest as the walls of the library came back into view.

Venn's hand grabbed the surface of the box just as the cloud of Bo's remnant disappeared, as though she could reach into it.

Faron pulled his hand back slowly.

"Venn," Kate whispered, trying to clamp down on the fear, "all that damage, and that was only the second time it opened. There was one more."

The aenigma box sat on the table, as vulnerable as the snowy rabbit next to it. The queen's remnant covered nearly every surface—it infected the books and permeated the room like a looming threat. The cavern fell both too exposed and too confined, and the nagging feel of being trapped tingled up the back of her neck.

Outside the cave was no different. The White Wood spread out around it, filled with elves with suspicious motives and plans. And past that, a foreign land stretched for endless days around her.

The box suddenly felt like prey, surrounded by predators. She picked it up, letting the faint thrum warm her fingers. "Crofftus." The rabbit twitched at her voice. "We need to make the bloodstone. We need to open the drawer and get them out."

"Who was that other person in the valley?" Faron asked. "Evan?"

"I don't know." Kate sorted through the books on the table until she found the one that described how to make the bloodstone. "But we need to get them all out before…" She glanced at Faron. "Before the mess with the queen and the elves and Home drags us back in and puts us all in danger. Again."

You might want to ask the king of the White Wood if he wouldn't mind lending you a wellstone as big as your thumbnail.

Faron raised an eyebrow. "We're a little low on wellstones at the moment."

"You were," Tribal said, "until you father found the drawer of them your mother had hidden, right in this cave."

Faron scanned the room. "Where are they?"

"Crooked King Thallion grabbed the entire drawer," Silas said, pointing to the table where the wellstones had been, "and left."

"I need one," Kate said.

Faron shook his head. "If there are wellstones, we need to figure out how many the elves need first. We've been low for decades. A century maybe. We have a lot of uses for them that we need filled."

"Then I'll go to the river and find another one." Kate grabbed her pack and tucked the box inside. "And I'm not letting this out of my reach until I get my brothers out." She leveled a glare at

Faron. "No more elven entanglements! I'm taking a wellstone from the Surn, and then I'm going to station dwarves at the doors of this room to turn it into a stronghold so we're safe from the mess of the White Wood for as long as it takes for me to make a bloodstone."

The pressure of homesickness she'd felt earlier squeezed around her, and an idea unfurled in her mind.

Silas straightened. "You're going to have the dwarves do what now?"

"We're not your personal guards, Twig," Tribal said.

The idea grew, thrumming with eagerness and a longing so fierce it tightened her hands on her pack.

In the midst of the foreign cavern and the foreign Wood and the foreign land, the thought blazed like a beacon. She clenched her hands on the top of her pack, sealing the box inside. It could be safe. Not just inside the fabric of a pack, but *really* safe.

The lienick formula lay open on the table. The neatly labeled jars of ingredients stood at attention on Renault's shelf, just waiting to be taken up and used. She could be to the river by noon and have a wellstone in hand by dinner.

"Crofftus," she said slowly, trying to keep her hope reined in. "If I find a wellstone, we'll have everything we need for the bloodstone, right?"

I believe so. If you go to the river, Fix and I can have the first step prepared before you return.

Fix looked alarmed at the idea of her leaving, but she set her hand on his shoulder.

"But it'll take days to make the lienick potion, even if we get it right the first time. Longer if we run into any problems." She glanced around the room. "I've noticed that it's been rare to have even a few days peace this close to the White Wood."

"Not sure we've had more than two at a time," Silas agreed.

"That's why…" Kate let her eyes fall to the box. "We should take everything we need to make the bloodstone…and leave."

The idea was met with looks ranging from puzzled to amused.

But this is where all the equipment is.

"And it's underground," Silas said, "which makes it far superior to any human hovel you'd drag us all to."

Tribal tapped his poker into the burning wood with a crunch. "And it has the forge for when we want to make more stonesteel."

"You already have stonesteel, and now that I don't need any, it's all yours." Kate studied the page in Renault's journal again, running over the things she would need.

Everything was right here.

She looked up at Venn, the eagerness inside her almost painfully strong. "Let's take the box and all the ingredients and leave! Let's get away from all the things here that keep trying to hurt us and it." The fabric of her pack dug into her palms as she squeezed it, and the box on the table fairly hummed with optimism. The hope from it grew brighter. "Let's go back to the Stronghold."

CHAPTER THIRTEEN

Venn's eyebrows shot up.

"What Stronghold?" Faron asked.

"The Keeper's Stronghold," Kate answered, her excitement bleeding into her voice. "My home. It's sheltered, has all the equipment we could possibly need, plus at least four Keepers who are bound to have more knowledge than I do, not to mention a seven-story library full of books we can use for research."

Venn began to shake her head.

"You can't leave," Faron said.

"I absolutely can." Kate grabbed Venn's arm. "We can go back through the dwarven tunnels. We'll be home in less than a week! Bo won't be in any more danger from anything here! We can work until we get the bloodstone right, then get him and Evan out."

What if we need another wellstone? Crofftus asked.

"I could find five in a single afternoon along the river here before we leave," Kate said. "Crofftus, come with me to the Stronghold. We can work there in complete peace."

To the Keepers! Absolutely not.

"Crofftus, your prejudices against—" Kate began.

"All the way back to the Stronghold?" Venn interrupted.

Tribal dropped his poker with a clang. "We're not taking you back through the tunnels."

"You started this trouble with Home by spreading rumors that there were diamonds in our woods," Faron said. "You are obligated to stay and help smooth that over!"

Kate felt a twinge of responsibility, but she shook her head. "Faron, since I've come to your woods, I've almost been killed by you, and I've had you steal the box. I've been bound to the Wood by your father, which almost killed me again, and had him order me shot in the chest. Then your mother attacked me and stole the box again. I am *not* risking it being stolen a third time. Or having some other elf try to kill me." She turned to Venn. "Please, Venn. We can actually keep Bo safe while we work this out."

Faron looked between them. "You are not leaving, Venn."

Venn gave him an incredulous look. "If you command me to stay—"

"Please come with me," Kate said to Venn. "We're stronger together to face whatever will bother us on our way. And in the Stronghold valley there are plenty of trees. You'll be fine. We can save Bo! You can end the life debt!"

"Venn has responsibilities to her people," Faron said firmly.

Kate grabbed Venn's forearm again. "I need to do this."

"I know." Venn met her gaze, and the reluctance in her gaze shifted to resolution. "I'm with you."

Kate's shoulders loosened, and she squeezed Venn's arm before letting go and turning to her pack.

"You cannot be serious," Faron objected.

"You had a debt to Kate," Venn said. "You know how it feels. Would you have let her travel away from here alone if you could have gone with her?"

Faron glared at her, then lowered his voice. "I need you here, Venn. Don't make me beg you to help your own people." He looked at Kate. "I..." He grimaced. "I need you too, Kate. I need help repairing the relationship with Home." His eyes drifted to the pack Kate clutched in her hands. "I understand why you two need to open the box, but you can do it here. I'll place elves around this cave to protect you. I'll swear that the box will not be taken or damaged—"

"Will your word bind your mother?" Kate asked. "If Naevys comes by, will any of your elves be able to stop her from doing whatever she wants? Will even a command by you stop her?"

Faron clenched his jaw shut.

Even from inside her pack, Kate could feel the humming warmth of the box.

The passageway with the pale lantern of hope came back to her mind, hovering just out of reach, as bright as a patch of moonlight in the dead of night.

It cast out glittering shards of light, sharp and piercing.

The lantern had moved closer—or she'd moved toward it, maybe. The walls crowded around her, lined with jagged ebony rocks, but the light was just ahead.

She blinked and met Faron's angry expression. "I am not unsympathetic to your situation, and I do feel some responsibility for the mess with Home, but my brothers have to be my priority. This isn't my home. These aren't my people. I was dragged into all of this because you attacked Bo. And I'm tired of being tangled up in the elven mess going on here. I can't imagine everyone leaving me alone here even for the few days I'd need." She looked at the dwarves. "I need help getting through your tunnels."

Tribal shook his head.

Silas frowned at her. "That's not possible. They'll be on the lookout. There's no way we could get through."

"Now, if you helped us reach that treasure in the carriage first," Tribal said, "then we would have a chance."

"That cursed carriage that almost killed us? No. No more delays. Venn, we were going to take the long way here. We can just do that."

"Four weeks of walking?" Venn said. "To get to a place where there are no more wellstones and half the ingredients we need don't grow? That's not the best idea you've ever had."

A surge of fury fueled by all the exhaustion and failures of the last weeks in the White Wood surged up in Kate. "I am tired of being pushed around by all the centuries-old turmoil that fills this entire place, Venn! I need to get my brothers safe, and no place here is safe. The only other place I know of where I can do what I need to do is the Stronghold."

Venn let out a breath that was almost a groan.

Kate tried to rein in her voice. "I understand if you can't come." At Venn's annoyed look, she raised her hand. "I do. I really do. There is a lot going on, and there's a dire need here for elves who can be trusted. If you want to stay, I understand. But I need to leave before some other part of the chaos hurts me or the box worse than it already has."

Venn strode across the room and pulled her cloak off a hook. "I'm staying with the box. And I'm hardly leaving you to fend for yourself alone for the month it's going to take you to get home."

"You did it alone," Kate said.

Venn gave her a flat look. "And you saw the condition I was in at the end of it."

"Venn!" Faron's voice snapped across the room. "You can't!"

"Fix the mess you made," Venn said sharply to him, but then her expression softened slightly. "Even after all this, I still want to think you can. That you can be the sort of king the White Wood deserves. I'll guess we'll see."

She picked up her pack and brought it over to the table. "Which ingredients do we need, Crofftus?"

The rabbit hesitated.

Kate squatted down next to the table, looking him straight in the face. "I know you're not excited about going to the Stronghold, but it's not the sort of place you think it is. And we can do this there."

I have no desire—

Kate set a hand on the rabbit's soft foot. "I need your help, Crofftus."

He tensed but didn't move. *All right, Katria.* The words tore out of him as if they cost him a great price. *I will come with you.*

She squeezed his foot with relief. "Thank you."

I do not promise to be polite to Milton.

Kate stood, grinning. "I can't wait to see how it goes when you're rude to him."

Venn. Crofftus hopped over next to the vials of ingredients. *Start with the three on the left of the top row.*

Silas frowned across the table. "You're leaving *now*?"

"It's still early in the day," Kate said. "We have a decent amount of supplies here. I don't see any reason to linger. We'll head straight downhill to the river and look for wellstones. If there aren't any this far south, we'll head north until we find some, but judging from how many I found while we were searching for Naevys, I don't think it will take long."

"We haven't shaped your stonesteel," Tribal pointed out, "and we haven't finished making the rest of it."

The pile of common steel next to the forge still held two hammer heads and an axe blade.

Kate felt a little pang of guilt. "You can keep the part that would have been mine, and you have enough extra for a couple of blades. If I get back to this part of the world, I'd be happy to make you more."

"If you get back?" Tribal asked. "Why on earth would you come back?"

Kate tucked the black leather book with the bloodstone instructions into her pack and sorted through the others on the table, suddenly wishing she had an entire wagon to fill with them. "Believe it or not, the question of what happened to the Kalesh emperor here is something I'd actually like to look into more. And Bo will want to too, once he's out." She ignored the massive series of events that would have to go right for that to happen and looked around the library. "Besides, I still haven't read all these books."

Faron's eyes locked on Venn. "You're actually leaving?" His anger was tinged with something pained.

Venn hesitated in the middle of wrapping a bottle. "I've been gone most of the last hundred years, Faron. What's another trip?"

He reached a hand out toward her, but she pulled away, and he let his hand drop. "Then I wish you safe travels." The words were formal, but he waited, as though expecting some sort of response.

Venn sighed and met his gaze. "You've always meant well, Faron, but that's not enough anymore. It hasn't been enough for a very long time. You need to decide what *you* think is right, and do it. Don't be swayed by what your father wants. Don't be swayed by the fact that Naevys is your mother. The two of them have caused a great deal of damage to the Wood and the lakes and the humans. It's up to you to fix it, and not to let them inflict any more." Her fingers twitched, as though she was about to reach out to him, but she closed them on the bottle instead. "Listen to Ayen and Evay and all the elves you've always respected. Your father has no hold on you anymore. Live like that's true."

Faron watched her for another moment, his face unreadable,

then he glanced at Kate. "The life debt is paid, but I still feel some connection between us."

Kate scanned through the golden haze emanating from Faron and found a thin strand of it stretching toward her, speckled with her own rust red. "What is it?"

He shook his head. "Maybe the echo of life debts linger." He gave Venn a troubled look before he refocused on Kate. "Keep yourself safe. I doubt I'll be able to reach you in time if you get into serious trouble."

With a sharp nod to both dwarves, he disappeared. The *vitalle* that puffed out of the space he left washed over Kate like a breath of fresh forest air. It was the alpine forest of the elven White Wood, and as it dispelled into the room and Venn's homier, more human-forest scents settled back in, Kate straightened her back.

Four weeks and she'd be home. The length of the journey stretched in front of her, impossibly long, but she tucked two more books of Renault's into her pack—the two with the most detailed descriptions of the box—and buckled it closed.

Fix crept out from a nook beside one of the bookshelves. Kate pulled on her cloak and slung her pack over her shoulders and squatted down next to him. "Do you want to come on a very long journey to a place that's…" She paused. "It's in a safe, lovely valley, and there are a few Keepers that live there, but it's very far away."

Fix hunched down, his face troubled.

"Or you can stay with us and help us get into some buried treasure," Tribal said.

The soft tread of Venn's footsteps came up behind Kate. "The way is fraught with danger, Kate," she said quietly. "It wouldn't be a kindness to bring him."

Kate set her hand on the gnoblin's bony shoulder. "No, I suppose it wouldn't. I'll miss you, Fix. Try not to let the Weasel

Brothers get into too much trouble. And just in general, stay away from the elves."

The edges of Fix's wide mouth turned down, and his eyes grew forlorn, but he nodded. He flicked his fingers at her questioningly. *See again?*

Kate offered him a smile. "I hope so. I really do want to come back. There are so many stories here I haven't sorted out yet. Besides, Venn will need company on her way back to the White Wood. When I come back, I'll try to find you."

One side of his mouth struggled to smile, but his shoulders slumped so dejectedly and the expression on his wrinkled green face was so miserable that Kate reached forward and pulled him into a hug. He flinched before slowly relaxing.

"I really will miss you." She pulled away, and the gnoblin stayed hunched on the floor. She stood, straightening her pack and feeling a pang of regret when she looked at the dwarves' identical faces. "You two watch out for Fix. No getting him into trouble."

"We would never," Tribal said, but there was more sincerity than indignation in the words.

Silas rose, a dissatisfied twist to his mouth as he rounded the table. "You don't need to hurry off."

Her pack felt heavy on her back, and the corner of something she imagined might be the box, even if it was actually a book, pressed against her back. She brought the idea of the lantern, hanging ahead of her in the darkness, back to her mind. The draw of the hope was too much to ignore. "Yes, I think I do. Thank you for everything." She held out her hand.

His thick dwarven fingers wrapped around her forearm. "Well, then, take better care of yourselves than we've seen you do so far. Neither of you seem too good at that."

"You're bloody awful at it," Tribal said, still sitting. "Especially the Twig. And when you inevitably get into a scrape, don't even try to let us know about it. We'll feel compelled to help you out *again*, which always interrupts our own plans."

Kate pulled the dragon scale out of her pack and handed it to him. "Keep this safe. When I see you again, we'll make more stonesteel."

He gave nothing more than a grunt of acknowledgment.

She smiled at him. "Goodbye, Tribal. I'll miss you too."

Kate started toward the door, glancing over her shoulder. "You should name the two knives you're making Kate and Venn."

Tribal gave an offended huff. "We want useful knives, not ones that are constantly causing trouble."

"Right." Venn picked up Crofftus and followed. "Because you two never want more trouble."

"We should make a new fire starter," Tribal said to his brother. "Name that after those two."

Kate cast one last look around the library. The call of the hundreds of books she hadn't read yet almost made her stop, but the box pressed heavy on her back. She shifted her pack and headed toward the chilly winter air seeping into the back entrance.

PART II

THE BOX

Having the box back in my possession was both reassuring and tortuous.

Tortuous because I couldn't open it, not safely. Tortuous because I knew the danger I had put my brothers in by opening the door to their pocket world twice without the amulet to protect them. Tortuous because it dangled a hope in front of me I couldn't quite reach.

But maybe more terrifying, as I look back, was how reassuring it was. Having it in my hands was like holding a dream. Like brushing up against a longing. It helped drive away the yearning I still felt sometimes for the White Wood, but that should have alarmed me more than it did.

I should have noticed how much the box was affecting all my choices. I should have noticed how smoothly it controlled me.

CHAPTER FOURTEEN

Another thick cluster of snowflakes landed on Kate's eyelashes in a clump of heavy white. She brushed it away, peering through a gap in the trees to her left, but the snow obscured the mountaintops beyond the edge of the forest. Everything past the hillside they trudged down was a flat white nothingness.

Crofftus had disappeared the moment they'd stepped back into trees to "find an animal more fit for travel," and aside from the quiet forest sounds of Venn's remnant and the faint shushing of their feet through the powdery snow, the forest was silent.

"How far to the river?" she asked.

"Less than an hour." Venn brushed her fingers over a large pine as she passed it. "Do you really think you'll find wellstones this far south?"

"They were spread fairly evenly through the stretches of river we searched earlier. I would assume some have made it this far." Kate paused. "No elf besides the Warden can find them?"

"The elders can find them in the smaller streams that run

through the White Wood, but I've never known anyone but Naevys to find one in the Surn."

A discomfort lingered on Kate's shoulders, as it had since they'd left the cave. Venn had been quiet since they'd begun. She hadn't looked back toward the White Wood as they passed out of it. She'd merely continued to touch the trunks they passed, even as they changed from the white of frost pines to the darker human forest.

The edges of the discomfort shifted to something that felt remarkably like guilt.

"I appreciate you coming," Kate said quietly. "I know you'd rather not."

"The White Wood has been fine without me for this long," Venn said. "It should stay that way a bit longer."

Kate paused. Had it been fine? She opened her mouth to say, *You don't have to come,* but the words stuck in her throat. The box sat vulnerable in her pack, the woods around them rife with the potential to lash out again and steal it. Venn's presence next to her felt like a shield. The thought of traveling all the way back to the Stronghold alone, keeping the box safe the entire time, was so daunting she closed her lips.

Venn glanced at her. "You're a mess."

Kate straightened. "What?"

"Humans are often messy. Often sad and relieved at the same time. Or angry and embarrassed. Your people's emotions, on the whole, are a jumbled mess."

"You can feel my emotions?"

"Not like before, but I am still an elf. I can sense your turmoil. I'm not sure I've felt you quite this much of a disaster since I first gave you the box and you were trying desperately to sort everything out."

Kate let out a breath that was almost a laugh. "Well, there's a lot going on."

"No, there's not. You have the box. Which should legitimately give you hope and legitimately give you worry about whether you'll be able to open it safely. You're right that the White Wood is too dangerous. Naevys is still here, doing who knows what. Thallion may not be king anymore—a fact he will certainly hold against you—but he's still incredibly powerful. And he knows that destruction of the box would wound you deeply. The humans in Home vacillate wildly between adoring you and hating you, so that doesn't feel like the safest place to be. And beyond all that, unless Naevys has taken her role of Warden up completely again, I don't think we've seen the end of monstrous creatures wandering into the woods. With Home being such a tasty-smelling target, I doubt their troubles are over."

Kate stopped. "You call that nothing going on?"

Venn paused beside her. "There's a lot going on, but nothing you should be concerned about. You were right. Home isn't *your* home. The White Wood isn't mine. I've spent so much time wrapped up with Faron and Thallion that I forget sometimes that my people are at the lakes. They have their own council of elders who are more than capable of sorting out the mess with Faron. What you and I need to do is get Bo and Evan out of that death trap they're in. And if it's not safe to do it in Renault's cave—which it clearly isn't—then the Keeper Stronghold is the next best option. So stop feeling guilty for the fact that I'm coming along. I chose to come myself." She glanced at Kate. "Faron has asked me more than once why I am choosing to stay with you over doing anything with him, and it's because it's been a very long time since I had a friend I could trust completely." She set a hand briefly on Kate's shoulder and started walking again. "Besides. I *like* to travel. Especially when elves around the White Wood are going to start looking for new leaders, or worse, a wife for their new king."

Kate took a deep breath, feeling marginally better. "I still feel some guilt over Crofftus."

"Because you're forcing him away from so many things here?" Venn asked wryly.

Kate laughed. "I doubt he cares about leaving here, but taking him to the Stronghold after a lifetime of him hating Keepers feels awkward."

"Maybe it's time he examines the prejudice he has against a man he hasn't interacted with in what? A hundred and fifty years?" Venn looked off into the woods. "Besides, you're taking him where he eventually wanted to go anyway."

"I know, and I know what he really wants is a human body again. I'm positive the Keepers will do everything they can to help, but..." She lowered her voice. "Where will we find a body that's not being used by someone else?"

"That is the most obvious challenge," Venn agreed.

They walked in silence for a few minutes while a question nagged at Kate. An irritating question. An obvious question. Probably, an important question. But today was for getting safely away from this area, not mulling over mysteries from the White Wood.

She made it another two minutes before it burst out of her. "She really just left the box in a clearing?"

Venn grimaced. "I know. I keep wondering if Faron lied."

"Surely, he could have come up with something more believable than that if it was a lie."

"He's certainly has enough practice to."

"So if he literally found it in a clearing—"

"As opposed to figuratively finding it?"

Kate laughed. "Yes, or his mother handed it to him, or he knows where she stashes important things, or Thallion does, or something. But if he literally found it in a clearing, then Naevys is either less sane than we thought—because she discarded today something she seemed desperate to have yesterday—or much more sane than we thought, and this is some elaborate plot to do…what? Who'd she think would find it in a clearing?"

"Faron, maybe." Venn looked thoughtfully into the trees. "If she's lucid, she'd know he'd be looking for her. But so would the rangers."

"So an elf would find it." The idea sat uncomfortably in Kate's mind. "But not you and I. And yet we have the box." She stopped. "Is that a problem?"

Venn drew up beside her. "How could it possibly be a problem that we have the box we need?" She narrowed her eyes. "Are you talking about some figurative problem?"

"No, a very literal problem." The forest around them was serenely quiet and still. "Not for us, but if Naevys wanted an elf to have the box, and now *we* have the box, is that going to turn into a problem for the White Wood?"

A line of worry creased between Venn's brows. "Do you want to stay and find out?"

The thought of bringing the box back into the dangers surrounding the Wood made Kate start walking again. "I want to take care of the problem we have before trying to help everyone else with theirs." The sentiment sat as uneasily as the questions about Naevys did.

From Venn's expression, it sat the same with her, but she walked alongside Kate, anyway. "Bo first," she agreed.

Another few minutes brought them to a gap between the trees. A patch of black water appeared far below them on the slope.

"Is that the river?" Kate asked.

Venn scanned the trees. "Yes. This is as far south as the elves patrol. Beyond here there is a spattering of humans, and we're only a short walk from the entrance to the dwarven tunnels." She offered a half smile. "You know, if we'd brought the Weasel

Brothers as an offering, maybe the governor would've taken us through his tunnels as a thank-you."

Kate laughed again. "I wish we'd thought of that hours ago." They walked in silence for a few more minutes. "Was Faron right? Is the connection you still have with the trees because of the betrothal?"

Venn didn't answer for a moment. When she did, her voice was quiet. "I think he might be. I'm not sure of another reason why I'd still have more connection than Ayen. And…" She fell quiet again.

"You can tell it's through him, can't you?"

Venn moved her head in the smallest nod. "I thought at first that I had returned to the way I felt the forest when I was young. When I first came to the White Wood, I could sense the trees, but barely better than any other elf. The Wood had a feel to it then. The northern feel that was so different from my old home. The more time I spent here, though, the more it drew me in. The more it lost that sense of foreignness.

"But now it's back to feeling very much like an alpine forest. Like it did when I was young, except…" She glanced at Kate. "When we were in the Elder Grove, when Naevys was choking Faron and I grabbed him to try to stop her—I smelled it then, too."

"It's his remnant. It embodies that forest in all its frost and snow and pine trees."

"After we saw how much Ayen had lost, I started to suspect. But when Faron came into Renault's cave, everything got stronger. I could feel the plants in the other cave the way I used to be able to. I could feel the normal connection I have to Faron, which was totally gone with Ayen."

"So if you broke off the betrothal…"

Venn's shoulders sagged. "I think I'd lose the little connection I have."

Kate paused before voicing her next question. "So, even though you can't make the trees listen to you right now, do you think you could call him and he'd hear you?"

Venn took in the forest around her. "This close to the White Wood, probably. I could call him and he could call me."

"Well," Kate said, "then let's get far enough away that you won't have to worry about that."

A half hour later, they came out of the trees at the top of an outcropping. From where they stood, it dropped down a rock-strewn slope that fell steeply, but not impassably, down to some trees before it reached the river. The outcropping itself headed north, sporting a faint trail along its top as it meandered downhill, eventually meeting up with the Surn.

Kate pointed along it. "The ravine is that way?"

"Yes. Can't say I'm sad we won't be visiting that place again."

"There are still a lot of puzzles there." Kate searched the trees, looking for any sign of the rockslide, but there was nothing but the treed bank of the river. "I do want to come back, Venn. I could spend a year in study between the ravine and Renault's cave." She sighed. "Maybe by then the elves and humans will have sorted themselves out."

"I doubt that."

Kate pointedly turned away from it. "Okay, I'm putting all mysteries from this place out of my mind until we free my brothers. Which way from here?"

Venn gestured along the top of the rocks, toward the ravine. "This drop-off is the edge of the elven patrols. The easiest way to the river is to follow the path along the top."

Kate felt an itch of urgency that rebelled against the delay of a path headed in the wrong direction. She glanced the other way. "Can we get around by heading the other way?"

Venn shook her head. "It moves away from the river and becomes a taller cliff the farther that way you go."

Kate looked over the edge. Past the slope below was a strip of forest, and then a bend of the river flowed past, wide and smooth. She traced the current, noting a sheltered, still spot. "Can we climb down here?"

Venn peered over the drop. "Are you serious?"

"It's only steep here at the top, and that curve in the river is the sort of place that wellstones were caught farther upstream. It's a great place to check." Kate moved closer to the edge. "There's a way down here. We'll head straight for the river." She sat on the edge and scooted forward, stretching until her feet brushed a wide rock, and she dropped down onto it, her foot slipping a little in the snow.

"Could you pick a route *more* likely to get one of us injured?" Venn asked, sliding down behind her.

"Yes. Anything anywhere near the White Wood." The next boulder was huge, but too far below her to reach, so she rolled onto her stomach, shimmied to the edge, and half jumped, half dropped the last foot.

Venn frowned down at her. "You're acting a little…"

Kate raised an eyebrow.

"Impulsive."

"Venn," Kate said, giving the elf room to land, "the only thing I need is a wellstone, then we can get the box somewhere *safe*. Why would we waste any time when every moment here could drag us back into some mess?"

Venn landed lightly next to her. "I'm not disagreeing with you. I'm just…"

Kate let out an annoyed breath. "Just what?"

"All these decisions feel a little…imbalanced."

A flicker of irritation rose in Kate. "Naevys is imbalanced. I'm resolved." She sat and slid over the side of the boulder, dropping a few feet to a small shelf. Her foot slipped in the snow, and she crashed to her knees, slamming her shin onto a hidden rock and letting out a groan of pain.

"Naevys is both imbalanced and resolved." Venn jumped down next to her, landing much more gracefully and offering Kate a hand. "The two things are not mutually exclusive."

Kate took it and pulled herself up. Her leg ached, but the little lantern of hope that the box offered was getting closer. She offered Venn a smile that was at least half grimace. "Maybe, but we're down the steep part. Just this rocky slope left—"

"That reminds me enough of the ravine to make this plan even less appealing."

Kate squinted down at the hillside. It did look a bit like the ravine. But it spread out to her right and left as far as she could see, so there was no way around it. "Let's not think about that."

She started downhill, clambering over the larger stones, occasionally sliding down an extra foot or two. Her legs, already soaked, grew wetter.

Near the bottom, the rocks ended, and she strode out onto a flat stretch leading to the last barrier of trees before the river. The snow had mostly stopped falling, but it was piled above her ankles on the ground. The sky was still heavy with clouds, and the trunks of the trees were steeped in darkness.

"Do you have any idea how deep the river is near here?" Kate asked. "Will we be wading in to get the wellstones or swimming?"

"I would guess—" Something big rustled in the trees ahead, and Venn stopped, grabbing Kate's arm.

A black shape moved in the shadows, and a shiver ran up Kate's neck. "Is that," she asked slowly, "a walking tree?"

The shape slipped closer, moving on undulating roots with an unnerving smoothness, shouldering itself through the trees by its branches.

Kate drew back. "Is that...Naevys?"

CHAPTER FIFTEEN

The creature, shaped almost like a birch, glided into the open. It was too thin and too fluid. Instead of bark, it was covered with a viscous liquid that shifted and churned, a dark, seething green flecked with embers of emerald that sparked into existence before flickering out. Carved into its trunk was a face. Not a human face, but two eyes that burned with dark green fire and a gaping slash of a mouth that hung open, letting out a chilling groan.

Venn swore. "*Naiwyn!*"

Another slid out of the trees a dozen paces to the left, this one churning with a dusky orange glow.

Kate's hand went to the small knife on her belt. "Who's *Naiwyn*?"

"It's not a who—it's a what. A tree sprite." Venn began to back up slowly. "A very rare tree sprite. Created from the spirit of an elder tree."

Kate stepped backward, trying to keep in the trail of footprints they'd just left. "Created?"

"To guard things. Do your best not to look threatening."

Kate forced herself to release the hold on the knife. "Created by who?"

"The royal family."

Kate gave Venn an incredulous look. "The elven royal family? So Thallion, Faron, or Naevys?"

Venn gave a wince for an answer.

The two *naiwyn* stopped a half-dozen paces from the trees, their branches shifting and groaning as though they were caught in a heavy wind. Their burning eyes bored into Kate, and she took another step back. "What are they guarding here?"

"I have no idea."

A quiet click sounded as Venn mounted a dart into her crossbow.

"Can you put them to sleep?"

"Probably not." Venn scanned the tree line ahead of them. "But it makes me feel better. I only see two of them."

Kate cast out. The wave rolled across the snow, setting bits of grass beneath it to glowing. When it reached the first *naiwyn*, the creature exploded into light as though it had suddenly burst into flame. Every root was a writhing mass of fiery green, the trunk as bright as the center of a forge, and each grasping tree branch its own flaming bough.

The second *naiwyn* burst into a torrent of deep, brooding orange. Their brightness nearly drowned out the light of the trees just behind them, which didn't appear to conceal any more.

"How do we get past them?" Kate asked.

"No one gets past the *naiwyn* when they're guarding something." Venn grimly started moving along the rocks in the direction the path above the cliff would have taken them. "They can draw on the power of the woods, but they obey mindlessly. Whatever they've been sent to guard, they will guard incessantly, but they aren't aggressive unless someone tries to get past them. We need to go around." The tree sprites held their ground at the edge of the trees, and Venn set out along the rocks.

She and Kate moved quickly, eyeing the tree line as they went.

Venn glanced over her shoulder, even after a rise had blocked the *naiwyn* from view. "I've never heard of them outside the White Wood." She frowned. "I've actually only heard of them being used once, and that was when they were set as a guard over the Elder Grove during an uprising not long after my people came here from the Wildwood." Her frown deepened. "Actually, that uprising was blamed on Renault."

"He tried to get into the Elder Grove?"

Venn shrugged. "I don't know the details. I wasn't even friends with Faron at the time. I just heard about it through rumors."

"What would they do to us if we got too close?" Kate asked.

"Their touch burns like fire. If they grab hold of you, they'll burn you until you die."

Kate raised an eyebrow. "They're made of fire?"

"*Ael'iza*, but in limitless amounts. Their form isn't really a body. There is no part of them that is critical. You could cut off limbs or roots or saw their trunks in half, and they would merely heal themselves."

"How does anyone fight them?"

"No one does." Venn looked up into the trees, as though looking for an answer. "The only thing that stops them is their creator cutting off the *ael'iza* feeding them." Her brow creased. "*Naiwyn* are a last resort. Creating one *kills* an elder tree. No elf would do this unless there was no other option."

Kate stared at her. "And you're *sure* that's what we just saw. Not some...common tree sprite or something?"

"If you'd ever seen a common tree sprite, you wouldn't ask that."

"Then what are they guarding? What's past that stand of trees?"

"Nothing!" Venn flung her hand toward the south. "Past that is a patchy human forest, the river, the entrance to the dwarves' realm and...nothing else. In a couple of days, we'll reach human settlements, but they're just small villages. There's nothing notable in that direction for at least a week."

Kate cast out several times behind them as they continued down along the rocky slope, but there was nothing beyond the tree line but trees.

When the trees drew closer, Kate cast out again, finding nothing unusual. "Do you think we can cut through these trees and get to the river—" She glanced at Venn. "They're not protecting the river, are they?"

"I don't know why they would. The river isn't elven."

"Could they be protecting wellstones in it?"

"Then why just here?"

Nothing moved by the time they reached the first tree, and Venn set her hand on it. She held it there for a moment before shaking her head. "They won't tell me anything."

"All right," Kate started between the trunks. "Let's try to get through quickly."

In a few minutes, Kate caught a glimpse of the dark river—and a glimmer of deep red shifted into view. She grabbed Venn's arm just as the elf skidded to a stop.

The *naiwyn* was shaped like a gnarled old pine but glided over the snow with an unsettling smoothness. Kate backed up. "Is that a third? Or can they change shape and color?"

"That's a third."

The glowing sprite slipped toward them, revealing a second just behind it, only slightly more orange than the one they'd seen earlier. The two creatures slid soundlessly between the trees, their surfaces churning and smoldering.

"Venn…"

"Run!" Venn sprinted back toward the edge of the trees.

Kate raced after, her feet sliding in the snow with each step.

They were passing the last trees when a flash of dark red whipped toward Venn. It looked like charred bark floating on a molten river. A strange shimmer of icy blue was interlaced through it all.

The end of the branch smashed into Venn just below her shoulder, sending her crashing to the ground with a cry of pain.

Kate dropped to her knees beside her, flinging up a shield of *vitalle*.

Another branch lashed out, crashing against the shield and sending pain slicing across Kate's palm. She flung up her other hand and poured more *vitalle* into the shield. Venn scrambled back out of the trees, away from the *naiwyn*, and Kate crawled backward with her.

The sprite stopped at the last trunk. Through the shield, which glimmered with a thin layer of Kate's remnant, the sprite stood like a roiling mass of blood-red fire and charred wood. The lighter-colored *naiwyn* hovered behind it, branches moving and groaning.

"Venn?" Kate risked a look over her shoulder.

"That hurt," Venn said through clenched teeth, gripping her upper arm.

Kate stood, holding the shield in place. The *naiwyn* didn't move. "Can you walk?"

Venn scrambled to her knees, then staggered to her feet, grabbing Kate's shoulder for balance.

"What do you say we back away slowly?" Kate said, stepping backward through the snow. She held the shield up for a dozen paces, but the *naiwyn* merely stood in the snow like fiery sentinels.

"What are they guarding?" Venn's voice was pained.

"I don't know." Kate dropped the shield. "But tell me you know of a route that goes very far away from whatever it is. And preferably stays away from the river for a while."

"We can avoid this whole area," Venn said, "but it requires a bit of backtracking. And you're going to get to see your ravine again."

CHAPTER SIXTEEN

Venn staggered again, her feet dragging over the snowy slope.

Kate pulled Venn's unhurt arm over her shoulder. "That's more than a burn, isn't it?" She cast out. The arm over Kate's shoulder was bright, along with the near side of Venn's body. But everything from her sternum to her other shoulder was dim, as though the *vitalle* had been sucked out of it. Even before Kate's wave faded, the area grew darker.

"My arm is cold, along with half my chest." Venn squeezed her eyes shut, leaning heavily on Kate. "It hurts to breathe."

Kate pushed some *vitalle* into Venn. It ran up against the dimmer part, and instead of driving it back, Kate's energy was absorbed into it, darkening along with Venn. She craned to look backward. The *naiwyn* remained where they were. Ahead, the cliff to their left continued to descend and shrink, until it disappeared entirely back into the forest. "If you can make it to those trees, we'll see if we can find a big tree to keep you from suffocating."

"Any tree," Venn said through her teeth.

Kate lengthened her stride as Venn's feet stumbled on.

The cliff finally ended near a broad fir tree. Kate cast out toward it but found no *naiwyn*. Kate half supported, half dragged Venn to it, where she collapsed, eyes shut, groaning in pain.

After another glance back to make sure no *naiwyn* were following them, Kate knelt and set her hand on Venn's shoulder, waiting to feel the *vitalle* from the tree pour into her.

A dozen small streams began, but the flow was slow and unfocused. Something almost like a quiet sob tore from Venn, and she squeezed her eyes tighter shut.

Kate stared at the trickle of *vitalle*, shocked at the difference from how the trees used to rush into Venn. "Here." She set her hand on Venn's shoulder above the burn, wincing at the hiss of pain it elicited from her. Pushing her own *vitalle* out, she gathered the energy from the tree and led it toward the coldness in Venn's chest. The *vitalle* followed her direction effortlessly, and the edges of the cold began to warm.

The *naiwyn* had burned through Venn's cloak and shirt, leaving holes as wide as Kate's palm, their edges charred. A strip of her shoulder about two fingers wide was an ugly, raw red, the top layers of skin gone.

Kate funneled her own *vitalle* to the burn, but there was nothing to do there. The coldness surrounding it was too dark. Venn's body wasn't trying to heal it. Kate refocused on the tree, drawing its power into Venn's back, leading it to the coldness that was now rapidly shrinking toward her shoulder.

When her whole chest was warm, Venn took a deep breath. "Thank you."

"The burn is..." Kate winced.

Venn twisted to look at it. "It doesn't hurt much." The coldness was completely out of her chest now, and the heat was pressing toward her shoulder.

Kate leaned closer to the burn itself. Along the very edge were glimmers of dark red and tiny specks of icy blue. "Venn! There's runelight here!" She stretched out a blade of her own runelight. "I think it might hurt soon."

Kate cut through the barrier, and the healing warmth flowed against the burn. Venn let out another hiss.

"Sorry." Kate funneled the *vitalle* from the tree farther down Venn's arm. The muscles of her arm were so dim Kate could barely see them, and she pushed the *vitalle* faster, lest the tissue die completely.

When Venn's entire arm and chest were nearly back to their normal brightness, Kate sat back and looked at the burn. The *vitalle* from the tree was crowded around the edges of the wound, working to bolster the healing that Venn's body had started, but...it was a burn. And burns were terribly slow to heal.

"That's going to take a while." Kate rummaged in her pack, pulling out the jar of yellow salve and a neatly rolled bandage. "Lucky for you, burns are one injury Keepers are well prepared for."

"Have you ever burned your hands this badly?" Venn asked, her face pinched in pain.

"No." Kate pulled out her water skin. "Hold your arm out while I try to clean this, or your entire sleeve will be soaked."

"Do you think I care about a wet sleeve?"

"Wet sleeves are horrible. Just do it." She helped Venn raise her arm and poured water over the burn. Once she'd rinsed it, she opened the jar. "It's hard to force yourself to use more *vitalle* when it hurts. I lose focus before I burn this badly." She scooped out a glob of the thick salve. "But there have been Keepers who have. Either the *vitalle* was pulled out of them by some other force, or they were desperate enough to continue. This is going to sting for a moment."

She wiped the salve on the burn, and Venn twitched away with a snarl of pain.

"But it should also numb it in another moment." Kate wiped on more, covering the whole burn.

Slowly, Venn's arm relaxed.

Kate wrapped a bandage around it, glancing over her shoulder again. "That'll take some time to heal, but I have plenty of salve. We should be able to keep the pain under control."

Venn stared back toward the trees where the *naiwyn* had been. "There are four *naiwyn* here. Why?"

Kate put the salve back into her pack. "Could it be Thallion?"

"I don't think he has the power to do it anymore."

"Then it has to be Naevys, right? Faron wouldn't do something like this, would he?"

"You expect me to know that?"

The oddness of the situation itched Kate's mind. Four nearly legendary guards keeping people from entering what looked like a perfectly normal part of the forest. Her fingers closed around her journal, and she almost looked for a pencil before her eyes fell on the box. She pushed the journal away and closed up her pack. "We'll ask Faron when we come back." She offered Venn a hand. "The box first."

Venn gave a slow nod, then grabbed Kate's arm, pulling herself up. "The box first." She moved her shoulder gingerly but winced in pain. "C'mon." She started north through the trees, paralleling the river but keeping it at a distance. "We'll have to head the wrong way for several hours."

The existence of the *naiwyn* quickly overrode any objection to the delay. Kate's mind wandered back to the sprites as they walked, mulling over the oddness of it all. Venn walked in a similar silence, the thoughtful frown on her face indicating her thoughts ran along the same lines. Several times, Kate almost opened her mouth to ask a question about them, but each time, she shoved it away. The box first.

As they moved through the trees, Kate cast out occasionally.

Venn glanced back at her after her third wave. "Nervous we'll be attacked again?"

"Yes, but also, the last time we were near here, the underground pathways Naevys was using to drain *vitalle* from the forest were so obvious. Like guides heading straight for the ravine. I could tell how close we were by the size of the pathways. But today everything is perfectly normal. There's nothing draining away at all. It feels exactly like a normal forest should."

"You say that as though it's bad."

Kate looked through the woods, searching for any sign of the ravine ahead. "Not bad. It's just…" She paused, trying to sort out what was bothering her. "The ravine was important to Naevys, and we don't really know why. Now that she's free from being trapped inside it, she just…stopped caring about it?"

The corner of Venn's mouth turned up. "You're upset that the ravine isn't special anymore?"

Kate allowed a smile too. "I know it sounds dumb. But the ravine *is* special. Isn't it? A lot of very strange things have happened there, and Naevys has been at the heart of all of them."

"I thought you were putting all mysteries from this area out of your mind until we come back."

"I am." Kate cast out again, finding the ground exactly as full of *vitalle* as it had been moments before.

Venn watched the wave spread through the forest, looking mildly amused. "Maybe it's connected to the *naiwyn*."

Kate stumbled to a stop. "Do you think?"

Venn let out a laugh. "No. It's just funny to watch your mind try to piece together puzzles that we have almost no clues about."

"Just wait until I start pestering you endlessly about Faron while we walk. I'm interested to know what kind of king you think he'll make."

"We are not talking about Faron for the next four weeks."

A clank sounded from up ahead along with a snippet of a cheerful voice.

Venn tilted her head. "You've got to be kidding." She strode forward.

Kate followed, and in a few minutes they came out of the trees and onto the river bank. Just upstream across the water sat the ravine. The familiar slope was covered in several inches of snow, each rock looking like a soft pile of white down.

Not a single line of *vitalle* led to it from the forest, but a quarter of the way up the slope, Tribal, Silas, Fix, Aislin, and Matlen all huddled around a section cleared of snow where the carriage was buried.

"Aislin and Matlen," Venn shouted across the river. "Why are you two not home?"

The entire group spun to look at them.

Aislin glanced at her brother, then wrinkled her nose. "Really, Auntie Venn, you can't expect us to follow directions like that. Not when there's treasure to uncover."

"You don't care about gold!" Venn strode along the bank until she came to the stepping stones and jumped quickly across them.

"You took a wrong turn if you're heading to Queensland," Silas said.

Kate scanned the slope for signs of remnants. A surge of frustration rose at the blanket of snow that hid everything from her sight. As though the secrets here were now buried even deeper.

Fix straightened from where he was fiddling with some rope and several long branches and gave Kate a wide smile. His body was wrapped in the slightly lumpy patchwork cloak he'd made, complete with a hood lined with wool from Kate's old glove.

"You come to help, Twig?" Tribal called down.

"No, our way back was blocked." She motioned to the two dwarves. "Don't try to get back to Rullduin any time soon."

"We don't intend to." Silas worked a thick branch between two rocks.

Aislin peered down the slope and then scanned the sky. "What happened to Crofftus? Is he still in that adorable bunny?"

"Probably not. He went looking for a better animal than a rabbit to travel in, but we haven't seen him since." Kate glanced at Venn. "What do you think would happen if he wandered too close to the *naiwyn*?"

Venn hesitated. "That depends on whether they see him as an animal or a human."

Kate felt a niggle of worry crawl up her neck. "Then let's hope he found some quick, skittish animal like a deer so he can get away from them." She glanced back the way they'd come. "And something smart enough to track us, or he's not going to know where we went."

"That rabbit seem jumpier than usual to the rest of you today?" Tribal asked, positioning another branch next to his brother's.

"Yes," Venn said. "He was nervous."

Fix's hands stilled on his ropes, and he met Kate's gaze with frightened eyes.

"The queen did almost kill him," Kate said.

Tribal and Silas heaved at their branches, and the rock shifted.

"Felt like more than that," Silas grunted.

Kate raised an eyebrow. "I didn't realize you two were so tuned in to emotions."

Tribal eased off his branch and resituated it. "We're tuned in to deception." He gestured to a small wedge-shaped rock near Kate's feet. "Could I have that?"

"Deception?" Kate handed him the rock, and he arranged it near his stick. "Venn, did it feel like deception?"

Venn gave a hum that sounded ambivalent. "He was certainly

wound up, but the rabbit was terrified. I just figured it was rubbing off on Crofftus too."

The gnoblin's hands clutched his rope.

"Fix, did anything happen between the queen and Crofftus?"

He hesitated, then made a hand gesture to the dwarves.

"Right," Silas said, "they talked. About not hurting books."

Fix gave a worried look and another sign.

"Longer? What else did they talk about?"

The gnoblin shrugged, touched his ears, and made a slashing motion.

Tribal frowned. "You couldn't hear anything they said?"

Fix shook his head.

"Naevys has a great deal of control over the animals in the White Wood," Venn said. "Maybe since Crofftus is in an animal, she can talk straight into his mind."

"He did say she sifted through his mind." Kate glanced behind them again, feeling a pang of guilt for not asking him more. "He didn't say that she hurt him."

"You think the stuffy old bag would admit to us if she did?" Tribal asked.

Kate straightened. "She touched him! When she touched me in the cave, she was suddenly inside my mind, searching it. If she grabbed the rabbit, could she have read Crofftus's mind?"

Venn looked thoughtfully back toward the woods. "I'm inclined to think she could."

"Then maybe that's what unnerved him." Kate followed Venn's gaze. "I hope he finds us soon."

Silas and Tribal heaved against the rock again. It shifted, and the wedge dropped into place.

"Now that you're here," Silas said, "you want to find some branches and give us a hand?"

She studied where the dwarves were working. "I think you're digging in the wrong place."

"You think you know better than us where to dig?" Tribal said with an incredulous look. "Never mind, we don't want your help."

"You're too low." She pointed higher on the slope. "The carriage was buried under the overhang of a huge rock, like that one."

"That big one is new," Silas said, grunting with the effort of moving the rock. "The old big one is now buried here."

She started up the slope toward them. "Let me see something. Even though Naevys's web of runelight is gone, I should still be able to sense the runes on the carriage." She reached them and cast out, looking for the faint line of etched runes that should be visible around the edges of the carriage.

Beneath the snow, the entire hillside burst into light.

She twitched at the same time as Venn, while Aislin and Matlen let out gasps and jumped back, clambering onto a large rock.

Running along the ground beneath the rockslide, ropes of *vitalle* crisscrossed over the slope, knotted together like a net. A hum rippled through it, spreading across the slope.

Shimmers of ruddy gold spread along every strand.

"What?" Silas froze in the act of leveraging a thick branch under a rock. "What do you see?"

"The net is still here!" Kate took a step back. "It's stronger than before!" She looked back at the woods across the river just as her wave washed into it.

"How?" Venn spun to take in the vivid web of light. "Where is all this coming from?"

The net was laid out under the rockslide, ending at the river on the bottom and the edge of the slide on the side where the carriage lay buried. The top of the slope was nothing but a rocky hillside, but the far side…

The trees looked normal, except for a patch, about halfway up the hillside, where a large pine stood dead, its needles all stripped away.

Kate pointed over the rocks to where the forest resumed. "Is this safe to cross?"

"Nope," Silas said. "The temperature's dropped too quickly. Things are bound to have grown a little unstable. Go up and around."

She looked uphill at the steep climb to the top. They stood barely a quarter of the way up. "Are you sure?"

"Yes," Tribal said, "we're sure. But by all means, risk your twiggy neck by choosing your own way."

Aislin leaned close to him. "The carriage is right here. I saw it light up."

"Of course it is," he grumbled.

"It's huge!" Aislin motioned to the ground. "I was expecting something little for the emperor to ride around in. This could have carried four people with room to spare! Maybe six!"

The ravine was unsettlingly like the Herald vision from earlier —the ravine caged in Naevys's web of protection. Kate's eyes dropped to the carriage again as she remembered the bright knot of *vitalle* that had sat over it. Images of Home burning and her friend's bodies lying on the ground flashed through her mind, bringing with them a ripple of dread and stoking the desire to get herself—and the box—as far from this as she could.

Silas shoved at his branch, and Kate set a hand on his arm. "Naevys is protecting this carriage for some reason. I don't think you should disturb it."

Fix shrank back from the rocks.

Silas raised an eyebrow at her. "You offering to stay and help?"

The unanswered questions buried in the ravine grabbed hold of her, but the creeping dread pushed them away. "No. And you should leave it alone. Messing with Naevys's treasure is the last thing I want to do right now." She glanced at Venn. "Were we headed up over this hill anyway?"

Venn nodded. "The path south is on the far side of this hill."

"Then let's go uphill, and before we leave, we'll see what she's using to fuel all this protection." Kate pointed at the dwarves. "You should absolutely leave this alone. Nothing good comes of disturbing this."

The two dwarves exchanged looks that were slightly troubled.

"Please try to stay safe." Kate started uphill with Venn. They'd gone a dozen steps before the questions became too much to hold in. "How is the net still in place? Naevys was drawing from everything across the river. There's nothing that powerful on this side."

"Maybe there's some source of power under the slope?" Venn asked.

"I don't think so. When we were inside the caves, it seemed like Naevys was drawing *vitalle* in from the outside."

The higher they climbed, the wider their view became. Behind them, across the river, the snow-covered forest rose up to the feet of the western mountain range, growing thicker and brighter as it shifted into the elven White Wood. When they neared the top, glimpses of hilltops to the north became visible too, covered by a thick, prickly carpet of pines. Above the rockslide, the slope lay undisturbed, and Kate started across it, watching the ground at her feet, tense for any sign of motion. Venn came behind her, with the dwarves, Fix, and the elf twins following too.

At the far side of the rockslide, the trees grew no more than a handful of paces from the jumble of rocks. She cast out, and the net covering the rockslide flared up again like a fiery web. About halfway down the slope—exactly where the dead pine stood—a blazing river of *vitalle* flowed into the rockslide, so bright that Kate drew back.

"Kate!" Venn grabbed her arm, pointing north.

More hills were visible from here, mostly speckled with greens and whites of the snow-draped trees. But in a jagged line heading north from the dead pine, a wide swath of the forest was grey. Dead trees stood bare of needles, with only thin lines of snow piled atop their branches. A river of death, rolling from hill to hill, leaving ash-grey husks in its wake.

Tribal came up to Kate's shoulder, swearing under his breath in dwarven.

"Are those...humans?" Silas asked, pointing to one bare, ashy patch where strange lumps were visible on the ground.

"Cattle," Venn said grimly.

"Too skinny for cattle," Tribal said, gripping his branch tightly.

"Withered cattle," Aislin whispered.

Kate stared over the long line of desiccated forest leading away from the ravine. It twisted and snaked over hills but always shifted back toward a single destination.

A valley with thin lines of smoke trailing up, from what could only be the town of Home.

CHAPTER SEVENTEEN

A shocked numbness filled Kate's mind as she took in the destruction. "She's taking *vitalle* from Home?"

"What are those patches?" Aislin pointed to several wide stretches of lifeless forest disconnected from the main line.

"I don't—" Venn stopped, her brow furrowing more with each section she studied. "I think each of those hills used to have a very old tree on it."

A piece of a puzzle fell into place in Kate's mind. "Like an elder tree?"

"There are no elder trees outside the elven woods," Matlen said.

Venn stared at Kate, her mouth open. "She wouldn't…"

"You said it took the life of an elder tree," Kate said. "But if Naevys wanted to create one outside the Wood, and she had to use an ancient human tree…?"

Venn's eyes slid shut. "It would kill a massive part of the forest. Just like that."

"Create a what?" Tribal asked.

"A *naiwyn*," Kate answered.

The elf twins' mouths dropped open.

"Which is...?" Silas prompted.

"A tree sprite," Venn answered.

"A murderous, fiery, single-minded, unkillable tree spirit used to guard things," Kate said, "which can both burn you and suck out your life at the same time." She gestured to the burned hole in Venn's cloak. "You really shouldn't try to get to Rullduin along the river anytime soon."

Tribal glanced at his brother. "Yet another way the elves will try to kill us."

"This settles it, Venn." Kate looked over the three barren patches. "It's Naevys, not Faron, who made them. Unless you can think of a reason Faron would want to power her protection over the ravine."

"I'm not even sure Faron *could* do this. To have this much sway over the forest outside the White Wood, it has to be the Warden." Venn turned to Kate. "Can you cut off the *ael'iza* flowing into the ravine?"

Kate's wave had long since faded, but she could still almost feel the massive stream of *vitalle* flowing into the rockslide. "No. There's far too much of it."

The words felt ashy on her tongue. Strictly speaking, it was true, but...

Kate shifted her pack. The corner of the aenigma box pressed against her shoulder blade, the blazing lantern of hope calling her toward it. Thoughts of Bo and Evan swirled through her mind. She had everything she needed to open the box. Glancing down at the river, she paused. She'd forgotten about the wellstones after the *naiwyn* attack, but there were almost certainly some right there. She could climb down, grab as many as she could find, come back up the slope, and follow the game trail over the top of the hill and into a different part of the world. A part that would, eventually, lead her back home.

Strictly speaking, she'd never be able to stop this powerful of a flow of *vitalle*.

She closed her eyes, and the lantern sprayed silvery moonlight through the dark path, so close she could almost reach out and take it. The hope stretched out toward her, catching at her and pulling her closer.

Her chest ached with the need to get the box safe, but she opened her eyes, and Naevys's river of death flowed over the hills with an unseen current, pulling her toward Home. It caught at the idea of leaving and unspooled it. Bo and Evan were joined by Yellow in his tavern. Nevin and Gerren, only just reunited now that Gerren's mind was healed. The faces of Home swam through her vision against the foreboding grey of the withered trees.

How much had Naevys already taken?

The pull of the box nagged at her, and the thought that she might lose this chance to open it almost made her stop.

But the threat from Naevys was too big to ignore.

She adjusted her pack again. "I can't cut off the flow of vitalle from this end. But most likely it's being built by smaller streams closer to Home, and maybe those I can stop."

She waited for one of the dwarves to make a joke about walking back into elven entanglements, but Silas started back down the hill. "I'll grab our packs."

"You're coming?" Kate asked.

Under his thick brow, Tribal's troubled gaze was focused on the smoke trails rising from Home. "Never going to get to our treasure until we take care of the mad queen," he said lightly, then glanced at Aislin and Matlen. "Might actually be time for you two to head to the lakes."

"Absolutely not," Aislin said. "We're coming with you to

make sure Home is safe." The glance she flicked at Venn held less certainty than her declaration.

"As far as Home," Venn agreed. "I don't want you two traveling alone around here. But if things look safe around the town, then you'll leave immediately, find Evay, and tell her everything that's happening. She definitely needs to know about this."

Aislin and Matlen gave quick nods.

Kate cast one last look at the trail that would lead eventually back toward the Keeper Stronghold, then set her shoulders and started down the slope toward the beginnings of Naevys's destruction. "Venn, it might be time to see if you can contact Faron. I think we're going to need some elven help."

Venn wrinkled her nose in annoyance. "We're too far from the White Wood, but the pine in the center of Home is over five hundred years old. I can contact him from there."

Kate trudged uphill through the snow, kicking up not only puffs of powdery whiteness but a disconcerting grey dust that reminded her of ash. The withered trunks around them stood like brittle husks. She reached up to push a branch out of her way. It crumbled at her touch, showering down snow and flakes of desiccated wood.

The desolation was wide enough for a half-dozen horses to ride abreast of each other. Kate resisted the urge to cast out again. Every wave she'd sent out had found absolutely no life along the path. No blades of grass, no small rodents, no insects. Not even the echo of *vitalle* that fallen leaves and needles clung to for a few days.

Aislin brushed a finger over a stick poking out of the snow, watching with a troubled look as it disintegrated. "She did all this since last night?"

"All of this," Venn said, "plus create four *naiwyn*."

"And fill the forest with the thorny frenbrush," Kate added.

"And set vine traps to capture dwarves," Silas added.

Kate frowned. "That is a *lot* of things."

"She had been sleeping in a cave for weeks," Tribal pointed out. "Maybe she was antsy."

"My point," Kate said, "is that maybe it wasn't all her."

Venn considered the idea. "Who else would help her? This"—she motioned to the withered forest—"could only be done by the Warden. Combine that with the *naiwyn*, and..." She shook her head. "All the strangeness we've encountered today feels like the Warden."

"Strangeness," Silas muttered. "That's a generous way of putting it."

Fix's head poked out of the top of the dwarf's pack, his hands clutching the leather as he took in the bleak trail.

At the top of the hill, at least twenty cattle lay dead, their flesh shrunken until each bone jutted against their hide. Kate cast out, but beyond her companions, nothing in the clearing lit up. There weren't even maggots on the cattle. They moved through, giving each carcass a wide berth. At the far side of the hilltop, the dwarves stopped, and Kate came up next to them.

Naevys's trail plowed through the forest with jagged edges and sharp angles, but it seemed to grow narrower the farther it went. The slash of bare trees on the hillside nearest to Home was no wider than a cart trail.

"Your story about the duke and the beetles is feeling less farfetched," Venn said.

Kate winced. "It is." She watched the distant scar closely, but it didn't appear to be growing. "Maybe Naevys's trail hasn't reached Home yet."

"The queen's route is as mad as she is if her goal was reaching the town quickly," Silas said, gesturing to the erratic path of dead trees. "If we leave it and follow that stream, we can be there in less than two hours."

The trails of smoke from Home rose into the air, grey against the white of the clouds. They looked much like they had every other time Kate had seen the town. Along Naevys's trail there were snowy lumps she couldn't identify. Most too big for a human. "What if there's more to see?"

"More dead trees?" Silas asked. "More dead animals? Seems pretty clear what the old bag was doing. She sucked the life out of everything in her way. I'm not sure I want to know if that included any hunters unlucky enough to be in her path."

"And we need to make sure Yellow and his log mead aren't..." Tribal waved at the cattle. "Like that."

Aislin let out a small gasp. "Naevys wouldn't do this to humans, would she?"

Venn kicked the snow out of the way to reveal a shriveled hawk lying on the ground. "I think it's fair to say we have no idea what she would do."

Kate pulled her eyes away from the withered creature, glancing around again as though she'd find Crofftus winging down to them. "You're right. I think we've seen enough of Naevys's handiwork."

Tribal started toward the stream, followed by Silas, the two dwarves' feet plowing a wide enough path through the snow that the slope was manageable. The water wound between several hills before bringing them to the edge of the wide valley containing Home. Fields began as soon as the land flattened. The snow over their long, straight rows was poked through with shorn-off stalks of grain. The fields led directly up to the town, which, aside from an unusual amount of activity along its outskirts, looked normal.

The trail of grey trees from Naevys was barely wider than a wagon at the edge of the field, but Venn squatted next to the nearest stalks and ran her fingers over them. "Dead," she said quietly.

Kate cast out, and her wave rolled over a wide path of lifeless crops that wound across the field before breaking apart into a dozen fingers that stretched around the town, none wider than a footpath. Both Aislin and Matlen watched with troubled expressions, unusually subdued.

"Aren't all crops dead in the winter?" Tribal asked.

"Dormant, not dead." Venn stood. "These, she's killed. They won't grow again in the spring or even fertilize the soil. Everything of value has been stripped from them."

"At least it doesn't look like she headed for the people." Kate started down a row in the field toward the nearest building. A crowd clustered in a street at the edge of town, lashing sharp sticks together, forming a bristling barrier that faced the field.

A shout rang out before they'd gotten close, and a handful of men lined the wall with pitchforks and heavy shovels.

"Merrick!" Tribal waved an arm. "Is that any way to greet your favorite dwarves?"

"Weasel Brothers?" a tall, broad man called out. "Get in here. Not a day to be out an' about in the hills!"

As far as Kate could see along the edge of the town, more barricades were already in place.

At the top of Silas's pack, Fix creased his brow in worry.

"You want to get down before we go into town?" Kate asked. At the gnoblin's nervous nod, she lifted him out of Silas's pack and set him on the ground. He scurried to the nearest lump of snow and burrowed into it.

As they drew closer, Merrick leaned a huge, long-handled hammer against the nearest house and stepped through a small gap in the barrier. "Venn," he greeted her with a nod. His gaze took in Aislin and Matlen, who were smiling brightly again, and landed on Kate. He inclined his head slightly to her before turning back to the dwarves. "Your hands'll be welcome here today."

"What's this for?" Tribal asked, reaching out to hold one of the stakes while a townsman lashed it into place.

"Did you see any more o' 'em in woods?" the townsman by Tribal asked with a wary note in his voice.

"Any more what?" Silas asked.

The man's brow darkened. "Pack o' wolves. Or something like 'em. Came late, in th' dead o' night. Broke into Mellron's house. Smashed his doors open, pulled apart th' place."

Merrick leaned on the end of the barrier and crossed his arms, which were nearly as thick as the dwarves'. He wore a blacksmith's apron, and his face had an open, friendly look. Despite his relaxed posture, his dark eyes continually scanned the hills.

"Was anyone hurt?" Kate asked the townsman.

"Not at Mellron's. He an' th' wife sleep in th' loft, but at Nevin's, one o' the creatures tore apart th' bed two o' his girls was sleeping in. Tore a chunk outta little Rellee's leg."

"Wolves?" Venn asked. "Broke into houses?"

"Wolves is the closest thing we can call 'em."

"Bigger than wolves should be," Merrick said, still focused on the hills, "with pelts more like ice than hair."

"*Gwerocs*?" Kate asked.

Venn's brow furrowed. "They don't travel in packs. How many were there?"

"Three, best we can tell." The townsman gestured into the town. "Most o' the buildings they tore apart were storage sheds or barns. They wrecked an old house just outside of town, but no one's lived there in a decade."

"Excuse me." Merrick lifted the end of the bulky blockade as though it were a tangle of thin twigs and pulled it back, making a wider opening. "Could you please come past the barrier, Keeper Kate?" he said, his voice calm and confident.

She blinked at the change of subject.

"Please," he said politely but firmly.

Kate hesitated. "Why me?"

"Because I've been tasked with keeping the humans behind the barriers along the southern end of town."

"Ah." Kate gestured to the elves and dwarves with her. "And they're not human." She looked over the empty fields. "Are we in danger?"

"Hard to say" he said, with a slight smile. "If you can assure me you know what dangers are coming and when they'll be here, I'll consider not insisting you step behind the barrier until it's closer to the time when they'll arrive."

"Behind your half-formed barrier?" Kate asked.

"A half-formed barrier is safer than no barrier at all. I would prefer if the Weasel brothers, Venn, and the other elves came behind it as well, but I was only charged with protecting the humans."

Kate fought to hold in an amused smile. "I don't really need…" She left the next words off, not wanting to insult the townsfolk for the work they'd done.

Tribal leaned forward with a grin. "What she means is that she's not a *common* human like you who needs a barricade. She's a *special* human."

Aislin let out a little giggle.

"Which means she gets herself in more trouble than the normal kind," Silas explained.

"I'm aware of the Keeper's skills," Merrick said, his voice unruffled, "and her propensity for running at dangerous things like wood trolls."

Kate raised an eyebrow. "The wood troll I helped put to sleep?"

"Have there been others?" he asked mildly.

Her other eyebrow rose. "Would it take more than one to

impress you?"

The smile was back at the edge of his mouth. "No. I was behind you, impotently holding a torch. I was suitably impressed. But, since it's evident that you're a valuable ally to our town, it would be irresponsible of me to let you stand in a more vulnerable place"—he gestured to where she stood—"when you could easily stand somewhere safer." He made a flourish toward the space inside the barrier.

Kate considered the man, who was remarkably well-spoken for a resident of a remote northern town. "You're not going to let this go, are you?"

His smile widened. "You haven't given me a good reason to."

She crossed her arms. "Who are you?"

"He's the blacksmith," Tribal said, moving past her. "And he's a bit stubborn. Maybe as stubborn as you."

Kate shifted her indignation toward him. "I'm not stubborn."

Venn gave a snort of laughter. "C'mon. Merrick's not the type to let things slide when he feels he's right."

"We're very happy to come in," Aislin said, stepping lightly past the barricade and surveying the townspeople.

Kate followed them in, catching the hint of woodsmoke in Merrick's remnant and the tang of metal that always lingered around fighters. She studied it, looking for any sign of brutality, but found none.

He moved the barrier back into place. "Thank you." He kept the smugness out of his voice, if not his smile.

"No," Kate said dryly. "Thank you. I feel so safe."

Merrick just gave her another easy smile.

"Where can I find the injured girl?" Kate asked.

He tilted his head curiously. "Can you heal her the way you fixed the boys' minds?"

"With a lot more ease."

He gave a thoughtful hum. "She's at the Blind Pig with our

healer woman. A good number of other folk are sheltering there too, especially the children and the old folks."

"Merrick," Tribal called from partway down the barrier, "if you've got an extra saw, we can get you some more stakes."

The blacksmith gave Kate a crooked smile. "If you'll excuse me, we have common human work to get done." He nodded to the elves, then headed for the dwarves.

Kate stared after him, half amused, half irritated. "What was that?"

Venn grinned at her. "I've always liked Merrick."

A cart rolled down the street toward them, creaking loudly, its top propped open and a colorful assortment of goods jostling inside of it. The short wiry old merchant who'd supplied the sleeping draught for the wood troll labored behind his handcart, giving them all a sunny smile. "Just making sure none of these hard-working folk are in need of anything!"

One of the wheels gave a long squeak as it was parked, and the merchant frowned at it. "You're going to need repairs soon."

"Hello, again!" Aislin said, traipsing toward him.

He took in Aislin and Matlen, and he grinned. "The elven twins! You two are astonishing!"

Matlen gave him a cheeky bow. "Not enough people realize that."

The merchant stroked his long beard as he stared at them. "Is there anything you want?" The question was asked absently, as though he'd asked it a million times and his mind was caught on something else.

"Just to look at all your interesting things." Aislin rummaged through his cart.

"Of course you don't want anything," the man said, almost to himself. "Elves rarely want anything, and elf twins!" At Matlen's curious look, he added, "It's just that elves are so connected to the woods that they seem to want for very little. On top of that, twins of all sorts are often very close to each other. With both, you two must be so connected to everything that you must desire very little."

Matlen gave a polite smile that showed no interest in the man's musings. Aislin picked up a woven red and green scarf and wrapped it around her neck. The pattern was lumpy and irregular, as though it had been made by a child, and Matlen let out a snort of laughter.

Remembering the merchant's remnant, Kate moved closer to him until the scents of the Wildwood of her youth enveloped her. The trees, the streams, the richness of the forest. A pang of homesickness rolled through her. "The town owes you for your help with the troll, and you're still offering to help more?"

He waved away her words. "When there's trouble, everyone should try to help." His smile turned self-conscious. The man's remnant sparkled with white, as though he were surrounded by stars. "Not that I have to tell a Keeper that."

Kate's desire to go home felt suddenly hollow.

"Is there anything *you* need?" he asked with a hopeful air.

She peered into the cart. "Do you have a magical amulet that helps open a puzzle box?"

He chuckled. "It's been quite some time since I've found a magical amulet that did anything. Did you enjoy the books I gave you?"

"What I've read."

He raised an eyebrow. "A Keeper has had new books for more than a day and hasn't read them all?"

She laughed. "Things have been…hectic."

"You know about Keepers?" Matlen asked.

"I've traveled quite a bit in Queensland." The merchant settled his hip on one of the handles.

"What are these?" Matlen pulled two small daggers from under other wares.

The merchant shifted to look at them better, and the cart let out a long groan. "Interesting choice. Those are magical dwarven knives."

Aislin took one of them, her face full of interest. "Magical?" She gave Kate a questioning glance.

The knives were slightly battered and plain. Kate cast out, and the elves lit up, but the daggers stayed dark. She gave a little shake of her head.

The peddler grinned. "There are more kinds of magic in the world than Keeper magic."

Kate's gaze strayed to the lifeless trail Naevys had left through the hills. "That is certainly true."

A bit of motion near the back of the cart caught Kate's eye, and Fix looked up at her with a skittish smile. He put a finger to his lips, then inspected the wheel that had been squeaking.

The merchant watched the elf twins closely, as though he were slightly perplexed. "Do you have anything to trade for the knives?"

"We don't have any coins," Aislin said.

"Doesn't have to be coins. It could be anything you have to trade."

Matlen sighed. "We don't have anything at all."

Aislin looked hopefully at Venn.

"The last thing you two need," Venn said, "is a pair of dwarven daggers. And it's time for you to go."

Aislin let out a groan.

Matlen pointed at the barricade. "But we could help, Auntie Venn."

"We'll do whatever you tell us to," Aislin said, looking desperate.

"This isn't a punishment," Venn said. "I need someone to get to Evay and tell her what's happening." Venn looked between the twins. "Please tell me I can trust you with this."

Aislin cast one last look at the men building the barricade and set the dagger down reluctantly.

"You can trust us, Auntie Venn," Matlen said. "I promise."

With a sad little smile from Aislin, the two disappeared.

The peddler blinked at the space where they'd just stood. "I like those two."

"Think they'll actually go?" Kate asked.

Venn just sighed.

The wooden cart gave a long creak, and the merchant frowned down at it, then leaned to see the far side. He drew in a surprised breath.

Fix met his gaze with wide, nervous eyes and, with a flash of green skin, disappeared into a hole in the ground.

The merchant pulled his cart back quickly, and the wheel moved silently. Kneeling, he examined the bit of wire wrapped around the hub along with a few other scraps of metal.

"That was Fix," Kate said. "He's a gnoblin, and, as his name implies, he's very good at fixing things."

The merchant looked at the freshly dug earth, which had collapsed behind Fix. "Wait! Let me pay you for the service!"

"He's shy," Kate said. "I don't think you'll see him again."

Venn started toward the square, and Kate fell in next to her.

"But—" The merchant sputtered. "I need to pay him! What does he want?"

"Give him something broken," Kate called over her shoulder. "If you can find him again!"

The sharp strikes of hammers echoed throughout the town as folk nailed planks over the windows. They passed the door of a large shed, hanging askew. Inside, the floor was strewn with broken bits of furniture and tatters of fabric. The door to a smaller closet in the back had been torn from its hinges and lay on the cluttered floor.

"That's the woodworker's house," Venn said quietly,

pointing to the house past the shed. "He has six children, all very young. Lucky the *gweroc* picked the shed instead of the house."

"Lucky, but a little odd, don't you think?" Kate asked. "Unless *gwerocs* are a lot less like wolves than they appear, wouldn't they go after homes with food and..." She cringed. "People. What is there in a woodworking shed?"

"And why were three of them looking for it together? *Gwerocs* are solitary creatures."

Kate shook off the memory of the icy creature stalking toward her on the outcropping. "Seeing as their fur is impervious to weapons and they're immune to magic, I can't imagine why they'd need a pack."

"I don't think they do. I think Naevys was controlling them."

"To what end? Is she just trying to terrorize the town?"

Venn looked over her shoulder at the shed. "I don't know, but I don't know anyone else who's capable of controlling them."

They entered the town square, and Venn grabbed Kate's arm, staring at the massive pine that grew in its center. "Cast out!"

Kate's wave rolled over the cobblestones, covered with trampled snow, finding nothing beyond a few hardy weeds lying faint and dormant between them. It reached the tree, and a stream of *vitalle* lit up beneath it, wrapping among the roots of the tree and flowing away across the square.

Venn rushed forward, under the branches of the huge tree, and slammed her hand against the bark.

The branches above her were covered in snow, but at the end of each cluster of needles, the green faded to a dry brown.

"No," Venn whispered.

"Naevys is draining this tree too?" Kate cast out again toward the roots. Life leaked from each root, thin threads of it joining together into larger strands until a wide stream flowed south under the cobblestones of the square. "These I can stop."

The sheltered ground under the tree was free of snow, and she knelt, setting her hand on the nearest root.

The trickle leaving it glittered with a thin shell of gold. Kate shaped a hook out of her runelight, reached under the stream, and pulled.

A shiver ran along the path of *vitalle*, and it stretched up, caught on her hook. A jab of pain shot into Kate's hand, and she let the hook dissolve. "The streams are encased in Naevys's runelight." She moved to the next root and found the exact same thing.

"Cut it off," Venn said sharply.

Her voice held such an urgency that Kate formed a runelight blade and sliced through the stream.

A lancing pain cut across Kate's palm, and a shockwave shot out from the root below her. A tremor ran along the stream, racing out of the square.

Venn spun to look down at the ground.

A thin blister crossed Kate's palm, and she shook her hand out. "That did *not* make the stream happy."

Venn flung both her hands back onto the tree. "Kate! Cut it off! Cut it all off! This tree is trying to..." Her brow creased in concentration, and she let out a growl of frustration. "He's trying to talk to me, Kate!"

"Talk to you? I thought the trees weren't doing that right now?"

"This one's so old. He's...desperate. She's killing him!"

"Venn," Kate said slowly, "the strands connected to this tree feel like the web over the ravine." She held up her blistered palm. "That was from breaking the thinnest thread. She does *not* want this broken."

"Can you do it?" Venn demanded.

"Maybe, but..." Kate scanned the square, taking in the

humans hurrying through it, and lowered her voice. "Do you really want to bring Naevys here?"

Venn spared a quick, troubled glance over her shoulder. "Kate, he's talking to me. I can almost hear him. He's connected to…I can't quite see it. But he's connected to so many things. Ancient things. Essential things! We need to cut her off!" Venn's voice was tight with fear. "Please, Kate."

Kate grimaced but put her hands on the next root. "This is going to hurt."

CHAPTER EIGHTEEN

Kate fashioned her runelight into another blade and slashed it across the second strand of *vitalle*. Searing pain shot up her arm like a spear of fire. The pain tore away her breath. Another ripple shot down the channel like an overly taut string had been violently plucked. The ground thrummed under her feet. She curled her fingers around the blisters on her palm and cast out. The root beneath her oozed like a bleeding cut, but the flow slowed even as she watched.

Naevys still leeched *vitalle* from eight other roots.

"Her power is fighting back." Kate rubbed her arm, the fiery pain still echoing along her bones. Her mind shied away from the idea of doing this eight more times. She glanced up at Venn to find her eyes filled with a deep, quaking fear. Not the worry of a moment, but fear on a foundational level.

Kate's own heart beat faster at the breadth of it. "It's that bad?"

Venn nodded with a small, desperate motion.

"All right." She needed some sort of shield. She held her hand out toward Venn. "I need your remnant."

Venn grasped her forearm without question, and Kate drew the elf's glittering green remnant into herself. The richer, brighter glimmers coated Kate's arm as she funneled them across to her other hand, focusing on the next root.

Kate could feel the larger channel of *vitalle* where the smaller streams met, flowing under the ground. It was far bigger than the ones she'd cut, but at least it was only one. She squared her shoulders and moved over it, trying not to think about what was about to happen.

Vitalle slid out of her fingers, infused with Venn's green and her own dark red, and she formed it into a shield, making sure the bottom edge was razor sharp.

She winced. "Brace yourself."

Venn's grip on her arm tightened. Kate closed her eyes. She lifted the shield and slammed it down into the ground.

Light exploded from the channel. A searing red bolt like lightning shot up into the shield and drove into Kate's arm like a spear of fire. Her vision flashed into blinding white nothingness, and she flew back, slamming into the trunk of the massive pine. The fire cut off, but the echo of the pain blazed inside her as though it had burned away her bones. The white faded, and the square of Home came back into view, tilting dangerously to the side.

Venn's hand landed on Kate's shoulder, and warmth seeped into Kate's back like sinking into a hot bath. It gushed into her, wiping away the pain, shifting it to a soothing heat.

Venn knelt by the tree, her forehead leaned against the bark, whispering fervently. After a long moment, she looked over with a relieved but weary smile. "Thank you."

Kate cast out into the ground. The roots of the pine lit up with *vitalle*, although slightly duller than she might have expected, but there was nothing trailing away from them. She felt nothing under the ground where the channel had been until her wave reached nearly the edge of the square, where a small, withered line of *vitalle* curled in upon itself.

Venn set her forehead back against the tree. "I can talk to him," she whispered. Relief and comfort filled her voice so thoroughly that, for a moment, Kate could almost feel it. The warm welcome of the woods. The acceptance, the deep, innate belonging. "I can talk to him, Kate. He was...trapped somehow."

A deep envy rose unbidden at the connection Venn held. Kate cleared her throat, trying to banish it. "Any chance you can also talk to Faron? Because Naevys is not going to ignore this, and the people of Home are going to need some help."

A smile crossed Venn's lips again. "I already did. And it was so good to use the trees to communicate that I almost don't care that it was with him. He and rangers are on their way."

Kate rolled her shoulders and pushed herself up. "Is the tree going to be okay?"

"With some care, I think so."

"Good, then let's go see to the wounded in the Pig."

Venn left her hands on the trunk for another moment before pulling away reluctantly.

The square rang with the sounds of hammers and saws as windows were boarded up and doors reinforced. The windows across the front of Yellow's tavern were already completely covered, and two men held the door open as they installed some braces that would help bar the door closed.

The interior was dark, but torches hung from every rafter. The now familiar smell of rosemary bread and coffee filled the air. Children's voices tumbled over each other from a cleared section of the floor to the left. A dozen elderly townsfolk looked up from the tables in the middle of the room as Kate entered. She offered them a smile, and a few smiled back through their worried wrinkles.

"Not more elves," an elderly voice complained, and Kate caught a glimpse of Griston and his perpetual scowl.

"You've got no place to talk," Maven snapped at him from the table near the door, her steel-grey hair tied up in a tight bun. She hunched over a steaming bowl of soup, her knobby finger pointing at him. "You've caused quite enough trouble around here."

"That weren't me!" Griston shouted. "The elves planted those diamonds in my packs."

"Enough with the elves," another man grumbled. "The only one who tricked us all is you."

Kate's smile turned to a wince, and she met Venn's uneasy look. A fire crackled in the huge fireplace to their right, and an older woman hunched over a boy, wrapping a bandage around his arm. Kate started toward them while Venn headed to the bar.

The healer's eyes widened when she caught sight of Kate, and she paused in her bandaging.

"Hello," Kate greeted her, looking over the handful of others resting in chairs near the fire. "I came to see if you need any help."

"You…" The woman dropped the end of the bandage in the boy's lap and grabbed Kate's hand. "You fixed our boys. I didn't think it could be done!"

"Yes," Kate said, patting the woman's hand. "Once I finally figured out how to."

The healer gripped her hand tighter. "And got assistance from the elven king."

Kate forced the smile to stay on her face. "Yes, the wellstone he gave me was the essential piece," she managed. "I heard there's a girl who was bitten?"

"Yes, Rellee." The woman nodded toward a girl of five or six years old lying on a blanket in front of the fire. "Took a chunk out of her calf. I've bound it best I can, but I'm afraid she may lose some movement."

Kate recognized the woman hunched over the girl as Gerren's mother—the boy who'd had his memory stolen by Faron. She reached the girl and said softly, "I can help her."

The woman looked up, and a dart of worry shot through Kate. But the woman who'd been so hostile toward her before now looked at her with nothing but desperation. "You can?"

Kate nodded. "Your family's had a hard time lately."

The woman let out a haggard breath, but a twitch of worry marred her brow. "I can pay you! For her and for Gerren! We have eggs or cheese."

Kate waved away the words and knelt down next to the girl. "Keepers never take payment for their help." Rellee's face was crumpled with pain and wet with tears. "Hi, Rellee, I'm Kate."

The girl's mouth dropped open. "The sorceress!"

Kate let out a short laugh. "I'm a Keeper. If you lived in my country, you'd know that means I can heal some wounds. Would you mind if I look at your leg?"

"You healed my brother!" Rellee whispered in awe.

"Is he still doing well?"

"He remembers everything," the girl's mother said, "except what happened when he was taken by the monster."

Kate pulled the blanket off of Rellee's calf, piling it around her knee to block the girl's view, then gently unwound the wide bandage. "Maybe that's something that's best forgotten."

Rellee gave her a somber nod. "I would like to forget the wolf." Her eyes fell to her leg, and her lip trembled. "Will it ever get better?"

Kate finished unwrapping the wound and worked to keep a grimace off her face. The young girl's leg was thin and wiry, but a chunk of muscle was missing from the meat of her calf. The lacerations through the remaining flesh were sharp and jagged. Kate cast out and found the bone unhurt. "I think we can help it get better." She funneled some *vitalle* into the leg, bolstering the little healing the girl's body was doing. "This might feel warm for a little bit." She reached her other hand toward the blazing fire and pulled *vitalle* from it, feeding that into Rellee's leg as well.

The deepest part of Rellee's muscle began to regrow, and Rellee gave a little whimper but stayed still.

Once the healing began, it took little effort to continue. The flow of *vitalle* tingled across her palms, stinging along the blisters from the pine tree. Kate looked up at the woman to distract herself from the pain.

"I've met your husband, Nevin, but I don't think I've met you yet."

"Rosia." The woman grimaced. "I'm sorry about the way I acted when you first came. It was—"

"It was understandable," Kate interrupted.

Rosia shook her head. "Still, I wouldn't fault you for hating me."

"It seems a bit foolish to be enemies when we've no real reason to be." A new layer of muscle began to grow.

"Coffee and bread are coming soon." Venn slipped into a chair at the nearest table, peering down at the wound. "How is it?"

"Fixable." Kate glanced at Rellee. "You know, Venn was bitten by wolves in almost this exact same place."

The girl turned alarmed eyes to Venn, who leaned closer and whispered, "It hurt. A lot." At Rellee's teary nod, she added, "If there's anyone who can fix you up, it's Kate."

The heart of Rellee's muscle finished knitting back together. Kate forced herself to hold her hand toward the fire, ignoring the growing pain across the blisters. The outer layers of flesh were always easier than muscle, and she gritted her teeth, forcing the *vitalle* to continue to flow. Rellee gave another whimper.

Venn glanced at Kate's hand stretched toward the fire and winced. "What do you need?"

"Any sort of distraction."

"For you or for her?"

"Both would be nice."

Venn looked around the room. "What kind of distraction?"

"A pleasant one. You know, tell a story." The pain flared in Kate's palm, and she bit back a groan. "Sing a song. Anything."

Venn gave her a flat look. "You're the storyteller, not me."

"An argument isn't a pleasant distraction."

Venn let out an annoyed breath, but Rosia's face was etched with concern, and a tear leaked down Rellee's cheek as she squeezed her eyes shut against the pain.

"All right," Venn conceded. "A story." She thought for a moment, then leaned toward Rellee. "Did you know Kate fought off one of those wolves all by herself?"

Rellee's eyes flew open. "But they're so big!"

Venn nodded. "And their fur is as hard as ice. No weapons or magic can get through it."

"I was hardly alone," Kate said. "You were there too."

"I was," Venn said, keeping her focus on the girl. "Our first attempt to put it to sleep ended up with him biting my arm and tossing me around like a flag on a windy day. He threw me off to the side and knocked me out."

Rellee's mouth hung open, and Kate shuddered at the memory of Venn's body hitting the ground and not moving.

Venn drew a dart from her quiver. "So Kate took one of these, created a magical bow, waited until the *gweroc* charged at her... then she shot straight into his mouth and put him to sleep."

The girl stared at Kate, awestruck. Her mother's expression was equally astonished.

"At which point he collapsed on me," Kate said with a wry smile, "almost suffocating me before I could shove him off."

One of the blisters on her palm tore open, and Kate yanked it away from the fire. The *vitalle* cut off abruptly, and the heat pouring into Rellee fizzled away. Kate cast out into the thin leg and found the muscle healed and the skin beginning to regrow over it. She sank back, letting her hands fall into her lap. "That's all I can do right now," she said. "I can try more later. If someone could bandage it again, that would be good."

Rosia leaned forward. Instead of a mass of torn flesh, it looked like a shallow wound. "You…?" She looked up at Kate. "How…?"

"You can see why people in Queensland are so fond of Keepers," Venn said, kneeling down and beginning to wrap the wound again.

"I don't really understand what a Keeper is," Rosia said, "but I'm very happy you're here."

"A Keeper!" a jovial voice said from behind Kate. The wiry little merchant who'd given Kate the three books after the troll attack leaned on the table, peering down at her. His white hair was combed neatly, as was his beard. "That race of plucky men" —he paused and bowed his head at Kate—"and women who lurk and tug behind the veil to smooth the surface of the earth."

She raised an eyebrow. "A quote from Flibbet the Peddler."

He gave her a bright smile. "Such a quotable fellow."

"I agree." She looked closer at the man. His features were rather indistinct, but there was something southern about the shape of his jaw. "Where are you from?"

He let out a chuckle. "Haven't been 'from' anywhere in a very long time. Just like to travel a bit."

"In Queensland?"

"I've certainly spent time there, yes."

Kate narrowed her eyes. "Because even in Queensland, not many people would know that Flibbet quote."

He let out an appalled huff. "Why on earth not?"

There was a slight commotion near the door, and a hush fell across the common room as Faron stepped through the door.

The bright snow from the square outlined Faron, but instead of just a dark silhouette, his skin glittered with a warm coppery glow.

"Oh!" the little merchant said. "Another elf! Delightful!"

CHAPTER NINETEEN

Faron scanned the room, giving the children a quick smile. Then, finding Venn and Kate, he strode toward them, his face etched in worry.

"Your Highness!" Magistrate Mirrow shoved his chair back and leapt to his feet. "The wolves! Have you found them yet?"

Faron paused to face the short, white-haired man, keeping his face polite. "Not yet, Magistrate. My rangers are right now positioning themselves around the town, though. If you'd be as good as to call a town meeting for tonight, we have some things to discuss."

"Oh, yes, I agree, Prince Faron," Mirrow said with a fast bob of his head. Faron stiffened at the title, but the magistrate hurried on. "So many things to talk about." He spun around. "Griffon, Teg, go spread the news. Town meeting an hour before nightfall. Everyone who can be spared from the barricades must come!"

Faron slipped past the man.

"Your Majesty," the little merchant said with a twinkling smile as he approached. Faron's eyebrows drew down at the appropriateness of the title, but the merchant merely offered a low bow.

"I'm blocking your table." He was starting to turn away when a little frown crossed his face. After a moment's hesitation, he added, "If there's anything you need that you think a lowly human merchant would have, please feel free to ask. I'm staying right here in the common room tonight for safety, but my cart is just out back in the stable."

Faron forced a polite smile. "Of course, thank you."

The merchant opened his mouth but closed it again and hurried off.

"That is an odd little man," Kate said, watching him take a seat next to Griston, who kept his scowl firmly fixed on Faron and Venn.

"You're glittering," Venn said quietly to Faron.

Irritation cracked through his calm facade, but the glow on his skin immediately faded. "It's hardly unwarranted. Are you two all right?"

"Hullo, Faron!" Yellow strode toward them, carrying a tray with three mugs and a plate of hot bread. He set the food onto the table. "Thought you might want something warm to drink."

"I appreciate that," Faron said with a sincere smile.

Yellow slapped a huge hand onto his shoulder. "Anything for the elves who help keep us safe."

Faron's smile grew slightly strained, but the innkeeper was already headed back to the kitchen.

The rest of the room was still quiet, all eyes turned toward them. Even the children were only whispering to each other. Instead of sitting, Faron stood stiffly and gripped the back of the chair.

"We have a lot to tell you." Kate tried not to shift under the attention of the entire room. "But maybe outside." She grabbed a chunk of the rosemary bread and her coffee.

"Please." Faron gave Kate a grateful look and picked up his drink. Venn grabbed the last of the bread.

"Magistrate Mirrow," Kate called, heading for the door, "could you send someone out to show us the buildings that were attacked last night?"

The cool afternoon air felt open and freeing after the smothering attention of the tavern, and Kate ate the last of her bread before wrapping her hand around her mug.

"What's happening, Venn?" Faron asked, his voice low as they headed toward the pine. "You sounded terrified. What do you mean Naevys is killing the woods?" He looked her over again. "Are you sure you're all right?"

"I'm fine. Naevys has drained the *ael'iza* out of a long strip of forest from the ravine to here."

His mug stopped halfway to his mouth. "What? Why?"

"To fuel a protective net she has under the rockslide."

"Why would she—" His attention snapped to the huge pine. "What happened here?"

"She was even draining this," Kate said.

He strode forward and set his hand on the tree.

"She was also trapping it somehow," Venn said. "At least that's what the pine said."

Faron's fingers pressed harder against the trunk. "Why would she hurt him? He's connected us to Home for centuries." He closed his eyes. "She did weaken you, didn't she?" he said softly.

From somewhere under the ground, Kate felt a tremor, as though a hundred small pathways leading toward the pine suddenly surged with *vitalle*.

Venn watched with the closest thing to approval Kate had ever seen her give to Faron. "I can't believe she hurt *this* tree."

A shiver of disquiet rolled up Kate's back. "Wait. Venn, you said this tree was old."

"Maybe the oldest on this side of the river," Venn said.

Kate's disquiet solidified into dismay. "So, this is the closest thing the human forest has to an elder tree?"

Venn's face paled. "She's trying to turn it into a *naiwyn*!"

Faron twisted to look at them. "What?"

"Naevys created at least four *naiwyn*," Venn said. "They're guarding…I don't know what, but you can't get past them south along the river."

"There's nothing there to guard," he said. "Are you sure—"

"I'm sure." Venn pulled the shoulder of her cloak forward, showing the scorched hole.

Faron dropped his hands from the pine and grabbed Venn's arm, taking in the bandage. "It attacked you?"

"They're blocking the line of trees past the southern edge of our patrols, and they don't want anyone getting past."

He looked between Venn and Kate, as though waiting for one of them to say they were joking. "*Naiwyn?*"

Kate leaned toward Venn. "I guess we were right that it wasn't Faron who made them."

"Me?" He pushed the hole in Venn's cloak aside. "Are you all right?"

Venn pulled her arm away with an exasperated sigh. "Stop asking me that. I'm fine."

He dropped his hands, then looked around the town. "What is happening? Why would she possibly create *naiwyn* to guard…" He dragged his hand through his hair. "There's nothing to guard there!"

"Is there anything in the ravine?" Kate asked pointedly. "Because she's definitely still guarding that too."

"No." Faron's gaze wandered up to the tree again.

Kate crossed her arms. "Really?"

He straightened under the scrutiny from both Kate and Venn. "No! What could possibly be in that ravine?"

"You tell us. You've watched it before."

"Because I was trying to find Bo." Faron grew exasperated. "I found traces of my mother near the ravine. Bo was interested in the ravine and…" He gave an annoyed wave at Kate's pack. "And he carried the cursed box that feels like Renault." He paused at that. "There have always been rumors that my mother knew Renault. Some of them are…less than complimentary to my mother, but regardless, anything that felt like the half-elf showing up was something I needed to investigate." He lowered his voice. "I was finding fewer and fewer signs of her by the day, and my father was adamant she be found. So yes, I was watching Bo, and when he disappeared, I was watching anyone who seemed connected to him or that ravine."

"But you didn't find anything in the ravine itself?" Kate asked.

Faron shook his head. "What is there to find in a hillside of rock?"

"There's something inside those caves," Kate said.

"What?" Faron asked.

"I don't know." Kate shuddered at the memory of the cave. "Naevys anchored herself there, drawing in power from the net she'd created. When Thallion tore her out of it, she left something behind. A knot of *vitalle* inside the rocks themselves."

"Something alive?" he asked, incredulous. "Inside the rock?"

"That's what it looked like."

He ran his hand through his hair again and let out a groan caught between frustration and misery. "I thought it would be hundreds of years before I inherited the throne, and I certainly never expected my first significant struggle to be against my mother."

The normal scowl Venn reserved for him softened slightly, but Faron had turned to face the tree. "I still have no idea what she's doing, but I can at least heal the injuries she inflicted here." He cast a nervous look at Venn. "I…could use your help. There are pathways below us that need to be rebuilt, and you have always been better at talking to the trees than I have."

Venn's eyes narrowed. "Even now?"

Faron looked between Kate and Venn, a slight vulnerability to his expression. "Even now. I have the authority now, and it feels...heavy. Like a weapon I don't want to use. And I can see the wood more, but there's..." He shuddered. "There's so much that it's hard to sort out." He gave Venn an apologetic smile. "So yes, if you could stay and help me talk to this old man, together I think we can heal him."

Venn set her palm on the trunk and nodded.

Faron's face registered a moment's shock, but he smothered it quickly and placed his hand next to hers.

From across the square, Merrick the blacksmith strode toward them. He looked curiously at the elves, then addressed Kate. "I hear you all are in need of a tour guide."

"Just me, I think," Kate said. "Our elven friends here have business with the tree."

Merrick looked up into the branches. "What sort of business are trees in?"

"Growing, mostly," Venn said over her shoulder. "And not dying. We're going to work on the not dying part."

Merrick looked like he wasn't quite sure whether she was joking, but when both elves turned back to the tree, he said, "Well, Mistress Keeper. The closest building that was harmed is Woodworker Glerrol's shed, which isn't far." The blacksmith gave her an easy smile, as though they were starting a simple walk on an average afternoon, and Kate fell in beside him, leaving the two elves to their work.

"I walked past the shed earlier, but I'd like a look inside. Can you see any patterns to which buildings were attacked?"

Instead of his normal quick reply, he considered the question seriously as they walked. "No. There's a shed, a house in town, a house on one of the nearby farms, and an abandoned home near the forest. Some parts of each are ripped up, other parts left alone. And as far as anyone can tell, nothing is missing."

They headed down the street toward the shed, and Kate eyed the sword he'd added to his belt, along with a wicked-looking war hammer. "I expected someone elderly or very young as an escort. Don't they need your help along the barricades?"

"I left the dwarves in charge. They know what they're doing and—unlike me—can be bossy to anyone in town without worrying about who'll take offense." The edge of a smile quirked up his mouth. "Magistrate Mirrow had picked Leonn, who is quite elderly and mostly deaf, to show you around. I convinced him that someone like you shouldn't be left with only Leonn for protection." He stopped in front of the shed and pulled the broken white door open with a creak.

Kate held his gaze for a moment, debating whether to try to convince him again that she didn't need any protection. But that mild yet determined smile hovered around his lips, and she didn't bother to argue the point.

Inside, the floor was riddled with splinters of wood. A table along the right wall was split in half, both parts tossed aside. Tools and broken bits of furniture lay everywhere. Across the room, what had once been a large closet was now only a broken wall. The door was ripped off, but the shelves inside, filled with rows of tiny carved figures, were unharmed. The left side of the room was perfectly intact. The cabinets were still closed, the counter on top of them laid out with tools and a half-assembled chair.

Merrick leaned against the doorframe, his arms crossed, surveying the destruction.

Her feet crunched over the floor as she studied it. The *gweroc* that had attacked her and Venn on the outcropping hadn't had a remnant, and she found no trace of one here either. Which wasn't surprising for an animal. "There was no food in here? No smell that could have drawn the wolves?"

"Nothing besides Glerrol's wood glue." Merrick pointed toward a sealed jar on the counter. "That stinks enough to raise the dead when he uses it."

"Can I see the next house?"

"That'd be Mellron's place." He stepped down the stairs and waited for her before he started down the narrow alley beside the shed. He gave her a sidelong look and, after a moment's hesitation, said, "I know your brother."

A tightness wrapped around Kate at the words, and she gripped the strap of her pack.

"He needed a chisel fixed," Merrick continued, "and we got to talking. He came several times to my forge, and we shared a few pints at the Pig." His eyes crinkled a little at the edges. "Had the entire bar in stitches telling us about some town he'd visited that was filled with only goats."

She let out a little laugh. "I have his journal, and I read about that. Sounded a little terrifying."

He glanced down at her with an earnest expression. "I like him." He rubbed the back of his neck. "I'm sure he's not..."

She felt a moment's gratefulness at the fact he hadn't said "liked him." "I know he's alive," she said quickly. "I just need to find a way to...get to him."

Merrick's brow furrowed at the vagueness. "Is he in danger?"

"Not imminent danger, I don't think. But..." She paused, suddenly self-conscious. Her complaints about being dragged into the problems with the elves and Home felt childish and selfish and, most irritating of all, irrational. Her brothers *weren't* in imminent danger. Time moved so slowly in the Runelight Drawer that it would take months in the outside world for any destruction to progress where they were. Wanting to turn her back on the people of Home and the White Wood, who seemed to be quickly running out of time, to save her brothers, who had plenty, was hardly rational.

Merrick gestured, encompassing the hills and Home. "But you've gotten dragged into trouble with trolls and elves and now *gwerocs* in a town you barely know."

She winced at how closely his words resembled her thoughts. "That's not terribly unusual for a Keeper. We travel a lot—usually in Queensland—and help where there are problems. But I admit that this time feels different. I'm distracted by Bo. I had the chance earlier to get him, but then more happened here…"

Merrick gave a noncommittal hum.

Kate glanced at him, grimacing. "Which is an incredibly insensitive thing to say to someone who lives here and is dealing with all these problems."

He shook his head as they reached the end of the alley. "No, the draw to help your brother is perfectly natural. It's just…"

"What?"

He shifted, looking uncomfortable. "I don't know the situation enough to comment. And, like you said, I have a vested interest in you staying and helping us."

Kate stopped and waited until he stopped as well. When he turned, she said, "Say what you think. I could use some new thoughts on the problem. I'm sick to death of my own circular reasoning."

He held her eyes and gave a reluctant half-shrug. "I'm not trying to be self-serving, but…" He rubbed the back of his neck. "I didn't spend a lot of time with your brother, but Bo doesn't seem like the kind of man who'd thank you for saving him at the expense of others."

The words sank into Kate like a slow punch, driving the air out of her chest. For a moment, she imagined explaining to Bo that she'd deserted Home in its time of need to get him and Evan out of the box. She could almost see the momentary confusion, then the dismay he'd feel.

"No," she said quietly. "He isn't."

Merrick started forward again. "Although," he added soberly, "if it was my brother missing, I'm not sure logic like that would change my mind."

Kate's pack pressed heavily on her back, and she shifted her shoulders. It wasn't only Bo. She pictured Evan, wondering what he'd think. But all she could see was the frightened boy who'd been sucked into the box all those years ago.

CHAPTER TWENTY

"Here we are." Merrick pointed at a modest half-timbered home sitting between its equally unremarkable neighbors. The only significant difference was that, like the shed, the white front door was barely hanging upright. The interior looked like a storm had torn through it. Cold air blew in, and snow dusted the floor. The home held a single room, bright with color. The walls were a warm yellow painted with clumps of wildflowers. The overturned table was light green. Steep red stairs led up to a loft.

"Mellron's wife paints," he said. "She always wanted to live in a city where people would pay her for it, but they have a farm outside of town, so she just paints everything she can get her hands on here."

Shelves dangled from the wall, their supply of crockery and cook pots heaped in a pile beneath them. The pantry at the back of the room was in shambles. Its skinny door, painted light blue, was tossed halfway across the room. She picked her way through the mess and ran her fingers over the gouges left by teeth and claws along the side of the doorframe. Inside, glass jars were smashed on the floor and a bag was torn open with a massive paw print, larger than her hand, left in the spilled wheat. But a string of smoked fish hung unmolested from the ceiling.

Kate considered the fish for a long moment, then turned back to Merrick, who leaned against the doorframe again. "What were they looking for?"

He scanned the room like a hunter scanning a forest, and she realized that he wasn't glib, just...very calm. "I don't see any pattern to it."

"Neither do I. How far is it to Nevin's place?"

"Not far."

They continued toward the edge of town, and Kate mulled over the odd destruction the *gwerocs* had left.

"Rumor is," Merrick said, interrupting the useless circling of her thoughts, "that it would take a whole month to reach your home."

She glanced up, her mind trying to catch up with the change of subject. "The rumor is true. Although, if there were a straight path through those mountains"—she gestured to the peaks towering to the west, past the White Wood—"and across the high desert past them, you could reach Queensland in a bit over a week. But I don't know if that route is even survivable."

He studied the tall peaks. "It'd be a foolish thing to try. You'd need a large, well-supplied wagon to survive the desert, and nothing like that would ever make it through the mountains."

He was at least a head taller than her, considerably broader with the muscled shoulders and arms of a blacksmith, and carried himself with a surprising amount of confidence that felt anchored in competence, not merely bravado. "You don't talk like you're from Home."

He gave her an amused look. "Was that a compliment?"

"More of an observation."

"Good, because if it was a compliment, then I think you just insulted all of my neighbors."

"Your neighbors all speak and carry themselves exactly as they should. Like folk living in a small, remote town. Nothing strange about that. What is strange is how you talk. Where are you from?"

"Born and raised right here."

"Then you must have traveled a lot."

"Not compared to the distances you have."

"How far have you gone?"

"Do you know where Donerten is?"

Kate raised an eyebrow. "It's a good-sized city at least a fortnight southeast of here."

He nodded. "Seventeen days. Bo knew where it was too. He'd been there, although more recently than I have. I was stationed there for two years."

"Stationed?"

"In my teens, I was a little restless. Told my father I couldn't settle down until I'd seen the world."

"And?"

"By the time I'd gone as far as Donerton, enlisted, and spent a few years in Lord Trenfold's army, I'd seen enough."

The scabbard at his belt was ringed with three lines of silver.

"Those denote rank, don't they?" she asked.

That earned her an impressed hum. "I was a captain."

"In just a few years?"

He made a dismissive sort of shrug. "I'm a fast learner." He walked beside her with a confidence that reminded her of the queen's personal guards, and Kate realized that even though she'd never seen him fight, she had no doubt he could. And that he could do it well. Despite her earlier objections, she found his presence—and his weapons—reassuring.

He was a curiosity in this small town. She felt the things she knew about him begin to arrange themselves into a picture—albeit one with a lot of missing pieces.

Kate gestured at the quiet houses around them. "Do many men here go south to join the armies?"

"Almost none. They're farmers and merchants who love it here and stay their whole lives."

"Then I see why they put you in charge of the defenses."

Merrick squinted at the barricade they were approaching, marking the edge of town. "I hope I'm not held responsible when they fail. Home is not an easily defensible town. We have seventeen streets or alleys that lead out to the farms, which we're barricading, but we barely have the people to man them all. And creatures like those wolves can obviously just tear the houses apart if we block the streets."

They walked in silence for a while before he looked down at her. "What's the farthest you've ever traveled?"

"Here, by far. I'd never been out of Queensland before this."

At the barrier, he led her along a rather winding path through the spikes of wood before they reached the edge of a field. He pointed to a farmhouse two fields away. "There it is." They started toward it, Merrick's hand resting on his sword hilt.

Naevys's work scarred the hills, and the box nagged at Kate. She shifted—for the tenth time at least—against her impatience to leave.

CHAPTER TWENTY-ONE

"Do you still get antsy here?" Kate asked Merrick.

His eyes slipped over the hills around the town. "No. I love it. Saw enough of fancy houses and busy places to last me for a lifetime."

"What's the fanciest place you've ever been?"

"A duke's house. It would've filled the entire square. The dining table sat thirty and was lit by a hanging chandelier that was probably worth more than half our town. Fancy dishes, fancy drinks, and food fancy enough that it tasted funny."

"Did you meet the duke himself?"

"Certainly not. Couldn't possibly expect him to speak with anyone lower than a general." He glanced at her. "Where's the fanciest place you've ever been?"

"Queen Madeleine's personal study. She invited me there for a meal. There are no fancy plates in there, but the food is spectacular, and she has a collection of books in there that are priceless."

Merrick slowed. "You ate with the queen?"

She nodded, feeling vaguely self-conscious. "Keepers are

advisors to the crown. I'm not at court too often, though. Is the duke the fanciest person you've ever been close to?"

He gave a little laugh. "No, I think you are." He considered her again, as though trying to figure her out. "Was that wood troll the worst thing you've ever fought?"

"Either that or the *gweroc*. One attacked Venn and me in the woods."

He raised his eyebrows. "And you both survived? I didn't see a weakness on them."

"In their mouths. We shot it with a tranquilizing dart."

His eyebrows stayed raised. "I'm impressed."

"You shouldn't be. We barely survived. It was messy and desperate."

"I've never seen a battle that wasn't."

"What's the worst thing you've ever fought?" Kate asked.

"Either one of the *gwerocs* last night or the Baron of Elswen." At her questioning look, he shook his head grimly. "He was a monster. The things that man did..." His face darkened. "Yes, Elswen was worse than the wolves."

They walked for several minutes with only the crunch of their feet in the snow until the blacksmith gave Kate an uneasy look. "Any chance Keepers fight dragons?"

Kate's steps faltered. "Please don't tell me you have a dragon around here."

He shrugged, but there was a worried crease in his brow. "Just rumors, at the moment. Have you heard of Yilfrist?" At her blank look, he let out a troubled breath. "Yilfrist is an ice dragon. Legend says he lives in the northern mountains, but every once in a while, he comes down to the human lands."

"I have never heard of an ice dragon. Only fire dragons."

"Oh, he breathes fire, but he's colored like ice. All frosty blues and whites."

Kate stopped. "Has someone seen him recently?"

"Not anyone from Home, but the merchants who travel hear whispers about him being seen." He shifted uncomfortably. "I bring it up because around Home, Yilfrist is known for…" He winced. "He's known for devouring mages. And you seem to be…mage-like." He looked away. "I just thought you should know the rumors are brewing."

Kate stared at him. "Is this the reason I'm honored with you as my personal guard? Because neither that sword nor that war hammer is going to stop a dragon."

"True," he said frankly, "but they're the best I have, so they're what I'll use." There was a note of humor in his voice, but also a steadfastness that reminded her of …

It reminded her of the other Keepers. A determination to stand up against whatever threats arose, no matter the cost.

An uncomfortable sensation rose in her, and she sought out Naevys's trail through the trees. This "mess" that Naevys had dragged her into was the sort of threat the Keepers stood against. Exactly the sort she'd always stood against.

For a moment, the desire to leave with the box rose up, but Merrick's quiet resolve woke something she'd been neglecting, and she turned her attention back to the people of Home and the danger they faced. She set her shoulders and refocused on Nevin's house ahead of them.

"Let's hope they're just rumors," she said. "Because I don't know of anyone who can fight a dragon. I know of a few who've tried to control one, but only temporarily, and with mixed results. They can be run off, occasionally, but I've never heard of one being defeated."

Merrick's face stayed clouded, but he nodded.

Nevin's timbered house stood in front of a large barn. Horses, goats, and a handful of cows grazed in a pasture nearby. This door, just like all the others, was torn off its hinges. The white wood lay on the ground where it had been dragged several feet from the building.

Kate paused at the sight. "Merrick, all the doors have been this white wood." She looked back toward the town. "But most of the doors in Home are dark."

The blacksmith straightened. "You're right. About twenty years ago, there was some flooding, and several huge frost pines washed down the Surn. Glerrol, the woodworker with the shed, took the wood and made all sorts of things out of it, but among them were four doors. All used in the four places the *gwerocs* attacked last night."

"Well, that's something." At Nevin's front door, Kate found the expected scene of destruction. Smashed furniture, broken crockery, the bed where Nevin's girls had been sleeping torn apart.

Three rooms were set off the back of the main room, their dark paneled doors opened, their contents undisturbed.

Merrick stood in the doorway, looking out toward the nearby hills, his posture watchful.

Kate glanced around Nevin's house one more time, but there were no remnants besides those of Nevin's family. "How far to the abandoned house?"

"All the way on the far side of town, at the edge of the trees."

"Have you seen it?"

He nodded. "The frost pine door was pulled off, but there was nothing inside it besides some rotting old furniture, and that was left alone."

"I don't think we need to go there. I think the doors are what's important. Maybe the elves will know why."

Kate followed him back outside, wondering what was so important about a few old doors made of frost pines.

The town was quieter by the time Kate and Merrick returned. Most of the windows around the square were boarded up, and the hammering from the barricades sounded from fewer directions. Kate moved through the trampled snow to where Venn and Faron still stood at the tree. Before she could ask how things were going, Ayen stepped out of the air.

Merrick flinched back but gave the ranger a nod of greeting.

"The rangers are positioned around the town," Ayen told Faron, "but they're spread thin. We could use more lookouts until the men of the town are done working on the barriers."

Faron looked critically up at the old pine tree. "I think we've done all we can here, anyway. He should recover, as long as my mother leaves him alone. We can help with whatever the town needs for the next few hours until the meeting."

"The barricades should be done by then," Merrick said. Some raised voices came from the outskirts of town, and he squinted toward them. "I believe that's my sign to get back to work." He looked over the elves and Kate. "Thank you, sincerely, for your help. We'd be in a tight place without you." With a polite nod, he jogged away toward the noise.

Kate watched him leave, guilt worming its way into her again. "We'll see if he feels the same after the meeting tonight when they learn Naevys is responsible for all this trouble, and we also tricked them about the diamonds."

Ayen winced. "We don't have to tell them everything."

Faron sighed but straightened his shoulders. "I'm not my father. I don't want everything I do to be wrapped in secrets and half-truths."

"Well," Ayen said dryly, "until they drive us out of town later, there are a few rooftops that are missing lookouts."

"Show us," Faron said. Ayen led them down a side street, and Faron fell in beside him. "How did three *gwerocs* get here last night without us knowing?"

"The paths all come from the east," Ayen replied. "I don't think they came through the White Wood at all."

Faron ran his hand through his hair again. "What *is* my mother doing?"

They reached a small forge at the edge of town. The smithy itself was open on three sides, allowing a wide view of the fields past it. Its round sign was made from a shield dimpled with hammer strikes until it rippled with the grey light of the cloudy afternoon. From the side of the smithy, the spiky barrier fence connected to the house across the street.

Ayen motioned to the roof. "The sentry here was pulled off Merrick's place to help with some wood cutting."

"I'll take this one." Kate peered up the ladder leading to the snow-covered roof. "I assume the plan is just to start shouting if we see anything?"

Ayen nodded. "We'll find someone to replace you when it's time for the town meeting."

He, Venn, and Faron headed farther east, and Kate climbed up the rough ladder. The snow had been trampled in a short path to the south-facing slope of roof, where enough had been cleared off the slate tiles for Kate to sit.

Straight out from the forge, several large fields stretched away, laid in neat rows to the forested hills. To her left, though, the forest drew closer, a mix of pines and bare birches only a stone's throw from the nearest building. Nothing moved as far as she could see.

Kate sat, pulling off her pack and settling it between her knees. The sounds of the barrier construction wafted over from a few streets away, but mostly the world was quiet and still. Her shoulders relaxed. She mulled the frost pine doors, kicking herself for not asking the elves about it, until she caught sight of the grey line Naevys had slashed across the distant hill, and a surge of frustration rose against the sight of it. Kate curled her fingers into the rough canvas of her pack, lifting her eyes to the hilltops farther south. The hills she'd be deep into by now if Naevys had just…stopped.

The pressure of Naevys's threat against Home rolled around her like the current of a river, pulling her farther downstream. Farther from the path she was trying to reach.

The resolution that Merrick had reminded her of faded in the face of the worry for her brothers. Merrick's comment about Bo and the goats made her pull open her pack and grab his journal. She flipped through some of the earlier entries, searching for those from last summer. He'd sent her a map of Donerton with his description of the large military headquarters. The Lord Trenfold whom Merrick had served under still lived in a massive fortress on a hill over the town.

A third of the way through the book, the word "Donerton" caught her eye.

> Ria,
>
> I don't envy the soldiers here in Donerton. They are quartered in a large, well-kept compound but seem to be sent out on endless campaigns.
>
> Lord Trenfold is complicated. I want to like him. He claims to stand for justice and peace, and some of his enemies in the past have been truly despicable men, yet I can't manage to be perfectly comfortable about him. Maybe because every time his men return from vanquishing an enemy, they return loaded with treasure.
>
> I spent last night in one of the taverns the soldiers frequent. They're a decent group of men, most having been drawn to the corps by a desire to stamp out evil.
>
> I spoke with one of the men whose name was Ravon. He must have not even been forty, but he wore his years heavily. He'd been in the army nearly two decades. After a few drinks, he confided that he'd never meant to stay this long. That back home, there had been a

girl he'd planned to marry, but once he'd enlisted and seen all the evil in the world, he'd felt compelled to stay.

I won't write down the horrors he told me about, because I don't need them fixed any more firmly in my mind, and you don't want them in yours. But suffice it to say that the eastern territories of this land remind me of the moors of Gringonn. Small warlords wage vicious wars against each other and rule what little they own with a stranglehold. They buy and sell their women like cattle, train their sons to fight from the moment they can hold a blade, and house their daughters with the goats and other livestock.

They're nomadic, so finding them is challenging, but when Lord Trenfold does, he sends his men with all speed.

He shows the warlords no mercy—and most of the eastern fighters choose death over surrender. But if any desire sanctuary, he offers it.

Which sounds noble until you learn that those are the only two choices he offers. Swear fealty to him and join his people (the men to his army, the women to house and feed the soldiers)—or be slaughtered.

You can see the toll it takes on Trenfold's soldiers. They are driven to rout out these monstrous men, but the ruthlessness they are required to show to do so seems to pull them apart.

I asked Ravon why he didn't leave years ago, and he reiterated that he felt compelled to help in the fight. But I think there's more. The riches these men capture all go into Lord Trenfold's treasury. The soldiers have free lodging and excellent food and drink in the compound. There's free entertainment and essentially anything they want. If they serve for twenty years, they get a significant allowance with which to begin their new life. Enough to live off of for several years in comfort. But if they leave the corps before then, they get nothing.

So to leave, they lose their home, their job, and their friends, and they have no money for even traveling home. They have the skills of fighters, but there are limited places in the world where those are useful. And so they stay. Some make a life here—marry, have a family—but most, like Ravon, seem to just drift along, fighting and waiting.

I find their situation sad. While Lord Trenfold's policy is to allow anyone to leave, very few men do.

The ones who do are revered almost as legends.

Ria, despite all their challenges, being near these men has made everything I do feel selfish. You, at least, are working with the Keepers, protecting Queensland, advising the queen, recording our history. What am I doing to help the world? If I cannot find Evan, will everything I've done be a waste?

I've finished exploring the local monastery, so it's time to move on, but I can't decide if I want to or not. These men here, in their endless battle against ruthless tyranny—do they make me feel free? Or useless?

I suppose they make me feel both.

A tangle of emotions sat inside Kate. She reread the last paragraphs, shifting under the idea the she was doing anything that wasn't selfish. She glanced up at the quiet fields, then back to his words. Yes, she was here helping Home, but it felt like an obstacle to get past, not some sort of heroic deed.

The corner of the box glinted from her pack, and she tucked Bo's journal back in before pulling the aenigma box onto her lap. In the vast emptiness, its bell tolled, filled with loneliness and longing. She closed her eyes, feeling it resonate in her chest. The metal edges dug into the palm of her hand, lancing sharply into her blisters. She kept the pressure on them, letting the pain feed the frustration simmering inside her.

The lantern of silvery hope still hung ahead of her, farther out of her reach than before. Almost out of sight beyond the winding walls of jagged black. The light called to her like the road south.

Offering answers. Offering her brothers. In her mind, she traveled distant roads, moving ever closer to home. To safety. To her desk. To the Stronghold and Gerone's honey bread and the Shield's wisdom. Toward the valley protected by vast cliffs and ancient magic.

Envy of that version of herself surged up like a wave. For a moment she could barely breathe. *That.* That was what she wanted. Not this. Not another elven danger threatening—

An especially sharp edge jabbed into the blisters on her palm, and she yanked her hand back. A shallow, narrow drawer poked out from the front of the box, high at the top on the left side.

The drawer was only half as wide as the box and sat high enough against the top that it didn't overlap the Hope Drawer or the Runelight Drawer, but it very obviously took up the same space inside the box as the Nostalgia Drawer should.

Slowly, she worked it open to find it lined with a dark red velvet, lush and soft.

Inside lay a thick ring of silver with a delicate pattern carved into it that caught the afternoon light. A faint remnant surrounded it, a delicate ripple of sound like a wind chime. Or the trickling of a tiny waterfall.

Kate cast out toward the ring. The edges of the drawer flashed with a near blinding brightness, but the ring itself did nothing. The pattern carved around it was one of waves, or hills, or merely curving lines that flowed in an endless pattern around the ring.

It was heavy for silver, and too bright. The surfaces reflected the indistinct light of the afternoon with flashes of white and the occasional glitter of green.

It showed no sign of tarnish or wear. The pattern was crisp, the edges smooth.

She slipped it over her first finger, and it slid all the way on, sitting with a reassuring weight against her skin.

Mesmerizing light played over the design, and she fed a

trickle of *vitalle* into it. The dribble merely ran along the edge of the metal and dissolved into the air.

She pulled the drawer farther out, but there was nothing else inside. "What opened you?" she asked quietly. "Envy, perhaps?"

A crack reverberated through the smithy, and Kate scrambled to her knees.

Huge tracks cut through the snow from the trees, straight toward the town.

She shoved the box into her pack and crawled to the edge of the roof.

Four huge brown bears crowded into the street alongside the smithy, lunging at the barrier. One stood up on its hind legs, its head nearly as high as the eaves. Black claws longer than Kate's fingers sank into one of the pointed stakes of the barricade and tore it off.

Wood splintered, and the center of the barrier sagged.

The other bears threw their weight into gaps between the sharpened sticks, ripping out chunk after chunk.

"Bears!" she shouted, clambering toward the peak of the roof. Her feet slid on the snowy tiles, and she dropped to her knees, her fingers scrabbling for purchase. "Bears breaking the barrier!"

From other rooftops, figures stood, then shouted down into the streets.

With a crash that shook the smithy roof, the bears tore through the barricade and charged into town.

CHAPTER TWENTY-TWO

Kate's fingers dug into the edges of the freezing cold slate as three bears tore down the street toward the center of town. She leaned over, searching for the fourth when a horrible splintering groan came from below her, and the roof shuddered.

Faron appeared in a gust of *vitalle*. "How many? Where did they come from—?" His eyes caught on the wide path through the snow from the trees, and he gave Kate a sharp, questioning look.

Guilt washed over her. "I…" The roof shook as the crack of breaking wood sounded from below.

He blew out an exasperated breath and disappeared.

Kate scrambled toward the ladder but caught sight of her pack and scrambled back over the slippery shingles to grab it. A low growl sounded from below. Faron responded with something soothing, too quiet for Kate to hear, and she raced back for the ladder. She climbed down enough to see into the smithy and found Faron facing the bear, a long stream of Elvish words rolling smoothly off his tongue.

The elf king's remnant enveloped him like a golden mist. The tendrils that held his authority anchored into the ground and reached out toward the bear like long, grasping fingers.

The animal let out a loud huff, swaying from side to side as it pawed one of its massive paws against the wooden floor of the smithy. Its low growl vibrated Kate's chest.

"Stay back, Kate," Faron said. He held out his hands toward the bear. "And you, calm down. There's nothing to do here. No one is threatening you. There's no food." He reached one hand toward the creature. The bear snapped its teeth, and Faron paused. "Why are you so mad?" he asked, his voice still pitched in a soothing tone. "There's nothing to be mad about. Feel the peace…let it in…"

Kate kept her grip on the ladder but cast out.

Faron burst into an explosion of light. Rivers of dazzling brightness flowed out of the ground and toward the bear. Faron's remnant reached the creature, and it flinched.

"Nothing to fear here," Faron continued. "Time to sleep."

He took a step closer and the bear spun, tearing out of the far side of the smithy and racing toward the center of town.

Faron swore and disappeared.

Kate dropped down off the ladder before the glittering remains of Faron's remnant had settled in a golden carpet on the floor. She raced through the smithy, through the cloud of citrus resin scent that Faron's remnant held.

The street on the far side was empty, but shouts and cries rang out from the direction of the square. She ran toward them. A body lay crumpled against a wall three houses down, and she dropped to her knees next to the man. His green tunic was drenched with blood, and his eyes were vacant. She cast out, but there was no trace of *vitalle* in him.

Swearing, she rose and ran again, her feet slipping over the snowy cobblestones.

She reached the square and slid to a stop. The massive shapes of four bears were spread across the square.

One slashed a vicious paw across a man's chest, sending him flying backward. Another tore through the door of a house while a child screamed from an upstairs window. Tribal barreled in after it, bellowing and holding his axe high.

To her right, a door was torn off the hinges, and sounds of destruction shook the building. A ring of men closed in on it.

A woman dragged a body toward a side street.

A man ran into the square, holding a burning torch and several more unlit ones, shouting for help.

Arrows flew through the air, sinking into the thick fur of the bears but seeming to do little more than irritate them.

"Spears!" Silas shouted from where he swung his axe at a bear's head. "We need boar spears!"

One of the men near him raced away.

"Just contain them!" Faron ran across the square. "The rangers will subdue them!"

He disappeared, then reappeared on the back of the nearest bear and thrust his hands into the creature's fur, just behind its head. The bear roared and twisted. Ayen stepped, appearing next to it and grabbing a wad of the animal's fur along its neck. Venn ran over, leaping through the air and landing on its back behind Faron.

The bear stumbled forward, its motions growing slower.

"Sleep!" Faron's authority shifted from soft tentacles to rigid spears that drove down into the bear's head.

Its legs collapsed, and Kate ran forward. Even lying down, the creature's back reached higher than her waist. She pressed her hand into its fur, pushing *vitalle* toward its mind. "*Paxa*," she whispered, pushing the desire to relax into the huge bear.

Faron's influence was struggling against its will, and Kate

slipped her own in, working to soften the determination the creature was caught up on.

She searched for the usual feel of an attacking animal. Hunger, defensiveness, or fear. But inside the bear, instead an animalistic mind consumed with a single thought, she found a tumult of emotions. Frustration, rage, and fear all warred with each other, driving the bear into a frenzy. But over every other emotion was an overarching hunger for…something.

A flash of daffodils filled Kate's mind. An entire garden bed of them, golden yellow, bending and bobbing in some spring breeze.

Faron's authority was slowly dulling the rage. Kate tried to help, but the bear continued to snap at anyone near it.

"Venn!" Kate called, holding out her hand. Venn grabbed it, and Kate funneled the elf's brilliantly glittering green remnant down her arm. The flow of *vitalle* surged brighter, and the bear's motion slowed. "*Dormio*," she whispered, willing the bear to sleep.

A sharp prodding of hunger jabbed into the bear's mind, and it shoved itself to its feet, throwing Faron off. He landed with a crash on the cobblestones, and the bear swiped a huge paw at Kate. She spun away, but it caught her with a glancing blow to the side and sent her sprawling into the snow, dragging Venn along with her.

The bear twisted to lunge at them, but Merrick leapt between them, shoving a torch in the bear's face. The animal reared back away from it.

Kate flung an arm toward the torch and pulled a chunk of fire off it, drawing it into her hand. The bear fell back into a low, swaying stance, its eyes fixed on the two fires.

The bear Tribal had chased into a home backed out the broken door, the dwarf's axe harrying it. Silas ran past, tossing a wickedly tipped spear to his brother. Tribal caught it and dropped his axe. With a shout, he charged forward. He slammed into the bear, and the spear sank into the furry chest. The bear gave a great bellow, but its legs gave out and it fell to the ground.

Silas circled around a third, an identical spear in his hands.

"No!" Faron cried. "Don't kill them!"

But the dwarf had already lunged, and his spear drove deep into the bear's back.

The bear in front of Kate drew closer, and she flung a line of fire out, blocking it off from herself, Venn, and Merrick. A ribbon of flame appeared, but it was thin, and the bear barely flinched.

"Venn!" Kate yelled again, and Venn grabbed her outstretched arm. The added strength of Venn's remnant fueled the fire into a blazing belt of flame that enclosed the bear.

It froze, and five elven rangers appeared inside the fire, all of their hands crashing onto the huge creature at once. The bear staggered, then collapsed to the ground, senseless.

All the elves stepped to the final bear.

Kate cut off *vitalle* to the ribbon of fire and let her burning hands fall to her lap.

Two of the bears lay dead, huge spears skewered into them. The last bear crashed to the ground, surrounded by elven rangers.

A long cheer rose up from the humans.

Merrick surveyed the square, settling his gaze on several men struggling to lift a fallen signpost off an unmoving body. He paused long enough to cast a quick glance at Kate. "Are you hurt?"

She shook her head, and his lips pressed together as though he didn't quite believe her. But all he said was, "Nice trick with the fire," before he ran toward the fallen post.

Venn rose and took in the wreckage. "How did four mountain bears get past your watch?" she asked quietly.

Kate winced, looking down at her hands. The silver ring still sat on her finger, surrounded by burned red skin. "Another drawer opened."

Venn raised an eyebrow.

Kate held up her finger. "Any idea what this is?"

"A ring that nearly got Home destroyed?" Venn offered her a hand.

Kate declined by showing her burned palms. She braced an elbow on the thick fur of the sleeping bear's haunch and staggered to her feet.

Faron appeared in front of them, searching Venn instantly. "Any injuries?"

Venn shook her head, and when he turned to Kate, she grimaced. "Only to my pride. I'm sorry. I got…distracted."

"That's what obsessions do," Venn said dryly. "Distract us."

A female elf appeared beside Faron, and Kate recognized her as the elven healer who'd helped take the wood troll out of Home. "There are no serious injuries on our part," Aylia said. "The humans, though…" She gestured to where a half-dozen men, each bloody, lay at the mouth of one of the streets.

"Go." Faron scanned the square and the two huge corpses. "What a waste," he muttered.

Kate started to follow after Aylia toward the wounded men, but Faron held up a hand. "She can heal them all easily enough. I need a word with both of you." He headed toward the large pine, and Venn, after a moment's hesitation, followed. Kate trailed behind the two of them, her feet heavy with exhaustion and guilt.

They reached the pine, and Faron moved into the shadows under its branches. Ayen crossed toward them, bringing Tribal and Silas with him.

Faron's expression was unreadable as he studied the destruction, but his hands were clasped tightly behind his back.

"It is confirmed," Ayen said quietly when he reached them. "The command that was driving all four bears was from

Naevys." At Kate's questioning look, he added, "When the Warden convinces creatures to return to the north, she buries a series of commands in their minds. Herion has unwound them a hundred times, once they get far enough into the mountains, lest they keep heading north forever. He says there is no question that this was her."

Faron's fingers tightened. "I need to understand what she is doing," he said in a low voice.

"She's trying to fight beetles," Silas said.

Tribal gave a nod of agreement. "It does seem that way."

"What are you talking about?" Faron asked.

Kate explained the story of the duke and the beetles. "We've just been wondering if she's trying to root out something we don't understand."

Ayen gave a thoughtful hum. "There *is* something wrong with the southern edge of the forest. Near where the Surn flows south, the forest darkens."

Kate nodded. "The shadows are too stark. And they feel... watchful."

"And there are thorny plants that spring up into walls, and vines that try to kill you," Tribal added.

Faron grimaced. "The shadows and the thorns have to be my mother. I remember one time when she was very angry with my father about something, and everything in the Wood was dark and thorny for several days." He rubbed his hand over his face, which didn't banish his worried look. "Tell me everything you've seen."

Kate explained the vines and the frenbrush, then the entire encounter with the *naiwyn*. Then the renewed protection over the slope of the ravine, the grey path of destruction through the hills toward Home, and ending with the draining of the pine they stood under.

"And then she has twice sent predators into Home." His face

was still impressive, but a pained confusion wasn't quite hidden behind his official tone. "Or I think it's safe to say she's the only one who could have sent the *gwerocs* in last night, in addition to the bears today."

"What does she want with Home?" Kate asked. "Surely, if she's after *ael'iza*, the White Wood holds far more than a human town."

"What were the bears looking for?" Tribal added. "The houses they tore into seemed random, and like the wolves, they mostly just destroyed whatever they could reach. Ate no food, just tore apart walls and ripped through doors."

The door the bear had ripped off lay outside the house, made of a pale wood. "There's something about the doors," Kate said. "The *gweroc* were drawn to doors made of frost pine."

"This one's not frost pine—it's birch," Venn said.

Kate paused. "Well, I was going to ask you what the meaning of the frost pine doors is, but now I'm out of ideas."

Ayen frowned. "The doors don't really make sense. Herion says they were driven by hunger. A drive to get to something he couldn't make out."

"Daffodils," Kate said. At their incredulous expressions, she added, "That's what was in the bear's mind. He was angry and scared, as though he were being threatened, and there was a hunger for a garden bed filled with daffodils."

"There will be no daffodils for months," Venn said.

"Does anyone in town grow them?" Kate asked. "It was a raised garden bed, absolutely full of them, just blooming in the sunshine."

Venn exchanged glances with the dwarves.

"Dunno of anyone who raises any flowers here," Silas said. "Not a lot of demand for bouquets in a little town like this."

"The bear was conflicted," Faron said. "I've never felt a wild animal so torn between things it wanted."

Kate nodded. "Maybe that was enough to make it go a bit crazy. Maybe the daffodils are just a random memory that it latched on to. I didn't get a chance to look in any of the other minds."

In an open part of the square, the townsfolk began piling broken wood into a long, low bonfire, while several men worked to butcher the bears.

Faron turned his back on the square and faced them all. "Regardless, Home is obviously not safe. I'm stationing rangers around it from this moment on until we find my mother." He grimaced slightly. "I've called for a town meeting, and I need to decide how much I want to tell the humans. Admitting my mother is behind all this is…not ideal, but hiding it feels like something my father would do. I think it's safe to say that whatever little faith the humans had in the White Wood is going to be sorely tested." He looked at Kate, Venn, and the dwarves. "I could use some help if you're staying."

Tribal set his axe on his shoulder. "You elves'll make a mess of it if left to yourselves, so we'll hang around for a bit."

Faron gave a nod with an edge of gratefulness and turned to Venn.

She met his gaze. "I'll stay for Home's sake, but as a resident of the lakes, not the White Wood."

With a stiff nod, he gave Kate a questioning look, and she shifted her pack. The square teemed with quiet activity, muffled by exhaustion and grief. Two bodies were laid near the wounded, including the man with the bloody green tunic. The pull of the box felt suddenly hollow, and another wave of guilt rolled over her. "I can't leave Home like this." Her eyes swept the square. "And I'm sorry."

The words were pathetically insufficient, but Faron merely nodded again and started toward the Blind Pig. "Then let's go make sure everyone's properly disappointed in my family."

CHAPTER TWENTY-THREE

Kate moved through the warmth and noise of the tavern, numbly returning nods and greetings with people she'd talked with during her time in Home and faces she didn't recognize. She shouldered through the crowd, trying not to slosh the mugs of coffee or drop the basket of bread Yellow had given her.

A few rousing "thank yous" were directed at her, and she ducked away from them, the truth of her failure with the bears sitting heavy on her shoulders.

Close to the fire, she found Venn, Faron, Ayen, and the dwarves at a table. None of them spoke beyond the occasional greeting to someone who passed.

"Magistrate Mirrow is coming," Kate said, handing Venn one of the mugs.

"Kate!" Rosia said, passing by the table and giving her a grateful look. "I think people in this part of the world are going to start understanding what a Keeper is!"

Kate was spared a response by Magistrate Mirrow calling for a chair to be brought to the front of the fireplace and motioning

Faron over. Rosia hurried away, and the room began to settle into their tables.

"What *are* Keepers?" Silas said to his brother. "Distractible?"

Tribal took a swig of his log mead. "Who knew they were so bad at seeing a herd of bears crossing the open ground?"

A twinge of guilt jabbed into Kate. "I…"

"You got distracted by the box." Silas reached over and tore a chunk off her rosemary bread, popping it into his mouth.

Kate glanced at Venn. "You told them?"

Venn raised an insulted eyebrow.

"No one had to tell us," Tribal said. "You're fairly observant—for a human—unless you're reading some ancient book or fiddling with that box." He pointed the top of his bottle at Kate's finger. "Since you seem to have come into possession of a dwarven vow ring in a style that was common at least sixty years ago, it's not a huge leap to figure you got another one of those nonsensical drawers open and found a wee bit of treasure."

The wavy pattern on the ring caught the lantern light and glimmered. Guilt washed over her, and she turned her palm upward, showing them the bright red skin on her palm and fingers. "Everything's a little tender to try to wiggle it off right now." The ring was such a useless thing. No clues to its story, nothing in it that should have distracted her so much. "It doesn't feel dwarven. I'd say it was human."

"Rings in that style were common for wedding vows," Silas said. "Looks like stonesteel, though, so it's a little nicer than most."

The ring was heavy on her finger, glinting balefully at her. "The drawer opened with envy, I think," she said quietly, pulling the ring against the red skin. The pain of it intertwined with the guilt in a fitting way. "I didn't even notice the bears until they were tearing apart the barricade."

Tribal leaned toward Silas. "If we ever travel with those two again, Twig never does watch by herself."

Silas nodded but kept his eyes on Kate. "That box is going to be the end of you. I don't want it to be the end of us too."

"My friends and neighbors!" Magistrate Mirrow called with a stiff formality from atop his chair. He again wore his black robe with red embroidery down the sleeves and around his collar. From this close, the wear on the cuffs and hems was too obvious to miss, but he wore it proudly. "Prince Faron assures me that the final two bears are being safely relocated away from the town, and the work crews report that the damaged barricade has been repaired."

The room quieted, and Mirrow gave Faron a polite bow. "We are grateful for the assistance of the elves today in fending off this new attack." He turned back to the room. "The good prince has requested to speak to you all and explain some new developments in the White Wood."

The short magistrate climbed down off the chair, and Faron moved up beside it, looking over the room. The light of the fire glowed behind him, but his face was still bright, shimmering with a copper tint. His expression was sober, and his hands were closed into fists at his sides. He glanced at Venn, who tapped her fingers on her cheek with a slight twist of amusement to her lips.

Faron let out a very quiet breath of frustration, and his glow dimmed. "Good people of Home," he began, looking over the room. "I wanted you to be aware of a change that has happened in the White Wood." His voice was even, but his hands stayed tightly closed. "My father, Thallion, is no longer king."

A ripple of surprise spread across the room.

"Is he dead?" someone called from the back of the room.

Faron flinched but shook his head. "No, but his authority was removed by the White Wood."

"For sending a troll at us?" Griston's scratchy voice called from the near the door. "And shadows and wolves and bears?"

"No," Faron began. "It was removed for…" He fell silent.

The tension in the room grew as Faron struggled for words.

Venn's hand tightened on her mug. Muttering began to crop up from assorted tables.

Kate surveyed the room, watching a dangerous sort of story begin to write itself. She pushed herself to her feet and rounded the table to stand next to Faron, raising her hand for quiet.

The rumble of voices grew, though, abuzz with anger.

Yellow banged his fist on the wall above the kitchen door, making it boom like a drum. "Let the Keeper speak," he said, glaring around the room.

Kate tried to ignore the way the title fit so ill on her shoulders. She cleared her throat and focused on the fact that this right here was what a Keeper would actually do. "The situation with King Thallion rose because of a conflict between himself and the elven queen, Naevys." The room focused on her, and Faron let out a pained breath. "It had nothing to do with Home. Thallion wanted Naevys to give up her role, as it was harming her health." A few of the faces softened, and Kate tried to keep her face neutral. "He went as far as to try to force her out of it. In the process, he overstepped the bounds of his authority. His crown was removed and given to Faron."

A new ripple of surprise ran through the room, and Magistrate Mirrow's face grew stricken. "My apologies for calling you 'Prince!'"

"I told you that old king was false!" Griston cried out. "And now he's sent monsters to kill us all! All our troubles are elven troubles!"

"No," Faron said over the rising hum of voices. "My mother really is ill. She was harming the White Wood before my father tried to stop her, and now, for reasons we don't understand"—he looked apologetically around the room—"she is targeting Home."

"Never trust the elves!" Griston shouted.

"The elves helped you just this afternoon," Kate called over the noise.

"After sending the bears in the first place." Griston shot to his feet. "They're always hurting us! Did the corrupt king overstep his authority when he drove us from the far side of the river? Is he hiding more diamonds there? Because 'twasn't me that started that rumor! Someone planted those gems in my wares!" He jabbed a finger toward the front of the room. "Th' magistrate's daughter was trampled! Girl lost the use of her right hand! And for what? So the elves can keep more riches on that side? What are they hiding?"

The magistrate's face had grown dark.

Faron raised his hands. "There are no diamonds in the White Wood."

"We saw bits of 'em!" someone shouted.

"Glittered just like diamonds!" a woman agreed.

Kate braced herself and then climbed up onto the chair Magistrate Mirrow had vacated. She pitched her voice over the crowd. "That was me!"

The room quieted.

"That was me," she repeated. "We had found Queen Naevys, and she was gravely ill. We needed King Thallion distracted for a time until she could heal." Magistrate Mirrow glared at her, and she felt a renewed surge of guilt. She directed the next words to him. "It seemed necessary at the time. All of the White Wood was suffering with the queen's illness, and when the elven wood suffers, the human lands do as well. I thought the idea of diamonds along the Surn would just provide a short distraction. I never meant for anyone to get hurt. I'm sorry your daughter was hurt. I'd be happy to look at her injury and see if I can help."

"What do you care if any of us get hurt, foreigner?" Griston demanded. "Everything that's happened here since you and that brother of yours came here has hurt Home!"

"Go back to your own land, Keeper!" a woman's voice called out.

"And we don't want no elves, either!" someone else yelled.

"You need help against these threats," Faron said loudly.

"Because the elves keep sending them!" Griston strode to the middle of the room. "Everything started with them!" He jabbed a finger toward Faron.

The room erupted into shouts. The anger and fear were almost palpable. Tribal and Silas had set down their bottles of mead and draped their hands casually on the hilts of their knives. Venn and Ayen sat straight-backed in their chairs.

The anger toward the White Wood grew, far past the point where a few words were going to quell it.

Kate searched for some answer, some way to keep the town protected, despite their mistrust of the elves—a mistrust she admitted was partially deserved. But the town needed the help of the elves.

Venn's eyebrows rose in apprehension, and Kate saw the answer.

She gave Faron an apologetic look. "Sorry about this," she said quietly. She held up her hands and funneled a little *vitalle* out of them, aiming at the four nearest lanterns. The flames flared brighter, and the noise in the room dulled. "Your troubles," she said loudly, before the quiet could dissolve, "have happened because of a select few elves from the White Wood. The elves who live at the lakes to the east, like Venn and Evay"—she motioned to Venn at the table, ignoring the indrawn breath from Faron—"have nothing to do with any of it. Would you accept help from them? Because the way things are going, you're going to need help."

"Is he king of the lake elves?" Magistrate Mirrow demanded, pointing at Faron.

"No," Kate answered. "They're a separate group."

"Venn and Evay have always been friends to our town," Yellow said. "I'd be happy to have more elves like them around."

Faron smoothed his face back into a polite mask. "I could send runners to the lakes asking for—"

"We trusted you both!" Magistrate Mirrow jabbed his finger toward Kate and Faron. "And you've both harmed our town. It's past time you left!"

Kate drew back from the viciousness in his voice.

"You don't want to kick out useful elves," Yellow said, his booming voice drowning out the other noises. "These two helped with the bears. Kate stopped the wood troll."

Mirrow crossed his arms. "They've hurt as much as they've helped!"

"It's time we fought back against the elves!" Griston raised his fist. "Find out what riches they are hiding!"

A surge of support rang out.

"There are no riches!" Faron called.

"Out!" Mirrow pointed at the door. "Out of our town!"

Yellow pounded on the wall again. "We're not driving out those who are helping us!"

"No one asked you, Yellow," Mirrow said.

"We're not driving out the elves." Yellow's voice was firm, and the room stayed quiet, looking between the two men.

Mirrow's brow creased. "Of course you want them to stay—you want their coin."

Yellow's jaw clenched. "Most of the town is here. Let's put it to a vote."

A ripple ran through the room, but Mirrow gave a dismissive flick of his hand. "There will be no vote. It is my duty to protect the town, and I take that seriously."

"We tasked you with keeping order in the town, Mirrow," Yellow said evenly. "Not running it." He addressed the room. "We've all been through a lot. Had dangers in town lately we could hardly have imagined. Some of it has clearly been the fault of some elves. And Kate, well, she's caused a bit of trouble too, but she also healed your men." He looked at Nevin and Rosia. "And your daughter. And she put a wood troll to sleep when a half-dozen of our men couldn't bring it down."

"Who's to say she didn't bring it here in the first place?" Griston shouted.

Yellow looked questioningly at Kate.

"She did not," Faron said, his voice even. "The troll is a symptom of my mother's illness. For centuries she's sensed when creatures have come out of the northern mountains and helped the elves send them back. But her mind is slipping." A flicker of pain crossed his face before he smoothed it away. "She no longer guards the border well. We've increased our patrols to compensate."

"So another problem that began with the elves," Griston grumbled.

"Some elves," Yellow corrected him. "Not all elves. We've had our fair share of trouble from humans, too. The bandits who plagued us last spring weren't elven. Or the band of warriors from Poluntchun who tried to take us over when I was a child." He paused. "I say we take Kate's advice and accept help from the lake elves."

"So they can endanger us too?" Mirrow asked.

Kate looked over the room. "Do you really want to weather whatever comes next without the help of any elves?"

"What are they sending against us next?" Griston demanded. "A plague?"

"These elves"—Kate motioned to Venn and Ayen and Faron—

"aren't sending anything. They're offering to protect you from Naevys."

"I think you've exhausted all the chances we're willing to give you," Mirrow said.

"A vote," Yellow called. "What does the town want to do? If tomorrow another threat arrives, do you want elves to help or not?"

"I am the magistrate!" Mirrow declared. "I will decide what we do!"

"Well, then let's see if your opinion is shared by everyone else," Yellow said. "All those in favor of driving all the elves out of Home, raise your hands."

Griston's hand shot up, along with an alarming number from tables around the room.

"And who's in favor of having elves from the lakes come and help?" Yellow asked.

A few hands rose quickly, then more, until the vast majority of the room held their hands in the air.

Yellow looked at Magistrate Mirrow. "That seems to be a majority."

"He is not your magistrate!" Mirrow yelled, pointing at Yellow. "He has no say!"

"Who thinks Yellow should be magistrate?" Nevin asked loudly.

The majority of hands rose again.

Mirrow glared at them. "You're all going to regret this!"

He shoved his way through the crowd toward the door.

"The elves'll end up killing you all!" Griston agreed, falling in behind the short man.

The tavern door opened, revealing the blue evening square, then slammed shut.

The eyes that turned back to Faron were wary. He cleared his throat. "While we mean you no harm, I understand your distrust. I will pull my rangers out of town, but we will continue to patrol farther out until the lake elves arrive."

The attention of the room swung back to Yellow, who fixed Kate and Faron with a hard look. "Don't make us regret this."

CHAPTER TWENTY-FOUR

Kate's bones felt heavy against the chair as she let Yellow's thick potato soup warm her. She reached for a piece of bread, and the pattern on the ring glinted again. The carved hills looked enough like the land south of Home that she felt another pang of regret that she was here instead of a half day's walk into them. She immediately shoved the feeling away. Home was in danger, and the nagging longing to leave felt invasive and irritating. Like a pebble in her shoe. Instead, she mulled the idea of what Naevys could be looking for in the houses of Home. Next to her leg, the quiet hum of the box called to her from her pack.

She squeezed a piece of the soft bread between her fingers, ignoring the itch to pull the box out. Upstairs later, she'd take it out and put together a timeline of what was required to open it. Creating the bloodstone would be easy enough. She'd copy out the instructions and begin making notes about them. She glanced around the tavern, as though she'd see Crofftus wandering through as a rabbit or a squirrel. It was a little odd that he hadn't shown up yet. Next time he was near, she'd need his opinions on a few of the steps.

The question of how many wellstones she should get nagged at her. She'd thought three, at the minimum, but to be sure she had enough, it was probably worth the time to find five. And if there was the possibility of using them for anything in the future, maybe she should stay along the river until she found ten.

The urge to take the box somewhere safe shoved that idea aside. No, she'd start at the bridge near Home then move downstream. She'd find as many as she could while they walked, but no more lingering.

Faron strode up to the far side of the table and set his hands on it, leaning toward Kate and Venn. "Will you come with me to the lakes?"

Kate's anger at Naevys flared toward him. "No. No more elven entanglements."

The common room was draining of people after the meeting. The men of town headed to their posts at the barricades, and the women and children hurried off seeking safe places to gather and sleep for the night. Ayen had left too, after quiet instructions from Faron to make sure every ranger he could find was stationed around the town, far enough away that the humans wouldn't see.

Faron worked to keep his expression calm. "I could use your help."

"The lakes aren't going to get angry the way Home did," Kate said.

"They'll be angry that we kept my mother's condition a secret," Faron said.

"They all know." Venn picked up a wide piece of cheese. "They have just been waiting for you to tell them."

Faron gave her a flat look. "They knew she was secretly draining the White Wood and also tinkering with the writings and inventions of Renault Half-Elven? And that she was capable of doing this to Home?"

"No," she admitted, "but you didn't know any of that either, so they can hardly hold it against you."

"We'll stay here," Kate said, "and attempt to smooth over things further."

Tribal nodded. "It might need some smoothing over. We're not the biggest fan of elves, but we still aren't paranoid enough to think the elves are out to get us all the time."

"You spent all morning complaining the wood was trying to kill you," Kate pointed out.

Tribal grinned. "Sometimes they're threatened by us. Can't blame them for posturing."

Faron slapped his hand on the table. "Enough! The lake elves rarely get involved with anything in this area. Venn, they think of you as a sort of ambassador already, and Kate, you're the sort of human who can convince them to help. *Please* come. Home can't be left open to Naevys's attacks, but I'm afraid the lake elves won't see this as a problem they need to get involved in. If there's another attack and my rangers try to step in, half of Home might attack them instead."

Kate glanced at Venn. "Is that true? Will the lakes refuse to help?"

Venn tapped her spoon on her bowl. "They are reluctant to enter into the sort of situations the White Wood involves itself in."

"Exactly," Faron said, "but they'll listen to you much more than they'll listen to me."

The familiar weight of responsibility began to press on Kate's shoulders, but she ran her thumb over the ring, trying to drive it away.

"You need to convince someone like Evay," Venn said.

"Who will also listen to you more than she'll listen to me."

Venn dropped her spoon into her soup. "I'm not part of your court, Faron. I'm not going to the lakes to plead on your behalf."

"It's hardly my behalf! Home is in serious danger, and my mother is—" He glanced around the room and lowered his voice. "Venn, I have no idea what my mother is going to do next. Home needs your help, both of you. And my mother needs your help, and"—he flung his hand around—"everyone needs your help!"

Venn gave an annoyed huff. Kate met her glance, catching a glimpse of the very recognizable battle between obligation and what she actually wanted to do.

The door to the tavern flew open.

Aislin rushed in. "Auntie Venn!"

"Unbelievable!" Venn pushed herself to her feet as Matlen ran in behind his sister. "Why are you two still here!"

The two young elves hurried across the room. Aislin grabbed Venn's arm. "You have to come! We were trying to get the trees to tell Evay what was happening when they gave a message to us! Auntie Venn, you've been summoned by the elder council!" She winced at Faron. "The council has also demanded an audience with Thallion and Naevys. Something about dangers in the woods."

"They were very angry," Matlen said, his eyes unusually serious.

Faron rose. "Is that enough of a reason for you, Venn?"

Venn's brow creased. "If the council called me…" She turned to Kate. "I need to do this."

Kate met her gaze. Light flashed from her ring with a glint of silver light like the small lantern, waiting in the darkness, beckoning to her, leaving her aching for all the things she truly wanted.

With an effort, she slid her hand off the table, dropping the ring into shadows and cutting off the glimmers of light. She reached for her pack, letting the soreness of her palm drive away the more elusive ache. "Then I'm with you. Let's get more bread for the road."

Kate forced her tired feet to keep moving through the powdery snow. The ragged ends of the day's clouds blew away to the east, and patches of moonlight lit the snowy ground. Faron stalked ahead of them through the woods, his back straight. Venn walked silently next to Kate.

"What does the council want with you?" Kate asked Venn.

"I have no idea. They summon me occasionally but never give a reason until I get there."

Aislin and Matlen traipsed along on Kate's other side, chattering tirelessly to each other and occasionally disappearing and reappearing somewhere off in the woods to investigate whatever struck their fancy. They spent several hours moving steadily north through the forest, and Kate suppressed a yawn, trying not to think about the warm bed back at the Blind Pig.

"Not far to the river," Aislin said cheerily. "And you can sleep in the boats for a few hours."

"It's irritating how long your kind can go without getting tired," Kate said.

Matlen popped into view beside her. "Aislin's right—just a few more minutes to the river."

"How long does it take you to reach the lakes if you can step?" she asked. "If you didn't have to wait for someone like me?"

"It'd shorten the trip to the river by an hour or so." Matlen tossed a pinecone at a nearby tree.

"But most of the trip is on the boats," Aislin said, "so stepping doesn't help."

Kate looked between them. "Could you teach me to do it?"

Aislin's eyebrows shot up. "Maybe! It's not hard."

Matlen jabbed her with his elbow and gave Venn an uncomfortable look.

Venn merely continued scanning the forest around them. "Do not expect intelligible instructions from those two."

Aislin leaned closer to Kate. "We've tried to help Auntie Venn before, but she's not quite convinced by our explanations."

"Because they make no sense," Venn said, but there was a slight smile at the edge of her mouth.

"They make perfect sense." Aislin held her hands next to each other, palms down, fingers out flat. "Stepping is a bit like overlapping leaves. If you wanted to walk from one little finger to the other, you'd have to walk all the way across both my hands. But if you overlap them..." She set one hand partially on top of the other. "Then the distance is much shorter."

Kate tried to wrap her mind around the description. "The ground is like leaves?"

"Of course not," Aislin said with a laugh.

"See?" Venn said.

"But you can overlap parts of it all the same." Aislin peered ahead. "See that funny trunk up there that splits and bends like it has elbows? To step there, I take the ground near that and overlap it with this."

Kate cast out just as a gust of *vitalle* puffed out of the young elf. Most of it hovered like a mist around her, but a burst of it appeared at her foot. There was a blur of warmth and light. Then the elf's entire body appeared far ahead, leaving only a cloud of *vitalle* dispersing into the air near Kate.

"It's not really like overlapping leaves," Matlen said under his breath to Kate. "It's like making a small jump into a big one, because the middle of the jump is just moving through air, and we all know air is nothing. So it doesn't matter how much of it you pass through during the jump."

"I don't think air is 'nothing,'" Kate began, but Matlen had already winked out of view with his own gust of *vitalle* and landed a few paces past his sister.

"Well, air is not trees," Matlen called back, as though that proved it.

Venn let out a tired laugh. "I told you."

"Come back here and do it again," Kate called. The twins reappeared near her side, and while she cast out, they both stepped again. "The *vitalle* is interesting. But they're moving too fast for me to see what's happening."

"Because air is nothing," Matlen said with a grin, "so it's very fast to get through it."

He has clearly never tried to fly. A grey bird with a white head landed on a branch above Kate, and the low rumble of Crofftus's remnant floated down.

Kate let out a breath of relief. "Crofftus! It's good to see you!"

Faron studied the bird with a frown.

I don't believe we've been officially introduced, Your Majesty. Crofftus's words were polite but cold. *And though you tried to kill me when I was a spider, I understand you helped to heal the eagle I inhabited before that, so I suppose my resentment and gratitude balance out to enough indifference that I will merely warn you that Katria and Venn are not part of your White Wood, and I do not see it going well for you if you attempt to control either of them again.*

"I have no intention of doing so," Faron said, without any sign of being intimidated.

Good, Crofftus snapped. *Because your family has caused them quite enough trouble.*

Faron raised an eyebrow at the hostility in his tone but didn't answer.

"Where've you been?" Kate asked Crofftus. "We've been worried."

I was doing exactly what I was supposed to be doing! he answered, irritated. *I have been searching the path you told me you were taking south through the hills. I spent all day searching for any signs of you and was nearly convinced you'd both been killed by those* naiwyn.

She winced in apology. "Sorry. We didn't have time to leave messages." She paused. "I'm relieved you knew what a *naiwyn* was. I was worried you'd stumble onto them."

I... The bird twitched on the branch. *I know a lot of things, Katria,* he said primly. *For instance, when there's suddenly smoke from Home that looks like a huge fire, I know that you have a propensity for being right in the middle of trouble, and I thought it best I investigate. But since I had exhausted the little nuthatch who'd already helped me search, it was some time before I could find another creature who could bring me this far north.* He fluttered to a tree farther along their path, the motion agitated. *When I saw the bear carcasses and the destruction, I...* His voice trailed away helplessly. *What happened?*

"Naevys attacked Home," Kate said. "First with *gweroc*, and then with bears."

The bird's wings flapped with a nervous energy. *But why?*

His voice sounded frightened in her mind, and she stopped under the branch he perched on. "Are you all right, Crofftus?"

The grey jay stilled. *Of course I am,* he said, annoyed. *This is all just...troubling, that's all.*

Venn peered at him dubiously. "You're just noticing this now?"

It feels worse now, he said roughly. He was silent for a moment, and when he resumed, his tone was calmer, even if the bird still shifted his weight. *I saw the barren strip of land leading from the ravine toward Home. Is that...* He shifted again. *Is that the work of the Warden?*

"It is." Kate told him about the net over the ravine. "Home knows that it's Naevys now, and they're not feeling particularly comfortable with the White Wood elves, so we're headed to the lakes to ask if they'll help protect the town."

I have always wanted to visit the lakes, he said with a bit more interest. *Although I'll find my own way instead of finding a creature who'd be happy to sit with all of you in a boat for hours.*

Matlen stepped and appeared under the tree, startling the bird.

Katria, I heard an elf say that stepping was like a mind jumping from one thought to another.

"Do you see?" Venn said in irritation, starting to walk again. "No one offers any explanation that actually makes sense. A mind does not literally leap."

"I don't think he meant literally," Kate said, "or the mind would come out of the body. The way his does."

"Well, my mind figuratively jumps all the time," Venn said, "and I never step. Crofftus, your explanation makes no more sense than the rest of them."

It makes perfect sense. Crofftus took off from the branch. *I'll see you at the lakes, Katria. Just…be careful.*

He soared away, disappearing through the trees.

Aislin looked after him, her mouth pursed in disapproval. "I think the dwarves are right. That bird thing is acting weird."

"He's always been a little weird," Kate answered.

"Not this weird." Venn started walking again.

Kate fell in beside her. "When do you think he heard elves talking about stepping?"

"I have no idea."

"Doesn't matter," Faron said. "It's nothing like a mind jumping. It's a stretching of the self and a shortening of the world."

Venn let out a sigh. "You are a part of the forest," she said in a decent, if fairly arrogant, imitation of Faron's voice, "and it is a part of you."

Instead of looking annoyed, Faron smiled. "Exactly. An elf is almost as much over there by that large rock as they are right where they walk." He stopped and faced Kate. "I think this is why humans don't step." His eyes trailed in the air around her, as though tracing something. "You're not truly a part of the wood." His brow creased. "Or you are, but more like an animal than an elf. You gain something from it. A nourishment that isn't food. It feeds something else inside you, and there is the awareness that when you die, you will be absorbed into it. But…" He shifted his attention to Aislin and Matlen. "These two are blurred into the woods. Their skin is so nearly the same as the bark of the trees that it is no stretch at all to believe they are there, or here, or anywhere. And so they can be."

"Are you saying I'm not connected enough to the forest to step?" Venn asked, her voice irritated. "Because until your mother ripped it away, I was far more connected than you."

"No, whatever issue keeps you from stepping, it's not connection." He looked around Venn again, and a sympathy crept into the edges. "She stole almost all of it, didn't she?"

"Perhaps a strong connection helps," Kate said, "but I think the problem you're having, Venn, is that you don't move *vitalle* as easily as other elves." She focused on a patch of snow three paces ahead and lifted her foot. Funneling some *vitalle* out of her toes, she sent it forward. The thread was weak and thin, and when it reached its goal, it merely brushed against the snow and found nothing to grab onto. Kate tried to push her foot along it. Her sole tingled, but when she stepped, her foot merely landed a single pace forward in the snow.

"All right," she admitted. "Maybe the connection matters. Maybe you should try, Venn."

"No," Venn said firmly.

"Kate's right," Faron said. "Maybe it's the *ael'iza*. If we could find a way to help you stretch some *'iza* out, you might be able to do it."

"We have somewhere to be," Venn said, moving past him, and

the hint of a smile crossed her lips. "Unless you're stalling because the river is near."

"I'm not stalling." Faron started walking again. "I was trying to give Kate an intelligible description of stepping."

He fell in behind Venn, his shoulders relaxed, his hands hanging loosely at his side. The rushing sound of a river filtered through the trees a few minutes later. Venn led the way forward, the reds and oranges of her hair bright against the white snow and dark pines. Faron followed a few paces behind, his own hair darker. His remnant flowed around him with a bright golden yellow, brushing past every tree with a gentle touch, dragging behind him like a cape, disappearing into the snow as though it was searching for a place to pool.

Everything about him seemed brighter. Lighter.

They reached the top of a steep decline and found the broad river flowing below it, the water black, the surface glittering with occasional glints of moonlight. On the near side, the trees grew sparse as they nestled up along the riverbank. The far side of the water was edged with cliffs that rose twice as high as the tallest pines before soaring up into a forested mountainside.

Venn passed into a stand of scraggly pines that clustered close together along the water. Kate followed her and found a narrow enclosure over a strand of pebbly beach. Moonlight slanted through the thin trees to fall on two narrow boats pulled up onto a tangled mat of branches. Each boat was made of wood almost as white as the snow.

Venn climbed into one and brushed the snow off a small bench spanning the back of the narrow craft. Kate stepped over the side and sat next to Venn. Instead of dragging the boat toward the water, Faron climbed in and cleared himself a seat on a second bench, while Aislin and Matlen clambered into the bench near the bow.

Kate looked along the floor, but there were no oars or poles in the boat. "How do you steer this?"

"Like this." Venn set her hand on the side. "Assuming the boats will still listen to me." The mat of branches below them shifted, making the boat shudder. Kate grabbed the side as the branches bent, lifting the little craft up and walking it down toward the water.

She leaned over the side to find limbs growing out from the planks themselves, as though they'd sprouted living branches. There were at least a dozen of them in varying lengths and thicknesses. Like an oddly shaped white insect, the boat crawled into the water. The branches beneath Kate dug into the stones along the bottom and pushed the boat away from shore. "You're doing that?"

Venn gave a hum of agreement and peered into the water as she directed it into the middle of the river. The full brightness of the moonlight fell on them, and Kate realized she could see the stones along the bottom through the crystal-clear water. The river was wide and surprisingly smooth. It wound in subtle turns along the base of the tall mountain to their left. To their right, the ground rose gradually into a tall ridge, dropping the river into a wide-based canyon.

The boat picked up speed and moved swiftly into the night.

CHAPTER TWENTY-FIVE

The boat rocked on the water, and a wave of tiredness rolled over Kate. She slumped lower on the bench before noticing how stiffly Faron sat ahead of her. His back was straight, and his fingers were wrapped tightly around the front of his seat.

"Are you all right?" Kate asked him.

"Fine," he answered shortly.

Venn let out a small chuckle. "He's not fond of these boats."

The wood under Kate's hand was smooth and nearly white. "They look like they're made from frost pines." She glanced at Faron's back. "Do you not like to see them used like this?"

He let out a short, nervous laugh. "I think the boats themselves are ingenious."

"He just doesn't like to ride in them," Venn said. "Elves from the White Wood don't swim. And while His Majesty is good at a great many things, directing these boats isn't one of them."

Faron cast a warning look at her over his shoulder.

Aislin spun around on her bench to face them. "Is it true that you got stuck on the river for a whole day, and Auntie Venn had to rescue you?"

"No," he said.

Venn leaned to the side to see Aislin better. "It's very true. He was coming down to the lakes to visit me—"

"I wasn't visiting you," he protested. "I had a message from my father to the elders."

"Ah," Venn said in a voice that held only amusement. "But he could only get the branches on one side to work with him. The others just hung like dead weight, scraping the bottom in the shallow parts, and turning the boat constantly to the left."

Faron shot her a black look. "It was fine."

Venn pointed to a little pocket of water tucked against the cliff face ahead on the left. "When he didn't show up, I came looking for him and found him stuck in a swirling bit of current just like that." She laughed. "All the longest branches were tangled together and stuck pointing straight down where they were surrounded by rocks. He was spinning and swearing and shouting at the boat."

Faron rubbed his hand across his face.

"How long had you been there?" Kate asked, trying to keep in a laugh.

"Half the day," Venn answered for him.

Kate looked across the river. "Why didn't you just step to the shore?"

"And leave the boat?" Faron asked, his expression rueful. "I'd never have lived that down."

Matlen grinned. "You may never live this down. I'm going to tell everyone I see about this."

Faron gave him a narrow-eyed look. "I will tell your parents to keep you on ice duty all winter."

"Like we haven't gotten out of that before," Matlen whispered loudly to Aislin.

"In Faron's defense, the shore is farther than it looks," Venn said. "The water is deep, and the current strong. Stepping that far would have been a risk."

"How'd you get him out?" Kate asked.

"Lake elves swim all the time. I swam across and climbed in."

"So not that strong of a current," Aislin whispered loudly.

Venn smiled widely. "Took a bit of work to untangle the branches before I could steer the boat back into the main current."

"Was he grateful?" Kate asked.

"Eventually," Venn said, still smiling and turning her attention back to the river ahead. "But he hasn't loved this trip ever since."

"Do you ever come this way alone now?" Kate asked curiously.

"Faron," Venn answered for him again, "actually is quite adept at stepping, despite what his nonsensical description of it might have led you to believe. I would imagine when he's alone, he walks it, stepping as often as he can."

"It's immeasurably better than one of these boats," he said. "But not as fast."

The boat rocked gently, and the shore moved quickly past. Kate leaned over the side to see the branches swishing back and forth in the water like long, white fish tails, propelling them downstream. Along the northern edge of the river, a huge mountainside rose into the air. The moonlight painted the snow-covered peak in silvery white. Above it, the sky was filled with stars. Kate traced the familiar constellation of the phoenix. It was one of the constellations that was visible out her bedroom window in the Stronghold on a clear winter night, and a pang of homesickness struck her.

Venn leaned against the stern of the little boat, trailing her fingers in the water.

"Isn't that cold?" Kate asked.

"Always." Venn's shoulders were loose, her face more relaxed than Kate had ever seen it.

Kate took in the beauty of the river and the forest and the mountains. "You love it here, don't you?"

"You can't tell right now," Venn said, her eyes tracing the outline of the slope beside them, "but it has all the right colors."

The mountain beside the river was covered with trees that rolled over every ripple of the mountain, like fur over the muscles and sinews of some great beast. "Then why do you leave here so much?"

Faron's head turned slightly, but he stayed facing away.

Venn refocused on the river. "Because there are other interesting places to see. And if you never leave, you never get to come home." The river widened, smoothing out. "We won't reach the lakes until dawn, if you want to get some sleep."

None of the elves looked tired, but a yawn crawled up Kate's throat. The sway of the boat was immensely soothing, and any objection she might have had was swallowed up by it. The floor of the boat was clean and dry, and Kate sat down in it, leaning against the side. Water shushed along the wood, the boat rocked gently, and despite the chill and the hardness of the wood, she sank quickly into sleep.

Brightness streamed into Kate's eyes, and she raised a hand to block it. Her back was stiff, and her shoulder against the side of the boat ached. She sat up and blinked into the early sunlight that slanted across the river. The mountain on the northern bank was blanketed with snow-clad trees. It rose so high that the top looked like a painting against the brilliant blue sky.

Along the riverbank, though, the ground was merely mottled with occasional bits of snow.

The sunlight cut into the water, landing on the bottom in wavery patches, revealing the rocks at the bottom in hues of purples and greys and yellows.

Faron lay curled up on his bench, awkwardly fitting his body into the small space, but his back rose in the long, steady breaths of sleep. Aislin and Matlen leaned on each other near the bow, fast asleep as well.

"You were right about the colors," Kate said, keeping her voice low. She stretched and rose to sit next to Venn, who still sat at the stern directing the little craft. The morning air was crisp and chill, and Kate drew her cloak tight.

Venn leaned easily back against the boat, her fingers resting on the side, her face lit with contentment. "Not far to the lakes," she said quietly enough not to wake the others.

An eagle swooped low over the river ahead, its talons skimming the water. Kate leaned forward, searching for Crofftus's remnant. There were no glitters, and it soared up into the sky, disappearing over the trees.

"Something is off about him," Venn said quietly.

Kate scanned the shore for any other animals. "He does seem...nervous since Naevys grabbed him. She must have really frightened him."

"He faced down Faron and Thallion and the whole mess in the Elder Grove without any obvious effects. For all his quirks, I wouldn't call him easily unnerved."

Kate glanced back at her. "There's a very strong argument to be made that Naevys is much worse than either Thallion or Faron. Maybe she hurt him somehow when she was inside his mind."

Venn was quiet for a long moment. "Or the dwarves are right, and it's not nerves—it's deception." At Kate's sharp glance, she shrugged apologetically. "They are good at spotting it."

The idea raised a simmering irritation in Kate. "What would Crofftus be deceiving us about?"

Venn gazed down the river. "I don't know, but Naevys knows how to leverage things. Maybe he told her things he shouldn't. There's something...guarded about him lately."

"She sifted through his mind. It's not like he could have hidden things from her."

Venn made a noncommittal noise. "Just...be careful around him."

They floated in silence as the boat rounded a turn. The possibility of Crofftus's betrayal needled at Kate. She wanted to dismiss it outright, but there *was* something odd about him. Still, aside from the dwarves' suspicions, which they'd pretty much always had about him, and Venn's vague feelings, there was no proof that he was anything more than his normal, enigmatic self.

She pushed the question away. When she saw him again, she'd worry about it. For now, she took in the pristine mountains, the wide river, and the colorful bed of rocks beneath the water.

She rolled her shoulders to loosen them. "I see why you love this place. We should have come here ages ago," Kate said, keeping her voice low. "Even Faron looks calm."

Venn's eyes dropped to his back, but she looked away quickly. "He's different," Kate added, "don't you think?"

"Who knew he'd be more relaxed as king than he ever was as prince?"

"It makes sense. I'm not sure he had any freedom at all before."

The only sounds for several minutes were the quiet lap of the river against the boat and the chirping of birds somewhere off in the forest.

"You think I should forgive him." Venn's words were more a statement than a question.

Faron's back rose and fell, his yellow remnant so strong it glittered, even in the morning sunlight.

"I don't know," Kate said slowly. "He spent one hundred and fifty years siding with his father against you, and then, to obey Thallion, he cut your tattoo and left you for dead." The prince's remnant floated past, the richness of the alpine forest feeling buoyant and rejuvenating. Kate sorted through it, finding intricate layers of growth and decay and waiting and relentlessness. It was too big and too complex to classify. "Whether or not you forgive him, I don't think you should trust him again."

Venn's shoulders sank a little, more in regret than relaxation. "I don't think I ever could."

The river narrowed, speeding up as it passed between two forested banks. Hemlocks and cedars rose among the pines here. Patches of thick green moss blanketed the rocks where they could be seen beneath the snow. The trees leaned over the water as though protecting it. One skinny pine had fallen partially across the water recently enough that it still held green needles. Venn steered around it. As they passed, she reached out and brushed it with her fingertips. Her remnant sank into it as though coming home.

Kate straightened, and Venn drew in a sharp breath.

"I can hear it!" Venn whispered, letting go of the boat and grabbing hold of the thin top of the tree. She held it as they drifted past, and the top of the tree bent along with them. "Kate! I can talk to it!"

The craft lurched slightly as it slowed and spun around the tree.

Faron jolted up, clenching his hands on the sides. Aislin and Matlen woke too, blinking into the morning light.

"You're not cut off from these?" Kate leaned over the side, watching Venn's remnant nestle in between the needles and brush along the wood.

"No! I can hear...everything!" The relief in Venn's voice was palpable.

"Uh, Venn," Faron said, his voice anything but relaxed. "The boat."

With Venn still gripping the tree and Kate leaning over the side, the little watercraft tilted dangerously to the side.

Kate moved quickly back, righting it somewhat. Venn squeezed the handful of needles one last time before letting go and setting her hand back on the boat. Faron flinched at the quiet groaning as the branches beneath them began swaying again, and the boat moved back into the middle of the river.

Faron kept a grip on the boat but faced Venn, his face hopeful. "My mother only cut you off from the White Wood?"

Venn's gaze traveled through the branches above them. "The White Wood and Kate." Her brow creased for just a moment before it smoothed again. "Although I suppose that was from the White Wood also."

"Cut you off from Kate?" Faron asked.

"We were in the Elder Grove together," Kate said, "using both our remnants to shield it from noticing Venn when...the shield failed. The Grove connected with Venn and somehow connected us. We could sense each other's emotions if we were near each other, and through Venn, I could also sense the forest. Not the way you all can, but I could feel the expanse of it. I knew how it lay over the hills and in the valleys."

"And that's gone?" Faron's question was tinged with sympathy.

The aching loss of it seeped into Kate from where she'd tried to shove it aside. "Yes," At the sorrow in the word, the elf twins' expressions grew commiserative, and Kate added, "But so is the bond with the White Wood your father forced on me, which continually tried to draw me in so completely that I would cease to exist. So it's not all bad."

The honey-gold remnants of the elf twins filled the air at their end of the boat, Venn's green glimmers were bright, even in the sunlight, and Faron's were so bright they were like golden sparks glowing. "It feels like I should be able to connect to you all," Kate said slowly. "I can see your remnants and I could connect mine to them, but it doesn't form the kind of connection Naevys formed between Venn and me."

Faron looked thoughtfully at her. "I can create some connections. Not as much as my mother, but I might be able to connect to you, at least partially."

Venn's eyebrows rose. "The king's powers are in his authority, not in his bond to the Wood."

"Mostly," Faron agreed, "but I can feel the links between elves and the forest better than before, and I know I can strengthen them—or weaken them. I'm more open to them than I used to be." He studied Kate. "Not as much with you, although I can feel you more than other humans."

Faron's remnant diffused out from him differently than the others. There was something open about it. Welcoming. Something stretching out into the world, gathering things toward him. "Yes, yours looks different," Kate said. "I could try to connect to you. I don't think it would be permanent."

His hand twitched on the boat. "How connected? Could we hear each other's thoughts?"

Venn let out a breath caught between a laugh and a sigh. "Have something to hide from her?"

Faron's brow furrowed. "No."

"Venn and I couldn't hear each other's thoughts, anyway," Kate said. "Just felt general impressions of each other's emotions."

Venn's distrustful look was back, and Faron held her gaze as he nodded. "All right, Kate. See if you can connect us."

"Yes," Venn said. "See what you find."

Kate glanced between the two of them while Aislin and Matlen sat silent and still, as though hoping no one would notice they were still there.

"This is bound to be less interesting than you're all expecting." Kate focused on Faron's remnant." It had grown considerably since he'd taken the crown. It was brighter and denser. Stronger. Different. Where Venn's was a pool of life around her. Faron's was the sea. Kate pushed her glimmers of red into it, and a sense of his vastness unfurled. She was a speck floating in an ocean of life. There was the impression of endless trees. Endless skies. All existing in him.

A jumble of emotions filled the space where he sat. Curiosity. Worry. The crushing weight of responsibility. Threaded through it all was regret. Insecurity.

Faron's attention shifted to Venn, and a deep old warmth rose. It was wrapped with thin strands of hope and thicker bonds of remorse and shame. It was so raw that Kate felt invasive, and she drew back.

But Faron leaned forward, his face bright with surprise. "I can feel you!"

A warmth flared up on his forearm, under his sleeve, and his remnant surged toward her, his gold engulfing her meager red glimmers.

The ocean rose, flooding her. She tried to pull away, but the vastness rushed around her, sending her tumbling. It rubbed against the edges of her mind, and her mind began to erode.

CHAPTER TWENTY-SIX

"Faron!" Venn's voice shouted from somewhere far away. The ocean receded, the emotions disappeared, and Kate reeled back, slamming against the edge of the boat. A hand gripped her shoulder as the chill morning air rushed around her.

"Kate?" Venn asked.

Kate shook her head, trying to banish the last of his boundless tumult. "That was *not* what it was like with Venn."

Aislin and Matlen stared at her and Faron with wide eyes.

Faron leaned closer, his hand outstretched but not touching her. "Kate? I'm sorry. I…"

She gripped the boat, which seemed to be rocking more violently than before. "You and Venn are very different."

"You're just figuring this out?" Venn asked.

"No, it's because he's king." Kate took a deep breath. "I connected with Thallion's mind once, when he tried to use a well-stone on me."

"You did?" Faron asked, his eyebrows raised.

"Didn't seem fair that he was the only one to try to get some memories." Kate studied Faron. "His mind was vast like yours. Connected to so many things. Feels almost like you're connected to the whole world. Naevys feels the same, too."

Faron paused, and his eyes flickered to Venn. "I told you—I can see everything, but it's more than that. I can feel the whole forest." His gaze moved to the trees. "Even here, I can feel it almost as strong as in the White Wood. I can sense..." When he turned back to Venn, there was something almost scared in his expression. "I can sense every tree and every elf and every creature in the woods. It's like..." His brow creased. "It's like that town we saw long ago. Everything is so busy. The trees are working so hard to grow, the creatures to build homes or find food. The elves are like entire cities in themselves, wanting and having and needing and giving." He shook his head, and his voice dropped. "I can't hold it all."

Venn's hand twitched off Kate's shoulder, as though she would reach toward him, but she merely put it back in her lap. "Maybe you're not supposed to hold it all. Maybe you're just supposed to be a part of it and let it talk to you if it needs something."

His eyes narrowed a bit, but he considered the idea. "Maybe," he allowed.

"What's on your arm?" Kate asked.

Faron's attention snapped to her. "What?"

"When you pushed your remnant toward me, your arm lit up."

Venn did lean closer now. "Kate, cast out toward it."

"Venn," Kate began, "if he doesn't want to tell us—"

"It's the runes, isn't it?" Venn asked. "The ones that let you use runelight."

Faron sighed. "I suppose it's not really a secret anymore." He pulled his sleeve up. Some white linen was wrapped around his forearm, clasped with a leaf-shaped metal pin that glinted in the shadowy light beneath the trees.

Kate glanced at Venn to see her response to the gift she'd given Faron centuries ago, but she merely tensed slightly.

"You have the runes woven on the fabric?" Venn asked. "How long ago did you do that?"

Faron unclasped the pin and unwound the linen, revealing the edge of a dark tattoo.

Venn drew in a breath. Aislin and Matlen whispered to each other and craned to see as more tattoos became visible.

They were ancient Kalesh, and Kate caught bits of their meaning. The most astonishing thing about them was how intertwined they were, complementing each other in complex, layered ways.

Venn stared at him. "You tattooed your runes?"

Faron finally raised his eyes to meet hers. "My father's idea once the fabric I'd had them embroidered on was damaged." He gestured weakly to her arm. "It seemed like something that had worked well in the past."

Kate kept herself from grabbing his arm to see the runes more clearly. "This is how you make the shadow."

"How many other elves use runelight?" Matlen asked.

Faron twitched. "Very few."

Kate leaned closer to the runes. "Your runelight cuts off *vitalle* with a shield—wait! You make two shields?"

"The inner one cuts off *ael'iza* and the outer stops light from leaving. I'm just standing there, but the light that would show you that is trapped inside with me."

She pointed to a set of three runes overlapping each other. "It reflects the light. Like a mirror, keeping it inside."

Kate funneled out *vitalle* into a round shield over her hand, then, glancing at his runes again, fashioned a second barrier outside the first. For that one, she focused not on *vitalle*, but on the morning light moving through the air. She strengthened the shield, making it more solid. The space around Kate's hand grew darker, while her leg beneath it brightened.

"You have to make sure you close it off," Faron said with a rueful smile. "Or all the light pours out the opening and just leaves things looking strange." He studied her closely. "You are surprisingly adept at elven forms of magic. I've never thought humans were capable of it."

"Renault could use both," Kate pointed out. "The things he made are a fascinating blend of human and elven ideas."

"Renault was half-elven," Faron said. "Are you?"

She let out a laugh. "No. Purely human. But I was born in the old Wildwood, and there's definitely a bit of elfishness left there. My entire childhood was surrounded by it."

"No human in Home has ever had the White Wood rub off on them," Venn said.

"No human has been bound to the White Wood either." Kate shrugged. "Maybe Naevys didn't sever every connection I have with it." She sank back onto her bench. "Faron, do you have any idea where we can find her?"

"No," he said, "but Virion might."

"That crazy old hermit?" Aislin asked.

"He's an elf who lives at the very edge of the lakes," Venn explained to Kate. "He keeps almost exclusively to himself. I've visited him twice with Evay, but it was very long ago."

"He lives alone now," Faron agreed, "but...he knew my mother when they were younger."

"A lot of elves knew your mother," Venn said.

Faron hesitated. "I think they were planning to marry."

Aislin let out a little gasp. "She wasn't going to marry Thallion?"

"This was before she was Warden." Faron grimaced slightly. "I'm sure plenty of older elves know about this, but I never did until I ran across a wellstone of hers once that had his *ael'iza* in it."

Venn's mouth fell open slightly. "I never heard her mention him."

"Neither did I. I think my father wanted it kept quiet. But when I asked her about the wellstone, she just stared at it for a moment, then took it and hid it away again without any explanation. I think he was close to her still when Renault was here." His expression turned guilty. "That same box that held the wellstone held some old letters, and there was one from Virion to my mother."

"You read her letters?" Venn asked.

"I was younger than them," he said, a note of defensiveness in his voice as he jabbed a finger over his shoulder at Aislin and Matlen.

"I would definitely read those letters," Aislin whispered to her brother.

"I don't know what I expected," Facon continued, "but something more interesting than I found. They weren't love letters or angry letters or anything particularly noteworthy. Virion just discussed some place Renault worked and wondered whether the half-elf could be entirely trusted."

"Let's definitely go talk to Virion," Kate said.

Sun glittered through a break in the trees ahead, and in a few moments, the boat floated out into a smooth, clear lake. The rocky bottom plunged down into obscurity until all Kate could see below them were the white trailing branches swaying behind them under the glittering surface.

Kate took in the forest that pressed up against the shore. The northern mountains soared up into the blue sky, the patches of white clouds matching their snowy peaks. "I can see why you like coming home."

"Only a few elves live here. Most are on the next two lakes."

Venn guided the boat across the water and into another wide section of slow-moving river. The edges of this one were rimed with a thin layer of ice.

"Do these freeze?" Kate asked.

"Eventually," Venn answered. "It'll be a few weeks until the larger lakes and the rivers do, but the smaller, shallower lakes are freezing already."

"Ice duty," Matlen said, "which Faron threatened us with earlier, is when perfectly innocent elves are tasked with keeping the rivers unfrozen."

"Travel is easier by water," Venn said, "but for a few weeks in the spring and fall, the rivers end up half-frozen and impossible to either boat through or walk over. So we try to keep them clear until it's cold enough that the freeze will happen quickly and completely."

"It's a miserable job," Aislin added.

In a handful of minutes, they emerged into a second lake.

This one was enormous, stretching into the distance before it turned and disappeared around a snowy hill. The rocky shore was topped by forests of pines and cedars. Birches, their branches bare of leaves, stood like white lace among the darker green.

A wide island rose out of the water ahead of them, blocking the center of the lake, holding its own forest. Venn aimed the boat around the side of it, and Kate realized what she'd taken to be merely trees included a structure. Two large pines emerged from its roof, and its walls appeared to be created by a complex arrangement of branches. Unlike the temporary shelters Venn had created, these limbs weren't just bent down from the trunk. These spread out like normal branches, forming a roof, until they split and dove toward the ground, making nearly vertical walls. The surface was a latticework of living branches covered in green needles, shaped around arched openings for windows and doors.

They rounded the shore and found the lake beyond it scattered with more islands, some small enough to only hold a dozen trees, others large enough to hold a village.

The boat floated under a thin bridge of woven green vines that stretched from a tall pine from the first island to the next. Kate set her hand on the side of the boat, feeling the subtle shifts in the wood from the branches down in the water propelling them along. While Venn navigated the stretch of lake, Kate made out a handful of additional homes. Some were built on the shore like the first one, others were nestled high up in the branches of large trees, and some sat out over the water, perched on roots that plunged down into the lake. Elves paused to watch them pass. Most raised a hand in greeting, and Aslin and Matlen called out cheerfully. Kate received long, curious glances.

Venn navigated the scattering of interconnected islands, floating under hanging bridges and skirting homes that grew out of the shores, until she steered the boat to a long floating dock on one of the largest isles. "We'll stop by my parents' home and send word to the council that we're here."

Matlen looked up brightly. "Do you think your parents will have any berry cakes, Venn?"

"They always have berry cakes," Faron said.

A young elf boy fiddling with a net on the dock stared at Kate for a moment before catching sight of Venn and scrambling to his feet.

"*Illease*," he said with a slight bob of his head to Venn, offering his hand to her while not taking his eyes off Kate.

Venn accepted his hand and climbed out onto the dock. "Thank you, Liall. This is Kate. A friend of mine."

Kate gave the boy a smile, but he merely stared at her. His wide eyes were the clear green of the lake, his hair a rich brown streaked with mossy green, and he looked to be around ten years old. Her smile turned slightly awkward as she realized that meant he was probably nearly a hundred. "Hello, Liall."

"And a friend of ours," Aislin said, climbing out of the boat.

Liall yanked his eyes away from Kate, but they only widened when he noticed Faron. "*Illean*," he said with a real bow.

"Good morning, Liall." Faron climbed out of the boat.

Liall straightened. "The council is waiting for you at the *grellise*."

"Already?" Venn asked.

"Yes, *Illease*. They have been there since dawn."

A look of resignation crossed Faron's face. "No berry cakes, then."

Kate moved to climb out of the boat, and the young elf twitched, then tentatively held his hand out. She took it and thanked him, but he made no acknowledgment beyond a slack-jawed stare.

Kate moved along the dock, catching up with Venn. "I assume few humans come here?"

"I can't remember another one. You're certainly the first one Niall has seen." Venn glanced at Kate, her expression slightly concerned. "Faron and I should go quickly. We'll drop you off at my parents'."

"I don't suppose they'd let a human come observe?" Kate asked.

"Not without an invitation," Venn said.

Faron raised an eyebrow at Venn. "Or being brought by you."

"That's enough?" Kate glanced back over her shoulder. "Oh." A few pieces of the interaction they'd just had fell into place. "*Oh*, Liall called Faron '*Illean*' and you '*Illease*.' Is that 'prince' and 'princess'?" Venn didn't answer, and Kate let out a short laugh. "Your grandfather was a prince. They call you princess here, don't they?"

Venn gave her a flat look. "The word '*illease*' has a considerable amount of nuance to it. 'Princess' barely scratches the surface of it."

"Sorry, Your Highness," Kate said with a curtsy, then grinned. "You're the reluctant princess!"

"What are you talking about?"

"It's another story by Flibbet the Peddler. The same man who told the story about the duke burning down his whole life to get rid of the beetles. Except in this story there's a princess from a fictional country who doesn't want to be princess, so she hides among the common people. It's very funny."

"I'm hardly hiding among the common people."

"What happens to this princess?" Faron asked.

"She gets herself into an inordinate amount of trouble because she won't use the authority she has," Kate said. "But eventually she realizes her people need a good leader. She goes back to the palace and helps run the country well. It's a much happier tale than the Beetle Duke."

Venn crossed her arms. "How is that anything like me?"

Kate paused. "I guess it's not, really. But just like the common people in that story, I keep being surprised with the amount of influence you hold. You could really bring a human into a meeting with the elders without any repercussions?"

Venn rolled her eyes. "You're a human, not some sort of monster. But..." She glanced at Faron. "In this instance, things are bound to be tense. Might be best if only Faron and I were there while we explain everything that's happened with Thallion and Naevys."

"You'd rather be with us anyway, Kate," Aislin said.

Matlen nodded. "Berry cakes."

The sun was already high in the sky. Each hour that passed added a slight pressure to the weight hanging on Kate. Her pack sat heavy on her back, and her mind kept drifting back to the box. Her fingers itched to pull it out. See if there was another option she'd missed. Something faster. Something that didn't leave Bo and Evan trapped a moment longer

Next to her, Venn adjusted her pack with a grunt of discomfort that almost perfectly matched Kate's feelings. She gave a quiet, matching hum.

Venn let out something that was far too tense for a laugh. "Regretting coming already?"

"I regretted it before I even agreed," Kate said. "What do you imagine the chances are that this council will move quickly and we can be on our way by lunch?"

"Slim." Venn looked into the trees. "Everything feels…heavy."

Kate's fingers tightened on the strap of her pack. "The life debt?"

Venn squinted ahead as though she could see an answer. "No, this is something else looming. The *grellise* is not far, and while it's not the Elder Grove, it has some of the same qualities. There's nothing here that calls to me, exactly, but I still feel like it wants to tell me something. Warn me." She shook her head. "Right now, I'd rather get Bo safe than risk us all in whatever this turns out to be."

Kate nodded. "If the lakes send rangers to Home, there's no real reason we need to spearhead whatever defense will be set up, is there? The elves can sense *vitalle* as well as I can. I'm useless in a fight, and you're not up to your normal skills with trees. I know we can't get back to the Stronghold with Naevys guarding the woods, but maybe we can go back to Renault's cave. We could at least make progress on the bloodstone there."

Venn nodded slowly. "That's true. We can let Faron do the job he's supposed to have been doing all this time." Her voice lacked conviction.

Some of the tightness loosened in Kate. Renault's cave still felt vulnerable, but at least they could be making progress on what really mattered.

They walked in silence for a few moments, and the thought of bears and *gwerocs* rampaging through Home and the *naiwyn* guarding the woods shined a light on that plan, showing it in a very selfish, very unflattering light.

Kate sighed. "A nice fantasy."

Venn sighed too. "It is."

Ahead, glimpses of a large clearing appeared between the trees. Faron led the quiet procession. His hair glowed with thin strands of deep red whenever he passed through a shadow, and when he ran his fingers through it, the skin of his hand was as bright as burnished copper.

"Faron's glowing again," Kate said quietly to Venn.

"He always does when he has something official to do."

"I wouldn't want to be him and have to explain all his father's recent decisions to the council," Kate said.

A hint of sympathy softened Venn's face, but her lips pressed together before she spoke. "Thallion was the instigator of it all, but Faron helped him."

"Do you really think he had a choice?"

"He had a choice." Venn's expression had resolved into its normal unyielding expression. "I had to obey Thallion, but I told him how much I hated it whenever I saw him. I told Faron I hated it. My parents know I hated it. As did Evay. Even you knew it before you'd known me a week. There is a very large gap between forced obedience and cooperation."

They followed Faron, Aislin, and Matlen onto a path that ran along the shore. The strange houses grew up sporadically along it. There were no streets between them, just paths that meandered through the trees.

They reached a house settled against the shore. Broad pine boughs stretched over it from three enormous trees that rose through the roof. Thin, arched windows encircled the first floor. A second floor grew up around the two trees to the right, and a third level circled the central tallest fir.

Venn's shoulders relaxed. "Welcome to my home, Kate."

CHAPTER TWENTY-SEVEN

Aislin, Matlen, and Faron disappeared through the front door, and a chatter of enthusiastic greetings rang out before it swung shut.

Venn sighed. "That is my parents' only flaw. They adore Faron."

"Are you going to tell them what he did to you?" Kate gestured to Venn's tattoos.

"I haven't decided yet." Venn pushed open the front door, which was made of a panel of thin branches woven so perfectly together that Kate couldn't see any light between them. She stepped in behind Venn and into a barrage of forest scents and sounds that filled the room.

It was like stepping into the heart of the forest. Springy green moss covered the floor, exuding a faint loamy smell. Branches and sprays of green pine needles formed the walls and ceiling, exuding a clean, crisp scent.

But it was remnants that infused the air. Trees and streams and snow and frost and pine needles and leafy ferns. Distant chitters of squirrels, the rustling of wind, calls from birds too far away to name.

Venn set her pack down beside the door, and Kate pushed the door shut, closing out the chill.

A long table filled the center of the room, made of smooth-barked wood that grew out of the ground. To the left, rocks were piled on each other to create a fireplace, which held a crackling blaze.

A jovial-looking older elf with silver hair that hung down his back thumped Faron heartily on the back. Aislin and Matlen were already standing over a plate on the table filled with pastries.

"Andovenn!" a female elf proclaimed from by the fire. Her hair was a mingling of reds and oranges, similar to Venn's but darker, with bits of silver woven through it. Her face was an older version of Venn's too—at least, it resembled Venn's current expression, which was relaxed and smiling widely. The elf brushed off her hands and hurried over to Venn, throwing her arms around her.

"Hello, Mother," Venn said, returning the hug. "I hope you don't mind that I brought some guests."

"Bah, Faron and the twins are almost family." The older elf glanced over Venn's shoulder, and her face lit even more. "You must be Kate! Evay told us all about you!" She hurried over, taking Kate's hand in both of her own. "It's wonderful to meet you! A Keeper! I've heard of you all but never managed to meet one before. I'm Lesille." The scents of Lesille's remnant wafted around Kate. The scent of the hills behind her childhood home. The rustle of moss under her feet. The feel of the maple bark under her hands as she climbed into a tree fort with her brothers. "Is it true you grew up in the Wildwood?"

Kate felt a pang of homesickness. "You remind me of it," she said with a smile.

At Lesille's questioning look, Venn said, "She can smell your soul, or so some dwarven friends of ours would say."

"Since when do you have dwarven friends?" Lesille said.

"Since not long after I met Kate." Venn crossed the room and hugged her father.

"I did grow up in the Wildwood,' Kate said. "I'm sure it's changed a lot from when you lived there, but compared to the other forests in Queensland, it's still among the most alive."

Lesille let out a nostalgic sigh. "That forest had the loveliest oaks." She blinked and refocused on Kate. "Please come and sit. Share a meal with us. This morning, you're part of the family, too."

"Thank you. I've never been in an elven house before. It's…" She gestured to the living walls and ceiling. "Breathtaking."

Lesille beamed at her. "Anreon has a way with trees. He's nearly as good at talking to them as Venn is, and he made all this." Her voice was tinged with pride as she looked fondly at her husband, then around at the rest of the faces. "Now, I have more cakes." She hurried back to the fire and grabbed a plate of pastries dotted with dark purple berries. She handed it to Venn and squeezed her arm, glancing at Faron. "All of you, sit! Eat! You look exhausted. It's been entirely too long since we've all been together."

Venn gave her a slightly exasperated look, but Lesille ignored it. Lesille leaned toward Kate and whispered loudly, "I haven't been this happy in years."

"I'm so pleased to play a role in that," Venn said dryly, but she gave her mother a slight smile and set the plate on the table.

Kate sank gratefully onto one of the wooden chairs made entirely of branches bent into smooth, comfortable sweeps. Faron nudged the plate toward her while Aisin grabbed another pastry off it. Kate took a cake, and the warmth eased into her fingers. It smelled of butter and tart berries. Her teeth sank into it, and she let out a little groan of appreciation.

"Aren't they delicious?" Aislin said, taking a huge bite.

"All right, niblings," Venn said, picking up a cake. "You two each take one more for the road and get home. No side trips, no adventures, just home. And don't come back near the White Wood until all this blows over."

Anreon looked sharply at Venn. Lesille hesitated but quickly wrapped up four cakes into a bundle and pressed them into Matlen's hands. "You each take *two* more." She steered him toward the door. "I'll let your parents know you're coming. No dawdling." Her voice had taken on a stern, motherly tone.

Matlen took the bundle with a resigned slump of his shoulders.

"And this time, make sure you get home," Venn said, firmly. "There's bound to be an assembly soon. I expect to see you there and hear you've been bored out of your minds between then and now."

Anreon tilted his head curiously toward Venn.

Lesille closed the door and came to sit next to her husband. "Not that I'm complaining, but why are you here?"

"We've been called to the council," Venn said.

Anreon's brow creased. "Is this because of the creatures from the north?" At the blank look from his daughter, he added, "Both an ice cat and a mountain drake have come out of the north in the past week. The rangers took them back, but it has everyone on edge."

Faron grimaced. "We've had similar trouble in the White Wood. But that's only a symptom of our bigger problem."

Lesille looked between Venn and Faron. "Which is?"

Faron let out a defeated breath. "Mostly my mother."

Venn handed her mother a cake. "If you'd like to hear about

the mess in the White Wood, you'll have to come to the council that's already waiting for us and hear King Faron explain."

The cake fell from Lesille's fingers as she and her husband stared at Faron.

Faron rose to his feet. "A lot is happening in the White Wood, but Venn's right—we need to go." He smoothed his tunic with a nervous motion.

Anreon rose too and, at Faron's questioning look, said, "Just because I don't usually fill it doesn't mean I don't still have a seat on the council. There's been some discomfiture around Naevys's absence. You might need a friendly voice."

The three grabbed their cloaks, and Kate itched to grab hers as well.

Lesille set a hand on her shoulder. "You can stay here with me. We'll eat, and you can tell me all about the Wildwood."

Venn gave her an apologetic look as she opened the door.

With a resigned sigh, Kate nodded. "Good luck."

"I think we're going to need more than luck." Venn followed Anreon and Faron outside, and the door swung shut.

Kate settled at the table in the quiet room, trying not to worry about how the lake elves were going to take the news that Faron and Thallion had hidden Naevys's condition.

Lesille patted her shoulder. "I hate being the one left behind as well."

"Does Venn often get invited to councils?"

"Not often, but sometimes." Lesille glanced worriedly toward a set of stairs along the back wall. "But things feel out of sorts lately. Evay was injured yesterday. Very badly, and she's not healing. She's upstairs but hasn't been conscious since they found her covered with burns and ice cold." Her voice dropped. "I thought she was dead when they brought her in. The healers and I have been trying to help, but…"

"Burns?" Kate asked, a spike of fear shooting into her. "And cold?"

Lesille nodded. "The burns won't heal."

"It can't be!" Kate pushed herself up. "All the way out here? Will you show me?"

At the urgency in Kate's voice, Lesille led her up the stairs and down a curving hall that wound between two of the massive trunks holding up the house. Lesille pushed open the only door that was closed.

The room sat above the kitchen, and the heat from the fire sifted up through the tightly woven branches of the floor. On a sling of vines lay Evay.

Kate cast out as they drew close, and Evay's body flickered with a faint echo of life. Lesille drew in a breath as the *vitalle* in the room lit up. The vines and the towering tree trunk that made up a huge portion of the wall blazed so much brighter than Evay that she was almost lost between them. A steady stream of *ael'iza* flowed from her hammock into Evay's body, but most of it swirled uselessly before dissolving into the air. Wide bandages covered her arms and her stomach. Another wrapped around her neck. Her skin was deathly pale, her russet hair limp.

Kate sank to her knees next to the hammock and laid her hand on Evay's shoulder. Her skin was cold and dry. Kate cast out into her again. The burns wrapping around Evay's arms and torso were dark, the edges of them as solid as a wall. The *vitalle* from the tree flowed up against them and was turned back.

Around the closest burn, what Kate had taken for darkness was actually speckled with glimmers of midnight blue. It encased the wound like a solid surface, keeping *vitalle* from crossing.

Like a shield.

"There's runelight here."

Lesille drew in a sharp breath. "That explains what's blocking me." Her shoulders slumped. "Then there's no hope."

Kate gave her a tight smile. "Actually, there's plenty." She stretched her remnant into Evay's arm, forming her own runelight into a spear. With a shove, she jabbed it into the deep blue surface. The shield shattered, and Evay's arm twitched. The healing energy from the tree flowed against the burn, and the edges began to heal.

Kate turned to the other burns, breaking each shield and letting the healing from the tree take effect.

With so many burns, though, the healing at each slowed to an agonizing pace.

When the last of the runelight was gone, Kate sank back.

"She's..." Lesille dropped to her knees near Evay's head. "She's healing!" Setting a hand on Evay's bandaged neck, she closed her eyes. A surge of *ael'iza* poured out of the tree, through the hammock, and into the wounded elf.

Kate cast out. Evay's body brightened, and the healing lit up like rivers of fire. "Very slowly."

Lesille looked between the glowing forms of Evay and the tree and Kate. "How do you do that?"

"It's called casting out." The warmth from the tree continued to flood into Evay like water into a vessel. "All Keepers can do it."

Lesille focused back on the wound as the wave began to fade. "Can you do it again?"

Kate did, infusing the wave with some of her remnant to hold it in place. A smile spread across Lesille's face. "That is very helpful!" She studied the wound in Evay's neck, and a stream of the healing shifted to ripple along it.

In mere moments, the deeper damage done by the burn was completely healed.

Kate leaned closer. "I've never seen anyone heal a burn that quickly."

"I've worked as a healer for centuries." Lesille moved to a

wide bandage on Evay's side. "It's why they brought her to me, but I haven't been able to make any progress until now. No one has." The flow of *ael'iza* from the tree shifted to eddy around this burn, and the innermost edge began to heal. "What did you do?"

"She broke through the Runelight." Evay's voice was thin and raspy.

Lesille kept one hand on the bandage but grabbed Evay's shoulder with the other, squeezing it. "You're back!"

Evay's eyes were barely open.

"It was a *naiwyn*," Kate said. "Wasn't it?"

"*Naiwyn!*" Lesille turned to stare at her.

On Evay's stomach, the burn shrank until it was only skin-deep, the tissue beneath it whole and bright again.

Kate nodded. "Naevys has them guarding the way south from the White Wood."

Lesille frowned. "Naevys? That makes no sense."

"Even when you hear what's happened, it still probably won't make sense." Kate gave a brief explanation of how Naevys had been missing, how Thallion had coerced Kate to help him, how he'd tried to take the Warden power from the queen, and how Naevys had escaped and gone mad, posting *naiwyn* at the edge of the White Wood and attacking Home.

Lesille listened, her mouth hanging open in shock.

Evay squinted, fixing Kate with a trouble look. "Why?"

"I don't know, but Venn and I saw four *naiwyn*. Yours was dark blue, wasn't it?" Kate moved to the door, pulling out the sleeve of Evay's cloak from where it hung. Ashes sprinkled to the floor.

"Yes," Evay answered.

Three long holes were seared through the fabric, the edge of them blackened and crumbling. Another long burn wrapped around the side of the cloak where Evay's stomach would have been. The other sleeve was almost in tatters, and the collar of the cloak had burned away.

The remnant along the burns glinted with a deep midnight blue, but Kate caught a glimmer of gold inside it, like a tiny star in a dark, shimmering night. There were no sounds—or at least nothing easy to hear. A sort of shushing or rustling seemed to emanate from the blue. Kate focused on the speck of gold and, for the briefest moment, caught the scent of Naevys's forest remnant. "There are traces of Naevys, too. She made it."

There was only one other impression: icy-cold mountains. Kate lost track of it before she could identify more.

"I was headed to the human town of Loerm," Evay said, her words weary, "which is about a day's walk past Cedar Lake, when the *naiwyn* blocked my path. There was nothing else nearby, and so I tried to circle it, but it blocked me again."

"Where's Cedar Lake?" Kate asked.

"A few hours' walk east of here. It's the last lake before the river turns and heads south."

"I know where that lake is," Kate said. "Small and teardrop-shaped, right?" More pieces fell together. "Let me guess: It's about the edge of the land you'd consider elven."

Lesille raised an eyebrow. "Yes."

"We found the others at the edge of what you'd consider the White Wood." Kate let the sleeve fall. "Why did it attack you?"

Evay let out a breath that was almost a laugh. "Because I decided to see if I could get past it."

"You decided to see if you could get past a *naiwyn*," Lesille said incredulously. The burn across Evay's stomach was mostly healed, and Lesille moved to the worst of the ones on her arm.

"I found a narrow ravine with no trees," Evay said, "and thought I might be able to step past it."

Lesille let out a long, exasperated sigh. "You're not three

hundred years old anymore, Evay. You're not running around the Kalesh Empire with Melia, evading human soldiers who don't understand stepping."

"Apparently." Evay lifted her head.

Lesille set a hand on her shoulder. "Stay still. There is still a lot of you to heal."

Evay's head fell back, but she shook her head. "I need to tell the council what's happening."

"The council is already meeting," Lesille said. "Faron and Venn are there now."

Evay frowned. "Why?"

"Faron," Kate said, "is explaining that he and Thallion hid Naevys's condition from everyone and updating them on her... Well, it looks a lot like madness. And Venn was called here because—" Kate paused. "I'm not actually sure why she was called."

"Probably because I was injured," Evay said. "I serve as a sort of ambassador between the lakes and the White Wood, and if I'm not available, they use Venn." She rolled and lifted herself onto her elbow with a grimace. "But they need to know Naevys is doing strange things here, too, so I'm going. Kate, you're coming with me."

Kate raised an eyebrow. "I'm not invited."

"I'm inviting you." Evay pushed herself up to sitting. "You know more about the *naiwyn* and are the one who can actually counter Naevys's runelight."

"Lie back down," Lesille said with a disapproving frown. "In an hour, I could have you feeling almost normal."

Evay fixed her with a flat look. "The queen of the White Wood just set a *naiwyn* to attack anyone leaving the lakes. This is an overstep of her power the likes of which we've never seen. The council needs to know this is not a problem that's far away any more." She rose but wavered on her feet. Kate offered her an arm, and Evay took it. They started forward slowly.

Evay took in the tattered fabric hanging by the door. "I think I might need to borrow a cloak."

CHAPTER TWENTY-EIGHT

Midmorning sunshine sliced down through the trees, striping the snow on the winding path with blindingly bright patches. The air had lost the cold bite of the night before, and Kate let her cloak hang open as they moved deeper into the island. The sky above was a vivid blue, and the sunlight, when they found a patch of it large enough to take a few steps through, fell warm on her cheeks.

The trees grew taller and thicker, and the trail began to rise. A different sort of weight settled into the air, pressing down gently on Kate's shoulders. A waiting. Or an expectancy. She caught a sparkle of light among the roots of a huge pine, but when she looked, there was nothing. No remnant, and not even any snow that could have reflected the sunlight.

Another glimmer made her turn the other way, but again she found nothing.

Evay walked with a determined expression, but her shoulders slumped wearily as Kate filled her in on all the details of the events in the White Wood and around Home.

At the end of the tale, Evay sighed. "A rogue Warden is…not good."

The ground rose, and they slowed. They soon reached a clearing with a sprawling gazebo made from four massive birch trees. Their branches wove together to form a roof over an intricately carved table that was shaped like a ring with a gap at the near side that led to an open center. At least a dozen elves sat around it, all of them with grey dusting their hair, if not silvering it completely.

Venn stood partway around the clearing, near the trees. Anreon sat in a tall chair along the near side of the table while Faron stood in its open center with every eye upon him.

Evay paused at the edge of the trees and set her hand on Kate's arm to stop her. Remnants flooded the clearing. Even this far from the elves, Kate could feel a tumult of wind through branches and lapping water on a lakeshore. There was the pattern of rain on treetops, the scent of ferns and tiny blooms, the crisp cold of pine needles. The crunch of fallen leaves. The entire table was shrouded in a cloud of glittering light. Silver and blue and shades of green floated around individual elves, but each spread out, mingling with the others until the hovering shimmer reminded Kate of the Elder Grove. The four birch trees glowed softly too, with their own sparkling white.

Venn caught Kate's eye, her expression full of questions.

"And so," Faron was saying, "the White Wood stripped my father of his authority."

An elderly elf rose to her feet, and where she touched the table, her deep violet remnant sank into the wood, spreading in a line along it. Her back was stooped, her hair hanging in long strands of glittering silver. Milky whiteness glazed her eyes, but she stared straight at Faron.

"You are not the prince." Her voice was low, but every elder paused. She walked smoothly around to the gap in the table and entered it to stand next to Faron.

He bowed his head toward her. "No, Allyesse. I am not."

A ripple of shock and suspicion flowed around the table. Bursts of light shot along the table between the hands of several of the elders like messages racing between them.

Allyesse lifted a hand, and Faron bowed lower until she could reach his forehead. "Hail, King Faron."

Gasps filled the clearing, and two elves leapt to their feet.

Faron raised his hand for quiet. "Yes, the crown has passed to me, but before we discuss that, I come with an urgent need. The human town of Home is in danger from Naevys and can't stand against her on their own."

One of the elven women who'd stood shook her head. "The human town is under your protection, and Naevys is your Warden. This is not our problem. We have our own here. Evay is terribly wounded, and her wounds will not heal. Our rangers are needed here to fight whatever hurt her."

"It was a *naiwyn*," Evay said, stepping forward.

"Evay!" The elf's expression was shocked. "You're healed?"

"Not fully. Not yet." Evay motioned to Kate. "But this is Keeper Kate from Queensland, and she broke through the barriers and allowed the healing to begin."

The attention of every eye fell on Kate with an almost physical force. Absolute silence met Evay's words, but the surface of the table flared with darts of colored lights passing between the elves' hands.

One severe-looking elf rose to his feet. His mouth drew into a tight line, and he slammed his hand down onto the table. A jet of his dark orange remnant shot along the tabletop, brighter and faster than the other streams. Every elf tensed and focused on Kate.

Evay crossed to the nearest birch and brushed her fingers over the trunk, and Kate caught a glimpse of burning orange light moving there as well. "Now, Elder Lymberon," she said, the hint of steel edging into her polite tone, "let's speak in a language our guest can understand. She is, indeed, human, but far from intruding, I invited her to this council."

"I can vouch for Kate as well." Venn said. The hint of a smile crossed her face. "Besides, I would imagine, given enough time and the ability to ask us each a thousand questions, she'd figure out how to listen to the sort of shout you just sent through the trees."

"You need to hear what she and Andovenn have to say about the *naiwyn*." Evay motioned the two of them toward the center of the table.

The coldness on Lymberon's face tinged with outrage, and at least half of the other elves looked displeased with the idea of Kate's presence.

Venn came alongside her and moved to the middle of the table, her fingers flickering by her side in the dwarves' secret language. *Stay alert.*

Kate scanned the elven faces and forced herself to stay relaxed. The eyes of the entire council followed her, studying and judging her every movement.

"Kate and I," Venn said loudly, drawing most of the focus back to herself, "encountered four *naiwyn* along the southern boundary of the White Wood's patrol range." She pushed her cloak back to show the bandage on her upper arm. "She helped me to heal."

"And she allowed Lesille to heal my wounds," Evay added.

An elf with hair so dark brown it was nearly black drew in a breath. "You broke the barriers around them?" she asked Kate. "Impossible. They were impenetrable."

Kate moved next to Venn, wading into a sea of glimmering colors. The scents of the surrounding remnants were so strong, and the swirl of lights so bright, she felt momentarily dizzy. She focused on the elf who'd just spoken. 'To an elf, yes. They were made of runelight."

Gasps sounded from all sides, and a trail of light shot out of the dark-haired elf's hand, racing around the table.

Faron frowned. "I believe Evay requested that we speak in a way Kate can hear, Payren."

The dark-haired elf's face grew hard. "You expect me to believe a human knows what runelight is?" she asked.

"She most definitely does," Faron said wryly.

"She not only knows what runelight is," Venn said, "she can also work with it differently than we can—and she doesn't have to have created it to affect it."

"The wounds held runelight?" Payren's eyes narrowed with suspicion. "Evay was attacked by an elf?"

"Not directly," Kate said. "The runelight was from the *naiwyn* itself."

An audible mutter passed around the table this time.

"How could you possibly know that?" Payren asked.

"Because Kate can see runelight,' Venn said. "It has distinct colors depending on who made it."

"And she can affect others' runelight?" Payren said, her voice dripping with disbelief. "Prove it."

Her light blue remnant blazed out of her and shot around the table.

Kate spun to watch it and caught Venn's fingers flickering again. *Shield.*

The blaze of blue with Payren's command reached an elf with golden hair the color of aspen leaves in the fall. He raised his hand, and dark red glitters coalesced around it. Kate poured *vitalle* into a shield, throwing it up around herself just as the air shimmered and a fist of something barely visible launched toward her.

A burst of icy cold air slammed into her shield like a boulder, sending a ripple of pain across her palms. She staggered backward, and the shield wavered, barely holding together. She threw more *vitalle* around herself.

Out of the corner of her eye, she saw Faron move toward her. Venn's fingers lifted, as though telling him to stop, and he did.

The golden-haired elf's brow twitched in annoyance, and he hurled another blast at Kate, the ripple of air twice as big as the first, easily big enough to tear through her shield. Bracing herself, Kate twisted the shield into a wedge, honing the front to a razor-sharp point. The frigid air slammed into it, but Kate's ruddier remnant tore into the darker red, splitting it in half, sending each part flying past her. Before it could reach the elves behind her, she tore her wedge into a dozen slivers and slashed into freezing air, shredding it into ribbons that broke up into nothing but cold wind.

The elf clenched his fist again, but Venn set herself between him and Kate.

"Since she is still standing, Terros," Venn said, "I believe the point has been proven." The elf didn't lower his hand, and Venn crossed her arms. "If you continue to attack my friend," she said mildly. "I'm going to take it as a sign of aggression."

An elf with a string of tiny white flowers laced into her braid stood. "That is more than enough."

Three other elves stood with her.

Payren gave a huff of disgust and took her seat again, waving for Terros to lower his arm.

"Since that has been settled," Evay said, "tell them who else's runelight was on the *naiwyn*."

Every eye fell on Kate with varying levels of contempt and curiosity. "Naevys's," she said. "She definitely created the *naiwyn*."

"And then stationed one near Cedar Lake," Evay added.

Lymberon was on his feet again. "Naevys is threatening the lakes? This is a grievous overstep!"

"Which is what they are saying," an elf with long, dusky-blond hair said. She stayed seated, but her pine-green remnant slid out of her hands, which were planted firmly on the table. Lines of it pushed through the other colored lights until she commanded the attention of the entire council. "They are admitting the problem and asking for help."

Faron gave her a grateful nod. "Thank you, Kaydryn."

"Help?" Lymberon's face reddened. "To control problems in their Wood?"

"Problems that are now affecting us," Kaydryn said.

Faron held up a hand. "It is our problem, but it has overflowed both to Home and to you. And we need help dealing with it."

"You have more rangers than we do," Lymberon said.

Faron hesitated, and Kate cleared her throat.

"King Faron explained to the people of Home that it's Naevys who is attacking them," she said, "and so they no longer trust the White Wood."

"For good reason." Lymberon took his seat again. "Neither do I."

Faron's shoulders stayed stiff. "I can deploy my rangers along your northern border to protect the lakes, but we need lake elves to help us protect the humans."

A sneer curled up the edge of Lymberon's lips. "Just use yours and tell the humans they're from the lakes. They'll never know."

Faron stiffened. "I gave them my word that my rangers would stay out of the town, and I intend to keep it."

"Your word?" Payren said. "Like the way you gave your word assuring us your mother was fine all this time?"

Faron's jaw clenched.

Venn faced Payren. "King Faron is not Thallion." Faron

twitched at the words but kept his face neutral. "He is attempting to fix things his father mishandled. Any issues you have concerning events from more than two days ago should be taken up with Thallion, not Faron. Now is the time for action, not complaints."

Faron's eyes locked on Venn's face, but she didn't look at him. Lymberon's expression hardened even further, but before he could speak, Kaydryn stood.

"You are right, Andovenn. Our grievances are with Thallion." She glanced at the trees around the clearing. "And apparently Naevys. King Faron, how many rangers are you requesting to aid you?"

"As many as you can spare."

Allyesse cleared her throat. "We will consider your request, King Faron." Her blind eyes shifted to Kate. "In our way."

Faron gave her a bow, then led the way out from the center of the table. Kate followed Evay after him.

Venn lingered for a moment by the elderly elf. "Elder Allyesse, the lakes barely ever involve ourselves with the affairs of humans or the task the White Wood has taken upon themselves to protect them, but the situation has changed. I am personally asking the council to listen to what King Faron has to say and offer him and the humans the aid they need." She took in the other elders, her posture almost regal. "Because I know the elves of the lakes to be honorable, I expect you all will find the compassion to lend your aid as well."

The hard bark of a fir pressed into Kate's back as she sat along the edge of the clearing. The late morning sun landed on her legs, warming them. Her thumb rubbed over the corner of a pocket on her pack where the canvas was frayed and soft. Her fingers itched to pull the box out, but the air of the clearing thrummed with the power of the elders' remnants. Glitters swirled past her like probing fingers. She shifted her pack, resting her knee against the top as though that offered any protection to what it held inside.

Venn and Evay both sat against a large tree next to Kate's, occasionally talking quietly to each other.

Faron paced on the ground in front of her, his face creased in displeasure as he shot another scowl toward the table where the elves sat silently, their hands resting on the wood and their heads bowed.

A needle of pain arced across Kate's sore palm, and she stretched her hand out, her burned skin pulling slightly. "For runelight being something Thallion has tried to discourage," she said quietly, "an awful lot of elves seem to use it."

"Certainly more than I expected." Venn studied the table of elders. "What did Terros throw at you?"

"Something very cold."

Faron's frown settled on the younger-looking elf. "I'm sorry, Kate. It was…" His hands tightened into fists. "I can't believe he attacked you."

"Payren and Terros feel the same way about humans as Thallion does," Venn said. "They weren't going to listen to anything we said or let Kate stay if we didn't prove who she was."

"Do the rest of the council share their feelings on humans?" Kate asked.

Venn shook her head. "A few of them. My father is a strong voice in support, as are at least half of the others. But there are a few whose views I don't know."

The elves talked on, and after the long night in the boat, the warm sunlight made Kate's eyelids heavy. She let them close, and the world spun slowly beneath her.

Next to her, Venn shifted. "If they don't offer help…" she said quietly.

"They will," Faron murmured.

Kate began rubbing the frayed edge of her pocket again. "How far is it to Virion's house?"

"An hour by boat, maybe," Venn said. "It depends on whether Cedar Lake has frozen yet. If it's thawed, the trip is quick in a boat. If it's completely frozen, the walk isn't bad. If the lake is just beginning to freeze, though, we'll have to skirt the entire thing, and that will take longer."

"Cedar Lake?" Kate opened her eyes and sat forward, looking between the two elves. "Where Evay was attacked?"

Venn paused. "I guess we have multiple reasons to go check on Virion."

"King Faron," Allyesse called out.

Venn tensed at the firmness in the ancient elf's voice.

Faron strode back into the center of the table, offering her a slight bow. Kate, Venn, and Evay rose to their feet.

"We will send three patrols of rangers," she said.

Faron's mouth fell open, and Venn blew out a breath of relief.

"Three?" Kate whispered. "Is that enough?"

Venn nodded, a smile touching her lips. "It's enough for you and I to extricate ourselves from the mess at Home if we really want to."

Kate sank back against the tree. "Finally, something good. Let's go see Virion this afternoon and get back to Renault's cave."

"Thank you," Faron said loudly, taking them all in.

Allyesse raised her hand to stop him. "But we have stipulations. The fact stands that you lied to us for years about Naevys's condition."

Faron stilled.

"Naevys pledged to be the emissary between the White Wood and the lakes, a duty she has neglected and is now obviously unfit for. Communications between the Wood and the lakes must be more candid and more frequent."

"I agree," Faron began, but Allyesse silenced him with a narrowing of her eyes.

"We require a new emissary. Were she well, we would name Evay, but as that is impossible, we name Andovenn in her place."

Venn stiffened.

Faron glanced at Venn for a heartbeat. "Andovenn has...some commitments she must fulfill before—"

"Andovenn will be our emissary, available at all times to both you and this council." Her words were as hard as steel.

Venn's shoulders sank.

"That doesn't sound like something we can extricate ourselves from," Kate said under her breath.

Faron opened his mouth, but Allyesse raised a finger to stop him. "Along with her, Keeper Kate will serve as an envoy between the elves and the humans. She will remain available to us and you and the people of Home until this conflict with Naevys has been resolved."

Faron darted a look at Kate.

"Definitely no extricating," Venn whispered.

The weight of Kate's pack leaned against her leg, but this was hardly a role to be refused.

She nodded.

"Our final stipulation is this," Allyesse continued. "The gap that Thallion has built between our two communities must be healed. The promise to do so has been in place for a very long time, but promises are now not enough. To gain the assistance of the lakes in your troubles and to ensure that no such division grows between us again, we require the marriage between yourself and Andovenn of the lakes be completed before the thawing of the ice this spring."

CHAPTER TWENTY-NINE

Venn froze.

Kate let out a whispered, "Noooo," that felt like a thunderclap in the quiet glade.

Faron stood in the center of the ringed table, his body tense, staring at Allyesse.

The white-eyed elf met his gaze calmly. "The three patrols are already being readied. We await only your agreement to our terms."

His mouth opened, then shut again. "I cannot speak for Andovenn," he said finally.

The attention of the council swung to Venn, who stood without moving.

Faron turned slowly, his face torn in apology but tinged with something pleading. Or hopeful. Or wounded.

Silence stretched out for a long moment, and Kate tried not to shift under it, searching for a way out of this for Venn.

"Kate…" Venn said under her breath.

"Agree to be the emissary," Kate whispered. "We'll figure out how to do that and open the box."

Venn ducked her head, her teeth clenched. "The emissary part is *not* the problem."

"I know." Kate's mind flipped the problem over. "Tell them the betrothal will stand, but you won't wed unless you know you have both Thallion's and Naevys's blessing."

Venn raised an alarmed eyebrow. "And if we end up with both of those things?"

Kate offered her a strained smile. "I'll help you sneak away and run. You can spend your life as a fugitive."

Venn stared at her. "That is a terrible plan."

"Can you think of a better one?"

"We *never* have a better one." Venn clenched her hands into fists. "Why do we never have a better one?" she whispered before addressing the table. "I accept the position as emissary—but only until Evay is fully healed."

There was a moment of silence before Allyesse gave a crisp nod.

"And I agree to the wedding..." Venn cleared her throat. Faron moved as though he would take a step forward, his mouth dropping open and one hand twitching as though trying to reach for her. "I will wed Faron once we have the blessings of both Thallion and Naevys."

Faron's fingers fell, and he let out a huff that sounded resigned and self-mocking.

A rustle of displeasure ran around the table, a handful of the elders' expressions darkening.

Venn kept her back straight. "As long as Naevys is alive, I will not disrespect her by marrying her son without her blessing."

Allyesse studied Venn for a long moment, and even though her eyes were clouded with white, there was an unnerving pressure in the stare. "She gave you her blessing when the betrothal was made."

Venn shook her head. "Naevys does not seem to hold to feelings she once had about many things. I would not presume to know her mind now."

Faron turned back to the council. "That is our answer," he said firmly. "Will you accept it?"

The elves around the table had their hands pressed to the wood. Even sitting, Kate could sense the *vitalle* racing between them as they argued silently.

Allyesse, though, did not touch the table, but gave a curt nod. "The rangers will be in Home by tomorrow afternoon. Since the people of Home trust you, Andovenn and Kate, your first duty as emissaries is to introduce Captain Tallinn to the humans and ensure the relationship between them begins on the most positive footing it can in such a time."

Payren shoved herself to her feet and, in a burst of blue remnant, she disappeared.

The other elders stood, some with irritation, some leaning forward to talk quietly to Faron. Within moments, only a few of them remained in the clearing.

"Back in Home by tomorrow afternoon?" Kate said to Venn. "Does that give us any time to see Virion?"

Venn's brow creased. "Enough time to get to him, talk quickly, and then leave from there. If we hurry, we need to walk the return trip anyway. Taking the boat upstream against the current is too slow. If we leave Virion's by mid-afternoon today and move quickly, we can make it."

Anreon came toward them, his face grim. "I'm sorry, Venn. I know that's not what you want."

Venn's jaw clenched for a moment. "I'm the one who let the betrothal go on this long. I couldn't expect it to be ignored forever."

Faron stepped up by Anreon's shoulder. "Venn, I didn't—"

She held up her hand. "Home needs our help, and so we'll do

what we need to do. But this changes nothing about how I feel, Faron."

He nodded.

"Faron," Kate said, "Thallion had sworn to protect the people of Home, and yet he harmed them. Is there any chance that's going to happen with these lake elves?"

Faron shook his head. "The elders are giving a command to the rangers that they cannot do anything harmful to a human, even in self-defense, for the next moon." He looked apologetically at Venn. "Allyesse has requested a longer audience to hear more details of what happened with my father and mother. I'll be here for at least the rest of the day. I'll come back to Home as soon as I can, though. I've already sent word to Ayen through the trees of what is happening. He'll help you with whatever you need."

Venn gave him a short nod, and after a moment's hesitation, he headed back toward Allyesse.

Anreon gave Venn a resigned smile. "Come by the house. We'll get you some food for the road, and you can be on your way by lunch."

Venn picked up her pack. "We have one more stop to make before we leave the lakes."

"More important than getting back to Home?" Anreon asked.

Venn grimaced. "In some ways, yes."

Anreon and Evay exchanged looks before Anreon fixed his attention back on Venn, his expression slightly wounded. "When were you going to tell your mother and I about the life debt?"

Venn stiffened, then let her shoulders fall. "I was hoping it would be done by now." She glanced at Evay. "You told them?"

Evay gave a half-shrug. "It seemed important."

"It is important." Anreon's expression was a mix of sympathy and worry. "Is there any way we can help?"

She started to shake her head, then glanced at Kate. "Actually, yes. You could tell us what you know about Virion. Was he really going to marry Naevys?"

"He was." Evay glanced over her shoulder at Faron and motioned to the path leading out of the clearing. "Let's walk while we talk, shall we?"

"Everything happened long before we came to this part of the world," Anreon said, his voice guarded as they started down the path winding downhill through the massive tree trunks.

"But we've pieced the story together." Evay gave him a pointed look.

His mouth tightened into a disapproving line. "Virion doesn't talk about his past. We shouldn't either."

"No one talks about it because it's a sad tale," Evay said. "But one that Venn might need to hear."

Anreon gave a resigned sigh.

Evay started down the path. "I've known Thallion, Naevys, and Virion all their lives. They were all close when they were young. Thallion's father was king, and Thallion spent a great deal of time in duties for him, but Naevys and Virion grew closer, and everyone expected them to wed." She glanced at Kate. "How much of the history of the Kalesh Empire do you know?"

Venn gave a quiet snort. "You'd be surprised."

"I've studied everything I can find on it," Kate said. "But I still feel like I only know bits and pieces."

"About four and a half centuries ago, the empire began to expand north." Evay touched the trunk of a tall spruce next to the trail. "They'd discovered the forests and began harvesting lumber for their southern cities. Their expansion was very fast, and the humans who lived here, who'd historically lived in isolated groups, banded together to stop the invasion.

"Thallion had only been king for a few years, but when he'd been prince, he'd interacted with the leaders of the people enough that when they were in need, they sent delegates to him begging for elven help."

"We knew of the empire," Anreon said. "If the human lands around the White Wood fell, the masses of soldiers the empire could send against the Wood itself would be nearly limitless. So Thallion agreed to send aid. The humans and elves made their stand near a city named Riekabrod."

"I know Riekabrod," Kate said. "It sits along the main river flowing down into the empire. The ford there has made it the focal point of a lot of military activity."

Anreon raised an eyebrow.

"She knows a lot of useless facts," Venn said.

"I know a lot of *interesting* facts," Kate corrected her. "I assume the empire needed the river to transport their lumber?"

Anreon nodded. "The battle was huge. Thousands of humans on each side. And Thallion sent an entire company of elves."

"How many is that?"

"One hundred and eighty." His voice was heavy. "Nearly all of the White Wood's rangers—Virion among them. It was a bloody massacre. On both sides. Only one out of ten humans from the north survived, but the empire's losses were even greater, and so the battle stopped the empire's progress north."

Kate looked between the three somber elves. "And the elves?"

Anreon sighed again. "Virion was the only survivor."

"Everyone had assumed he'd been killed too," Evay said, "because he didn't return for more than forty years."

"Forty years!" Kate asked.

"He'd been living with a human family all that time." Evay glanced at Venn. "Most believe he had a life debt to one of them. That perhaps a human saved him during the battle, and Virion stayed with him for the rest of the human's life."

Her voice lowered a little, even though the path around them was empty. "Whatever happened to him, he was changed.

He's…" The hint of a smile twisted her lips. "I've always thought the humans rubbed off on him. But he didn't travel back to see them. Instead, he settled down at the far end of the lakes."

"Really?" Venn asked. "That must have been a century before we arrived."

Evay nodded. "But a few years after the battle, all the White Wood knew was what a human messenger had reported. That the entire elven company had been killed. Not long after, Naevys became Warden and, thinking Virion was dead, married Thallion. Decades later, when Virion returned, he found her married and chose to settle alone by Cedar Lake."

"So," Kate said, "instead of living among the White Wood again, Virion settled alone by the lakes."

"Beyond them," Anreon explained, "the river turns south, and the land becomes more crowded with humans. This has always been considered the edge of the elven lands."

"So," Kate said slowly, "he chose to live at the very outskirts of his world rather than be near Naevys and Thallion?"

"Naevys," Evay said, "was devastated to learn Virion had been alive the whole time. She never would have married Thallion if she'd known. But by then, there was nothing left to do."

"That is pure conjecture," Anreon said, a note of sternness in his voice.

"It is very educated conjecture," Evay countered. "You know as well as I that Virion's return coincides with Naevys and Thallion beginning to live in separate parts of the forest."

"It also is not long after she became Warden," he said, "and Wardens almost universally isolate themselves from the busier parts of the Wood."

Evay leveled a flat look at him. "You think it's because she was Warden?"

"I think it's none of my business," he answered pointedly.

They fell silent, following the path until it led to his home.

Lesille met them with a hundred questions and a bustle to make lunch. While Venn and Anreon recounted the council, Lesille directed Evay to a chair by the fire, giving her a cup of tea and stern instructions to rest.

Kate set her pack on the long table and grabbed a notebook to write everything she'd just learned.

She had finished the notes and created a vague timeline along the edge of her page by the time Lesille was caught up. "Wait," Kate said. "Virion came back to the White Wood when? Almost four hundred years ago? Renault didn't come to this part of the world until a little over three hundred years ago."

"Renault Half-Elven?" Lesille said over her shoulder. "What does he have to do with it?"

"Naevys interacted with him a surprising amount," Venn said, "and we've heard Virion did as well."

Evay frowned. "I've never heard of a connection there."

"Well, we have a lot of questions about Renault and Naevys, so I hope Virion really did know him." Kate tucked her journal back into her pack, running her fingers along the edge of the box, feeling the quiet hum before fastening her pack closed again.

Anreon helped Venn wrap the last of the cakes, cheese, and some sort of steamed root that smelled like butter into a large bundle. When it was stowed in Venn's pack, he set a hand on her shoulder. "Please be careful."

"Yes," Lesille said, offering Kate a quick hug. "No more *naiwyn* or *gwerocs* or bears." She turned and enveloped Venn. "Get what you need from Virion and then get back to Home and let the rangers deal with whatever Naevys sends next."

"That's the plan," Kate said. "We need to free my brothers."

Anreon raised an eyebrow at Venn. "You expect us to believe you'll just let them fight for something like protecting Home, and you won't help?"

"Yes," Lesille said stubbornly. "That is exactly what we will believe."

Venn hesitated. "I do have a life debt."

"You have this whole time," her father said, "and yet you keep getting into scrapes that have very little to do with that."

Venn sighed. "We've noticed. How about this: We won't specifically seek out trouble."

"Somehow," her father said resignedly, "I doubt you'll have to. So please do be careful."

CHAPTER THIRTY

They walked back to the dock, where Liall greeted them again with marginally less shock than last time. Kate climbed into the boat while Liall untied it, and Venn took her place in the stern.

"Auntie Venn!" Aislin called, running toward the boat. "What happened?"

"The rangers are all assembling,' Matlen said. "Are they really going to Home?"

"Yes." Venn pointed a finger at the two of them. "And you two need to stay here."

Aislin's face wrinkled. "Oh, Mother took care of that. She heard what's happening at Home, and Faron told them we'd been there, and do you know what she did?"

"She marched us to Allyesse herself," Matlen said indignantly, "and had the elder actually *command* us to stay out of the fighting near Home and not even speak to the dwarves until this whole mess is done!"

"A binding command!" Aislin added.

"Really?" Venn asked.

"The kind that Thallion can give?" Kate asked.

Aislin nodded. "The council is the authority here at the lakes. And we can feel the weight of it." She pursed her lips. "We started talking about ways to sneak closer to Home, and suddenly everything felt very heavy."

Matlen gave Kate a wide smile. "We are not forbidden from talking to you, though. Allyesse seemed to like you. Something about not backing down."

"Go back home," Venn said firmly. "I'll send messages to my parents of how things are going so you can keep track here. And keep Evay company while she heals. When she wakes, she'll want to get up, but she should rest. You know how bored she gets having to stay still."

Aislin sighed. "If you gave us permission to come with you, even partway—"

"Absolutely not." Venn took the rope from Liall and set her hand on the side. The boat shifted and groaned quietly as the branches beneath it began to move.

"I hope I see you again," Kate said. "Thank you for all your help!"

"Wait! Come back and tell our mother how helpful we've been," Aislin said, raising her voice as they began to float away.

Kate offered them a wave and was met with disappointed faces.

Venn studied the twins, who stood on the dock, their shoulders slumped dejectedly. "I can't tell you how many times I've wished I had some actual authority over those two to make them stop throwing themselves into scrapes." She steered the boat away from the island.

The midday sun was surprisingly warm, but as the boat picked up speed, the breeze off the water chilled Kate's hands until she pulled them inside her sleeves.

The hills around the lake were reflected in near perfect images in the still water. The green of the forest branches were topped with daubs of snow. The brilliantly cerulean sky was clear except for a thick bank of clouds building up ahead of them. Kate leaned back, letting the sun hit her face, her mind skipping from thoughts of Virion to the bloodstone to the council to the agreements Venn had made.

Kate cracked an eye and found Venn's shoulders tense, her gaze fixed on a point along the distant lakeshore. Instead of lying still on the side of the boat, her fingers picked at a bit of rough wood, tearing off splinters.

"Thank you," Kate said quietly.

Venn glanced at her. "For what?"

"This." Kate gestured to the river. Venn didn't answer, but a low anger simmered in her face. Finally, Kate sat up. "Which is it? The emissary role or the wedding?"

Venn's fingers stopped on the wood, and she gave Kate an incredulous look. "I cannot believe you have to ask that."

Kate lifted a hand. "I thought it was the wedding, but then I realized being assigned a duty as an emissary might be like a command—the sort the twins got—and when I asked you to bring me to Virion, I was causing you to almost break it. Which seems like it might...cause some discomfort."

Venn shook her head. "They didn't command me. If I refuse to do it, I would incur the displeasure of the council, not to mention putting Home in more danger than it needs to be, but it wouldn't be like breaking a direct command from the council or Thallion."

"I'm sorry," Kate said, "about the wedding." The words sounded flat and useless.

Venn looked out across the water. "Kate, has he really changed?"

Kate paused. "In some ways, I think so."

Venn ran a hand over her face. "I know it's stupid to think that he and I could ever get back to what we once were, but…"

"It seems like a natural thing to wish for. Whether or not it will happen."

Venn nodded. "I don't think it can. There's been too much between us."

Kate tapped her finger on the side of the boat. "The quick timeline is certainly not going to help you figure it out. Although, maybe if we can put an end to this trouble with Naevys, the council will relent a little bit." She studied Venn's face. "If it comes down to it, will you marry him?"

Venn shook her head slowly. "I gave my word because we needed to help Home, but...I don't know if I can."

A cold wind blew into Kate's face, and underneath the growing bank of clouds, a curtain of snow greyed the hills at the end of the lake. Venn scanned the distant shore ahead and adjusted their heading toward a gap in the trees.

"Luckily," Kate said, watching as the snow obscured the edge of the water, "from the little we saw of how Naevys treated Thallion, if he gives his blessing for you to marry Faron, Naevys will deny hers just to thwart him." Venn almost smiled, and Kate added, "That's assuming she remembers who you are."

Venn's smile faded. "Or who Faron is."

"What happens if we never find her?"

"I would imagine that the rest of the council will agree with Allyesse. Naevys gave her blessing back when she was able to, and the marriage will go forward." Venn's thumbnail dug into the spot of rough wood again, even though her face stayed calm.

Wind from the approaching storm shoved against Kate, and low waves rose on the water. Kate gripped the sides as the water grew more turbulent. The veil of snow covered the lakefront ahead and moved quickly closer.

"Not if they can't find you."

Venn let out a breath that was definitely a laugh. "Right, the fugitive plan."

"Don't worry, if you run, I'll run with you. We'll find a way back to the Stronghold, free Bo and Evan, and...then just keep running."

"How reassuring," Venn said dryly, but her shoulders relaxed, and her thumb stopped worrying at the ragged spot of wood.

Their progress slowed as the boat struggled to move against the wind, and a splatter of wet snow hit Kate's cheek. Venn gripped the boat more firmly, but despite the steady motion of the branches propelling them forward, they seemed barely to move.

"This is taking too long," Venn said. "We should turn back and head toward Home. The rangers are going to get there long before we will, and that will cause nothing but trouble. We'll come back to Virion as soon as we can."

Kate's stomach dropped at the idea. She peered through the thickly falling flakes toward the shore, which had disappeared completely. "But we're so close to the river. Once we're there, the wind should lessen, right?"

Venn snorted. "You have no idea how close we are."

Kate smiled and drew her cloak tighter. "True. Are we close?"

Venn squinted forward. "Yes."

"Just to the river," Kate said. "Then, if it's still slow, we can turn around."

"Assuming we can find the river in this." Venn set her mouth into a determined line and held the side of the boat more tightly.

The dark shapes of trees emerged slowly from the formless white as the little boat struggled toward the shore. Venn peered at the unbroken line of pines before turning the boat to the right, where the wide river appeared. They floated into it, and the wind lessened to blustery gusts. Between the current and the branches propelling the boat, they picked up speed.

"See? We'll be fine." The current jolted them to the side, and a spray of ice-cold water shot into Kate's face. She gasped and sank lower.

Delicate sheets of ice grew along the edge of the river, and as they wound into the forest, the wind died down. The snow fell heavy and thick, washing out everything but the nearby banks.

Venn set her other hand on the side of the boat and whispered something. A hint of warm air brushed over Kate from the bench she sat on. It grew until the air around her felt like a sunny spring afternoon. Not far above her head, snowflakes reached an invisible barrier and melted, running down the domed top of the bubble of warmth.

"I thought you needed living trees to use their warmth," Kate said.

"These boats were made especially for these rivers, and it's often cold."

The river widened, and Venn kept the boat near the right-hand bank.

A strange noise came from up ahead, a sort of *veww* sound starting at a high pitch before quickly dropping into a low vibration.

"What was that?" Kate asked.

Venn made a hum as though she'd been expecting it and directed the boat over to the edge of the river. "Cedar Lake."

"The lake...talks?" The planks beneath Kate's feet groaned quietly, and she felt the watercraft slow.

"Sings."

They rounded a wide bend, and a lake came into view—completely frozen over. The snow obscured everything but the nearest trees and the flat expanse of ice stretching across the lake, which was lost behind a curtain of white.

Venn steered the boat to the shore, and the branches crawled out until they sat on the snowy bank. She grabbed her pack and climbed out.

The bubble of warmth evaporated from around Kate, and she pulled her cloak tighter as she followed Venn into the swirl of snowflakes.

"What do you mean it sings?"

"Just wait."

The snow crunched under Kate's feet, a layer of fluffy powder already building up over an older crust of snow. "How is this lake frozen when the others weren't?"

"Cedar Lake is so shallow you could almost walk across it in the summer. It freezes early, weeks before the deep lakes."

"Can we walk on it?"

"If we can't, we're turning around."

"What?" Kate said. "After coming all this way?"

"If we can't cross it by a boat, or by foot, it's two miles around through land that is filled with marshy wetlands. It's a miserable walk in the summer. In the snow, without being able to see a good path, it would take us half the day."

Venn set her hand on a tree and closed her eyes. When she opened them, she looked conflicted. "We can cross. It's far thicker than a handbreadth already."

"Is there a reason you don't want to see Virion?" Kate asked.

"No, Virion is fine. His house is actually really interesting. It's been ages since I've been there, but I remember his trees being very awake. I'm not sure we'll get much out of him, though. He lives as a hermit away from everyone, hasn't been close to Naevys in hundreds of years, and is a bit daft." Venn took a step out onto the ice. "On the other hand, the rangers are heading toward Home as we speak and are going to reach a very unwelcoming group of humans unless we get there quickly and try to smooth things over. So do your thing where you convince someone to trust you, then ask the questions you want." She pointed a finger at Kate. "But *only* the important questions. No researching irrelevant things. Then we get moving. We have a long way to go before we reach Home."

"Agreed."

"And," Venn added, "promise me that if Virion doesn't want to talk to you—about things he apparently never wants to talk about—then we leave right away."

Kate pushed down her curiosity about the elf. "Also agreed."

Venn looked marginally less concerned. "Then come on. Virion's house is on the far side."

Kate put a foot onto the ice, expecting it to be slick, but the surface was dusted with snow and felt more like hard, smooth rock than slippery ice. She followed Venn forward. Within a few dozen paces, the shore of the lake behind them was shrouded in white. Absolute silence fell. Even their footsteps were muffled by the growing layer of snow.

A crack rang out from under the ice, and a spike of fear shot through Kate. The same *veewww* noise shot across the lake under her feet like a ghostly call. It began high and dropped quickly to a lower thrum as it shot away. "What is that?" Her voice came out high and tense.

Venn didn't slow her pace. "The ice singing. Beautiful, isn't it?"

"Beautiful? It sounds like it's breaking! Why is the sound zooming around like that?"

"It's not breaking. But there are cracks in it, and when the weather changes, the cracks shift a bit. Like when a sunny day suddenly turns cold and snowy. The cracks shift against each other—" Another eerie call thrummed across the lake, the noise disappearing into the whiteness of the falling snow. "And it sings."

The sounds were definitely eerie, but beautiful. Otherworldly. The way they hurtled across the lake, the sound so fast she could barely follow, with swooping pitches that hummed and sent vibrations through the ice beneath her feet. It sounded like the song of stars, fallen to earth. Or maybe the call of the deepest seas.

The sounds echoed from unseen edges of the lake while huge white flakes spun lazily down, shrinking the world to this small stretch of humming ice.

"It sounds like crisp winter air," Venn said, "and clear, star-filled frozen nights. And freedom. And wonder." She glanced at Kate with a real smile. "Welcome to winter at the lakes."

Kate walked next to her, trying to soak it all in. "I like winter at the lakes."

Venn pointed ahead to where a murky shape was just visible through the snow. "Hail, Virion," she called.

The shape detached itself from the front of what must be a house and glided toward them. "It really is a human and an elf. How interesting." The tall form, almost too thick to be an elf, slid closer, stopping with a shushing sound when he was close enough to see them.

Venn offered him a slight bow, and Kate did the same. "My name's Andovenn. I met you twice before, with Evay, but it was long ago."

He was wrapped in a thick cloak of bear fur, and his boots had strange flat blades affixed to their soles, which slid smoothly over the ice. His remnant, a sparkling silver that shimmered like stars, flowed out behind him toward his home.

"I remember you, *Illease*," he said lightly. "You have a dead finger."

Venn held up her hand with a wry smile. "Two now."

His eyes crinkled with amusement. "At least it doesn't seem to be progressing too fast." His irises shone with a strange, piercing gold. His skin held a brown tint. He didn't seem particularly old, but his hair, which hung past his waist, longer than that of any elf Kate had seen, was as white as the snow. The braids in it were disheveled, as though he'd worn them for a very long time, and the ends were tied with small thongs of leather. There was something un-elven about them. Something almost dwarven. Or human.

While he didn't seem elderly, an agedness draped over him like a cloak.

"This is my friend Kate," Venn said.

He studied Kate for a long moment, his gaze so intense she readied a little *vitalle*. But his expression stayed genial. "Is any part of you dying?" he asked mildly.

Kate smiled at him. "Only my optimism that I'm ever going to accomplish what I need to."

He let out a chuckle and glanced at Venn. "Aren't humans adorable? Always trying to accomplish things. I hope you're teaching her how to live less..." He waved a hand, encompassing all of Kate. "Driven."

"Unfortunately," Venn said, "in this goal, I'm as driven as she is."

Virion tilted his head, considering Venn, and his smile faded. "A debt," he said, barely above a whisper. "You carry a debt to—"

Venn stiffened, but Virion's attention darted to Kate.

He studied her for a moment, then his brow furrowed in bewilderment. "Not to her. Not exactly."

Venn shifted her weight. "To her brother."

Virion took a probing step toward Kate before anger flooded his face. "You have something of Renault's!"

Kate's hand tightened on her pack. "A box."

"Why did you bring *that* here?" He drew back, jabbing a finger furiously at her. "He corrupted her. That box..."

Kate held out a hand toward him. "We know."

He stopped, his gaze shifting suspiciously between Kate and Venn.

"We know Renault did something to Naevys," Kate said. "She's changed. She's…"

"She's attacking the human town of Home," Venn said.

Virion's mouth dropped open, his anger shifting to confusion. "Why?"

Venn gave a small shrug. "We were hoping you could help us figure that out."

He closed his eyes. There was something resigned in the motion, but it was more complex than that. For a heartbeat, it held a bit of longing before it was tamped down.

"I hate that box." Opening his eyes, he motioned them toward his house. "It's dangerous, but bringing it inside won't make things any worse."

CHAPTER THIRTY-ONE

Five massive maple trees encircled Virion's house, their bare branches spreading out and down, forming solid walls of bark. A weak orange glow illuminated the windows and the front door, which was merely an open arch.

Kate pulled her cloak tighter, banishing a wish for someplace actually warm, and beginning to draw to mind the dozens of questions she wanted to ask the strange elf.

Venn leaned closer to her. "These trees are *very* alive. Almost like elder trees, except they're far too young." She gave Kate a pointed look. "I know you have countless questions building up, but remember we need to keep this visit short."

"Right. Short." Kate followed Virion in through the open doorway.

It was like stepping into summer.

Warm, rich air surrounded her. Green moss lined the floor in bright, springy softness. A vine crawled up around the doorway, hanging droopy violet flowers that gave off the scent of mountain meadows. Every wall was smooth and beautiful, created from woven branches. Sprays of maple leaves grew from the walls in vivid greens or blazing reds and golds, as though spring, summer, and fall all existed in this small space. The leaves shifted and fluttered as though stirred by a breeze that Kate couldn't feel. There was the slightest shimmer across the open windows and the doorway, like Venn's bubble of warmth on the boat.

The entire house was a single room. A fire crackled in a pit in the center of it. Along the far wall, a plush bed of moss was tucked up under a window. To the left, cabinets made of interlaced branches lined the walls. A wide table sat before them, littered with small wooden carvings. To the right was another table, tucked against a wall that was hung with tools.

The air was saturated with the sense of maples. Kate could feel the serrated edges of the leaves on her fingertips, hear the rustle as they shifted past each other in the mysterious currents.

The vibrancy of it caught at Kate. It was like the call of the White Wood when she'd been connected with it. She could almost sense the trees filling the room itself with their essence.

She let her cloak fall open so the warmth could seep in. From a pot above the fire, the scent of cinnamon and cloves wafted out.

"I always keep a little renberry wine on hand for guests." Virion moved over to the pot. His remnant glittered shockingly bright, as though a night sky's worth of stars had crowded into the room, but not just around Virion. Lines of it stretched out to every tree in the wall, merging with the subtle shimmers that traveled along each trunk. They were all nearly silver. A little lighter, or a little darker. One had a bit of gold.

"Nothing better than mulled wine on a snowy day." Virion glanced over his shoulder along the line of his remnant that connected to the large maple to the left of the door.

Venn flinched and looked up.

"Yes, Allorwyn," he muttered, "she's human. Stop gawking."

Kate glanced around the room. Virion went back to stirring

his pot. Venn met Kate's questioning look by pointing at the tree. "It's talking," she whispered.

"You can hear them?" Kate asked quietly. "Without touching them?"

Venn nodded, her eyes wide. "They're *so* awake."

"Hang your coats up." Virion motioned to some short branches jutting out from the wall near the door, then puttered over to the pot. "Take a seat, Kate." He nodded toward the only chair near the fire. It was, like everything else, created out of branches bent and smoothed. He hurried to the wall and picked up a small table, dumping a few miniature carvings off it before carrying it back to the fire. As he moved, the table shifted, stretching and bending. By the time he'd crossed the room, it was a second chair, which he held cheerily out to Venn.

She took it, her mouth hanging open in shock. Virion, who didn't seem to notice, scrounged up a small footstool from a corner and, in only a few moments, he'd yet another chair.

Kate held her hands out to the fire, letting the heat warm them. "The wine smells delicious."

"But we may not have time to drink any," Venn said, giving Kate a warning look. "I'm afraid we need to leave soon."

"Or we could just eat here while we talk," Kate said brightly. "Venn has a bundle of cakes we could share."

Venn gave Kate a flat look but dug the bundle out of her pack.

Virion took it and sniffed the fabric, and his face lit. "Delicious!" He quickly unwrapped them and set them on a metal grate hung rather high over the fire.

"They're quite good cold," Venn said.

"Nonsense, we'll just heat them a bit while the wine finishes." He arranged them carefully. "Violet berry cakes. You're missing out," he said toward the maple in the corner near his bed. "Maples," he said with a fond look. "Always wondering what it's like to be something they're not."

"They are?" Venn asked slowly.

"Aren't we all?" He twitched and shot an annoyed look at the first tree he'd talked to. "I am not stalling. You do realize what they brought." After a moment's silence, he turned back to Kate with an aggrieved sigh. "You might as well take it out and ask me whatever you came to ask."

Pushing down the familiar reluctance to show the box to anyone, Kate pulled it out of her pack and set it on her lap.

All the lightness in Virion's face faded to a somber sorrow. "It's stayed together nicely." Keeping his hands folded on his lap, he leaned closer. Kate twitched it back away from him, and he gave a chuckle. "It's got hold of you too, eh?"

"My brothers are trapped inside it."

Virion's eyebrow rose. "More people in there?" He frowned. "Of course, maybe they're safer than we are. It still seems exactly the same as—" He drew in a sharp breath. "She touched it. Recently."

"Naevys?" Kate's fingers tightened on the box. "You can sense her remnant?"

"Remnant is as good of a name for it as I've ever heard." He reached forward, and though Kate tried not to tense, the box quivered. "Don't worry. I don't want to hold it." He brushed his fingertips across the surface. His eyes pressed shut, and his fingers hovered a hair above the surface before he pulled them away. "Naevys had it." His voice was barely above a whisper.

"She did. I just got it back from her yesterday."

His eyes flew open. "You saw her?"

"Well, the box we found in the woods," Kate said. "But we did see her the night before that."

Virion looked up into the branches that made up his ceiling and gave a humming that could have been an acknowledgment.

"When you said the box was dangerous, did you mean for

us?" Kate asked. "Because my brothers are trapped inside, and the Runelight Drawer is crumbling."

He snapped his gaze back down to her. "You opened it without the amulet?"

The image of the sky cracking and crashing down filled her vision, and she squeezed the box, letting the edges of the metal dig into her fingers. "We didn't know."

He sank back in his chair. "Of course you didn't." He glanced over at the tree by his bed, and a hint of exasperation crossed his face. "Because it was hundreds of years ago when Renault used it." Venn tried to suppress a smile as Virion's exasperation grew. "Well, it's a long time for them!" He brushed a finger across the box. "It's a long time for me," he said, almost to himself.

"We actually came to see what you knew about Naevys and Renault," Kate said.

Virion's jaw twitched. "They spent a great deal of time together. She was very interested in his work." Virion took the pot of mulled wine off its hook. He carried it to the table and began filling three mugs, keeping his back to them. "But," he said without turning, "I didn't trust him."

Kate glanced at Venn. "Why not?"

Virion stood still for a long moment. Finally, he picked up two mugs and turned, his expression sorrowful. "He was brilliant, but obsessive." He handed a mug to each of them.

Kate wrapped her hands around hers, soaking the warmth into her still-cold hands. Bits of cinnamon and cloves floated on the top of the mug, mixing with the sweet scent of the wine and a hint of something citrusy. She breathed it deeply. The house wrapped around them like a cocoon. Outside the windows, the world was blotted out by the gently falling snow. No sounds came in the windows. Not even the hint of a breeze.

Virion returned to the table and picked up his wine, along with one of the little carvings that were scattered across the room. "He dragged her into his obsession somehow. The more time she spent with him, the more she…" He looked up at the trees. "Yes. The more she changed." Slowly, he came to sit back down by the fire.

"Naevys and Renault seem like an unlikely pair," Kate said.

"They weren't a pair. Not really. He was enamored with her, of course, but she never returned his interest." Virion glared up at the maple behind Kate with a pinched brow. "She would not love someone so fixated on one thing to the exclusion of all else. All family. All reality. All decency."

Kate glanced at Venn, whose eyebrows were high as she listened to whatever the trees said next.

"None of you were there," Virion said, irritated. He turned pointedly back to Kate. "She never returned his interest."

"I believe that," Kate said. "We found some old writing of hers. She seemed interested in his work, but anywhere from frustrated to incredibly angry with him as a person."

Virion glared upward. "See?" He took a drink, his face falling back into melancholy. "Still, he did change her. By the end, she had lost the peace she used to carry."

"By the end of what?" Venn asked.

"By Renault's death."

"Could you help us find her?" Kate asked. "We need someone who can get through to her and get her to listen to reason."

"She hasn't listened to me in…" Virion stared into the fire, rolling the carving between his fingers. "A very long time."

"She tried to drain the White Wood of all its *ael'iza*," Kate said, "and now she's attacking Home and draining it to fuel whatever she's doing in that ravine."

Virion sat unmoved, still fiddling with the carving.

Kate stared at it, trying to come up with some reason Virion should help them.

His fingers paused for a moment, and she realized the piece of wood was a tree. A maple tree with a small face on its trunk.

Naevys's face.

Kate straightened.

More carvings were scattered across his table. All maples. Several with their faces turned enough to see the resemblance to Naevys in every one of them.

Everywhere she looked, there were more. The house was made of maples. Virion spoke to them, lived in them, carved more of them.

Centuries ago, Virion had left the human world. And then he'd left the White Wood. The only thing he hadn't left were the maple trees that Naevys loved so much.

It wasn't age lying so heavily on Virion. It was grief. And waiting. Grieving for someone out of his reach. Waiting for something that continually felt less real. Kate shifted the box on her lap. How had she not recognized it in him before? Every time she touched the box. Every time she thought of the box, or Bo, or Evan. Every day for twenty years she'd felt that.

Virion was still lost in the fire, but she could feel the sorrow in him. She pointed at the carving in his hand and signed *treasure* to Venn.

Venn peered at the tree for a moment before understanding dawned.

Kate searched for something to tell him, something not about the world, but about Naevys herself

She leaned forward. "Thallion isn't king any longer." She could almost feel the spike of shock that shot through him. His eyes flashed up to her face, then to Venn's.

"He abused his authority," Venn said, "and the Wood stripped him of his power."

"He abused his authority," Kate added, "by trying to strip the Warden powers from Naevys."

Virion's mouth dropped open. "No!"

Kate nodded. "She nearly killed him for it. And Faron too."

"And several others who were nearby," Venn said dryly.

Virion dropped his gaze back to the fire. "Why would he do that?"

"Because he believed it was what was destroying her mind," Kate said.

"No." Virion dropped the carving and jabbed a furious finger at the box on Kate's lap. "Renault destroyed her mind. The Wood helped her stay sane."

He paused, staring unseeing at the far wall, almost thrumming with astonishment. "He's no longer king…" He dragged his attention to Venn. "For how long?"

"It was two nights ago."

A breath escaped him, almost a laugh. "That's what it was."

Venn leaned forward. "You felt his authority snap?"

Virion nodded, a smile crossing his face. "*That's* what it was…"

"Whatever Thallion commanded you to do…" Kate glanced around the house. "Wherever he commanded you to live, that's done now."

Virion sank back in his chair, a smile still playing on his lips. "I chose to build my house here, but…"

A piece of his story clicked into place. Kate reached down and picked up the delicate carving. "He commanded you not to speak of the past you had with Naevys."

Virion rubbed a finger over the little tree. "Naevys and I…" He said the words roughly, as though unused to speaking them, and then he paused, waiting. After a moment, his shoulders relaxed. "Naevys and I were wed." He paused again. "We wed in a small ceremony in a stand of maples." The words rushed out, a huge smile spreading across his face. The air around him vibrated with delight. "She was the most beautiful elf I've ever seen, and why she married me, I'll never know."

He rose and set his mug down on the table, crossing to his cabinets. A cluster of branches shifted to create a small opening.

Kate glanced at Venn, but she looked as confused as Kate felt. "I'm sorry," Kate said. "I don't understand elven ways very well, but how did she marry Thallion if she was already married to you?"

Virion's motions hitched in the process of pulling something out. He stayed with his back to them for a moment before turning, his smile fading to something more closed. "It wasn't an official marriage. We made vows to each other, but they're not truly binding unless they're made in the presence of the king. We meant to, but..."

"You ran out of time before you left," Venn said quietly.

A pained breath escaped Kate, and Virion flinched at the noise.

"I'm..." Kate shifted in her chair. "I'm sorry." The words felt woefully insufficient.

He didn't answer but returned to the fire, setting a box on his lap and wiping dust off its lid.

It was a miniature version of the aenigma box, complete with metal straps nailed along the edges and smooth wooden faces. Kate leaned forward. "Another one?"

"Not exactly. Yours does"—he wrinkled his nose—"many things. Mine"—he said the word with a possessive, adoring air—"is a single pocket world." Without a sound, a drawer appeared on the front of the box. Virion pulled it open, and a shimmer of gold wafted out, accompanied by the whisper of wind through branches, skimming across countless needles. The flutter of jagged maple leaves.

"Naevys." Kate leaned forward. The remnant felt pure. Simple. Freer than she'd ever felt it. "How old is that?"

Virion reached into the box and pulled out a thick silver ring set with a shard of wellstone. "Four hundred and fifty-two winters." He slipped the ring onto his finger, rubbing his thumb over the stone, everything about him radiating relief. After a moment, his brow furrowed, and he looked up at Kate. "You read Naevys's writings?"

"We found them in Renault's cave, along with a lot of Renault's journals and records."

Virion's head tilted slightly. "How did you find his workshop?"

"Faron led us to the cave entrance at the top of Reston Ridge," Venn said. "We managed to get past the traps set there. It's more like a library than a workshop now."

Virion handed Kate a warm pastry. "I don't know anything about a cave on the ridge. His workshop—where he made that box and this one, where he did everything—was hidden inside a pocket world."

Kate paused with the cake halfway to her mouth. "Where's the entrance?"

"It used to be in the woods south of Home, on the human side of the river. A bright door standing right in the middle of the forest. Inside it was full of books and the instruments he used to make his potions." Virion reached back into the drawer and pulled out a small pouch. He upended it, and a wellstone tumbled out into his hand. It flashed with light, and thin, hungry fingers brushed against Kate's mind, but not with much power.

"What does that hold?" she asked.

"Naevys and Thallion and I used it when we were young to record our adventures." He held it out on his palm. "Put your hands over mine. I'll show you what she used to be like."

Venn reached forward and set her hand on Virion's. After a moment's hesitation, Kate set hers on top. Memories washed into her mind from each of the three elves.

Naevys and Virion, their faces unlined and youthful, running through the woods.

A young Thallion grinning with an easy smile.

A wide vista where Thallion, Naevys, and Virion sat, watching the last of a sunset drain out of the sky.

Thallion, his hands grasping for purchase on a rock, looked up at Naevys and Virion climbing a steep mountainside. Naevys called out that they needed to go a bit higher. Thallion glanced over his shoulder, revealing a view that was partially blocked by tall frost pines.

Virion waded in the Surn, and Naevys triumphantly flung up a hand, sending a spray of water into the air. Her fingers pinched a small wellstone. Her other hand already cupped three more. Thallion shook his head in disbelief. Virion looked down and pulled his hand out of the water, only to reveal only a light yellow pebble. Naevys let out a laugh. "I'll tell the elders you both found some of these too."

A glen of maple trees surrounded Virion and Naevys as he held her hand and looked earnestly at her. "It's not your connection to the forest that I love — it's the way you hold that connection so sacred. How you see each tree and elf and creature as perfectly valuable.

"You'd be the best Warden our Wood has ever had because you really see everyone. You understand what they need, and you help them. You see me and know what I need. So many would use that for their own gain, but I never worry about that with you. I trust that you'll always care well for me and the elves and the Wood."

Virion pulled his hand back, and the memories faded. He rolled the wellstone between his fingers, his nostalgic smile shifting to something more sorrowful. "Haven't brought myself to look at either of these in...quite some time." He tucked it back into the pouch and set it back into the drawer.

A shimmer of blue was caught under the edge of one of the metal straps of his box, and Kate leaned forward. "Virion, has that been many places?"

"Only Renault's workshop and my cupboard."

"I have a potion that will show me memories from the remnants that were left on things. I see a bit of Renault's remnant on your box. Would you mind if I try to see what it holds?"

Virion hesitated, then held it out.

Kate pulled the solos potion out of her pack and dripped a single drop onto the remnant. A blue-tinged cloud rose up, and she pushed her hand into it. Venn reached over and did the same. Just as Virion's house began to fade around her, he stood and reached out as well.

> *Renault's hands held the small box over the smooth wood of a workbench. His fingers pressed against powdered wellstones that lined the edges of the drawer, dribbling power into them until they glowed.*
>
> *A door creaked and light streamed in over the table. His attention snapped up, and a surge of pleasure so strong it was almost painful shot through him.*
>
> *Naevys stepped inside, the sunlit woods behind her turning her to a dark silhouette before she pulled the door closed.*

Virion drew in a sharp breath.

> *She strode over to him, and he swallowed. "Good morning," he said when his voice was steady.*
>
> *The skin on her face was smooth and young. A crease of worry sat between her brows. "Just another small pocket." Her fingers fidgeted with something small and frosty blue.*

A shiver of irritation rolled through Renault.

Kate studied the room behind Naevys. Tall bookshelves covered the walls. Several other tables were situated under glowing orbs of light. Reflections bounced off dozens of glass bottles and vials. There was nothing cave-like about the space. It looked like a large room that might belong to a well-off merchant or a minor lord.

"I need to test the anchors." Renault turned back to the box. He leaned closer, and a large pendant around his neck thunked onto the table.

It was the size of his palm and glimmered with the bright silver of stonesteel. Runes encircled it, carved all the way around the edges, and a teardrop of glass was lodged into the center, full of blood-red liquid.

The Oziv amulet.

CHAPTER THIRTY-TWO

The memory continued as Renault pushed the drawer shut and set the box down. He raised his eyes to Naevys again.

"I have some stew from earlier..."

The Warden pushed herself up, her eyes trailing over things behind him, her expression torn between worry and frustration. "I will return to the woods."

A ripple of dissatisfaction rolled through Renault, and he rose, setting the box aside. "If you wish."

The words rolled off his tongue more bitterly than he'd intended, and he turned away from her to face a wall filled with books.

The image faded, and Virion's house came back into focus.

The elf sat frozen, his hand shaking over the box, his face torn with something too complex to decipher. "Can you do that again?" he whispered, the longing in his voice palpable.

The speck of Renault's blue remnant faded away with the end of the blue mist.

"No," Kate said. "Providing the memory uses it up." She handed the box back to him.

Virion let his fingers settle on it.

"Did Renault wear that amulet often?" Kate asked quietly.

"Always. Originally, it was just the topaz, encased in gold. It was meant to slow time for the wearer. If you touched the topaz, time drew nearly to a halt. He said it gave him time to think."

"That explains the strange gold cage around it." Kate tapped a finger on her leg, seeing the problems that would arise from such a stone. "Renault said no one should touch it for long. I suppose if time almost stopped for someone, they would never be able to actually get their finger off. They'd be stuck there for…eternity, I suppose."

"He was incredibly protective of it. Said if someone without any magical abilities touched it, it could kill them." Virion paused. "I think it's what hurt his daughter." He sighed. "That amulet, and the box you now have, became all Naevys wanted."

"Do you think she has the amulet now?" Kate asked.

"No. It's buried with Renault."

Kate sat forward. "Where?"

Virion shrugged. "Somewhere Naevys can't reach. I saw her walking the woods once, furious at him. Saying she should have taken it before he was buried."

Kate glanced at Venn. "Then why not just dig him up and take it?"

Virion gave a slight smile. "Renault wouldn't suffer to be merely buried in the ground. The man was far too arrogant for that. I'm sure he buried himself in one of his pocket worlds." He tapped his own box. "The one we just saw, if I were to guess. If he destroyed the entrance to it, he'd entomb himself inside with no way to reach him."

"That would explain some of Naevys's frustration," Venn said.

A frown creased Virion's brow. "You said Naevys had that box. If she'd finally gotten her hands on it, she'd never have given it up. How did you get it from her?"

"She left it in the woods," Venn said. "Faron found it."

"Impossible," he scoffed. "She'd never have left it anywhere vulnerable."

Venn gave Kate a troubled look. "Well, that's the story Faron told us, anyway."

Virion made a dissatisfied noise.

"Why did you say this was dangerous?" Kate asked. "For us? I know it's dangerous for those who are trapped inside it right now."

"Is it because people become obsessive about it?" Venn asked.

"I am not obsessive," Kate said.

Venn snorted. "You're a little obsessive."

"People absolutely become obsessive about it," Virion said. "It drives them to. Renault created it to be self-protecting. Whoever holds it wants to keep it safe. They feel something in it that calls to them with whatever they need most."

Kate shifted at the words.

"I would imagine, over the years, it's driven many men mad. But that's not the real danger. There is another aspect to the box. He used it to kill animals—and I think people sometimes. He called it the transference, and he labored for years to make it work."

"Transferring between life and death?" Kate asked.

"I never had him explain it to me, but that's the impression I got. It's the sort of idea he'd have treated as a puzzle instead of an abomination."

Kate considered the idea for a moment. "I've seen diagrams of his box, but never anything about that." She took a sip of her wine. "Do you know why Naevys protects that ravine south of Home?"

"She's there again?" Virion asked, his words sharp with worry.

"Right now we have no idea where she is. But she's protecting something there."

He nodded, his worry etched into lines on his face that looked well-used. "She has been for centuries."

"Do you know why?" Kate asked.

"No. But I've seen her there, watching it."

"Seen?" Venn asked.

Virion shifted, rubbing his hands together, suddenly awkward. "I...watch her sometimes. Make sure she's safe."

Kate glanced at Venn.

"How?" Venn asked. "Using the trees? Your connection with these is impressive."

He gave a self-effacing smile. "I've had a lot of time to shepherd them."

Virion's remnant still stretched out to the five maples that created his house. The trees themselves were shockingly vibrant. Their scents, the sounds of the leaves rustling against each other. Everything felt more immediate than regular trees. The feel of them suffused the air, strengthening around Virion.

Kate straightened, setting her wine to sloshing in her cup.

It wasn't strengthening around Virion—it was emanating out of him.

The vivid feel of the maples wasn't from the trees—it was from *him*. Kate took in the glitters of silver light around him. Everything in here was his remnant.

It so perfectly matched the trees themselves that she'd just assumed it was natural scents and smells—not that his remnant embodied a maple tree.

Her mind caught on the idea.

Virion's was by far the simplest remnant she'd found in an elf. It wasn't simplistic, though. The air was filled with the prickle of jagged leaves. The roughness of the bark scratched against her palms. The slightly sweet, mild, almost woodsy scent of fresh maple sap left the entire room smelling fresh.

But unlike other elven remnants that held disparate parts of the forest all in a single remnant, this one was exclusively maples.

Naevys's, by contrast, held the entire forest in its scope. Pines and wind and needles and sap and roots and creatures and a million growing things—along with a bright spot of maples that exactly matched Virion's.

"It's because of you," Kate said. "Naevys loves maples because of *you*."

He flinched and began to shake his head.

"Virion," Venn said, "help us. Maybe you can get through to her. She's turned away from everyone else."

Virion pushed himself out of his chair and moved to the table.

"I can't." His words were barely above a whisper. "You have no idea how agonizing it is to see her."

"Please, Virion." Kate stood. "She's going to destroy Home, and then maybe the White Wood."

"And then maybe the lakes," Venn said. "Evay was attacked by a *naiwyn* not far from here. One made by Naevys to keep anyone from leaving the area."

Virion kept his back toward them, standing perfectly still, his head bowed.

"Are you sure you won't come back with us?" Kate asked. "You have such a history with her that you could get her to remember who she is."

His forehead creased in confusion. "Remember who she is?"

Venn nodded. "When we saw her, she didn't remember Faron or Thallion or me. Her mind seems clouded."

"We had her own wellstone," Kate said, "and were going to use it to give her memories back, but Thallion took it from us."

"She doesn't even know Faron?"

"She desperately needs some help finding herself," Kate said. "If we find her, perhaps you could help with that."

Virion's eyes stayed locked on the pouch. He shook his head slowly. "She won't listen to me. I'm afraid I don't mean anything to her now. But..." He rubbed his fingers on the fabric before picking it up again. He held it out. "These are memories from happier times, when we had everything we wanted and all our dreams still felt possible."

Kate took it. "Thank you. Do you have any suggestions of where we should look for her?"

Virion sighed. "I can do better than that." He strode out the door, disappearing into the snow.

Venn sat for a moment in her chair, listening, and then stood. "The maples talk to him like...friends," she said in a low voice. "Until the end, when you said that Naevys loves maples because of him. Then they grew quiet for the first time since we got here." She looked up. "They say we should follow him. That he can find Naevys."

"At least someone can." Kate stood, setting the wellstone down next to her pack. She pulled on her cloak and followed Venn outside into a world of white. The edge of the lake, only steps from Virion's door, was nothing but a smooth, soft shelf of snow that disappeared within a dozen paces. The house itself was visible, and the nearest handful of trees, but those farther away quickly paled and disappeared.

Venn set her hand on the doorframe, then pointed to the left along the shore. "That way."

The moved through the silence for a dozen paces before Kate saw a dark shape settling into the branches of a massive maple tree. Its bare branches hung out over the ice of the lake, its trunk was wide as a dwarf, and its roots were gnarled with age.

Kate paused at the edge of the tree's canopy. Venn brushed

her fingers along one small branch, then drew it back quickly. "It's connected to...everything," she said in a low voice, "and it talks to him the way the house does."

"Is that normal? Are elves usually this close to trees they live near?"

Venn shook her head. "I've never heard trees talk like these." She barely touched a branch again, then frowned. "This will definitely take too long. He's searching everywhere. The lakes, the human forests, and the White Wood." She glanced up toward the sky, as though she could see the sun through the heavy snow. "We don't have an hour to waste."

Kate stared at her. "It'll take him that long?"

"At least. The area he's searching is huge."

"Could you do this?"

Venn let out a derisive snort. "I couldn't search a quarter of that area if I were given a whole day. But it doesn't matter how quickly he can do it. We should have left already."

"But he could find Naevys," Kate whispered. "Find her! We could get the rangers to go and actually deal with her instead of just waiting for her to attack Home again."

"I know," Venn said between her teeth. "But if he's not done in five minutes, I'm leaving."

"All right." Kate spent a moment gauging whether she could find her way back to Home on her own.

"And you're coming with me," Venn added.

Kate sighed. "Of course I am."

Virion sat in the branch his remnant flowing out from him and into the tree, stretching along its branches and trickling down its trunk.

A crash reverberated through the woods.

Kate and Venn both spun toward Virion's house.

Wood splintered and metal clanged.

Venn snapped a dart into her crossbow and ran for the house. Kate cast one last look at Virion, who hadn't moved from his perch, and raced after her.

More crashes rang out as they ran back to the doorway. Venn stopped on the threshold, aiming her crossbow inside.

The speckled grey and white back of a lynx sprang onto Virion's bed. Shimmers of a bronze remnant trailed behind it, along with the distant rumble of the ocean.

Kate stumbled to a stop. "Crofftus?"

Venn's crossbow faltered.

The lynx twitched and, without looking back, leapt smoothly out the window.

Venn hissed and ran across the room, bounding onto the bed and pointing her crossbow out the window. Kate stared at the empty opening where nothing moved but slowly drifting snowflakes. She dropped her gaze to the room. Virion's blankets were a tangled mess. Everything had been swept off the table. Mugs lay in puddles of wine. The carvings of trees had been flung across the floor. The cabinets were ripped open, branches dangling broken or lying on the floor. The door to Virion's closet was torn off its hinges, but the shelves inside were unharmed.

Kate took an unsteady step forward. "It was Crofftus?" The words felt foreign, as though she hadn't really said them.

Venn climbed off the bed. "It's just like Home."

"But...*why*?"

Venn moved over to lean back on the table, giving Kate a vaguely apologetic look. "This is Naevys's work."

A flare of anger rose up in Kate. "No. It's ridiculous to think he's working with her."

Venn took in the mess. "It doesn't feel so ridiculous right now."

Kate shook her head, even as the gesture felt childish. "But Venn, it's...Crofftus."

"Crofftus, who has avoided us a lot since talking to Naevys, has acted jumpy like he's hiding something, and who knew we were here, yet waited until we left with Virion to come in and ransack the place."

Kate sank down in her chair.

"Kate..." Venn waited until Kate met her gaze. "I don't need one of your story maps to put this puzzle together. Crofftus is working for Naevys."

The silence of the room wrapped around Kate for a long moment. "Why? Why would he do this?"

Venn leaned down and picked up one on Virion's carving. "What's missing?"

Kate found her own pack knocked over, her belongings dragged out onto the floor. She ran to it, dropping to her knees and scrambling through the blankets, books, and extra clothes until she caught sight of a metal edge of the aenigma box. She grabbed it and pulled it into her lap. Keeping the box close, she began to tuck the rest of her belongings back into her pack.

"Kate." Venn scanned the floor around her pack. "Where's Virion's wellstone?" She knelt next to Kate, and they searched the floor, but there was no pouch.

"Why take that?" Kate sank back on her knees. "Naevys already knows everything in it." She paused. "Do you think, if Crofftus is working for her, she can talk to him all the way here?"

Venn looked thoughtfully out the window where the lynx had gone. "Maybe. She's very connected to the animals of the woods. If that lynx was from the White Wood, I think she could speak to it. Enough that Crofftus could understand her, anyway." She rummaged through her own pack. "Nothing of mine is missing."

Kate tucked Bo's journal back into her pack, along with the three books from the merchant in Home and the books from Renault's library. Her hand paused. She shoved aside her blanket, but the last book was missing. Grabbing her pack, she dumped it out again. Her fingers tangled in the fabric of her clothes and bent the pages of Bo's journal as she shoved them aside.

"He took it!" A knot of panic tightened in her chest as she sorted through the mess again. "Venn! He took the book with the instructions for the bloodstone!"

CHAPTER THIRTY-THREE

Venn pushed aside the mess on the floor, but there was no black leather volume. "Did you copy it down somewhere else?"

"I was going to, but…" Kate sank back, the truth filling her chest with a cold shock. "We've barely had any time."

There was a rustle at Virion's door, and the elf stopped in the entrance, his mouth falling open.

"It was Naevys," Venn said, rising. "Rather, it was a lynx who is carrying the mind of a mage Naevys has convinced to work with her."

Kate squeezed her eyes shut.

"He took your wellstone," Venn said quietly.

Kate opened her eyes to see Virion's shoulders drop. "Well, I suppose we wanted to get it to her."

"Do you see anything else missing?" Venn asked.

"I have nothing anyone would want." Virion moved slowly toward the broken cabinets, scanning the room as he did. He peered into the gaps in the branches that used to be cupboard doors.

"I don't see anything else missing."

"He took a book explaining how to open the box without the amulet," Kate said, "so why didn't he take the box too?"

Virion began picking carved maple trees off the floor. "Maybe she doesn't want to open the box—maybe she just doesn't want you to."

"But why not? Using the bloodstone will destroy the pocket world, but I'm sure she knows that everything inside the box is mostly ruined already. She can't reuse it."

"True," Venn said. "But what other purpose would she have for the book?"

Kate began pushing her belongings back into her pack. "I have no idea. All it offered was a way for me to get my brothers out safely. An easy way. A way I could have done even back at the Stronghold—"

Two separate mysterious ideas suddenly fell together, and Kate felt the strange brightness of solving a puzzle. "The *naiwyn*..."

"What does the book have to do with those?" Venn asked.

"The book didn't just give me a solution. It gave me the chance to *leave*, and you with me. The *naiwyn* didn't appear until we wanted to leave. I'm not sure Naevys is keeping everyone from leaving. I think she's keeping *us* from leaving."

Venn shook her head. "But there's a *naiwyn* all the way out here. That can't be for us."

"If we hadn't seen the problems at Home and had kept finding the *naiwyn* blocking our path, wouldn't we have come this far?"

There was a moment of silence as Venn considered the idea. "Maybe. This feels like a stretch, though."

"I know, but in the Herald dream, she was coming for me. And in Renault's cave, she said, "Don't run," to us. I thought she was talking about that moment, but what if she wasn't? I have the box, but without that book, there's no way either one of us will leave."

"But..." Venn gave Kate a searching look. "What does she want us for?"

"You could ask her." Virion picked up his box and brushed it off. "She's in the woods south of Home." He looked at the two of them, his expression unnerved. "She's going to attack it. Right now, she's waiting for something to reach her. I could hear her talking to...something."

Kate stared at him. "Some*thing*?"

Virion picked up one of his carvings. He ran his finger along the cheek of Naevys's face, the motion broken. "Something."

Venn grabbed her pack. "How long do we have?"

Virion let out a breath. "She expects it at midday tomorrow."

Kate's stomach sank. "Midday... We can't get there by—"

Venn swore and started for the door. "Kate!"

Kate shoved the aenigma box back into her pack, her stomach dropping. She offered Virion an apologetic smile and gestured to his house. "Thank you, and sorry about all this."

"Kate!" Venn's voice snapped from outside. "Now!"

Kate's legs burned as she clambered up the last few feet before reaching the scratch of wagon wheels Venn had been calling "the north road" for the past couple of hours.

"This," Kate said, breathing heavily, pushing herself to match Venn's longer strides, "is not a road."

"It's road-like." Venn glanced up at the brighter patch of white in the sky where the sun must be. The heavy snowfall had tapered off, but the sky was still a solid mass of clouds. "And we should make better time now. If we walk until midnight, we can get a few hours' sleep before continuing tomorrow."

The exhaustion in Kate's body warred with the foreboding that nipped at her heels, and her mind turned back to the handful of ideas that had been churning through it since they'd left Virion's. Every single thought was irritating. There were too many questions, and nothing fit together.

It had been Crofftus in the lynx. There was no doubt. And yet, working for Naevys? The idea made no sense.

The obvious time he could have agreed to work with her was when they'd met in Renault's cave. But since then, he'd helped Kate make the solos potion. He'd helped collecting ingredients for the bloodstone. He'd been willing to go all the way back to the Keepers' Stronghold with her to help her further. None of that fit into him helping Naevys with whatever obsession she had with the ravine and now Home.

Then there were Virion's memories of Naevys and Renault. The relationship was still so odd. Nothing Kate ever learned made it less strange that Naevys had associated so closely with the half-elf. The image of the amulet flashed through Kate's mind, and she pushed away the illogical envy that rose. Instead, she focused on the one comment of Virion's that she couldn't quite shake.

If Naevys had sought the box for centuries, why, once she had it, did she just abandon it in the woods?

The question caused an uneasy prickle to crawl across Kate's neck that left her looking over her shoulder.

The one thing she'd been sure of since she'd reached the White Wood was that she didn't understand the whole story here.

Somehow, the fact that Naevys had abandoned the box drove that sensation home in a way that bordered on terrifying.

Kate's pack pressed against her back, leaving her sweaty despite the cold snow. She could almost feel the box sitting there. It was just near the top. She could reach it by just flipping open the flap and—

A flicker of annoyance at herself stopped the thought. *It's got hold of you too?* Virion's question prodded at her mind, shifting almost to a taunt. It was somehow insulting how deeply the box had anchored itself into her. Yes, it seemed to have done the same with anyone who possessed it, but it felt like she should be different. She wasn't some ancient Kalesh monk who'd secreted it away in a monastery. She could open its drawers. She could understand the magic that animated it. Could imagine how Renault had created it. Understand the time involved, the study, the massive amounts of *vitalle* required.

She could read the runes carved into the top—

Shaking her head, she tried to dislodge the image of the box from her mind, focusing instead on the snowy not-quite-a-road winding through the forest in front of her, pushing away Virion's words.

It didn't have hold of her. It was reasonable to feel protective of the box. Her brothers were in it. Until they were out, it made perfect sense to want to keep it close.

"Crofftus or Naevys?" Venn's words broke the silence.

Kate blinked and focused on her. "What?"

"You've been silent for hours. Which are you obsessing about? Crofftus or Naevys?"

Kate paused.

Venn raised an eyebrow. "No... Not the box again."

"I'm not obsessing."

"You are obsessing. When you think about something constantly and can't let it out of your grasp, that is obsessing."

A rush of possessiveness rose at Venn's words. "I don't want to talk about the box." Kate's words more waspish than she'd intended.

Venn gave her a gauging look but nodded. "Then ask one of the dozens of other questions you have swirling around in your brain. We're not stopping long enough for you to write them all out."

Kate shuffled through the mess of unanswered questions in her mind. "How could Naevys have gotten hold of Crofftus?"

"Because she's good at it." Venn pulled two berry cakes out of her pack and handed one to Kate. "When I first met her, she was renowned for getting people to work together. She always knew what they really wanted."

Kate took a bite. Even cold it was delicious. "So you think she still has that skill, but now uses it to manipulate others into helping her? What would she use Crofftus for?"

"He'd make an excellent spy. Except around you."

"He wasn't spying at Virion's," Kate pointed out.

"Not at the end."

Kate paused in her chewing. "You think he was listening before he ransacked the house?"

"Would you have heard his remnant if he'd stayed outside?"

"No. Virion's was too strong."

Venn kept walking, her shoulders tense. There was an air of guilt around her. Presumably at knowing she wouldn't reach Home as quickly as she should.

A rope of Kate's own guilt wrapped around her at the thought. It was her fault they'd gone to Virion's. Her fault they'd pushed on even when the snow had slowed them, and her fault they'd stayed.

Kate fought off the urge to rationalize it away. To point out that Virion had revealed interesting things. Instead, she focused on Venn's guilt. On the familiarity of it.

A wall of resistance wrapped around her. Excuses justifying herself sprang up. Bo and Evan's faces. She pushed them all away. The truth was, she'd put Venn in this position. "I'm sorry, Venn. I know the box gets in my head sometimes. I can't shake the feeling that if I just had the time, I could get Bo and Evan out. The thought gets…consuming."

Venn gave Kate's pack a gauging look. "I don't know if it's the life debt or the box, but it gets into my head too. Not as much as yours, but I think it affects everyone near it."

The glimmer of hope the box always held called to Kate, but she pushed it away.

"I'll be glad when we can get your brothers out and get rid of it."

A vague discomfort itched between Kate's shoulder blades. Once Bo and Evan were out, she'd… She didn't know what she'd do, but getting rid of the box didn't seem like the answer.

That was a decision for a much later time. "How close do we have to be before we can send a message to Faron or the rangers?"

"Through all these human woods? Pretty close."

Kate sighed. "That's what I was afraid of."

Warm midday sun streamed down onto Kate's head the next day, and she shrugged the rest of the way out of her cloak. Her entire body ached with exhaustion, and her breath clouded in front of her, even as sweat dripped down her back. "Please tell me we're almost there."

A wide valley spread around them, the snow dotted with lines of crops that had been cut close to the ground during harvest. The few hours' sleep under a larch last night had left a crick in Kate's neck and a tightness in her shoulder blades. The wind came in gusts and fits, chilling the dampness on her neck.

"On the far side of that hill." Venn's steps were unflaggingly quick, as they had been since yesterday afternoon when they'd begun this endless journey.

Kate took in the pristinely blue sky. "I don't see smoke from any chimneys."

"I'm hoping that's because it's windy." Venn angled to the side of the hill where a thin trail was visible through the trees. They hurried along the path that had been sorely neglected, fighting through crusty clumps of ankle-deep snow.

They rounded a corner, and the sounds of distant shouts wafted past.

Venn broke into a run. A surge of fear pushed energy into Kate's tired legs, and she followed.

The path spilled out at the edge of one of the fields on the western side of Home, and a cacophony of shouts and clangs filled the air. Smoke billowed out of a building to the south, the wind keeping it rolling along the ground instead of rising.

Inside it, something moved.

The smoke shifted, revealing a black-limbed *naiwyn*. It strode into the street like a massive, burning pine, seething with red fire.

CHAPTER THIRTY-FOUR

Venn swore and sprinted toward the town.

"A *naiwyn*?" Kate's mind scrambled to find any sort of defense against the tree sprite as she ran after Venn.

In the first street, she saw a woman rushing her children into a root cellar. "The elves are attacking!" she shouted at Kate before slamming the door closed behind them.

A flash of motion from the nearest house made Kate spin. The grey hind legs of an animal, short but fast, disappeared around the corner. She cast out after it, and the low, thickset shape of a badger slipped away along the building. Kate stared after it before the shouts and clashes of weapons echoing through the buildings set her racing after Venn again.

She skidded to a stop at the edge of the square. Elven rangers were spread out, fending off the humans who were attacking them with unbridled fury.

A man shouldered past her, holding a heavy hammer. "The trees and the animals and the elves are attacking!" he shouted. "Run!"

"The elves are here to help!" Venn ran toward a group of men attacking an elf.

Nearly a dozen other battles raged. The elves, travel-stained and weary, held off the humans, but they were sorely outnumbered.

Venn grabbed Kate's arm, her face draining of color. She lifted her other hand toward the pine in the center of the square.

Every needle on the massive tree was brown. The branches had shriveled. The trunk itself had withered into a thin husk.

"No," Kate breathed.

Shouts and clangs of weapons dragged their attention back to the fighting, and Venn ran for the nearest townsfolk attacking an elf.

Kate started toward another group. She didn't recognize any of the men. The elf gave up ground, not attacking them but holding off their attacks. "Stop!" she yelled.

The badger slipped out of a narrow alley close to her, its black eyes fixed on a child no older than four who cowered in the shadow of stairs leading into one of the larger houses. His face was streaked with tears, and he gaped through the open back of the steps at three men grappling with an elf.

Kate veered toward the creature. It froze, watching her, coiled to attack. She planted herself between it and the child, her back close to the steps. "Can you get inside?" she shouted over her shoulder.

The child curled up tighter.

The badger moved doggedly closer. Its body was close to the ground, but its claws—each almost as long as her fingers—scraped on the cobblestones. When it was only a couple of paces away, Kate drew some *vitalle* into her hand and reached forward. "Come here," she said, keeping her voice low, trying not to let it waver. "A little closer. Just let me touch you. We'll put you right to sleep."

It hissed and snarled, revealing viciously sharp teeth.

Another badger ran out of the same alley and lunged for the leg of the nearest man, sinking its teeth into his calf. He cried out and twisted. The badger dug its claws into him, scrambling up his leg to bite at his arm.

Kate pulled her attention back to the badger creeping closer to her. "Maybe no touching." She took the *vitalle* and stretched it out toward the badger, pulling the fiery glitters of her remnant with it until they brushed up against the creature's head. Her heart was pounding, and she blocked the chaos and shouts of the square out, focusing on the animal's mind. "*Paxa*," she whispered, pushing the *vitalle* into it.

The badger paused, and its snarl faded.

Kate funneled more *vitalle* out of her arm. "*Dormio*."

The badger faltered, then its eyes closed, its legs collapsed, and it sank onto the cobblestones. She stepped forward and set her hand on the fur of its grey-striped head. It felt coarse against her skin, and she funneled more *vitalle* into it, pushing its mind deep into sleep before turning back to the child. "Come on. Let's get you inside somewhere."

He didn't move. Kate glanced around the square, but the fighting wasn't lessening. Venn had untangled one skirmish between humans and an elf and had run to the next. But some of the fighting wasn't with elves. Two foxes attacked a young man near the entrance of the Blind Pig. A bobcat swiped at another. Small white-furred weasels shot through the chaos, biting and clawing at anyone they found. On the far side, a black bear charged a man who held an empty bow. Kate shouted, as though she could help, reaching out toward him.

Just before the bear hit, an elf barreled into the side of it, sending the bear and himself crashing into the wall of the nearest house. Kate caught sight of dark red hair before she saw Faron's face. He shoved his hands onto the bear's neck, and his lips moved in furious words. The bear slumped down, limp.

Kate dragged her attention back to the child. She squatted down and reached for him. When he didn't move, she grabbed his arm and pulled him out. He moved numbly, and she picked him up, searching for anywhere to take him. The door of the next house opened, and a woman motioned frantically. Kate hurried up the stairs to press him into her arms.

The woman's face was tear-streaked, and her hands shook.

"Keep the door closed," Kate said. "Bar it if you can." She spun back to the square as the door latched behind her.

Slowly, the humans were disengaging with the elves and turning their attention exclusively to the animals. There was one knot of fighting still, to the right, and Kate was about to start for it when she caught sight of a black dwarven beard backed up against a shop across the square. The chaos parted enough for her to see Tribal holding his axe ready, facing the muscled golden form of a mountain lion. Behind him, motionless on the ground, lay Silas.

The mountain lion stalked closer.

Kate was searching for a way to get to them when she caught sight of Venn's red hair only a dozen paces from the brothers.

"Venn!" she shouted. The elf stayed embroiled in a shouting match with several humans.

Kate cast out, shoving her remnant into the wave. "Venn!" She pushed the word through too.

Venn's head snapped up, and Kate flung a finger toward the dwarves. Venn ran toward them, and Kate's attention snagged on the sight of the slender threads stretching out from Venn in all directions. They weren't visible exactly. Or rather, they were in the way a ripple of heat is visible. More of an impression than a thing in itself.

The threads ran to the elf nearest her, to one over a dozen

paces who was cornering a mangy, slender prairie wolf. Connections ran to every elf in the square. Some led out of the square to places Kate couldn't see.

She froze for a moment, shocked that she'd never seen these before, until the reason struck her. These were lake elves. These were Venn's community. The ones she was intrinsically bound to.

Venn shoved her way toward the dwarves. The web followed her, unaffected by the chaos around her.

The complexity of the elven connections was staggering. Kate had known Venn was connected to them all, but seeing it like this…

She jumped off the stairs and ran toward the dwarves.

Another vibrant bond stretched across the square to the mouth of an alley, where two small figures lingered in the shadows of a building. Their matching golden hair and slim builds made her stomach drop.

"Venn!" She shoved the word forward again. Venn spun, and Kate jabbed another finger toward Aislin and Matlen.

Venn flung up her hands as though she could push the elf twins back. "Get away!" Her words were tinged with desperation, and they came through the commotion as though Kate stood next to her. "You were commanded!" Venn's voice filled with fear. "Get back!"

From only paces in front of Tribal, the mountain lion lunged.

Aislin and Matlen disappeared from the alley and reappeared next to the huge cat, crashing into it and knocking it to the side.

Venn broke into a flat run.

A fracture cracked through the air.

Every elf in the square flinched.

Faron spun from the foxes, searching.

Venn let out a cry, raw and broken, as the connection between her and the elf twins splintered.

Kate staggered forward at the vast emptiness that opened up in its place.

Faron appeared next to the mountain lion as it tried to scramble to its feet. He slammed his hands down onto it just as a dart from Venn sank into its haunch.

The creature collapsed.

Tribal threw his axe aside and grabbed Aislin, pulling her up. "What were you thinking?" His face was furious as he grabbed Matlen's arm and dragged him off the huge cat. "You're supposed to be somewhere safe!"

Kate sprinted toward them. The fighting had dwindled away to a few spots along the edge of the square where the last of the animals were being subdued. She jumped over the body of a small bobcat and reached the others just as Aislin wavered on her feet.

Venn stood staring at the elf twins, her hands reaching for them, shaking. "No, no, no, no, no…"

Matlen knelt on the ground, his head hanging forward, his hair covering his face.

Aislin's face was bone white.

Kate reached Venn, who trembled with terror and grief. The link between Venn and the other elves glimmered like a crystal spider web, but the air around the elf twins was unnaturally cold and empty.

"Are you hurt?" Tribal shouted, giving Aislin's shoulder a shake. "What kind of bone-headed move was that? You weigh less than one of its paws!"

Aislin let out a breath that was almost a sob and turned her terrified eyes on her brother.

Kate set her hand on Tribal's arm. "Stop."

The dwarf's face was drawn with fear. "What's happening? What's wrong with them?"

"They were commanded to stay away from here," Kate said quietly to him. "To stay away from you."

He scowled at the words for a moment before they sank in. He hurled a furious glare at Faron.

Kate tightened her grip. "Not by Faron—by their parents and the elders of the lake."

Faron let out a long, pained breath. "Which means they're now cut off from their parents and the entire community at the lakes."

"Aislin," Venn whispered, the word coming out broken. "Why?"

Tribal set a finger under her chin, raising her face to look at him. "What did you do?"

Her shoulders were drawn in, her eyes brimming with tears. She stood thin and vulnerable as though the emptiness was crushing her. "We couldn't let it get you," she whispered.

Faron set a hand on Matlen's back, his face drawn.

Venn grabbed Aislin, clasping the young elf to her chest. "You stupid, stupid, girl," she said into Aislin's hair. "You stupid, brave, *stupid* girl."

CHAPTER THIRTY-FIVE

Shouts came from down a nearby street, and Kate grabbed Venn's arm. "The *naiwyn*," she said.

Venn's face was creased with pain, but she pushed Aislin toward Tribal. "Get them inside. Keep them safe."

Aislin fell against the dwarf, burying her face in his shoulder, and he patted her on the back. "C'mon, trouble. You're freezing. Inside, like your aunt says." He wrapped his huge hands around her upper arms and pushed her upright. "You and your brother need to walk on yer own. Silas is gonna need a bit of help."

Silas groaned and rolled over.

"*Naiwyn*?" Faron asked. "How many?"

Kate glanced toward the withered pine, and Faron let out a gasp.

"We saw it down near the blacksmith's." Kate began running back across the square.

"Make sure there aren't any more," Venn called to Faron as she followed Kate.

In the street leading to the smithy, a crowd of townspeople were huddled together, blocking the way.

"Get back!" Kate pushed through them. "Don't go anywhere near that! Let the elves deal with it!"

The people backed away, their eyes following Venn with suspicion. Kate broke free of them. A few blocks ahead, the roof of the blacksmith's forge where she'd sat when the bears had attacked was engulfed in flame, pouring black smoke into the clear sky. Three men stood at the end of the street, facing the roiling red fire of the *naiwyn*. Two held swords while the third held a massive hammer.

One of the men hacked his sword at a root of the tree. It sank in, but the *naiwyn* showed no sign of noticing. It swung a branch at them, and the two swordsmen scrambled back. The other stepped smoothly out of the way and swung his hammer with a wide arc, catching the branch and slamming it down into the ground.

"Merrick!" Kate shouted. "Get back!"

He held his ground, and the two swordsmen struggled back up next to him, slashing out with strikes that were clumsy and mostly ineffective.

Kate ran toward them as the *naiwyn* crashed a branch against one of the thick posts holding up the roof of the smithy. The wood splintered and burst into flame.

"Get away from my forge!" Merrick picked up a heavy metal rod and hurled it at the sprite. It slammed into the trunk, and the *naiwyn* staggered back. The face on its trunk snarled in fury, and a half-dozen branches shot forward.

The three men dove out of the way as the branches crashed down.

Kate raced toward them, throwing out a shield that spread over all three. She slammed to her knees, shoving out every bit of remnant she could muster. The *vitalle* raced out of her palms in a fiery rush. Venn's hand clapped down on her shoulder, and her green remnant surged forward into the shield, mixing with Kate's fiery red.

The branches of the *naiwyn* slammed into the barrier like a battering ram but stopped, sliding away.

Kate stared through the shield at it, catching a discordant shimmer of icy blue laced in with the flaming red.

"I thought these things guarded something!" Kate yelled, grabbing the blacksmith's thick forearm. Merrick glanced up at her, and his eyes widened.

"They do!" Venn pulled one of the humans back. He spun in outrage, raising his sword again.

"Stop!" Kate shouted. "The elves aren't your enemies! They're here to help."

The man hesitated but didn't relax.

"Nolen," Merrick growled. "Look who it is. Listen to her!"

The other man took Venn's offered hand and scrambled back toward safety.

Merrick shoved himself to his feet, then pushed Kate behind himself, blocking her view of the *naiwyn*.

"This *naiwyn* isn't guarding! It's attacking!" Kate tried to step around him, but the man moved stubbornly in front of her again.

"Merrick," Venn said. "You won't be able to hurt it. Get back!" She ran to the other man, who was struggling to rise, and hauled his arm over her shoulders, pulling him down the street.

"I'm not letting it get any closer," Merrick said, picking back up his hammer and planting his feet.

"Maybe it won't!" Kate grasped his arm again. "Maybe it's guarding an exit from town. Get back!"

"It's destroying my forge!" He pulled his arm out of her grasp.

She set her hand on his arm. "Merrick, please back away. Just a little. I don't think it will follow."

He looked over his shoulder at her, anger warring with something else. Along the side of his neck was a long, thin burn.

"Please."

"Fine." He held his arm out, keeping her behind him as he slowly backed away.

She pushed at it, even as he corralled her backward. "What are you doing?"

"Just because you can shield us from that thing doesn't mean I'm going to let it get close to you."

Kate huffed out an irritated breath. "You have no weapons that can hurt it."

"Heavy enough iron pushes it back."

"And makes it angry."

He kept his eyes fixed on the *naiwyn*, which stayed by the forge, watching them. "Do you have a better weapon?"

"No one does," Venn said from just behind them. "Keep moving back."

Faron appeared next to her with a burst of *vitalle*. "Venn! Get out of here!"

"Me?" she snapped. "You get as far from that thing as you can!"

"Why don't we *all* back away?" Kate said.

The *naiwyn* still stood at the end of the road, blocking the way out to the fields and the forest beyond. It swayed slightly, its face curled in vicious determination.

"Venn," Kate said slowly. "I keep seeing an icy-blue remnant. This one had it, just a trace over its own. But the naiwyn we found in the south had it too."

Venn frowned. "Who's icy blue?"

"No one I've met yet."

Faron paused, considering the tree sprite. "I don't know who the blue remnant belongs to, but my mother had to be involved in making that. Maybe I can get through to it."

Venn spun and set her hand on his chest. "No. Naevys doesn't recognize anyone, including you—how could that thing?"

He glared down at her. "It could recognize me because I'm the king!"

"Not of *this* forest." Venn pushed him.

Three rangers appeared in the street behind Faron. "There are no other *naiwyn*," one reported.

"Then stand here and watch this one," Faron snapped, glaring at Venn. "What happened here?"

She opened her mouth but didn't speak.

"The tree started attacking," Merrick said, finally turning away from the *naiwyn*. "Then the elves joined in. By the time the warning bells were ringing, there were fights all over town. Then the animals started streaming in."

"Venn," Faron said, "I thought you explained to them—"

"We weren't here," Venn said with a hollow look.

"What?" he demanded.

"I asked her to take me to Virion," Kate said, before Venn could answer. "It's my fault. It took longer than we expected, and by the time we got here…"

The faces of the elves around them hardened.

Faron stared between the two of them. "You…" he said to Venn, a pained look in his eyes. "You accepted the role of emissary." His voice dropped. "I know you have other…obligations, but I thought we could count on you to…" He pressed his lips closed and shook his head. "Never mind. The life debt obviously trumps everything else."

"I…" Venn stopped, her face pale.

Noises filtered down the street from the square. Cries of pain, calls for assistance. The guilt rolled over Kate again as she thought of all the things that would have been avoided if they'd skipped Virion's and come straight here. The people and the elves could have been introduced. They could have faced the attack together. Injuries might not have happened. Lives could have been spared.

"It's my fault," Kate said. "Not hers. While we were at Virion's, Naevys sent"—she swallowed—"a lynx to attack his house, and we ended up staying too long." She made herself hold Faron's gaze. "Virion did say that Naevys is waiting for something that's supposed to arrive now, and she's in the woods south of Home."

Faron shifted his glare to her. "Anything more specific than 'south of Home?'"

Kate shook her head. "Can your rangers find her?"

Faron gritted his teeth and made a signal to one of the elves next to him. The ranger disappeared.

"And don't forget there are more *naiwyn* around," Venn said, her voice apologetic. "So be careful."

Faron raised one of his fists in front of his mouth, as though trying to bite back words. When he spoke, his voice was polite but strained. "Please stay here and smooth things over between the elves and the humans."

"Faron." Venn reached out toward him. "I'm sorry."

Ayen appeared at Faron's shoulder, and the king turned his back on Venn. "Let's go."

Faron and Ayen disappeared, while the other rangers moved closer to the *naiwyn*, taking up positions like sentries.

Venn swore under her breath.

Kate rubbed her hand over her face. "I'm sorry, Venn."

"Keeper Kate," Merrick said, stepping between her and the *naiwyn* again. "Can we move farther away from the fiery tree?"

"I'm fine," Kate assured him.

"I'm sure," he said blithely. "To the square, then?"

She crossed her arms. "Why?"

"I don't know how you just shielded me from the fire tree, but

I need to get back to the square, and I'm hardly going to walk away and leave you this close to that thing."

Venn let out a huff of laughter. "Looks like you found a bodyguard."

"I don't *need* a bodyguard."

Merrick didn't budge.

Kate narrowed her eyes. "All right, Merrick. You seem capable. Let's make a deal. When there's actual physical danger around, I'll do what you ask. But when there's magical danger, you will do whatever I ask."

He considered the offer. "I can live with that." He jabbed his thumb over his shoulder. "That's clearly a physical danger."

Kate took in the massive tree-shaped burning sprite. "Nice try."

He gave her his easy smile, even though his hand stayed curled on his hammer. "Were you headed somewhere besides the square?"

Kate let out a breath. "No." She caught up with Venn. Merrick's heavy steps followed them.

A bit of a smile played on Venn's lips.

Kate shook her head. "Shut up."

In the square, the humans were clustered in groups, tending to wounds or piling animals into wagons. Nearly every elf must have left to search for Naevys or join the guard at the perimeter of the town, because only two were still there, helping keep the surviving animals unconscious. Merrick strode toward the men trying to heave the unconscious mountain lion onto a cart.

"This doesn't make sense," Kate said quietly. "It's just another senseless attack. What does Naevys gain from hurting a few people? Half these animals were killed, more of them injured. What's the point of any of this?"

Venn took in the square, her gaze stopping on the massive pine.

Kate cast out. The people and animals lit up, but the tree itself towered up, taller than any of the buildings—and holding not a single spark of *vitalle*.

Venn walked under his desiccated branches and sank against his trunk. "What is happening, Kate?" she asked quietly. "Tell me you can piece some of this mess together."

"I wish I could."

From the direction of the forge, wood splintered and a puff of smoke rose up into the air. Townsfolk with buckets crept toward the fire, keeping to the streets the *naiwyn* wasn't in.

The mountain lion was lifted into the cart, which was then trundled toward the still forms of the foxes.

Venn studied the square, her jaw set in anger. "When is Naevys going to stop doing pointless, violent things?"

The details of the strange attack spun in Kate's mind, but she could see no reason for it. Beneath her feet, she caught a glimmer of Naevys's gold, and she knelt. "Venn, there's a bit of her remnant here along the roots." She set her hand on it and cast out. In the pine's roots, the faintest hint of *vitalle* lingered.

A narrow thread connected Venn to the old pine, thinner than any Kate had seen and dwindling even as she watched. "Venn!" She held out her hand, and Venn took it.

The feel of the tree, as faint as a dying echo, rolled past Kate, but along with it, a surge of Naevys's remnant.

An image slammed into Kate's mind. Venn flinched beside her. It was nothing but blurs of motion for a heartbeat until it coalesced into a single figure.

Standing in the center of the Blind Pig's common room—surrounded by people who were diving for safety—stood the dark, looming form of Naevys.

PART III

THE TRUTH

There's something a little bit satisfying that the explanation to every tragedy, every terror, every trouble that circled Home and the White Wood was found through research.

I'm not sure how I forgot the fact that much of the pain in the world is caused by someone who is in pain themselves.

Even those closest to Naevys didn't know the truth. Didn't know the depth of what she was suffering and fighting for.

Maybe, if there had been fewer secrets, there would have been less pain.

CHAPTER THIRTY-SIX

The door of the tavern burst open, and people streamed out.

"Elf!" a woman screamed, stumbling into the square.

Kate broke into a run toward the inn, Venn at her side. A dozen people raced out of the tavern before the door slammed shut. Venn reached it first, cracking it open and peering into the darkness.

Heavy footsteps pounded up behind them, and Merrick crowded close, looking over Kate's head.

Venn slipped inside.

"This is definitely magical," Kate whispered to him, shimmying in through the narrow gap. "Stay back."

Instead of seeing the common room of the tavern, she entered a small space, no larger than a closet, blocked off ahead and to each side with a wall of branches and pine needles that seemed to have sprung out of the floor itself.

All around them, voices cried out in fear and crashes shook the floor.

Every branch glittered with Naevys's golden remnant.

Kate cast out. The wall of branches lit up in front of them, each one originating from a knot in the wood of the floor. The walls on either side of them continued to the far side where Yellow's bar stood, completely blocking off both ends of the tavern. To the left, crowded back against the wall, at least twenty people huddled together while several more shoved tables over to form a barrier between themselves and the unnatural branches. To the right, people were pressed up against the bright *vitalle* of the fireplace or streaming up the stairs toward the sleeping quarters. Two men hammered at one of the windows, trying to break out the boards covering them.

Straight ahead, past the barrier of branches, Kate's wave rolled over the blazing form of Naevys moving toward the bar. It *was* Naevys, but she was too tall and too bright.

Her remnant filled the inn, pulling in the vastness of the entire forest. The breeze threaded through the branches, combing through needles. Roots dug and spread and spoke with each other. Creatures scurried in hidden trails.

And there were maples—Virion's toothed, fluttering leaves. The clean scent of sap. The reds and golds and vibrant greens.

Before Kate's wave faded, she caught sight of more branches growing closer to the people trapped in the ends of the tavern. They rose out of knots in the wood of tables and benches. More grew out of the floor itself. Some even sprouted from the thick shelf of the mantel.

Venn took hold of two branches barring the way to Naevys and closed her eyes. Slowly, the pine boughs began to lean away from each other.

"Merrick!" Kate grabbed two limbs blocking off the left-hand side. She pulled *vitalle* out of them, drawing the warmth into her hands. The pine needles browned, and the branches withered. "Here's something your hammer can do. Break through this and get those people out of here!" She pushed him toward the brittle branches as she ran to the right side. She heard his hammer crack into them as she drained the life from branches blocking the way toward the fireplace.

"Kate..." Venn stared through a thin gap in the wall.

Naevys towered above the bar. Her auburn hair flowed around her as though lifted by a breeze. Her hands were clenched at her sides, and her flowing mantle of mottled greens and browns fluttered around her, but her feet hovered nearly at the level of the tabletops.

Behind the bar, Yellow stood backed against the wall, a large cleaver in his hand.

An indrawn breath behind Kate made her flinch. Merrick stood at her shoulder, staring. "You're not going in *there*?" he whispered incredulously.

"Don't you even *think* about following." Kate pushed him toward the side. "Someone needs to get those people out." She gestured with a thumb toward the common room. "Promise me no one comes in here. Including you."

He grimaced.

"You swore to do what I asked."

He let out a growl. "Fine. But I don't like it."

"Noted."

Venn turned sideways and slipped through the branches. Kate followed, a spray of pine needles scraping against her neck as she shouldered through into a sea of Naevys's remnant.

The Warden moved closer to the bar, revealing the churning mass of vines holding her up. "You," she hissed at Yellow. "You stole it from me!"

The innkeeper's eyes dropped to Venn and Kate. "Get out of here," he shouted, gripping the cleaver tighter.

"Naevys!" Kate called.

The queen's vines stretched out, wrapping around stools and tossing them out of her way.

"Naevys!" Venn moved to the right. "What is it you want?"

"He stole it." The furious words echoed off the wall of branches.

"Yellow?" Kate called. "Are you hurt?" She stepped carefully forward next to Venn until she could see Naevys's face.

A rich copper sheen glowed from Naevys's skin. The gauntness that had filled it in the Elder Grove had been replaced with a power that radiated almost as brightly as her remnant.

"Kate?" Yellow said in a strangled voice. "I have no idea what she's talking about."

"Move toward the kitchen," Kate said as they continued to circle the Warden. They reached the bar, and Venn held out her arm toward Naevys, a dart loaded in her crossbow.

"There's no way a dart is going to put *her* to sleep," Kate whispered.

"I know. How many do you think it will take?"

Kate gave her an incredulous look and cast out. Her and Venn's forms lit up like little bundles of *vitalle*. Yellow's was slightly dimmer. The new walls of pine branches around them glowed warmly. But when the wave hit Naevys, light exploded as though the sun itself had burst into the tavern.

Venn lowered her arm. "Naevys!" she shouted. "Just tell us what you want. There's no need to hurt any more people. Or any more elves."

One of Naevys's vines yanked up a stool and hurled it at Venn.

Venn dove to the side, pushing Kate back, and the stool smashed against the bar where they'd stood. A splintered leg rammed into Kate's shoulder while most of the wood crashed down onto Venn.

"We need a better way to talk to her," Venn said between clenched teeth.

Kate pushed herself to her knees, and Venn did the same.

Naevys's vines carried her up to the bar. "Give me the entrance!" Her voice cut through the air with a command so heavy that Kate staggered back.

Yellow froze with one foot outstretched toward the kitchen door. "What entrance?"

"I have an idea," Kate said to Venn. "Naevys can sense what's in people's minds when she touches them, right?" At Venn's wince, Kate added, "And remember how I connected with Faron when we were in the boat?"

Venn's wince turned incredulous. "Remember how that went?"

Kate grimaced. "I do, but he could sense me. I think I can make Naevys sense me too." They crawled toward Naevys, and Kate stretched her fingers out, pushing her remnant toward the massive cloud of gold surrounding the Warden. Venn grabbed her arm, and the elf's green lights surged out with Kate's red. A hint of icy blue glittered on the surface of Naevys's gold.

Their joint remnant flowed into Naevys's, and Kate shouted, "Touch her!"

Venn shot out a hand and grasped the queen's ankle, and Kate cast out.

The web of connections surrounding the queen was breathtaking, reaching out in so many directions that it was like she existed inside a hazy mist. Kate grabbed for a strand that passed near her.

The tavern faded away and the world unfurled into a vast storm, raging through an endless forest. Kate tumbled along unseen currents, crashing into branches and scraping along the ground, of no more significance than a pine needle. Venn's grip tightened on her arm.

The storm seethed with fierce emotions. Fingers of envy dug into her, tearing bits of her away. A ruthless possessiveness coated every gust of wind and formed the backbone of every tree she careened past. A biting fury cut through the forest.

And every tendril of wind, every tree, every mote of dust was drowning in a desperate, driving need.

Kate gasped, clinging to the sense of Venn, trying to somehow right herself, find a place to stand amidst the turmoil.

"Naevys!" Kate shouted. "Stop!" But in the midst of the chaos, it was all she could do to hold on to herself. She had no focus left for getting Naevys's attention, and the words were swept away.

Then there was something else. Some*one* else.

Winding through the forest—but not a part of it—slid a sharp, unrelenting hunger. It was coated with lazy contempt and reveled in a well of power. Unlike the forest, the other soul fixed its attention on Kate.

A cold, calculated pressure wrapped around her, and an image slammed into her mind. Endless winter sky. Forests rippling over hills, crowding up against the unyielding spine of the mountains. Tiny homes filled a gap in the trees far below.

Little mage. The voice licked over Kate's mind with a hunger that drained away her warmth and left her shaking in the fathomless heavens.

She scrambled away and was in the forest again, buffeted by Naevys's desperation. Images flashed by.

A trail in the forest.
A crumbling stone archway between trees.
The yellow door, standing between two trunks.
Renault's workshop. The tables strewn with books and bits of woodwork. Potions simmering.
A net of light.
The buried carriage, glowing like a beacon.

A man striding across the workshop. His beard close cut and shaped to a cold point. His face etched with the haggard lines of obsession, his eyes glittering with it.

On his neck, a stonesteel amulet holding a vial of scarlet liquid.

The edges of Kate's vision blurred. The images jostled against the chaos of the forest. The biting hunger brushed past her, dragging nails along her mind, scraping it away.

The turmoil pulled at her, but she focused on the sensation. Wreathed inside of it was the sharp tang of fear and a prodding wedge of something familiar.

Kate! Venn's voice wove through the maelstrom. *This is not working!* The words were fraught with panic, but the tone was so familiar that something almost like laughter escaped Kate's lips. She grabbed for Venn and felt her presence like an anchor.

Kate dragged her mind away from the images and the swirl of emotions and focused on drawing in a breath. A real, physical breath. The edges of her mind were in tatters, fraying from the pull of Naevys and the other...thing.

Her fingertips burned, and she opened her eyes to see her remnant streaming with Venn's into Naevys.

Kate clenched her hand, cutting off the flow, and the tangible feel of the tavern crashed in around her.

She knelt on the floor, slumped against the leg of a table. Venn was on her knees beside her, her head hanging forward, her hand clamped onto Kate's arm.

"Venn?" Kate whispered. "She wants the door!"

The elf groaned and lifted her head.

"I will have it!" Naevys thundered, her voice vibrating the floor beneath Kate's knees. The Warden lunged forward, the vines holding her up slithering over each other and stretching up until she loomed over the bar. She stabbed her hands forward, her fingers curled like claws. Vines streaked out from beneath her, hurtling toward the wall behind the bar.

Yellow dove for the kitchen door.

The vines scrabbled against the sides of the yellow door mounted on the wall. Naevys twisted her hands, and tendrils wriggled behind it. She clenched her fingers shut, and the vines tore the door off the wall with a rending crack of wood. Plaster and splinters rained down from gaping holes in the wall. The vines pulled the door away, lifting it easily down to Naevys.

She brushed her hand over the faded, peeling yellow paint. A flicker of light danced along her fingertips, and she drew in a deep, exultant breath.

Letting her hand fall, she turned smoothly on the tangle of vines beneath her feet. The hunger in her face softened to something pleased. Her eyes fell on Kate and Venn, and she paused.

A small chickadee darted in between the branches and toward Kate. Crofftus's thundering remnant poured in with it.

Katria! Andovenn! Stay away from—

"Ah…" Naevys flicked her fingers and a vine lashed out, and a cage of her gold remnant burst into light around the bird.

Don't—

The cage slammed shut, and Crofftus's remnant and voice cut off abruptly.

"Crofftus!" Kate stabbed a knife of her runelight at the cage.

Naevys smoothly twisted it out of the way and pulled Crofftus close to her cold face. "I still have need of you."

Kate stretched out her hand and funneled more *vitalle* out, infusing it with her remnant and sharpening it as it raced toward the vine holding the caged chickadee.

A thick wall of runelight sprang up out of the floor in front of Kate, formed from the golden glitters. Kate's spear cut through it, but a second appeared while Naevys watched with an emotionless face.

The Warden's gaze scraped over Kate like claws over her skin.

At another flick of Naevys's fingers, dozens of vines shot out between the slats of the wood floor in front of Kate and Venn. Kate tried to scramble back, but they were behind her as well. They looped over her legs and around her waist before she could stand. In a moment, they'd bound her arms against her sides and anchored her tightly to the floor.

Only Venn's head was free of the green cocoon.

"Naevys," Venn said, her voice pleading. "Just take the door and go!"

The Warden leaned down, peering into Venn's face as though looking for something. "You used to be stronger." She reached a single finger toward Venn's forehead.

Kate tried to throw out a shield to keep Naevys back, but the queen's remnant was everywhere. In the vines, in the branches, filling the very air.

Naevys tapped Venn's forehead, and Venn's eyes flew wide open. Something flared up between her and the vines and every branch in the room. Between her and Naevys. An invisible cord. A connection.

Terror and shock and exultation rolled over Kate from where Venn lay.

Pushing aside the confusing swirl of emotions, Kate drew in more *vitalle*, pulling it from the vines themselves, trying to wither them. But even as she drained them, some force below the floor filled them again, keeping them tight against her.

Naevys's gaze followed something along the vines, and her mouth twisted in displeasure or contempt. She leaned down, and Kate tried to draw back, but the vines held her like bands of steel. Golden glimmers pooled around Kate. Naevys loomed above her like an inferno of *vitalle*. It wasn't just her body. She was barely taller than Kate, but her remnant didn't end with her body. It flowed seamlessly into the vines beneath her, like they were limbs instead of plants holding her up. It swirled in the vines holding Kate and Venn. It streamed along the branches that protruded from every knot of wood in the floor and tables in the common room.

The Warden drew closer until her face was only inches away. A wave of cold fear washed over Kate, and the muscles in her neck ached as she tried to pull back. Naevys's remnant swept around Kate, dragging her down, smothering her beneath the weight of endless trees.

Something rustled across Kate's mind, a breeze or an intrusion.

Can you feel it? Naevys's voice slithered into her head. *The hope? It's growing—clawing to get out.* Her eyes grew suddenly wilder, a hint of terror creeping into them. *Dare we let it?*

She reached out and set her palm on Kate's cheek. The queen's presence exploded inside Kate's mind. Kate tried to shove her back, to make a shield or a runelight blade or anything, but Naevys overwhelmed everything else. Fingers searched, probing and dragging out thoughts. Snippets of Kate's own memories were rummaged through, and a sharp pang of disappointment cut into her.

When the queen spoke again, it came out in a savage whisper. "Try harder, little mage." She twisted away, the vines under her roiling and carrying her to the wall of branches, which spread apart as she approached.

"Venn?" Kate whispered.

"It's back!" Venn's voice was hoarse. "Kate, it's back!"

The barely visible line between Venn and the vines wrapped around her suddenly made sense. "Your connection to the Wood?" Kate asked.

The vines loosened, and Kate fell forward, catching herself on the floor.

Naevys's mass of vines slid away after her, through the new

gap in the wall of branches, clutching Crofftus's cage and carrying the peeling, aged yellow door behind her like some treasured piece of art. She flicked her wrist, and the tavern door swung open.

A flurry of snow poured in from the square.

Kate shoved herself to her feet, hauling Venn up with her. "Snow?"

A piercing scream came from the square. Then another.

In moments, shrieks filled the air.

Naevys swept outside. Kate scrambled between the branches after her, grabbing the doorframe. Outside, the square swirled with snow. A few panicked, murky figures ran through it.

"Kate," Venn called from behind her. "Something's coming!"

Kate caught a glimpse of motion racing toward them through the chaos of snow.

Merrick burst out of the storm, barreling into Kate and driving her back into the tavern. "Not that way!"

She crashed back into Venn, and the three of them tumbled against the wall of branches.

Kate cast out. Past Merrick, a wall of *vitalle* blazed up blindingly bright. Flashes of ice blue raced past the doorway—glittering scales that looked like plates of crystalized winter. A reptilian foot shot through the door, so huge it cracked the frame. Claws dug into the wood floor, splintering the planks.

The rumble of winter storms poured into the room. Endless fields of ice, ancient and implacable. Moving slowly but inexorably across the earth, carving paths through mountains and earth and stone. Sharp blades of frost froze Kate's skin. Wind whipped sheets of sleet. Bone-chilling cold seeped deeper and deeper into the ground, freezing any snips of life ahead of it, driving creatures to shelter and still nipping at their heels.

Eons and eons of ice, so limitless and bleak that Kate drew back from the remnant.

In the tavern, frost crystallized on the broken doorframe and spread across the wall.

Merrick rolled onto his back, yanking a hammer from his belt and hurling it at the scales. It bounced off as though it had hit a stone wall.

Kate's wave spread. The creature was as long as the tavern and tall enough to block the first floor.

"Dragon!" someone outside screamed.

The lizard body scraped across the ground as the bright form of Naevys slid onto its back with the help of her brightly glowing vines.

The dragon's foot clawed out the door, tearing up the bushes and the stoop. The tail slid past in a blur and disappeared, leaving a thick smear of icy blue across the destruction in its wake.

A thick, massive icy-blue remnant, dusted with Naevys's shimmering gold.

CHAPTER THIRTY-SEVEN

Kate sank onto her back. Her wave hadn't even faded yet, but the air outside the door rang with emptiness. Venn sat against the branches and stared out the door. "Naevys," she said slowly, "just rode away on a *dragon*."

"Did that dragon just bring a snowstorm?" Merrick asked, his voice unsteady.

Kate rolled to her knees. Snowflakes settled to the ground outside, and a glimpse of sunlight cut through the white.

"That tree thing by my forge is gone." Merrick climbed to his feet and helped her up. "An elf told me it left just before the dragon showed up. Disappeared down a street so fast it was hardly more than a blur of red light." He stepped past her, holding out a hand to stop her from leaving as he scanned the square. "Not sure about the dragon."

"It's gone." Kate put a hand on his arm, pressing it out of her way. The ground along the front of the tavern was torn up. Old snow lay in piles with churned-up earth and the broken stones of the stoop. The clouds dissipated as she watched, revealing the crisp blue afternoon sky. The vivid blue remnant of the dragon coated everything. Endless ice fields stretched out beneath her, endless frigid skies.

Venn came up next to her, and Kate focused on the earthy, forest feel of her remnant.

"The dragon's remnant is icy blue." Kate sank against the doorframe, making it groan. Bright sunlight poured down on the brown and desiccated pine in the center of the square. "The same blue that's been on all the *naiwyn*."

Venn stepped out of the tavern, her face etched with disbelief. "How long has she been working with a dragon?" Her gaze caught on a skinny pine near the end of the inn, and she started toward it.

The square was empty, but a few faces peered from windows and street corners.

Something glinted by Kate's feet, and she reached down to pick up Merrick's hammer. "In case our earlier discussion of dragons didn't make it clear"—she held it out to him—"hammers don't really work against them."

He gave a self-conscious smile and tucked the hammer back into a loop at his belt, then peered at something by his feet. "Does it count for anything if I knocked a scale off?" He picked up a shard of silvery blue. It was shaped almost like a seashell, flaring out from one end into a wide fan. A ripple of snowy-white light skittered across the blue as he shifted it in his hands.

"Keep that," Kate said. "When all this is over, if we survive, I'll make you some stonesteel with it."

His eyebrows rose. "Only dwarves have stonesteel."

"Until now."

At the corner of the inn, Venn leaned her forehead against the skinny pine that rose up to brush against the second-story window.

Kate stopped a couple of paces away. "Venn?"

The elf didn't move. Her fingers were splayed on the bark,

and her shoulders rose and fell in deep, gasping breaths. "I can feel it," she whispered. "All of it. I can talk to them and hear them. Faron is hurrying back with his rangers. They must have heard the screams. I can…" She tilted her head to look at Kate, her cheeks wet. "Kate, I can feel it all again."

Venn's remnant spread from her hands and ran along the furrows of the bark. It flowed from where her head touched it. It flowed from the air around her. The rich green mist of shimmers wrapped around the tree as though trying to absorb it.

A shiver of uneasiness rolled through Kate, tainted by a hint of envy. "Is it like it's always been for you? Or like it was after you were in the Elder Grove?"

"Somewhere in between." Venn lifted her head. "It's like being whole again."

Kate tried to tamp down on the envy that rose in her as she stepped closer. A pool of contentment and relief and soul-deep joy washed around her. She drew back at the vibrancy of the emotions.

Venn looked up sharply. "It's back?"

Realization swept over Kate. "Naevys connected you to the forest again—but when she did, you and I were already linked, trying to talk to her." She took another step back, and Venn's emotions faded, along with a gentle whispering sound. She straightened and moved closer to the tree, putting her hand next to Venn's.

A whisper brushed across Kate's mind. She focused, and it came again. A word. A thought. An impression.

Icy-blue scales scraping past the branches.

Kate straightened. "Venn!"

"You can hear it!" Venn looked up into the tree. "This means we can track her. Figure out what she's doing."

Kate pressed her hand harder against the tree. "Where did she go?"

"I don't think she's landed yet. At least not in the woods."

"Venn!" Faron appeared in a swirl of *vitalle* and rushed forward, reaching for her. "Are you…"

Venn pushed herself away from the tree, a surge of complicated emotions rising in her. The strongest was relief, quickly followed by a sharp jab of betrayal. She crossed her arms tightly, and the relief was smothered out by a stiff resolve.

He slowed and stopped before he reached her, his hand falling to his side, even as he searched her. "Are you hurt? The trees told me what happened."

Venn shook her head. Faron opened his mouth, but then addressed Kate. "You?"

"We're both fine."

The elf king's eyes caught on the dry, dead pine in the center of the square. "I can't believe she…"

"A dragon?" Silas called, crunching across the rubble toward them. "A real dragon, and we were trapped inside?"

Tribal followed him. "Thought for a moment the rumors were true and it might have taken a mage." He gestured to Kate.

"Well, Naevys rode away on it after tearing the yellow door off the wall and capturing Crofftus."

"She took the door?" Faron said.

"And Crofftus?" Silas said. "Why would she take him?"

"Because he's working for her," Venn said grimly.

Faron's brows rose in shock, but the dwarves merely sighed.

Kate nodded toward the tavern. "Let's go see if there's anyplace left in there to sit. We've barely eaten or slept in two days. We have a bit to catch up on."

"I can't," Faron said. "I've called the elders to a council about my mother. Did she say anything to you?"

Venn shook her head. "She accused Yellow of stealing from her, captured Crofftus, stole the door, then…" Venn lifted a hand to her forehead. "She restored my connection to the woods."

Faron's fingers twitched as though he was going to reach for her. "That's... That's great, V."

The idea niggled a question in the back of Kate's mind. "Why?" At the confused looks from both elves, she added, "Why would she? Why does she care if Venn can talk to the trees?"

Venn set her hand on the tree, searching it as though it held some answers. "I have no idea."

"Well," Faron said, still studying Venn with a worried expression. "I'm leaving all my rangers here, along with the ones from the lakes. At least if more animals attack, they'll be able to help. If her *naiwyn* comes back, or the dragon..." He shook his head. "If the elders have any insight into any of this, I'll let you know."

Shouts rang out from along the front of the tavern, and Kate spun to see men crowded around a pile of rubble.

"It's Griston!" one shouted as two men pulled a body from under the rocks. "Dead!"

Kate ran toward them. "Let me see!" She cast out, but in contrast to the living people around him, Griston's body was completely dark.

One of the other men caught sight of Venn and Faron. "Stay back! Griston knew elves would be the end of him!"

Faron held out his hands. "This is a terrible tragedy. If anyone else is badly wounded, we have healers. I'm ordering every one of them to stay close until we can find and contain Naevys."

"How do we know they won't just hurt us worse?" the man demanded. "We keep trusting you, and more trouble keeps coming!"

Kate stepped between the man and Faron. "All these elves are here to help."

"While others attack us?"

"Don't be a fool, Petar," Merrick said from the front door. "You can't tell me you think all elves are the same. You obviously don't think all humans are. At least not the way you build your fences. They're twice as high between your house and Ren's because you think he's a bad neighbor. But Mer and Boren are fine. So it's not hard to believe Naevys is a bad neighbor, while King Faron isn't."

Venn's eyebrow twitched the slightest amount, but she said nothing.

"Every elf but one helped us today," Merrick continued. "Stop wasting everyone's time by causing problems where there are none. Now, get Griston somewhere more dignified, and I'll send word to Glerrol. We'll need a coffin."

Kate watched the men lift Griston's body and carry him across the square. "Are there any more dead?" she asked quietly.

"There weren't before the dragon," Merrick answered. "A few were badly wounded, but the elves were seeing to them." He paused. "There are a lot of smaller injuries, though."

Faron took in the square, his expression torn. "You have my deepest apologies for my mother's actions. Every available elf will be close by."

Yellow gave him a nod and headed back inside. With a slight nod to Kate and the dwarves, Faron disappeared.

"The twins are inside by the fire," Silas said in a low voice. "They're just...sitting there. Didn't even react much when branches started growing out of every surface."

Venn winced.

"You said the command they broke was from the elders and their parents," Kate said, "so it broke the connection with their parents. Does that mean they never get to see them again?"

"They can see each other again, but they'll feel the loss of their connection so strongly that it will be painful. Especially at first. Over time, it may dull a little and meeting them will be less distressing."

Tribal frowned. "You're saying elf children never disobey their parents without being cut off from them?"

"It's not a normal sort of disobeying," Venn said. "When an official command is given, it's a different sort of thing. It feels different. You can't accidentally break it. When Thallion commanded me not to speak of certain things, it was physically hard for me to do it. It was probably difficult for the twins to even get here. They definitely knew they were bumping up against the command, but…" She gave the dwarves a pained look. "Seeing you two in danger was enough to push them to break it anyway."

The two dwarves stood very still, their faces caught between shock and dismay.

Venn set a hand on Silas's shoulder. "Let's go see if we can find them anything to eat."

She headed into the inn, and after a moment's hesitation, the dwarves followed. A voice called for Kate, and she paused.

The merchant pushed his cart across the square toward her. "Are you in need of anything?" he asked, stopping next to her. "Are you injured?"

"No. You?"

He gave her a half-hearted smile. "I'm fine. I was hiding in a barn with some good townsfolk and didn't even catch a glimpse of the dragon." He sobered. "Earlier, I did see the little elflings being helped into the tavern. Were they hurt? I have some healing salves."

"They're not hurt. Not exactly." Kate glanced toward the inn. "They just…disobeyed and the consequences are severe." At the merchant's silence, she turned back to find him staring at the Blind Pig, his face pale.

"They disobeyed someone in authority?"

Kate paused. "You understand what that means?"

"They're cut off," he whispered. "From everything. From the forest, from their family, from their community." He looked up at her, his expression pained. "Can elves survive such a thing?"

"Venn says they can, although she's only known one who was cut off, and...I'm not sure he survived to a natural death."

His brow creased in concern. "Is there anything we can do?"

"I don't think so." Kate caught sight of the silver handle of one of the little daggers in the cart. "Although, do you still have both of those?"

He pulled out the pair.

"How much for them both?" she asked.

He studied her, settling against his cart while the wood groaned. "What do you have to trade?"

The silver ring she'd taken from the box right before the bears attacked was still in her pocket, and Kate pulled it out. "This?"

He took the ring and studied it. "It's stonesteel. This is rather valuable."

"Are you going to tell me that's magical like the knives?"

"No," he said slowly. "It's dwarven, like the knives, but I think it's just mundane metal."

"Well, I'd like to be rid of it, honestly." Kate gestured to the knives. "Will you trade?"

He shifted his weight on the cart, and it gave a long, low creak. His eyebrows furrowed, but he shrugged. "The deal is struck." He handed her the two knives and tucked the ring into his cart. After a short hesitation, he said, "I don't think a gift is going to help the elflings, though."

"I know." Kate ran her thumb over the ridged handle of one of the daggers. "But I need to offer something. Find a way to give them some sparkle of hope. Even if I know this won't really work." At his frown, she paused. "Do you disagree?"

"No, no." He ran his fingernail absently along a groove in the handle of his cart. "It's just..." He gave her a faint smile. "It reminds me of one of the books I gave you. It held conversations between Stonewall the Aged and Driscall the Crooked."

Kate gave a self-conscious smile. "I started it."

"It's well worth the read. The two men talk about hope in it. Stonewall begins by calling hope a glittering sword that can cut through the gloom of grief."

"An apt description."

"I thought so too, when I first read it. But both men were experiencing great tragedies. One was losing his father to senility, and the other's wife was gravely and incurably ill. As they walked through these difficult times, their definition changed. It was Stonewall who first corrected himself."

The merchant closed his eyes, and his voice took on the tone of a recitation. "'I cannot stop hoping. But it is not a bright, sparkling, unassailable thing. It is sharp and painful like a knife wound. Like fire burning me away. It is a form of torture, and yet I cling to it.'"

Kate shifted at the words that echoed the way hope had felt for decades as she'd searched for Evan.

"The part that struck me the hardest," the merchant continued, "was Driscall's response, which said, 'Hope is a stubborn, muddy, exhausted creature. Ragged too. Like something that has fallen in the filth and has to crawl out of it by sheer grit. Bloody and half-broken, but still crawling.'"

Kate gripped the daggers, feeling the visceral truth of his words.

He opened his eyes and gave a sad smile. "So perhaps you're right. Sturdy dwarven daggers might be a good gift for the elflings who will need hope just like that." A commotion from the front of the inn broke the moment's somberness, and he blinked up at Kate, and his expression cleared a little. "I hope you read the rest of that book."

"I will," she said, heading for the inn.

She'd nearly reached the door when he called after her. "Your little friend, the gnoblin. Do you know where he is? I owe him for fixing my cart."

She shook her head. "I haven't seen him since that day."

The merchant let out a frustrated grunt, and Kate raised the daggers in thanks before reaching the door.

Two men stood in the broken entrance, taking measurements as a young boy scurried out with an armful of pine boughs, which he tossed onto a growing pile.

Inside was a bustle of activity. Workmen sawed at the branches that had grown out of knots on the tables and the floor. Children carried the cast-off limbs outside. Despite the chill pouring in through the gap in the wall where the door had been, most of the men were stripped down to shirts, their heavy cloaks piled on the bar.

A blazing fire burned in the fireplace. In front of it, two golden-haired elves slumped on the floor. She watched them, her heart heavy for the long, lonely road they had ahead of them.

"What will happen to them?" Kate asked. "Can it be undone?"

Venn took in the two with a pained expression. "No. It's permanent."

"So what will they do? Can they even live at the lakes anymore?"

"They won't want to. The connection here will just feel empty, but if they were to go home, the loss of it would cause them pain."

"Did they lose their bond to the trees as well?"

"I doubt it. That's from being elven, not from their community. But I think it may be decreased. Everything about them will be weakened."

Kate started toward them. "I can't believe they disobeyed."

Venn crossed the room and knelt next to the elves. Silas and Tribal righted an overturned table, dragging it close to the heat, and Kate picked up enough chairs for them all to sit.

Venn pulled Matlen to his feet, set him into a chair, and caught

Yellow's eye. The huge barkeeper came over, his face still pale. "Are the young elves injured?" he asked Kate softly.

"Not physically. Any chance there's bread or something warm to eat?"

"Plenty." He looked morosely around the common room. "The kitchen, at least, is perfectly intact." He headed toward the bar.

Venn helped Aislin into a chair next to her brother. Her hands were shaking, and her face was pale.

The dwarves watched the young elf twins, their expressions worried.

"How can we help?" Silas asked. Neither of the elf twins showed any sign of hearing.

Venn shook her head. "There's nothing to be done. There is no turning back something like this."

"They're cut off?" Tribal said, his voice almost angry. "Forever?" Matlen's shoulders twitched at the word, and Tribal winced.

Kate sat down at the table and pushed the two daggers toward the elf twins. "The merchant was asking after you, and we struck a deal for these."

Matlen reached out mechanically and took one but just rested it on the table.

Silas picked up Aislin's. "These are dwarven." He twisted his wrist, watching the blade. "Well-made, if a little…" He gave a small smile. "Well, they were made for dwarven children. which makes them about perfect for your little hands." He slid it toward Aislin.

"Perfect," Tribal agreed.

Aislin managed a lift of her lips that vaguely resembled a smile.

Yellow came back to the table carrying three loaves of rosemary bread and a tray of coffee. He set it all down, then reached into the pocket of his wide apron and pulled out two very small, very brightly wrapped packages. He set them in front of the elf twins. "There's a merchant who comes through once a year from some city a month south of here. He brings these little candies. Calls 'em pulled molasses. You two look like you could use a little something."

Neither elf moved, and Yellow gave them all a tired smile and left.

Venn unwrapped one of the candies and held it by Matlen's hand. He took it, numbly, and ate a small bite. He blinked quickly and squeezed the soft pink wad gently. "Aislin." He pushed the other piece toward her. "Eat."

Aislin looked dully at the candy but opened the wrapper and nibbled at it. Her eyebrows rose.

Kate pulled a chunk of the soft, warm bread off the loaf and bit off a piece, barely holding in a groan at the buttery richness. "This is the best thing I've ever eaten."

"And Crofftus is really working for the mad queen?" Tribal asked.

Kate gave him a quick summary of the attack at Virion's house. "We think you were right, that he talked to her when she was in Renault's cave." There was a flicker of motion in the shadows of the fireplace and the glint from two wide eyes.

Kate leaned toward them. "Fix?" The gnoblin's wrinkled green face peered out from the shadows. "You want some bread?"

He crept forward, his eyes darting around the common room at the workers. Kate pulled a chair up, tucked between herself and Venn, and he scrambled onto it. He pulled off his warm cloak, and Kate noticed a few additional bits of fabric added from the last time she'd seen him.

"Welcome back," she said, and he smiled shyly.

"Did Crofftus talk to Naevys?" Venn asked. "Before we got there?"

Fix's smile faded, and his head twitched in a nod.

Kate handed him a generous chunk of bread. "What did they talk about?"

Fix's brow crinkled, and he picked a crumb of bread off the table, looking uncertainly at Kate. He made a hand gesture at Tribal and Silas.

"I don't know what that means," Silas said, a note of apology in his voice.

Fix looked around, then pointed at the fireplace.

"Fire?" Kate asked. Fix shook his head. "Flames? Heat?"

He waved away the fire and pointed out the front door, then at a torch lit on one of Yellow's posts, then back at the fire.

"Bright things," Kate said. "Light?"

Fix flashed her a wide smile.

"He talked to Naevys about light?" Kate glanced at Venn, who looked mystified.

The gnoblin bit his lip and held up his hands, touching each finger in order. Then he tapped the fifth one several times.

"Five?" Tribal asked.

Shaking his head, Fix stood on his chair, pointing to each plate on the table in order, ending at the one in front of Kate and tapping his finger on it.

"Plates?" Kate said with a wince. "I'm sorry. I don't…"

Fix gave a frustrated huff and pointed at each piece of bread on the table, looking up meaningfully when he reached the final one.

"Last," Aislin said quietly. "He's pointing out the last one of each thing he's counting."

The gnoblin gave a little hop of excitement and nodded at her, his smile so big that the corner of her mouth actually curled up a little.

"Light and Last?" Kate asked.

Fix pointed to the last piece of bread, then at the fire.

"Lastlight!" Kate leaned forward. "They talked about lastlight?"

Fix's smile died, and he curled back in on himself in his chair, his brow pinched with worry as he nodded.

"What's lastlight?" Aislin took another nibble of the soft candy.

"It's the idea that there is a lot of life in you, but you don't have to lose all of it to die. A person dies, and their body is still warm, their organs are still working, at least for a few minutes. There's not enough life in them to live, but it's certainly not zero. Renault said that what was left was a person's lastlight, and that it was made up by a large portion of the energy they had when they were alive." Kate grimaced. "He believed that if you could harness a person's lastlight at the moment of their death, you could get most of their energy."

She glanced at Fix. "It's how he made the big pocket world he put his wife and daughter into. The production of it killed a colony of gnomes, and he harnessed all their lastlight to fuel his creation."

Aislin's nose wrinkled in distaste. "That's gruesome."

"Why was Crofftus talking about it?" Venn asked.

Fix looked helplessly at them all. He pointed toward the wall where Yellow's door had hung.

"The door?" Kate asked. "Naevys?"

Fix gave her a quick nod and pantomimed reading a book.

"Naevys was reading," Kate said.

The gnoblin curled up like a bunny and pretended to hop, then read the book.

"Crofftus came up to her while she was reading? Did you hear what he said?"

Fix shook his head.

Kate sat back and looked at Venn. "If he spoke only to Naevys, he must not have wanted Fix to hear it."

"Or any of the rest of us who were coming back," Silas added.

"Were he and Naevys fighting?" Kate asked Fix. He shook his head. She set a hand on his arm. "That's what you were scared of when we came back, isn't it? Because Crofftus was talking to Naevys in a way that looked like he was helping her."

Fix nodded sadly.

"How long did they talk?"

He pantomimed turning three pages of the book.

"I don't suppose that book is still in Renault's cave?" Kate asked.

Fix shrugged with an apologetic frown.

"It's all right. I'm glad you stayed away from them." Kate looked into her coffee mug, a heavy knot sitting in her stomach. "I can't believe he's helping her."

"I sorta can," Tribal said, even though there was a note of apology in his voice. "I've never really trusted him."

"He's helped us countless times," Kate said.

"And clearly helped our enemies too." Silas pushed another piece of bread toward Kate. "Sorry, but it's not the hardest thing to believe."

Venn sat back in her chair. "I hate to agree with the dwarves, but of all the people we've had to change our thoughts about, Crofftus isn't the hardest." She reached into her quiver and pulled out two darts, both bent and battered, and offered them to Fix. His eyes lit, and he took them with a shy smile.

"Speaking of," Tribal said, jabbing a finger over his shoulder. "Why'd the mad queen—who we used to be trying to save but are now trying to stop—steal Yellow's door?"

Silas pointed a chunk of bread at Venn. "Do elves collect doors?"

Aislin gave a little giggle at the questions, although only the shadow of her normal laugh. "Most elven houses don't have doors. We use the warmth of the trees to keep the cold out."

The edge of Silas's mouth curled up. "Sounds like just the foolish sort of things elves would do. Anyone who knows anything knows that a well-made door is a piece of art."

Kate chewed her bread and studied the wall, pulling her mind away from Crofftus and bringing Naevys's actions back to her mind.

"The entrance…" Kate pushed herself out of her seat. "She said she wanted the entrance."

"The point of that door," Tribal said, "was that it wasn't an entrance to anything. That's why it was funny."

"Venn…" Kate shouldered through gaps in the irregular walls of pine branches until she reached the bar and climbed onto it. The empty spot on the back wall was at eye level but too far away to reach. She cast out toward it.

"You tried this when the door was still here," Venn said, climbing up next to her. "I thought you said there was nothing unusual about it."

"There wasn't." Kate's wave rolled across the wall, finding nothing. She drummed her fingers on her leg. "An entrance. She called it an entrance. Virion said that Renault used to have a workshop in the woods. There was a 'bright door,' but the entrance had disappeared. He thought Renault had gone into it to die and destroyed it, but what if someone *took* the entrance?"

"You think Yellow stole a magic door from Renault?"

Yellow strode out of the kitchen, carrying a tray of soup, but stopped when he caught sight of them. "That's what the top of my bar needed after today. Muddy footprints."

Kate glanced down and winced. "Sorry, we'll clean this up. Can you tell me again where you got that door?"

"In a deserted barn in the woods two hours south of town." He looked sadly at the wall. "Was just sitting in a horse stall, looking lonely."

"Could you tell us how to find the barn?" Kate asked.

"We tore it down for all this wood." He pointed his chin toward the common room. "Ain't nothin' left there."

"Still, could you tell us where it was?"

"Lemme drop this soup off for the workers, and if you've got a map, I can show you exactly where."

"Kate has maps and more maps," Venn said, climbing down. "And drawings and notes. I'm sure we can find something."

CHAPTER THIRTY-EIGHT

"There's a stream here." Yellow marked a line on one of Bo's maps of the trail between Home and the ravine. "It's small, and at this time of year will be dry, but there are four stepping stones across it. Just past the stream you'll see some wagon tracks heading east. Took a lot of trips to gather all that wood, so I'd worn a good path by the end. That hasn't been used in ages either, but it's hard for the forest to cover over a trail like that. You should still be able to see it. The path ends where the barn sat."

"Was there anything else in the barn?" Kate asked. "The frame for the door?"

"No. Just the door and…" Yellow made a distasteful face. "There was a skeleton. Always figured it was the barn's old owner. Musta been dead a long time to be nothing but bones. We buried them nearby." He tapped the map again. "You'll find the clearing it was in right there."

"Thank you," Kate said, and the innkeeper headed off to his other customers.

She studied the map. "Only two hours away. We have plenty of daylight left. I say we go see what's there."

"You think Renault built a pocket world in an old barn?" Silas asked.

"No, the entry to his workshop was between two trees. Venn and I have seen it. Twice now."

Venn frowned. "Virion's memories showed a stone arch as the entry to his workshop."

"From the inside," Kate said. "But pocket worlds must look different from the outside. Wherever Bo and Evan are, the exit can't look like the inside of a drawer. The doorways connect, but the inside and outside of it could be completely different from each other."

"Not to agree with the dwarves," Venn said. "But this feels a little like a reach."

Kate sat back, the pieces of this story shifting around each other in her mind. "I know. It does, except…I saw the yellow door three times. Once in the vision Herald from the White Wood, once in the Elder Grove when—" She grimaced. "When I was dying from that arrow in my chest. Both times Naevys was behind the door. Then I saw it again in the vision when Naevys was in Renault's cave. It's important—I know it is. And Virion said Naevys has been searching for the entrance to Renault's workshop."

The faces around the table were set in varying levels of dubiousness.

"I know it sounds crazy, but…it's right. I think Renault is in that workshop. Virion thought he might be buried there." She pointed at the dwarves. "But, as you've said before, there are an awful lot of rumors that give Renault credit for lengthening life. He could be using magic, or the pocket world could slow time. Either way, he could still be alive in there. And if he is…" She looked back at Venn. "He might have the amulet."

"You think Naevys wants the amulet?"

"She has in the past, and she's wanted Renault, and Virion says she wants into that workshop." Kate looked at Venn. "Can you talk to the trees enough to find it, if we get close? If Yellow found the door in a barn, that's the area where Virion said the workshop was. Maybe we can find the actual entrance."

"How will we do that?" Tribal asked.

Kate pointed to the empty spot on the wall. "What was that door always missing?"

"A doorframe," Venn said.

"Exactly. And Virion said the entrance to the workshop was a door between two trees. Maybe the doorframe is still there, and Naevys has been searching Home for the door itself."

"How would she know it was here?"

Venn paused. "Well, we did talk about it. After your vision, we discussed the door."

Kate straightened. "Oh! The door is bright yellow! She *has* been searching for it! It's what she sent the *gweroc* and the bears to find! But Crofftus said most animals don't see colors like we do. The creatures she sent tore off light-colored doors—maybe they couldn't tell yellow from other light wood." She looked back up at the wall. "If it's the door to a pocket world, it'll have runes carved into the edges. They wouldn't show up unless they were activated, which is why I didn't see them here."

"I think it still sounds a bit daft," Tribal said, "but I'm always up for searching for a secret room that powerful people have kept hidden."

Kate glanced at the elf twins.

"We can't leave them here alone," Venn said quietly, then patted Matlen's arm. "Are you up for an adventure? Apparently, Yellow will just stuff you full of candy."

The young elf tried to give her a smile, but it was weak.

"Great." Venn handed him one of the loaves of bread. "You two split that. Eat it all."

Yellow's wagon path was only the vaguest impression of parallel tracks winding through the forest. The grass to either side poked out of the snow, but along the old wheel ruts, the snow was mostly uninterrupted. The late afternoon sun slanted through the trees, leaving stripes of brightness amidst shadows.

Venn walked next to Kate, brushing her fingers along each tree, her gaze a bit distant.

Darkness clung to the underside of a thick branch, fallen long enough ago that its needles had all browned. Maybe it was just the contrast with the snow that made it feel so dark. The thought didn't ease the tension growing between Kate's shoulder blades.

"Anyone else a little leery about sleeping out here with the mad queen still on the loose?" Silas asked.

Tribal peered up through the branches. "And her dragon."

"I'll make us a shelter," Venn said.

"Oh, good," Tribal muttered. "A tree to protect us from the elf queen who commands the entire forest."

Aislin and Matlen trudged between the two dwarves, their faces dull and pale. Aislin held Fix in her arms, clinging to him tightly. The gnoblin, far from objecting, looked like he'd never been happier. Kate exchanged worried glances with Venn.

From behind the twins, Silas caught the look. "Tribal. If the mad queen comes for us in the middle of the night, you sacrifice yourself first."

Tribal's brow shot down. "Why?"

"Because you owe me."

Tribal stopped in the middle of the path. "For what?"

Aislin and Matlen stumbled to a stop too.

"For the thing with Pippi," Silas said.

Aislin blinked at the name.

Tribal's expression grew incredulous. "That was years ago."

Silas shrugged. "You still owe me."

"Isn't Pippi the governor's daughter?" Aislin asked.

"She is," Silas said, dropping his voice to a loud, confidential-sounding whisper. "And Tribal's fancied her for years." His fingers flickered by his side.

Tribal caught the motion, then his gaze shifted to the elf twins, who'd perked up slightly. He let out a breath that was more resignation than irritation and started walking again. "You volunteered to help with that thing," he threw over his shoulder.

"What thing?" Matlen asked.

"Well, Tribal's been taken with Pippi since..." Silas waved his hand in the air. "Forever. But with our mother being a wanted criminal for all her thieving, a good deal of which was from the gov'nor's personal stashes, the good ol' gov' has never been fond of Tribal. So to see Pippi, he needed a diversion."

"I did not need a—"

"He did." Silas moved up alongside Matlen, who wore the ghost of a smile. "The plan was that I was going to cause a ruckus just outside the gov'nor's gallery where he displays all his latest valuables."

"The gallery that our ma robbed at least four times," Tribal added with a grin.

"Exactly. Then, once I had gotten some attention, I'd escape through a small hallway just off the side. Tribal was to prepare by unlocking the back door while I was being noisy in the front. While the gov'nor came to investigate, Tribal was going to sneak to Pippi's window, help her escape, and treat her to a romantic dinner in Star Cavern."

"What's Star Cavern?" Aislin asked.

"A cavern with flecks of mica all over the walls and ceiling. If you bring a single torch in, it looks like you're under a starry sky." Silas glanced at the two elves. "Which is a bit of a novelty for dwarves. Anyway, I borrowed a friend's tunnel pig, which are obnoxiously loud when frightened, and set it loose outside the store room with a good smack on its haunch."

"Cousins reported hearing that pig all over the Upper Crust," Tribal said with a grin.

"Yes," Silas said. "*My* part went off like a gem."

Matlen gave Tribal a grimace. "You forgot to unlock the back door?"

Fix winced and covered his face with his knobby green fingers.

"Tribal," Silas said before his brother could answer, "was so besotted he forgot about me all together in his excitement. So, while I was being chased by guards down a dead-end hallway, then arrested, then interrogated for hours by the gov'nor, Tribal was off wooing Pippi under the stars."

Tribal gave a satisfied smirk. "It was a good night."

Aislin gave a little laugh, and Matlen smiled an actual smile. Venn let out a sigh that was both pained and relieved. She gave Silas a grateful nod.

He flashed her a smile, then turned back to the elf twins. "Nearly every time Tribal has tried to impress Pippi, at least one of us ends up in a bind."

Venn fell in close to Kate's shoulder. "Can you see any connections around them?"

Kate shook her head. "There's nothing around them. They're barely even connected to each other. At least not with those barely visible lines. Their remnants are unharmed and still merge so closely I can't tell where one stops and the other starts."

"I can't believe they…" Venn's words trailed off.

"You told me about Ulien, the elf who was cut off from the

Woods. You said the separation either killed him or made him give up the will to keep living."

Silas's voice continued, deep in some new tale, and Aislin let out another short laugh.

"They're young," Venn said, although whether she was trying to convince Kate or herself, Kate couldn't tell. "And they have each other."

They walked for a quarter of an hour while Tribal and Silas kept up a stream of outlandish tales, at least half of which sounded too implausible to be true. But the elf twins' shattered looks had softened slightly by the time Venn touched a tree and held up a hand.

"The glade is just ahead," she said in a low voice.

They slowed and crept forward. Birds chirped somewhere in the woods, but the air was so still there was no other sound beyond the crunching of their feet through the snow.

A clearing opened up. On the far side, a pine lay fallen, splayed on top of a flattened stretch of ground. A few pieces of broken wood poked up out of the snow.

Kate crossed to the meager remains of the barn.

"Yellow picked this place pretty clean," Silas said, kicking aside snow to reveal foundation stones.

"Venn," Kate said, "can you find the door from here?"

Venn was already crossing to the largest tree, a fir on the far side of the clearing. "This could take a few minutes. None of these trees are particularly old."

A collection of thick logs sat in a wide ring near the barn, and Kate swung her pack off and sank down onto it. Her arms felt heavy, her legs felt slow, and she wished the log were a nice soft bed back at the Blind Pig.

Her pack was open, and her fingers were reaching for the aenigma box before she realized what she was doing. *You are obsessing.* Venn's words echoed in her mind. *When you think about something constantly and can't let it out of your grasp, that is obsessing.*

Kate's thumb brushed the box, and a sense of relief washed over her. A desire to pull it out and hold it on her lap.

She fought it for a moment, but there was the *hope...*

With a feeling of relief, she gave into it and reached for the box.

CHAPTER THIRTY-NINE

A nail on the box glinted in the sunlight, and Kate forced herself to consider Venn's words. It was a reasonable description of obsession. But did it describe her thoughts on the box?

When you think about something constantly and can't let it out of your grasp, that is obsessing. Venn's words echoed in her mind. Kate's fingers tightened on the box as indignation straightened her spine.

She set the box on her lap. The distant, lonesome bell tolled, encapsulating the longing she felt. It was a beacon of hope. She closed her eyes, searching for the hint of lantern light in the way ahead. Searching for the only glimpse of hope she ever managed to stumble across.

The silvery light was there, but merely a shimmer, far in the distance. The search for Naevys and the ancient mysteries around the White Wood had dragged her back away from it again.

The words from the merchant came back to her. *"Hope is a stubborn, muddy, exhausted creature. Ragged too. Like something that's fallen in the filth and had to crawl out of it by sheer grit. Bloody and half-broken, but still crawling."*

Suddenly the lantern that the box offered felt hollow. She recognized the other form of hope on a much deeper level. In the years since Evan had disappeared, the drive to find him had felt like this. Like something that's fallen in the filth and had to crawl out of it by sheer grit. Bloody and half-broken, but still crawling.

She shifted at the thought. Before she'd touched the box, that was how she would have described the hope of finding Evan. Dogged. Stubborn. Yes, even muddy.

Yet the box seemed to offer something else. A longing that gnawed at her.

The log she sat on rocked, and she looked over to find Tribal settling next to her.

"When do we go to the carriage?" he asked.

She blinked at him, dragging her mind back to the present moment. "What?"

"You said you had a vision when the mad queen was in Renault's cave. She held the box and the amulet, and you saw the emperor's carriage that's buried under the rockslide. We've obsessed over the box and amulet—when are we going to focus on that carriage?"

An unreasonable amount of irritation rose at his words. "You want us to stop everything we're doing and go on a treasure hunt so you and Silas can find enough gold to bribe your way back into the governor's good graces?"

Tribal's eyes narrowed slightly. "You really think that's all we're after?"

A needle of guilt stabbed into her. "I just don't think the carriage is a high priority right now."

"Of course not. Because there's no way a carriage the mad queen has guarded for centuries in a ravine she's protected for centuries that's wrapped up in secrets that have been kept for centuries has anything at all to do with the mystery you're trying so hard to solve here."

Kate tried to stifle her annoyance. He was right. The carriage was involved, obviously. Not in a way she could explain yet, but it was definitely involved. So why was the thought of trying to dig it out so irritating?

Obviously, it was fraught with danger. Not to mention it would take an unreasonable amount of time.

The thought stopped her as the logic fell into place, answering her own question.

It was time she could be spending on the box. That was the source of the frustration.

The truth was unsettling. Yes, she needed to get Bo and Evan, but Tribal was right. That carriage was obviously important. Naevys protected it too closely for it not to be.

Still, her irritation lingered. "Fine." The word came out more waspish than she'd meant. "Unless we find some hugely compelling task we need to do in the workshop, we'll go investigate the carriage after we're finished here."

Tribal patted her shoulder with his broad, heavy hand. "Excellent."

"Kate!" Venn called from across the clearing. "It's close!" She gestured through the woods. "That way, just a few minutes' walk."

A surge of anticipation shot through Kate, and her fingers tightened on the box. If Renault's body was there…

She pushed the thought away, focusing on the obstacles in front of them. "How guarded is it? *Naiwyn*? The dragon?" She tucked the book and the box into her pack.

Venn hesitated. "It's not guarded. There's nothing near it. The dragon landed in a glen, Naevys put the door into a doorframe that was set between two trees and went inside. The dragon left and…" Venn tapped a finger on her quiver of darts. "The forest around the door is really young. I think the clearing used to be bigger, and new trees are starting to encroach on it. Their thoughts are disjointed. They all agree on the dragon, but their ideas are sketchy about Naevys."

"Did she leave?"

Venn spread her hands uncertainly. "Yes. But whether she came back again is very hard to pin down."

Kate stood and pulled her pack on. "It's weird that she isn't protecting it. Whether she's there or not."

"True, but they all agree the dragon left, and I don't think even young trees would miss a *naiwyn* standing near the door." Venn glanced at Aislin and Matlen where they sat against a tree, looking forlorn. "You two stay behind the dwarves, and let's stay quiet."

Kate moved up next to Venn, stepping close enough to feel the elf's apprehension.

Venn started through the trees. "You're entirely too excited about this."

"Virion thinks Renault is buried in there," Kate said, keeping her voice low, as though saying it out loud might make it less likely. "With his amulet."

"The amulet that Naevys would have already reached."

"True. But if she has it, then we can bargain. I will give her the box if she'll just let me use the amulet to open the drawer."

Venn squinted ahead into the trees. "I haven't noticed Naevys being in the frame of mind to listen to a rational bargain."

Frustration at the truth of her words flared up in Kate. "What should I do, Venn? Not try?"

"Of course you should try. *We* should try. Just...keep your expectations suitably low."

Kate grabbed her arm. "Venn, we're *so* close."

Venn let out a dry laugh. "Which is exactly when things keep going terribly wrong."

CHAPTER FORTY

"Any chance," Silas said from behind Kate, "that the trees have given any more clarity as to whether the mad queen is actually in this pocket world we're trying to get to?"

"No." Venn let her hand drag against another trunk. "Imagine trying to get a straight answer from a bunch of toddlers who are so distracted by things like a gentle breeze they can barely form thoughts."

"It's just..." Tribal grimaced. "Our group feels a bit...undersized for this sort of job."

"As much as I hate to say it," Silas said, "shouldn't we approach the mad queen with more...disposable companions? Like an entire elven army?"

"I sent a message to Ayen," Venn said.

"If you two are too scared," Kate added, "you're welcome to go somewhere else. We're going to scope out the door until the elven army arrives."

Venn held up a hand for silence and moved forward. A sliver

of daffodil yellow flashed between some trees, and Venn set her hand on another tree. "There's nothing there," she whispered.

Kate crept forward next to her, straining her ears. There were no bird sounds, no whisper of a breeze. A bramble to her right held a dark shadow in its center.

Venn stopped at the edge of a wide clearing, a dart loaded in her crossbow.

In the center, two pines, so young their trunks were no wider than Kate's palm, supported the yellow door. A matching yellow doorframe was attached to the trees with thin vines.

"Those trees are not three hundred years old," Kate whispered. "This is obviously not how Renault's entrance used to be."

Venn put her hand on the tree next to them. "There used to be old larches there." She nodded toward two long lumps along the ground. Each ended near their own mostly decomposed old stump about a door's width away from each other. "The trees remember Naevys digging the doorframe out of the ground and putting it there."

"How long ago?" Kate asked.

Venn shook her head. "Recently. Since the snow began to fall this year."

Kate cast out into the glade. Beneath the snow, dormant grass flickered dimly. The trees around the outskirts blazed up, along with the two trees next to the door. And then a brilliant strip of light flared out between the door and its frame.

When the wave rolled away without finding anything else, Kate took a step forward. Her gaze locked onto the door. There was something fitting about the way it stood between the two trees. "It wasn't exactly like this in the visions, but it was close."

Silas gave her an expectant look. "And what did it do in your visions?"

"The first time, getting close to it killed the entire forest. The second time, it opened to reveal Naevys."

Tribal sighed. "Why is it always something like this?"

Kate glanced around the clearing again. "Since there's nothing guarding it, I'm going to investigate."

Venn grabbed her arm. "Wait. Faron's on his way with the rangers."

"I'm just getting a closer look." Kate pulled away. The clearing spread around her, empty and vaguely threatening. The sun lit the trees on the eastern side, but the shadows along the western edge were growing steadily darker. Kate cast out again, trying to banish the feel of eyes on her from every direction. Her wave found nothing unexpected.

When she reached the door, a line of runes carved into the doorframe caught her eye. They were ancient Kalesh, and each was familiar.

"It's just like his other pocket worlds," she said over her shoulder to the others, who were moving warily forward. The construction was straightforward, and the rune that would open the door was located about halfway up the left-hand side, close to the doorknob.

Kate paused. In Yellow's tavern, the door hadn't had a knob, yet here was a copper knob covered in the blue-green signs of aging. She ignored it and looked back at the runes.

It was like a breath of fresh air. Runes she could read, calling for *vitalle* she could easily press into the correct place. No strange elven magic. No bonds that she didn't fully understand. No half-elven complications. This was human magic. Keeper magic.

Renault and his amulet could be on the other side.

Part of her mind raised the obvious issues with such a hope, but she ignored it. "I can open this."

Her eyes trailed along the doorframe, and the runes began to repeat themselves. Halfway down the right-hand side was another activation point, connected to the first through a long thread of runes.

"You want to open that door," Silas said, his voice low, "when you don't know if the mad queen is in there?'

"Because cornering rabid creatures is always such a good idea?" Tribal asked.

Amidst the yellow of the doorframe, the glitter of Naevys's gold remnant was smeared on the activation rune. A second smudge covered the right-hand rune.

Kate's fingers itched to touch them, but she forced herself to acknowledge the dwarves' point. She reached for the side pocket of her pack. "Let's see if she is in there." She pulled out the solos potion and dribbled it over the smear by the knob.

A fog of golden shimmers rose from the mark, and Kate pushed her hand into it. Venn did the same.

Naevys's finger pressed against the rune, her other hand reaching over to press the other one. There was a surge of heat, and the door cracked open outward into the clearing. Set just inside it was a slightly smaller stone arch.

The memory faded, but another cloud of remnant grew from a streak of her remnant that wrapped into the crack between the frame and the door. Kate adjusted her hand to that one.

The yellow door was pushed open from within, Naevys's hand gripping the frame. Outside, the bright sunlight of early afternoon landed in the clearing. She passed under the stone arch and out the door.

Kate pulled her hand away from the mist as it dissolved into the air and leaned closer to the runes. There didn't appear to be a second smudge from the Warden. "She's gone. She went in, then came back out." A thrill of excitement shot through her. "Let's go in."

She reached across the door to touch the other rune.

"Ah," Silas said. "What exactly will we find?"

"Renault's body." Kate set her fingers on both runes. "The amulet."

"Kate," Venn said, "this feels impulsive."

"Obsessive." Tribal turned the word into a cough.

The word thrummed inside Kate with a grating, irksome feel. "I am *not* obsessing," she said through clenched teeth. She spun to look at them all. "Do any of you really think the box isn't intrinsically connected to…" She waved her hand at the woods. "Everything that's going on?"

Venn frowned, neither dwarf said anything, and the elf twins just looked lost.

"Me neither." Kate faced the door. "So before it's used for whatever Naevys wants, I'm getting my brothers out. This is where Renault is supposedly buried, with his amulet. I'm going in."

"I thought you had a different temporary sort of amulet you could make," Silas said.

His objection fanned the irritation inside her. "Well, Crofftus stole that book, and I'd rather use the real amulet anyway."

"Twig," Tribal said almost gently. "If it's in there, do you really think the mad queen hasn't taken it already?"

The truth of it dug like a nail into Kate's gut. "Will you all stop pointing that out? Of course I think she has! But at least I'll know where it was a few hours ago! It's finally a place to start!"

Tribal pulled out his axe and hefted it, staring determinedly at the door. "As long as we all have reasonable expectations."

Kate focused on her two fingers touching the runes and tried to push *vitalle* out of them. The finger on her right hand warmed, and the rune beneath it flared, but the finger of her left hand did nothing. She pushed some out that finger, and the right side faded.

She let out an irritated hum.

"It's supposed to open," Tribal whispered loudly to Silas. "Right?"

"Shut up, Tribal." Kate shook out her hands. "I've never had to push *vitalle* out in two places at once before. It's surprisingly hard to concentrate on both hands at once."

"Connect them," Silas said.

Kate shot him an annoyed look. "I have to touch opposite sides of the door."

"No. Connect them in your mind. It's like fighting with two blades. You can't focus on one hand to the exclusion of the other—you have to think of them as the two ends of the single entity that is your arms. You're moving your arms, as a unit, with a blade at each end." He gestured toward the door. "Think of your arms as a single thing. Like a hose with two spouts that can shoot out magic or sparkles or whatever you do."

Kate mulled over the idea, seeing the connection of her arms to her torso, thinking of them as two outlets of the same well. "That's actually good advice."

"You sound surprised."

Kate imagined the *vitalle* in her chest welling up, flowing down both arms and out her fingertips.

Both runes warmed, and the door clicked open.

The dwarves, Fix, and all three elves flinched at the sound. Kate shifted to the side and turned the knob, pulling the door slowly open.

Inside the doorframe, the ancient stone arch lead into a dark room. Sunlight streamed through, landing on a rough stone floor and reflecting faint light onto tables and bookshelves and workbenches.

Kate cast out. The wave rippled oddly through the doorway but continued across the room, finding no sign of life until the shape of a small potted plant lit up along the far wall. The room was at least twenty paces across and equally wide.

Kate stepped into the room.

Prickles ran over her skin, like the jab of tiny pins, both icy cold and burning hot at the same time. Her foot landed on the stone floor with a dull thud and a puff of dust. Chairs were pulled up around three tables. Books covered their surface in piles or lay open as though someone were in the middle of reading.

Every chair was empty. There was no sign of a cot or a bed. She moved farther in. Behind her, Venn's light footfall landed on the ground, then the shuffling of the others. The room was set up for study or writing. Scrolls, loose paper, and a line of quills and pencils filled shelves along the walls. The sunlight glinted off a huge array of glassware at the far side of the room. An alembic sat in the center of one of the tables, with a selection of candles nearby. Instruments for measuring and stirring were placed neatly in their places.

Everything was designed for work, except for one nook along the lefthand wall with a large fireplace. The chair in front of it was tall-backed and upholstered with rich leather.

Kate started toward it, her hands feeling suddenly clammy. If Renault had died hundreds of years ago, whatever was sitting in that chair would be… At best it would be unrecognizable. At worst…

The room smelled of dust and must and something that might be rot. Or just old ingredients. A glance back at the glassware showed withered things hanging from the ceiling.

She reached the tall leather back and braced herself before stepping around the side of it.

The chair was empty.

CHAPTER FORTY-ONE

"What's there?" Tribal whispered.

"Just..." Kate stared at the chair, the emptiness of it seeping into her. "Dust."

Tribal shifted. "Like 'the half-elf died so long ago his body turned to dust' dust?"

Kate turned the chair to face them. "Just regular dust."

Venn lowered her crossbow, and the two dwarves lowered their axes.

"Does anyone see him?" Kate asked, trying not to lose the hope that had been growing in her.

Silas moved quickly through the room. "Not immediately."

The room was as chilled as the outside world, but wood had been laid in the fireplace with a healthy stack of extra in a recess beside it. Kate knelt and slipped her finger into the bundle of kindling in the center and shoved out a burst of *vitaile*. The fire flared up, and she stared into the flames.

Renault wasn't here.

She sent out a finger of *vitalle* and pulled a tongue of flame into her hand, cupping it in her palm. It warmed her skin, driving away the chill that had sat in her bones since...

How long had it been? Since Virion's? Had she been truly warm and comfortable since then? Rising, she dropped into the tall chair and sank into the plush cushion, watching the flame in her hand numbly.

Renault wasn't here, which meant—even if Naevys hadn't somehow found it already— his amulet probably wasn't either.

The truth of it weighed down on her, and she slumped lower.

"This," Silas said, coming up next to the chair, "is an excellent growlery."

She pulled her eyes away from the flame and frowned up at him.

"A growlery," he explained. "A refuge. A sanctuary to crawl into when you're feeling growly." He surveyed the nook and the fireplace. "You're doing it wrong." He took the arm of the chair and shoved it around until she faced the fire. "There. Now it's perfect."

The fire crackled loudly, warming her feet. Silas took a candle off the mantel, lit it, and used it to light a nearby lantern before disappearing into the rest of the room. Slowly, the ceiling and walls grew brighter, but she stayed staring into the fire.

Everything about her was heavy, as though she'd been walking uphill through deep snow for hours—for days. Constantly pushing back exhaustion, each step an effort. As though every time she'd lifted her foot higher, she'd just slid back down.

Renault wasn't here. Kate looked for any way around the fact or any clue to where he really was. Virion had thought Renault had buried himself here. Naevys had complained in a journal that Renault was out of her reach. It had made so much sense that he'd be here.

But Renault wasn't here.

And Naevys wasn't here.

The second thought felt stale. They'd been looking for Naevys for an eternity. Even when Kate had just been trying to figure out what had attacked Bo in the ravine, she'd been looking for the Warden—she just hadn't known it yet.

Frustration and impatience and the never-ending waiting warred inside her, and she glanced down at her pack. The box was right there. Right there! And yet she couldn't open it.

"Um," Tribal said from nearby, "do we just leave the door open?"

"Naevys is the only one I'd want to close out," Kate said, "and she knows how to open it. Let's leave it and enjoy the extra light."

The dwarf's feet shuffled uncertainly. "Do we need some sort of watch?"

Kate glanced at the open door dully, seeing the clearing beyond it. "If she comes back, it's not like we can stop her."

Rustles came from different parts of the workshop. Drawers opening, papers shifting. She sank back, too tired to ask what they were finding.

She held her hands out toward the flames, wondering how often Renault had sat in this chair and done the same.

"Where are you?" she whispered. "If you're not in your pocket world, where—"

The obvious answer hit her with an almost physical force. "You're not in *this* pocket world."

No. It couldn't be. He couldn't really be...

She yanked open her pack and wrapped her fingers around the warm hum of the aenigma box. "Venn! What if we have the wrong pocket world? What if Renault is in the box?" The idea shifted, filling in gaps in Renault's story. If he'd been close to death, what better thing to do than enter the pocket world with his wife and daughter and live in a time that moved so slowly that centuries in the outside world could pass before he actually died?

"Venn! He could still be alive!"

There was no answer, and Kate leaned around the side of the chair.

The room was lit with a half-dozen lanterns, the warm golden light filling it with an unexpected coziness.

Venn crouched in the far corner of the room, facing the side of a large bookshelf. "Kate…"

Kate pushed herself up and crossed the room.

Two small skeletons were huddled in the corner between the bookshelf and the wall. Neither would have stood taller than Kate's hips. For a moment, she froze at their childlike size, but their arms and fingers were too long, the bones too knobby, the skulls too wide.

"Are those…" She leaned closer. "Kobolds?"

One of the skeletons had its arms wrapped around the other.

Aislin and Matlen came up to Kate's shoulders, peering at the small figures.

A knife was crushed between them. Deep inside a nick in the blade, a glint of dark purple shone.

"There's a remnant." Kate set the box on a nearby table and went back to her pack, pulling out the solos potion.

Kneeling next to Venn, she let a single drop fall onto the notch on the knife. A cloud of deep, rich purple rose from it, and a lone toll of a bell rang out.

Kate sucked in a breath at the sound. "The bell!" It was the same tone as the box always held, except here, instead of feeling lonesome and lost in a vast emptiness, it was cheerier. Almost a bell of celebration. "The one I always hear in the box!" Kate thrust her hand into the cloud, and after a slight hesitation, Venn did the same.

A knife stuck out of his chest. Burning, tearing pain shot out from it. The worn, tattered green of his tunic darkened with blood.

Purple fingers scrabbled at the hilt, their knuckles like knots of a tree. Terror filled him, leaving his legs numb and twitching, bubbling higher in his chest until it rose into his throat, cutting off his air.

He looked up. Renault squatted close. His beard was cut close, shaped to a cruel point. His eyes were almost black, glittering with something hungry, even as a bit of sorrow creased his brow.

A warm rush of loyalty filled the kobold, nipping away at the edges of the blinding pain. The sharp stab of betrayal cut almost as deeply as the physical blade.

"If I had another option..." Renault said. "But I need to seal the door, and your mistlight is already so intrinsic to it all. Any other option would have been wasteful."

His hands gripped the aenigma box, the surfaces rich and new-looking. The metal shone with a burnished glow. Each rune on the top was carved in crisp strokes.

Horror and pain washed over every other emotion. The kobold tried to breathe, but a smothering weight sat on him. The edges of his vision grew dark.

"You should be proud." Renault leaned closer, his eyes searching the air around the kobold. "You've served my family so well. Go ahead," he crooned, the gentle tone nauseating against the backdrop of his hunger. "Let it go, Tumble. You're almost there."

His purple fingers grabbed for the hilt again, useless and clumsy, but his heavy arms fell to his lap.

Darkness raced in from the edges, searing the world away.

The black closed around the satisfied smile on Renault's face as he reached toward the knife.

Kate reeled back, taking gasping breaths as the purple mist

faded. Venn sank back on her heels, her eyes flashing with outrage.

A cautious step came up behind them. "What did you see?" Aislin whispered.

"Renault killed him," Kate said, slowing her breathing, "to get his lastlight." She pressed her hand against her sternum, the memory of Tumble's knife merging with the way the arrow had sunk into her in the Elder Grove. She rubbed at the spot, trying to banish the echoes of pain. "That was the kobold he'd used for years." Kate met Venn's appalled gaze. "The one his daughter loved. The one his wife thought he killed to make the pocket world."

"Which he did," Venn said.

A question pushed its way through the cloud of horror, and Kate's hand stopped. "But...why?"

Venn gave her an incredulous look. "To fuel that cursed box! Everything we learn about it makes it worse!"

A shiver rolled across Kate's neck at the thought, a repugnance at the way Tumble's life had been spilled. His essence drained away and infused into the box so strongly that hundreds of years later, his bell still rang in it. The thought of the warmth that permeated the box took on a more gruesome tenor.

Kate shook her head to banish the thought. "No, the pieces don't fit together. Why do all that?" She waved at the skeleton. "Lastlight is just a portion of someone's *vitalle*. They've already lost a portion of it by the time they die. That's the point. It's the energy that's left behind. Not enough to keep them alive, but still a good amount. So..." Kate grimaced at the sickening idea. "Why not just take it all? I can pull the *vitalle* out of someone who's perfectly alive. It would kill them, and I could take every bit they have. There is no chance that Renault was not capable of the same. Why stab Tumble and wait for death just to harvest only a part of the power his body contained?"

Venn stared at her. "Does it matter?"

Kate spun to take in the workshop. "It obviously did to Renault. He was vicious, yes, but in pursuit of his goals. Not needlessly. Why waste part of the kobold's *vitalle*?" She turned back to Tumble and caught a glimmer of green worked in between strips of leather on the hilt. Her fingers tightened on the solos potion. "Venn, there's another remnant."

Venn tensed. "Do we have to?"

"You don't." Kate took a bracing breath and let a drop of potion fall on the emerald speck. A haze of green rose from it. Slowly, she stretched her fingers into it.

Beside her, Venn shook out her hand and put it in as well. Aislin reached forward, but Venn gave her a pained look. "You'll feel the death."

Aislin's eyes widened, and she drew her hand back.

Crushing sadness crashed over her. A gaping hole of loss, torn open and left bleeding.

A trembling, green-skinned hand wrapped around the hilt and pulled it from his lifeless chest. Tumble's skin was grey, touched with faint lavender. His unseeing eyes were dull. His body slumped against the bookshelf, the front of his green tunic crusted with browned blood.

The green hand reached out and grabbed his shoulder, shaking him, then she looked wildly around the empty workshop. A bitter, gnawing grief dug into her.

"No, no, no, no," she whispered. Scrambling up, she stumbled to the shelves covered with glass bottles filled with liquids or powders or small objects. Pulling out a small jar, she uncorked it and dumped four dried berries into her hand. An acrid scent of vinegar filled her nose, causing a thread of fear to wind through the grief.

She cast aside the bottle and turned. Nothing moved in the room. Slowly, she raised her hand, her gaze skittering to the door, to the dark shadows, to the chair by the empty fireplace.

Fear and grief and resolution warred inside her.

When nothing moved, she let out a breath that was half sorrow, half soul-deep relief. "Really gone," she whispered. She brought her hand to her lips, and the bitterness of the berries filled her mouth. She swallowed quickly, and they burned down her throat.

She ran back to Tumble, kneeling and pulling him into an embrace, burying her face in the kobold's dry, wiry hair. "Hate him," she whispered viciously. "Hate him!"

Her stomach cramped, and a spike of fear shot through her. She gripped Tumble tighter. "I'm sorry," she whispered again. "I'm sorry. I'm sorry."

The pain lanced into her chest. The kobold squeezed her eyes shut. There was nothing in the blackness beyond the shuddering pain of her breaths, the limp stillness of Tumble's body, the metallic scent of blood, and the splitting grief tearing her apart.

A burst of pain exploded across her body. Then another. Then the sound of her breathing stopped. The feel of Tumble's hair grew faint, and everything faded.

Kate drew back, sucking in another gasping breath, feeling the air rush deep into her lungs.

"Twig?" Tribal asked, his voice wary.

"This one found Tumble's body, and…" She looked over at the shelves of glass bottles. One lay open on its side, nothing inside it but dark dust.

"Those were ferien berries," Venn said quietly. "Their poison is very quick." She swallowed down a grimace. "And very painful."

"Renault killed her too?" Aislin asked, outrage leaking into her voice.

"No." Kate corked the solos potion. "I think Renault was dead when she found Tumble. When she went to eat the berries, she waited, as though expecting to be stopped."

The two skeletons were so small crowded into the corner. So helpless. So hopeless.

"Occasionally," Kate said, "when someone cruel ensnares the loyalty of a kobold, they command them not to harm themselves as a deterrent from ending their enslavement early." She pushed herself to her feet. "The command is binding whether their master is close or not and lasts until the master's death."

"Then he's not in your box," Venn pointed out.

Kate nodded. "At least not alive."

A couple of quick knocks sounded from the middle of the workshop. Fix squatted on the tabletop near the aenigma box, rapping his fingers on the wood and pointing at an open book. Kate crossed over to him to find a drawing of Tumble, the knife in his chest. Beneath it, Naevys's writing filled the page in Kalesh.

Kate glanced at Fix. "How did you find this?"

He motioned to the table.

"It was like this?" At his nod, Kate turned back to the page.

Naevys's remnant was wiped along the edges of the page, bright and new.

"She was just looking at this." Kate glanced around the table. Bits of Naevys's remnant were caught between the slats of the table, deep inside cracks where they'd faded and grown old. On every surface there were signs of her having been here long ago, but the marks on this book were fresh. The sensation of wind and needles and maple leaves rustled around Kate as though Naevys were still here.

The queen's words were in faded old ink, and Kate translated them aloud.

Renault was a fool to use Tumble's lastlight. His wastefulness grows. His greed grows. Is it not enough to drain the White Wood? Must he continue to kill creatures who are bound to serve him?

His cruelty grows as well. I shudder, thinking what Tumble's last moments were like. Of course Renault used the knife. He'd need the struggle at the end, need Tumble's fear to grow his ael'iza. How could the scoundrel not be content with the amount the kobold would have had if he just killed him quickly?

I have never had the courage to ask him how he discovered that a violent, painful death gives off stronger lastlight than a complete quick death. I still do not.

His obsession grows.

I cannot fathom how it still grows.

In fresh ink at the bottom of the page, a note was added.

Now I can. Now I wonder that it didn't grow more.

CHAPTER FORTY-TWO

"Wait," Silas said, "the mad queen is claiming that she doesn't understand his obsession?"

"At the time when Tumble died, she was." Kate flipped earlier in the book until she found a date at the beginning of the entry about the kobolds. A dozen questions swirled in her mind, but her gaze was pulled back to the two skeletons in the corner. "I need to make a timeline, but first, does anyone know the burial practices of kobolds?"

No one answered.

"Because I only know detailed information about one kobold," Kate said. "Her name was Purnicious. She served the first queen of Queensland and her family for almost two centuries. When she died, she was buried in state in the royal tombs. But I don't know what other kobolds do. Are they buried under trees like elves? Under stones like the dwarves? In the ground like humans?"

"If I had to guess," Venn said, "I'd say they would do it in a pocket world. After all, it's where they go to hide from the world.

They're the experts on it. It's where Renault went to learn all of this."

Kate looked around the workshop. "I know Purnicious loved fabric. I have no idea if other kobolds are the same, but is there anything we could cover them with?"

"There's this." Matlen crossed to a shelf near the fireplace and pulled a richly embroidered blanket down. He shook it out, revealing the vibrant picture of a house in the woods, stitched into the fabric in bright reds and greens. The sky was vividly blue. The windows of the cottage shimmered in gold thread.

"It's perfect," Kate said.

Matlen and Aislin spread it over the bones, tucking it neatly around the edges. Then they both knelt next to the makeshift grave.

Tribal and Silas came over, standing soberly along the kobold's sides. Fix hopped to the closest table, squatting down, his eyes forlorn.

"We have a tradition," Silas said quietly, "for when someone's life is taken. Since the murderer deemed their lives less important than whatever goal they had, we gather and declare why they were more important." He looked sadly at the lumpy blanket. "Tumble was killed by Renault, and the other died of a broken heart, so as I figure it, Renault killed her, too." He shifted his weight. "Of course, it's always people who knew the cousin who speak, and none of us knew these unfortunate souls."

"I know a little about Tumble." Kate pulled out her journal, flipping to the page where she'd made notes on Renault's records. She found the section about Tumble and frowned. "Renault lied. He said in his reports that Tumble died while they tried to connect the pocket world in the box to the door, which matches the memory, but then Renault says he buried the body just inside the door to that pocket world. 'In a place no one would stumble upon it and be troubled.'" The disgust she already held for Renault grew, and she turned the page quickly. "That's not the part I was looking for. Here. Renault's wife wrote this."

> *He came home with a kobold! A lovely little thing named Tumble with skin the color of dark red wine. Miliene loves him, and he her. He's constantly making her little trinkets and dolls to play with, always conscientious to make it something she can hold. Her fingers won't grip well any longer.*

Silas knelt next to the bodies. "Rest well, Tumble. You were loyal and kind. Renault was wrong to take that from the world."

Tribal sank to his knees as well. "Rest well, Tumble's nameless friend. You loved deeply, and Renault was wrong to take that from the world."

Venn set her hand on the blanket and whispered something in Elvish. Aislin and Matlen bowed their heads.

Fix crept forward and placed a little black gem on the blanket.

"A black tourmaline," Silas said, his voice approving. "The traditional mourning stone."

Fix scooted back next to Kate.

The tangle of bones beneath the blanket was so small that it barely took up any space, and the tragedy of it sank into Kate. "Rest well, both of you. Your lives were valuable, and Renault was wrong to use them."

They stood for a moment in silence before Kate looked at her companions. "What do you say we find a way to stop Naevys from doing things just like this?"

"Yes," Venn said, stepping back from the bodies. "And quickly."

"All right. Naevys tore apart Home looking for that yellow door, then she came here. So let's figure out why." Kate started walking along the wall, surveying the shelves and cabinets mounted on it. "She definitely looked in that book Fix found, but I don't see any recent signs of her over here." A tall, luxuriously carved cupboard stood in the corner with a fresh smear of Naevys's remnant on the handles of the wide doors. Kate pulled at it, but it was locked. She cast out toward it. The doors appeared to be plain wood, but inside, a long shape like a knife lit up, hanging against the back wall.

Aislin and Matlen straightened. "What's that?"

"A weapon holding magic." Kate drew back. "Can any of you pick a lock?"

"Fix is better than we are," Silas said, pulling a chair in front of the cupboard. The gnoblin climbed up on it and peered into the keyhole. He pulled off his thick cloak before digging into one of his pockets.

Kate continued along the counter that ran all the way down the next wall. Books were piled along the back of it. Small contraptions littered the surface. Bundles of scrolls were tied together collecting dust, but any glimmer of Naevys's remnant was old and faded.

The last wall held the door, still open to the outside, a short line of shelves filled with more books and contraptions, and the nook by the fireplace.

On one shelf was an ornate box with a fresh smear of gold remnant on the lid.

Kate opened it and found it empty except for a piece of black velvet cloth with a round imprint on it the size of her palm—the size of Renault's amulet.

She stared at the emptiness for a heartbeat.

Naevys's remnant was wiped on the edges of the indentation, and a hint of old *vitalle* emanated from the box.

Kate's hands stayed frozen, holding up the lid. "She has it," she whispered.

Venn peered over her shoulder. "The amulet?"

Kate nodded, slowly letting the box close.

Silas let out a pained sigh. "Please don't tell me you're surprised by this."

Kate ran her finger over the swirling grooves in the lid. Dismay sank into her gut, pooling like ice cold water. "Not... entirely." Her finger paused on a Kalesh word carved into the wood.

Pruconet.

"Bridge?" Kate rubbed the thin marks. "I've never heard him call the amulet a bridge before."

"You haven't read everything the man ever wrote," Tribal pointed out.

"True, but I've read a bit about his amulet."

"It is a sort of a bridge, though," Venn pointed out, "between the real world and the pocket world."

"That's true." Kate cast out into the box, and some residual vitalle lit up. "There's still a...not a remnant, but a sense of power." Kate poured a little of her remnant into the wave to keep it in place while she studied it. The potency of the amulet rang out like an echo, but a strange one. This wasn't a seat of power that slowed time and held a potion that would stabilize a doorway. This was more tenuous. More fluid. "It is a connection. A binding."

"You say that like it's not what you expected," Venn said.

"It's not." Kate let the wave fade away. "I don't know what I expected, but this feels different. This doesn't feel like it would open the Runelight Drawer safely."

Venn's brow furrowed. "How do you know what that would feel like?"

Kate shook her head, trying to understand the vague sense coming from the box. "I don't know." Her disappointment and frustration swirled with a cloud of confusion. "But that feels wrong." She scanned the three large tables in the middle of the floor, but they were mostly empty. "And I don't see anything else Naevys touched."

The queen's remnant only glittered from four places: just inside the door, the floor beneath Kate's feet, at the table by the book, and in front of the cupboard. Naevys hadn't touched anything else obvious.

Kate studied the cupboard, a little bit of hope resurfacing. "Fix, when you get that unlocked, let's open it carefully."

The gnoblin made a few hand gestures.

"He says it's a complicated lock." Silas moved to the long counter and pulled a small box away from the wall, peering inside it. "Might take a bit."

Kate pointed to the open book. "That book mentions lastlight, and Fix says that's what she was looking for in Renault's cave as well." Kate rubbed her face, trying to drive away her growing frustration. The box labeled "Bridge" was just another piece of the puzzle that didn't fit. All the different pieces of Naevys's story lay scattered in Kate's mind, itching to be put into some semblance of sense. She closed her eyes, trying to get a hold of it all, but it was too jumbled. "Before, when I was trying to piece together what was going on with the Warden, I focused on Renault, trying to pin down his story, but it's Naevys's I can't sort out. There's a hole in it. A very big one." She grabbed her journal from her pack and sat at the table. "I want to construct a timeline of her actions. Venn, could you help with what you know of Renault? The rest of you…" She paused. "Not to sound obsessed, but could you look for the amulet?"

Silas frowned. "Didn't you just find its empty box?"

"I…" Kate gave a small shrug. "Just keep your eye out for it."

Tribal looked up from where he was rummaging through a drawer. "Look around a secret magical workshop for treasure? I suppose we could suffer through that."

"If you find the amulet," Kate said, turning back to her journal, "don't touch it. Virion said if someone without magical abilities touches it, it could kill them."

Silas's hands paused in the middle of shifting a pile of books on the cluttered countertop. "We'll let you touch it first."

Venn pulled up a chair next to Kate, her eyes lingering on Aislin and Matlen, who still sat hunched on the floor next to the remains of the kobolds.

Silas caught the look and cleared his throat. "Hey, skinny little elf twins, when you're done, can we borrow your skinny little elf hands? There's a broken drawer here that only opens a crack, and I can't reach what's inside."

The twins looked up at him, blinking slowly. Matlen rose, pulled up his sister, then the two shuffled over to the dwarves.

Venn sighed. "What do you need, Kate?"

Kate pulled off her cloak and hung it over the back of a nearby chair, working to settle the frustration inside her. She flipped to an empty page in her journal. "The problem with the relationship between Naevys and Renault is that there's too much time between when he was here and when Naevys decided to do..." She waved her pencil around, encompassing everything. "All this."

"That's hardly the only problem with it," Venn said under her breath.

Kate winced. "That's fair. But regardless, I'm struggling to keep their timeline straight. Let's start with a year I'm sure of. Emperor Sorrn came north looking for the amulet in the year 525 of the Kalesh Empire."

"Which was three hundred and five years ago," Venn said. "Because that is when my people came here from the Wildwood."

"All right, that's our anchor point. How long ago did Renault come to the White Wood?"

"I would say three hundred and thirty years," Venn said. "So the year 500."

"And we can assume Naevys met him around that time?" Kate began jotting notes.

"She was Warden by then, so yes. She'd have known of a half-elf settling at the edge of the forest."

"Renault's records from his cave covered several years of his work. But not too many. I think we can say that by 505, he'd created the box and the pocket world and the amulet."

"Which means"—Venn gave a subdued wave toward Tumble—"at that time, Naevys was still—not herself, maybe, but not as heartless as she has come to be by now."

"I agree." Kate looked at the page. "When do people think Renault died?"

Venn thought for a moment. "At least ten years before we came. But some think he'd been gone a lot longer."

Kate jotted a note. "So he died sometime between 505 when he made the box and 515." When Venn nodded, she continued, "Emperor Sorrn died in 525, and it took less than twenty years after that before the empire collapsed completely, and famine and war spread even up into this corner of it." She paused. "Famine and war that I always assumed came from the collapse of the empire, but which Thallion claimed was because the White Wood had been weakened by Renault."

Venn looked at the list. "Could both have contributed?"

"I suppose. It's an odd coincidence, though. The political collapse of an empire that had survived for centuries—a collapse that happened because the emperor died right here—coinciding with some rogue mage harming the White Wood?"

"Coincidences do happen."

The two events sat in Kate's mind with a disjointed feel. They were too connected to be unrelated, but too foundationally different to imagine they were linked.

She set aside the question for the more annoying one. "Here's the massive hole in Naevys's story. All of this"—she waved to the page—"ended around three hundred years ago. After Renault's death, Naevys definitely tried to redo some of his work, and she was frustrated with him that he hadn't taught her more, but she didn't really change then."

"No. I lived with her, on and off, from not long after the empire fell until about a hundred and fifty years ago, when I had my falling out with Thallion and Faron. During that time, she was…" Venn's unfocused gaze drifted to the far wall. "She was admirable. She negotiated peace between disagreeing elves, she…" Venn sighed. "I *thought* she fought off the weakness Renault had left in his wake. As far as I could tell, everything she did was for the good of the forest. I was preparing to someday be queen of the Wood, and I wanted nothing more than to do it as well as she did."

"Then when did she begin to change?"

"It's been within the last century that Evay began to suspect the role of Warden was wearing on her."

"So two hundred years pass with Renault gone and Naevys is normal, then suddenly she begins to obsess about him and his work. She then decides to protect a lifeless stone ravine while draining the White Wood. And then starts targeting humans in an effort to regain access to this secret workshop of Renault's." Kate circled the gap in her timeline. "What happened in these two hundred years?"

"I'm not the one to ask." Venn set her finger on the timeline. "For the past one hundred and fifty years, I've barely spent time in the Wood."

"Maybe Naevys is the one to ask." Kate pulled Naevys's journal closer and turned the page. A new entry started about an aging tree, coming to the conclusion that a tree did not hold the same sort of lastlight as a human.

She flipped more pages but saw no more smudges of Naevys's remnant. The entries stayed confined to noting things about the forest. "Or not." She let the book shut. "This ends while Renault is still alive."

"Will these help?" Silas dropped a short stack of books on the table. "No idea what they say, but they're in the mad queen's handwriting like that one, and they look like journals to me."

Kate opened one and found an entry from ten years after Renault's death. Like Naevys's other writing, it was all in Kalesh. Venn took it in and sank back in her chair.

"Too bad it's not in Elvish," Kate said, flipping through the pages. "Then you could help me read them."

"I'm pretty sure the point of using Kalesh was so elves couldn't read it." Venn picked up the pencil and turned to a new page in Kate's journal. "I'll note anything important you find."

Several entries discussed the weakness growing in the White Wood. Far from being concerned, Naevys seemed content to map it out. Kate flipped ahead until she found one dated from the year 525. Its content was unremarkable. She turned the page, and the writing changed from quick, flowing script to a heavier, more rushed hand. "Oooh, here's something. It's from the Kalesh year 525. Or about three hundred years ago." She glanced at the others. "It's when Emperor Sorrn was here." Translating, she read it out loud.

> *14th of Zemny, year 525*
> *They have settled in the ravine.*
> *The leader is someone important. He carries himself with the arrogance that human rulers wear. I waited to see if they would move on, but they have set up camp and pulled out tools.*
> *Tonight, I will command them to leave.*
> *A darkness lingers around their presence. A foreshadowing of trouble. They can't find it. They wouldn't know to look, and yet...*
> *It sits ill with me that they are so close.*

. . .

15th of Zemny, year 525

The man claims to be emperor, and his words have the ring of truth.

He invokes Renault's name. Claims the half-elf stole something from him. Declares he will retrieve it.

There's madness in his eyes. A madness that will not heed my warning.

He may be emperor, but he will stop.

16th of Zemny, year 525

The fool heeded nothing. They dig. In the wrong place, but they DIG.

17th of Zemny, year 525

The man is insolence itself. He is pride and pettiness and naked greed. I have appeared to him up until now cloaked. I have held my fury in.

No longer.

Because he is emperor, because angering the hordes of humans under him would be…inconvenient, I will give him one more warning tonight.

If he does not heed that, every human who knows the path here and searches in those caves will die.

Every single one.

They will not endanger everything. Not after all this time.

Kate turned the page.

18th of Zemny, year 525
It is done.
I have their minds, and their bodies rot in the sun.
The emperor himself is sealed in his grave.
None will touch him. Ever.

A chill rolled across Kate's neck, and she looked up to meet the wary eyes of her companions. "What is in that cave?"

20th of Zemny, year 525
Gone! They are gone!
He must have found them! I asked him what he'd found, and he lied to me. "Nothing," he said, as though treasures such as these were beneath him.
Nothing!
I searched the bodies. They are not there.
Did he send them away with servants before the end?
But then, why stay? If he found Renault's box and the amulet, what else was there to look for?
He must have stayed for greed. Hoping to find more.
He's double the fool.
It matters not. I will find them again.
Tomorrow, I hunt.

The next entry was a month later,

They elude me still. The humans are like insects—there are too many of them to track.
There will be fewer come summer when their crops fail and their animals wither.
They will not escape me if I have to search every corpse of the entire empire.

CHAPTER FORTY-THREE

"Sounds like you found your answer of how the famine started," Silas said.

"Naevys did it?" Venn's pencil hung motionless over the page. "It wasn't the weakness caused by Renault? It was her?"

"I guess you were wrong about her not going mad until recently." Tribal's voice was light, but his brow furrowed with uneasiness.

"And this explains why she was trying to make her own box instead of just using Renault's," Kate said.

Silas glanced toward the still-open door. "She's not coming back here anytime soon, is she?"

Kate turned to the next page of the journal, but there was another gap in time, and the next entry was a year later and made no mention of boxes or amulets or the Kalesh. It was back to notes on the health of the White Wood.

Kate sank back in her chair. "Emperor Sorrn took the box and the amulet." She considered the idea. "Naevys must have been keeping them in the caves in the ravine. This explains, at least, the history of the box. If the emperor had claimed it and sent it to one of his monasteries that kept his treasure, they'd have affixed the Kalesh seal to it, which it had when I first saw it. And I saw memories from the box once. It showed changing between hands a few times, different people secreting it away in different places until it finally came to the mine just across the river from my home."

She tapped her finger on the table, more pieces falling into place. "The men who took it from us wore Kalesh tunics, and they used magic. Bo has found several monasteries that still cling to Kalesh ideas. Maybe those men were from the last place the box had been hidden. Maybe they'd tracked it all the way to Queensland."

"But Naevys found the amulet?" Venn pointed her thumb toward the carved, empty box. "And brought it back here?"

The odd feel of the box itched at Kate's mind, warring with the hope that Naevys actually had the amulet and it was at least relatively close, if not actually findable. "Since I can't make the bloodstone that could work as a temporary amulet without the book Crofftus stole, I hope so." She tapped her journal. "Let's finish this mess with Naevys."

The rest of the journal was filled with ramblings about the forest. Kate grabbed another and found more of the same. Venn rose and moved to the shelves along the wall.

In the fourth journal, dated with the Kalesh calendar, she found the drawing of an ice-blue dragon. "Venn! This is from only eighty-five years ago."

> 3rd of Kyvet, year 745
>
> Yilfrist can sense them. Only the stronger mages, but that is all I need.
>
> Curse Renault for dying. Curse him for having such an odd assortment of abilities.

Yilfrist has caught two so far. The first, a mewling, spineless man who was less than useless. He could barely infuse runes with ael'iza, never mind help me create a box. The effort killed him in less than a day.

Yilfrist brings Renault up often. As though, when I introduced him, the dragon had anything but contempt for the half-elf. The kobold that Renault gave to him has died, though. Apparently, Yilfrist grew to like having a servant. Something about the ease of getting things from nearby settlements.

I told him to stop whining and go find another. He found several for Renault, after all. But he claims he needs help saving them. All he can do is put them in danger.

You would think the price I pay him is already enough. But the world is full of greed.

28th Madny, year 780
He has found another mage. This one holds promise. He can read the runes, at least.

1st Zemny, year 780
Who would have ever thought that Renault, with his conceit and waspishness, was unique? Why can none of these mages follow his work? This one read the runes, even understood the way the ael'iza would flow through them. But the smallest wellstone broke his mind.

Useless. They are all useless.

Just another suffusion for Yilfrist. I swear he brings me stupid ones just so he can absorb their power.

"So," Venn said slowly, "the rumors of a dragon hunting mages are true."

A shiver rolled up Kate's spine. "He spoke into my mind when we connected with Naevys."

"I heard it." Venn gave an apprehensive look toward the door. "He called you 'little mage.'"

Aislin and Matlen stopped rummaging through a pile of odd instruments and looked warily between Kate and the door.

Both dwarves stood shoulder to shoulder, leaning back against a counter that ran along the wall. Their gazes were fixed on Kate with equally troubled expressions.

"It's going to be the death of us," Silas said, "staying close to these two."

Tribal folded his arms. "The prospect of danger keeps growing on this treasure hunt, and the chance of finding treasure keeps shrinking."

"We were never on a treasure hunt," Kate said, flipping further through the book.

"*You* were never on one," Tribal corrected her.

"She didn't finish this journal." Kate turned to the last filled page. "But the final entry is only fifty years ago."

16th Myraz, year 782

Our current mage is from far to the south. So far Yilfrist was gone for nearly a month. But this one shows actual promise. He can read runes. And he can touch the wellstones, as long as he protects himself from the way they want to steal his mind. I think he can do what is necessary.

18th Myraz, year 782

He has done it! Perone has connected the runes! Finally! He claimed Renault's instructions were lacking a crucial step. I'm tempted to believe Renault would have done just that to thwart anyone who tried to come after him.

For now, Perone sleeps, having exhausted himself with the effort of completion. But tomorrow—tomorrow—we test it!

Can it be that finally the solution is within my grasp?

I cannot do it alone, but Perone should be able to do his part. We shall soon see.

I will let him rest a little. But not past dawn.

21st Myraz, year 782

Success evades me. Eighteen animals dead and nothing to show for it. Perone and I can each do our part, but doing them together never quite works. The host occasionally survives, but the guest dies every time.

I begin to mistrust Perone. He seems...wily. I catch him thinking, and it feels dangerous. Once or twice, I have detected the hint of an illusion around him. Yesterday, without me noticing, he found the notes on the others. I'm sure he has pieced together what happened to them.

I do not care. Let him fear the price of failure. He will help me complete this.

Success is so close.

It must be. Time is running out. I can feel it.

I can feel...everything. It pulls me out in thin strands, weaving me into the forest. I lose myself sometimes. In fact, it is only in here, with the door firmly shut, where I truly find myself again. But the price is too high. To find myself, I lose the Wood.

I cannot bear to be separated from it. But I also dare not fail. If I am lost, who will ever finish the work? Who could possibly stop the death? How could I let something so perfect die?

No. I must focus. We must succeed.

Kate looked up at Venn and saw her mystified expression.

So I stay and prod him. Curse him for not being Renault. Curse Renault for the frail humanness that led to his death. Curse me for not being able to merely do this myself.
The mage is tired. Another day of failure.
I am tired too. I will cage him for the night.
Perhaps tomorrow he will not fail.
Perhaps tomorrow I will lean on him harder.
<u>I cannot let death win.</u>

The final line was underlined with thick strokes that dug into the paper. Kate flipped past it, but all the rest of the pages were blank.

"That's an odd place to cut off," Kate glanced at the rest of the journals, but they were all from earlier times. "Unless…" She glanced around the workshop. A few faded glitters of Naevys's remnant were worked deep into the crevices of the table or glinted from the crease between the pages of her journals, but they were all old.

"Aside from this book," Kate said, tapping the journal with the kobolds and the lastlight, "nothing in here has been touched by Naevys in a very long time." She pointed at the open doorway that led to the forest. "Yellow said that door hung in his tavern for the past thirty years, and it was in an abandoned barn before that. What if this wily mage Perone"—she brought her finger back to Naevys's journal—"is our skeleton from the barn? What if he got out of his cage? If I were trapped inside a pocket world, I could get out of it. And knowing runes, I could probably remove the door and hide it somewhere in the woods."

"Without Naevys seeing it through the trees?" Venn asked.

"If he really was adept at illusions? Maybe." She turned to Aislin and Matlin. "You two convince the trees of illusions, don't you?"

Matlen nodded. "They're not particularly hard to trick." His shoulders fell. "Or they didn't used to be. We haven't tried yet."

"You've done it," Aislin said to Kate. "Haven't you? You made some sort of shield around yourself, and the forest couldn't tell what you were."

Kate nodded. "This entry was fifty years ago. Maybe Naevys never came back in here until today because she couldn't."

A shadow fell across the room, and Kate twisted to face the doorway. The dwarves and elves spun at the same moment, raising weapons.

Faron stood in the beam of sunlight, a handful of rangers visible behind him in the glade. He raised his hands in mock surrender and stepped inside, taking in the workshop. His eyes fell on Aislin and Matlen, and his expression grew pained. He crossed the room and set his hand on Matlen's shoulder. "How are you two?" he asked quietly.

Matlen gave a twitchy shrug. Faron squeezed his shoulder and came over next to Kate's chair. "We lost track of my mother again. I believe she's flying on the dragon." He rubbed a hand over his face. "Which is not something I ever thought I'd say." He looked down at the book curiously. "Is that why she came here?"

"She's been here a lot," Kate answered. "Although mostly a long time ago. Today, I think she only looked at—"

"Kate," Silas interrupted sharply. "There are more of those runes over here like there were around the door." He stood at the counter and held a lantern near the wall. The light glittered off a thinly carved design.

Kate rose and squeezed past Faron. "Venn can tell you what we've found."

"He can read it himself," Venn said, sounding irritated.

Faron gave some answer, but Kate leaned over the counter and took in the runes carved in a rectangle on the wall. "Definitely a pocket world." She set her finger on the correct rune, and the wall inside the runes disappeared.

Behind it lay a small stack of paper, each folded neatly. The entire bundle was tied with a gold and red cord. The papers, the cord, and the entire little cupboard were covered with Naevys's faded golden remnant.

"Treasure?" Tribal asked from her shoulder.

"I think it's letters." Kate pulled them out. Naevys's remnant covered every surface, as though she'd held them often. The top letter was addressed in Naevys's hand.

Kate paused and glanced at Faron. "Not sure we should read these. They look personal. They're addressed to Virion and dated from the reign of King Thorien."

Faron strode across the room. "That's my grandfather. These are well over four hundred years old!" He straightened at the writing. "They're in Kalesh?"

"All her journals and notes have been," Kate said.

"Why?" Faron looked around the room. "If those have nothing to do with Renault, why keep them in a language most elves can't read?" He stiffened and looked back at the letters.

"Yes," Kate said quietly. "So that most elves can't read it."

Faron stared at the letters, his face darkening. "Read them."

Kate hesitated. "Are you sure?"

Faron moved to the table across from Venn and sank into a chair. "A second person died from their injuries in Home."

Kate's fingers tightened on the letters.

Faron looked up at the others, his face stricken. "We have to stop her, and to do that, we have to understand what she's doing. Read them out loud."

Kate moved reluctantly back to her seat. Venn met her gaze with an uncertain look. The rich red and gold of the cord caught the lantern light as Kate sat and untied it. She picked up the first letter and held it toward Faron. "Maybe it should be you."

Faron folded his hands on the table, his expression strained. "Kate," he said, "please."

Kate opened the first one.

To Virion
951st year of King Thorien, 8th day of the White Moon

Both Faron and Venn looked up.

"That's the year of the battle," Faron said.

"Which battle?" Kate asked.

"Riekabrod?" Matlen asked.

Venn nodded and glanced at the dwarves, who had gathered around the table. "About four and a half centuries ago, a company of elves rode out with the humans to hold back the Kalesh incursion into the north."

"Virion was one of them." Kate read over the beginning of the letter. "This is while he was gone."

I have no way to send this to you, yet I am aching for a way to speak with you. So I will imagine you here while I write.

The snow grows deep. I hope you are south of it by now. Thallion thinks you all will be home by spring. I hope he is right, but even that is so long from now.

I have our seed. It is safe. Waiting for you to come back.

Venn's head snapped over to stare at the letter.

Faron hissed and pulled the paper out of Kate's hand. "They had a child?"

CHAPTER FORTY-FOUR

"A child?" The knot of questions Kate held about Naevys spread out in her mind.

"Elves grow from seeds?" Silas asked. "That explains a lot."

"To create a child," Venn said, ignoring him, "two elves bury a portion of their *ael'iza* beneath an elder tree, and it forms a seed."

"The Greenwood elves of Queensland do something similar. They're planted and grown." Kate paused and looked at Venn. "But the Wildwood elves are different, aren't they? I know the story of Leonis, who was half-elf. His mother was human. Can a human bury some of their *vitalle*?"

"Yes," said Venn. "With the help of a wellstone or a mage."

"Wait." Kate looked around the workshop. "Renault was half-elven. Was he from the White Wood?"

"His mother was Elianne," Faron said. "She left the woods to live with a human, and we lost her." He pushed the letter back toward Kate and sank back into his chair, a hint of betrayal in his expression. "My mother and Virion had a seed?"

Kate picked it up, mulling the idea. "I think you have a secret sibling, Faron."

His eyes flickered up to her, confused. "I don't."

"Well, you wouldn't know," Kate pointed out, "if it was secret."

"Faron would," Venn said. "We're too connected. Siblings are bound to each other. Actually connected. Elves are never lost or kept secret. We know who each elf is. If one was this closely related to Faron, he would know."

"You lost Renault's mother," Kate pointed out.

"When he says lost," Venn said, "he means she died."

A wave of irritation rose in Kate at the way Naevys's story refused to fall into place. She turned back to the letter.

I know our vows were unwitnessed, but I hold to them. Return to me quickly so they can be formalized.

Faron's mouth dropped open. "They wed? In secret?"

"Ooh!" Silas said. "The elven royal family just got more interesting!"

"They weren't officially wed," Venn said. "Virion told us their vows were informal. An official wedding between elves is sealed by the king," Venn said. "It's a symbol of the forest blessing the union. It is not truly binding until that point."

"True," Faron said, fixing Venn with an unreadable look. "Such a thing can be easily brushed aside."

Her lips pressed into a thin line. "Hardly easily." She turned back at Kate. "But a vow sealed before king and forest is a very hard bond to break."

"Even if one truly wants out?"

Venn rolled the cord between her fingers. "Because the forest seals the bond, the two are actually joined. Instead of two souls, they are, in some ways, one. They feel each other's pain and joy and needs. They can no sooner hurt the other than they could hurt themselves. It grafts the two together." She met Kate's eye. "Yes. It is a very hard bond to break."

An uncomfortable silence settled in the workshop.

Kate considered the pieces of Naevys's puzzle again, a few of them almost falling into place.

She turned back to the letter.

> *I have found the perfect place to plant the seed. There is a grove of maples that grows on an eastward-facing hillside. Everything about it reminds me of you.*
>
> *Return to me quickly.*

"I know that grove," Faron said, looking at his hands. "I found her there countless times."

"That was the first place Thallion took us," Venn said, "when we started looking for Naevys."

Kate pointed the letter toward Faron. "You gave your mother a shawl there last summer."

He looked up sharply. "How do you know that?"

"Thallion showed me the memory of the last time he'd seen her. He'd walked to that grove with you, and you gave her a shawl."

He nodded. "Whenever I looked for her, that is where I'd begin."

"Why did she need a place to plant the seed?" Kate asked. "I thought it was planted when it was created."

"No," Venn said. "It is created under the elder tree, then given back to the elves. But it is a seed. It is safe. Protected. Until it's planted, it just remains a seed."

"Sounds like an easy thing to lose track of," Tribal muttered to his brother.

Faron's brow creased in annoyance, but Venn let out a small

smile. "They're about the size of an apple, and immediately a connection forms between it and the parents. They are drawn to it, as long as the seed survives, which is about ten years. During that time, the elves find the perfect spot, then plant it in early spring when the ground thaws. They care for it all summer, and in the fall, an elf is born from the ground."

The picture that was forming out of the puzzle pieces in Kate's mind faltered. "What happens after ten years?"

"The seed decays and planting it does nothing."

Kate picked up the next letter. "This is from the next spring."

> *952nd year of King Thorien, 6th day of the Bud Moon*
> *The snow has melted. The maples' new leaves are vividly green. They smell like you.*
>
> *We have no news.*
>
> *No human in Home knows what has happened. Wherever you went is too far for the trees to see. I find myself watching the east every day.*
>
> *The horizon is always empty.*

> *952nd year of King Thorien, 19th day of the Wheat Moon*
> *The summer flowers bloom in the maple grove. The soil is too warm for planting. The season too far gone for seeds.*
>
> *I've tucked ours away. It is a daughter, I think. I know they say that cannot be known yet, but it is a daughter. I know it the same way I know you live. Next spring we shall plant her. I hope she has your hair.*
>
> *Thallion continues to declare you'll return soon. It eats at him that he was not permitted to go with you, but the duties of the White Wood govern most of his time now.*

Kate paused. "She didn't plant the seed when the time was right?"

"She couldn't," Venn said. "Both elves need to be there for the planting. They both share *ael'iza* with the ground when they plant it and continue to during the time when the seed grows." She sighed. "Since she had only ten years to plant the seed, and Virion didn't return from that battle for forty years, we know how this tragic tale ends."

The puzzle pieces drew closer, almost creating the story. The gap that had always been there shrank.

A seed. The maple groves. Wedding vows.

The ideas connected to others, hinting at answers to the questions that surrounded the Warden.

Kate glanced at the timeline in her journal. Except, like all things about Naevys, the timeline made no sense. "I think," she said, unfolding the next letter, "that we might not really know how it ends."

> 952nd year of King Thorien, 24th day of the Dry Moon.
>
> The human reached Home just as they finished bringing in the harvest. He was half-dead. The horror of your battle clings to him like the mud splashed on his boots and his pants and his cloak. It's in his hair and smeared across his face.
>
> Before he spoke, I knew what he would say.
>
> Every elf slain.
>
> Every human slain but him. He only survived because he was so gravely injured that the enemy took him for dead.
>
> The battle, he says with a great deal of bitterness, accomplished its goal. The Kalesh army barely survived, and they fall back to the south. For now.
>
> The Wood is in mourning.
>
> I...
>
> Virion, I find that I cannot mourn you. I know our vows were

not sealed. I know I shouldn't be able to feel your life or death, and yet... I do not believe you are gone. Thallion tells me it is mere fancy, although he words it kindly. But it is not.

I know you live.

Return to me, Virion.

Until you do, I will throw myself into caring for the White Wood. It is the only time my soul finds relief from the constant, endless waiting. I swear this waiting will be the death of me.

958th year of King Thorien, 25th day of the Fire Moon

I have made a new...I'm not sure I should name him "friend." Last month, a dragon with scales the blue of deep caverns in the glaciers approached the northern boundary of the Wood. He was lonesome and came searching for the Warden's help.

His name is Yilfrist—

"Yilfrist!" Faron stared at the letter. "She met the dragon over four hundred years ago?"

"Did the White Wood not know that?" Kate asked. "How could she hide a dragon?"

"She couldn't." Venn absently wound the cord around her finger. "It's not unheard of for dragons to come out of the northern range. They must have known."

Kate turned back to the page.

His name is Yilfrist. His brother died somewhere along the northern boundaries of the human lands, but he knew not where. He wanted the Warden's help to find his brother's bones. But Warden Ardryn continues to weaken, so I offered to help. My connection to the Wood has grown strong. I can even speak to the trees of the human wood, if they are old enough.

In exchange for helping him find his brother's bones, he agreed to fly me over the lands east of here. He claims to be able to sense beings with power greater than a human. He can find mages among them and is confident he could sense an elf.

Yilfrist points out that there's nothing in the human world that could stop you from returning if you were alive. I don't expect him to believe me. As long as he helps, he can believe anything he likes.

I have stopped telling Thallion that you still live. King Thorien grows very weak, and Thallion will inherit the throne soon. Much weighs on him now, including mourning your death. I do not like to add to his burdens.

Tomorrow I fly out to search for dragon bones and you.

Kate opened the next letter and paused. "This is years later."

3rd year of King Thallion, 1st day of the Ember Moon

This is the last spring, Virion. The seed already begins to weaken. I can feel her withering away. I wonder if you can feel it?

The healers say a seed this old might grow an elf, but it would be weak and short-lived. I hate that they say that.

Yilfrist and I have flown in all directions, searched everywhere, and have found no sign of you.

We found his brother's bones in the burned husk of a town, surrounded by human corpses. Yilfrist carried them back to wherever he lives in the mountains. I thought he would bury them. Instead, he absorbed them somehow. In the process, he gained his brother's power. He is faster. Brighter. Bigger.

I offer him sips of the power of the White Wood in exchange for more flights. The others do not know of our continued arrangement. Were Ardryn still a strong Warden, he would know. But he fades year by year.

This is the last spring, Virion, and since we have not found you, Yilfrist has offered an idea. The first time he suggested it, everything inside me recoiled. But the seed sits here by this paper. A tiny husk holding so much life. So much hope. So much of our future.

I cannot bear to let her go.
Will you forgive me for what I'm about to do?
I do not know.
And yet, I cannot let death win.

The words rang with familiarity, and Kate pulled over the journal with the pictures of the kobolds, staring at the final entry.

The mage is tired. Another day of failure.
I am tired too. I will cage him for the night.
Perhaps tomorrow he will not fail.
Perhaps tomorrow I will lean on him harder.
<u>*I cannot let death win.*</u>

"It's the seed." Kate breathed out the words as the puzzle pieces fell together, one after another. "All this time, she's been protecting the seed. That's what she's protecting in the ravine."

CHAPTER FORTY-FIVE

Venn shook her head slowly. "Kate, it's been hundreds of years. Far too long for the seed to survive." She looked earnest, but her words were missing their normal conviction.

"No." The pieces of Naevys's story tumbled into place. "It's her child in the ravine. That's what she's protecting." Before Venn or Faron could object, she grabbed the next letter.

> *3rd year of King Thallion, 2nd day of the Ember Moon*
> *Virion, it is done. I cannot stop trembling.*
> *Yilfrist explained that dragon eggs are soft when they are first laid. Too soft. The growing dragon can break out too soon, before it has grown enough or gained enough strength in the struggle to hatch. So the dragons harden the eggs. They encase them in a shield of what they call dragon stone. It keeps them safe and warm for centuries. The egg cannot be damaged or age.*

Venn made a pained sound. Faron leaned forward, his hands pressed into the table.

The dragon inside grows slowly, barely at all. But he grows strong before he can break out of it.

Our seed will not grow, of course, but she's protected. She will remain as she is for as long as we need. Until the first spring when you are home. I have sealed her in a cave.

I know. I can see your shock at the idea. But, Virion, the seed does not need the forest until you come back and help me plant her. This will just keep her safe. And secret.

I can't explain why I don't want the others to find her. She feels too personal. Our secret. Our hope. Our future.

Sitting here in this cave next to the dragon stone, my hope feels thin, though. It's been ten years, Virion. I know Thallion thinks I'm deluding myself, but I cannot shake the thought that you still live.

Virion, where are you?

Kate set it down and picked up the next. "This is twenty years later."

23rd year of King Thallion, 17th day of the Fire Moon.

I have not written since the day I entombed our seed in dragon stone. It sits ill with me. More and more so as the years go by. And yet, I cannot stay away from her. She is the only piece of you I have.

Is she the only piece of you left?

In three moons, it will be thirty years since you left. I confess that doubt creeps along the edges of my faith.

Is everyone right? Did you die with the rest?

I turn to the Wood as often as I can for distraction. It calls strongly to me. Almost as strongly as the seed. I know I told you I didn't want to be Warden, but there is a hole inside of me, and the Wood can fill it.

The more hopeless I feel about you, the more I consider answering its call.

. . .

24th year of King Thallion, 7th day of the Wheat Moon

I came to say goodbye. I have nowhere else to do it.

Spring has ended again. I cannot bear to wait for another. Holding this hope for you is too painful. It's tearing the life out of me.

This afternoon, I will offer myself to the Elder Grove. Warden Ardryn has lingered for decades, but he deserves rest.

And, I will admit this to you, if to no one else, I long to lose myself in the Wood. I long to end this cursed waiting.

So today, I'm laying it down. I'm setting aside the hope of ever seeing you again. I will take up the role of Warden, and it will consume me, and that is better than this.

Goodbye, my love. We should have had so much more.

Kate set the letter down slowly. Aislin blinked back tears, and Matlen squeezed her hand. Faron's outrage was tempered with pity.

Venn let out a long, slow breath and looked at the letter. "It was still fifteen years until Virion returned."

One last letter sat unopened. Kate unfolded it slowly.

33rd year of King Thallion, 1st day of the Pearl Moon

Others have graves to visit. Trees to lean against and talk to. I have nothing but a pile of unread letters. So here I am.

Thallion asked again if I would be his queen.

The crown sits heavy on him. You might not recognize this somber king if you were looking for the carefree boy he used to be. I have tried to help him. Tried to lift some of the weight.

It would be easier to do as his wife.

I told him of the vows you and I spoke. Of our intention to stand before the king when you returned. He was not surprised. I was, though, when it didn't make him take back his offer. He said he knew I loved you, and had you survived, he would have wished us all joy. But now, he claims I am his only true friend. The only voice he really trusts.

That may be true. He does not confide much in the elders. He speaks frankly only to me.

Will you hate me if I accept him?

Will I hate myself?

I do not love him, not the way I loved you. Not even the way I still do. But he has been my friend all these long years, and a partnership between the Warden of the Wood and its king would be a powerful thing.

He knows nothing of the seed, nor will he ever. She will remain, for all the long years, waiting for the one thing she can never have. She will wait as I wait. For you.

I will accept Thallion tonight.

If I cannot be happy, I will be useful.

Kate's mind reeled as pieces of Naevys's story clicked into place. The picture that emerged was tragic, stretching over centuries. Across the table, Faron dropped his head forward, his hands clenched together on the table. Venn's fingers twitched and then reached forward and took his hand. He flinched but, without looking up, shifted to grip her hand.

"She told me nothing," he whispered. "Nothing of the things that actually shaped her life."

Venn's hand tightened on his, and she looked at Kate. "This does explain everything."

Aislin and Matlen slinked lower in their chairs, as though feeling guilty for listening. Tribal and Silas turned back to the counter, as though that act could give Faron some privacy.

"Almost everything." Kate pulled the page with the timeline

closer. "It explains what she's protecting, but…" She glanced at Faron. "Naevys obviously never even told Virion about this."

"By the time he returned," Venn said, "she was already married to Thallion. What could she do?"

"True, there was nothing she could do. But this was four hundred years ago, and for most of that she's been Warden—a well-loved Warden. She's had a son. She was a respected queen known for negotiating fairly and bringing people together." Kate ran her finger down the timeline. "A hundred years after all this, when Renault appears, she discovers he's making pocket worlds where time slows in an effort to save his daughter. Naevys has a weakened seed that the healers say if it produced an elf at all, she would be short-lived.

"She didn't even confide in Renault." The loneliness and isolation Naevys had carried all these centuries wrapped around Kate like the cold of an endless night. "But here's a part I don't understand. Once Renault died, Naevys had his box and his amulet. She had them both until Emperor Sorrn took them. But she didn't use them? Instead, she secreted them away in the cave, where Sorrn was able to steal them."

Kate paused. "Wait. We've been thinking that Naevys wants the box for the Runelight Drawer, but she doesn't need time slowed. Her seed is perfectly safe." She tapped the queen's journal. "So what part of Renault's box was she trying to reproduce with Perone?"

No one offered an answer.

"Starting over four hundred years ago, she became Warden and spent centuries claiming to heal the White Wood from Renault's curse. But secretly she was using the power of the Wood to protect the ravine and try to create her own box, all while using the dragon to search for the original.

"Then, it wasn't until eighty-five years ago that she started using Yilfrist to find human mages to help her, and she apparently killed or fed them to the dragon when they failed. Why start then?" Kate glanced at Venn and Faron. "And how did she do all this in complete secrecy?"

"Evay always said she was closed off," Venn said. "She's kind and polite and funny, but she never talks openly."

"And everything she did was outside of the White Wood," Faron added. "So what elf would notice?"

Kate looked back at her notes. "So fifty years ago, she captures Perone, who helps her finally create…whatever she was after, but the two of them can't make it work. Perone escapes and cuts off Naevys's access to this workshop, and she…" Kate looked between Venn and Faron. "She what? What has she been doing the last fifty years?"

Venn gave a small shrug. "I haven't seen her much."

"She's been fading," Faron said quietly. "She's been lost in the White Wood more often."

Kate sighed. "So losing her chance with Perone made her give up, until Bo started digging in the ravine." Kate tapped the timeline again. "Which made her, understandably, angry. She attacked, was trapped under the rockslide, and inadvertently drained the White Wood by damaging the protection she had over the ravine."

Kate looked between Venn and Faron again. "But this doesn't explain what she's doing now. Why create *naiwyn* and keep people from leaving this area? Why drain a path toward Home? Why use Crofftus? Why destroy the elder tree in the square? Obviously, she attacked Home to find the door to this workshop and get the amulet, but…"

The most disconcerting question pushed to the surface in Kate's mind. "And above all else, why search for the aenigma box for centuries, then just discard it in the woods once she finally has it?"

Tribal cleared his throat and exchanged a look with Silas. "That's the sort of thing it's safe to assume is a trap."

Silas gave an apologetic nod. "Agreed."

"A trap for what?" Kate asked.

"My guess would be for you," Tribal answered.

"Or," Faron said quietly, "it just means my mother is losing her mind and no longer recognizes things that she used to value."

"Thallion thought she was merely sick," Kate said. "How could he miss all of this?"

"I..." Faron swallowed. "She has always been secretive, and he never pushed her for anything. With everyone else he's relentless, but if she didn't want to tell him something, he just...backed away." His gaze rested on the pile of letters. "I think he at least knew that she loved Virion, not him. I have always thought he was strangely reluctant to make her angry. I assumed it was because he was actually in love with her or that she had a way with him that no one else seemed to. But maybe he's been afraid for all this time that she'll break their bond and leave him."

Kate pushed back a shiver of sympathy for Thallion. Beside her, she felt a similar twinge in Venn before the elf stifled it.

"Maybe she was secretive," Venn said, "or maybe she had taken an interest in Home and the ravine, and he didn't bother to find out what it was because those are things he doesn't care about."

Faron flicked his fingers as though brushing the thought away. "Of course he cares about them."

Venn stilled. "Shall we talk about how he cares for the humans?"

He looked up at the anger in her voice, then let out an exasperated breath. "That was a hundred and fifty years ago, Venn."

"And I've been forbidden to speak of it ever since! Until now, because he is no longer king. And if I'm not bound, then neither are you, and we can talk about the thing you've refused to talk to me about. Let's talk about how he used those humans to lure that fire lizard into the open just to make it easier on his rangers. He sacrificed the humans, Faron, just to keep his rangers out of harm's way, and then he accepted the humans' gratitude like a hero."

Aislin's and Matlen's mouths fell open in shock as they looked between Venn and Faron.

"That's why you hate Thallion?" Matlen whispered.

"But the worst part," Venn said, keeping her eyes on Faron, "wasn't Thallion. By then I had come to expect that from him. But I didn't expect *you* to support him. I didn't think you would lie to those people about him!"

"It wasn't a lie," Faron said, his voice low and angry.

"You told them he *saved* them. Do you remember the names of the men who died? Renner, Doget, and Plan. Three men with families, all sacrificed senselessly, and you looked into their loved ones' eyes and *lied*."

Faron flinched.

Venn's breath came fast, her hand clenched on the table. "Why?"

Faron stared at her, his expression torn between fury and contrition. "You weren't the one who had to decide how best to confront a creature that dangerous and—"

Venn slammed her fist on the table. "Stop defending him!"

"He's protected Home for centuries!" Faron shouted. "Whether or not you approve of all his methods, that town still stands—days closer to the northern range than humans have any business being. He has protected it at the cost of our rangers. He protects it still! The Wood is empty of every ranger right now, Venn. I only called the advanced guard to protect Home. He pressed for them all."

Kate straightened.

A knife of shock stabbed through Venn's anger, and Kate froze. "What did you say?"

"I called every ranger I thought we could spare," Faron said, glaring at her. "He called for the rest of us to go to Home."

Venn's anger froze into something sharper, and she pulled back from the table.

Faron pointed a finger at her. "You question him at every turn. You question me at every turn, but you don't know, Venn, what it's like having to make these decisions."

"Thallion sent rangers to Home?" Kate asked. "Thallion?"

"You came to Home," Venn said, her voice low and dangerous, "because Thallion ordered you to?"

He raised his hand. "No, Venn. I came because you called me."

Her eyes dug into him, as though she could rip out the truth. "Where were you when I called?"

Faron hesitated. "He's my father, Venn. I just had the crown thrust on me. I'm going to talk to him sometimes."

An idea sprang into Kate's mind, and she glanced out the door, where she could see two rangers standing guard. Neither of them was Ayen.

"Faron," she said slowly, "why are you here? Venn called Ayen."

He shifted his attention to her.

Kate studied him, seeing a twinge of something like guilt cross his face. "You told us," Kate said, "you were going to a council with the elders."

Venn shoved herself up from the table, sending her chair crashing backward. "Did Thallion tell you to come find out what we were learning?"

"Venn…" Faron rose too, holding a hand out toward her.

"You…" Venn's voice was laced with rage. "When you came to Renault's cave asking for our help, was that your idea?"

Faron's mouth opened, but he didn't speak.

Kate's own anger rose. "Whose idea was it to bring me the box? Because if this is some trick of Thallion's—"

"It was my idea," Faron said quickly.

"Did you actually find it in the woods?" Kate demanded.

"Yes! Just like I told you, I brought it straight to you. I thought you deserved to have it after…everything. And I really did need your help."

"Wait…" A sliver of shock ran through Venn's fury. "Who thought I should go with you to the lakes?"

He didn't answer.

Venn's mouth dropped open. "*He* wanted me at the lakes, didn't he? You came to beg us for our help, but it was Thallion's idea."

"Venn…" Faron repeated, keeping his hand out. "It's not—"

"He wanted me named emissary, didn't he?" Venn took a step back. "You brought me there, and put me before the council, and made the whole show so that they'd realize they needed one."

"Everyone thinks that role should be yours, Venn," he said, his voice pleading.

"How convenient for you that Evay was injured," Venn answered, the air around her filled with seething fury.

Kate's hand clenched on the letter. "Did he plan that too?"

"No!" Faron's voice was fervent. "He was shocked to hear that there were *naiwyn* anywhere, and even more so that they'd attacked Evay."

Venn stared at him. "You don't deny the rest of it, though?"

"Venn," Faron began again.

All Faron's actions since he'd become king shifted, and Kate felt like she was seeing them for the first time. "Everything you've done has still been for Thallion."

He opened his mouth, but Venn stabbed a finger at the door. "Get out."

"Venn," he said, "you can't—"

"Don't you dare tell me what I can or can't do." She swung her finger around to point at him. "You and I are through."

Faron flinched. "Venn, stop." He started around the table toward her.

She backed away. "No. We are done." She swallowed. "I, Andovenn, declare my betrothal to Faron, king of the White Wood, terminated."

A thin strand of air between Faron and Venn snapped.

He flinched and staggered forward, his hand grabbing at the front of his cloak.

From where the strand had been, a burst of green and gold glitters puffed into the air, then faded away.

Venn's breath hitched, but she didn't move. "It's time it was formally broken. It's been broken in spirit for centuries."

"Venn," he said, the word strangled.

"Get out," she hissed.

Both dwarves started toward the king, their faces grim. Aislin and Matlen shrank down in their chairs, their eyes wide and alarmed.

Kate put herself between Faron and Venn, blocking him and drawing *vitalle* into her hands. Behind her, Venn's emotions settled into rage tainted with a deep, tearing loss.

"Leave, Faron," Kate said.

He looked past Kate, fury filling his eyes, but there was a ragged anguish behind it. His hand still clenched his cloak, as though he were trying to hold on to something. Behind Kate, Venn's emotions stayed determined.

With obvious effort, Faron smoothed his expression and offered Venn a shallow nod. "As you wish."

With his hand still pressed to his chest, he strode to the door, stepped out into the glade, and disappeared.

CHAPTER FORTY-SIX

From Venn, a crushing loss, both terribly old and agonizingly new—and so strong it ripped the air from Kate's lungs—tore open. Kate spun to grab Venn's arm. Her face was white, her eyes wet with tears. The furious determination that had carved her expression crumbled.

She took a staggering step.

Tribal tossed his axe onto the table and caught her other arm, guiding her into a chair. "Good of you to send him away," he said, his voice gruff. "Probably would cause some trouble if Silas and I killed the king of the White Wood." He let go of her arm but didn't back away.

Venn slumped forward, dropping her elbows onto the table and her head into her hands. Anger and pain radiated out of her, raw and jagged. Aislin gripped her brother's arm, both of them wearing shocked expressions.

Kate held on to the back of her chair, trying to push the pain and rage back, but it surged against her, almost feral.

Tribal's heavy hand fell on her arm. "Twig?"

The touch cut through the haze of emotions. "I'm fine."

He looked unconvinced but let go.

The room waited in uncomfortable silence.

"Didn't she promise the council she'd marry him?" Aislin whispered to her brother.

"I don't care," Venn snapped, and both elf twins winced.

Kate cast around for any way to help, settling on something that was bound to be ineffective but was better than nothing. "Fix, do you still have some of Yellow's coffee?"

In front of the cupboard, Fix dug into his pack, which sat on the chair next to him, and pulled out the cracked mug sealed with leather and the little belt.

Matlen pulled his worried eyes off Venn. "I'll make some." He took the mug to the fire.

Kate sank into the chair next to Venn's, and waves of rage rolled through the smothering loss that filled the space. Kate pulled the box closer and focused on the feel of the wood to keep Venn's emotions at bay.

The scent of coffee wafted over from the fireplace where Matlen worked, and Kate rubbed her thumb over the metal corner. Aislin still sat frozen in her chair. Tribal and Silas moved back to lean against the long counter, their axes in their hands. Fix crouched at the door of the cupboard, working long, thin tools into the lock.

"What now?" Silas asked quietly.

The book with the picture of the kobolds lay open on the table, along with the stack of Naevys's letters, but there were shelves to search, crates along the walls that hadn't been opened, drawers under the cabinets.

"We still don't know why Naevys needed to get in here," Kate said. "Fix, do you think you can get that open?"

He nodded, keeping his eyes on his tools.

Kate glanced at Aislin, and Silas caught the look.

"C'mon, nibling," he said to the young elf. "There are more nooks to explore over here."

Kate's gaze fell on the open book with the drawing of the kobolds. A flicker of irritation rose in her. Learning about Naevys's seed had filled in a great deal of Naevys's past, but it didn't explain her present. Nothing explained her letting the box go, or what was so important about this workshop.

Naevys's bright gold remnant was smeared across the page with the kobolds, but a glimmer of something darker shone in a blank space next to the picture. Kate leaned closer. Remnants didn't change color. She sifted through the impressions of forest and wind and maples. A definite line of darker shimmers lay on the page, more bronze than gold. A low rumble rolled out of it, like distant ocean waves.

"Crofftus!" Kate studied the page more closely. "His remnant is here." The familiar sound rumbled through her mind, bringing with it a wave of betrayal.

"Dirty traitor," Silas muttered from the counter.

Kate was about to push the book away when the shape of Crofftus's remnant suddenly became clear. It was a letter. Next to it was another.

"Kate," she said slowly.

Tribal glanced over. "You've been spending too much time thinking about the mad queen if you're starting to talk to yourself."

"No." She traced the lines of remnant. "It says 'Kate.'"

Venn shifted enough to look sideways. "Crofftus wrote you a note with his remnant?"

"Well, he wrote my name. I don't see any other words, just a few smudges."

Silas looked up from a box he was rummaging through. "The stodgy bug wrote a secret message only you can read and still felt the need to formally address it? Sounds about right."

Matlen set two steaming mugs on the table by Kate and Venn. The scent of coffee wafted out of silvery blue ceramic textured with dragon scales. The handles were shaped into long tails that curled up and coiled around the mugs.

"That..." Kate rotated her mug slowly on the table. "That looks expensive."

"All his mugs look like blue dragons." Matlen glanced at Tribal and Silas. "There are two more if you'd like coffee."

Tribal waved the offer away. "You niblings have it. But if you find any log mead, we're taking that."

"Did humans have log mead three hundred years ago?" Kate asked Venn.

The elf slumped to the side, freeing one hand to wrap it around the glittering blue mug. "No. Yellow was the first to brew it in Home."

"Poor old Renault was missing out," Silas said.

Kate took a sip, and the hot liquid flowed down her throat, bitter and nutty, soothing the edges of her frustration. She lifted the page of the kobold book carefully. "Why would Crofftus go to the effort of leaving a message if it only says my name?"

A bit of bronze remnant sat lower on the page, wiped across the words "White Wood." Another word past it was covered in his remnant, and the end of a word further on.

"Venn..." Kate flipped the page but saw no more smudges. "He marked these things. 'White Wood,' 'kill,' and the part of 'thinking' that says 'king.'"

Venn shifted to look at the page. "What?'

Silas shook his head. "Formal and morbid. At least he's consistent."

"And unclear," Tribal said, pulling a book off a shelf. "Is he telling you to kill the king? Or that he and Naevys are going to kill him?"

"Which king?" Aislin asked, her hands wrapped around a steaming mug.

"Good point," Matlen said. "If it's Naevys, does she know Thallion isn't king anymore?"

Something about the message niggled at Kate's mind. Silas was right. Why address a message only she could read? And after going through the effort of spelling her name, why leave the rest so cryptic?

"Could Naevys even kill the king of the White Wood?" Tribal asked curiously. "Couldn't he just command her not to?"

Venn looked at the page, her anger with Faron subsiding a little at the new curiosity. "It would be hard, but if she planned it right, she might be able to."

"How hard can it be?" Silas asked. "We almost killed the prince of the White Wood with one good swing of an axe."

"Faron wasn't the king." Venn said, "and he was in a cave. The king of the White Wood, while actually in the White Wood, is nearly invincible. The trees would heal any injury too quickly for him to even suffer. And then, yes, he could command the attack to stop or command other elves to protect him." She shook her head. "Most elves couldn't kill him, but the Warden might be able to. It still wouldn't be easy."

"Kate!" Tribal held up a book with an aged leather cover. "This has a drawing of your amulet." He brought it over and set it on the table. One corner crumbled away into dust, and he winced. "Sorry. There are two more volumes."

Kate opened the cover and found an image of the amulet and the title, *Exhaustive and Comprehensive Record of the Creation and Applications of the Oziv Amulet. Volume 1.*

"Tribal," Kate said as he set the next two thick books down gently. "This is amazing." Carefully, she turned the brittle page.

"More writing on an amulet we can't make?" Venn asked in a dull voice, staring back into her coffee. "Fascinating."

Irritation at her tone made Kate's hand twitch, and the paper tore. She glanced at Venn but bit back the retort that rose to her lips at the flurry of anger and pain still emanating from the elf. "Maybe this," she said, trying to keep her voice light, "will give better information."

Venn gave no response.

Kate flipped gently through the book. *Exhaustive and Comprehensive* sounded promising. Maybe the bloodstone wasn't the only solution for opening the Runelight Drawer safely.

The beginning of the book discussed the original creation of the amulet, which Renault had apparently made when he worked for Emperor Sorrn. Kate paused at the idea, but it fit. She'd never read outright that the two men were connected, but if Sorrn had traveled all this way to find Renault's invention, it made sense that they had at least known of each other.

Past that, though, were the records of the aenigma box's creation and the attempts to get the amulet to help access the door. There were more entries here of failures than in the book she'd found in Renault's cave. Every new one was a failure, though.

A loud click sounded across the room. Fix straightened and turned to grin at Kate.

"Very good!" Tribal said as both dwarves and the elf twins moved closer to the cupboard. Venn didn't even look up.

"Wait!" Kate stood and crossed to the cabinet. "Everyone stand back."

Tribal and Silas waited until everyone had backed up before they each took a handle and cracked the doors open, keeping themselves behind the wood. When nothing happened, they opened the doors farther.

Against the back wall, placed on elaborately carved pegs, hung a curved knife, almost long enough to be a short sword. Both dwarves let out appreciative hums at the sight. Tribal reached forward, but Kate set her hand on his arm. "There are runes."

She leaned closer and cast out again. This time, a line of *vitalle* ran along runes etched into the metal. "It's in ancient Kalesh and speaks of killing."

"A knife that kills?" Tribal said. "Shocking. Will it hurt me if I touch it?"

A shiver of disquiet ran up Kate's neck as she read the runes. "Not the hilt, but the blade might. The runes speak of a swift death if blood is drawn."

Silas gave a snort. "That's hardly unusual for a blade."

Kate glanced at Venn, but she was still staring blankly into her coffee.

Tribal reached forward and brushed his fingers across the hilt. When nothing happened, he wrapped his hand around it and lifted it off the pegs.

A shiver slid up Kate's spine again. "I don't like that knife."

Tribal moved away from the others and swung it. "It's incredibly light."

Inside the cupboard, Naevys's remnant was wiped across a second set of pegs, identical to the first.

"Look like there's a second knife." Silas glanced around as though they might have missed it on another shelf.

"Naevys took it." Kate searched for any other signs of her remnant inside the cabinet. A map of the White Wood was fastened to the bottom of the compartment. There were no gold glitters and the dust was undisturbed, but a short cut sliced through the parchment. Kate ran her finger over it and found a gouge in the wood, shaped like the tip of the knife, as though it had been stabbed through the map.

"Venn," Kate called. "Can you come—"

Venn shoved herself to her feet. "Get that away from Aislin!" she shouted, her face draining of color.

He paused in his examination of the knife and stepped farther back from the others. "This?"

"Where did you get that?" Venn demanded, rounding the table and pulling Aislin farther from him.

The dwarf pointed the tip at the cupboard.

Venn hissed out a breath. "I'd heard he had *nahquel* blades, but I didn't believe it!"

"What kind of blade?" Kate asked.

"*Nahquel.* They were created to kill elves. The power in the blade drains an elf's body faster than it can heal. It is said it only takes the smallest cut."

Tribal's bushy black eyebrows rose, and he moved carefully back to hang the blade in its place.

"That's alarming," Kate said slowly. "Especially if Naevys took the second one. What's here on the map?"

Venn stopped a pace back from the cupboard, her brow creased. "That's...Thallion's home."

Kate straightened. "Naevys is heading to Thallion's home with a knife meant to kill elves? I think that evens her odds."

Venn backed away toward the door. "We have to warn him."

"Thallion?" Kate asked.

"Not just Thallion. Faron lives there too."

Tribal narrowed his eyes. "The Faron we all hate?"

Venn turned to Kate. "The White Wood already barely has a Warden. It can't lose its king also!"

"But, Venn," Kate said, "it doesn't make any sense for her to go after Faron and Thallion. She only wants her seed."

Venn gave her an incredulous look. "Are you really looking for her to be logical? If they both die, there is no other king. The Wood will suffer, and the human world will suffer with it."

"Venn," Kate said, "we have no idea what she's actually doing. The only reason we think she's after anyone is a note from Crofftus—hardly a reliable source."

"And the knife stabbed through his house on the map."

"We have no idea how old that mark is. There's no sign of Naevys's remnant on it."

"Because she was holding the knife! Not the map!"

Kate shook her head. "We don't know what she's doing."

Venn paused, disbelief filling her face. "Are you serious? There is a clear picture here, a full story. I know you see it."

The frustration that Kate had been trying to contain pressed against the wall that held it back. "Every time I think we have the full story, we walk into some elven trap!"

"I am not risking the entire White Wood on the off chance you're right!"

"Well, I'm not risking me again! Or the box!" Kate gestured to the door. "Faron can hear you. Just go out and send him a message to be careful."

Venn glared at her for a moment, then stormed out.

Kate went back to the table and pulled the aenigma box closer to her book before sinking into her chair.

She turned the page to find the next entry labeled "Bloodstone - Instructions and Use."

Kate's hand twitched on the page, and the corner crumbled into dust. She gently set it down and grabbed her journal. The left-hand page held the instructions she'd found in the book Crofftus had stolen, and the right-hand side was filled with notes on the creation and use of the stone.

Barely daring to breathe, she began copying the instructions, forcing herself to work slowly and carefully.

A painfully bright hope rose in her, tearing at her focus and making her hand tremble.

"I can't find him"—Venn's voice cut through the silence from the doorway—"but the trees showed me Naevys's trail. I know where she entered the White Wood. We're at least an hour behind her, but if we hurry—"

"Venn, I'm so close," Kate said. "It's right here! Everything I need! I just need to copy it!"

"Then bring it."

"Bring it? I can barely turn the page without it disintegrating."

Venn whirled to face her. "Naevys obviously has the real amulet! We need to find her, not read some stupid book!"

"We don't know that! That box might not have held the amulet!"

Venn jabbed a finger at Kate. "You're willing to risk the White Wood on some vague hunch that something perfectly amulet-sized and obviously magical that Naevys wanted was not the amulet we know she's been after?"

Kate's frustration exploded through the wall. "What has the White Wood done for me?" she snapped back. "Hunted me? Imprisoned me? Tried to kill me? I am *done* putting aside what I need to do because I'm dragged into something for the White Wood, Venn! Just give me a few minutes!"

Fury radiated from Venn. "The fate of the Wood is at stake, Kate."

"So are my brothers! I'm not risking their lives on what will undoubtedly be another fruitless chase after something we don't entirely understand!"

Another fissure of betrayal opened up in Venn. "Never mind. You'd just slow me down." She stalked out the door, then disappeared.

Kate wrapped her fist around her pencil, trying to wrangle down the anger and frustration swirling inside her. Trying to focus on the book in front of her. The fury she could feel from Venn was receding, but whether it disappeared entirely was impossible to tell amidst her own.

Tribal's heavy tread came closer, and he stopped directly across the table, looking at her from under a dark, heavy brow. "What happens when you're done with those books?"

"Then I can finally get out of this place and save my brothers."

He waited for a heartbeat. "After we check out the carriage."

"The carriage?" Kate pointed her pencil at him. "You're the only ones who care about the carriage! We can't get into it! No one can get into it!"

"You could figure out a way. If you spent even a fraction of the time on it that you've spent on that box." He jabbed a thick finger at it.

"Time? You think all I need is a little time to figure out how to thwart a centuries-old elven curse? I didn't even know elves could curse things."

Silas crossed his arms. "Did you know mages could create secret pocket worlds where time was slowed? Because you seemed pretty surprised about that."

Tribal nodded. "If you can learn about pocket worlds, seems you can learn about elven curses."

Kate's hand tightened around her pencil. "It's not going to open! Bo tried, and Naevys killed all his men, then collapsed the mountainside. We tried and you two, and Crofftus, almost died!"

"But we got in," Tribal growled.

"Tribal! Let it go!" Her pencil snapped. "Find your hoard of gold somewhere else!" She threw the broken pieces down onto the table. "Or go steal it from someone—isn't that what you two usually do?"

He held her eyes, his expression hard. Then he turned away.

"C'mon." He motioned to Aislin, Matlen, and Fix. "You'll be safer with us than trapped in this dead end if the mad queen comes back." He stomped out the door.

Silas held out Aislin's cloak.

She took it with a vaguely apologetic look at Kate. "Where are we going?"

"We have stonesteel to forge." Silas lifted Fix and settled him on top of his pack before starting toward the door. "Not even a third of what we were promised, but at least it's something." He paused, looking at Kate disapprovingly.

"What?" she snapped. "Now you want me to stop and make more stonesteel for you?"

He waited until Matlen stepped outside then shook his head. "Told you that box would be the end of you."

He passed through the door, making the image of the clearing shiver. Fix looked at her with wide, sad eyes until Silas moved out of sight.

PART IV

THE TREASURE

I hold a lot of responsibility for where we were at that moment. Crofftus had been right that—Wait, I'm getting ahead of myself.

I can't look back on the day everyone left with anything but regret at how I acted and the danger I let Venn walk into alone.

I never realized, when collecting other people's stories, how much I'd want to change the facts of one I was in. If I'd sorted out the yellow door sooner, if I'd figured out about the seed sooner, if I'd understood Naevys's plan sooner, could Venn and I and the others have found some more peaceful solution? Could some of the loss at the end have been avoided?

The questions lead only to madness, and so I will set them aside and merely tell you what happened.

CHAPTER FORTY-SEVEN

Silence filled the workshop, disturbed only by the low crackle of the fire. The clearing was still and empty.

Kate gripped the box and closed her eyes against the sight.

They'd left. They'd all left. Now. When she was so close.

The words dripped resentment into the flurry of anger that swelled in her.

Crofftus had left her for Naevys—she almost choked on the bitterness of the thought. For Naevys! She'd told him she would help, and he'd thrown his lot in with the mad queen who'd tried to kill Bo? Who'd murdered people? And now the dwarves and Venn too. And Fix...

The sharp corners of the box dug into her fingers, and she squeezed harder, the pain fitting perfectly in with the seething anger and bitterness. The silvery lantern was barely visible, blocked by the jagged rocks of everything holding her back. Only a sliver of hope crawled through, desperate and lonesome in the darkness.

The box hummed softly.

Kate's anger shifted to cold determination. The others couldn't help anyway. They couldn't read Kalesh, couldn't understand the magic involved in opening the Runelight Drawer. They were only distractions. And what she needed was time to focus.

She opened her eyes—and found the box gripped tightly in her hands. For a heartbeat, shadows of something long and possessive stretched out from it, sinking into her fingers and coiling around her wrists.

She dropped it onto the table—and it was merely a box again.

The mournful bell tolled somewhere deep within, the endless sound of Tumble's remnant, trapped forever. The runes carved on it sat patient and silent, proclaiming the terrible hope and despair Renault had put into his creation.

But it was just a box.

She drew in a deep, unsteady breath but didn't pull it closer again.

The open page in the book described the properties of the bloodstone, but Kate's eyes slid over the words without seeing them.

They'd left. They'd all left.

Anger and indignation buffeted her like she stood in a strong wind. She rubbed her hands over her face, but her thoughts swirled and crashed together in her mind with a feverish clamor.

She flipped to a new page in her journal, grabbing her broken pencil in an effort to pin her chaotic thoughts to the page. Crofttus, the dwarves, Venn—all gone.

Her last entry was from what felt like ages ago. The evening before Thallion had bound her to the White Wood. She'd tried to set the facts aside and write about how she was feeling. The strangeness of being able to see remnants for the first time.

Every word of it rang true, and instead of listing facts, she took the emotions that were battering her and poured them out through the pencil.

I am alone. They all left me. Now, when I am so close. When did they become so selfish? None of us came here for the Wood or treasure.

The dwarves are going to kill themselves trying to get into that carriage, and Venn—I thought I could count on her. Not that she'd run off and do something as stupid as trying to protect Thallion or as hopeless as trying to stop Naevys.

Even as she wrote them, the words sounded hollow and petulant. The dwarves had most certainly come for treasure, and Venn had loved the White Wood for centuries.

Amidst her anger, a hint of uneasiness rose. She made herself reread the words. They were, she forced herself to admit, not entirely true.

A passage from Mother Gearts' book about the Darkest Night Festival that she'd read one night in Renault's cave while she was falling asleep came back to her.

I've applied this idea to other things besides failures. Anger, for instance. When I'm angry, truly angry with someone I love, and I can't even say why, when my mind races from reason to reason, none of them ringing true, I try to stop and see what my anger is saying. What is it that I value that I'm not doing? Or that someone else isn't showing?

It takes effort, every time, but I start by writing out the feeling, then everything true I know about the situation, regardless of how I feel about it. What were my motivations? What were the motivations of others? In the past, have they done this same thing? Or is it unique? Could I be misreading them? Did I give them reason to misread me?

Every time, I find something in myself that is at least partially to blame for my situation. I'm not foolish enough to think every-

thing is my fault, but I have yet to walk away from an argument and find myself blameless.

Kate set her pencil back onto the page, looking for everything she knew to be true.

Venn has repeatedly set aside her own goals to help save Bo—because she is driven by the life debt.

The words felt like a half-truth, and she forced herself to continue.

Her actions, though, have been more than that. She went to Virion's despite the fact that it was against what she wanted. She was willing to leave the White Wood and come back to the Stronghold with me. Yes, for Bo, but also out of friendship.

The thought formed a knot of guilt in her gut, and she moved to a different part of the page.

The dwarves are obsessed with treasure.

Those words were far less than half-true.

No, that is not fair. Time and again they have set aside their questing for treasure to help Venn and me, or to help the people of Home. They obviously want into the carriage, but can I blame them? It is their key to getting back into Rullduin. To their loved ones and their home.

She glanced at the box.

I suppose I cannot fault them for such a dream.

Still, the anger swirling in her didn't abate. It churned, searching for a target.

Her eyes fell on the box again, and she paused. *You're fairly observant—for a human—unless you're reading some ancient book or fiddling with that box,* Tribal had said after she'd missed the bears attacking Home.

They were accompanied by Venn's words that seemed to echo in her head too often. *When you think about something constantly and can't let it out of your grasp, that is obsessing.*

Kate set her pencil back onto the page, fighting back the resistance to admit the truth.

The box calls to me. I know it does. I feel it all the time.

A gentleness rolled over her at the thought. The tangle of hope that was carved into the runes on the lid, eternal and constant.

But it feels good. It's the only flicker of hope I can find in all this mess. And my brothers are in it. Trapped. Frightened.
Is it wrong that it calls to me? It does not feel wrong.

The question hung in the silent room, and Kate could almost hear the answers Venn or the dwarves would give. Or Crofftus— at least before he'd left.

But despite their silent censure, she left the box sitting where it was and returned to the book on the amulet. If it were their brothers trapped inside, they'd understand.

She dove back into Renault's writing, painstakingly copying the bloodstone pages.

Slowly, her anger and frustration were pushed aside by the work. The pointed concentration forced everything else back, and the world shrank to the scratch of her pencil and the dusty smell of the ancient book.

A candle in the center of the table flickered, and Kate looked up to find it had burned low. Four pages of her journal were filled with detailed notes. Since a single use of the bloodstone would open the door but destroy the pocket world in the process, Renault had declared it a failure. But first, he had tested it extensively, and there were still two more pages recording his thoughts.

A spike of uneasiness jabbed into her.

Something nagging.

A question she didn't have an answer to.

Her left hand rested on the box, and she tapped a finger on the runes.

What had changed for Naevys since the Elder Grove? The queen's journal still sat open on the table, and Kate sank back in her chair. Naevys had recognized the aenigma box and taken it. But why? She didn't need the Runelight Drawer—she must have needed something else.

What else did the box do?

There is another aspect to the box… Virion had said. *He called it the transference, and he labored for years to make it work.*

Transference. Between life and death.

The ideas shifted in Kate's mind, almost falling into place. Naevys had a seed that was hanging on the cusp of death. Did she need some way to bring it back to life?

Was that what she had wanted Perone for? To recreate the transference that Renault had been working on?

Kate gently turned the pages of Renault's book, scanning titles neatly penned across the tops of his pages until one stilled her hand.

The Bridge

Now that I have the time I need, I must create a solution.
Miliene is too weak to be healed.
That fact threatens to split me in two.
But I cannot ignore it.
It is not a healing of her body that I need, but a new body for her to live in.
The idea has lingered at the edge of my mind for years.
Using the lastlight left in someone's body at the moment of death, could I keep them alive long enough to transfer Miliene into them?
Could I use a host body and move Miliene into it as a guest?

Kate straightened at the words, which echoed Naevys's reports of what she and the mage Perone had worked on. *Eighteen animals dead and nothing to show for it. Perone and I can each do our part, but doing them together never quite works. The host occasionally survives, but the guest dies every time.*

She turned the page to find Renault's writing continued.

It has taken two weeks, but I did it.
The power needed for the transfer is easily held in the box, but the connection proved more complicated.
However, I have created a Bridge that draws from the box's power to connect two bodies. It uses vast amounts of ael'iza, but it works.

A sketch sat below the words. A metal disk marked with runes so intricate and complex it would take her ages to sort out.

I put my house cat into the body of a bobcat before it lost its lastlight. When it woke, it recognized me. Since the two cats are not really the same, the instincts of the bobcat's body eventually made it escape back into the wild, but I often see it in the woods nearby.

If I put a house cat into another house cat, I think the transfer would be perfect.

I need to create a casing of the Bridge so I can attach it to the amulet and the two can work together.

I am so close.

"The Bridge." Kate's voice echoed hollowly in the empty room. The queen's glitters shone from the book that had been on the table at first. The drawing of the dead kobold with Crofftus's strange message smeared onto it.

Life and death. Lastlight.

Naevys needed the Bridge to give her child a new body.

"Venn," Kate whispered. "You're right. Naevys already has the amulet. She just needed the Bridge." She glanced at the empty box. "And now she has it."

Another jab of uneasiness rolled through her, and she checked outside the door.

The glade was empty, the colors shifting subtly toward evening. A discomfort pulled her toward it, but she kept her seat. Venn was too far away to follow now, and the dwarves were probably in Renault's cave at this point, with more stonesteel than they'd ever imagined, even if they were disappointed they didn't have more.

Her frustration crept back in, but she turned pointedly back to the book. Two more pages.

She'd finished half of it when a third spark of uneasiness shot through her, so strong her hand twitched, and she marked a thick line across the page.

The disquiet was couched in anger. A deep, tearing anger that was trying desperately to fill a gaping chasm. The fury swirled around her, and her breath grew faster. Kate scanned the workshop and the open door again.

Everything was quiet. She glanced over her shoulder at the

blanket covering the two kobolds, but nothing moved.

A shadow shifted in the corner of her vision, and she spun back to the door.

The glade outside was perfectly calm and bright—but another shadow slid across the doorway. It was neither inside nor out, but it seemed to darken her vision itself.

She closed her eyes, and the shadows resolved into shapes. The snowy ground of the forest, scarred by a pitch-black hollow under a fallen log. A wide pine bough underlined with darkness like a line of ink had been drawn on the bottom of it. A pocket of night sky crouched among the branches of a thicket. The feel of the forest spread around her in an endless pool—and there was anger. Deep, simmering anger.

"Venn?" Kate's voice faded into the empty workshop.

But the image moved, as though Kate were slipping through the woods, skirting the darkest parts. Venn's hand came into view, reaching for a nearby trunk. The rough bark scraped against her fingertips, bringing the jolt of uneasiness again.

Kate opened her eyes, and the image faded against the brightness of the workshop. The trees were uneasy?

She covered her face with her hands to bring the woods back into focus. "Venn?" she called louder. "Venn! This is more than feeling you! I can see what you're seeing!"

There was no sign that Venn heard. The tree she touched offered the impression of Naevys passing by amidst a deluge of other sensations. Venn pulled her hand away quickly and continued, but in a half-dozen paces, a wall of thorny frenbrush as tall as her shoulders blocked her path. A flash of irritation rose, but it was tempered with something else. A deep, conflicted longing—and the dread that accompanied it.

Her fingers reached out and brushed the needles of the bush, avoiding the long thorns. The forest unfurled around her. It rolled over hills, endlessly connected. Gentle waves of its presence lapped against her, welcoming her back, drawing her in.

Kate gasped at the offered sense of belonging. It was the draw of the White Wood, the call of the Elder Grove, waking the soul-deep ache to join. To embrace the life that valued everything about her. To be part of something vast and eternal and thrumming with the power to heal and grow and renew.

Inside Venn, the anger and pain from Faron receded, drawing into a back corner of her soul, letting the peace of the forest replace it.

Kate dropped her hands. How was Venn's connection so strong? The wave of envy that rose in Kate almost drowned her, but she shoved it back, focusing not on how soothing it felt, but the price it would require from her.

The price it would require from Venn.

What had Naevys done?

Kate flipped to a blank page in her journal. Against the white page, the images from Venn were more visible. Kate searched the sense of the Wood around Venn, finding the river and the outcropping of rock where the *gweroc* had attacked them. Venn wasn't far from either, but she was very far from the point on the map where Thallion's home had been marked. Instead, she stood near a place all the trees bent toward. A massive old pine whose trunk was twice as wide as Kate and whose roots sank deep into the earth.

A tree in the direction Naevys had gone.

A chill ran up Kate's neck. It wasn't Venn's connection that was stronger—it was the call of the Wood. The same call that had bound Venn in the Elder Grove, more closely than she'd ever wanted.

"Venn!" Kate shouted. "She's leading you to an elder tree!"

Again, there was no sign that Venn heard her, but the elf straightened, drawing on a steely resolve. She dropped her hand

and skirted the frenbrush. A frost pine now stood in front of her with an empty, hollow teardrop-shaped knot. She started to reach for it but closed her fingers instead, pulling them back.

"Come back!" Kate's voice echoed hollowly in the empty workshop. "Something isn't right! She's leading you to the wrong place!"

With a bracing breath, Venn opened her hand again and reached for the trunk. "Show me," she whispered.

The tree flashed pictures of Naevys into Venn's mind, and at the same time, it gathered her in, warm and welcoming and relieved to see her. Venn's hand relaxed, and she leaned forward until her forehead rested on the wood.

The serenity of the forest flowed into her like warm water, soothing aches, dousing the knots of rage and betrayal that filled her.

It didn't touch Kate's own anger and frustration, but the old, deep fury Venn had held against Thallion cooled. Venn's long inhale filled the space with a pool of comfort and gentleness and rest.

"No..." Kate whispered. Her desperation to stop this weakened in the face of this much peace.

But Venn wouldn't want it. Not like this.

The steely resistance in Venn rose again, and she pushed herself away from the tree, stumbling around it. Ahead, the elder tree filled an open space, the sprawl of its branches blocking out the sky enough that the ground beneath it was bare of any snow or any growth.

"Naevys?" Venn's voice came out strained. "Thallion? Faron?"

There was nothing in the clearing but the tree.

Kate shoved herself out of her chair. Venn didn't have a shield. She had no way to hold back the draw of the forest. "Venn! She's not there!" She grabbed her cloak off the chair and shoved the box into her pack. "Back away, Venn! It's a trap!"

The power of the elder tree flowed across the ground and swirled around Venn, lulling her, speaking into her mind.

The words were elven, but Kate could almost make them out. The tree was pleased. Thankful. Comforted by Venn's presence. It drew her in like a lost child.

Venn sank to her knees, the sensation of the forest soothing everything inside her. With a sound like a sob, she curled forward, letting go of the last of her resistance.

"Venn!" Kate ran through the door. The tingle ran over her skin as she burst out onto the snow. The sunlight blinded her for a moment, and against the brightness, she saw a glitter of blue scales. She flung herself back toward the door, but the clearing was empty.

The scales glittered again at the edge of her vision, and Kate squeezed her eyes shut.

Naevys strode under the boughs of the elder tree. In her hand, she clutched a little wooden cage holding a tiny chickadee. Venn stretched out a hand toward her, the serenity of the forest smothering the fear and confusion swirling inside her. The Warden squatted down, her expression cold.

Elvish words flowed off her tongue, and Venn drew back with a spike of fear.

The queen posed a question, and Venn shook her head, a tiny bit of relief glimmering inside her.

With a snarl of anger, Naevys tossed the little cage aside and flicked her fingers at Venn. Frost-blue scales filled the space behind Naevys. The queen stretched one finger out and pressed it against Venn's forehead.

Everything went black.

CHAPTER FORTY-EIGHT

Kate's feet pounded up the hill, following Venn's tracks in the snow. Her breath came fast, and she pulled her cloak open, letting in the chilled afternoon air. Her legs burned with the effort, and her lungs felt raw, but a biting voice drove her on. *How could you let her go alone?* it asked for the hundredth time.

Kate pushed the thoughts aside. It couldn't be far now.

Shadows huddled under branches and among the roots of the trees. A stump, half-rotted away, jutted up out of the snow, but one side was caved in, filled with the dark of night.

Her foot slipped in the snow, and she slammed down onto her knee. She grabbed the nearest trunk and scrabbled back to her feet. The hint of something flowed out of the tree. Something expansive and rich. Kate left her hand on it, but the feeling faded. She started uphill again until she came to a long line of thorny frenbrush along Venn's trail. Ahead stood the frost pine with a hollow knot shaped like a teardrop. Inside the hole was nothing but blackness.

Kate stopped at the tree and peered around it into the clearing with the massive elder pine. There was nothing but trampled snow. She cast out, and her wave lit up the tree next to her in a blazing brightness. It rolled along the ground, lighting clumps of moss and dry winter grass until it hit the roots of the pine and blazed into light. The elder tree itself ignited into a towering pillar of warmth and golden light.

Buried in the trampled snow ahead, a dim flicker of life flared up. She caught the glitter of bronze remnant above it, and her anger flared back to life. She ran over, dropping to her knees to dig him out.

"Crofftus!" she growled, dragging up the cage with the snow-covered chickadee shivering inside it. "Where is Venn? What did you do?"

Katria. His voice was faint and broken. *Why did she come?*

"Because *you* left a message that Naevys was going to kill Thallion or Faron or both!"

Katria, he said weakly, *I didn't—*

"Where is Venn? Where did Naevys take her?"

I don't know! I tried to warn you—

"Warn us? When?" Kate shook the cage, and the bird crashed into the side. "When you deserted us for Naevys? When you hid the fact that you'd talked to her? When you tore apart Virion's house? When you let Naevys attack Home without giving us any warning? When—in all that—did you try to warn us, Crofftus?"

He shivered in the far corner of the cage, his feathers rumpled and caked with snow. *None of those times,* he said quietly. *Katria, I'm so sorry. Naevys talked to me in Renault's cave, she promised me...* He trailed off weakly. *She promised me a human body.*

Her fingers tightened on the cage. "I told you the Keepers would help you! Why would you trust her?"

The chickadee shrank back farther. *You didn't hear her speak,* he whispered.

"No, I didn't. Tell me what she said that made you betray us, Crofftus."

She picked up the rabbit, and—she was in my mind, Katria! Deep inside. She knew everything! She said that she could get me a body— easily—if I helped her. In an instant, she saw everything inside me. She saw the decades of longing.

She offered an end to always being on the outskirts of a mind. To never truly belonging in a body. To never being able to use hands or walk where I want or hold a book or a pen or touch something with fingers. I have felt paws and wings and antennae and fins. I've felt talons and claws and tentacles. But hands, Katria! Do you have any idea the privilege you enjoy by having hands?

He paused. *You know how much I want that. I've lived so long with the fear that I'll die somewhere in some forest, alone, because my host animal weakens and there is nothing else nearby to go into. Things die alone in the woods all the time, Katria.* The longing in his tone turned to contrition. *But it was the way she offered it. She knew what it was like. She'd been a tree and longed for legs and hands and a voice...* He gave a sigh. *I believed her. Believed every word. She knew everything. Knew you were going to take me back to the Keeper Stronghold. She said Keepers would never do what was needed, and that I already knew it was pointless to go with you—and I do, Katria. I know your offer is pointless. Keepers won't cross the line I need to cross.*

Something beneath Kate's anger snapped. A strand that had been holding on to something better. Some hope that Crofftus had just been deceived. "So you betrayed us?"

Katria, listen to me. None of that is important.

"Not important? How can—"

She has a child...or a part of a child.

"I know! A seed that's degrading and dying."

Yes. She says she has a way to transfer a mind from one body to another.

"With the Bridge, I know. It will somehow work together with the box so that she can try to put her child into another body"

Not just a body. She needed the right *body. Strong, healthy...well connected to the White Wood.*

Kate froze as the truth of it crystalized in her mind. "Venn?"

I didn't know what she wanted! He turned pleading. *She just waded into my mind and learned everything I knew of you both. So she lured Venn here, somewhere the power of the Wood could overwhelm her.*

Kate's fingers clenched again on the cage. "No, Crofftus, *you* lured Venn here."

No! I thought you would notice—

"You left a note meant to draw us out so we'd follow Naevys here!"

The tiny bird shrank even more, its body trembling. *I thought,* he said, his voice terribly small, *that you, of all people, would notice the name.*

The name...

A puzzle that had felt too small to bother with before suddenly grew clear. "It was addressed to 'Kate,'" she whispered. "Not 'Katria.'"

Naevys rubbed the bird's beak across the words. She knew you'd see it, knew you'd take it as a message from me, so I tried to warn you. I told her it would be hard for you to see my remnant among the brighter marks of hers. That she should write 'Kate' in an empty space to be sure you noticed.

"And...you never call me Kate."

It is not your name, he said simply. *You told Venn that Kate is the woman who studies and engages her mind, and Ria is the one who braves adventures. I've always thought both of those parts of you were essential.*

Kate sank back into the snow, the cold seeping into her legs, numbing her. "I knew there was something wrong with it. I just…" She lowered the cage to her lap. "There were too many other things. Faron is still serving Thallion. Venn broke their betrothal. She's…" *Broken.* The rope of guilt wrapped around her again like a heavy chain. "Naevys has a child with Virion. Two kobolds were murdered." *And the amulet wasn't there.* A humorless smile twitched up the side of her mouth. "I didn't keep myself in view, Crofftus."

Silence reigned in the glade.

I know, Katria, he said finally. *I have seen it. Naevys has given me tasks, but I have watched over you too, from far enough away that you wouldn't sense me. The box is…* He paused. *It is undoing you.*

At the mention of it, she became acutely aware of her pack on her back, the weight reassuring. Something sharp pushed against her, and she could picture the metal-wrapped corner.

"What am I supposed to do?" she whispered. "Not keep it safe?"

The problem is not that you're keeping it. His voice was surprisingly gentle. *It's that the box is keeping you.*

She clenched her hands into fists to keep herself from pulling it out of her pack. "I know. But I can't let it go."

The chickadee shifted. *Someone else could carry it for you.*

The idea sent a shock of possessiveness through her, followed by a jab of anger. "Who?" she asked bitterly. "Everyone else has left me."

A quiet sigh sounded in her mind. *Did they leave you? Or did you turn your back on them?*

Rage rose in her, but the around the edges, she caught the taint of failure. A deep failure she didn't want to look at. "I keep having to stop doing what I need to do." Her words came out furious. "I keep failing to get my brothers safe, Crofftus, and every time I fail, they end up in more danger."

None of the things you call failures were of your own doing. They were external forces keeping you from your goals. Limiting you. Your current situation with the box is the same. You cannot open it safely.

His words held the scholarly edge that he often used, and she almost threw the cage at the elder tree.

When I think of my failures, it is the same, he continued, his tone softening. *I have spent a hundred years in the bodies of animals, wishing for a human body. The failure to get one has haunted me all these years, driven me to even befriend a Keeper.*

She didn't smile at the wryness in his tone.

But those weren't really failures—they were just me fighting against outside limitations. My biggest failure was the choice I made to betray you to Naevys.

The words were softly spoken, but they cut through her anger like a knife.

Because that was not being unable to accomplish some goal. That was a blatant choice to go against what I valued. I could have given you the loyalty you deserve, told you everything Naevys said the moment she left. I could have been the friend you deserve. When he continued, his words were pained. *Instead, I stayed silent, and the moment I had the chance, I left to tell her you and Venn intended to leave the White Wood.*

Shock cut through all her emotions. "You did what? Is that when she made the *naiwyn*?"

I had no idea she would do such a thing! She'd asked me to report to her what you were doing. And so I did...For no reason other than some distant hope that she'd someday help me. The small bird sat hunched in the cage. *I'm sorry, Katria. I'm so sorry.*

But don't try to tell me that Andovenn and the dwarves all abandoned you. The relationships have been straining for some time, but I know as well as you whose fault that is. I know because my betrayal of your trust made me feel exactly how you look right now. Like you're angry just to keep your guilt smothered.

The truth of his words was too heavy to muster an argument against. "Betrayal sounds like I planned it."

No, you merely let yourself be led further and further astray by the hope you're clinging to in that box. As did I with Naevys.

A deep, painful shame rose in her, and an anger rose alongside it. But the anger felt...alien. Like strings pulling her in a direction she didn't want to go.

I heard a quote once. 'Love does not desert. If it missteps, it does not run. It returns, admits its error, and makes amends.' It's one I've been thinking of because I deserted you. I wanted to return when you were sitting on that log before you found the yellow door. When you were holding that box in your lap again, instead of helping the others.

Kate paused. "I had no sense you were nearby then."

I was very far above you, but eagles have excellent eyesight.

"You don't look much like an eagle."

I was in one. Naevys kept this bird caged, and sent me out as an eagle to spy for her. But the eagle is a creature of her Wood, and she controls it perfectly. He hesitated. *Even if she didn't, the animals adore her. They would willingly obey anything she asked of them. So when she called the eagle back, he obeyed. I tried to stay in the eagle so I could escape again, but...* The chickadee shuddered. *She killed it so I would have no choice.*

The slightest sympathy bloomed inside her, but she shook her head. "Why did she leave you here? More spying?"

My job was to help her capture Venn. She expected both of you to come, and when it was only Venn, she tossed me aside. I believe... I believe she wanted me as leverage in case you caused her trouble. When you weren't an issue...

Katria, he said, his voice low and shamed. *The only one who left you was me.*

She picked up the cage and funneled *vitalle* out of the little branches that made up the sides. They withered and grew brittle until she could snap them apart. The chickadee flapped out and flew up to a low branch.

Katria, he said, stricken, *I'm so sorry. I shouldn't have believed her. I should have told you everything.*

Kate shifted her pack, feeling the weight of the box. "If you'd stayed, I would have just driven you away as well, so I'm hardly one to judge."

The snow around Kate was trampled with Venn's footprints and Naevys's. The Warden's gold mingled with Venn's silvery green, and they were both smeared with the frost blue of the dragon, which spread across a huge swath of the ground.

"Crofftus, how are we going to find Venn?"

I have no idea. Naevys has shut me out.

A tendril of blackness flickered at the edge of Kate's vision.

She straightened and closed her eyes. "Venn?"

The impressions came faintly across her mind. Absolute darkness. A tight space. The slither of something beneath her. Pieces of metal sliding against each other. Everything dark and musty—a mustiness that smelled vaguely familiar.

"Venn!" Kate called again.

The sensation stayed the same. Venn was lying on her side in a cramped space, her legs curled up in front of her. Her mind moved sluggishly. She stretched her feet out, but they hit a solid wall. Her hands reached out, running into another wall. A desperate terror rose as she twisted, her hands scrabbling across the wooden slats above her. There were no gaps between the boards. Venn drew in a deep breath, trying to get the terror under control. Forcing her hands to slow, she probed every corner, searching for any gaps, but her arms felt like they were made of lead.

The wooden walls closed her in completely. Finally, she let her heavy arms drop onto the lumpy, cold surface below her. Her fingers fumbled against it, finding countless coins, cold and hard.

She picked one up and felt the profile of a man's face. Slowly, she flipped it over and felt the stamped image of a dragon coiled around a sword.

"That's a Kalesh coin!" Kate inhaled, as though she could physically smell more of Venn's air. "She's in some sort of box. It smells old and... Where have I smelled that before?"

You can see her?

"We're connected. Naevys connected her to the Wood again and—"

Venn pounded her fist against the box, and it let out a dull thud, the sound oddly dampened. It was a struggle to move her heavy arms, but she pounded again. "Is anyone there?" she shouted, her words slurred.

Only silence answered her.

Everything was dark, but there was the taint of something in the air.

Magic.

Powerful as iron, drenched in *ael'iza*. And old...very old.

The coin fell out of Venn's fingers, and the impression began to fade.

"Venn!" Kate called out.

The image dissolved away, the feel of the coins vanished, and the closeness of the space blew away into the openness of the woods.

Kate grasped after the feel of the magic and found the hint of a memory.

Runes.

Centuries-old runes.

Kate's eyes flew open.

That was where it had been—along with that exact same smell.

"The curse! Crofftus! Venn is trapped in the emperor's carriage!"

CHAPTER FORTY-NINE

"Venn!" The word sounded through the quiet of the snowy Wood. Kate squeezed her eyes shut again, dread washing over her at the thought of the wooden walls closing in around Venn.

How? Crofftus flew closer to her, alighting on the end of a branch. *How could she possibly be in there? It's sealed. Cursed.*

The question broke through her tumult of fear, and Kate grabbed for it, trying to concentrate on the logical question.

"I don't know, but it was the carriage. I could feel the curse. And it smelled just like it did when we broke the window." She climbed to her feet, her legs so cold she stumbled to get her balance. "Naevys can step. Maybe she could step inside with Venn and leave her there."

Did you sense Naevys?

"No, Venn was alone. Trapped in a very small box, lying on a bed of Kalesh coins."

Crofftus gave a troubled hum. *Sounds like something one would find in that carriage.*

Kate tried to get her bearings. "We need to get into it."

Impossible. We tried that before—with a lot more friends—and half of us almost died.

"Yes, but we got in. We just need to do it again. You can help me read the Elvish runes, and the dwarves can move the rocks." She paused. "Assuming I can convince them to forgive me."

She pointed past the elder tree. "That way to Renault's cave?" Her pants were cold and wet from kneeling in the snow, and she fastened her cloak tight around her again. The thought of Venn trapped in that small box made her start uphill with quick steps. "She must be in a chest or a crate. Why would Naevys take Venn just to hide her in the carriage?"

She was too cryptic for me to know her entire plan, but she's collecting what she needs, and I think she almost has it all. She needs a new body for the seed, which she now has. She needs the box, which she knows you have, and you can't leave the area because her naiwyn *won't let you. She also needs... She called it the key.*

"Key to what? Something more than the Bridge?"

Yes, it's something else that she still doesn't have. Something she's been seeking for centuries.

"She's been looking for the amulet for centuries. It's has been missing since Emperor Sorrn was here. In her notes, she said he stole it and the box and sent them away before she realized what he was doing."

No, the amulet doesn't quite fit. Whatever this key is, she's tried many over the years, but none of them have worked. It's a source of great frustration to her, and...There was something like shame in her when she spoke of it. But her words are so enigmatic that it's hard to tell if the shame related to this key or to something else entirely. The bird launched off the branch but only fluttered to the next one before landing.

Kate lengthened her stride. "So we need to get Venn out of that carriage before Naevys finds that key."

If she hasn't found it already. Something she said made me think she knew where it was—she just hadn't collected it yet.

"Well, then, we need to get Venn out before she collects the key or comes to collect my box." She paused. "If she needed it, why did she leave it in the woods? Did she just forget about it?"

No. She said it had a task to perform first.

"What task? Did she want me to get my brothers out?"

I have no idea. She's not the most coherent conversationalist. Or the most rational.

"Maybe she's not lucid enough to know what she's doing. Maybe she put the box down and just...forgot about it."

She knows exactly what she's doing. She's incredibly purposeful. If she left the box there, it was for a reason. She's putting together the pieces of some puzzle only she can see.

"What puzzle?"

That's the sort of thing you figure out, Katria. Not me.

The forest around them was quiet aside from the crunch of Kate's feet through the snow and the flutter of the chickadee's wings as it flew from tree to tree.

What is it that the dwarves need to forgive you for?

Kate stepped over a fallen log. "They..." Her mouth curled into a smile that was half grimace. "They wanted me to help them get into the carriage."

The small grey bird twitched to face her, and Crofftus let out a short chuckle.

Her smile faded. "All I ever wanted this box for was to get a clue to where Evan was. But looking back, I can see that as soon as I got it, it immediately became more. It felt natural. It linked me to Bo and must hold clues to Evan, but... It calls to me." She wrapped her hand around the strap of her pack. "Not with a sound. My hands just want to hold it." The weight on her back held the same comfort and longing the box always carried with it, but it was tainted slightly. The memory of Tumble's lonesome bell marred it with a greediness she couldn't shake. "There are so many mysteries in it that the desire almost feels natural. But it's not. Which you all have pointed out to me more than once, but I refused to listen to you."

Kate fell silent for a dozen paces. "Now the object I first wanted so I could get closer to those I cared about has done the very opposite. It's pulled me away from everything but itself."

The chickadee landed on a branch just ahead of her. *I'm not the one you need to say this to.*

"I know." Kate shifted her shoulders under the pack. "But it doesn't hurt to practice telling a story once you've figured out the truth of it."

They walked in silence past a line of thorny frenbrush harboring deep shadows underneath.

"It's Naevys making the forest dark, isn't it?" Kate asked. "Somehow, she's causing all these shadows."

It's worse close to her. The bird settled on a limb a little way ahead. *Everything about her feels dark, Katria. But the entire forest and every creature is still enamored with her.* The bird twitched, and Crofftus grunted. *Steady...* But the chickadee spread its wings. *She's calling the bird!*

"Naevys?"

The tiny grey chickadee spread his wings and took off, but his flight was erratic, and he dropped to the ground, barely getting his feet under him in time. *I can't fight it. Katria! I promise,* he said, his voice rough with the effort of keeping the bird down. *I don't want to return to her!*

He sounded sincere, but she shook her head. "I'm not sure it matters what you want if she can control any animal you're in."

I know. The bird trembled. *If you have a solution to my situation that doesn't involve me inhabiting one of the animals of her Wood, I would love to hear it.* The chickadee launched into the air, and Crofftus let out a hiss of frustration. *I'll be back!* His voice faded as the bird shot away through a gap in the trees. *Katria! I'll...* It faded away, leaving nothing but the quiet woods behind.

The break in the trees stayed empty as a knot tightened in Kate's gut. If Naevys didn't know already that Venn could communicate from the carriage, she would soon. She could just pull it from Crofftus's mind. He wouldn't even have to say anything.

The thought snagged in Kate's mind. Would he talk anyway? Willingly?

She pushed the question away. She was hardly the one to question someone's loyalty.

Starting up the slope again, she tried to formulate what she would say to the dwarves. By the time she reached the edge of the trees, the words she'd said to Crofftus about the box had settled into a logical order. An apology that, while humiliating to admit, was honest. More honest than she felt like she'd been about herself in a long time.

She reached the tree line beneath Renault's cave and paused to get her bearings before striking out to the left across the slope that was covered with an undisturbed blanket of snow. A few minutes' walk brought her to within sight of the gaping dark front entrance, and not far past it, the snow was trampled in a path to the back entrance.

Crofftus's remnant rolled down from the sky above her, and she looked up to see a grey and white bird flying toward her. When he didn't appear to be heading to the ground, she held out her arm. He landed on it smoothly, the bird's tiny weight feeling like it was made mostly of air. It turned inquisitive black eyes on her, and she leaned back.

This little fellow won't hurt you. The bird looked away from Kate, unconcerned, eyeing the ground around them. *Grey jays aren't afraid of people. He's more likely to snatch a snack out of your hand and take it back to his hoard than to bite you.*

Kate relaxed her arm. "What happened to the chickadee?"

I got him to land in a tree with this fellow and transferred before he could take off again. I'd imagine he's back with Naevys by now.

"Do you know where she is? She's not waiting next to the carriage, is she?"

The little bird twitched in what might be the shake of his head. *No, we were heading farther north than the ravine.*

Kate's hand tightened. "Toward Home?"

Not that far north. Somewhere in between.

"Like Renault's pocket world?"

That's a possibility.

Kate started up the path toward the back entrance. "Won't she just call this bird back to her too?"

She might, but I'm hoping it takes her a little while to find me.

Kate followed the trail up the rock face and started toward the pile of rocks she could see ahead, marking the shaft that would lead into the back of the cave. "Are you sure you want to come in here with me? The dwarves never really trusted you in the first place. Now…"

The bird's talons tightened on her forearm. *I'm with you, Katria. Whether we're facing Naevys or a pair of surly dwarves.*

"Even if I can never find you a moral way to get back into a human body?"

Sometimes, it's hard to remember my humanity. Animals are concerned first and foremost with survival. Whatever action will keep them alive is the one they'll choose. Some know the concept of loyalty. They'll mate for a season or a lifetime, and decisions about their survival will become decisions about their family's survival. But I managed to forget even that. The pull to be safer, to be stronger, to be independent was too much.

I'm in this condition through my own selfish blunders. I don't want to become human again at the cost of my humanity.

Kate straightened. "All right, then, let's go see how forgiving dwarves are."

The rock wall was rough under Kate's hand. She paused just before the library door, listening to Silas's low voice rumbling in an instructive tone, the words too quiet for her to make out. Tribal answered with his usually dry sarcasm.

Just on the other side of the doorway, the bookshelf was still in disorder from Naevys's rummaging. The lantern light warmed the browns of the leather covers and the yellowed edges of the pages. The dry, whispery vanilla scent of the books smoothed the edges of Kate's tension, like walking into the Stronghold library. Like coming home.

Except there was more than just the look and smell of the books. The queen's remnant was still sprinkled everywhere, but the darker copper of the dwarves glittered from the floor by her feet, interspersed with the lighter honey-colored remnant of the elf twins. Venn's green glinted alongside Kate's own red and the barest hint of Crofftus's aged bronze. Around her, the scents of roasting meat and spiced ale intertwined with those of sap and moss and forest breezes, wrapping around her like a comfortable blanket. A blanket she'd torn—maybe torn to tatters. A blanket she couldn't quite wrap around herself, like she didn't fit in it any longer. Like the tight bands of guilt wrapped around her held it at bay.

A vast hollowness opened up inside her, and she stepped into the doorway without meaning to.

The dwarves squatted in front of the blazing forge, the matching silhouettes of broad shoulders and bushy beards so familiar she could have drawn them from memory. The elf twins leaned over them, peering into the fire.

The top of Fix's head was visible as he hunched off to the side.

The steel the dwarves had gathered for her to turn into stonesteel still sat in a pile. The unread books were still stacked in the piles they'd created: *Ignore, Maybe,* and *Read.* The Read pile still held five volumes, and the Maybe stack had three times as many.

The homeyness of the room felt distant. The anger that had filled her in Renault's workshop was back, but this time it was aimed at herself. She wanted to move forward, but her feet were rooted to the floor. She didn't quite fit in here now. The speech she'd prepared circled in her head, sounding pathetic and defensive.

Love does not desert, Crofftus said quietly into her mind. *If it missteps, it does not run. It returns, admits its error, and makes amends.*

"Then let's hope there's love on their part as well as mine," she said under her breath.

Without giving herself any more time to think, she entered the room. Her speech dissolved, replaced by a longing to feel a part of this place again. "You're right," she said.

The dwarves, the elf twins, and Fix all spun to face her, both dwarves gripping their knives.

Kate took another step forward. "This box will be the death of me if I drive everyone else away just to protect it. I'm sorry."

Aislin's and Matlen's faces broke into smiles, but their cheeks and eyes still looked wan. Silas shoved his knife back into his belt and crossed his arms, scowling. Tribal noticed the jay, and he let out a growl.

Kate shifted her shoulders. "I…"

Silas turned back to the bellows and began to pump them slowly. "Haven't seen her speechless often."

"Figured she'd have some speech made up," Tribal said, still watching her from beneath an angry brow. "Long and logical, having finally sorted out the story of how wrong she's been and how right we always are."

A small smile twisted up the edge of Kate's mouth. "Do you want to hear it?"

Tribal let out a snort. "Please, spare us. It's enough to know that we were right and you were wrong."

"If that's what you're saying," Silas said over his shoulder, "you can stay, but the bird is not welcome."

I fell for Naevys's lies, Crofftus said, quietly. *I was stupid, and I'm sorry.*

Neither dwarf answered.

"I've spoken to Naevys," Matlen said. "When she speaks, you just...*want* to believe her."

Aislin nodded. "She found us convincing the trees that a band of human had dammed the river with furniture." At Tribal's amused snort, a bit of her old mischievousness surfaced. "We didn't really know what human furniture looked like, so we made it look like elven furniture. Well, some ranger immediately assumed the humans had raided an elven house, and there was a bit of trouble brewing when Naevys discovered us."

Matlen's smile was rueful. "She actually convinced us that we didn't want to cause trouble like this. And we actually didn't. For an entire fortnight."

"A fortnight?" Tribal said. "The mad queen must have near miraculous powers."

She does, Crofftus said.

Silas studied Kate, his bellows moving again. "By way of apology, if you made the stonesteel you owe us, it wouldn't go amiss."

"I can't yet," Kate said. "I need your help."

"When doesn't she?" Tribal muttered, but he stayed watching her, and Silas's bellows paused.

Kate swallowed. "Naevys took Venn."

Aislin grabbed her brother's arm. "What?"

Tribal sheathed his knife. "She took our elf?"

"Naevys lured her into the woods with that ruse in the workshop, right to an elder tree where Venn would be overcome. Then Naevys and the dragon appeared and took her."

"The ruse..." Tribal pointed his knife at Crofftus. "The one you made."

Crofftus's wings fluttered in agitation. *Unwillingly, I swear.*

Aislin peered at Kate worriedly. "Why does she want Auntie Venn?"

"To kill her and use her body and her lastlight to provide a new body for the child in the seed." At their horrified looks, she added, "It was in Renault's writings. It wasn't the amulet Naevys took from the workshop. It was the Bridge. A disk that attaches to the amulet and transfers one person's life into a new body."

Silas pulled the bellows away from the fire. "Where does she have our elf?"

Kate grimaced. "Trapped inside the emperor's carriage."

"The carriage?" Tribal asked. "Our carriage?"

Kate tried to nod, but it came out more like a twitch. "I need your help to break into it." She shifted at both dwarves' incredulous looks. "I recognize the irony."

Silas rose and grabbed a bag off the table, dropping a handful of something that looked like bolts into it. "How do you know this?"

"Venn and I were connected when Naevys gave Venn back the power to talk to the trees. Somehow we still are. I saw, through Venn's eyes, when the dragon came. Now she's trapped in some small box inside the carriage. I need your help to get her out."

"Well," Silas said with a small smile, picking up a stack of metal disks, "this saves us some trouble at least. We were about to go find another human mage to help us open it."

Tribal grabbed a bundle of rope and stuffed it into his pack. "But since you're here, I guess we can use you."

Matlen moved to what looked like a disassembled handcart and picked up a pile of metal brackets.

Aislin looked thoughtfully at the ceiling, as though she could see outside, then began gathering lanterns. "Might be dark by the time we get there."

Their remnants fused seamlessly with the scents of the library now, gliding effortlessly through the hollowness to wrap around Kate. "Thank you," she whispered.

"If anyone's gonna lock that elf up underground and threaten to kill her," Tribal said lightly, "it's gonna be us." He tucked a wrench into his pack.

"What is all that?" Kate asked.

"It will be an ingenious pulley system that will help us move rocks," Silas said, "which is much better than its former life when it was a handcart for moving books around." He swung his pack onto his back, and it landed with a heavy thump. "Any idea how long we have 'til the mad queen murders the princess of the White Wood?"

Kate shook her head. "Crofftus says she's keeping her safe until she has everything she needs."

"Which is?" Tribal asked.

"She has Venn and the Bridge. I think we have to assume she also has the amulet. So she just needs the box and some sort of key. But we don't know what that is."

Silas stopped in front of Kate, giving her a flat look. "The box she just left in the woods a few days ago?"

Kate gave a half shrug. "We're not really sure why she did that."

"Might be a good thing to not have with us when we go to the carriage she guards," Tribal said.

Kate gripped the straps of her pack. "I'm not leaving it unprotected somewhere."

"Never imagined you would." Silas walked quickly past her out the door. "But you know I'm right. Let's not dawdle."

Aislin offered Kate two lanterns and gave a sympathetic look. "If my brother was in it, you'd have to kill me to get it out of my hands." She patted Kate's arm and followed the dwarf.

Tribal hefted his axe. "What sorts of things you figure the mad queen'll have left to guard the carriage?"

"Let's hope it's massive bears or *gwerocs* with fur impervious to axes," Kate answered. "And not the *naiwyn*."

He squinted at her, then raised his voice. "We need to find friends with weaker enemies, brother."

"She can make stonesteel," Silas called back.

Tribal grunted. "Suppose that's something."

CHAPTER FIFTY

Kate's feet slid on the snowy hillside for the hundredth time, and she threw her hand out to the nearest trunk to keep herself from falling. Without slowing, she hurried after the dwarves. The image of Venn trapped—the feel of the confined space—closed in around Kate like a solid cage of dread.

Her mind darted again through the different possibilities of what they might find in the ravine, but every option was terrifying. The dwarves were handy in a fight, but Fix was nearly useless and Crofftus still inhabited the jay. The elf twins kept the quick pace without any obvious effort, but they barely spoke and still seemed almost curled in on themselves, skirting around each tree instead of touching it.

The walls of fear rose up around her, close and cramped, and her breath came faster, both from the speed of their descent and from the foreboding crowding around her.

Weapons. They needed weapons. The concrete thought drove the claustrophobic feeling back. Her own *vitalle* could put to sleep one creature, or maybe two, depending on how driven they were, but none of that would be enough. Venn's crossbow was a significant loss, as was the lack of any elven backup. But not only would Faron probably refuse to listen to a call from them, no one in the group had the ability to make one.

They'd come far enough downhill that she found herself continually searching through the trees ahead for any sign of the river as she mentally rummaged through her pack, searching for any weapon she'd overlooked.

"What do we do if Venn is guarded by *gwerocs*?" Aislin asked, her voice low.

The fear closed around Kate again at the thought of the massive wolves. "I don't know. Last time, we needed Venn's darts."

Matlen skidded down a stretch of snow next to her, his pale face the only indication this wasn't just an afternoon adventure for him. "If it's the bears again, though, you can put them to sleep."

"I don't know that either. Faron had trouble with them. I'm not sure I could do it alone. And if I can, it won't be quick."

"And if it's the dragon, or a *naiwyn*..." Aislin said, her voice lower.

"It's not gonna be," Tribal said over his shoulder.

Matlen frowned up at him. "How do you know?"

"Because if it is, we can't get to our elf." Tribal strode down the hill without slowing. "And we need to get to her."

Kate tried to reach out toward Venn, tried to sense anything from the elf, but there was nothing.

Crofftus's remnant came from above them, and the grey jay flew down, alighting on a branch. *Gwerocs! Three of them! They're guarding the carriage!* He fluttered to another tree. *Watch yourselves —you're almost in view of the ravine.*

Tribal slid his knife out of his belt and slowed, moving almost silently through the trees. Silas motioned for the elf twins to hang back and followed his brother.

The forest thinned, and the two dwarves stopped before they reached the end of the trees. Kate's feet slid on the last bit of snow behind them, and she grabbed Silas's wool sleeve to steady herself. Ahead, the river lapped against the ice along its edges. The sun had just fallen behind the western horizon, and the clouds in the eastern sky blazed with orange light, turning the snow in the ravine into a rippled surface of tawny gold.

Along the right-hand side of the rockslide, three glittering shapes like shaggy beasts of ice paced among the lumps of rock.

She gripped Silas's arm. "Their fur is as hard as solid ice. Your blades and axes will be no use. Last time we had to shoot one of Venn's darts into their mouth."

"I don't suppose you have any of those," Silas said.

Kate started to shake her head, but Fix rummaged into one of the many pockets in his cloak and pulled out three little bits of wood that looked like smoothed-out acorns.

"From her broken darts!" Kate took them and cast out. They were empty of *vitalle*, but when she pushed a little in, it held. "All right, I could rig these so they'll put the *gweroc* to sleep, assuming we can get them into their mouths."

"If you distract them," Matlen said to Tribal, "Aislin and I could step up close and shove them in."

"That's a terrible plan," Silas said.

"None of the rest of you are fast enough to do it," Aislin said firmly.

Tribal opened his mouth to object, but Kate spoke first. "She's right. We don't have time to figure out another way. I'll prep these, and we'll all move together. If we come up from the right, we can keep them backed against the rocks, which should limit their movements."

She focused on the wooden nodes in her hand and began to

funnel *vitalle* into them, infusing them with the will to make the creatures sleep. It was odd to push the magic into the tiny holding chamber instead of into a creature, but she finished all three within a matter of moments while the dwarves whispered adamant warnings to the elf twins to be careful with themselves.

"Everyone ready?" Kate handed each of the elf twins one of the nodes. "Just get this into their mouth. They're fragile enough that they'll break under a single bite. Make sure your arm isn't part of the same bite."

"Anything else we should be aware of besides three nearly invulnerable giant wolves?" Tribal asked Crofftus.

Not that I saw, but I will check again. The jay flew back up into the sky.

Silas watched him go. "For the record, I'm not comfortable trusting the bird."

Fix's large eyes followed the jay until it disappeared over the trees.

"I do think he's sorry he trusted Naevys," Kate said.

Silas grunted. "So he says."

"Yes, just like I said that I'm sorry I focused on the box too much, and you started trusting me again."

"That's pushing it," Silas said with the edge of a smile. "But you're easier to keep track of. We always know what you look like."

"And that you're always slow and weak and not terribly bright," Tribal added.

Kate glanced at Fix. "Do you trust him?"

The gnoblin curled in on himself at the question, then gave a little half shrug and pointed at Kate.

Kate rolled the node between her fingers. "I think I do."

Fix gave her a smile that was more determined than cheerful and flicked his fingers in a dwarven signal.

Tribal sighed. "Fix says he will too." He shook his head. "Not sure that's the best idea."

"Well, let's focus on the enemies we know we have." Kate started forward.

Tribal grabbed her arm. "Anyone slow and weak and not terribly bright stays in the back."

Silas nodded and started forward.

The *gwerocs* turned to face them when they emerged from the trees, but the massive wolves didn't leave the snow above the carriage, which the dwarves had trampled a few days ago.

"Calm and steady," Silas said, heading for the stepping stones that crossed the river.

"Would we see *naiwyn* if they were here?" Aislin asked, her voice tight with worry.

"They blend into the trees well when they want to." Kate studied the edge of the forest that sat about a hundred paces to the right of the rockslide. "But when I saw them, they were protecting the trees. I would think if they were protecting the carriage, they'd be stationed by the carriage." Still, she cast out, funneling her wave toward the nearest tree line. The trunks lit up in solemn columns, but nothing like the blazing *vitalle* of the *naiwyn* appeared. She cast out again across the slope of the rockslide, but aside from the glimmering net of *vitalle* that Naevys kept under the rocks and the three searingly bright forms of the *gweroc*, there was nothing alive there either. "I don't think there's anything else."

Aislin gave a troubled sort of hum. "You know what isn't here? The dragon. And it hasn't been."

Matlen nodded. "You can tell by the snow. Nothing that big has been here."

"Told ya," Tribal said, walking steadily up the hill. "No dragon. Nothing to worry about."

Kate took in the undisturbed snow. "How'd Naevys get Venn here, then?"

"Our elf's not that heavy," Silas said. "The mad queen could have carried her."

The thought was reasonable, but it nagged at Kate's mind. "I suppose she would have had to step into the carriage to get Venn in anyway."

"That's dangerous," Aislin said. "Stepping to somewhere you can't see."

"Unless she's very familiar with it," Matlen agreed, "it's a ridiculous thing to try."

"Somehow I think Naevys is very familiar with every part of this ravine," Kate said. "But something still feels off."

"Has there ever *not* been something off in this ravine?" Tribal asked.

They moved away from the water and silence reigned, broken only by the crunching of their boots in the snow. The *gweroc* now stood still, gauging their progress with emotionless grey eyes. Each wolf-like creature was huge enough that their shoulders were taller than Kate's waist.

"Fix," Kate said quietly, pulling him from her shoulder and setting him down, "find a place to burrow in and stay safe until this is over."

The gnoblin hesitated before hunching over and digging into the cold ground. Within the space of a few moments, he was gone.

The rest of them neared the spot where the carriage was buried, and Kate cast out into the ground. The shape of it lit up, outlined in the runes of the elven curse that kept it undisturbed—and kept her wave from passing through.

"We're coming, Venn," she said, keeping her voice low.

"Niblings," Silas said, "be ready. Aislin with Tribal, Matlen with me. Hang back at first. We'll attack enough to get the beasts to open their mouths, then you step in and out. Fast. Absolutely no one gets their arms bitten off, is that clear?"

The two dwarves crept forward, shoulder to shoulder. The *gweroc* watched them without blinking. Two moved to the edge of the rocks. The third, the largest of the three, stayed back. There was something unnervingly intelligent in his eyes.

Naevys is controlling the big one. Crofftus flew down and settled on a rock uphill from the wolves.

"So the mad queen knows we're here?" Tribal asked, still moving forward.

Yes.

"No time to waste, then." Silas lunged forward, swinging his axe at the *gweroc* on the right. It danced back before leaping forward, snarling. Matlen appeared in front of it, then disappeared so quickly Kate barely saw him.

Tribal charged the second wolf, smashing the dull side of his axe into the wolf's shoulders and sending it stumbling to the side. It scrambled back to its feet and hurled itself at the dwarf. Aislin blinked into sight in front of Tribal before reappearing by her brother. Both wolves slammed into the dwarves, driving them backward, but even as they growled, the noise grew less vicious, and the creatures' motions slowed.

The third *gweroc* took in the elf twins and Crofftus before his flinty grey eyes fell on Kate's hand with an almost physical weight. It stepped over Silas's leg, stalking closer with a calculating set of its head.

Before she could cry out, it lunged at her. She held the node out, but it twisted its muzzle past her. Sharp, solid, jagged fur crashed into her arm, knocking the node of *vitalle* out of her hand.

Aislin screamed, and Crofftus shouted something urgent.

The spiky, ice-crusted fur of the *gweroc's* head barreled into her chest, jabbing into her ribs like a spiked cudgel. She fell backward, slamming onto the ground and knocking the breath from her lungs. The creature landed on top of her like the mountain itself was trying to bury her. Her arms were pinned against the *gweroc's* chest where she'd foolishly tried to hold it back.

"Twig?" Tribal's voice was muffled as he struggled to get out from under his own creature.

Kate thrust *vitalle* into the wolf, but the icy fur was like a stone wall, blocking every attempt she made.

With a snarl, he stretched his maw open. His fangs, wet and wickedly sharp, drove toward her throat.

CHAPTER FIFTY-ONE

G rey feathers swept in and battered against her face, screeching and pecking at the flesh of the *gweroc's* nose.

Shouts rang out from the dwarves, and she caught the glimpse of an axe swinging before a heavy blow shook the creature's body. The wolf's massive jaws snapped shut around the bird, and Crofftus's remnant cut off. With a twist of its head, the *gweroc* tossed the limp bird away and shot toward Kate's neck again.

Crofftus's remnant suddenly rolled out from the wolf, as loud as if Kate stood at the ocean, watching high waves crash against the shore. The wolf's head twitched, and instead of tearing into Kate's throat, it slammed its muzzle into the ground next to her ear.

Get the node! Crofftus's voice came strained through her mind. *Hurry! I can't hold him long! Naevys is here—she's trying to push me out!*

Kate shoved against the *gweroc*, but he weighed too much for her to even budge him. "I dropped it near my feet!"

Aislin and Matlen scrambled down by her legs.

"Got it!" Matlen clambered back up to the *gweroc's* head. "Open its mouth!"

Crofftus gave a long, strained groan, but the wolf's mouth opened slightly.

Matlen jabbed the node in and yanked his hand out as the jaws snapped shut, leaving a long bloody scrape along the elf's forearm.

The *gweroc* snarled again, dragging its face back to Kate's, but its eyes grew unfocused.

"Crofftus," Kate managed, gasping for air. "Get him off me!"

Can't! Naevys is fighting me! Need...another...animal! Crofftus grunted.

The wolf's movements slowed, and its body sank limply onto Kate. Her arms ached from pushing it, but she could barely get it to shift. Aislin and Matlen threw their shoulders into its side, and it toppled off.

Kate sucked in a lungful of air and struggled to her knees. "Jump into one of the other *gweroc!*"

Naevys is blocking me! Can't hold on... Crofftus's voice grew fainter. *Need a new host...* The rumble of his remnant grew quieter.

Kate cast out, but there were no creatures nearby except the *gwerocs*. "Do you sense anything?"

Too late... Crofftus's remnant faded until it was so quiet she could barely hear it. *Thank you, Katria, for trying.*

"Wait! We'll find you something!" She scrabbled to her feet and cast out again, searching for even the tiniest trace of *vitalle*. A beetle. A worm. Anything.

The ground around her was empty of life.

Glimmers of bronze mistlight drifted up from the senseless *gweroc*, forming into a ragged cloud.

"Crofftus!" Kate sank down next to the creature. "Use me!"

We would drive each other mad within moments, he said softly. *It's all right, Katria. This was always going to be my end.*

Kate threw out a shield around the mistlight, keeping it from drifting away, but the motes of light flickered out one by one.

Both dwarves staggered closer to the sleeping *gweroc* on the broken body of the jay.

I did think, Crofftus said, his voice so faint she could barely hear it, *that I would die alone. It is better this way.* The edges of the bronze cloud grew darker, turning to specks of ash. *Thank you for letting me be part of all this.*

"Well, you did stalk us," Tribal said, but the words were kind, "so we had no choice, but you did well saving Twig."

"'Twas brave of you," Silas agreed. "We all know she never manages to save herself."

Crofftus let out a huff of laughter. *Try not to let her kill herself now.*

"Crofftus!" Kate held the shield steady, even as the flecks of bronze continued to darken. "There has to be another way!"

Not without hurting one of you, and I don't want to hurt someone else to save myself. I lost sight of that for a moment. He let out a grunt, and the *gweroc* twitched. *Katria, listen to me. Naevys is growing more crazed as she nears her goal. She will act soon—*

His voice cut off as a surge of bronze glimmers spilled out of the *gweroc*. Crofftus's rumbling remnant cut off abruptly.

"Crofftus!" Kate tightened her shield around the fading glints of his mistlight.

A spray of dirt hit Kate's foot. Fix clawed his way out of a new hole in the ground and scurried up onto the icy-crusted fur. He jabbed his bony fingers toward his own head, hopping on the sharp fur, his eyes wide and pleading.

"Crofftus!" Kate grabbed Fix, her hands sinking into the warm coat that enveloped him. His buckles clinked as she lifted him up into the thinning cloud of mistlight. "Come back! You've been in Fix before! You said he has space in his mind where you can fit!" She tightened the shield around the gnoblin. "Come to Fix!"

The bronze lights swirled around Fix's green face for a moment before they began to drift closer.

A hint of ocean rumbles sounded from the gnoblin. Fix's gaze darted fearfully around, and Kate set him down gently on the ground. He squatted lower as the sound of Crofftus's remnant grew. Slowly, bronze glitters seeped out of Fix's skin, mixing with the gnoblin's pale yellow.

Thank you. Crofftus's voice was barely audible.

"Are you…" Kate studied the gnoblin. "Are you both all right?"

Fix's round eyes still twitched, as though looking for something he couldn't see, but he nodded.

I will be. Crofftus paused. *Fix, there's all this space in here where, if you were a goblin, the hive mind would be. I can stay back here.*

The gnoblin's shoulders relaxed, and a small smile quirked up the edge of his mouth. He made a series of hand gestures.

Crofftus. Family, a quiet, thin voice said, the tone rough and unsteady.

Fix's pearlescent eyes widened, and his wrinkled face filled with surprise.

Kate reached out to touch Fix's thick sleeve. The dwarf and elf twins all straightened.

"Was that you?" Kate asked the little gnoblin.

He met her gaze with a mixture of elation and alarm. *Yes.* His mouth spread into a wide smile, even as he ducked his head.

Kate squeezed his arm gently. "I'm so very happy to hear your voice."

Katria, Crofftus said, *we must hurry.*

Kate looked over her shoulder at the quiet ravine. "Right."

"How long are these beasts going to sleep?" Tribal set his foot against one and rolled it over.

Kate cast out and found the *gweroc's* minds locked in sleep. "Several hours, I think."

"Then let's get these rocks moved." Silas started toward the nearest trees. "This elf isn't gonna free herself."

Blue-grey dusk settled over the ravine as the dwarves used their small crane to lift the first rock. A disquieting creak groaned from the thick branches they'd collected and affixed to each other to hold up their pulley system. While they worked, Kate scanned the trees in every direction, her mind turning their situation over again and again. The fear that had pushed her since Venn had been taken felt worn out, and a growing exasperation shouldered it aside. "This isn't right."

Silas stopped, his hand steadying the large rock swinging slowly from their crane. "What's wrong?"

"Everything. Everything about this place is always wrong." Kate paced downhill, studying the forest across the river. "It's driving me mad. Never once since I came here have I had any idea what is truly happening. I learn one piece of the story and all it does is reveal another dozen questions I can't answer.

"First, I was sure the box would lead me to Bo and Evan, when it, in fact, contained them. Then I was sure I was saving a wounded Faron from the shadow, when he *was* the shadow—a severely wounded and weakened one, until I healed him. I was sure Thallion was destroying the White Wood and killing Naevys, when it was all her doing. And now, when I'm sure Venn is buried here, I can't come up with any reason that she should be."

Silas heaved the rock to the side, and Tribal turned the crank, lowering it slowly onto a growing pile off to the side. "You saying the elf's not in here?"

"No, she is. I'm sure she is—" Kate let out an annoyed laugh. "I should say I *think* she is. But *why*? Naevys has a thousand places to hide her in the woods. Why bury her in an ancient carriage?"

It's one place you can't get to easily, Crofftus pointed out. *I think you keep surprising the elves with your skills. Maybe it was specifically to keep you from rescuing her.*

"I can't talk to the trees. She could have hidden Venn anywhere."

"But Aislin and Matlen can," Silas said.

"Maybe it's about Auntie Venn, not us," Aislin said thoughtfully. "With her trapped in there, she should be unable to contact anyone. Naevys restored Venn's connection to the trees and made it strong. But under normal circumstances, if she hadn't been so strangely bound to you, Kate, being in that carriage would have ensured that she couldn't contact anyone. Not even Faron." She winced now too. "If they were still betrothed."

Kate started back up the slope, casting out for the hundredth time at the net of protection Naevys had spread over the ravine. "Something's still off."

"Light the lanterns!" Tribal said, leaning down to peer into the hole they'd created in the rockslide.

Aislin lit one and brought it over. In the flickering light, the black side wall of the carriage was visible along with the corner of the window they'd broken last time they'd tried to get into it.

Kate cast out into the hole, and the surface of the carriage lit up, the trail of runes lying across it like a blanket, outlining every surface. The carriage was still positioned how it had been when they'd found it, on its side with part of the top crushed in. The door was buried in the ground beneath it, and the single broken window faced upward with a glimmer of *vitalle* stretching across it. "The curse is still very much in place." She cast out again, this time with a strong wave straight into the gap of the window, but the runes stopped it from going farther. "I can't tell what's inside. Don't reach through the window until we can find a way to disable the curse."

"One more rock to move," Silas said, climbing down into the hole. He gingerly set a foot on the side of the carriage, but nothing happened. Tribal hung the sling down, and Silas fastened it around the rock that was blocking the rest of the window. With a heave, the dwarves shifted it slightly, watching the rocks around it closely. When nothing else moved, Tribal threw his weight onto the crank and lifted it out of the way.

Kate slid down to kneel on the carriage. The window was nothing more than a few jagged pieces of glass along the edges, but she brushed her fingers across where the rest of the glass should be.

The moment her skin touched the invisible surface, a jolt of *vitalle* was yanked out of her. Her fingers grew ice cold even as the rush of energy burned the tips of each, and she yanked her hand back, rubbing her fingertips. "Definitely don't touch the window."

Kate cast out again into the carriage, but her wave rolled up against the curse and was deflected to the side. It ran instead around the side of the carriage and into the ground, lighting the net across the surface. She sent the wave rolling up the slope, and most of it faded quickly as it sank into the rocky ground, but uphill from the carriage, a section of it passed into what must be a cave. Tendrils of the net ran into the cave along each wall, collecting along one of the walls into an oblong object the size of a melon. "The seed!" Kate focused on the pale light she could sense. It was not the brightness of an elf, or even a human. It wasn't even as much *vitalle* as an animal would carry. It was barely as bright as a fern. "It's in a cave." She pointed to the hillside twenty paces above them. "I think it's very weak."

A small rock rolled down onto the carriage by her feet with a crack, and she jumped. "Let's get Venn out before Naevys comes to take her." She refocused on the wood beneath her feet. The protective net and the curse still held the grating, corrupted remnant, but threaded through it all she could now feel Naevys's. She knelt down on the wood. The queen's remnant was everywhere, but woven into it were glimmers of other colors. Yellows, silvers, greens—a hint of sky blue. Kate leaned closer and drew out the sense of the blue remnant. Summer wind. Windswept hills.

"It's Bo!" Kate looked over the surface of the carriage and caught a coppery glint that smelled of spiced ale.

Tribal paused. "Where?"

"His remnant is part of the shield around the carriage. As is Silas's."

Silas frowned down at her. "Why?"

"I think because you stuck your arm into it and the curse stole some of your remnant. Bo must have touched it too while he was trying to unearth the carriage."

The corruption came from other strands of remnant that were blackened, left the tang of vinegar on her tongue, and smelled of rot. She braced herself and pulled one out from the rest. It was decidedly human. Thinner than an elf's and more isolated. The one next to it was someone different. As were the half-dozen intertwined with them. She sank back on her heels, looking over the slope. There were dozens of humans' remnants here. A hundred, maybe.

"It's not just you and Bo," she said to Silas. "The net protecting this place is made from the remnants of all the people she killed. I would guess these are Bo's workers and Emperor

Sorrn's soldiers. And anyone else we've never heard of who she's killed in this ravine."

I don't doubt there are more, Crofftus said.

"So how do we get into this carriage without her sucking more of our life away?" Tribal asked.

There was a gust of *vitalle,* and Thallion stepped onto the snow next to Kate. "You can't. It's impossible."

CHAPTER FIFTY-TWO

Kate spun to face Thallion just as Faron appeared behind him. "What are you doing here?" she demanded.

Faron took in the hostile looks around him. "We're here to help you find my mother."

Kate pointed at his father. "Does he know what's actually happening?"

Thallion gave her a withering look. "More clearly than you do, I assure you. She must be stopped."

Kate paused. "You know about the seed?"

"He has my mother's wellstone," Faron said, his expression troubled. "He took it from Fix in the Elder Groves, remember? He's delved into her memories. He knew about Virion and the seed before I arrived to tell him."

"So you left us and ran straight to him?" Tribal said with a growl.

"Seeing as we'd just learned some shocking news about my mother," Faron said coldly, "it seemed appropriate."

Thallion looked down into their hole derisively. "You think the Warden is buried in this ravine again?"

"No," Kate said. "Venn is. And we're getting her out."

Faron took a step forward. "What? How? I knew I couldn't feel her in the woods, but I thought she'd just gone back to the pocket world."

Thallion let out a breath of understanding. "She's chosen Andovenn as the new vessel."

"Something we're not comfortable letting happen." Silas shouldered past the two elves and dropped into the hole next to Kate.

"You're wasting time we don't have," Thallion said dismissively. "Naevys needs four things. A new host—she could use any elf, so removing Venn from her clutches is pointless—Renault's amulet, the box you carry"—he pointed at Kate—"and a mage who's part elven to help her with the transfer process."

"A part-elven mage?" Kate asked. "That's the key she needs?"

Makes sense, Crofftus said slowly. *She's been trying to find the right sort of mage for a very long time, but she said she'd found her key already. And we don't have a—*

"You cannot truly be so blind," Thallion said, watching Kate as though she were a broken tool he was forced to use. His eyes were narrow and piercing, as though he could dig into her and pull out the truth he was looking for.

"I have no idea what you're talking about."

"As much as you've denied being related to Renault," Thallion said, "you can't ignore the fact that you have a remarkable aptitude for elven magic."

Kate raised an eyebrow. "You think I'm part elven?"

"Give me some of your blood and I'll see."

She stared at him. "Last time you took some of my blood, you bound me to the White Wood."

"I could hardly do so again in the middle of a rocky hillside. Why do you think Naevys is suddenly moving ahead with her plans? What has changed from the past, besides your appearance?"

"I…" The idea of elven blood felt irrational. She wanted to throw the idea out, and yet something about it caught at her.

"If you can't tell if she's elven," Silas said, "how would the mad queen know?"

Thallion shrugged. "The Warden might have an inkling just from meeting you, but she would need your blood to know for sure."

Kate set her hand on her cheek, where Naevys's thorn had dug into her skin and torn out a bloody scrap of flesh. "She did take some…"

Thallion held out a knife. "Your palm, please. I only need a drop."

"You didn't get enough of my blood before?"

"I wasn't looking to see if you were elven."

If he's right, Katria, Crofftus said, *the queen needs you as much as she needs Venn. If you're not elven, then Naevys found someone else, which seems unlikely.*

"Well, you're not taking it from my palm." Kate took the knife and set the tip against the back of her forearm, pressing it in until the tip pierced her skin and a drop of red blood swelled up.

Thallion reached out his long, thin fingers and wiped it off her arm, rubbing his thumb over it, smearing the blood on his fingertips. He let out a breath that was half-laugh, half-defeat. "No wonder you've caused so much trouble here. It's far back in your lineage, but there's definite elven blood." He held out his hand for the knife.

"I'm not…" Kate offered it numbly. "There are no elves in my history."

Thallion held up his red-smeared fingers. "There most definitely are. You must leave. Now."

Kate shook her head. "I'm not leaving. We're getting Venn out."

"You have two of the things Naevys needs," Thallion said. "Staying here is foolhardy."

"Even if I wanted to leave, which I don't, Naevys has the way south blocked by *naiwyn*. She's keeping everyone from leaving."

Thallion cocked his head to the side, his expression growing troubled. "Or she's been keeping you from leaving."

Kate considered the idea. Naevys had created the *naiwyn* when Crofftus had reported that she and Venn were leaving. "Doesn't matter. I'm not leaving Venn here."

Thallion looked down at the exposed side of the carriage. "No one can get through that curse. You especially cannot if you're elven. Leave this useless task and get yourself and your box away." The words made an uneasiness tickle across Kate's mind, but he continued, "Or better yet, find where Andovenn really is and prepare her again to be Warden, because the role must be taken away from Naevys."

Frustration drowned out the uneasiness. "You tried that already. It didn't work well."

"It didn't work because you didn't believe me that Naevys shouldn't be Warden." Thallion flicked his long fingers in a gesture that indicated the ravine and all the woods around it. "Now do you see? She has too much power. She'll drain the woods in her madness. The White Wood will suffer, but the human world could be utterly destroyed." His eyes scraped over the hillside. "Is she inside the caves now?"

"Not that I can tell." Kate cast out into the rockslide again, and her wave passed into the caves above them, lighting the queen's net of protection feeding the pathetically weak seed but finding no other life. "We don't know where she is."

"Well, we do know that she needs you and that box." Thallion took a step toward Kate. "If you won't take the box away from here, I will."

He stretched out a hand toward her.

Faron grabbed it. "No. We've taken enough from Kate already. You won't take this from her." The green bands of his remnant stretched out and wrapped around his father.

Thallion stiffened. "You dare to command me?"

Faron's expression twitched, but he straightened. "It is my duty to protect the White Wood, those who are a part of it, and those whose lives are affected by it from any who would harm them or take from them."

"You've always been spineless." Thallion tore his arm out of Faron's grip. "But I didn't know you loved your mother so little."

A flicker of fury crossed Faron's face. "I love my mother deeply, but if she is the one hurting what I need to protect, I will stand against her, just as I will stand against you when you do the same."

Thallion's mouth curled into a sneer. "The Wood needs a stronger king than you."

Faron let out a breath. "Undoubtedly, it does. Regardless, I'm staying here to help free Venn, and then we'll do what we can to stop my mother."

"You're staying here?" Thallion said, his voice thick with disbelief. "Trying to save the elf who rejected you so thoroughly? Who threw away whatever love she had because she didn't understand what it means to rule?"

Faron's uncertainty shifted to a cold resolution. "I do not love Venn because she loves me back, Father. I love her for who she is, and I have loved her for my entire life." He took a step closer to his father until their faces were mere inches apart. His jaw tightened. "I deserve what she did. I spent centuries bowing to you, betraying what I felt was right because I was too afraid to stand up to you. I'm a coward, because it took you losing everything before I had the courage to make my own choices. And even when I had the chance to escape you, I ran right back, spinelessly doing what you wanted." He set a finger on Thallion's chest, and shadows gathered around his hand. "No more. You are not king of the White Wood. You gave that up to chase your own selfish greed. The crown has fallen to me, and I swear I will do everything I can to deserve it. Everything I can to make reparations for the harm I've caused serving you." He held his father's angry gaze for a long moment, inky blackness wrapping around his hand and up his arm. "So help us free Andovenn, or leave."

"You're a fool," Thallion whispered. He disappeared with a rush of *vitalle* that lit Faron like a candle.

Except for his hand, which was wreathed in blackness, where no light or signs of life crossed his runelight.

Kate stared at the darkness as the *vitalle* faded and Faron dimmed back to himself in the dusky light. "Faron! I know how to get into the carriage!"

CHAPTER FIFTY-THREE

"We can use your runelight!" Kate knelt next to the window. "Your shadow keeps everything from crossing it." She focused on her hand, shaping her remnant into the double-layered shield that he used, feeding *vitalle* into it. Shadows enveloped her fingers, and she pressed against the shimmer of light covering the window—they passed through.

The *vitalle* of the curse flowed around the shadow like water around a rock.

She looked up at the dwarves. "Could you lower me down?"

Silas raised an eyebrow. "Through that tiny window? That would be a tight fit."

Lower Fix and me in, Crofftus said.

Fix's eyes widened.

"Fix'd fit," Tribal said. "And he'd be better than you, Kate, at opening any locked crates."

Kate met the gnoblin's gaze. "Fix?"

The gnoblin swallowed then nodded. *Help Venn,* his thin voice said quietly.

And we should do it quickly, Crofftus said. *Thallion is not wrong. We should get Kate and Venn and the box far away from here as soon as we can.*

Kate held her hands over the window and fed *vitalle* into the shadow, trying to spread it into a tunnel wide enough to let Fix fit through. No matter how hard she pressed, though, it stayed close to her skin.

"I can only create it around myself," Faron said. "I don't know how to put it around anything else."

Kate took in the open window and the bits of carriage wall visible around it. "What if we kept it a little around my body and a little around yours?" She held her arms out to either side of the window and let the shadow stretch up them and across her chest, forming an arc of darkness.

Faron took her hands with warm fingers, squeezing her tight enough that she winced. "Sorry," he said, his brow creased with worry. Shadows flowed out from him until their arms enclosed a circle of darkness. Where Kate's remnant butted up against Faron's, a thin seam pierced the blackness. Kate pushed her remnant into his, feeling the vastness of the forest seep into her. The seam sealed up, and Kate closed her eyes. Focusing on the lower edge of the shadow, she stretched it downward into a column. It passed through the window without effort.

A puff of cold, dry air blew up the path and into Kate's face, the exact scent from Venn's vision. Aislin held a lantern up, and through the inky black tunnel, the heart of the carriage was visible. A tumult of papers lay everywhere, sprinkled with glints of gold coins.

"Venn!" Kate called.

Nothing but silence came back.

She tried to cast out, but too much of her concentration was taken up with the tunnel.

Quickly! Crofftus said, and Fix scampered up the crane and climbed into the sling. Aislin handed him a lantern, and Tribal began to lower him down.

Kate's palms tingled from the *vitalle* coursing through them, but Faron showed no sign of effort. He stared down into the tunnel, his expression near frantic with worry.

"How do you know she's here?" he asked in a whisper.

Fix kept his arms wrapped tight around himself, watching the wall of shadows warily.

"Naevys somehow linked us together when she restored Venn's connection to the woods. When she was taken—for just a few moments—I could sense everything she could. She's in a crate, lying on top of a lot of Kalesh coins, and it all smelled like this carriage. Beyond her, I could feel the elven curse."

Faron met Kate's gaze skeptically. "You're linked to her? What is she feeling now? Can she hear us?"

"I think she passed out a few hours ago, and I haven't sensed anything from her since." The anxiety she'd been pushing down rose at the words, and she refocused on the shadow.

In the carriage, Fix climbed off the sling and crouched, holding out the lantern.

It's very stale down here, Crofftus said, his voice tight. *I don't think the curse lets air through. Please don't shut us in here.*

Kate tightened her grip on Faron's hands. "We won't. What do you see?"

There's... Crofftus's voice was low. *It's a mess. There are papers everywhere, Emperor Sorrn is here.* He made a noise that sounded like a cough of distaste. *He died from a blow that crushed his head, if you were curious. There are books, Katria, and fabric. And shoes. Why does the man have so many shoes?*

"What about a crate?" Kate called down.

Fix held the lantern up and squinted toward the back of the carriage.

Yes, but... If she's in that, Katria, it will be a very tight fit.

"Can you get it opened?"

Fix crept forward, stepping over papers and coins and what might have been Emperor Sorrn's arm, before he moved out of sight. The motion of his lantern sent his shadow darting across the mess.

Can you get that open, Fix? There was a moment's silence.

Can open. Fix's voice floated through Kate's head confidently.

"I don't like this," Silas said quietly from where he stood with his back to Faron, facing out toward the nearest trees. "Gettin' harder to see out here. These lanterns are about to be a beacon declaring exactly where we are."

"Naevys already knows," Kate said. "And so does Thallion."

He let out a displeased hum. "I still don't like it."

Aislin held a lantern up, and the light caught on the elven runes carved on the surface of the carriage beneath Kate's knees. "Faron, what does the curse say again? It starts with 'You are cast out.'"

He nodded. "The full curse is:
You are cast out, isolated, left in outer darkness.
You shall remain as you are, forever.
Locked away, unseen, unfound.
Those who seek you shall never find you.
If they persist, the shadow of death shall come for them."

Kate paused. If the elven curse kept everything inside it from changing at all, maybe she hadn't heard from Venn in hours because Naevys had resealed the curse after getting Venn into the carriage.

The uneasiness she'd felt when Thallion had been here tickled at her mind again. Something was off. The curse…

"Faron," she said slowly, "is your father right? Could no elf get past this curse?"

He nodded. "The 'those' in 'Those who seek you' means elves."

"Could you? Using your authority?"

He considered the question. "I don't have the authority to stop myself from being an elf. I suppose I could wrap myself in a shadow and go in the way Fix has, but I don't know of any other runelight that blocks *ael'iza* like this. I don't think anyone but you or me could get through."

Kate's stomach began to sink. "Even Naevys?"

"I don't know of any power she has that could allow her through."

Katria! Crofftus called. *Fix unlocked the chest!*

Kate peered down into the carriage, her uneasiness turning to dread. "Could she have stepped past it?"

Faron's hands tightened on hers. "No. Stepping uses a path of *ael'iza*."

The truth landed heavily on Kate. "Then she couldn't have—"

Katria. Crofftus's voice was full of disappointment. Kate winced even before he continued. *She's not here.*

Kate tried to fit the facts together. "But..." She'd seen Venn here, felt the box and the curse. How could she have sensed all that? Unless... What had Crofftus said about Naevys? *She just waded into my mind and learned everything I knew of you both.*

If Naevys had done the same to Venn, she'd know about the bond. Could she have made Venn think she was in the carriage? How would she—

The answer was obvious. Venn had memories of the smell of the carriage and the feel of the curse. Could Naevys have trapped Venn in some crate, then dredged up her memories of the carriage? From Crofftus's experience, there was no doubt she could have, but why would she?

Katria... Crofftus breathed.

Kate's mind spun at the questions. Why would Naevys feed her a fake message that would—

Fix! Crofftus said cautiously. *Pick it up carefully!*

"Wait!" Kate shouted. "Don't touch anything!"

Katria! Crofftus called. *It's here!*

Kate leaned forward, warping the side of the shadow. "Don't touch anything! I think it's a trap!"

The lantern light inside the carriage wavered erratically, then grew brighter until Fix came into view, his huge eyes glinting brightly in the dim carriage.

On his hand, on a piece of embroidered blue fabric, lay Renault's amulet.

CHAPTER FIFTY-FOUR

The stonesteel disk glinted around the glass vial of blood-red lienick potion. Exactly how it had looked when it hung around Renault's neck.

"That's..." Kate's hold loosened on Faron's hands.

"Not yet!" He tightened his grip. "Get Fix up!"

Silas leaned over the edge of the shadow as Fix climbed into the sling. "Is that the amulet?"

Tribal began to haul Fix up. "*The* amulet?"

Kate couldn't bring herself to answer. A rabid, feral hope rose in her as Fix creaked his way higher.

As soon as the gnoblin was above the level of the window, Kate dropped the shadow. The cool night air rushed around her hands and arms. She took the fabric cushioning the amulet from Fix's hands before the dwarves even swung him away from the window.

Could it really be the amulet? It was heavier than she'd expected. The stonesteel disk was as wide as her palm, catching the lantern light along its smooth edges and the thin band of runes carved into it. In the center, the delicate glass holding the lienick potion was teardrop-shaped.

She cast out toward it. The amulet flared into light. The potion glimmered brightly, and the runes on the stonesteel glowed like they were filled with molten metal, but beneath it, a blazing light shone out. Kate reached out gingerly and touched the edge, turning it over slowly and laying it back down on the cloth.

A lip of stonesteel along the outer edge held an elaborate cage of golden wire in place. Thin strands of gold wrapped in from the side, twisted together and curled into sweeping designs that brought to mind flames or the curls of a fresh green shoot in the spring. Nestled in the middle of it was an amber topaz, glowing as if it held a sliver of the sun.

Kate's wave faded, and the amulet dimmed to mundane silvers and golds, but the topaz continued to swirl with a luminescence like it held motes of burning gold. In front of the topaz, the metal cage spun into a spiral that Kate touched gently. It gave way but pushed her finger back out quickly. Renault's spring. The device he'd created to ensure no one touched the topaz for too long.

Silas knelt down and peered into the carriage. "Tribal..." He held his hand out for a light, and Aislin handed him a lantern.

A rumble rolled through the ground. Kate's gaze snapped up, and she set her hand protectively over the amulet

"Are these rocks about to move?" Matlen asked nervously, moving toward the edge of the rocks with his sister.

Tribal set his hand on the nearest stone, frowning.

"That didn't feel like a rockslide," Silas said.

"Then what was it?" Kate asked. Everything remained still, but she started after the elves.

"Tribal!" Silas dropped to his knee. "You're not going to believe this! I think I see Dirthor's crown!"

"What?" Tribal rushed over to the window.

"That is definitely stonesteel, and look at that ruby!"

"Fix!" Tribal called. "You need to go back in there!"

"What's Dirthor's crown?" Matlen asked.

"The crown of the last High Dwarf to live in Rullduin!" Tribal said, his voice excited. "It was lost in a collapse that drove the dwarves out of the caves. No one knew what happened to it, although there have been theories that it was washed down the river to this side of the mountains."

The elves and dwarves chattered on, but the amulet glinted in the lantern light, and Kate focused on it. It couldn't *really* be Renault's amulet, could it? She studied the topaz, watching the glowing honey-colored lights swirl inside it. There was one way to check...

She set her finger on the spiral of wire and pressed in.

The ground beneath her feet trembled again, but her fingertip touched the topaz, and—everything disappeared

She floated in a velvety blackness. The ravine was gone, along with her companions. There was nothing but an endless expanse of darkness. The worry for Venn and the thrill of finding the amulet faded away like smoke on a breeze.

Glimmers of light burst into existence. An entire night sky, not untouchably distant, but surrounding her, swirling past with endless glitters of blues and greens and vibrant white. One star near her grew brighter, expanding and turning golden red before shrinking again to a small, tight blue. Another off to her right grew suddenly and exploded in a burst of light shooting out into the endless sky. It rang with the endless hum of eternity.

She was a tiny speck of dust in the vast universe. Thin strands of every color shot past her, moving both forward and backward at the same time, and each glimmer of light held a tone, a hum. The different pitches flowed over each other, joining and growing or intertwining before pulling away. Somehow, she could see the distant past and the unimaginable future, all in a single moment.

It was like the pull of the White Wood. An embrace of something so vast and eternal that any question of belonging or purpose faded away. She was part of this. Not just now. She always had been. And like the White Wood, it began to tug at the edges of her, pulling grains of herself away, drawing them into the beauty of the stars.

She fought against the idea, pushing the stars away, and the ravine suddenly came back into focus.

Everything was perfectly still. Tribal still held his hand on the stone, his brow creased. Silas was kneeling. Matlen stood off the rockslide looking worriedly uphill, while Aislin was frozen mid-step moving toward him. The flame in her lantern was unmoving. The only thing that still moved was the swirl of golden light inside the topaz.

Kate tried to pull her hand off the amulet, but a pale, ghostly image of her fingers separated from her actual hand before snapping back into it. Panic rose in her at the idea of being trapped here—until she saw a shift in her finger as it sat against the gem. Her hand was moving, just incredibly slowly.

Kate stared around the frozen ravine, her panic turning to wonder. The amulet worked! It slowed time for whoever touched the topaz. She forced her thoughts into order. Naevys had brought Kate here, to this carriage. Where the amulet was hidden.

She tried to spin and pull the aenigma box out of her pack, but her physical body didn't move. *Time to think.* That was what Renault had created it for. Time to stop everything else and think.

All right. Think.

Why would Naevys go through all this trouble to get Kate here? She must have known the amulet was buried here. Her notes had said she knew the emperor had it, though she'd thought he'd sent it south to be protected. She'd searched for ages. When had she realized that she'd buried it with Sorrn when she'd killed him? Buried it in a carriage she'd cursed so even she couldn't get into it?

A strand of light stretched away from the topaz with something that looked like shapes in it. She focused on it, and the thread came closer to her. In it was an image of her own face. Farther away from the amulet, she caught a glimpse of Fix's face, his wide eyes glinting like pearls, surrounded by the dark walls of the carriage as he picked the amulet up. She moved forward and saw, from the amulet's point of view, Fix holding it out and moving under the shadowy tunnel. Kate's and Faron's faces looked down on it in shock.

This was the past! Kate slid the string of images closer, moving forward and backward along it, watching Fix discover the amulet and bring it all the way to her.

She pulled more of the fiber closer, past the image of Fix opening the box, but there was only darkness. She pulled faster, and the darkness remained. The more she concentrated on the strand, the clearer it became until she could see it extending infinitely far into the past, encased in the lightless box.

On the other side of the topaz, more subtle than the thread leading to the past, a handful of threads stretched away. These held images as well, each beginning with Kate's face. She concentrated, and they grew more visible.

In the brightest of the threads, the entire world seemed to shake, and she saw the ravine from the vantage point of the amulet itself.

> "Definitely not a rockslide." Tribal stood and pulled his axe out.
> In the flickering light of Aislin's lantern, a massive form burst out of the ground.
> It was like a worm, except a thousand times too large. The front of it burrowed out of the ground with an explosion of dirt, and its front dropped down onto the ground. The rest—consisting of

pinkish ridges of flesh, glistening in the firelight—wriggled out of the hole. The top of its head was as high as Kate's waist, and it opened a round, gaping maw at Tribal. Three circular rows of teeth lined the opening, each razor sharp and dripping with some liquid that looked green in the lantern light.

Fix cowered down in front of it.

Tribal swung his axe into the side of the worm's head. It sank in with a squelching noise, but the creature twisted, its dripping teeth still lunging for Tribal. Kate's fingers gripped the sides of the amulet, but she slapped her other hand into the worm's side, shoving vitale into it. Faron appeared beside her, pressing his hands onto the pink flesh and shouting commands in Elvish. The creature slowed slightly but closed its jaw around Tribal's shoulder.

Silas charged at it from the far side, sinking his own axe deep into its side. The worm tore away from Tribal, leaving bloody streaks through the dwarf's ripped coat. It slammed its head into Silas, hurling him backward.

"It's not listening to us!" Faron shouted.

Kate nodded. "Naevys is controlling it!"

Aislin screamed, and Kate spun to find a second worm launching out of the ground at the elf twins. Aislin disappeared, reappearing on the back of the creature, but the rows of teeth bit into Matlen's leg, and he let out a scream. Aislin stabbed a small knife into it, shouting for her brother. The worm flung Matlen away and shifted to charge at Silas.

The first worm crawled toward Faron, and he went down. The massive pink body rolled over his foot, crushing it.

Faron blinked out of sight and reappeared next to Aislin, favoring one leg and driving a long knife deep just behind the gaping mouth.

The worm twitched, throwing Aislin off. Faron held on, jamming his other hand onto its head and continuing to command it in Elvish.

> *Kate, still holding the amulet, came closer to the first worm, which was thrashing on the ground. Kate swung her other hand back into it, and it slowed.*
>
> *A dozen vines shot out of the ground around Kate's feet, winding up, wrapping around her legs and her body, lashing her arms—and the amulet—to her sides.*
>
> *Her body was jostled from the back.*
>
> *Naevys stepped in front of her, eyes glittering, her hand closed around the aenigma box. "Thank you." She reached out a shimmering copper hand and hung the amulet around her neck. It sank into the silvery fur of her cloak.*

Kate stared at the strand, terror gripping her. There was nothing but the silver fur stretching ahead until the thread became too faded to make out.

Next to it was a second thread, almost as bright. It began with the rumble and the worm bursting from the ground. This time, Tribal dropped his axe to grab Fix and toss him out of the way, and the worm's massive jaw engulfed his entire head. Kate slammed her hand onto it alongside Faron, and Silas buried his axe into the creature's side. But this time, when the worm beneath Kate's hand stilled, so did Tribal. Aislin and Matlin battled the other, and Faron moved to help them.

In the shock of the moment, the vines appeared, followed by Naevys. The elf queen dug the aenigma box out of Kate's pack and plucked the amulet from her hand. With a "Thank you," she slid it over her neck and disappeared.

Kate grabbed for the next strand, and the next. Each possible future played out in variations of the same events. Some horrifically tragic, some leaving only wounds and terror.

But every one of them ended with Naevys taking both the amulet and the box.

Kate's heart beat faster, and a long, impossibly slow rumble started beneath her feet. The spring on the amulet had already started pushing her fingertip away from the gem.

"No!" Kate searched for another possible future, but while there were many other threads, they were too dim to see. "Wait!"

Her finger pulled away from the topaz, and the rumble in the ground thundered beneath her.

"Watch out!" She flung a hand toward where the ground shifted at the edge of the rocks just as the massive worm breached the surface and shot toward Tribal and Fix.

The dwarf glanced at the gnoblin.

"Fix!" Kate shouted. "Run!"

As the little creature dove out of the way, Tribal hefted his axe. The maw opened and Tribal drove his blade into the side of it.

Instead of slamming her hand onto the worm's side, Kate lunged for Tribal, yanking him out of the reach of the dripping teeth.

"Faron!" Kate scrambled back to put her free hand on the creature's pale, oily skin. "Put it to sleep! There's another one coming! Aislin! Matlen! Move back!"

The elf twins disappeared and reappeared a half-dozen paces away, but when they did, they staggered and grabbed each other for balance.

Silas plunged his axe into the side of the worm, as he had in every future, and the creature shuddered. *Vitalle* raced out of Kate's hand, and she funneled it into the beast, searching for anything that was like a mind. There was something not far behind its mouth, and she shoved her energy toward it, feeling Faron's coming alongside. It rolled toward them, pinning and crushing Faron's foot before he stepped and appeared a few paces away, his face creased in pain.

The second worm shot out of the ground, a little uphill, chasing Aislin and Matlen.

It must feel our footsteps! Crofftus called from where Fix scrambled up a huge rock.

The elf twins disappeared and reappeared a dozen paces away. But this time, Aislin fell to her knees. The second worm didn't chase them but spun and wriggled closer to the first.

The worm next to Kate thrashed its head to the side and caught Tribal's leg in its teeth, dragging him through the air. The dwarf's body hit Fix, who tumbled off the rock toward the carriage. Silas slammed his axe in again, closer to the worm's head. It dropped Tribal and turned. Its motions were slow, though, labored, and another axe stroke from Silas stilled it completely.

The second worm snapped its jaws just as he lunged out of the way. Its teeth caught on his back, leaving a bloody tear in his cloak. Faron stepped again, appearing at the creature's side, pressing his hands to its flesh as Aislin and Matlen leapt onto its back, digging small knives into its head.

Kate spun around, searching for—

Naevys appeared inches from her, eyes glittering darkly. Kate tried to dive to the side, but vines shot out of the ground, wrapping around her and spinning her until her back was to the queen. Her pack jostled as Naevys sliced the top open.

"Stop!" Kate shouted, trying to turn away. "Naevys! Stop!"

The queen appeared in front of her, her copper fingers clenched around the aenigma box. The sight of it in Naevys's hand felt like the thrust of a knife. Like the tearing open of a wound. Kate tried to twist the amulet away, but the vines were too tight.

Faron materialized next to Kate with a burst of *vitalle*, not putting any weight on his right leg. "Mother! Stop!" He grabbed Kate's arm and wove a wall of shadow around it. The blackness grew, blocking out Naevys's face.

A thin whip of vine sliced through the darkness and slashed

down across Faron's forearm. It tore through his cloak and sleeve and into his flesh—right where his runes were tattooed.

His shadow dissolved almost instantly.

He let out a cry and dropped to his knees, gripping his arm as blood welled up between his fingers.

Naevys barely spared him a look before touching Kate's hand. A warmth rolled out at her touch. The queen's presence washed over Kate's mind, rummaging almost carelessly through her thoughts. Involuntarily, each finger relaxed. Kate tried to shove a shield out, but Naevys's magic worked too fast. Kate's fingers went numb, and the amulet tumbled out of them.

With a complacent smile, the queen plucked the amulet out of the air before it fell and hung it around her own neck.

She pulled out a silver disk from a pocket, and Kate felt the same fluid sense of connection she'd found in the empty box in Renault's workshop.

The Bridge.

It snapped onto the amulet with a click, completely covering the side with the lienick potion.

Naevys drew in a long breath, closing her eyes and gripping the amulet and the attached Bridge. When she opened them, she stared into Kate's face with an unreadable expression. "Thank you."

Without another word, she disappeared.

PART V

THE TRAGEDY

The farther I get from these events, the more tragic they feel. They felt tragic then too, of course. How could they not? But the older I've grown, the more I've seen this pain echoed in other places. The sort of pain that breaks the soul and warps the mind.

We don't speak about this sort of loss. We shy away from it at every turn.

A book I brought back from Home has a discussion about loss by Driscall the Crooked. He says:

> *The moment we begin to love, our loss begins. We may not feel it at first as loss. Possessiveness, I think, is the first sign. Then an uneasiness that the loss might happen. Then abject fear. Because how can one survive the loss of something we truly love?*
>
> *We were not built for loss.*
>
> *Everything inside us rebels against the very idea of it.*

That is the lesson the White Wood taught me. We were not built for loss.

CHAPTER FIFTY-FIVE

The vines went limp, and Kate staggered forward, casting out as though the queen's trail would somehow be visible.

A flicker of brightness appeared higher up the rockslide before winking out.

The pack on her back felt too light. The lumps against her back were wrong. The absence of the box like an open wound.

Her hand felt too empty. The haunting grandeur of the endless sky in the topaz pulled at her. The longing to hold it again was like a physical pain.

Gone. Naevys was gone with Bo and Evan. And the amulet that could actually save them.

Everything is gone. The empty place on the fabric where the amulet had been lying was like a physical thing. A tangible *lack*. A hole that gaped wide open inside her.

Underneath it, cold dread hardened at the fact that Kate had no idea where Naevys had taken the box or the amulet. Or Venn.

She took a step uphill. "Where did she go, Faron?"

He still knelt, gripping his arm. Blood soaked through his sleeve, but no longer dripped onto the red-stained snow.

"We have to find her!" Kate's fist closed around the fabric. Naevys had played her perfectly. Drawn her to the carriage the queen couldn't open herself, tricked her into figuring out a way into it. Kate's mind reeled at the sheer number of questions the thought raised. How had Naevys known she could get into it? It wasn't even Kate's magic alone that had provided access—it was Faron's too. Granted, Faron's elven magic wouldn't have been able to cross the barrier. No elf could have broken through the curse alone. It had needed her human magic too.

And...why not just ask? Naevys could have told Kate the amulet was in the carriage, and Kate would have tried just as hard to get it as she'd tried to save Venn. "Why all the secrecy?" she whispered. "Why all the games?"

She cast out again, feeding her remnant into it so it would linger. But no luminous elf queen lit up.

Next to her, though, Tribal groaned. Clusters of *vitalle* crowded around the long gashes that bled from his neck to his elbow. At each wound, some corrosive power ate into his flesh, driving back the healing.

Silas lay on his side, the exhausted elf twins hovering over him, feeding *ael'iza* into him in an attempt to stop the blackness climbing up his leg from the jagged bite marks.

And Fix was...

Kate spun, looking for the little creature. He'd been pushed by the worm toward—

She scrambled to the carriage. Through the window, Fix's pained, frightened face peered up at her. She could hear no sound of his remnant or Crofftus's.

She shot one last look after Naevys and shoved down her fury. Turning, she grabbed Faron's shoulder. "Both dwarves are wounded, and Fix and Crofftus are trapped in the carriage. They'll run out of air if we don't get them out."

"She cut my runes." Faron's voice was tight with shock, and he was still gripping his forearm.

Between her anger at Naevys and the memory of Venn gripping her own tattoos just the same way after he'd cut them, any sympathy Kate had felt dissolved. "Well, it's not going to kill you." Faron closed his eyes, his face stricken, and Kate rubbed her face, trying to banish her panic. "Can you heal it?"

He gave a nod.

"Good. I need your help getting Fix out." She cast out at the two dwarves again. Tribal's wounds were more severe, and she knelt next to him. "Aislin! Come lend me some of your *ael'iza*!"

The young elf hurried over, and with her help, Kate funneled *vitalle* into Tribal's body, shoving back the poison, pushing it out to the surface where it dripped out of his wounds in a yellowish pus. The healing moved painfully slow, and blazing heat grew on her palms. Kate cast glances up the rockslide and to every bit of trees visible in the meager moonlight. Naevys was getting farther away by the moment.

The lantern light flickered over Tribal's face, though, and the alarming paleness of it dragged Kate's attention back to her work. She continued until the poison was out and the gashes weren't terribly deep.

The bite on Silas's leg was at least clean. The worm had punctured him, but not torn great gashes out of his flesh. Faron had begun the healing already, with Matlen's help. Kate funneled her own *vitalle* and Aislin's toward the wound as well, ignoring the pain in her hands. Though every minute took an age, the poison finally finished oozing out of him, and the wounds shrank.

Kate sat back, shaking out her hands. "That's all I can do for now, or I won't have the strength to get Fix out. Faron, how's your tattoo?"

He held out his hand, showing the runes completely healed, and shadows emanated from his skin.

"Excellent." Kate pushed herself up and moved over to the carriage. Fix's round eyes caught a little light from where he huddled on the floor. His face was pale, and from the shimmer of the curse that blocked the open window, she caught a glimpse of Fix's yellow remnant and a glitter of Crofftus's copper.

Faron grimaced and pushed himself to his knees, crawling toward the carriage, his right foot twisted at an unnatural angle.

"Faron?" Kate took a step toward him.

He waved her away. "The gnoblin first."

She held her aching hands out to him and winced when he took them. Before she could think too much, she fed *vitalle* out again. Searing pain shot across her palms, but she constructed the shadow tunnel, combining it with Faron's remnant until it passed through the window space.

Thank you! Crofftus's voice was sapped but relieved. *The curse weakened Fix a lot.*

Aislin and Matlen dropped the sling down.

"Just climb into it," Kate said, trying to ignore the pain in her hands.

"Bring the crown out with you," Tribal called from where he still lay.

"No," Kate said as the edges of the shadow began to tatter. "Just hurry and get out!"

The elf twins hoisted the gnoblin out, and Fix collapsed next to the wagon. Kate sank to the ground, taking in her exhausted and wounded companions gathered among the lumps of dead worms.

"Aislin and Matlen," she said, "are you two all right? When you stepped, you seemed injured."

The twins exchanged troubled looks.

"It was...hard," Matlen said. "Stepping even that small distance was exhausting."

Silas frowned at them. "Because your bond to the elves was broken?"

"Venn thought you might suffer in other ways for a little while," Kate said. "But she thought things like that would come back in time."

Aislin shrank a little lower, and Matlen took her hand and squeezed it. Silence reigned for a minute.

"Did I see Naevys in the midst of all that chaos?" Silas asked finally.

"She took the box," Kate said, her fury returning. "And she took the amulet. I watched her attach the Bridge to it."

Tribal stared at her. "That's...not ideal."

She now has the body she needs in Venn, Crofftus said in a defeated tone, *the box for power, and the amulet and Bridge to control it.*

The breath that hissed out of Kate's lungs was soaked in frustration and self-reproach. "I gave her everything..." She sat up. "No, she doesn't have everything. She needs the seed!"

Tribal lifted his head. "The one that's buried under all this rock? The one she could probably step to and reach at any moment?"

Matlen shook his head. "Not unless she's very familiar with the caves."

"We found her lying in them when she was still half-tree," Kate said. "I think it's safe to say she's familiar with them." She cast out into the hillside. The dim bit of warmth she'd sensed before lit up in the cave above them, but without any sign of Naevys. "But she hasn't gotten it yet." She turned her weary head toward Fix. "Is there any way you could tunnel into those caves?"

Fix stayed on the ground but made a hand signal.

Falling through the window took a lot out of him, Crofftus said. *It took a lot out of both of us, but he'll look for a path of earth that leads inside. He knows they are threaded through the rocky ground.* Slowly, Fix pushed himself up and shuffled off a little way away from the rockslide, looking intently at the ground.

"Do you think Auntie Venn is in there too?" Aislin asked.

"There's no one that alive in there. Just the seed, which is very, very weak." Kate started to stand, but a thought struck her, and she paused. "Venn was able to get a message to me—even if it was just the message Naevys wanted her to send. I've been waiting for another, but maybe *I* can talk to *her*."

Kate closed her eyes, thinking about the ways she'd contacted Venn in the past. Anger at Naevys boiled around her, pulling her focus off time and again. She clenched her hands, trying to ignore it, and focused on opening herself up to Venn's thoughts.

A different surge of anger swirled in from outside of Kate, followed by a jab of shock.

Images of Renault's pocket world workshop flashed across Kate's vision. The door, the tables, a large cupboard in the corner.

"Venn?" The anger around Kate receded slightly, pushed back by a wave of hope. She let out a breath that was too exhausted and bitter to be a laugh. "It's *your* anger I've been feeling." She filled her mind with the idea of herself and the others coming to the yellow door and felt Venn's surge of relief.

"Venn's in Renault's pocket world," Kate said.

Silas pushed himself up with a grimace. "At least we know where that is. Let's go save the elf. Again."

"I'm coming." Faron rose, but when he tried to stand, his right ankle crumpled, and his face drained of color.

"That's broken," Kate said. "It's too big of an injury for me to heal."

Faron's mouth pressed into a thin line. "It's too big for anyone to heal. I need the White Wood." He glanced at Kate. "I'll meet you at the pocket world."

Silas raised an eyebrow. "Surprisingly, your help would be useful, but how are you going to find it?"

"I'll follow your trail. It's easy to find dwarves in the woods."

Kate rubbed her face. "We have another problem, though. Renault's workshop is probably where Naevys has gone, and we've proven several times that we can't fight her."

Silas squinted across the ravine in the general direction of Renault's workshop. "Can you tell for sure?"

"No." Kate thought for a moment, an idea taking shape in her mind. "But if she is, I know a sure way to get her out of there." Fix had disappeared into a hole in the snow, and Kate bit back a grimace at how small it was. "I'm going to try to extricate the seed from the cave. That should bring her here, and you'll have time to get into the pocket world and rescue Venn. Aislin and Matlen, did you see how I opened the yellow door?"

The elf twins nodded.

"Hang on." Silas limped past her to pick up his knife. "You're the one Naevys needs. Bringing her right to where you are seems like a bad idea."

"Except the mad queen didn't take Twig," Tribal pointed out. "So maybe Thallion, the lying, conniving, dethroned king, is just lying or conniving again."

"Regardless," Kate said, "without Venn, she'll still not be able to do the transfer. Get Venn out, then Aislin and Matlen can hide all of you in the woods so Naevys can't find you again."

"Hide us from the elven Warden with the crazy forest magic?" Tribal asked. "In the forest?"

Kate turned to the elf twins. "Can you two still convince the trees of things?"

The two young elves exchanged looks.

"I *think* so," Matlen said.

"Then convince them you're not there. Naevys only knows what the trees know."

"What about you?" Aislin asked.

Kate paused. "I don't know. Once I see what condition the seed is in, I'll figure out something. Just get Venn somewhere safe."

"That is not much of a plan." Tribal rolled onto his uninjured side and leveraged himself up. He looked Kate over, his expression worried, but all he said was, "Dirthor's crown is in that carriage, and you still owe us treasure." He pointed a finger at Kate. "Don't die."

"I don't plan to," Kate said. "When all this is over, assuming Faron agrees to help, we'll get every single thing out of this carriage. You can have the crown and all the gold."

Faron pushed himself up. "Help me get Venn safe, and I'll do anything you want."

Silas squinted at him. "Still not sure I trust you fully, but telling off your father was a good start."

Kate heaved herself to her feet, brushing off her hands. Her legs felt unsteady and her head heavy. She took in the massive worms. "What *are* these?"

Faron shook his head. "I have no idea."

"Tunnel serpents," Silas said. "They live deep underground. Haven't ever seen one in real life before."

Aislin peered at the worm in distaste. "What do they eat underground that makes them grow this big?"

"Other things you wouldn't like to run into," Tribal said. "And occasionally dwarves or gnomes or goblins."

"The Warden of the White Wood called up creatures from beneath a mountain?" Kate glanced at Faron. "Is that normal?"

His hand gripped his blood-soaked sleeve. "Nothing about my mother seems normal."

"You should get moving," Kate said.

Tribal gave one last look of longing at the carriage, then

started toward the river, gingerly holding his shoulder. "Let's go steal our elf back."

CHAPTER FIFTY-SIX

Kate watched them trudge downhill, a line of lantern lights bobbing into the night. Bringing the last with her, she followed the thin footprints Fix had left in the snow. A dark hole opened in the slope a dozen paces uphill from the worm carcasses and barely wider than her torso.

She squatted to look into it. "How does it look?"

There is a path, Crofftus said. *He's just widening the final part.*

Memories of the last time she'd crawled through a narrow hole out of these caves rushed back into Kate's mind. "When you say 'widening,' do you mean actually making it wide enough for me? Or just wide enough for Fix?"

There was a moment of silence. *He's insulted. It's actually ingenious, Katria. He digs and reinforces the hole at the same time. It's astonishing how skilled he is at it.* Crofftus's voice sounded more impressed than Kate had ever heard. *He's finished. You can come now.*

Kate peered into the narrow black hole and shook out her hands. It was wide enough for her, but she shrugged off her pack. After a moment's thought about what she might encounter dislodging the seed from the cave wall, she dug out the solos potion and tucked it into the pocket of her pants. Deciding her cloak would make it even more awkward, she pulled that off, too. The cold night air running over her neck and bleeding through her clothes helped her overcome the last of her reluctance, and she shimmied into the tunnel on her elbows. The burrow was taller than she'd expected, and while she had to duck her head, she only brushed against the top of it once, sending a spattering of cold earth down on the back of her neck. She tried to shake it off, but the chilly dirt just shifted lower on her back. Gritting her teeth, she wormed her way forward.

"Fix?" Her voice came out higher than she'd intended. A sprinkle of dirt ran down her face, some of the grit landing in her mouth, and she tried to spit it out. "A little light wouldn't go amiss…"

A scurrying noise scraped through the smothering darkness ahead, and Fix's yellow remnant appeared from around a turn. He held a bit of mosslight in his hand, and the dim glow showed his weary but encouraging smile.

It seems to be difficult for him to put words together, Crofttus said, *but you're a third of the way through. It's surprising how cozy this feels. Fix is perfectly at home here. He can almost taste the differences in the soil, and he seems to be able to sense when he's nearing a rock. It's fascinating.*

Kate's hand crushed something that had too many legs and gave a wet crunch. She yanked her hand back and wiped it on the earthen wall. "Cozy is not the word I would use."

The weak light from the gnoblin crouched ahead of her in the tunnel was both reassuring and terrifying. The outlet felt infinitely far behind her, and the mosslight showed nothing but earthen walls. She moved forward, her fingers caked with the damp, cold earth. Something sinuous and as long as her finger curled out of the wall next to her before disappearing into a shadow. She drew her elbows in closer and moved faster.

There were two turns and one tighter spot where the walls shrank in to graze her shoulders.

There are rocks there, Crofftus explained. *He couldn't widen them more, but you're almost out.*

After a hundred more terrifyingly rapid heartbeats where she crawled downhill—a decidedly unpleasant sensation—Fix's yellow glow moved out of the burrow into a wider space. Kate spilled into a thin tunnel and scrambled to her feet, brushing the dirt off her hands and out of her hair. A clump of earth fell out of the bottom of her shirt, and she stepped away from it as though it were going to try to climb back in.

Fix's eyes glowed with curiosity and something very close to amusement.

Kate wiped more dirt off her face. "Fix, I'm terribly grateful for your skills. I admire them greatly, but can we *please* widen that before we need to get out?" He gave her a bright smile, and she cast out. The feeble light of the seed lit up through the wall to her left. "It's that way about a dozen paces. Can you get us to the cave that's there, Fix?"

He nodded and motioned her to follow him. His remnant left a faint yellow trail as he moved slowly and tiredly down the tunnel, which ran, as far as Kate could tell, parallel to the surface of the ravine.

A cave soon opened to their left, the floor cluttered with fallen rocks. Deep gouges in the walls and floor showed where Naevys's branches and roots had once been anchored.

Kate cast out.

Low along the wall where Naevys had lain wounded and still half-tree, a faint knot lit up—melon-sized and buried behind a thin, rough layer of stone. The barest hint of a pale blue remnant glittered on the surface. A familiar frosted winter blue that held impressions of vast sweeps of ice and the jaggedness of frost amidst a bleak, gnawing cold.

"The dragon stone egg." Kate probed at the edges of it, finding a solid barrier of rock infused with Yilfrist's remnant. Inside it lay something smaller.

"Seed" was an appropriate name for it. It glittered with gold over the rather flat, oblong shell, sharp at one end. Whatever life there was—which wasn't even as bright as the glowing mosslight—was contained inside.

Kate picked her way through the fallen rocks and knelt, pushing her remnant into it. Her glowing flecks of light slid so brightly among the dragon's blue that they looked like flaming embers spreading across an empty winter sky.

From the seed, long, hair-thin paths of *vitalle* stretched out toward the surface of the ravine like threads of a spider's web. Power from the net over the rockslide trickled into it, but at least half the *vitalle* dribbled uselessly away over the surface of the seed and dissolved into the rock, the way healing energy slipped around a part of a body too damaged to heal.

The feel of the hard floor beneath Kate's knees faded as she closed her eyes and focused on the seed. She searched through the dimness for something to connect to. A slight brightening filled the center like a captured speck of moonlight. Around it, the remnant was as pearlescent and elusive as mist. There were no distinct smells or sounds. No sensations of anything but a vague warmth and waiting, so faint they were more like echoes or memories.

Kate searched for any sense of a consciousness. Any sense of a single individual.

She caught the idea of a young girl, but it felt invasive. Like a concept thrust onto it, rather than coming from the seed itself. She studied it again and realized the surface wasn't gold—it was covered in a shimmer of Naevys's light, protecting it. Along this thin skin from the queen, the idea of the daughter was firmest.

The *vitalle* from the hillside fed it slowly, dripping in life, fueling the survival of the frail mist inside—but there were pockets of darkness too. Patches where the remnant had cooled to darker flecks.

"It's barely alive," Kate said quietly. "If it's alive at all. If it's detached from the net, I think what's left will fade away in moments."

Then how will we move it? Crofftus asked.

The idea struck a discordant note inside her. Taking this seed from here felt like a violation. The way it had felt when Naevys had taken the aenigma box. The familiar longing to hold the box rose in her, the permanent ache at not being able to save her brothers.

Suddenly, the sense that the seed was a girl didn't feel invasive. It felt...hopeful. Painfully, desperately hopeful. The way Kate felt every time she imagined freeing Evan. The terrible longing to see his face, even knowing it would be too young and too much like it had been the last time she'd seen him.

"I can't move this." Kate sank back on her heels. "It's Naevys's child—or its very fragile remains. I can't take that away from her."

There was a moment of silence.

If she comes back and takes the seed—and you—Venn will die.

Kate rubbed her hands across her face. "I know. But she took my brothers from me, and it felt like she tore open a wound. I can't do the same to her." Kate looked back at the seed. "Maybe we shouldn't take it. Maybe we should strengthen it. The *vitalle* from the rockslide is unfocused. Maybe I can help, and Naevys won't need Venn's body."

She set her palms on the rock, closing her eyes.

Sending her own *vitalle* out to meet one of the trickles coming from the slope, Kate guided it more completely through the dragon stone egg and into the seed. She moved to another and another. In a handful of minutes, the life from the slope was pouring straight into the thin mist. It flowed in such minuscule amounts that it was impossible to tell if the seed was strengthening.

Kate opened a channel through her palm and pressed some of her *vitalle* in.

"The seed holds nothing but a white mist," Kate said. "Its surface is protected by Naevys's runelight, and there's another layer of stone around it with the dragon's remnant."

The dragon was here? Crofftus's voice was wary. Fix skittered back behind a pile of rocks.

A ripple rolled out of the egg and over Kate's fingers. It spread along the back of her hand and up her arm, followed by a strange, tingling warmth.

The red of her remnant brightened slightly, taking on a fiery aspect against the icy-blue specks along the stone. A shiver of uneasiness rolled up her spine at the strange new radiance.

Kate pulled away, but the skin of her palms and fingers was fused to the rough stone.

She tried to leverage one hand off, but it wouldn't budge. "I can't let go!"

Kate tried to cut off the flow of her *vitalle,* but it continued, as though the channel had been locked open. Only a dribble of warmth, but it was persistent.

"The dragon egg is an elegant solution, is it not?" a soft voice asked.

Kate twisted to see Naevys standing at the back of the cave. Her tall, thin form was wreathed in the glitters of her bright gold remnant. She moved forward, and the mosslight caught the warm copper tinge of her skin. Her eyes were clear, her cheeks no longer gaunt. Her silver robe flowed around her like water.

With a sinking feeling, Kate looked back at her own arms. Her remnant wasn't brightening after all. Naevys's gold was sprinkled through it, stretching over Kate's skin, creating a sleeve that bound her to the stone. "What are you doing?"

Naevys moved reverently closer until she sank down next to Kate. The vastness of the White Wood pulled Kate along endless hills. The breeze drawing though pine needles like it flowed through a comb. The web of roots and plants and tiny creatures burrowing into the ground. The barely audible thrum of the heartbeat of the entire forest.

Kate focused on the hard ground beneath her, trying to banish the boundless remnant.

The queen's eyes were locked on the seed, her expression lifted by hope and softened by adoration. "Without Yilfrist's egg, she never would have survived this long." She reached for the wall, hesitating just a moment before setting her fingers on the rough rock. "It took you a very long time to come."

The words were laced with accusation, and it took Kate a moment to realize they were directed at her. "Me?" She slid a shield out from her hands to cut off the *vitalle*.

"Why *did* you come?" Naevys flicked her fingers, and the shield shattered.

Kate flinched at the ease of it and started to create a blade that could cut through the sleeve holding her hands on the stone. "I was looking for my brother."

"No," Naevys said dismissively as she brushed away the blade as well. "It is more than that. Did you hear my call all the way from your home?"

Kate's mind scrambled for another way to unlock her hands from the seed, a wave of helplessness growing in her. "I heard nothing."

Naevys focused on Kate's hands, and a golden sleeve brightened around them and the seed. "I thought you were related to him," the queen mused, "but I don't think so any longer."

"My brother?"

A twitch of irritation marred the queen's brow. "Renault. But your blood is of the lake elves."

Kate shook her head. "Impossible. My family has lived in Queensland for—" She paused, understanding dawning. "We've always lived in the Wildwood. Which is where the lake elves came from."

Naevys gave a hum that could have signified agreement. "Your elven heritage is very diluted. It could have been centuries ago that it entered your family." Gold glitters slid out from the queen, covering the egg and trailing up the wall along the streams of *vitalle*. "Thallion is a fool for not noticing, but even a fool can occasionally do something right. When he so crudely bound you to the White Wood, he awoke your blood." She dropped her gaze to Kate's hand. "A true connection is an elegant thing. A melding, a gentle, intricate grafting that makes two creatures into one. His barbaric blood bond was merely an enslavement. As easily broken as a leash is cut."

The queen stroked her fingertips over the stone wall, and a fond smile lit her face.

"What do you want from me?" Kate asked.

A sharp crack rang out from down the tunnel, muffled and deep. A rumble followed, shaking the ground beneath Kate's knees. She ducked as dust and small rocks pelted down from the ceiling.

Naevys kept her eyes fixed on the stone. "Your blood."

CHAPTER FIFTY-SEVEN

"It is honorable of you to try to heal her." Naevys's fingers slid gently over the rough wall. "Misguided and useless, but honorable."

Kate tried to pull away again, her helplessness growing. "Then why not let me remove my hands?"

Naevys let out a breath that was almost a chuckle. Instead of answering, she leaned her ear closer to the stone. "I can still hear her heartbeat," she said quietly. "Although not as strong as it once was. There was a time when I heard nothing"—a smile grew across her face with the brightness of a sunrise—"but then it beat." Her smile faded. "And now it sighs, or..." Her brow furrowed. "Or I sigh." She pressed her palm against the egg. "What if it is my own heartbeat?" Her words were so quiet Kate could barely hear them, and Naevys's brow stayed creased with confusion. "Or before, perhaps mine was silent?" The queen's gaze grew unfocused. Her voice quieted until it was no louder than a breeze on a distant hill. "Was it I who woke?"

Another crash vibrated the floor of the cave, but the queen gave no indication that she heard it. Her eyes drifted to the wall.

Kate glanced toward where Fix and Crofftus had been, but wherever they were, they were well hidden. "It was here, after I drove the humans away and came close to her, that I *then* heard her heart."

Bo's journal entry came back to Kate's mind. The tree attacking his men, killing them with a wellstone that ripped out their minds. How the creature—Naevys—had stumbled into the cave where Bo hid—this cave—and collapsed against the wall, speaking in a language he couldn't understand.

"You think," Kate said warily, "that you ran them off? You killed all but one."

Naevys continued as though she hadn't spoken. "Her heart beat with mine, as it always should. I could almost feel her, like my branches could dig into the stone and hold her. My skin aches to hold her close, but I can't pick her up. Can't take her from this protection. What if my touch hurts her? What if she needs more than I can give? This gap between us might as well be a chasm. I can't *touch* her." She finally turned her eyes to Kate. They were hollow and broken. "A mother is made to touch her child. My arms are weighed down with their own emptiness. It is too painful to imagine her gone, and yet I can't bear to hope for her to come back to me. What if the pressure of that hope smothers her?"

Kate slowly pushed another shield out of her hand, slipping it between her smallest finger and the rock. Instead of cutting off the flow of *vitalle*, her shield slid through it as though it didn't exist. She spread it out, but until the shield stretched outside of the golden sleeve Naevys had wrapped around Kate's hand and the seed, it was like trying to cut with mist.

"And so I linger in this liminal space." Naevys laid her cheek against the rock and closed her eyes. "Not daring to hope, but unable to despair."

The pain and endless waiting dripped from her words, so familiar they caught at Kate's chest.

Naevys opened her eyes, their blackness deep and consuming. "I see your pain," she whispered. "The loss that you can't let go. I know it." Her expression turned hungry and desperate. "Is it too late to hope?"

The question Kate had asked herself for twenty years no longer felt old and stale. It ached like a muscle strained too far. A ligament stressed until the fibers inside it began to tear.

The queen settled against the stone, rubbing her thumb over a jagged edge. "Or is this the time to hope?" she asked quietly. "Is hope really *hope* if it's still reasonable to expect that it might come true?" The queen's gaze landed heavily on Kate. "Because we are long past that point, you and I."

Kate began to shake her head. Naevys fixed her with a piercing gaze, and Kate braced for the queen's intrusion into her mind. But the edge of Naevys's mouth merely twitched up in a hollow imitation of a smile. "I know your thoughts." The words slid through the cave like a knife. "I know what you've hoped for. I know how tenuous your plans are. I feel your loss and the madness nipping at the edge of your mind."

A shiver rolled across Kate's neck. She ignored it and searched for where the queen could be hiding the box.

Naevys's eyes closed again. "The entire world calls it madness," she whispered. "But it's not. It's what hope does to the soul when you push it far beyond its limit. It becomes something else. It is purified, refined until only its core remains. An eternal, expectant love."

She sat back, giving Kate a smile that was tinged with sadness, and a reckless, unhinged hunger.

Naevys wrapped her fingers around Kate's wrist, her skin hot. "But it matters not. This is not the time for hope. It is the time for resolve. You worry for your friend Andovenn, but that fear is new. So fresh. Such a pale shadow of what you know it could grow into—the real fear. The terrible, corrosive waiting."

Naevys straightened. "It is time to end the waiting. We've choked on hope until it's curdled within us. Unable to grow. Unable to die." She faced Kate. "Let us end it."

The floor of the cave shook again. The grinding of stone against stone assaulted Kate's ears as she ducked. A rock the size of her fist tumbled onto her shoulder, sending a shooting pain across her back.

The little of Fix she could see disappeared behind the rocks.

Naevys didn't flinch, even as dust and small pebbles bounced off her back. "Good," she cooed quietly, leaning closer to the egg. She set both hands on it, spreading her fingers wide. A knife of her remnant formed effortlessly out of her glitters and sliced through one of the strands of *vitalle* coming from the net out on the hillside.

The thread snapped and sprang back, leaving a strand of darkness like the afterimage of a light.

"Naevys!" Kate said. "Whatever is in the seed is very weak. I'm not sure it's even—"

"*She* is alive." Naevys's voice was as hard as steel. "And you will keep her so until we reach the workshop."

A long, low scraping echoed down the tunnel, which now was filled with a faint grey light. The impression of endless glaciers swept into the cave, massive slabs of ice carving their way through mountains. Biting, pelting sleet. Soul-deep cold, freezing the air and the earth.

The rimy blue of Yilfrist's snout came into view, and frost spread across the floor where his massive clawed foot scraped over it. The dragon's remnant blasted through the cave like a winter gale. It barreled into Kate as she fell against the wall, twisting her arm awkwardly.

He moved closer, sliding his belly along the floor, his wings pressed against his sides. The two rows of spikes along his back reached nearly to the ceiling. Dim mosslight sent ripples of white flitting across his scales. His slitted eyes were a dark, hungry, cavernous blue.

Crystalline patterns of frost spread across the floor from his touch. The frigid air chilled Kate's neck and turned her breath into white clouds.

Kate dragged her shoulder away from the wall. Every part of her ached with cold—except her palms, which were still warmed by the flow of *vitalle* leaving her and dribbling into the seed. A terrifying hopelessness crept over her as she tried again to pull away from the wall.

"Yilfrist." Naevys stayed against the wall, unmoved by his appearance. "It is time. Remove the dragon stone."

A flicker of resentment flashed in his eyes—but it was so quickly erased it might have been a trick of the light. The massive dragon shouldered his way forward. Naevys's fingers grazed the rough stone lovingly before she pulled away. Yilfrist moved his head between Kate and Naevys, his chin scraping over the rocks scattered around the floor, the top of his snout almost level with Kate's shoulder where she knelt.

Arctic cold poured off of him. Kate shivered as she tried to pull away again, but her hands stayed glued to the dragon stone.

Little mage. Yilfrist's voice licked over Kate's mind with a gnawing hunger, and he inhaled.

Air slid over Kate's hands toward his nostrils, and with it he syphoned *vitalle* out of her hand and forearm, leaving a slicing cold behind as though spikes of ice had been driven into her skin.

"No." Naevys's voice was quiet, but the command cut short the dragon's breath. "Just melt the stone."

The dragon stayed perfectly still, but he blew out a gust of air as hot as an oven.

His shadowed nostrils were only inches away, and Kate strained to see any sign of the coming fire. Trying not to imagine flames engulfing her hands along with the stone.

"Naevys!" she said, her voice anxious as she pulled her body as far from him as she could.

The dragon exhaled, but instead of fire, a rush of *vitalle* poured out of him. It washed across Kate's hands like hot water, leaving them unharmed—but the rock wall beneath her fingers dissolved into dust. The particles fell away, revealing the yellow egg.

The golden sleeve of light connecting her to the still-hidden seed pulled Kate's hands tight against the smooth surface.

Yilfrist blew out another hot breath, and the egg grew rough and gritty under her palm. A final breath disintegrated it into sand. Some skittered down the wall while the rest of it pooled into a pile of yellow dust cushioning the seed.

The sleeve drew Kate's hands firmly against the shell of the seed, which nestled down onto its little beach of yellow. It reminded her of a grape seed, although big enough to fill her palm. The surface was a warm brown, rounded on one end and tapered on the other.

Kate shifted her hands until they were cupped beneath it.

Naevys reached out but stopped before touching it. "What can you sense?" she whispered.

"A mist." Kate brushed her thumb over the seed. It was warmer than the cave, and now that there was no dragon egg between it and her hands, her *vitalle* flowed faster.

Naevys hunched over the seed, her hand still outstretched, a desperate hunger radiating from her. "What else?"

Kate focused on the wisps of white. "Nothing else. There are no sounds or smells. It is just…mist."

The queen dropped her hand. "Soon there will be more." She

wore several green rings, and she pulled one off. Vines stretched out of it. They wrapped around Kate's wrists and fingers, binding her cupped hands beneath the seed.

"What are you doing?" Kate started to step back, but Naevys reached inside her cloak and pulled the amulet over her head.

The amulet spun slowly, one side showing the topaz set beneath the spring, the other side covered in the disk of silver inset with intricate runes—the Bridge. The sight froze Kate to the spot. She reached out, as though her bound hands could snatch it from Naevys's grip. But the queen merely set the amulet gently atop the seed.

Kate extended her fingers to reach it, but they were bound tight. More vines grew, binding the amulet to the seed, almost obscuring the swirl of honey-gold light from the gem.

With a wave of her hand, Naevys tied the shoots around Kate's shoulders, bending her arms up until they were pressed against her chest.

"Naevys," Kate said, struggling against the bands. "I know what you want to do with Venn's body. But you can't! You can't sacrifice Venn for this!"

The queen flicked her finger, and a thick vine curled across Kate's mouth like a gag.

Kate tried to shout past it, but her words came out muffled, and Naevys turned away.

The green tendrils grew, Naevys's golden runelight animating each strand. Kate stabbed a blade of runelight into them, and Naevys's runelight snapped, but before it could disappear, Naevys healed it.

Kate sliced at another, and another, but as fast as she cut, the queen repaired, all the while adding more cords around her.

Another wave of helplessness rolled over Kate, but a blaze of anger flared up behind it, burning it away.

Instead of a knife, she shot out a dozen claws of runelight, slicing into every vine.

The plants loosened.

Naevys gave a little chuckle and set her finger under Kate's chin. "You fight well, little mage, but save your strength for battles you can win." The vines exploded around Kate, wrapping her in a cocoon of Naevys's runelight.

It lifted Kate off the floor, floating her and the seed up near the ceiling, over the sharp spines that rose in two long rows down Yilfrist's back. Between them, near his wings, was a narrow flat spot, barely wide enough for her. Naevys lowered her into it.

Kate shoved out more claws of runelight, but Naevys's just shifted or healed, keeping Kate bound tight.

She thrashed against the bands and bit into the gag. A dribble of bitter juice ran into her mouth, stinging her throat. Shouting into it, she strained against her bonds, but they felt like metal. Faster than she could follow, they stretched out and intertwined around the spikes like a net, pressing Kate down flat on her stomach and anchoring her to the dragon's back. The bands around her shoulders were pressed against the spines while frigid scales beneath her sucked away the little warmth she had left.

Another set of vines lifted Naevys off the floor, and Kate braced for her to try to fit into the crowded space. But the queen merely surveyed the bundle on Yilfrist's back. "Take them to the workshop and keep them safe until I arrive."

With a rumble deep in his chest that vibrated Kate's entire body, sounding somewhere between a growl and an acquiescence, he twisted his body. He folded back on himself like a snake, and his scales slid over the rock floor with a quiet hiss, crushing small rocks as he crawled into the tunnel along the back of the cave.

His motions were unnervingly smooth, and Kate twisted

against the constraints, but she could barely move. A faint light appeared, and the dragon turned into another cave, heading toward a gaping opening torn through the rockslide. She pulled back, as though she could stop him. Stones had tumbled into the cave, but he crawled over them, shoving effortlessly through until he broke out into the night.

CHAPTER FIFTY-EIGHT

Yilfrist's muscles rolled beneath Kate, and cold night poured around the vines binding her. The chill bit through her tunic, and she wished fervently for her cloak, which still lay outside of the tunnel Fix had dug.

Kate tried to look back over her shoulder into the cave to see if Naevys followed, but she couldn't turn far enough.

The dragon's wings unfurled, stretching to a half-dozen paces each, and with a single mighty beat, he shot into the air. The speed of his ascent shoved her down against his scales like a huge weight had crashed onto her. The unyielding vines dug into her hips and ribs and shoulders.

Any feelings of helplessness or anger fled in the face of the crushing weight and the need to draw in a breath. She twisted her head to the side and gasped in some freezing air before it was stolen again—this time by shock. The ground fell away at a dizzying rate. The black hole they'd climbed out of shrank along with the lumpy surface of the rockslide. In the time it took her to gasp again, the boulders looked like nothing more than pebbles.

Cold air howled past her ears, whistling through Yilfrist's

spines. Forested hills spread out from the ravine, their trees a mottled etching of silvery snow and black shadows. Moonlight glinted off a curve in the Surn, bright against the black water.

Yilfrist's massive wings beat downward with a roar of air that thrust them up toward the endless sky dusted with glittering stars.

She was anchored so tightly to his back that she couldn't move, and she let herself relax slightly, taking in the world below.

It was like the most precise, detailed map she'd ever seen. The flow of the hills was clearly visible in highlights and shadows from the moon. The smaller streams feeding into the Surn wound like black threads in their valleys. The long slope rising toward the White Wood rolled over ripples in the earth that would have taken her hours to traverse but that now looked like nothing more than waves on the sea.

She squinted into the wind, her eyes watering, scanning uphill until the forest gained a lighter aspect, the shadows giving way to the glittering white trunks of the frost pines.

The wind blew cold against her face, but a warmth grew in her belly as she tried to commit the view to memory. She twisted, looking over Yilfrist's right wing to catch sight of the flickering lights from Home nestled in the hills to the north.

With effort, she dragged her mind away from the stunning splendor below her and focused on her current dilemma. She was bound, and Yilfrist was taking her to Renault's workshop, where he would guard her until Naevys came. Once Naevys had everything in the workshop with Venn, the chances of overpowering her or disrupting her plans in any way went almost to zero.

The heat spread down the front of her thighs and along her forearms where they touched the warmth of Yilfrist's scales.

The thought dragged her attention back to the beast carrying her—the beast with ice-cold scales.

The heat wasn't from his scales—it was from the threads of *vitalle* he was drawing out of her.

She slammed a shield into place between them, and the heat cut off abruptly, leaving nothing but the blistering winter cold. The dragon's deep laugh rumbled in her mind, easily heard despite the rushing wind.

You think you could stop me from feeding if I really wanted to? His voice sounded inside her skull, low and rumbling like the grinding of ice over rocks. A force brushed her, so immense that she flinched and poured more *vitalle* into her shield, even as she recognized that she could never hope to stop him if he attacked.

But the dragon did nothing beyond fly over the woods, and Kate's mind spun around the question his threat raised—because he obviously *did* want to.

What is surprising, she thought, *is that Naevys can stop him.*

She doesn't stop me. His voice echoed coldly in her head.

Kate stilled. *You can hear my thoughts?*

When we are touching. There was a sense to his mind. The same feel as his remnant—a vastness that stretched over countless centuries.

A vastness that might even overshadow Naevys's.

Kate continued to tug against her bonds, her mind teasing at the edge of an idea. All this power, and yet Yilfrist had obeyed Naevys instantly in the cave when the queen had ordered him not to take *vitalle* from Kate. How could the Warden of the White Wood command a dragon of the northern mountains?

Naevys's words from her letter to Virion came back to Kate's mind. *I offer him sips of the power of the White Wood in exchange for more flights.*

"She fed you from the Wood." Kate's voice was lost in the wind, but a twitch ran down Yilfrist's wings, making his entire body shudder. *How much did she give to you,* Kate thought toward the dragon, *before, as the Warden, she could exert control?*

She does not control me. He tucked his wings and dove.

Kate rose off his back, terror clawing up her throat and choking off a scream as only the vines held her in place. She clenched every muscle, squeezing her eyes shut and trying not to think of the ground rushing toward them. He leveled out, and she settled back onto the comparative safety of his frozen scales.

Naevys and I have an understanding, he said mildly.

Kate took several breaths, swallowing down the terror, her limbs hollow and tingling from the fear. "I know. She'll find you the bones of the other dragons if you help her find mages."

You're brighter than most I've found, little mage. He dipped his right wing, and they began a slow, lazy spiral toward the ground.

The moonlight landed in a snowy clearing below that could be the one with Yellow's abandoned barn, and Kate's heart sank. Time. She needed time to think. There must be some way to convince Yilfrist to defy Naevys.

Perhaps it is because you are part elven, the dragon mused, seemingly only mildly curious. *You smell of the forest the way they do.*

Elven blood!

The amulet could offer time, and the only thing keeping her from using it was the vines binding her hands—but elves could manipulate vines.

Kate reached her mind toward the strands of plants wrapping around her. Ignoring Naevys's runelight that coursed through them, she focused on the essence of the plants. Fibers ran along each tendril, curving and flexing around Kate. Instead of cutting the runelight, Kate sent the idea of relaxing into them, just like she would do to calm an animal.

Nothing happened.

Wind pulled strands of hair from her braid and snapped them against her neck. She cast out into the green tendrils around her. There wasn't a mind to connect with, merely long fibers that curled everywhere they touched her.

Each held a sort of longing to wrap around an object. A need to climb and grow.

Kate pushed a new desire into the plant. An urge to wrap around the dragon's scaly back.

The vines loosened slightly.

Kate shimmied her hand—and slid it around until she reached the spring over the topaz.

The ground grew closer, and she pressed her finger against the stone.

The wind cut off abruptly. Every sensation of motion ceased.

She floated weightlessly in an endless black.

CHAPTER FIFTY-NINE

Stars exploded around Kate. Not the distant pricks of light like the night sky, but blazing orbs of blinding light swirling past her, growing and shrinking. Each somehow within reach but also infinitely far away at the same time. A song filled the air, lulling and beautiful, carrying her away on languid harmonies.

Strands of light in colors she couldn't name raced past, calling her, enveloping her, drawing out the fear that filled her. Replacing it with the gentle embrace of belonging.

It pulled at the edges of her, unspooling her mind.

She rebelled against the lure, and the darkness shattered. The song ceased.

The dragon came back into view, hanging suspended above the ground, banked to the side. Looking down his wing, Kate could see the small glen with the yellow door. In front of it stood a flaming green *naiwyn*, and facing it were four figures—two stocky dwarves and the slighter forms of two elves.

What is this? Yilfrist's voice thundered through the silence. A ghostly image of his head detached from his physical one and twisted to look back at her, his milky-white eyes filled with rage.

"You're here!" Kate lifted her spectral head. Between herself and Yilfrist, a thin white line stretched, connecting them in a way that reminded her of how Thallion had connected her to the wellstone.

Where are we? Yilfrist demanded.

"We haven't moved, but time has slowed almost to a halt." A lock of Kate's hair shifted slowly in the air.

Another thread of light connected her to the amulet—no, not to the amulet. It extended beneath the amulet to the wisp of pale light.

"The child!" Kate leaned closer, trying to make out a form, but the wraithlike brightness had no distinct shape.

Something shifted behind her, and Kate turned to see the hazy form of Fix, wedged between two spikes on Yilfrist's tail. "Fix!"

Did you expect us to stay behind? Crofftus's voice was tense, and Fix's face was frozen somewhere between stubborn determination and fear.

"Yes!" The gnoblin's body looked like it might slip off the dragon at any moment. "You were hidden!"

He made a dismissive noise. *This amulet is fascinating!*

Kate turned back to the amulet, trying to set aside her fear for them. "Just...hold on tight."

That was our plan.

The topaz rested in its amulet. The thin lines of the possible futures spread out from it, and she grabbed the brightest. The image of her own face looked back at her, the sky behind her spinning as Yilfrist landed.

> The branches of the naiwyn seethed an eerie green glow in the moonlit clearing, a simmering, glowing viscous liquid covering every surface. It roiled with the dark green of the deep seas, laced

with flecks and sparks of emerald. Its lopsided gash of a mouth hung open below irregular eyes that glowed with a verdant fire.

A blazing branch slammed into Matlen, knocking him to the ground. He lay still with a scorch mark across his chest. Tribal bellowed and slammed his axe into the tree. A branch snapped off, but the naiwyn didn't pause.

"Back away!" Kate shouted.

Silas flung a knife, and it sank into the glowing green trunk.

The tree sprite swung another thick branch, catching the dwarf in the chest and sending him flying back. He landed next to a bundle of cloth—the broken form of Aislin.

Kate shoved at the vines shackling her, pouring every bit of vitalle into them she could, loosening them enough to wriggle out. But by the time she leapt down from Yilfrist's back, Tribal lay in the snow, a pool of red growing beneath him.

Kate dragged her eyes away from the topaz and looked down into the clearing. The figures of the dwarf and the elf twins were clearly visible, Aislin frozen mid-stride as she ran toward the *naiwyn*.

"No!" Kate grabbed for other threads. The same scenario played out in each one.

They should not engage. Yilfrist's thought rumbled through her mind. *The sprites cannot be defeated.*

"Unless Naevys cuts them off from the power of the forest." Kate twisted to look back toward the ravine, as though she could see Naevys approaching.

The Warden is not close yet.

"Wait!" Kate swung back to the dragon. In her first encounter with the *naiwyn*, it had been laced with blue glimmers—*frosty blue.* "*You* helped her make them! That's how she could create them from the human woods—you gave her some of your power!"

The dragon's milky eyes focused on her. *You are perceptive for one with so much human blood.*

"Will you cut it off now?" Kate asked.

Yilfrist let out an amused snort. *No.*

Why not? Crofftus asked. *Naevys wants it, not you. I've never heard of a dragon so completely controlled.*

"Neither have I," Kate said. "Not without complicated, powerful magic. You're not actually a creature of her Wood. You don't have to obey her."

I am not obeying. Yilfrist's words were cold with disdain.

"Right," Kate said, searching the other futures. "You have an *understanding* where you help her find what she needs, and she feeds you from the White Wood until you belong to her."

Yilfrist looked away, unconcerned. *How long will we be frozen here?*

Kate's finger sat firmly against the topaz, but the spring was already pushing away. "Not long. What would it take to get you to help me?"

Something you cannot give.

"Try me."

He let out a derisive snort. *Can you give me my mother? She lived in these mountains long ago but died far to the south. Naevys has sworn to help me find a piece of her.*

An image poured into Kate's mind—a dragon, so dark green she was almost black. She moved through a massive cave, dimly lit by an opening high above. When the light caught on her scales, ripples of deep blue skittered across their surface.

The impression of immense mountains crashed into Kate. The endless weight of rocks, the cold, implacable immortality of the earth.

Kate straightened. "I know that remnant!"

His head twisted again to look at her. *How?*

The remnant faded, but it was undoubtedly the one she knew.

Kate glanced down at the clearing below them. "I've felt it before."

The dragon was silent for a moment. *You lie.*

Kate pulled to mind the first time she'd felt the dragon scale in Renault's cave. "No. The gnoblin had it."

> Fix reached into one of his pockets and pulled out a chip of something dark green. The flickering lantern light sent ripples of deep blue light skipping across the surface. He held it out to Kate.
>
> The moment her fingers touched it, the echo of a remnant as large as a mountain rolled out of it. Not so much a sound or a scent as the feel of endless tons of rock, solid and eternal.

She pushed the memory along the strand of light to Yilfrist, and his ghostly form grew as still as his physical one.

"Neither Fix nor I have it any more," Kate said, "but I can get it for you if you cut off the power of the woods to the *naiwyn* and swear not to hurt me or my friends."

Yilfrist's eyes bored into her for a heartbeat, and Kate felt her finger slipping away from the topaz.

"Unless," she said, "you really are under Naevys's control, and you have no freedom."

His expression didn't change, but he inclined his head. *As soon as time resumes, I will cut the tree sprite off, and you will give me the scale.*

"One of my friends down there has it. So they need to survive, and you need to kill the *naiwyn*."

Cutting a naiwyn *off from the woods does not kill it — it merely makes it killable.*

"Killable?"

It will not be able to heal from any injury inflicted upon it. But I will not help you fight it. It is the Warden's creature.

Kate took in the glowing sprite casting a green light across the clearing. The dwarves had only axes, and the elf twins had no weapons at all. "I would need to be off your back and unbound when we land."

I can loosen your bonds, but I must have that scale. If you and your companions die, I still need it. Tell me who has it.

She paused. "You swore not to hurt any of them."

He growled, and even as a ghostly shape, she felt his back rumble. *I do not need reminding of my vows.*

Do not trust him, Katria, Crofftus warned.

Kate gave her companions below one last look. "There's no point in hiding it now. One of the dwarves has it in his pack. How will you get it if we're all dead?"

Yilfrist turned this attention to the ground. *To gain my mother's memories, I need to devour it. It matters not what I devour with it.*

Kate's finger slipped off the topaz, and the wind roared past her ears. The frigid cold of Yilfrist's back seeped into her again as they lurched back into motion. Below, the dwarves and elves slowly approached the *naiwyn*.

Yilfrist tilted further, tightening his spiral as he raced toward the clearing.

Matlen and Aislin spun to look up, grabbing Tribal and Silas and shouting words lost in the rush of the wind. The four scattered, diving back toward the trees.

Yilfrist's wings flared at the last moment, and he slowed so fast Kate was crushed against his back, her breath driven out of her. Before she could draw another, the vines shifted, lifting her over his spines and dropping her behind his left wing.

She slammed into the ground just as her bonds loosened. Even through the cushion of the ankle-deep snow, pain shot through her shoulder and hip. Yilfrist strode toward the *naiwyn* as Kate gasped. Her hands still locked against the seed by Naevys's golden sleeve of runelight, she shimmied out of the vines. Fix scampered up beside her, tugging at the bands to help her out.

"Twig!" Tribal whispered from behind her. He grabbed her arm and lifted her to her feet, dragging her backward.

"I need the green dragon's scale!" Kate pulled against him, trying to stop their progress.

With only a moment's hesitation, he dug into a pocket of his fur-lined vest and produced the fragment. Moonlight sent flashes of midnight blue over the dark green, and the colossal weight of its mountain remnant rolled over her. He held it out, looking doubtfully at her hands gripped around the seed.

"Bring it." Kate took a few steps toward the dragon.

"For what? We need this to make stonesteel."

"No, we need it for payment. That was Yilfrist's mother's scale."

The dwarf's black brows rose, and he looked warily at the dragon. "Ah... In that case, he can have it."

Yilfrist slid smoothly between the *naiwyn* and the nearest trees. Kate cast out, and the tree sprite lit into a blazing mass of *vitalle* with more pouring into it from the forest. The dragon flared up just as brightly. His foot slashed down, and his silver blue claws ripped through the streams of *vitalle* like tearing paper. The paths vaporized.

The *naiwyn's* branches shuddered, and it grew dimmer. Yilfrist crawled smoothly around it toward Kate, his gaze hungry.

"Twig..." Tribal said, an uncharacteristic note of wariness in his voice.

She gestured for Tribal to hold the scale up. "It's right here."

Yilfrist stopped only paces away and drew in a breath that tugged Kate's hair forward. The slits in the dragon's eyes dilated, and his body grew perfectly still. *Throw it here.* The command whipped out, and Tribal flinched.

Kate nodded to the dwarf, and with a pained sigh, he tossed it through the air. It glinted with flashes of deep blues and green before Yilfrist snaked his head forward and caught it in his mouth. A shiver rolled down his neck and along his back, reaching all the way to his tail in a ripple of frost white along the glacial blue.

Our bargain is complete. The trembling continued in his legs.

Kate took a step back. "Agreed."

Without another word, the dragon snapped his wings out and shot into the air like a fragment of winter torn from the snowy ground.

CHAPTER SIXTY

Silas approached, his boots making his progress through the snow even quieter than it should be. "I have no idea what just happened, but I did think the dragon was going to do more than dance around the tree monster and claw at the air."

Tribal nodded. "Either kill us all or kill the creepy tree."

"He weakened it," Aislin said, her voice just above a whisper.

"It can't heal itself now," Kate agreed. "But we still need to get past it."

Matlen peered into the edge of the forest. "Is Naevys coming?"

She can travel quickly, Crofftus said, *But not nearly as fast as the dragon. She'll be here soon.*

"Is that..." Tribal gestured to Kate's hand.

She nodded. "Naevys's seed and the amulet. I can't take my hands off them." The thought snagged at her mind. She hadn't been able to take her hands off while Naevys had been there to overcome the runelight shield. But now...with Naevys far away...

Kate formed a shield over her palms, and Naevys's golden sleeve dissipated into the air. "I guess her power weakens when she's far away." Kate slipped the seed into her pocket and hung the amulet around her neck. She tucked it safely inside her shirt, the weight reassuring despite the chill of the stonesteel against her skin.

Weren't you supposed to stay touching the seed? Crofftus asked.

"I still am." The seed, driven by its tiny hunger, continued to draw trace amounts of *vitalle* from Kate's leg, but barely enough to notice.

"Is that the *real* amulet?" Silas asked.

"It is. I used it." Kate tilted her head toward the *naiwyn*. "I saw you all fight it and lose." The memory sent a shiver up her spine. "You can't let it touch you."

"That's gonna be tricky," Silas said. "It has a lot of limbs."

Kate studied the sprite, which stood firmly a half-dozen paces in front of the yellow door. "It's guarding the workshop. If Aislin and Matlen step to the door, it should focus on them, then Tribal and Silas can attack it from behind. It can't heal now." She gestured to the dwarves. "So you make some wounds, and I'll drain it of life."

The four of them looked at her with dubious expressions.

"Just that easy?" Silas asked with a raised eyebrow.

Kate offered him a smile that was little more than a wince. "Just that easy."

What should we do? Crofftus asked.

"For the moment," Kate said, "just stay away from it."

"Well, it won't get done by standing here." Tribal pointed his axe at Aislin and Matlen. "Keep moving. Don't do anything stupid. Just get its attention, then step out of reach."

"Quick, erratic steps," Silas agreed. "We already have one elf who needs rescuing. Don't give us any more."

Aislin began to wave away their worry, but Kate set a hand on her arm. "Don't exhaust yourselves."

The young elf gave her a bright smile. "A few steps over short distances will be fine."

"And we're getting better," Matlen agreed.

Both dwarves' expressions stayed mildly disapproving.

"Nothing stupid," Silas said sternly.

The elf twins nodded dutifully and disappeared, reappearing on each side of the *naiwyn*. The sprite's branches snapped out at them, but the twins blinked out of sight, stepping out of reach and closer to the sides of the yellow door.

The *naiwyn* faced them, and the dwarves moved forward on quiet feet. Kate followed, wincing at the noise of her own boots in the snow. "Can you create one big wound?" she whispered. "It would be easier to drain one large hole than a lot of small ones."

"Oh, sure," Tribal said dryly. "Hitting a moving target that's trying to kill you in the same place more than once? Simple."

The elf twins blinked out of sight before the sprite's branches crashed into the ground where they'd stood, transforming two patches of snow into steam.

"You first," Silas said to Tribal.

"Why?"

"I have better aim than you."

Tribal shot him a dark look. "Absolutely no one believes that." But he slipped smoothly forward, and as the *naiwyn* turned toward where the elves had reappeared, he slammed his axe into the nearest large root.

The sprite's branches swept toward Tribal, but he sprinted away. The tip of a branch brushed his pack, leaving a scorch mark.

A deep gouge marred the root, bleeding a bright green light.

Kate cast out, pouring her remnant into it until her red glitter filled a path between herself and the sprite. She anchored it to the root and pulled *vitalle* out of it. A thin trail of energy trickled out. "I need it bigger."

Aislin and Matlen appeared next to each other, pressed against the yellow door, and the *naiwyn* twisted again.

"Aislin! Above you!" Silas shouted as the *naiwyn* raised a huge branch. He darted forward and slammed his axe straight into Tribal's mark.

The end of the root snapped off, and while Silas raced out of the way, Kate yanked at the *vitalle* in the creature. It gushed out like a flood, drenching the ground in front of it with a viridescent pool of light that melted the snow and sank into the earth as the tree grew dimmer.

"That's big enough!" Kate grabbed for more of the sprite's *vitalle*.

"Niblings!" Silas shouted. "Get out of there!"

But Aislin and Matlen stood in front of the door, leaning heavily on each other.

Before the elves could move, the *naiwyn* swung its branches toward them.

Aislin buried her head in her brother's shoulder, and Matlen threw his arms around her.

Kate dropped her hold on the *vitalle* and shoved a shield toward the elves, wrapping it around them just as the branches crashed together.

Fiery limbs slammed into the shield, sending searing pain across Kate's palms. The green *vitalle* of the *naiwyn* ate into the surface of the shield like a hot poker scorching wood. Kate gritted her teeth and strengthened it as the sprite squeezed tighter.

The dwarves sprinted forward, shouting and slamming their axes into any branch or root they could reach.

The *naiwyn* thrashed and let go of the elves.

Kate dropped the shield, and Aislin and Matlen staggered back around the door, limping, their cloaks smoldering. "Run!" Kate yelled.

The dwarves dove closer before the sprite turned back around. Four roots and as many branches were hewn off, their ends dripping green light, and it moved haltingly.

Kate focused on the wounds, ripping *vitalle* out. The tree sprite shuddered but set itself in front of the yellow door again, its branches ready to attack.

The green light poured out of the axe wounds, pooling around the roots. It grew dimmer, until, with a flicker, it disappeared.

Kate sank to her knees in the cold snow, dropping her aching hands into her lap. Tribal and Silas came cautiously closer, their axes held at the ready. Matlen helped Aislin around the door, both limping. Fix crept out from behind a nearby tree.

"Is it gone?" Tribal asked.

Kate nodded. The two dwarves were singed, their clothes soaked with melted snow and darkened with dirt. The elves looked worse, their hair and faces smudged with soot, their clothes charred in a handful of places, and their expressions weary. They stumbled to the nearest pine, which was young and thin, and leaned against it.

Kate cast out. Their bodies were dim with exhaustion, and the tree barely trickled any *ael'iza* into them. She turned to the dwarves. "Get the two elves to bigger trees than these so they can heal."

"Silas can take them." Tribal faced the yellow door. "I'll help you get our elf out of there."

Kate shook her head. "If you go in with me and something goes wrong, you won't be able to open the door again and get out. The elves are in bad shape. Get them somewhere safe." She paused. "Actually, it really would be helpful if Virion came here.

See if you can help them summon him. He has the best chance of getting through to Naevys, though I doubt he'll reach us in time."

Tribal set a heavy hand on Kate's shoulder, and she tried not to stagger under the weight. "Be careful, Twig. Get Venn and get out of there."

"That's the plan."

He raised an eyebrow. "How often do your plans work?"

Kate gave him a tired smile. "Almost never. Thank you for… everything. I couldn't have done any of this without you two."

His expression dropped into a scowl. "Don't say things that sound like goodbyes. We'll see you soon."

He trudged toward the elf twins, and Kate moved to the yellow door. She reached out both hands and touched the runes on either side of the frame. A little push of *vitalle* was all it took for the door to click open.

Fix came up next to her leg.

We're coming with you, Crofftus said. *And for once don't argue about it. I can read runes, and Fix and I could open the door to get out if we needed to.*

Kate raised an eyebrow. "You said you can't move *vitalle* anymore."

I said it causes my host pain and unravels my mind if I do too much. Activating a single rune is quite possible.

Fix gave her a determined smile.

His face and Crofftus's voice were familiar and reassuring, and she reached down to set her hand on the shoulder of Fix's thick cloak. "I'm not going to lie—I'm happy to have you two with me."

She stepped inside.

The tingle like tiny pinpricks washed over her skin as she crossed the threshold, crossing under the stone arch that sat just inside the yellow door. Two of the lanterns from earlier still burned, casting dim light through the large room. Her footsteps on the floor echoed dully in the silence.

"Venn?" she called quietly.

She cast out.

The wave rolled through the room, passing over the tables and chairs and shelves like nothing more than a gust of air.

No living thing lit up.

CHAPTER SIXTY-ONE

The fireplace held nothing but white ash. The dry paper scent of books and musty old herbs mingled with the residual smoke like echoes of activity.

There was no sign of anything disturbed.

A glimmer of Naevys's remnant—newer than when Kate had left this afternoon—now coated the floor against the far wall in front of a space filled with nothing but a few empty coat hooks and a shallow shelf.

Kate pulled the yellow door closed. The moment it latched, it shifted to dark, aged wood reinforced with wrought-iron bands, lodged tightly against the stone archway.

There was no reason to stay quiet, but disturbing the silence felt dangerous, and Kate crept quickly and quietly across the room. Behind her, Fix's footsteps were silent. At the side of a panel in the wall, Naevys's remnant was dusted over a round knot in the wood. Kate pressed it, and with a click, the wall swung open like a door, revealing a closet.

The hidden space was lined with shelves of books, trinkets that reflected the lantern light with the warm glow of gold, and a huge trunk set against the back wall. The latch glittered with Naevys's gold, as did the floor in front of it. Kate dropped to her knees and cast out. Thinly carved runes of protection and preservation sprang into light all over the surface.

Kate reached for the latch and caught the green of Venn's remnant smeared across the crack where the lid rested. With another glance over her shoulder at the silent workshop, she slowly raised the top.

Venn lay curled up on top of a bed of gold and silver coins with barely any room to move. Her eyes were closed, her body limp, her breath long and slow.

Her warm winter cloak was gone, as was her crossbow. The sleeve of her tunic was torn off, revealing the complex runes tattooed onto her forearm.

Kate set her aching palm on Venn's forehead and pressed *vitalle* into her. "Venn! Wake up!"

Venn's eyes fluttered open as a groan escaped her lips, and Kate felt a surge of fear from her. Venn's fingers scrambled for purchase on the edge of the box, and she heaved herself up. "Where's Naevys?" Her words came out rough and raw.

"On her way." Kate pushed back the vividness of Venn's emotions and grabbed her arm, helping her climb out. The elf staggered, and Kate ducked under her arm, steadying her. "Let's get you out of here." She started out of the closet. Venn stumbled along, her head hanging forward, her arm heavy on Kate's shoulders.

"You were right before," Venn said, the words slow and slightly slurred. "We should have taken the box and run." Her feet dragged with each step.

Katria, we need to move faster. Once we're out of here, Naevys will still be able to track us.

Kate paused and reached up to funnel more *vitalle* into Venn's forehead. "Wake up a little more. We need your feet to work better."

Fix scampered to the workshop door, motioning for them to hurry.

Venn's eyes cleared slightly, and she focused on Kate. "What do you have? I feel something powerful."

Kate pulled the amulet out of her tunic and felt a jolt of shock run through Venn.

"Where...?"

"Inside the emperor's buried carriage." Kate pulled Venn into motion again, heading around the tables toward the door. "Naevys made me think you were there, but she just needed a non-elven mage to get past the curse and retrieve the amulet." Kate turned the pendant to show the silver Bridge, covered with complex runes, that Naevys had attached to the back.

Venn's dread grew, and she hurried her steps. "Then we run now! We need to get the box and the amulet away and get your brothers out! Kate, we need to get you away from here!"

A jab of guilt shot through Kate, and Venn looked up sharply.

Kate grimaced. "Naevys has the box."

Venn stumbled.

"I'm sorry." The lack of the box sat like a rock in Kate's stomach. "She attacked us at the carriage. She actually took the amulet and the box but gave me the amulet back when the dragon helped us free this." She pulled the seed out of her pocket.

Venn stared at it for a moment, then pulled Kate to the door. "We need to get that and you away from here."

"Me?" Kate stepped away from Venn and touched the stone archway, pushing *vitalle* into it until the runes lit up. "She wants to kill *you*, Venn."

"I know." Venn leaned tiredly against the wall next to the door. "She showed me her plan."

Kate glanced at Venn. "She told you she's going to sacrifice you to save her child?"

A flicker of uneasiness crossed Venn's face. "She wasn't exactly...rational. I'm sorry I ever doubted that Naevys is like that Flibbet the Peddler story."

Kate found the two runes she needed to open the door. "The duke and the beetles?"

Venn nodded. "She's willing to burn down everything around her for this." She set a hand on Kate's arm. "But she can't do any of it without you, so we really need to get *you* out of here." She let out a tired laugh. "Your elven blood explains a few things. Like the Herald visions and Thallion's ability to bind you to the White Wood."

"It does." Kate set her fingers on the runes—but before she could activate them, the markings flared and the door swung open.

Fix dove out of sight.

Naevys stood in the moonlit glade of trampled snow, glittering with her golden remnant and holding the aenigma box in her hand.

Her remnant flooded the room: the immensity of the woods, the interconnected roots and creatures and brush, the sheer, overwhelming power.

The queen moved inside, and slithering green vines pulled the door shut behind her. At her hip hung the *nahquel* blade. Kate grabbed Venn's arm and pulled her back, Venn's dismay melding with Kate's own.

From a knot of green in the queen's hand, vines exploded outward, wrapping around Venn's body.

"Naevys!" Kate slashed into the green plants with a knife of runelight, but Naevys's golden strands that were animating them healed instantly. "Wait!"

Venn struggled against the tendrils, desperation and fear

seeping out of her, but they wrapped her arms tightly to her body and pinned her legs together. The green cords lifted her up and laid her on the table on her back. "Naevys!" Venn called before another wrapped across her mouth, reducing her voice to muffled shouts.

Kate grabbed at the bonds, drawing *vitalle* out to weaken them, but it was like trying to drain the water from a raging river.

Naevys held out her other hand, holding a second knot of vines. One shot out and wrapped around Kate's waist, yanking her into the nearest chair. Kate tried to free herself, but they coiled down her legs and up to her ribs, binding her tightly to the chair.

Venn twisted, fear creeping into her eyes.

The queen stepped up next to the table, and her remnant saturated the air.

Kate could taste the sap. Her skin prickled with the brush of pine needles and maple leaves. She lost herself for a moment in the delicate carpet of moss, the tangled roots of the low plants covering the dirt.

She shook off the impression just as Naevys set the aenigma box down gently next to Venn. Shoving at the chair, Kate tried to pull herself out of it, but the bands pinned her to the seat. She grabbed at the table, but the chair was also anchored to the floor. Everything from her ribs down was locked in place.

One small tendril snuck into her pocket and pulled out the seed. The snip of green held it up, and Naevys's face softened. "It's time, my love," she crooned quietly. "Finally time." The vine stretched over and laid the seed on Venn's chest, setting it down as gently as if it were made of glass. "No more waiting." New strands from around Venn spread out and enveloped the seed. "I told you I would save you."

The faint white mist was barely visible amidst the deluge of Naevys's gold remnant. Kate cast out, and the queen straightened at the light that burst from herself and Venn and the aenigma box.

Resting atop Venn, the seed was a spot of darkness among the runelight-filled room.

"Naevys," Kate said, keeping her voice low, "this is not your child. It's not what you think—"

"You might have confused Yilfrist enough to help you." Naevys's voice whipped out like a knife. "But you will not sway me. Not when I'm this close." A new shoot wrapped around Kate's arm, forcing it out, pressing her hand against the top of the aenigma box, pulling it closer until it sat right in front of her.

A surge of golden *ael'iza* flowed out of the queen, along the vine binding Kate, and she felt the heat of it seep into her body, then flow into the amulet hanging on her chest. A channel opened up into it, and Kate's *vitalle* slipped into the heavy pendant too. The metal disk of the Bridge warmed.

A violet glow seeped out of the amulet like a luminescent fog. It wiped chilled fingers across Kate's chest, leaving an icy coldness in its wake. The mist spread until it brushed against Venn, and a shiver ran through it. As though driven by an unseen breeze, the haze condensed, forming a narrow pathway between the amulet and Venn. It settled on her chest, enclosing the seed as well.

Naevys surveyed the connection, spread like a web over the table. It encircled Kate and Venn and wound up against both the aenigma box and the amulet. A frantic hope glinted in the queen's eyes, but she paused, scanning the room itself.

Kate caught sight of Fix, crouching in a dark corner, his opalescent eyes shining warily in the gloom.

"Cold," Naevys muttered. "Too cold." Setting down her knotted ends of the vines, she stepped and reappeared at the fireplace. "You should be warm when you wake," she muttered. "Safe and warm by the fire."

The amulet thrummed against Kate's chest, and a spark of

hope grew. "Venn..." she whispered, gripping the amulet with her free hand and staring at the box.

Venn's quiet, indrawn breath sounded so loud that Kate cast a glance over her shoulder. But Naevys still knelt at the fireplace, arranging wood. Turning back, Kate met Venn's desperate look.

"Hurry!" Venn mouthed.

Kate pulled the amulet closer to the box, her fingers trembling. At a sudden thought, she leaned closer to Venn. "Renault could be in there, too! He could help stop Naevys!"

"You actually think Renault would work *against* Naevys?" Venn's brow furrowed. "No. It's safe to assume he won't be on our side."

Kate swore. "Good point."

"Do it anyway," Venn said, "before she comes back."

"But anyone I get out is just going to be trapped in here with us. And her."

"At least they won't be destroyed because she tries to do too much with the box." Venn glanced toward the fire. "Stop dawdling, or you won't have enough time to figure out what you're doing."

Kate glance down at the amulet. "Time is not a problem." She leaned toward the box, and the amulet pulled toward it like a magnet.

Carefully, she poured *vitalle* out of her hand and infused it with her remnant, creating a pool of runelight that swirled around the box and the amulet.

The slightest hint of a crack appeared in the front of the box, and Kate squeezed the amulet, shoving her thumb onto the spring until it touched the topaz.

Everything went black.

CHAPTER SIXTY-TWO

Kate hung in an endless midnight sky, flung with thousands of stars. She was a speck in the infinite universe, surrounded by the hum of an eternal melody that swept around her, welcoming her, drawing her in. It tugged the edges of her mind, unraveling her, drawing her out into nothing but light.

She pulled herself away from it, focusing on the idea of Bo and Evan.

Renault's workshop came back into view, perfectly still. Kate's physical hand was frozen on the amulet, Venn watched Naevys with tense eyes, and the box looked just as old and worn as ever.

But along its front, hovering between her face and the barely opened drawer, was a tunnel made of mist and shadows and the stars themselves. It drew her in, and for a moment she was falling toward the pocket world.

She caught herself and, like swimming against a strong current, dragged herself back out.

At the far end of the tunnel, the valley was choked with

clouds of dust. It rolled up toward her, and dust and grit filled her mouth.

A terrible, deep groaning vibrated through the pocket world. The needles on a scraggly pine tree near the door trembled, and a spattering of dirt tumbled down the nearest slope.

Through the haze, she could barely make out the blue sky—or what was left of it. A quarter of the way across the long valley, it cut off abruptly at a jagged edge. Beyond it was a hollow blackness that howled with wind, swirling the clouds of dust that rose from the devastated valley below. Massive blocks of what had once been sky lay broken on the ground. The green hillsides were buried in rubble, the forests drowned in a thick sea of dust and dirt.

She stared at the swirling dust for a long moment, shocked at how fast it moved. She'd expected to peer into a world where everything moved at a glacial pace, but the amulet not only connected it to the real world, but somehow matched the flow of time between them.

The ledge she'd seen in Bo's and Evan's memories sat at the end of the tunnel. Something moved to the left, and Bo staggered into view along a thin path, carrying a young girl. Behind him—

Kate's breath caught.

Behind him came Evan, still the slight boy from twenty years ago. Chunks of earth were caught in his mop of red curls, and his face was smeared with dark brown earth—but it was him. Exactly the same.

Something wrenched in Kate's chest, and she stared at him, staggering up the hill, an injured woman's arm over his shoulder.

"Evan!" The word tore out of her, tense and scared.

Both of her brothers' heads snapped up.

Bo's face was filthy, his whole body coated with a layer of dusty brown. "Ria!"

Evan's mouth fell open, and his feet stopped. He searched

Kate's face, hope warring with an obvious lack of recognition. His expression was terrified, helpless, like a trapped creature. His arms were still long and thin from how fast he'd grown over that winter twenty years ago. His feet and hands still too big for his growing body. He supported the woman beside him, but it was clearly a struggle.

His face was still so round and innocent. He was still so much a *boy*.

She looked into the ruins, and guilt swept over her. She'd put Evan there twenty years ago, opening the drawer without the amulet and beginning the destruction of the entire pocket world. She'd surrounded the box with runelight and opened the door again while fighting Faron, crumbling more of the sky. That must have only been…

She counted the days. In the pocket world, it must have been less than an hour ago. They must have been running from this destruction ever since, climbing to the only place that might be safe.

Bo twisted to look at the valley, but the remaining sky stayed in place. He let out a long exhale of relief. "I knew if anyone could find the amulet, it would be you!"

Kate dragged her eyes back to him, the question of how he knew about it dying on her lips when she realized that the girl in his arms was weak and sickly.

Miliene. Renault's daughter. And the woman with Evan must be Naome, Renault's wife. Of course they'd explained how the box worked. All four of them must understand perfectly why the valley had collapsed.

Evan started forward again, an uncertain smile on his face.

Kate searched past him for any other person, but there was no one. "I'm sorry I didn't find it sooner."

A sound from Renault's workshop made her glance over her

shoulder. Naevys was turning toward her from the fireplace, almost imperceptibly slowly, her eyes burning with fury.

"Come quick, Bo! I can't keep the door open long!"

Bo hurried forward with a pronounced limp. "Evan! Run!"

A wave of *vitalle* swept over Kate from the empty space beside her in the workshop. A blur appeared on the floor, coalescing into Naevys's foot, followed quickly by her legs and torso and head as she stepped into view. Her face contorted in rage.

"Bo!" Kate shouted. "Hurry!"

Naevys's arm appeared a hair's breadth away from Kate's hand on the amulet.

Bo stumbled across the rock shelf toward her.

Naevys's hand crashed into Kate's, shoving her thumb away from the topaz.

"No!" Kate reached into the tunnel, but Renault's workshop blazed back into motion.

The queen grabbed the amulet and wrenched it out of Kate's grip, snapping the chain and pulling it away.

The tunnel shuddered, and Bo staggered to a stop, drawing back at the sight of the furious queen, twisting to shield the girl in his arms.

"Naevys!" Naome's voice came weakly through the tunnel from where she limped closer beside Evan. "Help us!"

Bo looked between Naevys and Kate. "Ria?"

"Stay close to the door!" Kate shouted at him. "I'll—"

Naevys shoved the Runelight Drawer shut, and the tunnel vanished.

Kate's fingers scrabbled for the drawer, but it disappeared into the box with a flicker of *vitalle*, leaving nothing but a blank surface.

Her breath came out in a rush, like she'd been punched in the stomach. Dust still tickled her throat and coated her tongue, and the absence of the tunnel left a void in the sounds of the workshop.

Venn let out a pained groan, and her wave of disappointment washed over Kate.

"It's not time for that." Naevys shot a vine out, and it slithered between Kate's fingers and the box, wrapping tightly around it, leaving no room for the drawer to open.

"Naevys!" Kate grabbed for the amulet. "Let them out! There's no reason for them to suffer like—"

"They suffer," Naevys said, holding the necklace out of reach, "because their suffering is of no importance. These events"—she gestured to the table—"the *important* events, began centuries ago, and they have finally drawn near." She looked at Kate with a hungry, calculating air. "For hundreds of years, I have searched for a mage who was part elven—and here you came straight to me. The land, the world, history itself have brought this moment to me. Nothing else matters." She turned back to Venn. "It is time for *my* work."

Naevys's mouth tightened into a resolute line, and the hope inside Kate guttered out. She lowered her outstretched hand. The thought of the crumbling pocket world paralyzed her for a moment before she shoved it away, trying to figure out a way to fight.

A question rose in her mind. "Where's Renault?"

Naevys raised an eyebrow. "Did you think he was in there?" She let out a derisive laugh. "He's long dead. Buried in an unmarked grave that no one will ever find." She held up the amulet. "But I don't need him. I have you. I've been searching for a way to get to this for centuries. I never imagined that sniveling emperor would keep it with him. He sent every other bit of treasure he found away from me. But I cursed his carriage before I realized he'd kept this. Cursed it so even I could not enter it." She set a finger under Kate's chin. "I spent centuries capturing mages and having them try to break into it, but they never could."

Kate twitched away from the queen's finger.

"But it's not only that." Naevys's eyes bored into Kate, and she felt a rustle in her mind like she had last time Naevys had stepped into it. "You can see the lastlight. Your mind is like his."

Kate shook her head, trying to dislodge the queen. "Naevys, I know what you want to do, but it's not going to work. The seed is too—"

"The seed is dying," Naevys said, the words rushed and blunt. "But her spirit is strong. I can feel it. Andovenn's body is all she needs."

An idea flickered to life in Kate's mind. "But Venn isn't healthy. Her hand is poisoned. She's constantly in danger of it killing her."

"Her tattoo is her most appealing attribute." Naevys drew the bronze-hilted dagger out of her belt. "It continually heals damage done to her hand. It cannot truly fight off the *nahquel* blade's power, but its healing will slow the progress, so *you* can see the exact time of her death."

Kate shook her head again, this time in refusal. "I won't help you—"

"I don't need your help," Naevys interrupted, "but if you do help the *ael'iza* flow smoothly, there will be less...collateral damage. You'll be connected to it all, and through you, I will direct the transfer."

"I *won't* help you kill Venn and my brothers!"

"The transference power of the box is not connected to their pocket world," Naevys said dismissively. "If your brothers perish, it will be because you weakened the box by foolishly opening the drawer without the amulet so many times. As far as the transfer itself, there is nothing you need to do. I merely need your blood to connect it all. I will direct everything, and I will see it all through your eyes."

"At the cost of Venn's life?"

"There is always a cost," Naevys said simply.

A vine wrapped around Kate's hand, pinning it to the box. Naevys set the amulet next to it, the face with the Bridge disk pressed against the box. A quavering hum emanated from where they touched, along with a faint violet glow.

"No." Kate tried to pull her hand away. "I won't."

Naevys let out an annoyed sigh. "Yes, you will. Human magic and elven magic are very similar, but not identical. The transfer process creates connections and directs life, both things that work within the natural order that elven *ael'iza* can accomplish. But moving that life into a different body is unnatural—and only human magic is good at forcing the unnatural into existence.

"I can create the web of connections needed, but the transference is delicate. The elven magic and human magic fueling it must flow seamlessly from a single mind who can meld them together. Two cannot work in unison to accomplish something so sensitive. You will be the conduit." She smiled at Kate with genuine gratitude. "Because you can do both." Her smile grew biting. "So help me willingly, or I'll force you to, and it will be messy. Your elven blood I can control, but your human power... Well, if you won't give it to me, I have access to all the human lives in Home. Their power is crude and weak compared to your own. At least a hundred of them will die for the same amount of power you could give me easily, but I *will* make it work."

Kate drew back, but Naevys merely leaned closer. "If you do help me willingly, I'll give you the box and the amulet to save your brothers. But make it hard on me, and Home will suffer. Then when we're done, I'll destroy the box and everyone inside."

Naevys's eyes became piercing. "It will be better if you don't fight." The queen's power moved more fully into Kate's skull.

Kate tried to shove her out, but Naevys was implacable. Unmovable. Naevys rustled across Kate's thoughts, fingers probing her mind. With a simple prodding, Kate felt her *vitalle* begin to flow into the amulet. She tried to cut it off, but Naevys's presence in her mind overwhelmed every other intention.

Naevys studied the stream of energy, then nodded. "Good," she whispered. She paused and gave Venn a slight nod. "Thank you for your sacrifice."

Venn struggled against the vines, but only the one around her hand loosened. Naevys stretched out the *nahquel* blade. A frisson of fear tore through Venn as the queen nicked the back of Venn's hand with the tip.

CHAPTER SIXTY-THREE

Venn gasped. Blood swelled up, dripping out of the wound. A shadow oozed out of the blade as well, reaching her hand and crawling along her skin, drowning out the green of her remnant. The color bleached out of the skin on her hand, spreading quickly with the shadow to her wrist. Kate's fear was surrounded by the cloud of Venn's.

A blaze of *vitalle* shot out of the amulet in a ball of violet light.

Naevys picked up the two knots at the end of her vines. Within moments, a web of energy flowed across the table. *Ael'iza* raced from the queen through the vines and into Kate. It merged with her *vitalle* and coursed down her arm, connecting with the Bridge on the amulet. The violet band of light coupling Venn and the seed to the amulet flared and solidified into a humming leash.

Kate tried to reel in her *vitalle*, but the rush of Naevys's power shoved any of her autonomy aside.

Naevys's breath came faster with the effort of holding it all together. The tabletop was crisscrossed with Kate's *vitalle* connecting Venn, the seed, the box, the amulet, and Kate herself —all held together by the queen's runelight-infused vines.

Venn's mouth pinched with pain, and she closed her eyes, struggling to tamp down her rising terror.

The paleness moved so fast along Venn's skin that Kate could see its progress. The creeping shadow from the *nahquel* blade moved along with it, leaving her skin grey and dark. When Venn opened her eyes, they held a grim acceptance.

"No..." Kate whispered. Venn's arm held no glitters of green, and the last glints at her shoulder flickered out.

Bound to the top of the box next to Kate's hand, the topaz swirled with the hint of amber light, calling to her like a beacon of hope. A beacon of time.

Slowly, Kate worked her first finger toward the gem.

Naevys closed her eyes, her brow creased in concentration.

Before she opened them, Kate twisted, stretching her free hand out to grab Venn's shoulder, and shoved her finger onto the amulet, pressing the spring until she touched the stone.

She fell into the velvety black, and the dread of the workshop evaporated. The longing to be enveloped by the swirling stars barely tickled Kate's mind before she shoved them away and the workshop came back into view.

The motion of the *vitalle* stilled, and the flame in the nearest lantern barely shifted.

The milky-white shape of Venn's face rose out of her body, looking warily at the motionless room. "What is this?"

"The amulet. It slows time for whoever touches it." Kate gestured to her physical finger. "As long as they're touching the stone." She peered around. "Naevys?"

Venn straightened. "She's here?"

"I don't know. She's in my head out there." Kate studied the queen, who was standing perfectly still next to the table. Her face was creased in concentration, her hands clenched with the effort of holding her web. "But I don't think she's in here." There was no sign of another presence in the frozen moment—except a smudge of white rising from the seed.

Unlike Venn's ghostly shape or Kate's own, the child's was formless. A mist. An exhaled breath frozen in the moment before it fades.

"That," Venn said softly, "does not look really alive." She met Kate's gaze with a haunted look. "Is she killing me for nothing?"

"No. Because we're going to stop her." Kate tried to infuse the words with confidence. From Venn's expression, she hadn't succeeded. She leaned closer to the topaz, searching for the threads of possible futures. She caught sight of a handful of bright ones. "Look at this. The topaz shows options of what could happen next. Maybe we can find a way out of this mess."

She drew up the most vivid line, and Venn gasped at the clear image of the workshop from the point of view of the topaz.

"The brightest strands are the most likely to happen." Kate lifted the thread.

Venn lay on her back, features creased in pain. Kate gripped her shoulder, a rising hopelessness filling her face, and Naevys stood, her attention tied to the small seed, hope lighting her eyes with a feverish light.

Kate pulled it closer, and the image moved ahead.

Venn's body drained of color. Kate gripped her shoulder tighter, shaking her head and shouting at Naevys to stop. The queen grabbed the back of Kate's neck as her eyes rolled up until only whites were visible.

Kate's body stiffened, and her head froze, pointed straight at Venn. She was silent, tears streaming down her cheeks, and then Venn's head lolled to the side.

A breath like a sob tore out of Kate's lips.

Naevys's eyes refocused on Venn, and a manic smile stretched her lips back, baring her teeth. "Now!"

With a flick of her finger, the vines around Kate's wrists dragged her away from Venn and snapped her palm down onto the amulet.

A light blazed out from where the box and amulet touched, glowing like a miniature violet sun. Kate gasped and twitched as light poured out of her hand too. As Venn's skin greyed, the glow enveloped her and the seed.

White mist seeped out of the seed and into Venn's body.

The light grew brighter, and Kate turned away, meeting Venn's horrified gaze as the elf shielded her face from it.

When it faded, Kate looked back to the strand to see Venn's chest rising in a shallow breath.

Naevys shoved Kate out of the way and cupped Venn's face in her hands. Her copper fingers stood out starkly against the paleness of Venn's cheeks.

Kate swallowed. No, not Venn—Naevys's child.

"My love..." Naevys's voice was a gentle whisper, a breath of life. A hint of healthier golden brown slipped into the cheeks. The eyelids fluttered and cracked open, revealing Venn's honey-brown irises.

Naevys gasped, as though she'd clawed her way to the surface of a deep lake that had been drowning her. "Amyra!"

But the eyes slid shut, and the skin beneath Naevys's fingers paled again.

The chest twitched with one last struggling breath, then stilled.

"NO!" Light blazed around Naevys, and she funneled it into the lifeless body.

Kate shuddered and tried to pull away, but bright lines of vitalle raced out of her.

Naevys crawled up onto the table as light continued to stream out of Kate and the box—and into Venn's body.

Naevys screamed, and a long vine lashed out toward the door, sparking with vitalle. It crashed into the rune on the doorframe, and the door burst open.

Faron stood in the doorway, but before he could move, a river of vitalle hurtled through him and into the pocket world. It swirled through the room and slammed into Kate, flooding her with faint bands of light that reminded her of human remnants. Dozens of colors churned wildly together, crashing into Venn's body, spilling recklessly over the table and dripping onto the floor before fading uselessly away

Faron stayed trapped on the doorstep, convulsing as his vitalle joined the flow.

His body drained of life, and he toppled to the floor.

"Faron! No!" Venn's hand reached toward the thread. "What is all that *vitalle*?"

"It's Home!" Kate whispered. "She's draining Home! She'll kill them all!"

Fix appeared at Kate's side, his mouth twisted in fear. He shuddered as vitalle ripped out of him. With a cry, he collapsed out of view.

Venn's lifeless body grew more grey, and Naevys's screams grew more ragged.

A new stream of light entered the workshop—green and brimming with the life of the forest.

"The White Wood!" Horror filled Venn's face. "She's draining the White Wood!"

Kate dropped the strand, stunned. "Like she did after

Emperor Sorrn died? Because that time she crumbled an empire and brought deaths to hundreds of thousands!"

Venn stared at the *ael'iza* storming into the workshop. "This time, I think she'll kill the elves too."

With a shaking hand, Kate picked up the strand again and pulled it farther. "It's madness to kill so many others just to have the chance to save one."

Naevys threw back her head and screamed. The sound tore through the workshop. The rivers of vitalle from Home and the White Wood surged brighter and thicker, rushing into Venn's still body and finding no purchase. The light broke apart and cascaded off the table, churning in a growing pool on the floor that spread and cooled and darkened until the life inside it dissolved, leaving only fading glints of countless remnants.

Light glowed from seams in the aenigma box. Cracks spread across its surface, and dribbles of light trickled out, growing quickly to thick streams until the box fractured and the vitalle inside it poured out, racing toward Venn's body.

The flow from Home thinned like a river whose source had run dry. Fix pulled himself weakly into Kate's lap, his face etched in pain as he huddled into a tight ball against her stomach. The trail of faint yellow light leaving him ended, and his body went limp.

Kate curled over him as she withered, shrinking until she toppled lifeless onto the table.

Naevys gripped the body on the table, burying her face in its shoulder. The workshop grew dimmer until even the ael'iza from the White Wood thinned.

Finally, when all was dark, she collapsed, weeping.

Kate dropped the strand, the bleakness leaving her cold. She met Venn's eyes, the elf's shock and dismay matching her own.

"Look through the other futures," Kate said, her voice tense. "How do we stop this?" She grabbed a second bright strand leaving the topaz and dove into its possible future as Venn grabbed another.

Kate's scene began again, except this time, she shoved Naevys away and grabbed Venn's cut hand, trying to heal it.

But the blood continued to flow, and Naevys returned, wrapping Kate completely in vines as the agonizing scene played out just as before, leaving nothing but Naevys sprawled in the center of a sea of death.

Kate grabbed another, and another. Venn did the same, her grim expression filling slowly with despair.

The fifth line had ended in failure before Venn spoke.

"Kate..." Her voice was quiet, her eyes pained. She held up a thread, so dim it was barely visible. Kate took it and watched the process begin again, just as all the others had, until...

Kate threw a shield up between herself and the amulet. Instead of stopping the flow, all the vitalle grew tumultuous, splashing out in all directions. Some of it was wasted; some still flowed around the shield and into the amulet.

Naevys gave a tired sigh and flicked her fingers.

The vine opened the door and the river from Home surged into the workshop, killing Faron and slamming into Kate. She tried to hold the shield against the rush, and a devastatingly large amount of vitalle sprayed out uselessly into the room.

Naevys gave a frenzied scream and the flow increased, sweeping through Kate and washing her shield away.

"Kate," Venn said weakly. "You can't stop this."

The words Kate was shouting at Naevys died on her lips. "I can!"

"Kate," Venn repeated. "Enough."

Kate felt her finger begin to lift off the topaz, and she pulled the thread forward faster, watching a short argument between herself and Venn while a knot of dread grew inside her.

"Stop fighting her," whispered Venn. "Help her do this."
Kate's face was torn with despair, but she gave a broken nod.
With a cry of frustration, she dropped the shield. Instead of fighting the queen, she pushed her own vitalle into the web to help.
In mere moments, Venn's body stilled.

Kate looked up at the ghostly visage of her friend, a feral anger growing inside her. "No."

Venn pointed at the thread in Kate's hand. "Keep watching."

The workshop was calmer than other strands, the river from Home thinner, and no flow appeared from the White Wood.

As soon as Venn's body went limp, Kate thrust her hand onto the amulet, and Amyra's mist flowed into its new home.

The weak energy from the seed still took only two breaths before growing still, and Naevys threw herself in the futile attempt to save the life that had been lost centuries ago.

But her frenzy was less, and while Faron and Fix still fell lifeless, Kate still leaned heavily on the table, and some of the *vitalle* from Home was still uselessly spilled, Naevys collapsed in grief before any of the White Wood was destroyed.

Kate shook her head. Something that felt like some sort of beast snarled inside of her, raging against the idea. "Venn. No."

Venn gestured toward Kate's finger, which the spring had pushed almost far enough to lose contact with the topaz. "We're out of time. You know that's the best option."

Kate looked at her in disbelief. "I'm not helping her kill you to save myself!"

Venn gave her an annoyed look. "You know it's more than that. It protects at least some of Home and all of the White

Wood. And Kate..." Venn's look turned pleading. "Look at the box."

The aenigma box sat unharmed on the table, the amulet resting on top of it.

"No." The creature inside Kate began to pace. "We don't know this will work."

"We know it works better than fighting her!"

Kate gestured to all the strands. "Once I do something as different as helping her, none of these possibilities exist. Infinitely more strands will appear, and we won't be in here to see them. Any of a dozen futures could play out." She pointed at the strand they'd just watched. "We have no idea if *this* is the one that will. Things could go even worse than the others."

Venn gave her a flat look. "Worse than the entire world being destroyed?"

Kate shook her head again. "There has to be a different way."

"Do you see one?" Venn asked quietly. "I'm already cut by the blade, Kate. I'm already dead. At least this way it could be worth something."

Kate grabbed for another thread even as her finger's connection to the stone weakened.

"Kate." Venn's voice was almost too quiet to hear. "This is how it should be. My life for Bo's. This is what the life debt is."

Kate's mind scrambled for other options. She stared at the new thread, rushing to the end to find darkness and death.

"It's not your choice," Venn said, her voice determined, even if the edges of her eyes were still full of fear. "It's mine. Help Naevys, and when I'm gone, get your brothers out of that box."

Kate's hand stopped before picking up another thread. "Venn, I can't..."

"You can." Venn took a deep breath. "And so can I. You're constantly trying to sort out how stories fit together. Well, this is the way this story needs to end, and you know it."

The truth of Venn's words drove into Kate's chest like a dagger, and she curled forward, frantically searching for a different option.

But every other thread was too dark to make out, and before she could come up with an answer, her finger slipped off the topaz.

CHAPTER SIXTY-FOUR

Vitalle swirled through the workshop—toward the seed, toward the amulet, toward the box, toward Venn.

Green glints of the elf's remnant drifted away from her chest and flickered out. Venn stopped struggling. "Do it, Kate." Her eyes held the same terror-laced resolve she'd had in the topaz. "Please."

The creature inside Kate lashed out against the horror of the plea—but Venn was right. There was no other way. With an audible growl, Kate shoved the creature back, driving it into some sort of cage as it railed against her.

She met Venn's gaze. "I'm sorry." The words barely made a sound.

Venn's head shook weakly. "Don't apologize. The life debt has been heavy for a long time."

Kate tightened her grip on Venn's shoulder, and the cold limpness of it made her shudder. Blinking back tears, she focused on the web of energy Naevys had created and bent her mind toward making it flow more smoothly and more quickly.

Vitalle rushed into the amulet, and Venn's eyes squeezed shut, her face creased in pain. The violet glow brightened around the seed, growing like a blister as glimmers of green remnant peeled away from Venn.

Naevys stood a pace away, studying the vines and Venn. Her presence hovering over Kate's mind, keeping everything flowing.

Kate searched for any way to break the queen's control. To break Venn away. To break any part of this horrible web.

Venn's breath grew shallow.

Everything in Kate rebelled. She formed a blade of runelight, looking for the linchpin holding the knot of power together.

Maybe if she severed the connection between the seed and Venn—or between the amulet and the box—or between herself and the amulet—

She froze at the memory of Venn's words. *She can't do any of this without you, Kate.*

Kate's hand tightened on the box. *I'm the linchpin.*

Next to the box, the *nahquel* blade lay on the table, well within reach.

"Kate..." Venn's voice was barely audible. "For once, stop trying to find another solution. This story is done."

"No," Kate said. "There *has* to be another way."

"There isn't. No matter how many times you insist there is." Venn's face was ashen, her eyelids heavy. "I should have died outside your Stronghold the day we met. A pointless death, leaving the life debt unpaid. This is better."

"There is nothing *better* about this!"

Venn let out a thin huff. "There is, and you know it. When you finally do write all this out, I know you'll do it justice."

Kate shook her head, *racing* to think through the different futures she'd seen. But all she could see was herself, alone, while Naevys killed Venn, Fix, Faron, and—

Faron!

The door to the workshop was still closed.

What can we do? Crofftus's voice came from beneath the table by her knee. *Katria! What can we do?*

"I need to be free so I can open the door! Faron is outside! He could help, and if we don't let him in, Naevys will open the door soon, draw in *vitalle* from Home, and it will kill him!"

You'll never get free of all that, Crofftus said. *But...*

Fix straightened and tilted his head, as though listening. His face scrunched in fear, but he gave a quick nod.

We'll open it.

"That'll hurt you!" Kate whispered.

Are you saying that in the futures you saw, if we don't open the door, we're all safe?

Kate squeezed her eyes shut to banish the image of Fix's lifeless body on her lap.

That's what I thought.

Fix crept toward the door, staying out of Naevys's sight.

We can do this.

The gnoblin reached the door while Naevys stayed focused on the seed. Standing on tiptoes, he touched the thin rune near the doorknob. The rune lit up, and Fix gave a hiss of pain, yanking his hand away and staggering backwards. Crofftus's cry of agony echoed through Kate's mind.

The door clicked. Fix's fingers were blackened, but he used his other hand to shove it open wider.

The glade outside held nothing but the moonlight over the snow.

Kate searched the shadowy trees for Faron but caught no sight of him.

A blur of motion by the aenigma box caught her eye.

Not far from the blade of red runelight she still held—the drawer was cracked open.

Kate swore and banished the blade, but the runelight had already triggered the box, and the drawer stayed open, the tunnel made from the proximity of the amulet appearing again.

Vitalle from the workshop raced into the drawer, and the sky crumbled.

Bo threw himself over the cowering forms of Naome and Miliene.

Evan pounded on the edge of the opening, shoving at it. He caught sight of her and a spark of hope grew in his wide, pleading face. "Ria! Help! Open it more!"

Kate threw up a shield to protect the box. The action caused a ripple in the flow of *vitalle* swirling through the room, and Naevys let out an angry hiss.

Kate's free hand yanked at the edge of the Runelight drawer, but the vines blocked it from opening. She thrashed against the ones holding her. "Evan!" she shouted, shoving runelight out of her hand, through the shield, forming a hook that could pull the drawer open.

"Bo!" Kate yelled, wedging the hook into the drawer and trying to pry it open. "Get ready!"

"Stop!" Naevys's command whipped against Kate, and the hook wavered. "If you fight me," Naevys snarled, "I *will* take what I need from others."

Kate ignored her, tugging at the hook again.

"Remember," Naevys said, her voice as cold as ice, "*you* caused this." She thrust her hands out toward the door and clawed her fingers. With a heaving motion, she pulled them toward the table, and the river of *vitalle* from Home hurtled into the room.

Fragments of human remnants raced past Kate to dash against the turbulent swirl of power around the amulet. replacing the *vitalle* Kate had pulled away.

Kate's shield shattered under the force of it. In the box, debris rained down onto Bo's back as a massive slab of blue sky tumbled down, slamming against the edge of the rock shelf and plunging into the valley. Beyond it, there was nothing but clouds of dust and patches of empty, gaping blackness where the sky should be.

"Ria!" Evan's voice was high with fear, and his fingers scrabbled at the edge of the crack she could see through.

Kate shoved the runelight hook deeper into the drawer and shoved all her will at it, bending the *vitalle* near her to help.

The flow from Home was tumultuous. Naevys's web of light began to tatter, and undirected *vitalle* spilled out across the table.

Naevys let out a growl, and the flow from Home doubled.

The scent of fresh-tilled earth flowed past. A grassy remnant that felt familiar. At least a half-dozen more were entangled with it. Turquoise, sage green, the dark blue of a night sky, a blaze of orange like a sunset. Smells of homes. Sounds of family and farming and cooking and building.

Her own words echoed hollowly in her mind. *It's madness to kill so many others just to have the chance to save one.*

A deafening crash sounded from within the Runelight Drawer.

"Evan! Bo!" Kate screamed into the billow of dust that filled her view.

The rush of life from Home raced past her shoulder, buffeting her with the terrible cost Naevys was inflicting.

Evan stumbled back into view, coughing, his face and hair coated with dirt. Behind him, the hazy form of Bo staggered closer, carrying Miliene, with Naome clutching his arm. Their white, terrified eyes looked out from faces covered in the destruction of the world around them. Blood trickled down Bo's temple from a wet patch in his hair.

"Ria!" Bo called, his voice hoarse.

The scent of almonds shot by, and Kate imagined Yellow, staggering against the bar in his tavern as his *vitalle* was sucked out of him. A hint of Merrick's woodsmoke escaped the flow, and she could almost see the blacksmith collapsing on the floor of his forge.

It's madness to kill so many others just to have the chance to save one.

The beast inside Kate snarled at the bars around it, and fury rose in her.

Venn lay still and grey on the table, the barest glimmers of remnant clinging to her.

Tears carved paths down the dirt on Bo's cheeks, and the sight slammed into Kate like a punch, knocking out her breath.

Evan pounded at the crack between worlds.

After everything—after all the searching and hoping and struggling—they were so close.

But the price to save them was so terribly high.

Too terribly high.

A cold emptiness grew around her as Venn faded, and her runelight hook hesitated.

"I'm sorry," she whispered to her brothers. "I can't."

Evan's eyes widened, and he threw himself against the crack with more desperation. "Ria! Help!"

Confusion crossed Bo's face until the moment he realized something had changed. He sank to his knees, clutching Miliene to his chest. He held Kate's gaze as his expression sank into resignation.

"I love you," he mouthed.

Kate tried to answer him. To say she loved him. That she was sorry. That she'd been railing against this ending for weeks, but the grief and guilt raced up her throat and choked off every word.

With a last, grief-stricken look at Evan, she let the hook dissolve.

CHAPTER SIXTY-FIVE

With the dissolution of Kate's runelight, the flow of *vitalle* smoothed again.

"Enough!" Naevys gritted her teeth against the massive power she was controlling. Her skin glowed with a burnished bronze. Her hair darkened to a deep red and seemed to rustle in an unseen wind. "Finish it."

Another vine snapped around Kate's free arm and lashed it against the top of the box. Beneath it, the Runelight Drawer was still opened a crack, the tunnel from the amulet still showing her the chaos her brothers were trapped in.

"Naevys," Kate choked out past the tightness in her throat. "Stop. Please. This won't work. The seed is too far gone. I've seen it in the amulet."

Naevys hesitated, but she shook her head. "Finish it."

Kate drove back the furious creature inside her again and took a bracing breath, not looking at either Venn or the box. "Only if you stop drawing *vitalle* from Home."

Naevys glared at her, but with a flick of her fingers, the river of life stopped.

Kate let out a breath, trying to dislodge some of the guilt over deserting her brothers, but it sat in her chest like a boulder. Her hands flexed against the *vitalle* around them, but Naevys's power pinned her in place.

With another resolute breath, she forced her mind to focus on the flow of *vitalle*, directing it, letting it connect the seed to Venn and the amulet to it all. The light from the Runelight Drawer called to her, but she pressed her eyes shut, lest she see their faces again and destroy everything to save them.

With a pained exhale, she let Naevys take control of it all.

Bo doesn't seem like the kind of man who'd thank you for saving him at the expense of others.

Kate clung to Merrick's words and let the *vitalle* flow.

Fix's small hand landed on her leg, and he climbed furtively into her lap.

What can we do? Crofftus asked.

Kate fought against the pull of all the *vitalle* and shook her head. "There's nothing to do."

Fix's eyes, growing wider and filling with horror, flickered between Venn and the box. They settled on the aenigma box, and with a look of sympathy, he touched Kate's arm.

A shock of *vitalle* jolted out of her and into his hand, and he yanked it back.

There has to be a way! Crofftus's voice was determined.

"There's nothing." Kate pulled uselessly at her arms, but Naevys's control was complete. "It's too late."

Fix crouched in her lap, his brows knit in worry.

The box... Crofftus's words were somewhere between a question and sympathy.

Kate kept her eyes from the sliver of brightness around the Runelight Drawer. "Saving them had too high of a price. If she can't do this, she'll kill everyone in Home and the White Wood."

Fix curled into a tighter ball.

Can you convince Naevys the same is true about her seed?
Kate shook her head. "She doesn't care about the price."
Then make her care!

Kate desperately thought back to all her interactions with Naevys. In the Elder Grove, there had been a moment when Kate had pushed the remnants of those Naevys had loved back into her when she'd stopped fighting and actually seen the elves around her. She'd grown lucid, if only for a moment.

But now was different—Naevys had turned away from everyone. Venn, Faron, Thallion. Even the White Wood meant nothing to her any longer.

Fix shifted in her lap, cringing lower, and his foot pressed on something hard in her pocket.

The solos potion.

A hint of hope sprang up in Kate. If Naevys could see what the seed truly was—see what it had become—maybe that would rouse her from this madness.

Kate tried to pull her hands away from the box and the flow of *vitalle*, but she couldn't move.

The queen's web of *vitalle* continued to flow through her, blazing a hot trail up her arm, across her chest, and down her other arm. And her body was locked in place, unable to break free.

"Mother!" Faron's voice rang out from the doorway. He squeezed past the edge of the stream of vitalle racing in and ran in. "Stop!" He crashed against the table, his hands grabbing for Venn, his fingers tearing at the green bands around her.

His yellow-gold remnant poured out as he funneled healing *ael'iza* into Venn's body.

Thorns emerged from Naevys's shoulders and arms, pitch black at the base, their tips blood-red. Barbs ruptured out of the vines, too, jabbing into Venn and into the air.

Faron yanked his hands back, blood oozing from a half-dozen punctures on his palms. "It's Venn! This is madness!"

Naevys's skin was now a seething bronze, her hair so dark it was almost black. Sparks shot from the ends of her hair like crackling charred embers.

Faron's hands froze as he took in her fury. "Mother…?" The whispered word was almost lost in the churning chaos of the room. He looked between Naevys and Venn, and his jaw clenched in resolve. "No." The golden filaments that showed his authority drove into her. "Stop." The command snapped through Naevys's web of control, and the stream of energy pouring into Venn ruptured.

But the power of Faron's authority couldn't sever Naevys's runelight that held the vines in place. He yanked at the bonds, ignoring the thorns bloodying his hands, but they didn't move.

The full force of Naevys's fury swung toward him. While Naevys was distracted, Kate flung out a blade of runelight and sliced through the vines, snapping her golden core. Venn's constraints went limp.

Faron tore them off Venn and shoved the seed off her chest. It tumbled over to land at Venn's side. A flood of *ael'iza* poured out of him, gushing into Venn, shoving the dark mist back and infusing her cheeks and neck and shoulder with the slightest hint of warmth.

But the shadow from the *nahquel* blade pushed back, and her shoulder greyed again.

He stared at the progress in horror, then caught sight of the blade itself. "No!"

Shadows exploded from his hands and streamed out from himself, cascading over Venn until both of them were enveloped in a churning wall of blackness, as though a blanket of night wrapped around them.

The feel of Venn's dwindling fear cut off abruptly, and Kate flinched at the emptiness that filled the air in its place.

Naevys poured her runelight back into the vines and flung them at his shadow, but her runelight couldn't harm his any more than he could harm hers. The tendrils slid over the surface like water over a rock. The thorns slid along the edge without showing any sign of damaging it.

Naevys threw her head back, and a feral scream tore out of her throat. She curled her hands into claws and thrust them toward Faron, struggling as though with a great weight. Her face contorted as she strained, and the massive flow of *ael'iza* from the White Wood thundered in.

It barreled across the space and slammed into Faron's shadow. The scent of elven remnants exploded into the room. Forests and trees and streams and pines and earth and prickly brush. Skies and wind and rain and snow. Dew and frost and fog. The raging river carried streams of colors of every hue—and when they hit the shadow, they ricocheted into the air, dissolving silently—the vivid lives of elves fizzling out like a spark from the fire.

The flow from Home grew again too, scents of homes and shops and forges mingling together in the last moments before they blinked out.

Kate sat pinned to her seat, the vines now limp, but her hands were still locked on the box and the stream of *vitalle* still raced through her, trying to reach Venn through Faron's shield.

Naevys's hand shot out toward the seed, which sat just at the edge of Faron's shadow, but she froze inches away from it.

She won't touch it! Crofftus's voice cut urgently through the chaos.

"She knows!" Kate tried to yank her hand off the amulet, but the flurry of *vitalle* held her fast. "She won't touch it because she'll connect too closely to it, and she knows what she'll find!" She thrust blades of runelight at the web, but there was too much of it to cut. "I need my hands free! I have the solos potion! I can show her what the seed is! Make her see it!" She twisted her body, but she might as well have been shackled in iron.

Fix straightened in surprise and then shrank back again. After a moment, his mouth tightened into a determined line, and he nodded. He climbed up onto Kate's lap.

With a grimace, he reached out and grabbed the box right next to Kate's hands. His little green body shuddered, and he sucked in a terrified breath.

The flow of *vitalle* coursing through Kate dwindled, and Fix's body stiffened.

"No!" Kate tried to jostle him away. "The *vitalle* will hurt you!"

Fix gritted his teeth and shook his head stubbornly.

"Crofftus! Just opening the door caused Fix pain! Moving this much *vitalle* will tear apart your mind!"

Not immediately. His voice sounded strained. *I can still do enough to direct this* vitalle.

Fix let out a small whimper but kept his hands tight on the box.

She felt the river of *vitalle* lessen. "Fix, let go!"

Help Kate. Fix's voice said quietly into her head. Thin but resolute.

Let go, Katria, Crofftus said. *Free yourself and stop her.*

Kate shook her head violently. "You can't handle all of it!"

If you can't stop her, what happens to us? Crofftus asked bluntly. *You've used the amulet, haven't you? You've seen the endings.*

Kate kept shaking her head.

We all die, don't we?

Fix sank lower in her chair, but he kept his grip on her hands.

"Crofftus, I can't leave you to—"

Katria, he said quietly. *It's the obvious answer and you know it.*

There was a beat of silence.

Fix, Crofftus said, *thank you for the nicest home and the best company I've had in a very long time.*

Fix gave a shuddering breath. *Crofftus family.* He turned his wide eyes up to Kate. *Kate family.*

"Fix…"

He gave her a little smile. *Fix help Kate stop queen. Fix hero.*

The chaos from the White Wood and Home churned through the room. Faron's shadow still encased himself and Venn's body, and Naevys screamed at it all, hurling more and more *vitalle* at her broken web.

Kate bit down another wave of guilt and resistance. "You both are." With a pained groan, she loosened her grip on the box.

Fix flinched before steeling himself again.

"Thank you, both," she whispered in his ear. "And I'm sorry."

Gritting her teeth, she let go of the box, and the flow of *vitalle* cut off. She shoved her hand into her pocket, pulling out the solos potion, then dove for the seed. Twisting the cork out of her vial, she dribbled serum onto the smooth brown surface.

As the white mist rose, bright against Faron's dark shadow, Kate grabbed Naevys's outstretched arm. Thorns jabbed into Kate's palm like needles, but she dragged Naevys's hand into the fog.

CHAPTER SIXTY-SIX

Naevys wrenched her hand back, but Kate grabbed it tighter, ignoring the thorns digging deeper into the flesh of her palm.

With the contact, Naevys's mind surged into Kate's. Not with the controlled rustle that had happened before, but with a gale-force wind racing through her, tearing away every thought. Surrounding her like she'd been tossed into a stormy sea.

The queen's desperation pounded at Kate, drowning out her own emotions.

Some small part of Kate recognized the loss of it all—how the devastation at the stillness and emptiness where Venn's presence used to be didn't matter now. Nor the trembling form of Fix, tears streaming down his cheeks as he clenched his blistering hands adamantly around the box.

There was nothing but the anguished frenzy to save the seed, the smooth surface tucked against her palm, its warmth almost gone.

Kate focused on it, desperately clinging to her goal, even as

Naevys's feral hope tried to wash out every other thought. Kate forced Naevys's fingers to stay in the mist.

A shape rose in the haze, and the queen froze.

A faint light appeared, then a rustling. Dirt fell away. The white boughs of frost pines came into view, interlaced beneath a pale blue sky. Naevys peered down, a blazing smile on her lips. Beside her, Virion's face was filled with wonder and a joy so fierce it almost looked like fear.

"It's perfect," Naevys whispered.

At the core of the seed was a knot of ael'iza. It had no remnant, no emotions. No expectations or fears. It was merely a speck of possibility. A possibility so vast it could encompass the universe. But so fragile it barely had the strength to remain a speck.

Naevys hissed an indrawn breath and stopped struggling against Kate's grip. The thorns sent jabs of pain into her hand, but Kate kept her hold firm. The *vitalle* racing in from Home and the White Wood dwindled until they both stopped.

The starry night spread overhead. In the cold, Naevys and Virion spoke with their breath hanging in the air, clouds of wishes masquerading as promises. Their words flowed long and low and with desperation lacing every whisper. He gave her a cloak, and even in the moonlight, the fabric was dappled with the reds and oranges and golds of a maple in autumn. The seed was clutched to Virion's chest, its light flickering like some distant star, bright and hopeful and tenuously delicate.

"We'll plant you in the spring," he whispered.

Something almost like a sob escaped Naevys. She stared at the seed, her face drawn in agony.

The broken net of *vitalle* roped across the table faltered and fizzled out.

Fix's hands came free, and he collapsed on his side.

The vines around Kate fell limply away.

Naevys stood on a ridge, her face turned eastward into the long shadows of evening that stretched across the endless human lands. She clutched the seed in her hand—its light noticeably dimmer—her cloak wrapped around her against the wind, the colors as vibrant as the clouds staining the western horizon.

"Where are you?" she breathed. "Why do you not come?"

In the early morning light, she clutched the seed with both hands, holding it tight to her stomach as the tattered edge of the cloak fluttered around her. She stood at the edge of a forest. A human city was just waking across a narrow valley. Smoke trails rose from chimneys. A cart slowly wheeled along a dirt road heading south.

She set her hand on the nearest tree, and her question rolled out through the forest.

No answer came back.

The queen's hand trembled.

On the table, Faron's shadow lightened, and Kate caught a glimpse of him, his hand stretched out, his finger brushing the edge of the seed's mist.

Naevys sat in Renault's workshop, bent over the seed, which lay nestled in the faded and patched cloak. The light in it was dim. Ragged around the edges as though it were slowly eroding away.

A cave. Dark and lifeless. Naevys held the seed against her chest for as long as she could. Inside it, the light blinked out for a moment before reappearing. She didn't look at it, but her hands tightened each time the light inside it flickered.

Yilfrist's icy-blue head slid up next to her, and she set the seed gently in a nook of the wall. Her hands lingered on it for another moment before she pulled back and nodded.

The dragon exhaled a long, cold breath, and a hazy blue light coalesced around the seed. It grew smooth and round like an egg, and when Yilfrist stopped, it settled into a pale-yellow stone.

From deep inside, the flicker of light slowed to a sluggish flutter. Naevys sank down beside it and buried her head in her hands.

In a long, silent darkness, the light dwindled. Fading. Shrinking. Until with one last almost imperceptible glimmer, it guttered out into nothing more than the memory of hope.

Naevys's hand grew still. The thorns on her skin inched outward, growing longer and more vicious.

One pierced deep into the flesh by Kate's thumb. She let go of Naevys's wrist, and the storm of her emotions subsided. Blood welled up in the wounds, and Kate shifted her fingers until they hovered in the faint white mist that remained.

The darkness stretched on, endlessly, until Yilfrist breathed again, warming, melting, freeing. Naevys looked down, her face aged and desperate. Kate, her eyes wide with fear, drew out the husk, dark and empty, holding only the exhale of its last breath, long ago spent.

"No," Naevys whispered, the word dragged out like the long rasp of a sword sliding clear of its sheath.

The mist faded away, leaving the seed mundane and brown.

Faron knelt on the table, his body hunched protectively over Venn, his fingers reaching into the last of the white haze.

Kate lowered the seed to the table. "Naevys," she said, reaching toward the queen's arm but stopping before touching the long, blood-red barbs. "I'm so sorry."

Naevys's head began to shake, the motion small at first, then growing more frantic. More violent. "NO!"

The rush of *vitalle* from Home thundered back into motion, along with the green torrent from the White Wood.

Vines exploded out of the knots she'd set on the table.

Kate grabbed Fix and yanked his limp body out of the way as three vines impaled themselves on the boards where he'd been. Another pierced Kate's arm as she dove away. A half-dozen more shot toward Faron. He curled over Venn, and the vines stabbed deep into his back.

He screamed in pain. "Mother! Stop! Please! There is more than the seed! Can't you see what you're doing?"

See what you're doing....

The amulet still lay on the box. Kate tucked Fix's still form safely under the table and lunged for it.

Vines slammed into the table, splintering the wood. They hurled Kate's chair across the room and tore apart books, shredding the pages and sending them scattering across the table. Thorny vines lashed Faron's back, reducing his cloak to a shredded, bloody mess—until he fell limp.

Kate gripped the amulet and reached for Naevys.

The bands had unraveled from around the aenigma box, and it had been shoved farther away until it was pressed against Venn's hip.

In the midst of Naevys's storm of runelight, another glint of light came from the cracked-open drawer.

More vines spiked with long, vicious barbs rose above the aenigma box and began to careen toward it.

The ragged desperation in Kate stopped her in her tracks. She reached toward the box, and a scream tore out of her throat, feral and unhinged—and so much like Naevys's that a cold wash of shock raced over Kate.

In the split second before the thorns descended, she saw the hope of saving them for what it was—untenable.

Can't you see what you're doing? Faron's question echoed in her mind, directed at her. And she knew the answer. The price to save the box was still too high. She didn't need the amulet to show her those futures.

There was no saving anything while Naevys sought to destroy it all. The end of the hope Kate had clung to all these years shattered.

A gaping wound opened in her chest. The one that had been there for twenty years—the one she'd pointedly ignored, busying herself with research and projects so she wouldn't have to face the awful truth.

She could not save her brothers.

And she knew it would haunt her for the rest of her life.

Evan's face, his desperation as he called for her help.

Bo's confusion, then worse—his comprehension.

Knowing they'd die never understanding why she hadn't saved them.

She whispered one last broken apology and lunged for the queen.

Before the vines landed, Faron's body shifted, and Venn shouldered out from under him.

Her eyes widened at the box's impending destruction.

"Bo! No!" A wave of fierce determination rolled out of her, and she curled around the box just as the thick vines slammed into her, driving their spikes into her body.

Along with the explosion of fear and pain from Venn, something snapped.

A bond. A weight. An oath.

Kate briefly registered that Venn's life debt was broken before she wrapped her arms around Naevys. Thorns dug into Kate's arms and chest and the side of her neck.

Pain burst everywhere in Kate's body, and the sense of Naevys's presence swept through Kate. An ocean of it, pouring around Kate, unmooring her mind.

Before she lost sight of her goal, Kate pressed her finger onto the topaz, and the world went dark. She fought off the draw of the stars that flung themselves into existence and clawed her way back to Renault's workshop, where everything was frozen.

Naevys's white face curled in fury. "Get me out of here!"

"Not until you look at what you're doing." Kate pulled the brightest thread of the future closer to Naevys.

The queen tried to shove it away, but Kate grabbed her arm. Even in the ghostly version of the room, the thorns in Naevys's flesh bit into Kate's hand, and she winced.

"Look!"

> Chaos reigned in the workshop.
> More vines buried themselves in Faron's back. His shirt was soaked red with blood, and when the next vine skewered into him, his body didn't react.

"That is your son, Naevys!" Kate said. "Your living, breathing son."

The queen stared at the thread, fury warring with agony in her face.

> Venn wrapped her arms around the aenigma box, hunched over it, shielding it from damage.
> A vine snatched up the seed and shoved it onto Venn's back. Naevys poured her power toward it, and a light blazed out from the box and the amulet, glowing like a miniature violet sun. As Venn's skin began to grey, the glow enveloped her and the seed.

White mist seeped out of the seed and into Venn's body.

The light grew brighter, and when it faded, Venn's chest rose in a shallow breath.

Naevys shoved Kate out of the way and cupped Venn's face in her hands. Her copper fingers stood out starkly against the paleness of Venn's cheeks.

"My love..." Naevys's voice was a gentle whisper, a breath of life. A hint of healthier golden brown slipped into the cheeks. The eyelids fluttered and cracked open, revealing honey-brown irises.

A choked cry came from the queen, and she spun to Kate, her thorns growing longer, stabbing into Kate. "Get me out of here!"

Kate gritted her teeth against the agony. "Not until you see it all."

Naevys gasped as though she'd clawed her way to the surface of a deep lake that had been drowning her. "Amyra!"

But the eyes slid shut, and the skin beneath Naevys's fingers paled again.

The chest twitched with one last struggling breath, then stilled.

"NO!" Light blazed around Naevys, and she funneled it into the lifeless body.

"I'm so sorry, Naevys," Kate whispered. "I'm so sorry."

The queen's eyes were locked on the thread, her features contorted with pain.

Naevys screamed and crawled up onto the table. The vitalle from Home hurtled into the room and crashed into Venn's body.

Naevys gripped the body, burying her face in its shoulder—but it didn't move.

The flow from Home thinned like a river whose source had run dry. Hundreds of human lives spilling out uselessly onto the table, dripping onto the floor where they dissolved into nothingness.

"That's the entire town of Home." Kate squeezed Naevys's arm, ignoring the jab of the thorns. "Every human, Naevys. Dead!"

A hint of horror crept into Naevys's expression.

The queen sobbed, shaking the lifeless corpse.
Even the blazing stream of ael'iza from the White Wood thinned. The scents of the forest faded. The sound of the wind in the trees died.
The queen's screams filled the new silence.

Naevys shuddered at the sound.

"Please," Kate implored her. "Can you see what you're doing? Can you see the price this is costing?"

Outside the door of the workshop, moonlight fell on the withered husks of the forest.

Naevys's gaze turned to Venn's body, curled on the table, and she shrank back.

The spring on the amulet pressed Kate's finger away from the stone. In the moment before it was pushed off, the image settled into a single scene.

The workshop grew dimmer as every source of life dwindled away until there was nothing but darkness and the endless echoes of Naevys's cries.

Kate's finger slipped off the topaz, and the workshop spun into motion again.

Rage blasted out of Naevys, sending Kate tumbling through the sea of the queen's presence. Deep under the surface were currents of something broken and jagged. Kate clung to the feel of the amulet in her hand as the fear and grief scraped against her, grinding away the edges of her mind.

Kate threw up a shield around herself, and the grinding stopped

"Please don't destroy everything else!" Kate dragged the memories from Virion's wellstone to her mind and shoved them toward Naevys the way she'd shared the memory of the scale with Yilfrist. "Can you remember the other things you love?"

It was like trying to launch a paper boat into raging rapids. They were torn apart in an instant. There was a brightness anchored in Naevys's maelstrom, and Kate tried to push the memories toward it again. But holding the shield around herself took too much of her effort.

Kate could vaguely make out the forms around her in the workshop. Fix curled up on the floor, Faron lying still on the table, and Venn huddled around the box—the unharmed box.

Kate clenched her hands. Naevys *had* to remember.

"Take care of them, Venn," she whispered, and she dropped the shield.

The turmoil swept back in around Kate, Naevys's presence eroding her mind like water rushing past a sandbar.

Kate clung to the memories she'd seen in Virion's wellstone and grabbed Naevys's shoulders, forcing the queen to look at her. With a heave, Kate funneled the scenes toward Naevys's bright center.

Naevys and Virion, their faces unlined and youthful, running through the woods.

A young Thallion grinning with an easy smile.

A wide vista where Thallion, Naevys, and Virion sat, watching the last of a sunset drain out of the sky.

Naevys gasped, and the thrashing vines in the workshop slowed.

Thallion, his hands grasping for purchase on a rock, looked up at Naevys and Virion climbing a steep mountainside. Naevys called out that they needed to go a bit higher. Thallion glanced over his shoulder, revealing a view that was partially blocked by tall frost pines.

Virion waded in the Surn, and Naevys triumphantly flung up a hand, sending a spray of water into the air. Her fingers pinched a small wellstone. Her other hand already cupped three more. Thallion shook his head in disbelief. Virion looked down and pulled his hand out of the water, only to reveal only a light-yellow pebble. Naevys let out a laugh. "I'll tell the elders you both found some of these too."

The queen let out a shuddering breath.

A glen of maple trees surrounded Virion and Naevys as he held her hand and looked earnestly at her. "It's not your connection to the forest that I love—it's the way you hold that connection so sacred. How you see each tree and elf and creature as perfectly valuable."

The vines stopped, and Naevys stretched out a hand, as though she could reach into the memory.

"You'd be the best Warden our Wood has ever had because you really see everyone. You understand what they need, and you help them. You see me and know what I need. So many would use that

for their own gain, but I never worry about that with you. I trust that you'll always care well for me and the elves and the Wood."

Naevys's eyes closed, her brow creased with pain and longing. The thorns slid back into her skin, leaving small bloody holes.

"I'll miss seeing your face every day, and I already can't wait to get back to you."

An angry hiss caught in her throat and tumbled out as a sob.

Her head drooped, landing on Kate's shoulder as she let out one last trembling breath and began to weep.

PART VI

THE ROAD HOME

And so, the events around Home did have an explanation. A more far-reaching explanation than I'd expected. A more melancholy one. But at least, finally, the story had an ending.

Well, that part of the story had an ending. I suppose most stories that are lived don't actually end. They shift and move in different directions. The people in them separate and begin new stories, their lives changed but not ended.

One thing I didn't expect when I stepped out of the Stronghold with Venn, holding the aenigma box I didn't understand and thinking we were on a simple rescue mission to find Bo, was that by the end I'd have gained two roguish dwarven brothers, a pair of elf twin niblings, and the nephew/uncle that Fix/Crofftus had turned into.

When I stepped out the door that day, even after hunting for Evan for decades, I don't think I fully understood the lengths one would go through for their family. The one they were born into—or the one they stumbled into.

I understand it now.

CHAPTER SIXTY-SEVEN

Naevys's presence enveloped Kate. The queen's anger cooled, shifting to thick, smothering guilt and rending loss. The emotions dragged Kate down, and she sank. The edges of her mind dissolved into the vastness.

The queen's weight lay heavy on her shoulder, and Kate slumped against her. The workshop dimmed. Vaguely, as if from a great distance, she saw the swirl of *vitalle* racing through the room begin to slow. The air stilled. The tangle of vines fell limp on the table.

Venn's body was still wrapped around the aenigma box, the Runelight Drawer now closed. A dart of longing to open it shot through Kate, but the sea of pain smothered her, drowning it out. She tried to fight her way closer to the box, but it was too far away.

Some small part of her knew that while something had ended, there was still more to do. Things she cared deeply about. But Naevys's sobs were like the wind through the forest. Washing over everything else. Blowing every other thought away.

They pulled her away from the small wooden box on the table, and Kate couldn't remember why that mattered.

It was a relief to let go of her nagging worries and troubles.

Something snaked between her and the queen. Jostling. Burrowing into the space between them. A green vine wrapped around Naevys's shoulders, dragging her upright, and a hand grabbed Kate's arm, unwrapping it from around the queen.

The moment the contact was broken, Naevys's flood of pain fled, and the sights and sounds of the workshop rushed back in.

Kate's arms ached where Naevys's thorns had pierced her skin, her palms ached from the *vitalle* that had been pulled through them, and a fogginess filled her head. She sucked in a long breath and found Venn lying on the table. One hand rested on the vines that were gently leaning the weeping queen against the table, and the other gripped Kate's shoulder.

"Thank you," Kate whispered.

A scuff sounded from the door. Virion stood in the doorway. "Naevys?" The queen flinched and lifted her head from the table. He disappeared and reappeared at her side.

"Virion..." Her face was creased with guilt and regret, and she pulled away from him.

His eyes fell on the smooth seed that sat in the middle of the table, and he flinched. Picking it up, he held it between himself and Naevys. "You kept it all this time?" he whispered. "Why didn't you tell me?"

"I..." She dropped her head into her hands, and a broken sob tore out of her. Still holding the seed, he gently turned her toward him and wrapped his arm around her shoulders.

Venn pulled her hand off the vines that had been holding the queen up.

The memory of Venn's remnant drifting away and the grey shadow of the *nahquel* blade rushing up her arm made Kate spin to face her. The elf's skin was pale, but green glimmers hovered around her. The cut on her hand from the *nahquel* blade was gone, and, aside from looking exhausted and weak, she seemed healthy.

"Venn! How are you…?"

"Twig?" Tribal called, entering the room cautiously from outside, holding his knife and scanning the destruction. Silas followed, drawing his knife.

"Auntie Venn!" Aislin pushed past them, running toward the table. "Are you hurt?"

Venn shook her head, letting go of Kate's arm and pushing herself up to her elbows.

"You should be." Kate cast out toward her, but there was no sign of either the cut or any weakness. "How are you not dead?"

"It was—" Venn's eyes widened, and she twisted to face Faron.

The elven king lay still on the table, the back of his cloak soaked with blood.

"His shadow stopped the power from the blade!" She rolled him over, and his body moved limply.

His skin was covered with the dark grey shadow from the *nahquel* blade, and Kate cast out at him. His arms and legs were dark, and his torso only held a few guttering points of brightness. Inside his head was a dim core of light, but it faded even as her wave passed through it.

"No!" Venn grabbed his shoulders, and his eyes cracked open. "No! You idiot!" Her voice broke on the words, and a flood of anguish flowed out of her.

Aislin and Matlen drew back, gripping each other's hands and staring horrified at him. Both dwarves lowered their knives.

Kate's wave faded, but she stared at his body, the memory of the death filling it paralyzing her. "What did you do? Your shadow should have blocked what the *nahquel* blade was doing. From both you and Venn."

"It did," he said weakly. "But the blade had already connected to Venn, and when I cut that off, it was searching for another victim. So I gave it one."

Kate's mind grappled with the idea. "How?"

He let out a faint laugh. "I *am* the king of the White Wood, Kate. I do have abilities you haven't catalogued yet."

"You *are* the king!" Venn shook his shoulders. "The Wood needs you!"

"Who else would you have had me direct it toward, Venn?"

Venn's grip tightened. "No one! But, Faron! You're the *king*! You can't just throw yourself into something like this!"

"I didn't exactly stop to think it out. But if I had…" One of his shoulders rose in the hint of a shrug. "The crown has never meant anything compared to you, V. I forgot that for a while." His eyes slid shut. "I'm so sorry."

"Kate!" Venn set her hand on Faron's cheek. "Help him!"

Kate pushed herself up. Her legs were weak, but she moved around the table, slowly shaking her head. "Venn, there's nothing to—"

"Heal him!" Venn snapped.

Faron's eyes opened. "It's a bit late for that, V."

"Kate!" The word tore out of Venn's throat, ragged with desperation.

Kate set a hand on Faron's chest. It rose in slow, shallow breaths. Reluctantly, she cast out again, and two small spots lit. One near his heart, the other in his lungs. Every other part of his chest and gut were devastatingly dark.

Any hope she'd had left faded away.

This was not a body trying to heal. It was far beyond that. It was clinging, as all bodies do, to the last bit of life it could, but even that was failing.

Venn stared at the dimming spots, and the misery filling the air around her made Kate push some *vitalle* into Faron. It swam to the quickly dwindling bits of light near his heart, but there was nothing for it to help. He was too weak to heal, and Kate's *vitalle* merely faded into darkness.

Kate met Faron's eyes and saw the resignation there.

"I'm sorry." She left her hand on his chest and pushed the *vitalle* toward his head, trying to dull his pain and clear his mind.

He offered the ghost of a smile. "That feels warm." His eyes flickered to where his mother was collapsed against Virion. "Thank you, Kate, for stopping her."

Venn shook her head, the motion desperate. "Kate, there has to be something you can do!"

"You know there's not, Venn," Faron said quietly. "This isn't Kate's fault."

A futile fury rose in Venn, and she grabbed fistfuls of his shirt. "No, it's yours!" Tears leaked out of her eyes. "How could you do this? *Why* would you do this?"

Faron's hand twitched as though he would raise it to touch her, but his arm stayed limp on the table. "I've loved you my whole life, Venn. I've done a thousand things wrong. Given you a thousand reasons to hate me. I owe you this a thousand times over, and that still wouldn't be enough." He dropped his gaze to her hands on his chest. "I never could manage to be as strong as you thought I was."

"Faron?" Naevys's voice trembled as she pulled herself away from Virion, recognition filling her eyes. "What have I done?"

Venn flinched at the queen's approach, but she didn't let go of him. "Can you heal him?" she whispered.

Naevys took Faron's limp hand, and a sob escaped her as she shook her head. "I'm so sorry, Faron."

Faron attempted a smile. "I love you, Mother. It's good to see you again...really *see* you. I thought I might not get to—" His body convulsed, and he cried out.

Kate shoved more *vitalle* into him until her palms burned, but it dissolved away without dulling his pain. Faron curled into a ball and cried out again.

"Kate!" Venn's voice tore out of her.

An idea flashed into Kate's mind. "Venn, give me your hand!"

Venn dropped her grip on his shirt and grabbed Kate's hand. There were barely any gold glimmers rising from Faron, but Kate pulled Venn's green toward them, connecting the two.

Faron's dread and anguish rushed into the bond, crashing into Venn's. The torrent of emotions from the two of them merged, and Kate caught the edge of it. Grief. Sorrow. Remorse. Shame. Love.

"I should have trusted you more." He gasped. "Let you in. Let you help."

"Let me in now," Venn pleaded.

Faron pressed his eyes shut and he twisted in agony as the well of his emotions opened. Every feeling was laced with fear and suffering. Venn pulled at it, drawing it into herself and replacing it with something gentler.

Admiration. Fondness. Love.

Faron let out a sigh of relief, and his eyes opened, the well of peace growing inside him. "I love you, Venn."

Venn leaned her forehead down to his. "I love you."

She pulled a rush of pain and sorrow and grief out of Faron, and for a moment, all he held was peace. Then even that faded away.

Venn's head dropped onto his shoulder, the lastlight of his remnant clinging to her for another moment before it disappeared.

Kate let go of Venn's hand, and the workshop fell silent. Venn's shoulders shook. Naevys's face was stricken. The dwarves stood a few paces back, their knives hanging useless at their sides. The elf twins had drawn back and clung to each other.

Virion still stood watching Naevys, his shoulders sagging with sorrow.

A memory from the chaos Naevys had caused rushed back into Kate, and she dropped to her knees. "Fix? Crofftus?"

Beneath the table, the gnoblin's small green body lay on the floor. His arms were spread out awkwardly.

He's badly hurt. Crofftus's words were faint.

Kate crawled over to him. Fix's knobby hands were blistered and raw. The cuffs of his sleeves were charred. Lines of burns snaked up his arms.

"Oh, Fix." Kate set her hand on his shoulder and pushed *vitalle* into him. It moved sluggishly through her aching palms. Aislin crawled under the table and set her hand on Kate's, funneling more *vitalle* into the gnoblin. Along the less severe burns on his arms, his skin began to heal, and he let out a thin sigh of relief.

Crofftus, Fix's voice said quietly, *took it.*

"Took what?" Kate directed the healing lower down Fix's arms.

I tried, Katria, Crofftus said. *I tried to shield him from the pain of it, but I couldn't stop it all.* His voice had a strange timbre to it. Thinner. More fragile.

Kate straightened. "Crofftus, how badly hurt are you?"

Crofftus hurt, Fix said. *Crofftus very small.*

It just wore away a bit of me, Crofftus said. *Will Fix be all right?*

"This will heal." Kate pulled a little more *vitalle* from Aislin, but the progress on Fix's hands slowed. "It will take time, though. I'm sorry I can't do more right now. Aislin, if you bring me my pack, I have some salve that will dull the pain."

The young elf crawled away just as another scuffle sounded from the doorway, and Kate looked through the legs of the table to see a squirrel on the doorstep. Behind it hopped a snowy-white rabbit. A raven flew in, circling the room before landing next to

Naevys and sidling up next to her. The rabbit hopped in cautiously until it reached Naevys's foot, where it pressed the side of its head against her ankle. The squirrel followed, scampering up her chair and her back, curling itself around the back of her neck like a scarf.

Naevys let out a shuddering sob. A jay winged in and landed on the table beside her.

There, Fix, Crofftus said with a note of relief. *I can give you your mind back. That rabbit will do nicely.*

The bronze glimmers of Crofftus's remnant that hovered in Fix's sparse yellow one didn't move. Crofftus gave a small grunt of annoyance, but the sparkles and the sound of distant waves stayed firmly anchored to the gnoblin.

Kate, Crofftus said, his voice nervous, *could you bring the rabbit closer?*

The rabbit was within arm's reach, much closer than Crofftus would normally have needed, but Kate scooped it up. Crofftus gave another grunt, but his remnant didn't move.

Crofftus too small, Fix said, his voice sorrowful.

I... Crofftus let out a small groan. *Katria, I can't do it.*

"Are you too weak?" She touched the rabbit to Fix's leg. "We can keep this little fellow nearby until you've rested."

I don't think rest will help. There's nothing left for me to grab with. I used to be able to reach out, but now, there is nothing to reach. A note of horror crept into his voice. *It whittled me away, Katria! A part of me is...gone. Permanently gone.*

Fix made a sad sound and nodded. *Crofftus very small.*

I'm so sorry, Fix. Crofftus's tone turned agitated. *I can't leave! You're stuck with me! I never meant for that to happen.* His voice broke. *You were so generous to let me in for a short time, and now... you're shackled with me. I'm so sorry!*

Fix let out a breath that sounded almost like a chuckle. *Fix not shackled. Now, Fix not...* The gnoblin's brow creased, as though trying to find the words. *Have room for family. Always empty before. Now Fix not empty. Crofftus give Fix family. Give Fix voice.*

Crofftus was silent for a moment. *I'm not great company, Fix. I'm cantankerous and bossy. No one wants me as family.*

Fix wants Crofftus. The gnoblin's voice was filled with a nervous entreaty. *Does Crofftus want Fix?*

Do I...? Fix, of course I do. You're the cleverest, kindest, most welcoming and amazing body I've ever been in. Leaving you would have been a terrible sacrifice.

Fix's mouth spread in a tired smile. *Good. Kate can let bunny go. Crofftus stay.*

CHAPTER SIXTY-EIGHT

Aislin crouched down by the table, and Kate handed Fix to her and showed her the salve for his burns before crawling out.

Tribal offered a hand to help her up. Venn curled over Faron's contorted body.

"How did the elf king die?" Tribal asked quietly.

"Saving Venn from the *nahquel* blade." Kate motioned to the dagger, which still sat on the table.

Silas picked it up gingerly and took it back to the cupboard it had been found in, tucking it away. The dwarf twins glanced at each other, then Tribal gently pulled Venn away from Faron's body.

Anguish and sorrow still rolled off her in waves. Her cheeks were wet with tears, her expression broken, and she pulled against the dwarf's grip.

"Just for a moment," Tribal said gently. "Faron should be given a little more dignity than this."

The elf's actual name sounded strange coming from the

dwarf's mouth, and Kate spent a moment wondering if she'd ever heard either brother use it before.

Silas straightened Faron's legs and shifted his shoulders until he lay on his back. The dwarf set Faron's hands on his chest until he looked like a king lying in state.

Tribal guided Venn back to him, and she took Faron's hand again. From this close, Kate could feel the gaping void his loss had left in Venn. Like a massive tree had been ripped out by the roots, leaving a torn, bloody chasm.

Kate took a step back, barely able to breathe through the agony of it.

Ayen appeared in the doorway and walked cautiously into the room. His eyes fell on Faron, and he froze.

Naevys shifted and looked over her shoulder at Ayen, searching his face as though trying to remember who he was. "I took the Warden preparation from you..." She pressed her eyes shut for a moment. "I shouldn't have." Without rising, she flicked a finger toward Ayen. "Another should be ready."

A shimmering band of light shot across the workshop and slammed into Ayen, knocking him to the floor. Kate straightened, but no one else seemed to notice the light.

No, it wasn't exactly light. It was a flow of something so thick it was almost solid. It was hot and vast and held countless remnants. Trees and rivers and wind and grass. Elven mistlight, the shimmer of fairies. The entire forest distilled into one essence.

It was the elven *valoryl*, the power of the Warden.

Kate grabbed the table. "Venn! Naevys is giving up her Warden powers!"

Venn raised her head, but the flow stopped almost as soon as it had started, and Ayen was left with shimmering green eyes and a glazed look. Kate's grip on the table loosened. "She just prepared him for it again, didn't she?"

Venn nodded and turned back to Faron. Naevys dropped back

into her chair, burying her face in her hands. Virion wrapped an arm around her shoulders again.

On the table, the aenigma box sat plain and still, Renault's amulet discarded near it.

Kate's heartbeat quickened, and she pulled the box close. With trembling hands, she picked up the amulet.

Katria, Crofftus said, *do you need help?*

"I can open the door for them, but along with my brothers, Renault's wife and daughter are both there, and they're both hurt." Kate glanced at Tribal and Silas. "They might need help getting out."

The dwarves positioned themselves next to her.

The stonesteel amulet felt heavy in her hand, and she squeezed it before setting it down on the lid of the box, over the runes Renault had carved so many years ago. The king on his knees, the fear that the safe battlements he'd built around his wife and daughter were crumbling, the endless hope and fear and worry.

Kate glanced around the workshop one more time, her gaze lingering on Naevys, but the queen was hunched over the table.

Venn dropped Faron's hand and came next to Kate, shoulder to shoulder. Her grief was raw and vast, but there was more now. She was determined. Protective. "Let's get them out."

Bracing herself, Kate pressed some of her remnant out of her hand, feeding *vitalle* into it until she held a sphere of runelight. She pushed it against the box, and a crack appeared along the top of the Runelight Drawer.

The amulet's tunnel of mist and shadows and stars emerged from the box, and Kate dug her fingernails into the edge of the drawer, prying it all the way open. A strong current tried to drag her in, but she fought against it.

At the end of the tunnel, the rocky outcropping swirled with dust and debris.

Evan still stood near the end of the tunnel, his expression still terrified, and she realized that for him, it had only been a few seconds.

"Evan!" she called. "Climb out!"

Shock filled his face, then relief. He pulled Naome away from Bo and propelled her toward the tunnel. The woman's dark curls were tangled, and her face was covered with dirt. Blood stained the side of her dress. She reached back for her daughter, but Bo waved her away.

"Go!" He climbed to his feet, staggering forward. "I have Miliene!"

Naome scrambled into the end of the tunnel. When she'd nearly reached the end, Kate grabbed her arm. For a moment, Naome's skin felt transient, as though Kate could squeeze her fingers and pass through it, but Naome struggled forward and her arm solidified. Kate pulled, and the woman tumbled forward onto the table. Kate caught the scent of cinnamon and spices from the woman's clear blue remnant.

Silas caught Naome's arm, steadying her and helping her onto the floor as Evan climbed into the tunnel. His mop of curly red hair was matted over his face. His eyes locked on Kate's with a scared desperation, and she reached in to grab him. His arm turned solid—the thin, wiry arm of a boy—and she yanked him out.

He clambered off of the table, and she wrapped her arms around him. "Evan!" She cast out into him but found only small injuries. Scratches and bruises, but nothing serious.

"Ria? Is it really you?" He clung to her, his head a few inches shorter than hers.

His fiery orange remnant glittered brightly around him, and she sucked in the scent of pine trees after the rain. It was even more fresh and lively than she remembered, and a lump rose in her throat.

"She's hardly ever speechless like this," Tribal said. "But she's been looking for you for a very long time."

Evan's mouth fell open in shock at the sight of the dwarf.

"Welcome back to the real world," Tribal said with a grin, pulling on his arm. "Let's step away from your sister and the door until your brother's out."

Evan let Tribal pull him away, his eyes growing wider the more of the room he took in.

Bo moved into the end of the tunnel, carrying Miliene's limp body. The wind howled, driving pebbles and twigs and dirt against him like tiny weapons. The valley behind him was dark and choked with dust.

"Bo!" Venn called, the air around her humming with nerves. "Take my hand!"

"Venn?" He blinked up at her. Blood dripped down his temple. Venn reached farther in, and her hand grew insubstantial. She began to topple forward.

Kate grabbed her shirt. "Venn! Don't go any farther!"

Bo stumbled again, his strength waning.

"Bo!" Venn called again. "Give me your hand!"

He shook his head. "Take Miliene!"

Bo lifted up the girl, and Venn grabbed her. Kate dragged the two of them back until they emerged from the tunnel. Miliene looked no older than nine. Her arms and legs were painfully thin, her cheeks gaunt, her eyes scared. Tribal took her gently and carried her to where Naome sat on the floor, leaning weakly against a table while Aislin and Matlen examined her leg.

Naome took her daughter, and Miliene sank against her with a sob.

Bo was on his knees in the tunnel, his shoulders heaving, blood running freely down his cheek, his eyes bleary.

"Bo!" Kate shouted, climbing back into the tunnel.

"Kate, wait!" Venn scrambled after her. "Give me your hand!"

Kate reached back and gripped it tightly, venturing farther into the tunnel. The air tingled and her skin hummed, pulling her forward.

Bo crawled forward, his movements heavy and unstable. Behind him, a huge slab of rock slammed down on the outcropping. Kate crawled deeper into the tunnel, and Venn's fingers sank into her skin, as though she were turning to mist.

"No farther, Kate!" Venn called.

Bo threw himself forward, reaching for Kate, and she grabbed his wrist and pulled.

The motion dragged her forward, and she felt Venn's fingers sink deeper into her.

"You're all going the wrong way!" Tribal called.

Venn was yanked backward, and Kate was dragged back with her. She clung to Bo's wrist, pulling him against the current. Another heave from Venn brought Kate hurtling out of the tunnel, Bo coming with her.

Kate tumbled onto the table, and dwarven hands steadied her.

Dust billowed out of the pocket world, obscuring the valley. "Is there anyone else in there?" Kate cried over the sound of the wind.

"No!" Bo gasped, scrabbling to his feet on the floor. "Close it!"

Kate shoved the drawer shut and cut off the sphere of runelight. The tunnel dissolved, leaving nothing but the plain, aged box on the table. She climbed off the edge of the table and pulled Bo into a crushing hug. The feel of his broad shoulders, the grip of his arms. The solidness of his presence was like a balm, soothing the last of the worry she'd carried for so long. She pulled back to look him over. "Are you all right?"

He offered a half-hearted smile. "I'll let you know when the room stops spinning."

Kate cast out toward him and found the gash above his temple to be more messy than deep.

Venn sank into a chair, and Bo gave her a crooked smile. "I assume dragging me out of there cancels out that life debt?"

Venn laughed. "Actually, I broke that a few minutes ago when I saved the box from being destroyed. This was because you're Kate's brother, and we've been trying for a *very* long time to get you out of there."

Kate took hold of Evan and dragged him closer, wrapping her arms around both brothers, burying her face against them. Their remnants pressed against her. Bo's windswept summer hills and Evan's rain-drenched pines. The fiery orange specks from Evan mixed with Bo's sky blue, and Kate drew them all into her own ruddy orange glitters, breathing in the warmth of their presence.

The knot of worry that had sat in her gut for Evan for twenty years finally loosened, and tears sprang to her eyes. Evan clung to her the way he had when he'd been scared of thunderstorms when they were little, and Bo's larger, stronger arms crushed both of them.

"I can't believe you're both finally here!" Kate whispered.

Evan pulled his head back, and gave a wry smile. "It has been a very long three weeks."

Kate let out a laugh. "It's been a little longer for some of us." She let go of Bo and cupped her hands around Evan's cheeks. "It is so good to see your face again."

He wrinkled his nose and leaned away. "Ria, stop being so gushy. Bo already hugged me for an hour when he showed up."

Bo scuffed his hand through Evan's hair. "It was hardly an hour, and I deserved a long hug after searching for you for twenty years."

"As do I." Kate dragged Evan close again, and despite his grimace, he returned her hug.

Naome cleared her throat, and Kate let him go, turning to take in the rest of the room.

"Naevys?" Naome asked in a tremulous voice.

The elven queen flinched, and her gaze fell on Miliene, slumped against her mother. Naevys's face creased again in sorrow. "Hello, Naome. Hello, Miliene."

Naome's eyes drifted around the workshop. "Bo's right, isn't he?" she asked quietly. "Renault has been dead for a very long time."

Naevys nodded, the motion so small it was barely perceptible. "For more than three centuries." She considered Miliene. "He worked unfailingly to find a cure. His every thought was bent on it." The queen's brow furrowed, and she leaned closer. "Miliene is bonded to the amulet."

Miliene's eyes grew clearer, and she looked around. "The amulet? It's here?"

Naome frowned. "You can't have it, Millie." She glanced at Naevys. "Renault believed that touching the amulet is what made her sick in the first place. She saw stars, and they…called to her. She couldn't forget them."

"I've seen the stars," Kate said, "and felt the draw of them. Without magic, it would be nearly impossible to pull away from them."

"Can you see the bond?" Naevys asked Kate.

There was nothing immediately visible from Miliene to the amulet. Kate cast out, and besides the forms of everyone around her, a tenuous silver line stretched from the young girl to the amulet. More lines stretched out from the Warden. Between her and Virion was one as thick as a cord. Another connected her to Venn. Another to Ayen. Between the queen and Faron's body was nothing.

Leading away from Miliene was a different sort of line. It was hair-thin and as clear as glass. Like a strand of spider web, but glimmers of light moved along it, all flowing from the young girl to the amulet.

"It's draining her." Kate forged a knife of runelight and tried to sever the connection, but her blade passed though it as though nothing was there.

"Can you not see? It is stardust," Naevys said quietly. "It is anchored in the liminal space where the stars live and die. It cannot be broken from here. But in there…"

Kate rose and picked up the amulet. The thread from Miliene passed straight into the topaz.

Naevys's hand shot out, and her fingers wrapped around Kate's wrist. *This was the beginning of it all.* Her voice echoed in Kate's mind. *Everything started with this. Everything Renault did was to save this child. The box, the pocket worlds, the slowing of time. The death of the kobolds and the other creatures. All the swaths of forest he drained. Until his dying breath, he strove to break this thread.*

Naevys's gaze lingered on Faron and swept to the seed that now sat in her other hand. *I finally understand. I know what it's doing to her. What it wants.* She looked up at Kate. *I can break it, but I need your help. You said you would help me save my child. Would you help me save Renault's? Can we end all of this? Finally?*

"Why do you need my help?" Kate asked.

Because you are different. Like Renault was different.

Kate swallowed. "What do you need from me?"

"Twig." Tribal's voice rumbled from behind her. "What are you doing?"

"Take me into the amulet," Naevys said. "Inside, we can break what shackles this girl."

"And then she could heal?" Naome asked eagerly.

"And then she would have the chance to." Naevys's eyes were clearer and more pleading than Kate had ever seen.

Virion shifted. "Naevys, what are you doing?"

The queen didn't look away from Kate. "Renault caused so much pain with these creations, and for hundreds of years, I've made it worse. Here, at the end, maybe we can right something.

Finally use this for the good that was intended." Her eyes grew distant. "Maybe I can finally do something right."

"The draw of the stars in the amulet is strong," Kate said. "It won't give her up easily."

"It is the same magic that imbues the Elder Grove and the sacred spaces of the world." Naevys gave a sad smile. "It will let her go if I ask the right way."

Kate's hands ached from the *vitalle* that she'd already moved, and her body was heavy with exhaustion. But Miliene's face was drawn, and she could barely lift her head off her mother's shoulder.

"All right." Kate picked up the amulet and hung it around her neck. She sat on the floor. "Naome, let her rest on me." She wrapped her arm around Miliene's shoulders and pulled the young girl close. "Don't touch her while I'm using the topaz, or it'll pull you in too." She glanced at Silas, who gave her a short nod and moved behind Naome in a position to pull her back if needed.

"How long will it take?" he asked.

"For all of you, it should be instantaneous."

Naevys let go of Kate's wrist and set her hand on Virion's cheek. "It should have been different between us," she said quietly. "I wish it had been different."

Virion's brow quirked, but before he could speak, Naevys turned away, took hold of Kate's wrist again, and nodded.

Kate pressed her finger into the spring until the flesh of her fingertip touched the topaz.

CHAPTER SIXTY-NINE

Blackness spread out around Kate, then countless stars were flung across it. Unimaginably distant. Close enough to touch. Growing. Shrinking. Aging. Regressing. Lines of light blazed past her, threads of stardust so thin she could barely make them out.

Each star and glimmer of light reverberated like a bell ringing in the darkness. The notes swelled and merged, falling into harmonies that vibrated through Kate. The exhaustion and worry still tangled in her loosened. The expanse wrapped around her, cradled her. Called her to join it. It stroked the edges of her mind, dragging away bits of her with a sensation so lulling she sank into it.

An impression of Naevys appeared beside her, and Kate shook off the splendor of the sight, focusing on why they were there. Miliene's eyes widened as she leaned against Kate, her face shining with joy, as though she'd just found the home she'd lost long ago.

The queen stood tall and a little apart, her eyes taking in the stunning splendor with an odd resignation. "I still have never seen anything as beautiful as this."

"I'm back," Miliene whispered. The thread of light from her was just like the others arcing through the endless sky. Like a strand of shattered rainbow connecting her to all the vast glory.

And down the connection, bits of Miliene's daffodil yellow remnant flowed.

"You can't stay here." Kate reached out and took hold of the thread. It felt like a wire of steel. "It's killing you."

"I don't want to leave," Miliene whispered.

Kate tried to snap the connection, but it might as well have been made of diamonds. "Naevys! How do we release her?"

"I can break it," Naevys said, her face unlined for the first time. "But you must take her out."

The draw of the stars grew, and Kate struggled to keep her mind on Miliene. "Why couldn't you and Renault have saved her hundreds of years ago?"

Naevys's gaze followed a dart of light through the sky. "I didn't know enough then. I didn't understand what the amulet was doing to her. I hadn't learned to understand our connections well yet. I couldn't see what I do now." A hint of nostalgia creased her brow. "And I don't know that back then I would have been willing to pay the price."

"What price?" Kate could faintly sense her physical finger beginning to be pushed away from the amulet.

"The same price the White Wood asks of me. The same price the amulet is taking from Miliene, even now—everything." Naevys turned to her. "It will push you out, and the girl. Make sure you don't lose your hold on her, or she will be lost in here forever, never waking in the outside world."

Kate paused. "What about you?"

"I will join it," the queen said. "When I do, there will be a moment when I can control the connections. I will break Miliene's, and you can take her back to her mother."

"How do you know?"

"Because I've spent a very long time swimming in the magic of the Elder Grove. I know its currents. I know everything it connects to. I can feel its wants, and this is just the same. In the end, we will all join it, and all live in the beauty of it."

"As soulless stars?"

"Not soulless, and not stars. You cannot see it yet. I can only barely see it, but these are not stars. They are souls raised to a glory we cannot begin to understand. We can barely even see it, but they *belong*. Do you feel it? They understand where they are and who they are, and they are part of eternity. They are…*more* than we are."

"You can't stay here, Naevys."

"Why not?" She turned to face Kate. "What do I have to go back to? The world I damaged? The son I killed? The daughter I never let live? I can never atone for what I've done. I have little time left anyway—I can feel it. The White Wood has taken the best of me, and I squandered the rest. If I return, it will be for a brief time where I will never be able to right any of the wrongs I've done. But here, now, I can right something. I helped Renault. I hurt others with him, all to save this child. It was our first failure, but not our last. So many of my failures are irreversible. Elves dead. Humans dead. Trees sucked dry and used up.

"But this—right here"—she pointed at Miliene—"he gave her life until now, and I can finally set her free. *This* is something I can do." She set her finger under Miliene's chin, lifting her face. "At least one mother will get their child back today."

Naevys turned her back on Kate. "As soon as the strand breaks, take hold of her and get yourself out of the stars. I'll only have a moment to help you. Longer than that, and it'll draw us all in."

Miliene stretched out a hand toward a star, her face blissfully vacant. Kate gently pulled it down and wrapped her arms around the young girl.

Naevys spread her arms out and raised her head. The lights racing past bent toward her, spiraling into her until they shot through her body. The queen began to glow. More threads coalesced around her, welcoming her, drawing her deeper into the stars.

She tilted her head slightly back toward Miliene and clenched one hand into a fist.

The glittering tendril of light connected to Miliene shattered, and the girl drew in a shuddering, horrified breath.

Even as Miliene struggled, Kate spun the girl to face her and shoved back against the stars.

Darkness clung to her like honey, but she squeezed her eyes shut against the beauty. "Not yet. This girl has more life to live." Kate thrust out a shield, and the darkness fractured.

Renault's workshop flashed into view around them, everyone frozen in time.

The hazy form of Naevys appeared next to them for a moment, her arms outstretched, her head flung back. The ghostly image grew brighter until it exploded in a burst of light. A shockwave slammed into Kate, and her finger slipped off the topaz.

Miliene let out a gasp, and the shockwave blasted into the workshop.

Naevys's physical body tumbled back into Virion. The nearest lantern burst. The aenigma box flew off the table. Everyone staggered back as dust and small chunks of the ceiling rained down.

"Miliene!" Naome scrambled toward her daughter. The young girl blinked. Her eyes were clearer, and she reached for her mother's hand.

Kate released the girl and cast out. "Naevys broke Miliene's connection."

The floor trembled beneath her feet, and Venn grabbed Kate's arm. "What was that shock?"

"It was Naevys. She…" Kate glanced at Virion, who was shaking Naevys's shoulders. The queen's body was limp, and her chest rose in a shallow breath.

Virion stared at her for a moment, then raised his eyes to Kate. "She's not coming back, is she?"

Kate shook her head.

Virion caught Naevys as the last breath escaped her lips and she toppled to the side.

Ayen cried out and fell to his knees. A rush of *valoryl* raced out of Naevys's body and plowed into him, knocking him to the floor, senseless.

A chunk of the ceiling crashed down, revealing a thick root.

"Time to leave," Silas said, pulling Bo to his feet.

A deep crack split the ceiling above the fireplace. The floor shook under Kate's knees. Another root protruded through the fissure, bone white.

"I think this pocket world is underground," Tribal said, propelling Evan toward the exit. "Matlen, grab Fix. It's definitely time to get out of here."

Kate stood and helped Naome lift Miliene. Tribal swept the girl up and started for the door amidst crumbling chunks of falling ceiling.

Silas heaved Ayen over his shoulder. The flow of *valoryl* dwindled, and Ayen, though senseless, began to glow.

Kate pulled Venn to her feet.

"Faron," Venn said, her words desperate. "He needs to be buried beneath the trees."

Kate motioned to the dozens of frost pine roots now visible above them. "I think he will be!" She pushed Venn toward the door. "Virion! Time to go!"

The elf was kneeling, clinging to Naevys. A block of the

ceiling crashed down onto the table, sending a blast of broken rock at the elf, and he flinched. Kate grabbed his arm.

She spared a moment to look for the aenigma box, but it was lost in the rubble. She tugged on Virion, and he let go of Naevys, his face wet with tears. Together, they dashed for the door.

Kate ran outside with Virion as the ceiling of the workshop collapsed. Dust and debris rolled out of the doorway, pelting the huddled group with bits of stone and wood. Moonlight lit the cloud to a hazy grey, and they all scrambled farther back. The stone archway inside the door caved in, but instead of showing more rubble, the entire pocket world disappeared, leaving nothing but the blue of the nighttime forest visible past the yellow doorframe.

The rumbling cut off abruptly, and Kate scanned her companions. They were dusty, leaning heavily on each other, but at least they were safe.

Virion stared through the empty doorframe, his face bleak. "Where did she go?" he asked quietly.

"She joined the stars," Kate said. "She said it was the same magic from the Elder Grove. That it was beauty and glory and belonging." She paused. "She said she could never make up for what she'd done, but by joining the stars, she could free Miliene from them and do some good."

He stared up into the dark sky. "Was she at least at peace?"

Kate nodded. "I think so."

Virion digested the words for a moment. "Thank you," he said sorrowfully as he stared into the woods.

Aislin and Matlen knelt by Miliene, their hands on her shoulders, their heads bowed. Even in the moonlight, the young girl's cheeks seemed to be regaining some color.

"How is she?" Kate asked.

"Healing," Matlen said. "She's weak, but I can't see anything else wrong with her. I think given time, she'll be fine."

Kate gestured at the empty yellow door. "I'm sorry all of Renault's things in there are lost," she said to Naome.

The woman shook her head. "I never wanted any of his research or inventions. I know he meant well, at least at first, but his work took all the best of him away from us." She looked around the woods, her expression lost. "I've been waiting for Renault to come get us for a very long time. Now what do I do? I'd always thought we'd live near Home when we got out, but Bo says the town hates Renault."

Kate winced. "They do. They blame him for anything they don't understand. I'm not sure how they'd react to you two coming back. It'd probably be best if you found a different town."

"You could come stay with me for a bit," Virion said quietly. "I live on the far eastern edge of the lakes. It's quiet and safe, and I have plenty of room. Miliene could recover there, and if you decide you'd like to move to a human town, there are a couple I could take you to."

Naome looked at him cautiously. "Why would you take in two humans?"

"Miliene isn't fully human," he said, "and it might help her to be near elven trees." He paused, his face mournful. "But more than that, I've lived alone for centuries waiting for something that was never going to happen. And it feels like maybe you have too. Maybe we can stop waiting and figure out how to start living again."

Naome looked uncertainly at Kate.

"Virion is well regarded by the elves," Kate said.

"I would trust him," Venn agreed.

Naome gauged the white-haired elf for a moment, then nodded. "Thank you."

Kate looked curiously at Virion. "How did you get here so fast?"

He turned his eyes back to the empty yellow doorframe.

"After talking to you and Venn, I decided maybe it was worth it to find her and try to help." A weary, sorrow that held centuries filled his face. "The young elf twins found me not too far away."

Kate set a hand on his arm. "I'm so sorry about Naevys, but I'm glad you got to see her before the end."

He twitched his head in what might have been a nod.

Out of the corner of her eye, Kate caught Evan staring at her, leaning on his back foot, wringing his fingers together, an expression on his face so familiar that it stole her breath. It was the look he had when he was trying to figure out a situation that he thought everyone else understood. He'd given their mother that look when he was trying to gauge if he was in trouble the day he'd let the pig out and it had rooted through the edge of her vegetable garden but had also scared a fox away from the chickens. The look he'd given Kate when he'd smashed a spider that had been crawling toward her but had broken her cup in the process.

A smile peeked out from his lips, but his eyes kept scanning her, twitching with something like confusion.

Something in her chest loosened at the sight of him. He was here. Right here. Yes, he was the same age he'd been last time she'd seen him, but he was *alive*. He hadn't been dragged into years of slavery or tortured by foreign men. He was right here. Everything she'd ever thought of saying to him dissolved at the sight of his round cheeks and boyish mop of hair. A weight fell off her shoulders—a weight she'd carried for so long she hadn't known it wasn't just a part of her. He was here, and he was safe.

She swallowed and reached a hand toward him before dropping it. "Evan." Her voice came out barely above a whisper. "I'm so sorry."

His brow creased in confusion.

"It was me," she said. "I'm the one who opened the box that

day outside the mine. I didn't know what I was doing. My magic was just waking up, and I was trying to save you, and—"

Bo straightened in surprise.

Evan's eyes grew wide. "It was you who pulled me from the water, wasn't it!? I was being dragged down under the river, and then something grabbed me and lifted me back out. Something I couldn't see!"

Kate blinked at him, dragging that part of the day long ago to her mind. "Yes, that was me too."

He wrinkled his nose at her. "And you're apologizing?"

"Not for that, but for trapping you in the box, yes."

He shook his head. "The valley wasn't bad. It took a little while to get over the shock of being there, but Naome was nice and took care of me, and Miliene..." He dropped his voice so Naome and Miliene couldn't hear. "Poor Miliene was so sick. There was nothing I could do for her but try to make her laugh. But Naome said it made her happy." He pointed at Kate. "You saved my life in the river, got all of us out of the box safely, and healed Miliene too. I can't really see what you have to apologize for."

Kate opened her mouth to object.

"He makes good points," Bo agreed.

One of Evan's impish grins spread across his face. "It is weird, though, how much you look like Ma."

Kate raised an eyebrow. "I do not!"

Bo slung his arm over Kate's shoulders and laughed. "She does. And she's bossy like Ma too."

She jabbed him with her elbow. "Shut up! I am not!"

"She's very bossy," Tribal said.

Evan scanned the strange assortment of dwarves and elves before he turned back to Kate, his smile disbelieving. "Are you really..."

"He doesn't believe that you're a Keeper," Bo said. "Even

though he's the one who thought you had a magic nose that day in the mine."

For the first time in twenty years, the thought of the mine didn't sober her. "You thought I could smell gold, like a goblin." The idea pulled a laugh out of her, and it felt like she hadn't laughed in years.

Evan bit his lip. "Can you do some magic right now?"

Kate plucked a tiny spray of pine needles out of his hair and set her fingertip against them. She pushed *vitalle* in, and a wisp of smoke rose. Evan inhaled in amazement. A tiny flame grew, and Kate plucked it off the pine needles and held it in her palm.

His mouth dropped open, and he reached his finger into the flame, yanking it back with a hiss. "That's real! What else can you do?"

"Asks the boy who was just rescued by her because she made a magical tunnel that led to a magical pocket world," Silas said, "and dragged him out, then did something weird with time where the elf queen died and this young girl—who's been sick for centuries—actually seems to be getting better."

Kate pulled Evan into a hug again, exhaustion rolling over her. "I'll do whatever tricks you want after we get some sleep. We've been looking for you for a *very* long time, and now that the search is finally over, I think we could all use some rest."

Ayen groaned and sat up. "Naevys?"

"Gone," Venn said, holding out a hand to him. "You're the Warden now."

He blinked up at her with eyes that shone with a strange green light as he grasped her hand. "I noticed."

She pulled him up, but he staggered into her. "I think you should get to the Elder Grove. It might help the transition."

He turned his face up to the trees. "I can feel that she's gone. There's...damage. The Wood has been damaged, but I think it can heal now." He set a hand on Venn's shoulder. "Very soon, come find me and explain everything that just happened. The elders of the Wood will need to hear of Naevys's and Faron's death." With a small nod to Kate, he disappeared.

"There is a stand of maples not far from here," Virion said. "I can make a shelter that will keep us warm until morning."

"Whoa," Tribal said. "This is not over."

Silas nodded. "We still need to get back into Emperor Sorrn's carriage."

Bo's head snapped up. "You've been in the carriage?"

Silas grinned at him. "That's where we got the magic amulet. But there's more in there. So much more! There's an ancient dwarven crown that we thought was lost, and so much gold."

"Any papers?" Bo asked, excited. "Emperor Sorrn was said to keep notes on everything! He might have all sorts of information about life at the peak of the Kalesh Empire."

Tribal sighed. "He's just like his sister," he said to Silas. "They are entirely too excited about paper."

"Did someone say there was gold?" Evan asked. "Like actual gold?"

Silas patted the boy on the shoulder. "There's one person in your family with their priorities straight. Let's go."

"Go where?" Kate asked.

Tribal gave her an incredulous look. "To the carriage, of course."

"Naevys is dead," Kate pointed out, "but the curse is its own thing. It will still be unbroken."

"That's all right. You can get past the curse and open a hole, we'll get everything out, *then* all this will be done."

"It must be nearly midnight," Kate objected, "and the ravine is an hour away."

"A half hour at the most," Silas said. "And we're not letting you head off to do anything else. You know you'll get distracted and our carriage raid will be put off *again*."

Tribal pointed at Kate. "You have promised us this multiple times."

"The carriage, Ria!" Bo said, his eyes bright. "It's barely midday for Evan and me! Let's go! Don't you want to see what's in it?"

"I do!" Matlen said, his voice excited.

Venn's eyebrows rose, and a flash of pleasure cut through the sorrow that had surrounded her. "Because you care so much about gold?" she asked with the shadow of a smile.

"Because it's somewhere secret," Aislin said, her eyes shining. "And that makes it fun."

The elf twins' faces were more animated than they'd been since their bond with the elves had broken. Venn exchanged hopeful looks with Kate and asked, "Are you up for one more adventure tonight, Kate?"

Bo, Evan, both dwarves, and the elf twins all looked at Kate eagerly. Even Fix lifted weary eyebrows expectantly.

Kate laughed. "Fine. Let's go break into Emperor Sorrn's carriage. Again."

Evan let out a whoop and spun around. "Excellent! Which way?"

CHAPTER SEVENTY

Kate's footsteps crunched through the snow as they moved up the side of the moonlit ravine. Even with Naevys gone, her web of runelight still covered the slope. The carcasses of the massive worms lay on the ground, a dingy greyish-pink in the silver light.

Bo hurried up the hill with the dwarves, picking his way around the worms. He peered into the window of the carriage. "I can see his foot!" He reached toward the window.

Tribal pulled him back. "You don't want to reach through there. That's what your sister is for."

Kate skirted one of the worms. "We have a problem, though. I couldn't create the tunnel into it without Faron's help. I needed to make a circle with his arms so we could wrap the shadow around that."

"The shadow?" A hint of wariness crept into Bo's voice. "What kind of shadow?"

"The exact kind of shadow you're thinking of," Kate said. "Faron was the shadow creature that was tracking you. He was searching for his mother and thought you might know something about her."

Bo's look turned puzzled. "The elf prince?"

"He became the king," Tribal said. "But yes. We have mixed feelings about him."

"But he stepped up in the end," Silas said, "and died saving Venn, which forgives a lot of his bad choices."

Venn shook her head at Bo's questioning look. "It's a long story."

The moonlight fell into the carriage, lighting the emperor's slipper, a jumbled mess of paper, and the edge of a silver crown. "We'll need more light."

Silas set about lighting a lantern.

Kate knelt next to the window. "Venn, can I borrow your arms?"

Venn knelt across from her and held out her hands. Her emotions were more controlled than they'd been in the workshop. The grief was now a tight ball, sitting in the center of a pool of numbness. "I'm not Faron."

"No, but I think I can mix our remnants enough that the shadow can be convinced you're part of me."

Bo glanced at the dwarves, elves, and Fix. "Is this making sense to any of you?"

Katria has learned, Crofftus said, the professorial tone back in his voice, *that the remnants she can sense can actually be manipulated and shared even—*

"They can see things we can't," Silas interrupted. "Don't bother trying to figure it out. Just let her do whatever idea she has. She occasionally fixes things."

Evan smacked Bo on the arm with the back of his hand. "I said that about her in the mine! You drag us into crazy places, I get us into trouble, and Ria fixes it all."

"That mine was twenty years ago for us," Bo said, "but it's still pretty true."

Tribal grimaced. "Except when she occasionally makes things worse."

Evan looked expectantly at Kate. "Are you going to make more fire?"

"The opposite." Kate took Venn's hands. Their arms formed a circle over the carriage window, and her red remnant slid onto Venn's green. Venn peered down into the window, letting her curiosity fill some of the empty space inside her.

Kate focused on the layers needed for the shadow, and slowly the darkness coalesced around her and Venn's arms.

Bo drew back slightly as the tunnel formed, stretching down through the window. "Is that hard to make?"

"It takes some effort to create," Kate said, ignoring the heat in her palms. "But then it's easy to hold."

Tribal and Silas moved to the wooden crane that still stood next to the carriage. Aislin set Fix down next to Kate's leg before she and her brother joined the dwarves.

"Lower me inside," Matlen said, climbing into the sling. "Then you can hang Aislin near the window, I'll hand things to her, and she can give them to you."

Bo moved closer again as Matlen was lowered into the tunnel. The light from the lantern shone off bits of gold and bright folds of fabric. "Can I go in too?" he asked, breathless.

Matlen smiled up at him as he climbed off the sling. "There's plenty of room. And so much stuff!"

They lowered Bo down, then Aislin, who stayed hovering inside the tunnel, keeping her arms tight to her body to avoid the walls around her that churned with shadows.

"Ria, there are maps!" Bo said, excitedly. "And—Oh, I just stepped on Sorrn's hand!" He stumbled back into view, shuddering. "The old man is in remarkably good shape."

"The curse preserved everything in there," Kate said. "Can we start pulling things out, please?"

"Matlen," Silas called, "by your left foot is a silver crown. Pass that up first."

The elf passed it up to Aislin, who handed it to Silas. The two dwarves stared at it for a moment, turning it slowly.

"It's really Dirthor's crown!" Tribal's voice was almost reverent.

"How'd emperor Sorrn get it?" Bo asked.

"I'm guessing the same way he got the rest of this treasure," Tribal said. "Stole it from someone." He held the crown up in the moonlight. "Silas, there is *nothing* this won't buy us."

"I think this is a bag of gold," Aislin said, holding up a pouch. "It's very heavy."

"Then that's for the gov'nor." Tribal took the bag and peeked inside, grinning. "I love this carriage."

"Ria!" Bo's voice came from out of view. "I think I found pages of Sorrn's journal! And books!"

"Pass them up!" Kate called.

"Forget the papers," Silas whispered loudly to Aislin. "Bring up more gold!"

Less than an hour later, several heaps of assorted treasure were laid out around the outside of the carriage. One held gold that the dwarves had organized into some sort of classifications. Another was a pile of gems and trinkets of silver that Evan was happily rummaging through. The third, sitting next to Kate and taking up a good amount of her attention, even though she was still holding the tunnel open and couldn't read any of it in the dark, held stacks of paper set out on a blanket to protect them from the snow.

Near Kate's foot was an ornate wooden box, exactly sized to hold Renault's amulet.

"That's everything but the good old emperor." Bo grimaced up at Kate. "Think it's a fitting burial for him to be left in his very fancy carriage? I don't really want to pick him up, and I don't think he'd fit up the tunnel anyway."

"He should stay there," Kate agreed. "The curse is intact. He'll stay just as he is forever."

The dwarves lifted Matlen out on the sling and lowered it back down for Bo.

"There is artwork on all the walls." Bo held the lantern out. "Ria, I think this is the palace on the sea!"

"Bo," Kate said, her arms feeling heavy. "Be done. Please."

He glanced up at her and gave a crooked smile. "Right. We have enough out there to look through."

When he'd been lifted out, Kate dropped Venn's hands, and the shadow dissolved. She sank onto the blanket. The moon drifted high overhead, and her breath clouded above her. She picked up the ornate box, pulled the amulet off her neck, and tucked it inside. It fit perfectly into a circular depression in the velvety interior of the box. "Now that we have all this out, how are we supposed to transport it anywhere? It's too much to carry."

Silas looked up from where he rummaged through the stack of gold. "Since everyone around here thinks this ravine is cursed, there's probably no safer place to leave it. No one besides us ever comes here. We'll cover it up well enough that even if they do, they won't see it. We can go to Home tonight to get some sleep. Tomorrow, we'll get a wagon to carry all this into Rullduin."

Tribal held up Dirthor's crown. "We'll keep this with us, though."

"Is that to pay off the gov'nor?" Aislin asked.

"No!" Tribal pulled the crown close to his chest. "Horgoth's hairy beard, no! The gov'nor's insufferable enough without this sort of power. We'll give him the gold. This is for us. With it, we'll have influence. So much influence."

"All because you have a crown?"

Silas nodded. "If we possessed this crown, we could do

anything."

"Like run Rullduin?" Matlen asked.

Silas wrinkled his nose. "Who wants to do that?"

"Like impress that governor's daughter you like?" Aislin asked Tribal.

Silas laughed. "Yeah, if Tribal had the crown, there's no way Pippi's father would object to him."

Tribal glanced at Silas. "We could make sure they route the new cart tracks past the beryl mine because we have the crown."

Silas grinned. "We own a quarter of it. That would triple its value. And you can court Pippi now. Because we have the crown."

"You could send Brustol to the salt mines." Tribal said. "Because we have the crown."

"Tempting. You could hire Felbor to make you an entire set of throwing knives," Silas countered.

"I don't understand," Aislin said. "This crown will make you the rulers? You can command all these people?"

"No," Tribal said, "we'd have to pay for all of it, but they'd listen. Everyone would listen. Because Dirthor was a great High Dwarf, and his crown has been lost for hundreds of years. It's gained a legendary status. It is said it will come back to the most noble among dwarves. The one most worthy of admiration and respect."

"In this case, the two most worthy," Silas said.

Venn gave a snort. "But they all know you two."

"Doesn't matter," Tribal said. "We have Dirthor's crown. Everything in life just got easier."

Silas picked up a stack of gold coins and a handful of silver ones. "We'll take a few of these with us, too." At Evan's hopeful look, he pointed to a dark gem set in a ring. "If you want something valuable, take that. It'll buy you a mansion back in Queensland."

Evan grinned and picked it up.

"Is this enough gold?" Aislin asked Silas. "Can you buy your way back into Rullduin?"

"This is ten times more than we'd need," he answered. "Twenty times, maybe."

Aislin and Matlen exchanged nervous glances. She picked up a small gold coin and fiddled with it. "Is it enough to buy our way in too?"

The dwarves both stopped and stared at the elf twins.

"That's a terrible idea," Venn said.

"You two want to come with us?" Silas asked slowly.

Aislin and Matlen nodded quickly, their faces hopeful.

"We don't have anywhere else to go," Matlen said. "The forest feels strange, and the lakes aren't home anymore. I don't think we'd like to stay in caves all the time, but you two don't seem to do that."

"And, well…" Aislin gestured to the two dwarves. "You feel a bit like the uncles we never had."

Silas's fingers twitched, and Tribal, after a moment's hesitation, nodded.

"You can't go with them," Venn said. "These two dwarves are —surprisingly—all right, but the other dwarves in Rullduin aren't. They do not want a pair of elves coming—"

"Yes, it's enough to bring you in, too," Silas said lightly. "Enough money can buy anything in Rullduin."

Venn rubbed her hands over her face.

"Dwarven tunnels!" Evan said. "Can we go with them, too?"

"What tunnels?" Bo asked.

"The dwarven realm of Rullduin is under those mountains," Kate said, pointing to the huge silvery slopes to the west. "They actually connect to Queensland. Come out not far from where we grew up."

Evan straightened. "They could take us home? We could see

Ma and Dad?"

The question was so childlike, so eager, that Bo met Kate's eyes. "We could read all this on the way," he said. "I wouldn't mind being home for a bit."

"Is there enough to pay our way through too?" Kate asked.

"Yes," Silas said. "But we're taking that out of your cut."

Kate's gaze strayed across the valley toward where Renault's cave was hidden. "As long as we get a wagon big enough to bring a few things from Renault's cave as well." She glanced at Venn. "Are you up for some traveling?"

Venn gave an annoyed shrug. "I'm still ambassador to the White Wood. I can't leave until Evay is healed."

"Right." The idea of leaving Venn made Kate pause. "I forgot about that." Her mind jumped to the betrothal and how at least being forced to marry Faron wasn't a threat any longer.

From Venn's bleak, complicated expression, her thoughts followed a similar path.

Kate knelt to help Bo organize all of Emperor Sorrn's papers and books, fighting off a deep sense of sadness. She'd always known that, eventually, she'd go back to Queensland and Venn would stay here, but somehow it had always seemed further in the future. There were still all the books in Renault's cave to read.

Kate caught sight of the youthful hope in Evan's face, and she pushed her curiosity about Renault's library out of her mind. Of course Evan wanted to go home. He was still a child, and as far as he was concerned, he'd been trapped in a strange world for weeks, only to come out of it and find himself in a different strange place.

Bo covered the papers with a heavy blanket and weighed it down with a couple of rocks. He glanced at the clear sky. "Those should be safe until tomorrow." He stood. "There's a great inn in Home, the Blind Pig. The log mead there is fantastic." He glanced at Kate and Venn and the elf twins. "Well, some of you might not like it, but you two would." He gestured to the dwarves before scooping up a handful of silver coins. "Emperor Sorrn can treat us to some."

Tribal grinned. "If I'd known how much I was going to like you, I'd have obsessed with your sister about getting you out of that box."

"Let's get started," Kate said, pushing herself up. "It's still a long way back to Home."

Aislin nudged Evan with her elbow.

"Ria," he said, a note of hesitation in his voice, "Aislin and Matlen told me most of what's happened, but while we walk, will you tell us what happened with Naevys in the workshop?"

A wave of sorrow rolled out of Venn, and Naevys's broken face came back to Kate. For a moment she wanted to say no. To plead that she was too tired.

But Evan's interest was mirrored in Bo's face, and the faces of the elf twins and the dwarves.

"It's a story we don't know the end of," Tribal pointed out. "And we know how much you dislike that."

"Do you want to know the ending," Kate asked, "even if a lot of it is sad?"

Aislin bit her lip.

"From what I know of this story," Bo said, "the sadness has been woven into it for a very long time. I can't imagine it ending without a good bit of sorrow."

Kate picked up the box with the amulet. "True. I don't think it could have ended without some." She looked at Evan. "I'll tell you this if you tell me everything that happened to you since the mine."

He gave a quick nod.

"Good." She gestured to both of her brothers. "Do you know about the seed?"

"Yes!" Evan said. "We know up to when Aislin, Matlen, Tribal, and Silas left to rescue Venn from the workshop."

"After that," Kate said, starting down the slope next to him, "Fix burrowed a tunnel into the caves for me." She tried to suppress a shudder, but it didn't work.

Fix's tunnels are amazing, Crofftus said. *Brilliantly constructed.*

"They are." Kate leaned toward Evan. "They're also tight and terrifying. Although crawling through it didn't turn out to be the most terrifying part of the night."

His eyes were wide in his freckled face. "What was?"

"Riding on the dragon. Or maybe being under Naevys's control. Or thinking I was watching you and Bo die in the box." Kate shook her head. "There are a lot of contenders for most terrifying. I'll let you decide once you've heard them all."

CHAPTER SEVENTY-ONE

Kate's eyes were gritty with exhaustion as she blinked into the light pouring into the common room of the Blind Pig the next morning. The forest of branches Naevys had grown from the floor and the tables had been sawed off and stacked outside. The broken tables and chairs had been removed, and the remaining furniture felt sparse in the large room. But the fire burned brightly, and the scent of rosemary bread wafted out of the kitchen.

Bo waved her over to a table where he sat with the elf twins, Yellow, Venn, and Merrick.

"We've been telling Yellow what happened," Aislin said brightly. "And how his yellow door is now just standing in a clearing in the woods if he wants it back."

"I'll get some lads to help fetch it." Yellow pointed to the empty spot on the wall above his bar. "Can't leave it bare like that." He turned to Kate. "I always thought the door was odd, but I never imagined it opened a secret magical room."

"I didn't either." She looked closely at Yellow. Last night, when they'd arrived long after midnight, he'd told them how the town had been beset by weakness. Everyone had collapsed, feeling more and more drained as the minutes passed. But then it had stopped. Two elderly men who'd already been sick had died, but everyone else was left just exhausted, as though they'd been ill for a week. "How are you and everyone else this morning?"

"Recovering." He stifled a yawn. "I'm still knock-out tired, to be honest, but I feel marginally better than last night."

"Good." She took a piece of rosemary bread from a plate on the table. "Is there a wagon in town we could rent today?"

"I have one," Merrick said, "and the horse to pull it. I can drive you wherever you need."

"It's some heavy things the dwarves found, and we just need to get it to the entrance of Rullduin. It should only take a few hours."

"I can do that. But before you go, I believe you promised me some stonesteel."

"Yes," Silas said, coming down the stairs. "You owe us stonesteel too. Merrick, you have a dragon scale?"

Merrick pulled the icy-blue scale out of his pocket. The firelight sent ripples of frost-white light over the surface.

"Perfect," Tribal said. "We'll use your forge and have plenty by lunch."

Behind them, Helron the storyteller came down the stairs. "Keeper Kate, you also owe me the story of the troll fight."

Kate winced. "I did promise you that, didn't I?" She rolled her neck. "Can we do all this at once? Helron, come to the forge, and I'll tell the tale of the troll fight and the whole rest of this mess while we make the stonesteel."

"Will your story explain all the chaos that's happened in Home?" Merrick asked.

Kate nodded.

"Perfect." He stood. "I'll get the forge hot. I'm looking forward to having some explanation for all this."

Venn pushed herself back from the table. "I'm going to contact Ayen and see how everything stands in the White Wood. I'll be back by lunch."

Merrick's forge was open to the cold morning air, but the fire was so hot that Kate pulled off her cloak as she sat next to the crucible of molten steel.

The dwarves and Bo sat nearby, examining several of the weapons Merrick had forged. Evan had woken just as they were leaving the tavern and was exploring every inch of the smithy. Helron sat at a table near Kate, a journal in front of him. He opened to a page with notes jotted in different places, connected by lines and arrows. Large blank places sat between them, waiting to be filled.

Kate raised an eyebrow. "I like your story map."

"I hate not knowing the whole story," he said.

"Me too. I promise by the time we're done here, we should have filled in most of your blanks."

"Can I listen too?" The little merchant parked his cart next to the forge with a sunny smile. "I promise not to interrupt."

"The more, the merrier," Kate said.

Helron flipped to a new page and looked expectantly at her. "I assume this story begins when Bo came here?"

Kate held the dragon scale over the glowing steel with some tongs. She brushed a finger of *vitalle* across the blue surface, and tiny nodes of the scale sprinkled down into the crucible. "No, it actually begins almost four hundred and fifty years ago."

Helron's eyebrows rose, and the merchant gave an "Ooh!" of excitement.

Kate began telling how Virion and Naevys had created a seed.

It was past midmorning before she reached the collapse of

Renault's pocket world. Helron had filled a dozen pages in his book. Bo, Evan, the merchant, and Merrick had long since abandoned any activity aside from listening in amazement to the story.

Kate cast out into the crucible, and the steel lit up with the essence of the dragon scale. "That should be good, Merrick. I think you have one more batch? We'll do that while Helron asks me the dozens of questions I can see spinning in his mind."

Helron scribbled some more words down. "Give me a moment."

Kate set down the tongs and stood, stretching. "Gladly. I need to stretch my legs."

Merrick carefully moved the crucible, and the dwarves drew close to help him prepare another batch of steel.

Rising, Kate weaved through the smithy and out into the road, stifling a yawn. The town of Home was blissfully quiet, with only the normal sounds of rural life floating down the road from the direction of the square. Outside of town, there was still the ugly scar across the hills from Naevys, and two of the houses along the street had boarded-up windows and doors. But the sense of danger was gone. The snowy landscape around her felt peaceful instead of menacing.

Venn strode toward her from the end of the street, with Fix walking beside her. His hands were wrapped in bandages over the burns, but he was almost back to his usual scamper. "Ayen is doing well. Still a little dizzy from the Warden power, but he's in touch enough with the Woods to have directed the rangers toward any lingering creatures who shouldn't be here. He says the area around Home is safe, and he's sending more rangers down to the lakes to make sure there's nothing amiss there too."

"Any news on the *naiwyn*?"

"Apparently they disappeared when Naevys died," Venn said, holding out a wedge of cheese, "which is good, since tracking down Yilfrist to help destroy them all would have been difficult. Ayen says the dragon has gone too far east for him to track."

Kate took a bite of the sharp cheese. "And what is the Wood doing now that Faron is gone? Is there another king ready?"

"The elders are conferring." Venn's gaze ran along the scarred hills to the south. "Thankfully, Naevys gave the Warden power to Ayen before she died. If the Wood had been without a king and a Warden at the same time, I think it might have suffered. But Ayen is already doing a good job. And shockingly, Thallion has been helping heal the edges of the forest that Naevys damaged."

Kate raised an eyebrow. "That's...surprising. But good to hear."

"He's lost everything now. His crown, Faron, Naevys. I guess all he has left is the White Wood. And I suppose he probably always has loved that." Venn glanced over Kate's shoulder, and Kate turned to find the wiry merchant approaching.

He opened his mouth before his eyes fell on Fix. "You!"

Fix scuttled behind Venn while the merchant hurried to his cart.

"Kate said you like broken things." The man pulled open the lid and rummaged inside. "And I owe you for fixing my squeaky wheel. Aha!" He stood, holding up a complicated contraption. It was vaguely cylindrical, with gears and arms and wires connected in a dizzying fashion. A handful of pulleys held a string taut, even as it wove through the apparatus.

Fix froze, staring at it.

The merchant pushed off his cart, and it made a long, low groan. He let out a sigh of relief and held it out. "There. The deal is struck."

Fix's mouth sagged open as he took it, turning it slowly in his bandaged hands.

The merchant tucked his wares back into his cart and closed

the lid. "Thank you for letting me hear your tale," he said brightly to Kate. "It's been so long since I've seen a Keeper being so...Keeperish. I've missed it."

Kate gave a snort of laughter. "That is not what happened here. I was wrong at nearly every point. I misunderstood almost everyone, and I was constantly focused on the wrong thing."

He patted her arm fondly. "You all think you're doing a terrible job. I believe it's the curse of those doing the right thing to always fear they're doing it wrong. Milton has struggled with it for years."

Kate straightened. "Milton? You know the Shield?"

He chuckled. "The Shield is such a big name for such a small person."

Kate looked more closely at the man. There *was* something familiar about him. "Have we met before? Before Home?"

"Yes, although you were quite young."

"How young?"

"Probably twelve. That's usually when new Keepers appear, isn't it?"

The memory fell into place, and Kate's mouth dropped open. "You were at Will's wedding! At the palace in Queenstown! I remember because you were an odd addition to all the Keepers who were there." She pointed at him. "You were talking to the Shield."

He smiled fondly. "How is he doing?"

Pieces of a puzzle Kate hadn't been trying to solve fell into place. "You're an odd little merchant...and you know the Shield... You're Flibbet the peddler!"

"The one with the beetle story?" Venn asked.

"And a thousand more!" Kate's mind reeled at the idea. "You're really him?"

Flibbet bowed with a cheeky smile, then pointed at her. "But when Milton accuses me of interfering—again—tell him I did *not* come here for you. I just came for the festival." He leaned closer. "It was great fun watching you, though."

Kate stared at the man, the sheer number of questions she had paralyzing her.

"I've literally never seen her this speechless," Venn said.

"Kate," Merrick called from the forge. "The steel is ready."

"Well." Flibbet headed for his cart. "You're needed, and I have places to be. I was just on my way out of town when I heard you'd be telling the tale of what happened, and I couldn't resist stopping by to listen." He lifted the handles of his cart and gave it a push toward the square.

"But wait!" Kate took a step after him. "I have so many questions!"

"You always have questions," Venn said.

"Be sure to tell Milton I wasn't interfering, " Flibbet said with a wave. "Tell him I miss him, and he should be proud of you!"

"Come back with us!" Kate called. "The Shield is aging! Quickly! Come visit him yourself!"

Flibbet looked hopefully at his cart, but he hit a small rock in the road, and the wood gave a sharp creak. He sighed. "I wish I could. I really do. Safe travels, Mistress Keeper! It's been a pleasure."

"Wait!" Kate called again. But the peddler waved again and trundled his cart away toward a bend in the road.

"Kate?" Bo came up next to her. "The steel's ready. We can finish this by lunch and be on our way." He dropped his voice. "Evan is trying to hide it, but he's anxious to get home."

Kate watched the disappearing merchant for another moment. "Right," she said absently. "We should get him home."

Kate pushed the front door of the Blind Pig open near midday to find the room warm and smelling of bacon and stew and the familiar rosemary bread. In a cluster around the tables near the fireplace, a handful of people from the town were gathered along with Aislin and Matlen and Evay.

"Aunt Evay!" Venn crossed the room quickly.

"You look better than last time we saw you," Kate said.

"Thanks to you." Evay smiled at the two of them before her face sobered. "Aislin and Matlen told me what happened with Naevys and Faron. Their bodies are gone?"

Venn nodded. "The pocket world seemed to be under the White Wood somewhere. When it collapsed, there were frost pine roots coming through the ceiling."

Evay sighed. "They both would have been glad to be given back to the trees." She set her hand on Venn's shoulder. "I'm sorry. I know you and Faron had your disagreements, but..." She paused. "I didn't always agree with the decisions he made either, but I didn't envy the position he found himself in with Thallion. And if Faron could have picked a way to die, it would have been protecting you."

Venn closed her eyes. "I don't deserve it."

"He thought you did. And, while his death is a tragedy and a blow to the White Wood, I admit I'm glad he felt that way." She squeezed Venn's shoulder and offered her another smile. "In happier news, I'm here to officially take the position of ambassador from you, Venn, and remind you, Kate, that your role was only for as long as Naevys threatened Home, so you are also released."

Venn straightened. "I'm free to go?" She spun to face Kate. "I'm coming with you." At Evay's questioning look, she said, "Kate's taking her brothers back to Queensland and I'm going along." She glanced over Evay's shoulder. "Did the twins tell you they're going into Rullduin with the dwarves?"

Evay's mouth dropped open in shock. "I know it would be too painful for them to go back to the lakes, and too painful for their parents, at least for a while, but Rullduin?"

"Surprisingly," Kate said, "the Weasel brothers are very fond of them. They're offering some of their treasures to bribe the dwarven governor into letting all of us pass through the tunnels."

The dwarves arrived with Merrick and his horse-drawn cart. Yellow loaded two crates of food into the back, along with three large bottles of log mead, for which he was handsomely paid with Kalesh gold.

Kate gave him a hastily drawn map of where his yellow door was now sitting in the woods. "Thank you for your hospitality and for being kind to us even when the town's opinions of us wavered." She paused. "What happens now? Is Magistrate Mirrow still officially the magistrate? Or are you?"

"I'm not sure the town needs a magistrate," Yellow said, "but Mirrow's gone. He packed up and left the morning after he was voted out. So I guess we'll just see how things go from here."

Merrick climbed up into the wagon and started the horse forward.

"Next time any of you are near Home," Yellow said, looking at the rest of them, "I expect to see you."

Bo clapped the innkeeper on the shoulder. "I will find a way to get back to have more of that rosemary bread."

Evan fell in next to Kate. "So we pick up all that treasure now, and then we get to go home?"

She draped an arm around his shoulder. "One more stop. But you'll like it—I promise."

The wagon crunched over the layer of snow on the trail, drowning out the voices of the dwarves ranging ahead, Bo and

Merrick talking animatedly in the wagon, and the elf twins and Evan, who were engrossed in some sort of game that involved running, hiding, and hurling snow.

Next to Kate, Venn walked quietly, her emotions calmer than yesterday. Although the calm was more numbness than peace.

To their left, Evan leapt out from behind a tree and hurled a powdery wad of snow at Matlen, hitting the elf squarely in the back. Matlen spun, disappeared, and reappeared in a branch above Evan, shaking the tree and sending the snow in its branches tumbling down.

A smile crossed Kate's lips, the hundredth since they'd left Home. Everything about Evan was both surprising and familiar, and hearing his shouts and laughter again after all these years was slowly healing something inside of her that had been wounded for a very long time.

A bit of pleasure emanated from Venn as well. "It's nice to see the twins happy again."

Aislin stepped, appearing a branch higher than her brother and dumping a handful of snow on his head. She let out a peal of laughter and disappeared again.

Kate straightened. "Venn! In the workshop, while I was using the amulet, Naevys stepped from the fireplace to right beside me. And since time was slowed for her, I saw it! I think I know how it works!"

Venn's eyebrows rose and a hint of interest flickered inside her.

"Faron and the twins were right," Kate said. "It involves both being connected to the world—which you're good at—and the ability to move *ael'iza*—which I'm good at. I think together we might be able to do it!"

Venn's interest rose. "How?"

Kate moved off the road so the wagon could pass. "Take my hand." She mixed their remnants together around their clasped hands until both their arms held glitters of green and red. "Let's start small. That stump just ahead? I'm going to push out a path of our remnants to it from the toes of our right feet." She did, and a shimmer of red and green light stretched through the forest.

The red and green remnants reached the stump. Venn's green sank into it like meeting an old friend, and she raised her eyebrows. "I can feel that."

"Good. Now, I'm going to push some *vitalle* into the path, and you anchor us to that stump, then we're both going to step with our right feet." Kate shifted her weight and, at Venn's nod, pushed *vitalle* toward the stump.

She raised her foot alongside Venn's and focused on the far end of the path.

The line of remnants brightened, and Kate's foot stretched forward. The world pressed in around it, squeezing it in a vice, but she was already moving forward. The pressure moved up her leg, then her stomach. It shoved the air out of her lungs and crushed her arms to her sides. Her back leg was squeezed and—

Kate's foot landed next to the stump beside Venn's.

The pressure vanished with the abruptness of a rug being pulled out from under her feet. The cold air slammed back in, and a wave of dizziness rolled over her. Kate stumbled forward, and the world began to slide sideways.

Venn dropped to her knees, grabbing the stump to steady herself and Kate's arm to steady her.

Kate gasped.

"You stepped!" Aislin cried, appearing next to them and clapping her hands. Behind her, Evan stood open-mouthed next to Matlen, who was grinning broadly.

Venn let out a groan.

"Is it supposed to feel like that?" Kate shook her head, trying to dislodge the dizziness.

"It doesn't feel good at first," Matlen said brightly. "Once you get used to how to brace for it, it gets easier." He popped into view in front of Kate. "See? No dizziness! You just need to practice."

The vertigo began to subside, and Kate pushed herself up. "Maybe later."

"Yeah," Venn said, rising gingerly. "We'll practice again later. I saw what you did, Kate. Next time I can help." She shot Kate a smile that held actual happiness. "But we did it."

Kate felt her own smile grow. "We did it."

Merrick's wagon, loaded down with treasure from the carriage, was tucked safely in a dense copse of trees downhill a ways, and the afternoon sun was starting to drop into the west by the time Kate clambered down the rock chimney into the back entrance of Renault's cave. Bo and Evan came on her heels, their excited voices echoing over each other in the stone tunnel.

When she led them into the library, Bo stopped dead in his tracks.

"Renault wrote all these?" he asked, slowly taking in the room.

"Some of them. Others are ones he collected, or Naevys wrote, or…" Kate gestured to the bookshelves she'd never even touched. "I don't even know what most of them are."

Evan picked up a book and crinkled his nose at the writing.

"A lot are in Kalesh," Kate said to her younger brother. "Although a few you'd be able to read." She pointed at a doorway. "Through there you'll find a very interesting room."

Evan put the book down and started for the door.

"We'll come with you!" Aislin said, skipping after him. "It's our favorite part of this place."

Bo still stood, staring almost hopelessly at the shelves. "So, whose are all these now?"

"No one's." Kate picked up one of the books Naevys's remnant still lingered on. "Renault's gone, Naome doesn't want it, Naevys is gone—everyone who wrote anything here is long gone. The elves don't care about this, and none of the humans can move *vitalle* or read Kalesh."

He picked a book up off the table. "I see why you wanted to spend months here."

Kate looked after her younger brother. "Somehow I doubt Evan feels the same. You know, aside from Thallion, the only people who know this cave exists are right here. I don't think Thallion cares about any of it, and this isn't the sort of treasure the dwarves hoard. Venn will need to come back home sometime. We can come back with her and bring a big wagon, a lot of boxes, and maybe an armed escort. We'll take all these back to the Stronghold where they can be studied at will."

"Agreed," Bo said quickly. "But we can take a few now, right?"

"Oh, we're definitely taking a few."

CHAPTER SEVENTY-TWO

Kate sat on the bench next to Merrick as the wagon trundled up the narrow path in the darkening gloom toward the blackness of the cave ahead. A wide, quick-flowing river poured out of its mouth, running downhill toward the Surn.

"Is this really the entrance to dwarven caves?" Merrick asked under his breath.

Kate nodded. "I wouldn't spread that knowledge around, though. There are guards inside who wouldn't take kindly to humans coming to explore."

"We've had enough problems with the elves lately," he said. "I don't think we also need to irritate the dwarves."

Tribal signaled for Merrick to stop and, from the wagon, pulled out a small pouch that clinked when he hefted it. "Wait here. Silas and I will go in and make arrangements with the good cousins manning this door."

The two dwarves tromped inside. Evan, Bo, Aislin, and Matlen stood ahead of the wagon, peering into the darkness.

Venn leaned against the side of the wagon with her arms crossed. "Days underground. Again."

"We'll get you some moss when we get in there," Kate offered. At Merrick's confused look, she added, "The tunnels have moss that glows when it gets wet. Actually, the river has glowing plants in it too. Grass, flowers, little bushes. It's amazing."

A bit of yearning crept into his expression. "If there weren't several families in Home waiting for things to be fixed, I would ask the dwarves if they could fit one more human in to their party."

Tribal and Silas reappeared and motioned them closer.

"Let's get this stuff loaded up!" Silas called. "We have three boats. Should be plenty of space."

"Well," Kate said to Merrick as she rose, "it was very good to meet you." She extended her hand, and he took it, but instead of shaking it, he just held it.

"It was nice to meet you too, Kate." He paused, then added, "You know, if all of the *gwerocs* and bears and killer tree sprites and dragons had given us a breather"—he gave a little laugh—"and if you weren't a famous Keeper who dines with the queen, I would have asked if you wanted to have dinner with me."

The calluses on his hand were rough, but Kate squeezed it tighter. "If we'd had a breather, and I didn't have a brother to get home, I would say yes."

"Twig," Tribal called from the back of the wagon. "Do you care how these books are packed?"

Kate twisted to see him picking up a box. "Yes! The greenish crate has to be on top!" She gave Merrick an apologetic look. "I'd better go." She squeezed his hand again. "If you're ever in Queensland, come find me."

He let go of her hand. "I will. I figure I can just ask anyone on the street and they'll know where you are."

She gave him a self-conscious smile. "They can at least point you in the right direction."

The boat rocked gently, making Kate's notes messy as Bo finished recounting his time in Home and inside the Runelight Drawer. He'd spent a total of six hours in the valley with Naome, Miliene, and Evan. Long enough to find out their stories and tell his own. And try to escape the destruction that kept growing worse.

The recurring quiet splash of the paddle wheel had faded into the background, like the voices of her companions echoing off the tunnel walls.

The three boats were tied together, bow to stern, close enough to step from one to the next, and the dwarves took turns manning the paddle wheel in the front boat. The train of boats traveled slowly upstream, tethered to the wire hanging from the ceiling that kept them on course.

"Knew you'd come," Bo said finally. "I knew if Venn actually took you the box, you'd come and figure out all the strange puzzles."

"Really?" Kate asked. "Because I did a very poor job of figuring it out."

"To be fair, how could anyone have guessed what was actually happening? Ancient mages and ancient elves fighting to save children we'd never heard of? Magic that even you have never encountered?" He paused. "I am a little sad the aenigma box was buried."

The itch to hold the box still tickled Kate's fingers, and she rubbed her hands together. "So am I. At least partially. The other part of me is glad it's gone. It had too much of a hold on me."

He nodded. "Still…a magical box! I doubt I'll find another one of those anytime soon."

Kate's eyes strayed to Evan, who sat in the middle boat floating behind them, his head leaning close to Aislin and Matlen. The three of them had spent most of the trip upriver talking and laughing and playing elaborate games that involved glowing moss and thrown pebbles. "I never imagined we'd find him so… unchanged."

Bo nodded again. "I know you need to go back to the Stronghold when we get to Queensland. But I think I'll stay with Ma and Dad for a bit. See how Evan really is. See what he wants to do next."

"We're almost to the docks," Silas called over the noises of the river, from the front boat where Tribal paddled.

"What about the horrible Drain that we had to go through last time?" Venn asked.

"What's the Drain?" Evan asked.

"A narrow set of rapids just downstream from the dock," Venn answered. "I can't imagine how we'll get up that."

"No need to." Silas pointed to where the wire above them split in two directions. "Downstream boats go through the Drain. Upstream boats go around it to the old docks, through that smaller passage. Then they're portaged back to the new docks where we got on last time. We'll unload at the old docks and make our way through the tunnels on foot." Silas stood with his hand on the long pole that held the hook looping over the wire. When they reached the fork, he made a series of deft jiggles, and the hook bounced perfectly onto the wire to the right.

Once it was set, he headed back to the third boat, loosening the knife at his belt.

Venn raised an eyebrow at the action. "How much trouble are you expecting at the docks?"

Silas gave a tight shrug. "Probably a good amount. The cousins at the entrance had to report us. They'd have been punished for not doing it."

"Report us how?"

"There are signal wires that can send codes."

Kate narrowed her eyes. "From your nervousness, can I infer that you're not expecting a warm welcome?"

Aislin let out a nervous giggle. "No, not warm."

"Just how bad was your last trip here?" Kate asked.

Matlen winced.

Silas rubbed his beard. "It'll be fine," he said, his voice not terribly convincing. "We just need to talk to the gov'nor."

Tribal continued to paddle, and the boats slipped smoothly up the smaller channel.

"How much are you going to have to pay him?" Bo asked.

"That depends on how mad he is," Tribal said. "We have several options ready." He nudged a set of pouches by his feet. "He's holding a grudge against Silas and me, but a handful of the larger gold coins will pay for those crimes. The presence of the rest of you is tricky, though. If we can convince him to see the advantage of helping an elven princess and a human who advises the queen, it might cost only a few more coins to get you all through. If he's more sensitive about the fact that we brought you..." He tapped a much fatter pouch. "It'll cost a bit more."

A few moments later, they rounded a gentle turn and came in sight of a wide pool lined with docks. A handful of small warehouses stood on the shore. There were only two dwarves in sight, both carrying large sacks at a far dock.

Tribal and Silas exchanged looks but steered the boats between two of the docks. Tribal climbed out and tied up the first boat. Kate had grabbed a post to follow when heavy footsteps vibrated the dock. A dozen heavily armed dwarves marched out from behind the nearest building, lining the docks on either side of the boats, knives and axes in their hands.

One guard grabbed Tribal by the arm, while the rest leveled their weapons at the boats.

Kate raised her hands.

"I didn't believe it," a low voice rumbled. The guards parted, and a dwarf strode forward. He was nearly as broad as he was tall, a rich gold brocade vest stretching to cover his enormous girth. "They sent a message up that the Weasel brothers were back, but I thought they *must* be mistaken."

"Hullo, Gov'nor Rumolt," Tribal said, giving an awkward nod while the guard twisted his arms behind his back. "We were just coming to see you."

The gov'nor's black eyes were nearly hidden beneath his shaggy brown hair and thick beard, but they ran over Kate balefully, and she shivered at the hatred in them. His face turned an ugly red, and he strode up to Tribal and grabbed a fistful of his shirt. "After that last stunt you pulled, you dare to come back again, with more humans and more elves? You're all going in the rift this time! You'll die slowly in the blackest pit of the earth!"

"Wait!" Tribal said. "These are influential humans and elves! One's an elven princess, and one advises the human queen."

The gov'nor leaned forward and snarled into Tribal's face, his voice so quiet Kate barely heard it. "Do you know the trouble you've caused? Every noble has turned against me. I've emptied my coffer trying to soothe them!" His eyes bored into Tribal with a burning hatred. "I have to pick between Pruston and Grummdor!" The two names came out dripping with loathing.

"Those two swine?" Tribal's lip curled in contempt. "What could you possibly have to pick between them for?"

"For my daughter Pippi's hand in marriage!" Rumolt ground out between his teeth.

Tribal's expression turned dangerous. "No."

"I have no choice!" Rumolt spat the words, still speaking quietly. "You stripped me of all my power with your defiance!" He raised his voice. "You parade outsiders through our realm like you own it! Well, now you will pay, and so will they!"

"We *can* pay!" Tribal said. "We can pay a *lot*. More than your coffers held before!"

Rumolt glared at him. "Can you buy back the respect I once held? Because that is gone, and no amount of gold will bring it back." He flung a hand at the boats and shouted, "Kill them! Kill them now! We'll drop their bodies in the rift!"

Guards lunged forward. One grabbed Kate and yanked her up onto the dock, a knife pressed into her side.

Another wrapped his huge hand around Evan's thin arm and dragged him out of the boat, raising an axe above him.

Venn flung up her crossbow at the dwarf approaching her. Bo landed a punch on his guard's cheek, snapping his bearded head to the side.

"Stop!" Silas bellowed. "Venn! Put it down. Bo! Stop fighting!"

Aislin and Matlen pulled their dwarven daggers from their belts and stood back to back, their faces fierce. Two guards rushed them, easily overpowering them and dragging them onto the dock.

Silas lunged forward, drawing his knife and pressing it against one of the guard's throats. "Stand down, cousin," he growled.

"These are elves and humans," the guard snarled.

"Yep," Silas said, "but they're *our* elves and humans. Hands off. Now."

"Do not take your hands off them," Rumolt shouted.

Silas and Tribal exchanged glances, and Tribal grimaced but gave a short, tight nod.

With a growl, Silas spun, picked up a sack bulky enough to hold a huge portion of the dwarves' gold, and held it out over the water. "Gov'nor! Call them off! Or this goes into the river!"

The gov'nor's eyes narrowed, but he raised a hand, and the guards paused. "What is that?"

Tribal's jaw ticked, and he squeezed his eyes shut for a

moment before gathering himself. "It's a gift, for you. You *don't* want Silas to drop it in the river."

"Why not? I'm sure we can recover whatever it is."

"True"—Tribal lowered his voice—"but it's unlikely it will be recovered by *you*. And trust me, you want to be the owner of that."

The gov'nor's eyes narrowed.

Kate twisted her head to see the sack. It was the right size and shape for—

"These good people actually helped us find it," Tribal said. "They're emissaries from the humans and the elves, offering this gift." He leaned closer to the gov'nor. "You want to take a look at it before you do anything…regrettable."

Rumolt glared at him for a moment before letting go of his shirt and motioning Silas to come. Silas yanked his arm away from his guard and climbed up onto the dock, shouldering past dwarves who glared at him as though they'd like to rip his beard off.

He reached his brother, and Kate caught just the slightest flash of regret in his eyes before he held out the sack. "We all felt that a leader like you deserved something this valuable," Silas said, his voice almost sounding sincere. "A ruler who cares for the dwarves in Rullduin with a level hand and allows a few select outsiders not only to survive coming into the caverns but to pass through them, unmolested."

Rumolt's face darkened. "There's not enough gold in the world to pay me to do that."

"Good thing this isn't gold, then." Tribal reached in the sack and pulled out Dirthor's crown.

Aislin gave an audible gasp that echoed through the silent cave.

Rumolt's mouth dropped open, and he reached slowly for the thick silver crown. "It can't be."

"Look at the inscription inside." Tribal turned it.

Rumolt's hands closed on the silver. "It is," he breathed. "It's really Dirthor's crown!"

A ripple went through the guards on the docks.

Tribal kept his grip on it. "Show yourself as Dirthor's heir," he whispered, "and all the disrespect goes away."

Rumolt looked at him sharply. "Why give me this? You two hate me. Why not keep it for yourselves? You could've ruled with this."

"We don't want to rule," Tribal said. "We want the freedom to come and go as we please, and the freedom for these outsiders to do the same."

The gov'nor considered the boats shrewdly. "If they're caught stealing or harming anything, we'll kill 'em."

"They're not here to cause any trouble. Just want to see the wonders of Rullduin and pass through your amazing realm." He glanced at the elf twins. "As often as they like."

Rumolt's eyes fell on Kate again.

"Advisor to the queen and an elven princess?" he asked. "Then the humans and elves know we're here?"

"You're missing the point," Silas said. "The elven princess and the advisor to the queen are declaring your legitimacy."

Rumolt's eyes were drawn back to the crown. "You'll try to take it from me."

"You have our word we won't," Silas said. "You'll have nothing but support from us."

The gov'nor gauged the dwarf twins. "And in return?"

Tribal's voice grew grim. "Have your guards take their hands off our friends. And make sure no one else in all of Rullduin harms them. In any way."

Rumolt looked between the prisoners and the dwarf twins, his expression slightly disbelieving. "You two have changed."

"Do we have an agreement?" Silas asked.

Rumolt's gaze dropped to the crown again, and a rabid hunger filled his eyes. "We do."

Tribal let go of the crown.

Rumolt snapped his free hand at the guards. "Release them all."

The knife stayed tight against Kate's side, and none of the other guards moved.

Tribal let out a short, regretful sigh before raising his voice. "All hail Dirthor's heir!" he shouted.

Rumolt raised the crown and set it on his brow.

Kate's guard's grip loosened, and his knife came away from her side.

"All hail Dirthor's heir!" Silas called out.

A ripple of uncertainty passed through the guards until one yelled, "Hail Dirthor's heir!"

The others joined in, lowering their weapons and crowding back toward the gov'nor.

Tribal and Silas both watched with forlorn expressions as Rumolt strode away, his arms flung up in victory.

Kate stepped up next to them.

"Not a word," Tribal growled.

Kate placed a hand on his arm and squeezed. "Thank you."

"That was two words, Twig."

CHAPTER SEVENTY-THREE

Within an hour, a small one-wheeled handcart had been loaded with the rest of the dwarven treasure and Kate's books. The gov'nor had penned a declaration of pardon for Tribal and Silas, given them a stern warning that it wouldn't cover future crimes, and left the docks with his entourage of guards.

Tribal watched him go with a sigh.

"You gave up your fancy crown," Aislin said by his elbow. "The one that could have brought you anything you wanted."

Tribal set his huge arm over her slim shoulder. "It did buy us what we wanted, nibling. Now let's get moving. We can drop most of the gold off in our treasury, then head east."

"You have a treasury?" Evan asked, his eyes bright.

Tribal nodded. "Secret treasury. But seeing as how none of you will ever find your way around Rullduin without us, there's no harm in showing it to you. If we don't dawdle, we can get through the tunnels in three days, but if we take four, you'll get to see a lot more interesting places."

Evan shot his hand up into the air. "I vote for more interesting places!"

"Me too," Aislin chirped.

Tribal gave Venn a questioning look.

She tucked one last piece of moss into her pack. "As long as we keep finding moss, an extra day isn't a problem."

"The longer route is better lit. There'll be moss everywhere." Tribal turned to Kate. "Twig?"

"For once," Kate said, "I'm not in a hurry to get anywhere. Show us whatever you want to show us."

The dwarves' treasury turned out to be a room hidden behind a secret door, holding furniture, a large fireplace, a tremendous number of gadgets made by their late father, and piles of gold and gems.

Kate stood in the doorway, surveying the treasure. "Why on earth did you need more treasure to buy the governor's favor if you had all this?"

"This is what you'd call...tainted goods," Tribal said easily.

"Most of it is things our mother stole. And most of it is recognizable." Silas picked up a necklace with an enormous green gem. "We can't exactly bribe the gov'nor with Lord Turgoth's heirloom emerald, can we?"

"Then what do you do with it all?" Evan asked.

"Besides admire it?" Silas selected three rings from a pile on a small table. "We take them out of Rullduin and trade them to humans for all sorts of things."

Tribal brought in the last crate of gold and set it in the corner. "The loot from the emperor's carriage, though, can be put to good use here in Rullduin." He grinned. "We have ideas of what we'll spend it on, but we'll sit on it a bit for now."

"Besides, Tribal needs some time to figure out how best to woo Pippi with all this treasure," Silas said with a grin. He picked up a handful of coins and handed them to the elf twins, Bo, Evan,

Venn, and Kate. "There, now we're not worried any of you will starve to death once we're back in the human realm."

Traveling through Rullduin without needing to be stealthy was a vastly different experience from the covert rush during their first passage, and Kate quickly filled the last blank pages of her notebooks with descriptions and sketches. Tribal and Silas took them through caverns that shimmered with gems, past chasms so deep no sound returned when Evan tossed a stone over the edge, and through ornate halls constructed by dwarves, with intricate carvings covering the walls and the ceilings.

Four days later, daylight—actual bright, fresh daylight—poured into the mouth of the same cave Kate and Venn had followed the dwarf twins into when they'd first met. Venn hurried past the rest of them into the daylight, turning her face up toward the sun. Everyone else filed out onto the jumble of rocks on the side of the Marsham Cliff that hid the dwarven entrance.

Unlike the snowy entrance near Home, this more southern door in Queensland opened up into a view of early winter. The trees in the forest below were bare of leaves and the grass was brown, but there was no snow to be seen.

"Kate." Venn held out her hand. "The dizziness will be worth it to reach the trees faster."

Kate took her hand and cast out, sending a trail of green and red remnants from their toes to the base of a huge oak at the bottom of the slope. Venn directed her green lights to connect with the tree, and Kate pushed *vitalle* through the connection.

The thread lit, and they both stepped forward.

The world pressed in, then fell away, taking the air with it, until Kate's foot crashed down onto the dirt next to the oak, and she gasped. Venn grabbed for the tree to steady herself, and Kate sank to her knees as the wave of dizziness crashed into her.

Venn's remnant sank into the tree, and the *ael'iza* in the trunk flowed smoothly into the elf. Venn let out a breath of relief, leaning her forehead against the bark. "That wasn't quite as bad."

Kate blinked into the forest that wouldn't stay quite upright. "Still not great, though."

Aislin and Matlen appeared beside them, their faces bright with excitement at the view of the forest, and without the slightest sign of any disorientation.

"That time was a lot farther! You're getting better!" Matlen said encouragingly before the two of them scampered into the trees.

Bo and Evan clambered down the slope, each carrying one of Kate's boxes while Tribal and Silas lowered the cart carefully down the rocks with a set of ropes. Fix sat on Evan's shoulders, his knobby hands gripping Evan's forehead, his eyes wide with wonder as he took in the forest that only held a few pines.

When the cart was on the ground and the boxes packed safely under an oilcloth, Kate climbed onto the back of it to rest, and Bo sat next to her.

His gaze drifted through the trees around them. "It's good to be home."

She pushed her shoulder against him. "It's good to have you home."

Evan and the elf twins were embroiled in some game under a huge oak tree, their laughter echoing through the trees.

Tribal finished coiling up his rope. "Where to first? The Wildwood or your Stronghold?"

"They're in opposite directions." Kate pointed southeast. "Our home in the Wildwood is a day's walk in that direction. The Stronghold is a day and a half straight north along the cliffs."

Another peal of laughter came from behind the oak tree.

"We can do both," Bo said. "Ria, you and Venn can take the books to the Stronghold, while Tribal, Silas, and I take the elf twins and Evan home."

Kate shook her head. "We met the dwarves very near here. That night we were set upon by twenty bandits who burned the dwarves' cart to the ground. It'll be easier to protect Evan and the elf twins and the books if we stay together."

Tribal crossed his arms. "You think we can't protect some children from a few humans?"

"There were *twenty* of them, Tribal," she said.

"All the more reason to get the books back to the Stronghold quickly," Bo said. "The bandits are only here in the south. You two can head north without any danger."

"And you?"

"We'll head northeast to Milford. The road from there is a little longer, but Duke Tunnerin's men protect it, and there are plenty of inns. We'll be perfectly safe there. We'll be home by lunch tomorrow." At her worried look, he rolled his eyes. "You realize I've traveled in far more dangerous places than the Wildwood for the past ten years, right?"

"As have we," Silas said.

"They have a point," Venn said. "And if something happens to these books, you're going to be insufferable."

The crates in the cart did feel vulnerable, and Kate nodded reluctantly. "All right. But once we've delivered the books to the Stronghold, I'm coming to Ma and Dad's." She climbed off the cart and crossed to the oak tree. "Evan, I need to go get these books safe. Venn and I are going to the Stronghold, but we'll meet you at home soon."

His smile faltered, and some of the fear that had haunted his eyes when she'd seen him in the Runelight Drawer crept back in. "You'll be careful?"

"I will. You be, too. Listen to Bo and the dwarves." She

wrapped her arms around him, squeezing his shoulders. "I'm so happy to see you again, Evan. I'll be home in less than a week, and we'll all be together."

His grip around her was tight, like a frightened child, but when he pulled back, he forced a smile. "Do I get to come to the Keeper Stronghold sometime?"

She grimaced. "I promise you would not like the path to get to it." Turning toward the oak tree, she called, "Fix! Do you and Crofftus want to come to the Stronghold?"

The gnoblin paused in the middle of a little caper and turned slowly to face her. Fix's face was eager, but Crofftus's voice came out tense.

We both know that the Keepers don't have a way to get me my own body.

Fix's brow creased with indignation. *Crofftus has body.*

I know, Fix, and I love it here. But are you sure you don't want your autonomy back?

Fix crossed his arms. *Minds are for family. Crofftus is family.*

Crofftus was quiet for a moment. *All right, then, I don't need another body, so I really have no reason to go to the Stronghold.*

"Except to meet the Shield," Kate said. "And heal whatever rift is between you two that has kept you bitter for more than a hundred years."

Venn nodded. "You really should meet him. He's not the man you think he is."

Fix hopped from one foot to the other, his eyebrows high with hope.

Crofftus sighed. *If it will make you happy, Katria, I will go talk to Milton.*

"Excellent." Kate patted Tribal on the shoulder. "We'll see you at my parents' house in a week."

∽

The day moved on, and Kate traded off with Venn at pushing the cart along the narrow trails they found in the woods. Near lunchtime, they trundled into a clearing with a wide patch of wilted brown brush covering the ground.

This is where we met, Crofftus said from where Fix sat on the wagon. *The fox was there, in the middle of the dead brush, when you saved it from the vimwisps.*

Kate glanced up into a tree where a small vimwisp nest sat snugly in the fork between two branches. "Look, Venn! The branch that looks like a pig's snout. The one you shot when I was just using it to give you some directions."

Venn rolled her eyes. "You were being unclear."

"You were being grumpy."

"We were being stung by huge vimwisps!"

I'm very grateful, Crofftus interrupted as the cart rolled out of the clearing, *that you stopped to help the fox.*

Fix smiled widely. *Fix happy too.*

It was nearly noon the next day before Kate turned the handcart off the great northern road and onto a barely visible trail leading toward the Marsham Cliff. The moment they entered the trees, the forest darkened, and Venn tensed.

"This will lead us to the Stronghold," Kate said, "but it's guarded by ghosts."

Ghosts? Crofftus asked.

Venn shuddered. "They'll taunt you with all your fears."

"Just stay on the path and keep moving." Kate shifted her grip on the cart. "They can't actually hurt you, but if you run, the woods will funnel you back out to the road, and we'll have to try again."

They taunt you with your fears? After everything we've been through, that doesn't sound too bad.

"It is."

Venn picked Fix up off the cart and held him tightly, her eyes searching the trees ahead.

Kate straightened her shoulders and strode forward. "Just remember, keep moving."

For several long minutes, the forest was quiet. Kate's ears strained for the sounds of wolves howling, which sometimes ushered in the ghosts, but there was nothing.

A flicker caught her eye on a trunk ahead, and her hands tightened on the cart. As she reached the tree, a milky-white face slid out of the bark. It was Evan, his eyes dark holes of fear, his skin gaunt. "You sent me there!" he whispered. "Everything I suffered was because of you."

Kate flinched away from the face, but the words didn't stab into her the way they would have weeks ago. "You told me yourself I also saved you," she whispered.

Behind her, Venn hissed, and Fix let out a moan.

Kate hurried the cart on, and Bo's face emerged from the next tree. "You opened the drawer twice without the amulet," he whispered, contempt dripping from his words. "We almost died because of you."

The sentiment pressed on Kate, but not with the weight she was braced for.

"Evan went through that horror because of you," another Bo said.

Voices peppered her, flinging failure after failure at her, but unlike other times she'd walked this trail, the words didn't cut into her. There was some truth to them, but they weren't the whole truth.

She broke out of the woods and into a clearing set against the base of the Marsham Cliff, and the ghosts faded. Venn stumbled out behind her.

I did not like that, Crofftus said in a strangled voice.

Fix nodded vehemently, even as he kept his face covered.

Venn's face was pale, but she gave Kate a perplexed look. "They tried to taunt me with the same fears as last time. How I was helpless against the elves ruling the White Wood. How I was just a pawn. How they would always drag me back and take my freedom. Except…"

Kate nodded. "They chose my old ones, too. They blamed me for Evan being trapped and tortured and how I'd almost destroyed the pocket world with my brothers still inside, but…" She let out a little laugh. "Every other time I've walked this path, I've had some big unknown in my life. Something I was terrified of. But right now, things feel…settled. We didn't perfectly save my brothers, but we did save them. And the White Wood. And Home."

"Maybe we haven't developed new fears yet," Venn said.

"The Shield always says that the truth is far more complicated than these ghosts ever make it seem," Kate said. "This is just the first time I've actually been able to believe it."

"So you're saying next time we walk this path, it's likely to be worse?" Venn asked.

"Undoubtedly."

Fix peeked out at her and offered a weak smile.

Kate gave him a real one. "But we're past the bad part. Now we get good food, good friends, and a lot of books."

A blank rock wall sat against the bottom of the cliff, and Kate moved over to a barely visible rune carved into its surface. The rune was coated with the remnants of Keepers who'd passed before. She pressed her hand to it and fed some *vitalle* in. "*Aperi.*"

The wall next to her shifted, the rocks moving to create a wide opening into a smooth-walled tunnel. Fresh air blew out of it, and Kate gestured them inside. "Welcome to my home."

CHAPTER SEVENTY-FOUR

She pushed the cart quickly down the long tunnel that ran beneath the Marsham Cliff and moved out into the sunlight again in the hidden valley that lay behind it. The hills of grass had browned as winter approached, and the trees at either end of the valley were bare of leaves.

The white tower of the Stronghold rose toward the sky, and the scent of bread floated on the breeze, bringing a grin to Kate's face. She was most of the way to the door of the low kitchen along the base of the tower when Kellen emerged from the door.

"Kate!" He hurried forward, holding a half-eaten slice of bread and bringing with him the fresh, healing scent of tree sap. The familiar smell of his remnant was now also surrounded by a glittering yellow that fit him perfectly. "And Venn! You're back!" He stopped when he saw Fix. "And...another friend?"

"This is Fix." Kate gave Kellen a tight hug, which he returned awkwardly. "He's a gnoblin."

"What's in the cart?" Kellen asked.

"Books and papers from the last emperor of the Kalesh Empire," Kate said, "and writings by an ancient half-elf mage named Renault who created really unique magic. He's the one who created the aenigma box, and an amulet that slows time."

Kellen's eyebrows rose. "I'll get these inside!"

Gerone appeared in the kitchen door, his white hair cheerfully disheveled, his face split in a wide smile. The scent of baking bread, both real and from his remnant, swirled out from him, and he was wreathed in amber shimmers of light. "Kate! Come in! There's bread and avak jam, and we still have some apples in the cellar!" His eyes fell on Venn, "Ah! You're back! Glad to see you two didn't kill each other!"

After a quarter of an hour's bustle, they sat around the table in the kitchen. The elderly Mikal had joined them, his normal stoicism ruffled enough to smile at Kate and say more than once that he was "very pleased" that she was home. The scent of his remnant, sweetness mixed with the tang of vinegar, fit so perfectly next to Gerone's that Kate couldn't help smiling at the two of them. Instead of eating, Mikal dove into the crates Kellen had set on the table, sorting the papers, creating piles, and occasionally muttering exclamations that sounded almost like delight.

Gerone was slicing more bread for them when there was a rustle at the door leading to the Stronghold, and the Shield stepped in. His remnant swept in with him. It was so much stronger than the others. Not as strong as an elf's but close. It smelled like hearths and sounded like crackling flames. Before, she'd gotten a golden impression from it, but now, she could see glitters of shimmering gold all around him. They enveloped him and reached out to brush along the walls the way Venn's reached out to trees.

In contrast, his face was thin, his skin pale, and he had one hand on the wall to steady himself. Still, his smile was as wide and bright as ever. "Kate," he said warmly, "and Venn. Welcome back."

Kate rose and crossed the room to give him a hug, soaking in his remnant. His shoulders felt bony and brittle, and she curbed her enthusiasm enough to make the embrace gentle. She met Gerone's eyes, seeing a sorrow and resignation that squeezed her heart.

The Shield patted her arm. "Don't look so glum, my dear. It can't possibly be a surprise that I'm aging."

Fix sat hunched on the bench next to Venn. The Shield's eyes fell on the creature, and his bushy eyebrows quirked. "A gnoblin! It's been a *very* long time since I've seen one of you!" He took Kate's arm and shuffled toward the table. "Welcome!"

Hello, Milton. Crofftus's words were cold, and the Shield drew to a stop, his eyebrows shooting up high on his bald head.

Mikal, Gerone, and Kellen all froze, their eyes wide.

"The gnoblin is Fix," Kate said. "We met him in a cave near the town of Home. And living inside his head is a mage named Crofftus, who, as you can tell, can speak directly into others' minds."

There was a moment of silence before the Shield took a stumbling step forward. "Crofftus? It's really you?"

"You know him?" Gerone asked.

"From long ago..." The Shield's face turned contrite. "We knew each other when we were very young. But, Crofftus, you left!"

Left? I stayed in town while you *left to become a Keeper.* The words were laced with bitterness.

"I...I searched for you." The Shield shuffled over to the table and used Kate's arm to lower himself onto the bench. "I searched for you to tell you how sorry I was! I was so threatened by you! It took the Keepers several years to get it through my thick skull how selfish I'd been." He let out a breath that was half-laugh, half-despair. "Honestly, it's still a struggle every day. But I'm *so* sorry for how I treated you! It was unpardonable."

"You really were as awful as he says?" Kate asked.

The Shield nodded. "Maybe worse."

We began working together, Crofftus said. *But there was only one place to be filled in the Keepers' Stronghold. Not two. And so, when the Keeper came to our town...*

"I sabotaged you," the Shield said softly. "And took the spot. I'm so sorry. I don't deserve your forgiveness for that, but you should know that I've regretted it my entire life." He looked sadly at the gnoblin. "I've often wondered what you did with your life."

Fix shrank back, shifting uncomfortably, and Crofftus said nothing.

"Crofftus learned how to inhabit animals temporarily," Kate said.

"Really?" the Shield said, impressed.

"But one day," Kate continued, "his animal went too far from his human body, and it died."

"So you've lived in animals ever since?" The Shield's voice was awed. "Amazing."

It has been, Crofftus said softly.

The Shield studied the gnoblin for a long moment, and Kate got the impression that he wasn't looking at the gnoblin at all. "And lonely, I would imagine."

It was. Until I met Katria and Andovenn.

"I'm so very glad you did," the Shield said. He straightened suddenly. "Animals! You must be intimately acquainted with all sorts of animals!"

When Crofftus didn't answer, Kate said, "He is."

"Would you..." The Shield rubbed his hand over the back of his neck in an unusual show of nervousness. "Would you help me with something? I have a project I started years ago involving communication with animals, but I gave it up as lost because I couldn't imagine anyone would know enough about animals to help me. But you...You!" He let out a bemused laugh. "You've done the impossible!" He leaned closer to Fix. "Would you come look at my notes?"

Fix's eyebrows rose, as though he were waiting for an answer.

When Crofftus spoke, his words were quiet. *You know I've hated you for years.*

The Shield's shoulders sank. "I deserve it. I deserve to have you hate me for years more, but I'm afraid I'm almost out of those." He paused. "You have every right to walk away. I wouldn't blame you at all. But you've always seen magic differently than I have, and even if you can't bring yourself to work with me, I'll be gone soon. Perhaps you can find a place here after I've left."

Fix sat very still.

A place? Here? Crofftus asked warily. *I'm not a Keeper.*

"You can manipulate *vitalle* and have spent your life in study and exploration of the world. That sounds a lot like a Keeper to me."

I can't manipulate vitalle, Crofftus admitted. *Not anymore.*

The Shield waved the objection away. "There was a Keeper not long ago named Rett. He suffered a terrible injury and was much the same. You have the skills to be one of us, and Katria clearly trusts you, or she wouldn't have brought you here. That's enough for me."

A hopeful smile curled up Fix's mouth, and he waited expectantly until Crofftus finally spoke.

I would very much like to see your notes, Milton.

Fix gave a little hop of happiness.

The Shield grinned. "Do you speak, Fix?"

Crofftus helps me. Fix's voice came shyly.

"Excellent!" The Shield patted the gnoblin on the shoulder. "Shall we go to the library?"

Kate spent the rest of that day and the majority of the next telling the story of the White Wood and the aenigma box to Gerone, Mikal, and Kellen. She answered their endless questions, showed them her journals, and let Venn explain to Mikal every aspect of the elves that he could think to ask about.

The Shield and Crofftus holed themselves up on the third floor of the library, surrounded by books on animals and communication. Fix scuttled over tables, opening books for Crofftus to read and munching happily on snacks that Gerone continually brought them.

On the morning of the third day, Kate walked out of the Stronghold to find the air crisp and cold. The sense of snow tickled at the edges of her mind, as though forests in the mountains to the north were already catching drifting flakes.

"You and Venn have bonded closely," the Shield said from behind her. He sat on a bench against the tower, so short that his feet hung above the ground. His eyes followed something in the air around Kate.

"The White Wood bonded us together," Kate said, coming to sit next to him. The strange remnant of the tower itself wrapped around them. Too many scents and sounds to sort out, and very faint glitters of light in every color. "After that was broken, Naevys bonded us again." She frowned. "I haven't been able to tell you much of what happened."

"Each night, Mikal's been telling me what you told him of your story" At her frown, he waved her concern away. "I don't sleep much anymore. It's been very nice to have such a fascinating tale to entertain me. But your bond is more than that." He smiled at her. "I suspect it's because you're not fully human."

She looked sharply at him. "Did you know that because of Mikal? Or because you just know a lot of things I don't think you should know?"

He patted her hand with his thin dry one. "I've always

thought you had something slightly...mystical about you. I attributed it to your childhood in the Wildwood, but since hearing your tale, I did a little digging in the genealogies and discovered something interesting." He pulled a thin scroll out of his black robe. "You remember Leonis? The half-elf who helped the first queen, Sable, to unite Queensland? Well, after his adventure with Sable, he settled on the edge of the Wildwood and ended up marrying a human woman. They had three children, and their descendants settled outside a town called Welsley."

Kate straightened, unrolling the scroll. "That's close to where I grew up."

"From what I can tell," the Shield continued, "no other elves married humans in that area. It's a strange enough occurrence that such a thing is usually noted. So while I can't trace a direct line from Leonis to you, it certainly makes sense that he's your ancestor."

Kate stared at the Shield. "Leonis? I've always liked him in the old stories." She digested the information for a moment and found it...reassuring. Eventually she looked at the old man next to her, tracing the lines of weariness in his face. "You and Crofftus have been busy."

The Shield smiled. "He's been remarkably helpful. And it's been good to see someone from so long ago."

"Has he brought up how much he'd like a human body again?"

"He has, and we've discussed it at length. But he's right. There's no way we can think of to do it without killing someone. And that feels morally questionable. Besides, Fix is genuinely distressed by the idea of Crofftus leaving, and I think the two of them make a very good pair."

"Good." She straightened. "Did Mikal tell you I met Flibbet?"

The Shield's smile turned fond. "How is the old peddler? You know," he said thoughtfully, "Flibbet knew Leonis."

Kate dropped her hands to her lap. "He can't really be that old. He just seemed like a strange elderly man."

"He's definitely that old. He interfered with that whole business with Sable just like he was interfering in the White Wood with you."

Kate laughed. "He said you'd say that. Told me to tell you he was merely there for the winter festival and barely did anything at all. Oh, and before I had any idea who he was, but after he helped us fight off the wood troll, he gave me a book for you. It's buried in my pack, but I'll get it for you. It's by Stonewall the Aged and Driscall the Crooked. He says it will continue a conversation you two have been having for a very long time."

The Shield's bushy eyebrows rose. "Did he really?" He sighed. "I would have liked to chat with him one last time." He looked at Kate closely. "What else did he say?"

"That he would have liked to come see you."

"Anything else?"

Kate paused. "He said you should be proud of me, that it had been a long time since he'd seen a Keeper do such Keeperish things."

The Shield patted her hand kindly. "I am very proud of you, my dear. A whole new part of the world now knows what a Keeper is."

Kate felt a worm of guilt in her gut. "I did a lot of things wrong. I think a lot of people suffered, and maybe died, because I didn't figure things out fast enough." She let out a breath. "I just…couldn't see the whole picture. I tried. I kept thinking I'd figured it out, but I kept getting it wrong."

"Real life, as it's happening, is a messy, complicated thing," he said, letting his gaze roam over the quiet valley. "I think one of the hardest things I ever had to learn was that in the moment, it's nearly impossible to see the whole picture. Sometimes, later on, you can look back and make some sense of it. But while it's all swirling around you..." He squeezed her hand. "Sometimes we just have to embrace not knowing."

"I hate not knowing."

He laughed. "As do I." He sobered. "I'm glad you're back, my dear. I was afraid you wouldn't return before..." He swallowed. "I can feel myself weakening by the day. My mind is slowing. My joints hurt. My fingers struggle to hold a quill or a book. It's time for me to pass on. I can't even be upset at that, because I've had a hundred and fifty years. Far more than most." He squeezed her hand again. "And they've been good years. But my mind is consumed with figuring out what comes next, and I hate that I cannot know."

He rested his head back against the white tower. "I have spent a lot of my life trying to figure out the stories and make history make sense. But this, this great eternal question... This I can't answer."

Kate covered his hand with her own. "What can I do to help you?"

"You've already done it. You went and saved a great number of people and elves, and you came back, so I was selfishly able see you again and hear your tale." He leaned against her. "Now, don't look so forlorn. I'm not leaving today or tomorrow. Or even this winter. This lingering has the feel of something slow." Across the rolling grass, Venn moved under the distant trees. "She's getting antsy."

"To be honest," Kate said, "so am I. I want to get back to my brothers and see how they are."

"And then?"

Kate considered the question. "I don't know. Will you be disappointed if I don't come straight back here? If Venn's not anxious to get back to the White Wood, I thought maybe we could travel Queensland a bit. Maybe with Bo. I have the itch to gather stories."

He gave her a broad smile. "If I were a hundred years younger, I'd join you."

∼

Kate caught up to Venn at the base of a particularly large bare oak tree that sat near the southern edge of the valley. The elf's emotions had settled into a low, steady calm interwoven with sorrow.

"I see what you like about this place," Venn said, setting her hand on the wide trunk. "The trees are...they aren't elven, but they're something. I think living near Keepers for centuries has rubbed off on them. This whole valley feels like...well, like the rest of you Keepers feel."

"Thank you for being patient while I sorted things out here."

"Last time it wasn't the Stronghold that was bothering me. It was the life debt." Venn gave Kate a rueful smile. "And I was wounded and tired and angry that I owed Bo anything. But it turns out that saving Bo's life was the beginning of some very interesting events."

Kate winced. "Sorry I wasn't more gracious to you."

Venn shrugged. "I've been told I have the ability to be a bit surly."

Kate let out a laugh. "A bit." She leaned back against the tree trunk and looked toward the tunnel leading out of the valley. "What do you say we leave this afternoon? Go see how Evan and Bo are doing. And see how my parents are handling two dwarves and two elves in their house."

"I would love to." She paused, and a bit of curiosity edged into her emotions. "I find I have some sort of lingering connection to Bo. It's not the life debt anymore, but we're still connected somehow. And I'd like to figure out how." A smile crossed her face. "And I'd love to explore the Wildwood again. Just the edge of it the other day spoke of secrets and mysteries that still linger in it."

Kate straightened. "The Wildwood still talks to you?"

Venn let out a breath of laughter. "It didn't literally speak, Kate. Couldn't you feel that there were things to explore there?"

"Oh." Kate grinned at her. "It's usually you who takes things too literally. But yes, it did feel that way. Of course, it's always felt that way to me." She tapped her fingers on her leg. "You know, while we've been gone, there have been more reports of bandits along the southern part of the Wildwood. I don't like the idea of them there."

Venn frowned. "Neither do I."

"Maybe we should look into it. I think Crofftus will want to stay here, but do you think the Weasel brothers and the twins would help?"

"Undoubtedly," Venn said with a grimace.

"And Bo will probably want to help as well."

"That's not a lot of fighters to take on what will undoubtedly be violent bandits," Venn pointed out.

"True, but we're a resourceful group. We did save the White Wood from an evil king and queen bent on destroying it."

Venn gave a snort. "Barely."

"It still counts. I'll say goodbye to the others. Gerone will pack us some food. Then I'll just need to get some—"

"Blank journals," Venn said. "You're going to stop often to write down everything we find, aren't you?'

"Of course. And I also have a list of questions about elves that Mikal has prepared for you that he hasn't asked yet."

"That man asks even more questions than you do."

"I know. Isn't he great?" She looked at Venn's green remnant sinking into the tree. "How long do you want to be away from the White Wood?"

"At least a season or two. I'm not even sure what is waiting for me there, and I don't need to know right now. The elf twins need at least that much time to adjust to their new situation anyway. We should take them back eventually, but not yet."

"Well, then." Kate pushed away from the tree. "For once, let's just wander a bit. No shadows hunting us, no kings forcing us to serve them, no queens terrorizing the land. Just a few straightforward bandits to root out." She started back toward the Stronghold.

Venn fell in beside her, the elf's green remnant, forest scents, and cloud of emotions feeling like a bit of home traveling along with them. "You think it will stay that straightforward?"

Kate gave her a grin. "Definitely not."

THE END

ACKNOWLEDGMENTS

Thank you so much for reading the final book in Kate and Venn's quest to open the aenigma box! I appreciate you picking these books up more than you could ever know.

Thank you Laura Josephsen for your editing jujitsu. I'd like to think I'm getting better at commas, but we both know that's not true.

Thank you again, Dalton, for the talks in the car about plot questions. Thank you Belle and Liam for the random questions I've thrown at you about the series, trying not to spoil anything. Thank you Jason for your endless support and encouragement of this career.

Thank you to Melissa for the Indiana Jones memes that helped me stay sane and Constance for the world's fastest Omega read. You were both more helpful than I can express. Sorry to both of you about that thing with Bo.

ABOUT THE AUTHOR

JA Andrews lives deep in the Rocky Mountains of Montana with her husband and three children.

She is eternally grateful to CS Lewis for showing her the luminous world of Narnia.

She wishes Jane Austen had lived 200 years later so they could be pen pals.

She is furious at JK Rowling for introducing her to house elves, then not providing her a way to actually employ one.

And she is constantly jealous of her future-self who, she is sure, has everything figured out.

For more information:
www.jaandrews.com
jaandrews@jaandrews.com

facebook.com/JAAndrewsAuthor
x.com/JAAndrewsWriter
instagram.com/jaandrewsbooks

Made in the USA
Middletown, DE
01 September 2025

13443101R00449